Gods of Opar
Tales of Lost Khorkarsa

Gods of Opar
Tales of Lost Khokarsa

Philip José Farmer
and
Christopher Paul Carey

SUBTERRANEAN PRESS • 2012

First Edition

ISBN
978-1-59606-471-3

Subterranean Press
PO Box 190106
Burton, MI 48519

www.subterraneanpress.com

Table of Contents:

Map 1: Ancient Africa circa 10,000 B.C.
Key: **1.** Mukha; **2.** Miklemres; **3.** Qethruth; **4.** Siwudawa; **5.** Wethna; **6.** Kethna; **7.** Wentisuh; **8.** Sakawuru; **9.** Mikawuru; **10.** Bawaku; **11.** Towina; **12.** Rebha; **A.** Klemqaba country
(A description of the maps follows on page 561)

Map 2: Island of Khokarsa

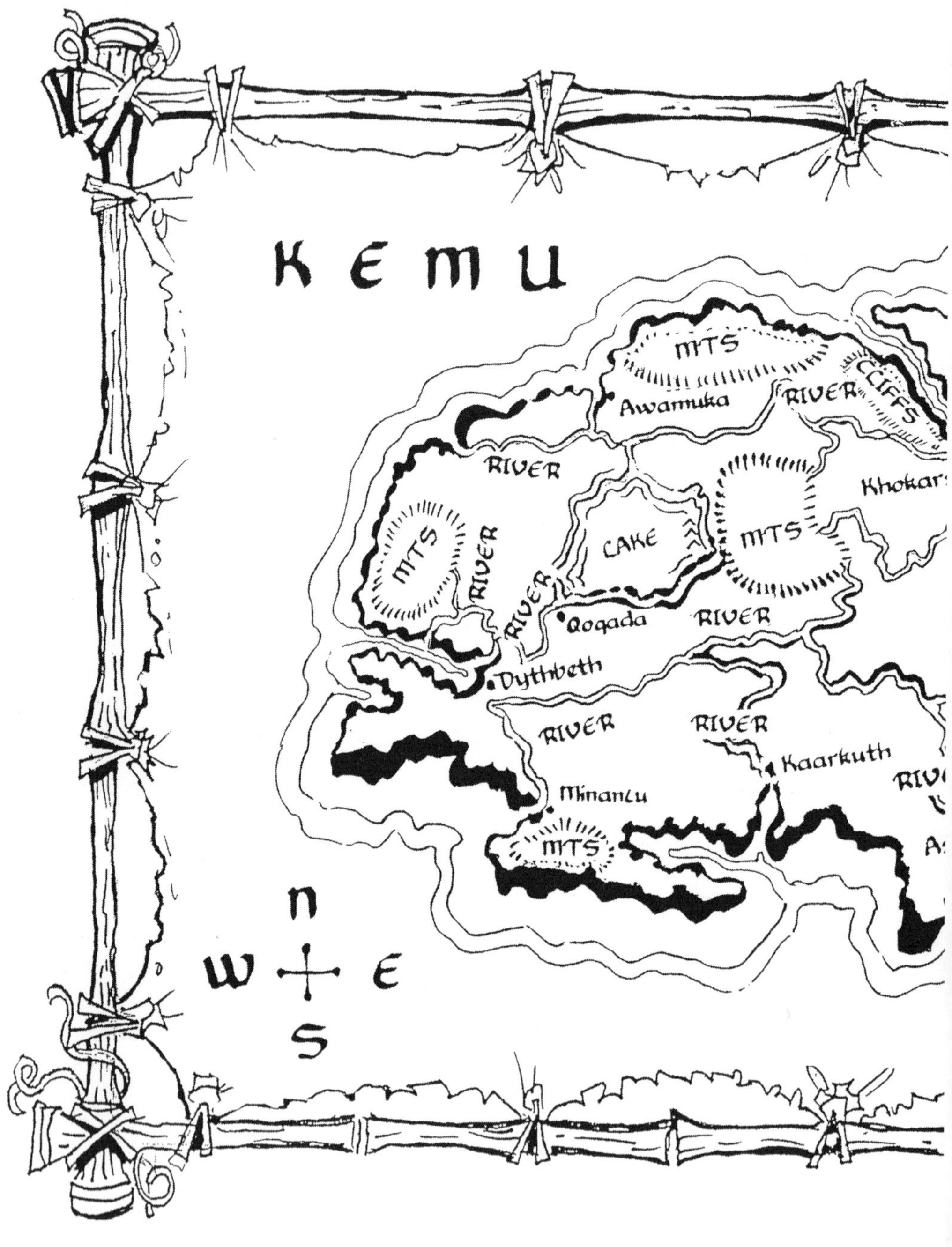

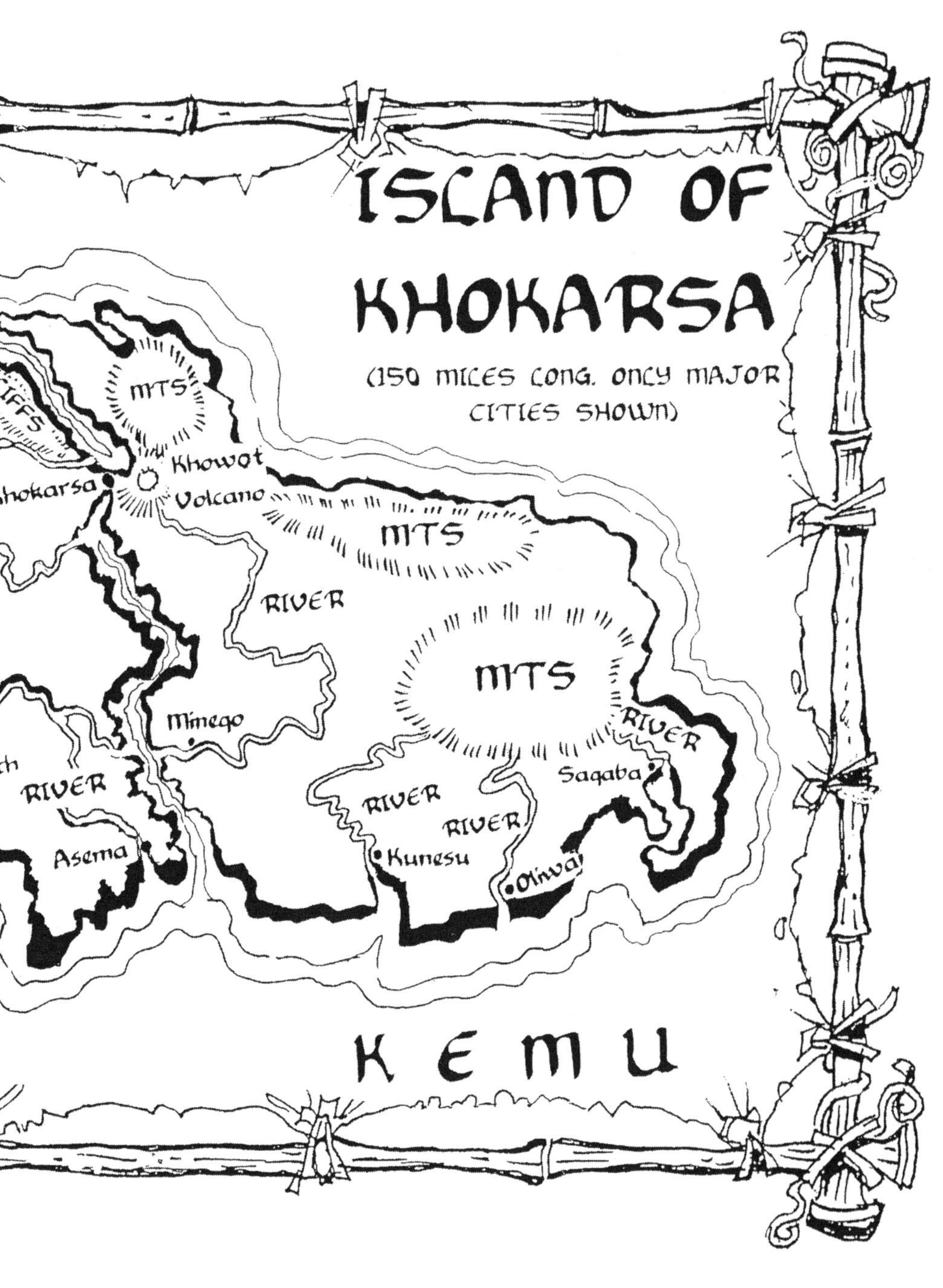
ISLAND OF KHOKARSA
(150 MILES LONG. ONLY MAJOR CITIES SHOWN)
CLIFFS
MTS
Khokarsa
Khowot Volcano
MTS
RIVER
MTS
Mineqo
RIVER
RIVER
Saqaba
RIVER
RIVER
Asema
Kunesu
Oinwa
KEMU

Map 3: Central Section of City of Khokarsa

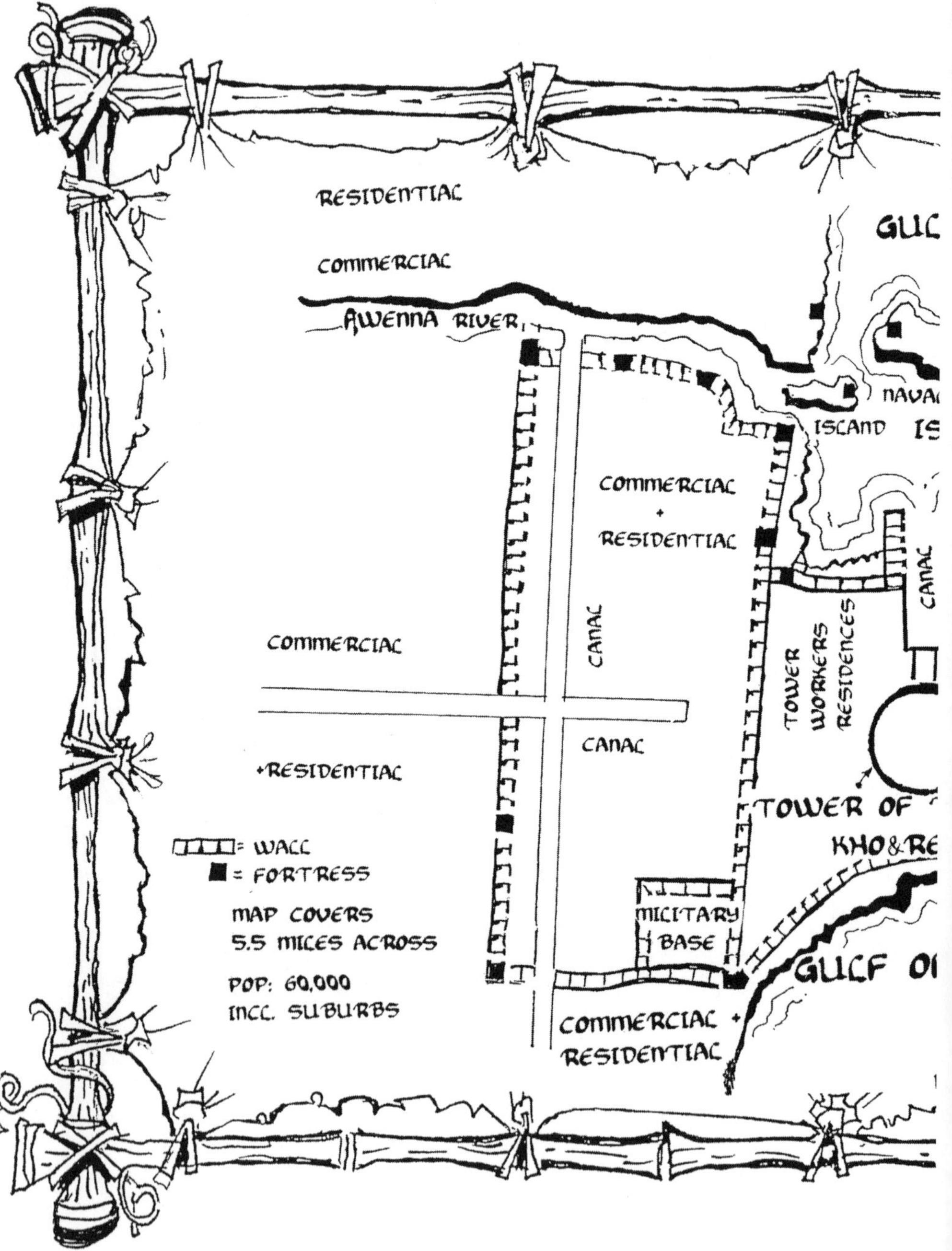

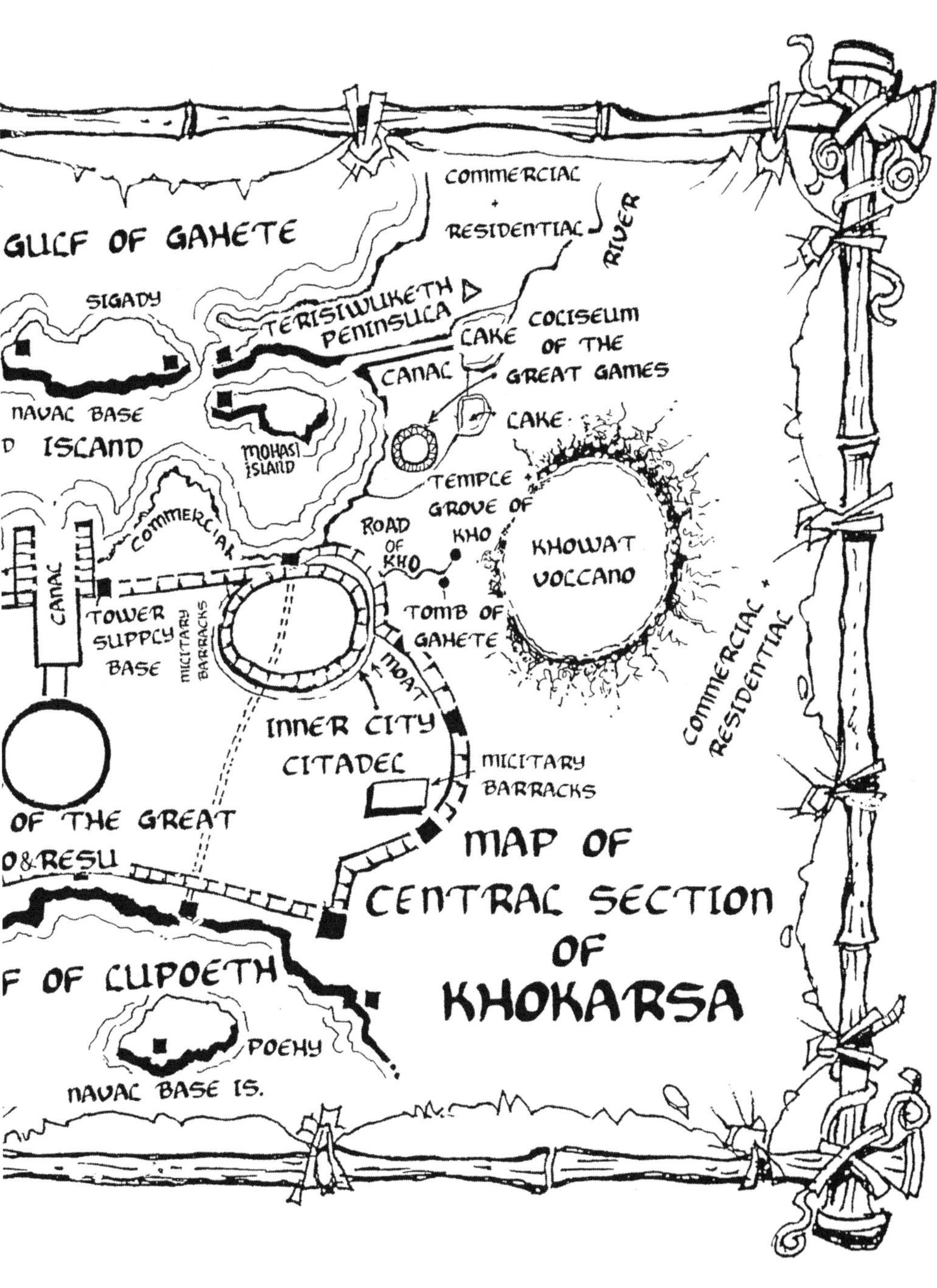
GULF OF GAHETE
COMMERCIAL + RESIDENTIAL
RIVER
SIGADY
TERISIWUKETH PENINSULA
LAKE
COLISEUM OF THE GREAT GAMES
CANAL
NAVAL BASE
ISLAND
MOHASI ISLAND
LAKE
TEMPLE + GROVE OF KHO
ROAD OF KHO
KHOWAT VOLCANO
COMMERCIAL
CANAL
TOWER
SUPPLY BASE
MILITARY BARRACKS
TOMB OF GAHETE
MOAT
COMMERCIAL + RESIDENTIAL
INNER CITY CITADEL
MILITARY BARRACKS
OF THE GREAT
O&RESU
MAP OF CENTRAL SECTION OF KHOKARSA
F OF LUPOETH
POEHY
NAVAL BASE IS.

Hadon of Ancient Opar

Philip José Farmer

Dedicated to HULBERT BURROUGHS in gratitude for his permission to write of Opar, that hidden city of "gold, and silver, ivory, and apes, and peacocks" and of the civilization which founded it.

ACKNOWLEDGMENTS

I am grateful to Frank Brueckel and John Harwood for writing the article which sparked the inspiration to create Hadon of Opar and the Khokarsan civilization. I thank Hulbert Burroughs for his kindness in permitting me to launch this series of novels. The basic debt, of course, is owed to Edgar Rice Burroughs, without whose tales of Opar and other lost cities this book would never have been written.

—P.J.F.

1

Opar, the city of massive granite and little jewels, quivered and blurred. Solid with great stone walls, soaring slender towers, gilt domes, and eight hundred and sixty-seven years of existence, it wavered, bent, and dissolved. And then it was gone as if it had never been.

Hadon swallowed, and he wiped away his tears.

His last vision of glorious Opar had been like a dream dying in a god's mind. He hoped that it was not an evil omen. And he hoped that his fellow contestants were similarly affected. If he was the only one to have wept, he might be mocked.

The longboat had traveled the curve of the river, and the jungle trees had moved between him and his native city. He still saw it in his mind, its towers like hands raised against the sky to keep it from falling. The little figures on the stone wharves—among them his father, mother, sister, and brother—had dwindled in his sight, though not in his mind. It was they who had brought the tears, not the city.

Would he ever see them again?

If he lost, he would not. If he won, years might pass before he took them in his arms. And his beloved Opar might never greet him again.

He had left it twice in his nineteen years. The first time, his parents had been with him. The second time, he had lived with his uncle, but Opar had not been far away. He glanced at the young men standing by him. They were not looking at him, and he was glad, because tears were running down their cheeks, too. Taro, his friend, grinned with embarrassment. Hewako, a dark lump of stone, scowled at him. He was not crying; stone did not cry. He was too strong for tears and wanted everybody to know it. But then, he had nothing or nobody to grieve for, Hadon thought. He felt sorry for him, though he knew the feeling would not last long. Hewako was such a surly, arrogant brute.

Hadon looked about him. The river at this point was about half a mile wide, and brown with the mud it was ferrying from the mountains to the sea. The river was walled with green vegetation except where mud banks shoved out like fingers testing for another advance of the trees. On them lay grinning sacred crocodiles who rose up on short legs as they became aware of the lead boat and slid oilily into the brown water. Parrots and monkeys screamed at the boats from the green. A blue-yellow-and-red kingfisher flashed from a branch, falling like a feathered star. It checked, swooped along the surface, and lifted with a small silvery fish in its talons.

The twelve oarsmen grunted in unison with the chunk of wooden blades in the river and the bronze stroke of the coxswain's gong. Short, squat, thick-necked, bar-browed, first cousins of men, second cousins of the great apes, they pulled and grunted while sweat matted their hairy bodies. Between the oarsmen, on the narrow deck, lay chests of gold ingots and diamonds, boxes of furs, carved figurines of goddesses, gods, monsters, and animals, of herbs from the rain forest, and piles of ivory tusks. Five soldiers in leather armor guarded these with spears.

Ahead of Hadon's boat were six boats carrying oarsmen and soldiers only. Behind his boat came twenty-three more, all heavily loaded with the precious products of Opar. Behind them were six craft forming the rear guard. Hadon watched them for a while and then began pacing back and forth, five steps at a time, along the crowded poop deck. Keeping in shape was vital. His life would depend upon it during the Great Games. Hewako and Taro and the three substitutes soon imitated him. Three in Indian file paced back and forth, and the others did setting-up exercises. Hadon watched with envy the flexing pythonlike muscles of Hewako. He was said to be the strongest man in all Khokarsa, except for Kwasin, of course. But Kwasin was exiled, wandering somewhere in the Western Lands with his huge brassbound oak club on his shoulders. Had he been a contestant, it was doubtful that anybody else would have entered.

Hadon wondered if he would have dared. Perhaps; perhaps not. But though he did not have the body of a gorilla, he did have long legs and speed and endurance and a swordsmanship that even his father applauded. And it was the final contest, that with the sword, which decided.

Still, his father had warned him.

"You're very good with the *tenu*, my son," he had said. "But you're not a professional, not yet, and a man with experience could chop you to pieces despite your long arms and your youth. Fortunately, you'll be up against green youths like yourself. It is ironic that there are many men who could easily best you with the sword, but they are too old to win at the other games. Still, if some old man of twenty-eight should decide to try for the prize, he just might squeak through, and then Kho help you!"

His father had felt the stump of his left arm, looked grim, and then had said, "You have never killed a man, Hadon, and so your true temperament is unknown. Sometimes, a lesser swordsman can defeat a better because he has the heart of a true killer. What will happen if you and Taro are the finalists? Taro is your best friend. Can you kill him?"

"I don't know," Hadon had said.

"Then you shouldn't be in the Games," his father had said. "And there's Hewako. Beware of him. He knows you are better with the *tenu* than he. He'll try to break your back before the final test."

"But the wrestling matches are not to the death," Hadon had said.

"Accidents happen," his father had said. "Hewako would have cracked your neck during the eliminations if the judge had not been watching. I warned her, and though I am a lowly sweeper of the temple floors, I was once a *numatenu*, and she listened to me."

Hadon had winced. It hurt him to hear his father speak of the old days, of when he had two arms that could wield a broadsword more expertly than anyone else in Opar. An outlaw sword, swung from behind, had severed his father's arm above the elbow during that struggle in the dark tunnels below Opar. The king had been killed in that murky fight, and a new king had ascended the throne. And the new king had hated Kumin, and instead of retiring him honorably on a pension, had discharged him. Many a *numatenu* would have committed suicide then. But Kumin had decided that he owed more to his family than to the somewhat nebulous code of the *numatenu*. He would not abandon them to poverty and the dubious charity of his wife's relatives. So he had become a floorsweeper, and this, though a lowly position, put him under the special protection of Kho Herself. The new king, Gamori, would have liked to expel Kumin and his family into the jungle, but his wife, the chief priestess, forbade that.

Kumin had sent Hadon to live with his brother, Phimeth, for several years. This was to give Hadon a chance to learn swordsmanship under the tutelage of the greatest wielder of the *tenu* in Opar, his uncle. It was in the dark caves where his uncle lived in exile that Hadon had met his cousin, Kwasin, son of Phimeth's and Kumin's sister, Wimake. Wimake had died from a snakebite some years before, and so Hadon had lived for four years without a mother or an aunt or any woman whatsoever. It had been a lonely time in many ways, though delightful in others. Except for Kwasin, who often had made Hadon miserable.

Just before the Flaming God, Resu, disappeared behind the trees, the longboats tied up at docks which had been built some hundred years before for the overnight stop. Half of the soldiers took their stations behind the stone walls enclosing all but the riverside of the docks. The other soldiers built cooking fires for themselves, the officers, and the contestants. The oarsmen made their fires in some corners of the walls. A fine boar and a great drake were sacrificed, and the best portions were tossed into a fire as offerings to Kho, to Resu, and to Tesemines, goddess of the night. The legs of the pig and the remnants of the duck were cast into the waters to placate the godling of the river.

The swift current carried the legs and the body away in the dusk. They traveled to the bend, where the shadows fell from the branches of trees. Suddenly the waters moved, and the legs and the fowl went under the surface.

One of the oarsmen murmured, "Kasukwa has taken them!"

Hadon's skin prickled coldly, though he felt that crocodiles, not the godling, had seized the sacrifice. He, with most of the others, quickly touched his forehead with the ends of his three longest fingers and then described with them a circle which swept out and over his loins and ended on his forehead. A few of the grayhairs among the officers and the oarsmen made the old sign of Kho, touching their forehead first with the tips of the three fingers, then the right breast, the genitals, the left breast, the forehead again, and ending up on the navel.

Soon the air was thick with smoke and the odor of cooking pig and duck. Most of the party belonged to the Ant Totem, but a few were members of the Pig Totem and hence forbidden to eat pork except on one day a year. They supped on duck, boiled eggs, and pieces of dried beef. Hadon ate sparingly of the pork, millet bread, goat cheese, the sweet and delicious *mowometh* red-berries, and raisins. He refused the sorghum beer, not because he did not like it but because it would put fat on him and reduce his wind.

Though the smoke fell over them in the still air, made them cough, and reddened their eyes, they did not complain. The smoke would help keep off the mosquitoes, the evil little children of Tesemines, now swarming from the forest. Hadon rubbed a stinking oil over his body and hoped that this and the smoke would enable him to get a good night's rest. When dawn came he would oil himself with another repellent for the flies that attacked as soon as the sun had warmed the air.

Hadon had just finished eating when Taro pulled at his arm and pointed downriver. The moon had not yet come up, but he could see a great dark body on the bank across the river. Undoubtedly, it was a leopard come to drink before hunting.

"Perhaps we should also have sacrificed to Khukhaqo," Taro said.

Hadon grinned and said, "If we sacrificed to every deity and spirit who might possibly harm us, we would not have room enough in the boats for all the animals we would need."

Then, seeing by the firelight Taro's offended expression, he smiled and slapped Taro's shoulder. "There is good sense in what you say. But I wouldn't dare suggest to the priestess that we offer to the leopard goddess. She wouldn't take it kindly if we stuck our noses into her business."

Taro was right. Late at night, Hadon was jerked from a troubled sleep by a scream. He leaped up and grabbed his broadsword and stared bewilderedly around. He saw a black-and-yellow body leaping over the wall, a screaming oarsman between its jaws. And then both were gone. It was useless and dangerous to pursue the leopard. The captain of the guards raised hell with the sentinels, but it was merely to relieve his own fear and anger.

Somehow, the leopard goddess had been offended, and so they made haste to placate her. Klyhy, the priestess, now sacrificed a pig to Khukhaqo. It would not bring the poor oarsman back, but it might prevent another leopard from attacking. And the blood of the pig poured into a bronze bowl surely would please the ghost of the oarsman and keep him from prowling the camp that night. Hadon hoped so, but he did not go back to sleep. Neither did the others, except for the oarsmen. The labors of the day ensured that almost nothing would keep them awake long.

At dawn the priestess of Kho and the priest of Resu stripped and took their ritual bath in the river. The soldiers looked out for crocodiles while the rest of the party bathed in order of seniority. They ate a breakfast of okra soup, dried beef, hard-boiled duck eggs, and the unleavened millet bread. Then they pushed out into the river again. Four days later, in midmorning, they heard the rumble of the cataract. A mile above it, they docked their boats, unloaded the cargo, and began traveling slowly along the road. This was paved with huge granite blocks. The vegetation along it was cut back at regular intervals by jungle rangers. It curved away from the falls and then terminated at the edge of the cliffs. Here the party followed a narrow, steep, and winding road cut into the face of the mountain. Soldiers preceded and trailed the caravan. The oarsmen huffed and puffed, carrying the boxes, chests, and tusks. The herdsmen moved behind them, calling out or prodding their squealing charges with pointed sticks. The ducks in the cages on the oarsmen's backs quacked. The sacred parrot on the priestess's shoulder screamed and chattered, and the sacred monkey on the priest's shoulder hurled shrill insults at invisible enemies in the jungle.

What with all the noise, Hadon thought, they could be heard miles away. If any Kawuru pirates were waiting in the dense forest below, they would have plenty of warning. Not that there was much likelihood of an ambush. An escort of soldiers from the seaside fort would be at the foot of the mountains. But the Kawuru had been known to slip past these.

Presently, the priest's swearing was added to the racket. The monkey had relieved himself on the man's shoulder. Nobody except the priestess dared laugh, though they couldn't help grinning. When the priest saw them grinning, he swore at them. A soldier brought a jug of water, and he cleaned off the mess with a linen cloth. After a while the priest was laughing too, but the monkey rode the rest of the way on an oarsman's shoulder.

At dusk they came into a cleared area near the bottom of the falls. Here fifty soldiers waited for them. The party bathed in the thunder and the coolness of the waters, sacrificed, and ate. At dawn they were up, and two hours later were loading the cargo into longboats. They had a three-day journey ahead of them. This would have been tense enough. But a fool of an oarsman increased their nervousness. He declared that on the last trip he had glimpsed the river godling.

"It was Kasukwa himself! I saw him just as Resu went to bed. He rose from the waters, a monstrous being four times as big as the biggest bull hippopotamus you ever saw. His skin was as thick and brown as a hippopotamus', though it was warty. The warts were black and as large as my head, and each of them had three eyes and a tiny mouth filled with teeth as sharp as a crocodile's. He had long arms like a man's, but where hands should be were the heads of river pigs, with red eyes that flamed. He stared at me for a moment, and my bowels still turn to okra soup when I think of his face. It was a hippopotamus' except that it was hairy, and he had only one great scummy-green eye in the center of his forehead. And his teeth were many, and like spearheads. And then, while I prayed to Kho and also to G'xsghaba'ghdi, the goddess of our forefathers, and thought I would faint, he sank slowly back into the river."

The other oarsmen grunted in affirmation, though they had not seen Kasukwa.

"We will sacrifice an especially fine boar to him tonight," Klyhy said. "Even if, as I think likely, your vision was inspired by beer."

"May Kho strike me dead, here and now, if I am lying!" the oarsman cried.

Those near him jumped back, some looking upward and others downward, since Kho can strike from the earth or the sky. Nothing happened, and everybody breathed relief. Hadon suggested to the captain that he should tell the oarsman to shut his mouth before the entire party was in a panic. The captain said that he resented youngsters giving him advice, even if they were to be heroes. Nevertheless, he spoke sharply to the oarsman.

Grim and horrible Kasukwa was not seen during the journey to the sea, though he disturbed the sleep of many, and the oarsmen turned pale every time a hippopotamus surfaced near their boats. Late in the evening of the third day, they rounded a bend. There, beyond the wide mouth of the river, was the sea, the Kemuwopar.

On the northern bank were docks and the great galleys and warehouses, totem halls, houses, and the stone fort. The coxswains stepped up the beat of the bronze gongs. The oarsmen, though weary, grinned, showing their thick blocklike teeth, and summoned strength in their massive and hairy arms for the final lap. For a while they would be safe from the Kawuru, the leopard goddess, and the river godling. And tonight there would be a feast in their totem hall, followed by a beer-sodden sleep.

But not for Hadon. Stuffing the belly with food and beer was not for a youth who must keep himself light and swift for the Great Games. However, Klyhy had promised to receive him tonight in the little temple of Kho by the fort. She was ten years older than he, and a beautiful woman, if you could overlook the beginnings of a beer paunch and the sagging of the large breasts, and Hadon could. Besides, it was a great honor to be accepted by a priestess. And if her sister priestesses stationed here liked his companions, they would not sleep much tonight either.

Hewako was not pleased by this. He had hoped Klyhy would take him in her dark bronze arms and that those big gray eyes would be on fire with love of him. When he had heard Klyhy say yes to Hadon, he had scowled and flexed his massive biceps. He did not dare say anything while Klyhy was in hearing. Hadon had grinned at him, but the thought of the long sea trip ahead was not pleasant. Though he had an easy nature, Hewako's jibes were rubbing it away.

2

Whether Hadon won or lost the Games, he would be a hero. If he lost, however, he would be a dead hero, buried in a mound of earth under a tall pointed marble monolith. Passersby would pray to him and pour mead or wine on the earth. Much good that would do him. And when he considered that he would be pitted against the strongest and the swiftest youths of the empire, he felt his confidence bending and shaking as a reed in the wind. He had a strong ego, otherwise he would not have become a contestant. But only an egomaniac would take it for granted that he could go through the other contestants as the farmer went through the millet with his scythe.

Nevertheless, the ceiling-high bronze mirror this morning showed him a man who looked like a hero. Even if he said so himself. At six feet two inches, he was the tallest man in Opar. This was due to his Klemsaasa ancestors and, no doubt, to the gods who had been his forefathers—although, now that he thought of it, there were few men of the upper classes in Opar, or in the empire itself, who could not claim from one to a score of gods as ancestors. All his foremothers had, as was their holy duty, resided in a house of god for a month as a temple prostitute. Though theoretically they must accept any male worshiper, in practice they had ensured that only a king, a hero, a great merchant or soldier, or a *numatenu* was admitted to their cubicle. The children of these unions, if any, were supposedly fathered by the particular god of the temple. Hadon could recite the names of twelve gods, not to mention two score of godlings, who had been many times his ancestors. Theoretically, that is. Few educated people believed that conception was due to the intervention of divine Kho Herself. It was admitted by all but the most die-hard conservatives that the human male himself was responsible for pregnancy. But this made, in theory, no difference. The male's body was taken over by the god of the temple during the holy coupling, and the child was the god's, not that of the man. The man was a mere vessel.

Hadon was not a temple child. His oldest brother, his mother's first child, had been fathered by the great Resu himself. But Resu had not favored him. He had died at three of a fever, the first of seven brothers and sisters to go as children to the arms of Sisisken, grim ruler of the shadow world.

Hadon's curly red-bronze hair indicated that the Flaming God was his grandfather. His large hazel eyes showed that he was of Klemsaasa stock. At least, they were supposed to do so, though he had observed that many of the old Khoklem stock had hazel or even blue and gray, eyes. His features, which he immodestly admitted were exceptionally handsome, were those of the people who had come down from the Saasares mountains eight hundred and sixty-four years ago and seized the city of Khokarsa. His forehead was high and narrow, though swelling at the corners. His ears were small and close to his head and slightly pointed at the tips. A prominent supraorbital ridge was mounted by thick eyebrows which almost joined. His nose, though straight, was not as long as most of those supposed to be descended from the Klemsaasa. Just as well, since many also had beaked noses. And his nostrils were more flaring than the Klemsaasa's. No doubt this was due to his Khoklem ancestry. But then, no one was pure-blooded, however much the Klemsaasa denied being mixed with the shorter, darker, heavier-bodied, snub-nosed, straight-haired aborigines.

To complete the roster of pleasing features, he had a short upper lip, full but not thick lips, and a chin strong and deeply clefted.

His body was, he told himself in his more critical moments, too lean. Still, his shoulders were very broad and heavy. His was the physique of the long-distance runner, though he had never been beaten in the dashes. His legs were extraordinarily long, and so were his arms. The former gave him his speed, and the latter were a great advantage in swordsmanship. Indeed, they were so long that he had often been accused of having a great-ape grandfather.

Hadon thought of the many fights he had had as a child because of this insult and the many more because his playmates had jeered at his father's missing arm and lowly status. But most of the jeerers admired and envied him now. Only Hewako among them had succeeded in becoming a contestant from Opar. Hewako still made remarks about long-armed men with monkey ancestors and about floors that needed sweeping. But he always looked away from Hadon when he said this, and he never mentioned names. So Hadon had determined to ignore him until they got to the Games. Then he would get his revenge. Of course, realistically, Hewako might be the one to get revenge. But Hadon preferred not to think about that possibility.

He combed and brushed his shoulder-length hair and shaved with one of the recently introduced iron razors. An hour later, wearing only a loincloth and a rosary of electrum beads, he was jogging along the dirt road that paralleled the shoreline for many miles. Behind him ran Taro and the three substitutes. They passed many farms where millet and sorghum were grown and many pigs and goats were raised. The farmers and their wives, clad only in conical straw hats and animal-skin loincloths, straightened from their labors to stare at them. Seeing the red-dyed hawk feather tied to the hair above the right ear of each, the mark of a Great Gamester, the farmers bowed.

Hadon felt good again. His legs were getting the stretching they needed, and his wind was not as weak as he had thought it would be after the long journey. He wasn't as strong as be would have liked to be, but Klyhy had not let him sleep until an hour before dawn. Not that he minded.

When the four, sweating and blowing, returned to the docks, they saw Hewako working out with weights. He scowled at them, and he did not offer to join them in throwing javelins or slinging stones. Instead, he ran off to do his roadwork alone. Hadon shouted after him, "The farmers' daughters had better look out!" but Hewako ignored him. Hadon was referring to Hewako's rejection by a priestess. When he had bruised her with a too passionate hand, she had kicked him out—literally. Perhaps he had then gone to the totem hall of the oarsmen, the Gokako. They practiced group marriage and were free with their wives, who were not above taking money for the use of their bodies. But it would have been socially demeaning for Hewako to join them. And if some drunken Gokako happened to be in a bad mood, it could be dangerous. Once Hewako entered the hall, he would leave behind him any protection of the law. Should a Gokako stick a knife in him, that was the end of the matter. Besides which, a man would have to be hard up to bed one of those short, squat, and ugly women.

The others laughed at Hadon's remark and resumed their exercises. They ended with a wooden-sword fight while wearing helmets, cuirasses, gloves, and armguards of leather. Hadon beat them all, though he did get a nasty whack across his forearm from Taro. Taro was almost as tall as Hadon, and more muscular. And he was, Hadon reflected, a splendid acrobat and a great javelineer, one who consistently beat him when throwing at a target. He could still be in the Games while Hadon was lying on a granite slab.

The thought that they might have to try to kill each other saddened him. They were lifelong friends, but they would soon be trying to shed each other's blood. All for the glory of being the husband of the queen of Khokarsa.

Three more days passed. The cargoes were loaded on the morning of the second day, but the captain of the merchant vessels wished to wait until the next day. And that day had dawned, a lucky day, the first sea day of the month of Piqabes, goddess of the sea, in the Year of the Green Parrot. There was no more propitious day for starting a sea voyage unless it was in the Year of the Fish-Eagle. But that would not occur for seven more years.

The day was bright and cloudless. The wind was blowing from the southwest, and the waves were not high. The sacrifices had been made, a heron flew across the ships from the right (a very good omen), and everybody filed aboard in a good mood. A drunken sailor fell off a gangplank and had to be fished out, but the fleet's priestess, Simari, said that that wasn't a bad omen.

The army band on shore played a song in honor of Piqabes; their drums, flutes, harps, xylophones, marimbas, and gongs boomed, shrilled, twanged, tinkled, rattled, and clanged in a similitude of rhythm and melody. Simari, the last aboard, danced around and around, whirling a booming bullroarer at the end of a cord. A tall fat woman, she wore a fish-head mask and, over her pubes, the stuffed tail of a fish. On one large breast was painted a giant sea turtle and on the other a sea otter;

a crocodile and a hippo were painted above and below her navel, which was circled with blue. Hadon and Taro waved at Klyhy and Taro's lover, the beautiful Rigo. The gangplanks were swung off, and the oarsmen dipped their blades in the shallow water and pulled. Simari, panting behind her mask, went to the prow of the ship, just above the huge bronze ram, and chanted while she poured out a libation of the best Saasares wine into the sea. The captain, Bhaseko, invited the priestess, the first mate, and the future heroes to the poop deck for a cup of wine. Hadon could not refuse this, but he drank no more than one cup. His fellows did not feel so restrained.

Hadon felt hot in his bronze helmet and cuirass, but presently the wind became stronger and cooled him. The captain began bellowing orders. The great purple sail of the only mast, placed near the bow, was hoisted. Simari went into her cabin, set forward of the captain's on the poop deck, to change and to wash off the paint. The others went down to the main deck and walked to the foredeck, where their quarters were in a cabin. Its roof was only two feet above the deck; they had to go down into a small room with bunks. The portholes were open except in time of storm or cold, and then they were closed with heavy wooden shutters.

Hadon stored his armor and his *numatenu* sword and a small chest of belongings under his bunk. Below him rose the grunting and squealing of pigs and the bleating of goats. The odor that rose from the pens was something that would have to be endured for a long time.

He went back out on deck with Taro, whose wine-flushed face was almost as red as his hair. By now the fleet was in formation, the merchant ships, the bireme, and two uniremes forming a V in the center. Ahead were two uniremes, on each side was a bireme, and behind were two uniremes. The fish-eagle-head standard of the Khokarsan navy fluttered from the mast tops of each of their escort. The gong of the coxswain clanged, the oars chunked into the sea and pulled out dripping, the oarsmen grunted and sweated and stank of sweat and millet beer, the officers shouted orders, the animals squealed and bleated, the pet fish-eagle of the priestess screamed down from the mainmast, the green waters rolled into the muddy beaches a mile off, and they were well on their way.

Their ship, the *Semsin*, was a long, narrow vessel with two tiers of oarsmen. The main deck ran from the poop deck to the foredeck, both of which were six feet above the main deck. Along both sides of the main deck were open portions. The heads of the oarsmen were just level with the main deck. Each tier had twelve oars on a side, two men at an oar. The lower tier was so close to the upper that the top oarsmen could touch the heads of the lower with their feet if they wished to. Below the lower tier was the deck where the cargo, the supplies, and the animals were kept. Also on this deck was the sick bay and a room where the wounded were treated during a battle.

The galley carried two catapults, one on each of the two highest decks.

The *Semsin* was steered by a rudder, which had recently been invented; two sturdy sailors manned the rudder handle.

The sailors, oarsmen, and marines slept on the deck or in the hold.

The quarters for the ship's officer were forward of the cabin that the contestants shared. The galley was forward of the priestess's cabin on the poop deck. Though it had a breezeway, smoke from the stone fireplace often filled the priestess's and captain's cabins unless the wind happened to be favorable.

Hadon had made one trip before, when his parents had gone to Khokarsa to live for two years, and he wasn't looking forward to this trip.

Five days later, they passed rugged and sheer cliffs. Halfway up one was a huge and dark hole, the entrance to the caves in which Hadon and his cousin Kwasin had lived with their uncle, Phimeth. Hadon purchased and sacrificed a small boar and prayed that the ghost of his uncle would find the blood pleasing.

The days and nights passed as best they could under the conditions. Bored and wishing to get more exercise, Hadon asked the captain if he could help row. The captain replied that this would be socially degrading. Hadon said that his companions would share the oar with him. He wouldn't be working alongside a common fellow. Besides, this was for exercise, not pay, which took it out of the category of manual labor.

The others were not eager for the task, but Hadon explained that if they did not row, they might be in a weakened condition when they arrived at their destination. After the first half-hour at the oar, Hadon wished that he had never thought of the idea. His palms were rubbed raw and bloody, and he was sure that his back was going to snap. On the other hand, he now knew that he was not in such excellent condition as he had thought. He gritted his teeth and rowed, staring at the broad, hairy, sweating back and bull neck of Hewako, working at the oar ahead of him. Hewako was the most powerful man Hadon had ever seen, but evidently he was hurting. Hewako swore for fifteen minutes, then quit to preserve his lungs. Hadon grinned through his pain and weariness and vowed that he would not give up before Hewako. He did, but only because his nerveless hands could no longer grasp the oars. Hewako fell over about three minutes later.

The oarsmen, all rude and impolite fellows, laughed at them. They asked if they were the type of heroes being sent to the Games nowadays. Now, in the old times... Too exhausted even to feel shame, Hadon staggered off to his bunk. For the first time, the uproar of the beasts below did not keep him awake.

He was back at the oar next day, though he had never hated to do anything so much. By the time they sighted the red city of Sakawuru on top of the black cliffs, he was able to row two hours at a stretch, three times a day. His hands were building up a heavy callus, and his chest and arms seemed to have added an inch. He worried that this type of labor might interfere with his swordsmanship, but he had to have the exercise. Besides, if he quit he would be mocked by the rowers.

At the red-granite city of Sakawuru, the ships resupplied, and the crew was given four days' liberty. Hadon spent his time either touring or running along the dirt roads outside the city. He felt tempted to drink the cool beer available in the hall of the Ant Totem, but he decided not to. Hewako apparently fell prey to his great thirst. Hadon saw him once staggering out of the hall of the Leopard Totem.

The fleet set out again. The lookouts in the crow's nests were still alert for pirates, though the chances for encountering them were less than in the waters just crossed. They stopped at the city of Wentisuh for one day to disembark two sick sailors and hire replacements. Hadon had never been in Wentisuh, so he and Taro wandered its narrow, crooked streets, listening to the exotic tongue of the farmers in the markets and the common citizen. Hadon was a superb linguist, and in Opar he had taken the trouble to gain some fluency in Siwudawa from the family of a Wentisuh merchant. These people were a strange one, noisy and volatile among themselves, grim and silent when strangers were among them. Their skin was a brownish-yellow. Their hair was coarse and straight and black. Their noses were long, thin, and beaked, and many had a slight fold of skin in the inner corners of their eyes. Though they worshiped Kho and Resu, they had many aboriginal deities, the most prominent being Siwudawa, a parrot-headed androgyne.

The fleet left Wentisuh and traveled in a straight line for the city of Kethna. The wind changed direction then, and the sails were hauled down. Clouds, the first of the rainy season, covered the face of Resu; the seas became choppy; the rowers had to work twice as hard to maintain the same speed; the shifts were changed to an hour apiece. Then the rains struck. The storm, lasting one day and night, was hell for Hadon. He got seasick and spent most of his time on the railing giving to the sea the pork that he had eaten that morning. Hewako whooped with laughter at the sight, but in half an hour he was hanging on the railing by Hadon's side.

Hadon had recovered by the time Kethna appeared, but he swore that he would never again consider the navy as a career. Kethna was a city of high white-stoned walls and black towers and domes, perched on a cliff five hundred feet above its port. Kethna was fifty miles from the Strait of Keth, where it kept a large fleet. Its rulers paid tribute to Khokarsa, but it ran local maritime affairs with a high hand. Every merchant ship that passed through the strait had to pay a heavy tax for the privilege. Nor did Kethna officials bother to hide their arrogance. They treated the Khokarsan fleet as if it came from a conquered province.

"If our king would quit occupying himself with the building of that great tower," the captain said, "and pay more attention to business, he'd teach the Kethnans a bloody lesson. They need taking down in the worst way. It doesn't make much sense for Kethna to send tribute to Minruth with one hand and take away from him with the other. Why should we pay a tax to these hyenas?"

Why indeed? Hadon thought. But he had more important matters to consider. Hewako's veiled taunts and his sneaky tricks were about to set Hadon afire. He had even thought about complaining to the priestess so she would impose a ban of silence between him and Hewako. He felt, however, that this would be unmanly, even if it was the rational way out. He couldn't challenge Hewako to a duel, because fighting between contestants for the Great Games was forbidden. This was a wise rule, since so many contestants in the old days had picked fights in order to eliminate competitors before the Games started. Even if this rule had not existed, the challenged had the right to pick the weapons, and Hewako was not fool enough to choose swords. He would want a barehanded battle, and Hadon knew that he would lose that. Of course, he might be wrestling with Hewako at the Games, but that event was for points only.

Then, the night before they were due to arrive at the strait, Hadon awoke to find himself smeared with pig dung. He sat quietly in his fury, thought, and then went outside to dip a bucket into the sea and wash himself off. On returning, he looked at Hewako. The hippopotamuslike fellow seemed to be sleeping. He certainly was snoring, but Hadon believed that he was just pretending, that he was laughing inside himself. He forced himself to lie down, and after a while he fell asleep.

He was, however, up and about before any of his bunkmates. He went into the galley, found that the cooks were down in the hold, and ate a quick breakfast of bread, hardboiled duck eggs, and cold okra soup. Then, taking a bucket, he disappeared into the hold. He emerged while the drums for awakening the morning shift were beating. He took all of his cabinmates aside except Hewako and spoke quietly but fiercely to them. They sniggered and promised silence and cooperation. Two of them agreed to delay Hewako a minute or so by "accidentally" spilling hot soup on him. None of them liked the surly, arrogant man. Besides, they thought it only fair that Hadon pay Hewako back in kind.

Hewako arrived late at the oars, cursing, his legs red with a slight burn, and swearing vengeance on the soup-spillers when they got to the Games. He found his bunkmates at their positions and the man he was to relieve angry because of the delay. He grabbed the oar handle, then swore and sputtered, but the gong of the coxswain sounded the first stroke, and he could do nothing but stay at his post.

Taro was Hewako's oarmate, and Taro had complained that though the joke would be on Hewako, they would all suffer.

"The air for a mile around is going to be bad for everybody. Hewako won't be the only one gagging."

"Yes, but only Hewako will have his hands in it," Hadon had said.

Hewako kept his indignation and fury down to a mild roar, but after two minutes he decided that he had had enough. He bellowed out for a replacement. The gong master yelled back at him to keep quiet, that he had had his chance at sick call. Hewako shouted back an insult. The gong master screamed that if there was another word from him, he'd have him up before the captain for a lashing.

Since the youths had been told that they would have to accept oarsmen's discipline when on duty, Hewako became silent. At least, he said nothing to the gong master, but he threatened Hadon under his breath. Then he pleaded with Taro to trade places. Taro said he'd sooner drown. After a while Hewako had no breath for anything but his labor.

All might have gone as planned if the first mate had not walked by Hewako. He stopped, wrinkled his nose, and said, "Whew? What's that?"

Nobody answered. He sniffed around until he located the source of offense. He stood for a moment, leaning over and looking down at Hewako, before he roared for the gong master. The master turned over his gong to his subordinate and hurried down the deck. When he ascertained what the trouble was, he requested that the captain be summoned. The captain passed from irritation because his breakfast was interrupted to anger when he saw—and smelled—the cause of commotion. By then Hadon had quit grinning. He hadn't thought that anybody but he and Hewako would be involved, except for the breathers in the immediate area, of course.

The captain sputtered and then shouted, "You future heroes can horse around among yourselves all you want to, as long as it doesn't interfere with the operation of my ship! But this does it! A rower can't be efficient if he has to handle a slippery oar, nor can those around him be efficient if they are sickened! You all report to me at the end of the shift! Gong master, douse this man with water until the dung's all gone! And you, Hewako, make sure all traces are gone before you report!"

The result was that Hadon had to confess. The captain had promised to have every one of the youths lashed if the culprit did not declare himself. Hadon, at high noon, had his hands tied above him to the mast. A burly oarsman struck Hadon's back five times with a hippopotamus-hide whip. Hadon had thought that the humiliation would be worse than the pain. But it wasn't. The whip cut to the muscle, and blood ran down between his legs. He clamped his teeth, refusing to cry out, and he slept on his face for many nights thereafter.

It was some, though not much, consolation when Hewako got three lashes. The captain did not ask Hadon why he had played the trick, since Hadon would have had to refuse to answer and he would have received more lashes. He investigated and found a watchman who had seen Hewako in the pig sty and had also seen Hadon washing himself off. Hewako confessed and shortly afterward had a bloody back. Later, in the privacy of the cabin, Hewako said that he was going to get the captain someday. Hadon replied that he didn't exactly love the captain, but he did respect him. If he had failed to do his duty because the culprit might someday be in a position to execute him, he had no business being the captain.

"I'll get you during the Games," Hewako said.

"You'll only be trying to do what everybody else will," Hadon said. "But, in the meantime, why don't we lay off each other? If we keep this up, we'll wear each other ragged. And a ragged man has no chance in the Games."

Hewako did not reply. However, thereafter he spoke to Hadon only in the line of duty. Though their backs were on fire, they returned the next day to the oars. The priestess rubbed a soothing ointment on the wounds, though it was not soothing enough. She advised them to wash their backs every two hours with water and soap and watch carefully for infection. Fortunately, there weren't any flies at sea, but the cockroaches would nibble at the wounds at night unless they also smeared on a repellent.

"And stay out of the pig sty," she said, and slapped them playfully on the back. Caught by surprise, they screamed, and the priestess laughed uproariously.

"Boys will be boys," she said, "but you're men now. By Kho, if I weren't married to the captain, I'd see just how manly you two are!"

Hadon was glad of that. He didn't care for fifty-year-old fat women, and he would not have dared refuse her invitation.

3

The high rugged cliffs continued to rise from the sea. The galleys kept away from them by two miles, since there were reefs close to them. Many a ship had been driven against them by storms and all hands perished without a trace. Then the strait itself appeared, a narrow break in the cliffs, and the fleet put into a port that had been built at great expense of money and life. Two stone breakwaters curved out from cliffs, against which a floating great raft was moored, and on this raft were the headquarters of the Kethnan strait fleet. The Khokarsan fleet was obliged to put in here and to submit to another search. The captains of the merchant and naval vessels fumed, but they could do nothing.

"Fifteen years ago, Piqabes destroyed this place with a great storm," the captain said. "Would that she'd do it again! Though not while we're here!"

At dawn the next day the fleet put out, its path curving outward so that it could enter the strait head-on. The strait was a gloomy chasm created by some enormous riving of the mountains in the distance past, perhaps at the creation of the world by Kho. It was the only water connection between the two seas, the northern Kemu and the southern Kemuwopar. It was unknown to the civilized world until the hero Keth led two galleys through its awesome darkness, and they burst out into a great bright sea. That was one thousand and ninety-nine years ago. A few other explorers had followed, but there was no active colonization until two hundred and eighty-six years later, when Kethna founded the city named after him. Fourteen years later, the priestess-heroine Lupoeth discovered diamond-bearing clay and gold at the site of Opar, and the southern sea became worthwhile considering by the rulers of Khokarsa.

So narrow was the strait that at a distance of a mile its entrance looked merely like a darker vein of stone in a dark cliff. Then, as the first of the naval vessels, a bireme, plunged into it, it seemed to gape like the foaming mouth of a stone monster. Hadon's vessel was the third to enter. One moment they were tossing on the choppy waters in the bright sun, and the next they had been swallowed up. The waters rushed through, carrying them between sheer walls so high that the sky was only a thin ribbon. The dusk rapidly settled about them, so thick as to seem palpable. There was no turning back now, because there just was no room to maneuver.

They must either go ahead or go down under the waters; there was no other choice. A signalman stood on the prow, above the bronze ram, and called back to the first mate, who relayed instructions to the gong master. Torches guttered on the prow and along the side of the vessel; the oars lifted and dipped, their blades only a few feet from the black hard walls. The chunk of oars, the dripping of water as they lifted, the voice of the signalman and the mate, and the clang of the gong were the only sounds. The orders were for everybody else to be silent, but that was not necessary. Nobody felt like talking, and even those who had made the passage many times felt what Keth and his men must have felt the first time they dared it. Truly, it seemed to be a gateway to a world of the dead, of the queendom where dread Sisisken ruled over her phantoms, pale citizens of the greatest empire of all. No wonder that Keth had had to put down a mutiny before he could lead his men through this twilit passage.

The strait did not go as a measuring stick, but curved back and forth. Several times the walls moved in closer, and it was necessary to ship the oars while one side of the vessel touched stone. Though the contact was not hard, it would have crushed the fragile hull if bumpers of mahogany had not been put up before the vessel entered the strait.

Hadon and his companions stood before the fore deckhouse and watched. They had been relieved of their duties during the traverse, since the captain wanted only professionals at the oars. Hadon and Hewako were happy about this, because their lash wounds were far from healed. But their happiness was tempered with apprehension. They kept looking upward and muttering prayers. There were said to be ogres who lived in caves along the cliffs, and if they heard a ship coming, they would stretch down their long arms and snatch up a mariner and eat him. And sometimes the wild Klemqaba would hurl large rocks at the vessels.

Presently clouds shut off the blue line far above, and they seemed to be crawling through the night. The captain ordered more torches lit, but these were soon sputtering in a heavy rain. The wind, which had been only a soft fingertip on their necks, suddenly became a heavy cold hand. The contestants went into the deckhouse and put on caps and ponchos of animal skin and then came back out on the deck. They did not want to be trapped in the house if the vessel should be pushed hard against a cliff. Not that much could be done if the ship did sink. They would be crushed between hull and cliff if the following vessel tried to pull them out of the water. Still, it was better to die in the open.

The strait twisted for fifty miles, and it took two days and nights to get through. The rain stopped, the clouds moved off, in the middle of the noon of the second day the walls suddenly fell away, and they moved onto a broad sea in golden light. Simari sacrificed the finest of the boars and poured the best of wine into the blue waters, and the rowers chanted a thanksgiving song. Everybody smiled, and those not working capered. Hadon felt so good that he drank two cups of wine. The steward, a dour little man, noted the cups down in his records. The city of Opar was paying for the expenses of Hadon's trip, since he was too poor to bear the cost himself.

The captain consulted the lodestone compass card to check that the lead naval vessel was on the proper bearing, and the bireme turned north by north-northwest toward the island of Khokarsa. The last lap, the longest, lay ahead of them.

Days and nights passed. The broad blue-green Kemu was the only thing they saw except for birds and an occasional ship.

Several days out of Khokarsa, they sighted fishing fleets. These consisted of small ten-man sailing ships and a mother ship which prepared the fish and salted them. Clouds of birds, fish-eagles, sea vultures, and white birds with hooked beaks, the *datoekem*, swirled around the boats.

And then came the day when a long dark line lifted on the horizon. Sea-girt, cliff-girt Khokarsa was rising to meet them.

The fleet rowed into the broad bay of Asema, passed its red-and-black walls and white towers and domes on their port, and by nightfall were in the long arm of the sea, the Gulf of Lupoeth, that cuts the island almost in half. The traffic became thick with naval vessels putting out for years-long patrols; merchant vessels, some of them gigantic triremes; fishing-boats; and the trade boats carrying cargo between the cities of Khokarsa or river boats ferrying the products of the inland plain cities to the coastal cities, where they would be transferred to the seagoing merchant vessels.

It took three days until the sea arm began to narrow, but before that they saw the peak of the great volcano, Khowot, the Voice of Kho, which lies just east of the capital city. Then they saw the top of the Great Tower of Kho and Resu, two-thirds completed, centuries in the building, its construction often abandoned during times of tribulation.

The captain had by then run up the great linen flag bearing the red ant, the sign that this ship carried contestants from the treasure city of Opar. The flag ship of the fleet saluted the merchant ships, and the naval vessels veered toward the port on the naval-base island of Poehy. The merchants continued, bearing east of Poehy and proceeding slowly through the thick traffic. Presently they were docked, while an army band played, and the contestants filed off the gangplank to be greeted by the officials who would take charge of them.

Hadon was very excited, though he hoped that it was not noticeable. He was dressed in his finest hippo-hide sandals, a kilt of leopard skin, a bronze cuirass bearing a relief of the great red ant, his bronze helmet with its plume of hawk feathers, and a broad leather belt supporting a bronze scabbard in which was the long, square-ended, slightly curving broadsword, the *tenu*. There seemed to be thousands waiting along the docks, and in the narrow streets beyond, more thousands hoping to catch a glimpse of the Great Gamesters. They waved and shouted and cheered, except for some rowdy drunks who booed. Doubtless, these were partisans of contestants from other cities.

Things went swiftly after that. The officials took over the youths from the priestess Simari, and then, the clangorous band leading, they were marched through the city. Hadon had hoped that they would be presented to the king and his daughter. No such thing. They passed near the high black granite walls of the Inner City, but after a while it was evident that they were to go straight to their quarters near the coliseum of the Great Games. Their progress was slow because of the crowds, which threw petals on them and tried to touch them. Their route led through the commercial and residential area of the east, lined by two- to four-story-high buildings of adobe brick with a thick covering of white plaster. Many were tenement buildings. Though the city of Khokarsa was the richest in the world, it also held the most poor people. Evidently many of them neglected their daily ritual bath, because the stench from them in the hot narrow streets was strong. Added to that was the odor of rotting garbage on the pavements and barrels of excrement waiting to be shipped out to the rural areas for fertilizer.

After a mile, the street began climbing, and suddenly they were going by the residences of the well-to-do and the wealthy.

These were large two-story buildings set behind high walls and guarded even in daytime by men with spears and swords. Here the crowd thinned out, consisting mostly of wives of the wealthy and their sons and daughters and the servants and slaves. Hadon saw one beautiful girl who made his pulse beat faster. She wore only a kilt, but it was of the finest linen, embroidered with red and blue flower patterns, and a necklace of diamonds fell between her breasts. A large scarlet flower adorned her long blond hair. If there were more girls like her, he thought, he might enjoy his free time. If he had any. He had no idea what restrictions he faced during the training period.

The street kept winding up and up, and soon they were so high that he could look down on the Inner City. He could see the moated and walled citadel in the northeast corner, the rocky hill on top of which were the palaces, the temples, and the main government buildings. Beyond was the great tower, a ziggurat now five hundred feet tall, its base covering half a mile. Dust hung around it, dust stirred up by thousands of men and oxen laboring there.

The street began to descend again, and they were crossing the Road of Kho, the wide stone-block-paved highway that meandered from the wall of the Inner City up the steep side of the volcano. Above them, glittering white, was the tomb of the hero Gahete, the first man to land on this island, almost eighteen hundred years ago. Up beyond it was the plateau on which was the great temple of Kho and the sacred oak grove. But he could not see them.

They passed through another wealthy residential area, crossed a bridge over a canal, and then, coming onto a broad field, saw the coliseum. Hadon's heart beat even faster than when he had seen the beautiful blond girl. Inside the high circular granite walls his fate waited for him. But he would not see its inside today. He was marched into the barracks reserved for the youths and assigned a bed and a closet. He was glad to remove the hot bronze armor and to take a shower.

4

A month passed before the contestants were received by the king and his daughter, the high priestess. In the meantime, the youths spent the daylight hours training and the evenings talking or shooting dice. Everyone trained by himself; there were no practice matches among them; but they carefully watched each other, making evaluations. Hadon had been mildly shocked to discover that there were three youths taller than he, two of whom were much more thickly muscled. The third, Wiqa of Qaarquth, was the man who might beat him in the 440-yard dash and the two-mile run. He wouldn't know until the day the races came, of course. But Wiqa was fast, very fast. He also seemed to be a swift swimmer, though Taro thought that he could beat him. Hadon didn't believe this, but he did not say so. Taro, who had always been so jolly in Opar and on the voyage, had become glum. It was evident that he regretted now having entered, and it was too late to back out. There was no law forbidding him, but he would be thought a coward if he did, and he could never return to the city of Opar.

Hadon had his own moments of doubt and gloom. It was one thing to be the tallest and the swiftest in Opar, but here he was, a rube actually, up against the pick of the mighty empire. He could not quit, though he could manage to disqualify himself during the field and track events. If a man did not pick up enough points from these, before the dangerous events, he would be eliminated. And doubtless others before him, losing heart, had done just that. He hoped that Taro would do this. He could not. When he was in a contest, he had to do everything he could to win. He wouldn't be able to live with himself if he deliberately lost. And suicide, unless committed under honorable circumstances, assured one the most miserable of existences in the empire of dread Sisisken. Whereas if he died fighting bravely during the Games, he would be buried as a hero, and his pylon would rise along the Road of Kho.

He kept his doubts to himself. When he wrote long letters to his family in Opar, he tried to convey the idea that he was sure of becoming the victor. By the time the mail had been delivered—if it were, since the ship bearing it might be intercepted by pirates or sunk in a storm—he would long since have been buried or become the husband of Awineth and the new king of kings of Khokarsa. That is, he would be if Awineth accepted him, because she had the right to reject anyone who did not please her. And it was possible that Awineth might marry her father. Rumor had it that Minruth had wooed her but that she had said no. Minruth would not wish to give up the throne, and he had precedent for his suit. Three kings of Khokarsa had married their sisters or daughters to retain the crown.

Meanwhile, whatever happened elsewhere, Hadon had to consider the immediate goal. Wiqa was a threat in the races. Gobhu, a mulatto of a family that had been free for a hundred years, was a threat in the broad and high jumps, and he seemed to be very fast in the hundred-yard dash. There were at least three men who seemed destined to win in the wrestling. Hewako, he thought, would finally prevail, though a bull of a man from Dythbeth, Woheken, was immensely strong and very quick. Hadon watched the youths wrestling with professionals. They all seemed to be very impressed by Hewako and Woheken.

Hadon wondered what the *numatenu* with whom he worked out, using wooden swords, thought of him.

They always beat him, though never by more than four points, and he thought that they respected him. The only contestants who seemed to be as skillful as he were Taro and Wiqa. The sword fight was the most important, because it was to the death. But, as his father had said, the man with the most killer's drive would probably be the winner. And all the youths were untested; none had ever killed a man in a sword fight.

Hadon made his evaluations of his competitors and was not overly worried for a while. Then, one day, it struck him that some might be deliberately holding back so they could surprise their opponents. And he had trouble getting to sleep because of worrying about it.

The day came when they were to be presented at court. They rose at dawn, bathed, sacrificed, and ate. Clad in full armor, they marched behind a band to the Road of Kho and over its ancient marble blocks to the city. Again they passed through cheering crowds. They halted before the fifty-foot-wide moat and the hundred-foot-high walls that ringed the base of the acropolis of the Inner City. They marched across the oaken drawbridge, the massive bronze gates at the other end opening as they did so.

Beyond was the steep granite hill of the citadel, a truncated cone two hundred feet high and over a half-mile in diameter. Around its perimeter was a wall of massive granite blocks fifty feet high. The heroes walked up the steep marble staircase lined with diorite and basalt statues of the *r"ok'og'a*[1] and waited at its top for their elders to catch their breath. Then they passed through a twenty-foot-broad and forty-foot-high gateway. Above this were two carved fish-eagles in profile, a massive diamond set in the eye socket of each. They walked down the wide straight

1 Probably a now extinct giant reptile, the dragonlike *sirrush* depicted on the Ishtar Gate of ancient Babylonia. In Hadon's time they could be found in the jungles along the southern sea.

Boulevard of Khukly, the heron goddess, past crowds of government officials and workers. They halted once more, this time before the thousand-year-old palace of the rulers of the empire of Khokarsa. This was, next to the Tower of Kho and Resu, the largest building in the world. It was nine-sided, built of red-veined white marble, and capped by a dome plated with gold, the base of which was inset with patterns of diamonds, emeralds, and rubies. They walked up the nine wide steps, each dedicated to a primary aspect of Kho, and came to a portico. Each of its colonnades was carved in the stiff style of the ancients; each was a representation of a beast, plant, or hero of the nine-year Great Cycle: a fish-eagle, a hippopotamus, a green parrot, the hero Gahete, a sea-otter, a horned fish, a honeybee, a millet plant, and the hero Wenqath.

Hadon was awed by all this. By the time he had marched into the central room, where royalty sat and the great men and women stood, he felt very small and humble.

The bronze trumpets blared, bullroarers throomed, and their escort grounded the butts of their spears with a crash.

The herald cried out, "Behold, priestess of Kho and of her daughter, the moon, the heroes of the Great Games! Behold, king of kings of the empire Khokarsa and of the two great seas, the heroes of the Great Games!" And he finished by three times reciting the passage that must end all official greetings in this palace. "And remember that death comes to all!"

Awineth sat on an oaken throne on whose high back was perched a chained fish-eagle. The throne was unadorned, though the woman it held was adornment enough. Her hair was long and jet black, her features were striking and bold, her eyes were large and dark gray, her skin was white as milk, her breasts were full and shapely, and the legs were slim and rounded. Certainly she left nothing to be desired physically, though her hips might have been a little broader. It was said, however, that she had a hellish temper.

Her throne was a half-step higher than the king's, a superiority which Minruth was supposed to resent very much. His throne was, in contrast with hers, a splendor of gold and diamonds and emeralds, its back topped by a diorite carving of Resu, the Flaming God, as a crowned eagle of the mountains. Minruth was a man of medium height, but he had broad shoulders and a big paunch. His features were much like his daughter's, except that his nose was larger and slightly curved. Fat now hid the muscles that had enabled him to win the Great Games thirty-eight years before. Still, he did not look as old as most men of fifty-six. He did, however, look unhappy. His thick dark eyebrows, so much like his daughter's, were bent in a scowl.

Near him, a huge black lion, chained, lay on the marble dais and blinked sleepy green eyes.

Awineth spoke in a strong but pleasant voice. "Greetings, heroes! I have watched you unseen and have listened to your trainers. You are all men of pleasing physique, though I'm not too sure about the quickness of wits or of speech of some of you. I would not want to bear children to a man of dull mentality, so let us hope that none among you who fit that description becomes the victor. I would not marry such a man! However, it is seldom that a slow-wit wins, so I am not troubled much by thoughts of having to reject the victor."

She made a sign, and the herald thumped the butt of his staff and cried, "Does the king of kings, the father of the high priestess, wish to speak?"

Minruth spoke in a harsh, rumbling voice. "Yes. I have seldom seen such a sorry bunch of heroes. Now, when I fought in the Great Games, I was pitted against men! I am sorry that my daughter must have such a bad lot to choose from. If, that is, she does so choose."

Hadon's face burned with shame.

Awineth laughed and said, "It is always thus—the good old days, the good old days, when giants walked among us. Well, there is one among you who specially pleases me, and I have prayed to Kho that She give him the victory."

"Is it I?" Hadon thought, and his heart leaped.

Awineth arose and said, "Dismiss them."

Hadon was startled. He had thought that there would be more to it than this, a banquet perhaps, during which he might get to talk to Awineth. But no. They were to be herded out after their long walk, marched back hot and thirsty to the barracks.

Hewako, behind Hadon, muttered, "If I ever get my hands on that beautiful bitch, she'll not be so arrogant."

Taro, beside Hewako, said, "She'd probably rather marry a gorilla. Didn't you hear what she said about the lamebrains among us?"

"And you, Taro, I'll break your back," Hewako said.

"Silence, there!" the herald said in a low voice. Hewako shut up, the band began playing again, and they started the march back. As they emerged from the palace, they saw that the wind had shifted, and clouds of dust from the works around the great tower were powdering everything. Hadon thought that it must take an army just to keep the palace clean. Also, the odor from the thousands of workers and beasts, and the clamor, must be disturbing to the palace occupants when the wind blew their way. But they would not be the only ones unhappy about the Great Tower. The expense of building it was a heavy burden to the taxpayer, and diseases often broke out among the workers. Minruth would do better to stop its construction and to spend money on destroying the pirate city of Mikawuru and humbling the arrogant Kethnans. But it was said that he was mad and that he was intent on finishing the tower in his lifetime. Now, if he, Hadon, became king of kings, he would slow down the work on it, enough to relieve the tax burden but not enough to anger Kho and Resu. Then he would devote money and energy to proper matters.

That was the last the youths saw of Awineth and Minruth until the first day of the Games. But they heard rumors of events in the Inner City. The most exciting was that a man, the sole survivor of an expedition across the savannas and mountains to the far north, had returned. And had brought word that he had seen, actually seen, Sahhindar, the Gray-Eyed God!

This was electrifying news. Sahhindar, god of plants, of bronze, and of time, had long been exiled by his mother, Kho. The priestesses said that he had incurred

Her wrath when he taught the first men to domesticate plants and animals and to make bronze. She had planned to do that Herself when the proper time came, but the Gray-Eyed God had disobeyed Her and showed men too soon how they might become better than the beasts. And so She had thrust him from the land, and She had taken away his ability to travel through time, to go back and forth between past, present, and future. Sahhindar, thereafter, was doomed to keep pace with time as all but Kho Herself must. And he was doomed to wander the jungle and the savannas outside the borders of Khokarsa, on the edge of the world itself.

Yet here was a man, Hinokly, who claimed that he had met the god, had talked to him, and had been told that someday he might come back to Khokarsa. Could it be true? Or was it some wild tale?

"I know the deities walk among us," Taro said to Hadon. "But do you know anyone besides the oracular priestesses who have ever seen a god or goddess? Have *you* ever seen one?"

"Only in my dreams," Hadon said.

"If this is true," Taro said, "it might mean that Kho has forgiven Sahhindar. Or it might mean that he is coming back despite her ban. In which case, Khokarsa will suffer from the wrath of Kho. It is always the mortals who get hurt most when the deities quarrel among themselves."

"Perhaps Hinokly is a liar?" Hadon said.

"No sane man would dare make such a lie. Kho would strike him down."

"Then he may be insane. It is said that he suffered terribly in the Wild Lands."

Wiqa said, "I will deny it if you quote me. But I've heard that the priests of Resu would welcome the return of Sahhindar. They say that he would ally himself with his great brother, Resu, and chain up Kho until She acknowledged that they were master. And I've heard it said that Minruth would be pleased if Sahhindar returned. He would then remain king, force his daughter to marry him, and he would raise the status of men."

Hadon and Taro turned pale. Hadon said, in a low voice while he glanced around, "Don't repeat such things, Wiqa! Do you want to be castrated and then thrown to the pigs?"

He stared suspiciously at Wiqa. "Or are you one of those who think Resu should be paramount?"

"Not I!" Wiqa said. "But it's no secret that Minruth believes that Resu should be chief and master. And it has been said that he has been heard to say, while talking with the priests of Resu, that he who controls the army and navy is the true master of Khokarsa. Spears are to be feared as much as, if not more than, the wrath of Kho, according to him."

"It is said that Minruth drinks much and talks boldly when in his cups," Hadon said.

"Minruth is a descendant of the Klemsaasa, who seized the throne and did away with the custom of sacrificing the king after he had ruled nine years," Wiqa said. "If one custom can be changed, so can another."

"I'm a descendant of the Klemsaasa, as you are," Hadon said. "But I abhor the idea of blaspheming against Kho. If She becomes offended, then we may have another Great Plague. Or She may speak with fire and lava and earthquakes and destroy this ungrateful land. It is said that Wimimwi, Minruth's wife, prophesied just such a thing if the priests of Resu did not abandon their efforts to make Resu chief of creation."

"Here comes Hewako!" Taro said. "For the sake of Kho, let's drop this kind of talk. If he should report us, he would be rid of three of his chief competitors."

"I've said nothing to be ashamed of," Hadon said.

"Yes, but by the time the priestesses determined that, the Games would be over."

It was Wiqa's turn to become pale. It had suddenly occurred to him that Hadon and Taro could eliminate him if they reported his words.

"Don't worry," Hadon said. "Getting you into trouble would not be honorable. Besides, you only passed on rumors and hearsay. But Hewako would report you."

And then the first moon day of the month of Adeneth, goddess of sexual passion, in the Year of Gahete the Hero arrived. On this day the crowds streamed out to the coliseum, which could hold 150,000. At the ninth hour of the day, the high priestess and the king arrived and took their seats under the canopy. The gates were closed, the trumpets flourished, the drums beat, the bullroarers throomed, and the heroes marched out to hail Minruth and Awineth and to pour out libations to Resu and Kho. The herald announced the first event, and the Games had begun.

There were three champions from each of the thirty queendoms of the empires. The first event was the hundred-yard dash. Deciding the winner from ninety contestants was a lengthy procedure. There was room abreast for nine men on the quarter-mile track that circled inside the coliseum. The contestants from three cities, Opar, Khokarsa, and Wethna, ran the first race. Hadon, atremble to go, crouched, clad in only a doeskin loincloth, waiting for the yellow linen cloth to strike the ground. The crowd fell hushed as the trumpets blared, the starter gave the directions, the cloth fell, and all nine hurled themselves down the track. However, a clang of gongs summoned them back before they had gone a few paces. A man from Wethna had made a false start.

On the second fall of the cloth, they started true. Hadon was happy at the end, because he had passed the finishing post first. Taro was second, a man from Khokarsa third, and Hewako, surprisingly, the fourth. Though squat and massive, he could pump his short legs like a hippopotamus', which can run swiftly indeed for short distances.

The winners of the first four races were then matched. Up until the last moment, Hadon thought that he was going to win that. He was a slow starter, behind the other three for about fifty yards, but then his long legs gobbled up the earth, and he passed Taro, then Moqowi of the city of Mukha. He drew even with Gobhu of Dythbeth and was exultant for several seconds as he thought he was going to pass him. But Gobhu put on a burst of speed—evidently he had been saving some strength—and he beat Hadon by a foot.

Hadon wasn't depressed. He had done better than he thought he would. The hundred-yard dash was not his forte.

He looked up at the box in which Awineth sat. Was it his imagination, or did she look disappointed? Probably it was the former.

The second-place winners of the first races were then matched; after them, the third-place winners. Gobhu was given a gold crown to wear in life and in death.

The second event was the quarter-mile dash. Hadon felt more confident now, but even so he was beaten by about six inches by long-legged Wiqa. This did not depress him, even though this was the first time that he had ever lost this event. Considering the competition, he had not done badly. And he did win first place in the race for the second-place winners.

Hewako, he was pleased to see, won nothing. But then, the fellow would pick up many points in the wrestling, boxing, and javelin-throwing.

Late that afternoon, the two-mile race was run. This was to be done in four heats at first, twenty-two men in each race. Two had been eliminated on points in the previous races, reducing the number of contestants to eighty-eight. The two disqualified walked off with hanging heads, but Hadon thought that one of them looked relieved. He wasn't going to be king, but then he wasn't going to die either.

Twenty-two men made a very crowded track. Moreover, for the first quarter-mile, pushing and tripping was allowed. Hadon took the outside curve at first. Though this would require him to cover more distance, it kept him free of the shovers and the trippers. He trailed along behind Wiqa and Taro and a tall fellow from Qethruth, and then slowly increased his speed the second mile. At the third quarter of the last mile, he crept up behind the three still in the lead, and in the fourth quarter he drew up even with Wiqa but was still on the outside. Then, in the last half of the last quarter, he burst into a pace that brought him four paces ahead of Wiqa. He could have gone faster, but he wanted to save his strength. And he was glad that he had eliminated Wiqa, his chief competitor, in the first heat.

An hour later, his wind was recovered, but he was not as strong as he had been in the first-two miler. Still, he sped along the outside. This time, however, the others, knowing that he had won the first race, tried to gang up on him. Someone shoved him hard from behind, and he fell on his face, skinning it and his knees. Angry, he jumped up, overtook the last man by the end of the first mile, and then stepped up his speed. He went agonizingly slowly, but he did not want to burn himself out. In the final quarter-mile, he drew on strength which he had not known existed in him. That golden crown glittered invisibly at the end of the track, and he won it by ten paces.

Was it his imagination that Awineth was smiling because she was pleased that he had won, or did she always smile at the winner?

Hadon slept heavily that night while torches flared along the walls of the great hall and guards prowled softly among them. In the past, contestants had sometimes done things to their fellow competitors—poisoned them, released venomous snakes on their beds, or poured itching powder on the bedclothes so the contestant would lose his vital sleep. The guards were here to ensure that nothing like that happened. And outside, more guards watched, because relatives and friends of the Gamesters had been known to attempt similar deeds. The guards themselves were watched by others, because guards had also been bribed.

Thus Hadon slept deeply, knowing that nobody—such as Hewako, for instance—was going to try to cripple or kill him.

The next day was a day of rest, during which he worked out very lightly. The day after, the Games were resumed with the broad and high jumps. In these, the contestants knew fairly well beforehand what the results would be. They had watched each other during the workouts. But the information had been kept from the crowds, or at least was supposed to be kept. Actually, the big gamblers had been spying and had bribed the officials for advance information, and they were now making bets with the suckers. The big money was on Gobhu in the broad jump, with, significantly, none on Hadon or Kwobis as second-place winners. These two had jumped equal distances so many times during practice that the professional gamblers did not care to chance their money on the second-place winners.

In the high jump, those in the know were backing Hadon of Opar, with Wiqa of Qaarquth in second place.

However, man proposes and Kho disposes.

The wind was tricky that day, with intervals of calm and sudden gusts. Each contestant was given only one broad jump, and so was at the mercy of chance. It was Gobhu's bad luck that the wind was against him but with Hadon and Kwobis. He came in third, with Kwobis first and Hadon an inch behind him.

In the high jump, each man could stay in as long as he did not knock the bar off. The bar was set at five feet ten inches, however, and the contest quickly became one among Hadon, Wiqa, Taro, and an exceptionally long-legged man from Qethruth, Kwona. At six feet four inches, Hadon was the only one to clear the bar. His feat was remarkable, considering that the jumpers were barefoot. The record was six feet five, and the betting became furious in the stands while the bar was set at that height. Hadon waited for the wind to die down and then made the greatest effort in his life. He lightly touched the bar as he rolled over, but it remained on its pegs. Amid cheering from the winners of bets and groaning from the losers, he made ready for an attempt to beat the record. The wind suddenly blew again, but this time it was behind him. He ran at the bar, gauging his steps so he could leap ahead of the usual mark; otherwise the wind might carry him too swiftly and against the bar. He knew as he left the ground that he was going to make it—Kho was with him—and though he again touched the bar, and it seemed that it would quiver off, it did not fall. And so he got a double golden crown that afternoon, one tier for being the winner, one tier for breaking the record.

The following day was one of rest for the youths. The next day they marched out behind a band to the lake, while good-looking girls strewed their path with petals. They found the stands packed with people, most of whom had made heavy bets, whether they could afford it or not. The first event was one of endurance, a swim across and back the quarter-mile-broad lake. All eighty-eight Gamesters lined up, and when the starter's trumpet blared, they dived into the water. Hadon trailed along behind half of the swimmers. He knew his own pace, and he did not want to burn himself out. At the other end he had passed many and had only about ten ahead of him. After touching the baton of a referee on the dock, he turned and began to increase speed. Halfway back, he was a little behind Taro, a youth from Dythbeth, Wiqa, Gobhu, and Khukly. The latter was from the pile city of Rebha and had spent more time in the water than anybody else. He had heavy shoulders and exceptionally large hands and feet and was the one Hadon had worried most about. Now Khukly, deciding to turn on the power, drew even with the others and then passed them. Hadon felt as if his lungs were burning, and his arms and legs were becoming as stiff as driftwood. This was the time when the spirit had to be strong enough to overcome the body's pain, and he urged himself on, though it would have been so pleasant to quit. He passed all but Khukly and drew even with him and lashed himself on, on, on. The crowd's roar mingled with the roar of his blood in his head. And, suddenly, it was over and he was panting like a cornered boar and so weak that he almost accepted an offer to pull him out. Pride prevented him, and he hauled himself up onto the dock and sat down until he could recover his wind. Well, he had almost made it. If the distance had been about twenty yards more, he could have passed Khukly. His endurance was greater. But the lake was not longer, and so he had been beat out by half an arm's length.

Two hours later, the first of the youths climbed up a seventy-foot ladder to a narrow platform hanging over the middle of the lake. He wore a bonnet of fish-eagle feathers and his face was painted to resemble a fish-eagle's. Around his ankles were fish-eagle feathers. He poised on top of the platform while the crowd fell silent. When the trumpet blared, he soared outward. The crowd roared as he cut the water cleanly, though the bonnet and the ankle feathers were torn off.

The high dive was a feature of the Games founded on an ancient Fish-Eagle Totem ceremony, when the courage of youths during the rites of passage was tested. The betting was the heaviest so far, though it was not on the winner, since there was no gold crown for this. The money was down on whether the diver would survive without injury, and since no practice dives had been made, no one knew what the ability of the individual divers was.

The third youth hit the water with his body turned and leaning outward. The crack of flesh against the surface was heard by everybody, and the youth did not come up at once. A boat put out from an anchored raft nearby, and divers went down after him. They pulled up a corpse.

As the sixth youth fell, he was struck by the wind, still tricky, and he hit the water sideways. He wasn't killed, but broken ribs and injured muscles had eliminated him.

When Hadon's turn came, he waited for a few seconds after the trumpet call. Many in the crowd booed him because they thought he had lost his nerve. But he was waiting for the wind to pass, and when it did, he jumped. He was just in time to avoid the second trumpet call, which, if sounded, would have disqualified him for the rest of the Games. And he would have been open to accusations of cowardice.

He entered the water cleanly, but nevertheless came up slightly stunned. Years of practice had paid off.

At the end of the contest, the crowd went away pleased, except for the lovers, relatives, and friends of the dead and the injured, of course. Five were among the latter and four among the former.

The next day, the dead were buried in their earth tombs, and pointed marble monoliths were erected over the mounds. The contestants strewed white petals over the tombs, and the priestesses sacrificed bulls so the ghosts could drink blood and go happy to the garden that Kho reserved for heroes.

The next three days were devoted to boxing. The youths' fists were fitted with thin gloves that had a heavy layer of resin-impregnated cloth over the knuckles. In the preliminaries, they were matched according to height, so Hadon found himself facing Wiqa. Hadon had great confidence in his pugilistic ability, though he dreaded the wrestling, which would come after the boxing. Wiqa, he quickly found, was also confident, and with good reason. Hadon caught a right to the jaw and went down. He waited until the referee had counted to eleven and then rose. Less cocky, he boxed more cautiously. Presently, after an exchange of hard blows, he shot his long left arm up through Wiqa's guard. Wiqa tried bravely to get up but just could not make it.

The odds went up on Hadon when the crowd saw his whiplash left.

Hadon fought twice more that day and won, but that night he nursed a black right eye, sore ribs, and a sore jaw.

The next afternoon, his first opponent was Hoseko, a short, powerful man from Bawaku. Hoseko was outreached by Hadon, but his thick body and heavy-boned head absorbed punishment as a bull elephant absorbed darts. Hadon ripped his face with a series of slashing blows, but Hoseko, blinking through the blood, kept on boring in. And, suddenly, a sledgehammer left caught Hadon on the jaw, and his legs crumpled as if they were made of papyrus. He got to his hands and knees after hearing the referee, unaccountably far away, count to seven. By eleven, he was on his feet again.

Hoseko advanced slowly, chin down, shoulders hunched, his left fist out, his right eye blinded with blood. Hadon, his legs still crumply but slowly regaining their power, circled Hoseko. Hoseko kept turning and advancing. The crowd booed Hadon, and the referee cracked his whip against the ground. Fight! Or feel the whip against your back the next time!

Hadon continued circling, jabbing at Hoseko but not connecting. Out of the corner of his eye he saw the referee lift the whip handle again. The hippopotamus hide traveled back, back, over the referee and behind him, the arm jerked forward, the tip sped toward Hadon; timing himself exactly right, he ducked. The tip whistled above him, going inward past him, and it cracked against Hoseko's face. Hoseko cried out with pain and surprise; the referee shouted with surprise; the crowd roared protest. But Hadon had taken advantage of Hoseko's confusion and the dropping of his guard. Hadon's left came from far out and ended against Hoseko's sturdy chin.

Hoseko's eyes crossed; he staggered backward, his hands falling down to his sides; Hadon buried his left in Hoseko's solar plexus; Hoseko fell down doubled up onto the ground and was there long after the count of twelve.

There was a delay. The referee summoned the two judges, and they talked for a few minutes, gesticulating and looking frequently at Hadon. The crowd, becoming restless, booed the three men. Hadon, panting and sweating, stood unmoving. He knew that the three were discussing the admissibility of his trick. Was it valid for a boxer deliberately to cause the referee to use his whip, dodge it, and cause it to strike his opponent?

The referee and the judges were in a difficult situation. This had never happened before. If they ruled that Hadon's trick was admissible, then they could expect other contestants to try it. Not that it would be easy to pull it off again. Every referee would be on his guard from now on. If anybody was foolish enough to try it again, he'd get his back laid open to the shoulderbones.

Possibly it was this that decided the judges. The referee, scowling, lifted Hadon's right arm. The crowd cheered and then laughed as rubbery-legged Hoseko was carried off between two officials.

Hadon's second fight late that afternoon ended when Hadon sank a whiplash left to his opponent's solar plexus. He had taken so much punishment, however, that he walked off in a daze. Taro grabbed him, sat him down, washed and bandaged his facial cuts, and dabbed cold water on his face.

Hadon opened his eyes and became aware that an old man, one of the trainers, was standing by him.

"Why are you staring at me?" Hadon said.

"You got a lot to learn yet," the old man said. "But I haven't seen a left like that since the great Sekoko. He was before your time, kid, but you must have heard of him. He was boxing champion of the empire for fifteen years. He was tall and slim like you, and he had long arms like you and a left that murdered them. I'll tell you what, kid. If you get eliminated on points, don't feel bad. I can make you champ in a few years. You'll be rich and famous."

"No, thanks," Hadon said.

The old man looked disappointed. "Why not?"

"I've seen too many punch-drunk boxers. Besides, I intend to be king."

"Well, if you don't make it, and you're still alive and healthy, see me. My name's Wakewa."

On the third day, Taro was carried off senseless in his second match. But he had enough points to stay in the Games. Hewako had knocked out his opponent's front teeth and smashed his nose in two minutes, and now he rested. As Hadon walked by him toward the circle, Hewako called out, "I hope you win this one, floorsweeper's son! Then I'll have the pleasure of mangling that pretty face before I break your jaw and eliminate you from the Games and send you in disgrace back to Opar!"

"The jackal yaps; the lion kills," Hadon said coolly. But he felt that there was an excellent chance that Hewako might be able to make good his boasts. It was plain that he expected Hadon to be better than he in the final contest, the sword fight. Hadon had better qualifications—height, arm length, and most important, many more hours of practice with the *tenu*. Hewako had also worked out from childhood with the wooden sword; there wasn't a healthy child in the empire, male or female, who didn't. But Hewako had known that his talents were in boxing and wrestling, and so he had devoted more hours to them than to the *tenu*. He wasn't a professional boxer by any means, but he was closer to being one than Hadon.

It was obvious that he hoped to so cripple Hadon that he would not be able to continue competing. Whether or not he did cripple or perhaps even kill him, he had to win the match on the following day. Either Hadon or Kagaga would win today's match, but whoever won, Hewako had to win tomorrow. He did not have enough points to stay in unless he did so. But if he won the boxing and then went on to win the wrestling, he would have enough points to stay right in to the finish. Provided, that is, he wasn't crippled or killed before then.

Hewako was hoping that Hadon would win today so he, Hewako, could eliminate him the hard way tomorrow. Hadon could afford to lose today, since he had accumulated so many points. And this was why the man who hated him so much was rooting for him.

Kagaga meant Raven, and Kagaga certainly looked like one. He was a tall, dark, stoop-shouldered, long-nosed youth from some small town above the Klemqaba coasts. He had a croaking voice and a pessimistic temperament. But he was a very good boxer. And he charged Hadon as if he meant to batter him to a pulp within a few minutes. Hadon retreated, but he danced in now and then and flicked at Kagaga's face or hammered his arms enough to keep the referee from using his whip on him. Kagaga called to him to stand still and fight like a hero, not a wild dog. Hadon merely grinned and back-pedaled or sometimes suddenly advanced to jab Kagaga lightly on the face before retreating again. The crowd booed, and Hewako bellowed accusations of cowardice. Hadon paid attention only to the referee and to Kagaga. He kept dancing in and out, using his longer reach to thump Kagaga, not too hard, on his forehead or nose. And, suddenly, Kagaga's right eyebrow was cut and blood was streaming down into his eye.

"Now, I suppose, you're going to run around him while he bleeds to death," the referee said. "Get in there and fight, or I'll flay you."

Hadon had hoped to drag the fight out until both he and Kagaga were too tired to lift their arms. Then Kagaga would win on points because of his aggressiveness, or Hadon would lose because of his lack of aggressiveness. Neither would be badly hurt, and Hadon could rest tomorrow while Hewako wore himself out on Kagaga. But this was not to be. Hewako might get his chance to cripple him tomorrow after all.

Reluctantly, Hadon attacked. There was a fierce exchange of body blows, thudding of fists, gruntings, and then one of Kagaga's fists slipped through, rocked Hadon's head back, and Hadon fell to his knees. He tried to get back up—no one was going to say that he had deliberately taken a dive—but he could not make it. He heard the referee count to twelve, and a few seconds later he rose shakily to his feet. Kagaga was looking dazed at his sudden good luck, and Hewako's face was as red as a baboon's bottom.

A minute later, Hadon, walking unaided to the showers, grinned at Hewako. Hewako's face became as red as if the baboon had been sitting on a hot rock.

The single event the next day was the match for the boxer's golden crown. Kagaga adopted his opponent's tactics of the day before, since he knew he could not last long in a toe-to-toe slugging fest. Unlike Hadon, he failed to gauge the limits to the referee's patience. The whip caught him by surprise across the back; he jumped forward into Hewako's fist; he fell senseless with half his front teeth knocked out.

After the ceremony, Hewako approached Hadon and said, "Day after tomorrow the wrestling starts. I didn't get a chance at you in the boxing, but you're not going to get away from me in the wrestling. And when I get my hands on you, I'm going to break your back."

"If you do, the referee will knock you silly with his club, and you might be eliminated," Hadon said. "Of course, I don't blame you for your eagerness to get rid of me now. You know that if we ever face each other with swords, you're a dead man. Though I may just chop off your nose to teach you a lesson."

Hewako spat at Hadon, though he was careful not to hit him, and he strutted away wearing his gold crown.

"Why does that man hate you so?" Taro said.

"I don't know," Hadon said. "I never did anything to offend him, not in the beginning, anyway. It's just one of those things, where you dislike a person for reasons you don't know."

Hewako never got his hands on Hadon. Hadon was eliminated after two victories by a bull buffalo of a youth from Mineqo. Hewako looked disappointed; Hadon merely grinned at him, knowing that that would infuriate him. And Hewako almost lost the golden crown. During his last contest, he grabbed his opponent's fingers and tried to twist them back. This was illegal, and so the referee slammed his billy against the back of Hewako's head. He lost his senses long enough for his opponent to pin him, and Hewako came close to losing the third fall. Hadon, standing on the side, grinned again at Hewako when he winced as the gold crown was placed on his head.

He sobered up when he thought about the next seven events. Except for the last, no golden crown would be awarded. A man either survived or he didn't. From now on, there would be no referees to ensure that the rules were abided by.

And there was Taro. What if the final contestants were Taro and he? One would have to kill the other, and he certainly did not intend to be the corpse. The thought of slaying Taro depressed him. As he had done several times, he wondered why he had ever entered.

The answer was obvious. He wanted to be the greatest man in the kingdom. And Taro had also volunteered, knowing that he might have to face Hadon with a sword.

Two days later the crowd was again assembled in the stadium around the lake. The centers of interest were, first, the huge and hungry sea crocodiles that slid through the waters. The second was two ropes stretched across a part of the lake between two sturdy poles. One was farther out than the other and at a lower level than the first. One end of a third rope was tied to the middle point of the nearest rope running over the lake, and the other end was held by an official standing on a tower high above the edge of the lake.

The band blared; the crowd roared; vendors passed among the crowd selling fruits, cakes, and beer. Then there was a flourish of trumpets, and the crowd fell silent. Hadon, as the one with most points, had the honor of being the first contestant. He climbed up the high ladder to the platform, where he was handed the end of a rope. This was attached at the other end of the rope which ran at right angles across this corner of the lake. Beyond that rope was the lower parallel rope. And below were the crocodiles, the great gray armor-plated, many-teethed saurians.

Hadon looked at the canopied box in which Awineth and Minruth sat. They were far away, tiny, so he could not see her expression. Was it fear and hope for him? Or, like that which must be on Minruth's face and on most of the crowd's, did it show a desire that Hadon would fail and that he and the crocodiles would provide a brief but entertaining spectacle?

He hated the crowd at that moment. Crowds were people who had lost their individuality, who had become no more than vultures. Less, in fact, since vultures acted by the nature given to them by Kho, and by so doing were performing a useful deed. Yet, if he were in the mob, would he be any different from the others?

The starter's trumpet screamed. The crowd's roar subsided. He bent his knees, grasped the rope with both hands, and waited. The trumpet screamed again, as it had so many times in the past two thousand years, because this, like the high dive, was an ancient Fish-Eagle Totem custom.

He pushed out, clinging to the rope. The water swooped toward him; he drew up his legs, though the crocodiles could not reach him, and he curved up and out. Then he reached the end of the arc and fell back. He jerked his body on the return and swung back out again. Twice he increased the height of the swing. The third time, as he arrived just before the top of the arc, he prayed briefly and let loose. He soared out toward the rope before him, fell, and his hands closed on the outermost rope. And he was dangling while the crocodiles bellowed below and whitened the water with their furious lunges and thrashings of tails. He was too far away to be reached, of course, but his ordeal was not yet over. He had to go hand-over-hand along the rope until he got to the platform at the end. Then—he hated to think of it—he must take a balancing pole and walk the rope back to its other end.

He had no difficulty getting to the platform, though his palms were sweaty. An official handed him the pole after he had recovered his breath, and the trumpet screamed the third time. He stepped onto the rope, which was not as taut as he would have liked, and walked slowly, his bare feet lifting and gripping slowly. Below, the crocodiles thundered.

Hadon had practiced tightrope walking since he was two. But the crocodiles made a dangerous trick even more dangerous. If he lost his balance and had to grab the rope, he would not be eliminated. But he would have to go back to the platform and start all over again.

The rope swayed, and he strove to balance his weight so that the rope would not go into an increasing oscillation. The cheers of the crowd and some boos from ill-wishers reached him faintly, but the bellowing of the hungry beasts below was loud. He would not look down at them. He must concentrate on getting across.

When he reached the other platform, he almost collapsed. Suddenly, he was shaking and weak. But he had done it and would not have to do it again.

He climbed down and took his place among the contestants, who were sitting on benches near the edge of the lake. Beyond them was the bronze-wire fence put up to keep the crocodiles from coming ashore.

"How was it?" Taro said.

"Not bad," Hadon said, hating himself for his bravado. It would never do for a hero to confess that his guts had turned into a beast trying to claw its way out through his belly.

The third man lost his balance, grabbed the rope, and hand-over-handed back to the platform. The second try, he fell with a scream, and the water roiled around his body. Hadon felt sick for him but glad for himself.

Hewako had to make two attempts, but he got across. His skin was gray beneath the bronze as he climbed down.

The man who followed him missed the rope when he let loose of the swinging rope, and he fell to his death.

By the time the last of the contestants had reached the ground, the sun was quartering the west, and ten were food in the bellies of the crocodiles.

The funerals the next day were curious in that they lacked the presence of the deceased. Stone statues representing the dead, all with the same stylized faces, were lowered into the graves, and earth was mounded over them and the monoliths set above them. Hadon watched the weeping relatives and wondered if his parents, too, would have occasion to grieve for him.

The next day the youths competed in the javelin-throwing. Each had a small round shield for defense but could not step outside a small circular fence. Each contestant was given three javelins to throw and had to endure three cast at him by another contestant from a distance of a hundred feet.

Twelve were wounded seriously enough to be eliminated; two were buried the next day; one man disgraced himself by jumping out of the ring. He hanged himself that night, and so saved himself from a coward's grave.

The games of the next three days were tests of the youths' skill with the sling. On the first day, Hadon was among the initial group of contestants to enter the field. There were ten of them, and each wore only a loincloth and a leather belt. The belt supported a dagger in a sheath and a leather pouch. The pouch held three biconical molded lead missiles. In the hand of each youth was a sling made of soft dwarf antelope leather. The youths marched to the center of the field and halted when a trumpet blew. The crowd fell silent. Another trumpet blast. A huge door in the wall which they faced swung open. Presently, thirty male gorillas, blinking in the sunlight, growling, nasty-eyed, emerged.

The crowd began yelling and cheering. The ten youths arranged themselves in a line facing the gorillas. Hadon was at its extreme left. The trumpet blew for the third time. Each youth tied one end of the sling's strap to one of the four fingers of his throwing hand. The other end, knotted, was then placed between the thumb and forefinger of that hand. With his other hand, the youth removed a lead projectile weighing three and one-half ounces from the pouch. He placed it in the pad which formed the pocket at the end of the two straps.

The gorillas, meanwhile, nervously ran back and forth on all fours or stood up and slapped their chests with their open palms. Though fearsome-looking beasts, they were naturally timid. However, for the last thirty days trainers had been trying to condition them to attack human beings. The trainers had pelted them with stones and poked them with sharp sticks until they had driven them into a fury. Eventually, the gorillas had gotten accustomed to taking out their frustrations on dummies in clothes stinking of humankind. For the last twelve days they had been tearing these apart, apparently with vast satisfaction. And so it was hoped that the gorillas would attack the contestants now. Especially since their trainers, safe on top of the wall, were throwing stones and pointed sticks at them. The giant anthropoids, however, for the moment seemed only bewildered and frightened.

The trumpet blew again. Hadon, with the others, held the ends of the sling above his head with one hand and the missile in its pocket in the other. Then he released the pocket end and began whirling the sling counterclockwise parallel to his body. Around and around, four times, the sling whirled, deriving most of its speed from wrist movement. At the part of the circle closest to the ground, he released the free end of the sling. The lead projectile, traveling more than sixty miles per hour, hurled in a parabola toward its target three hundred feet away. This was a huge reddish gorilla with a broken right canine and scarred face.

The thud of missiles sinking deep into flesh or smashing against the stone wall could be heard over the entire stadium. Six of the giant apes fell backward under the impact, and none of them moved after that. The crowd roared as the youths placed their second missiles in the slings. By then ten of the apes were advancing toward the youths, roaring, slapping their chests, picking up blades of grass and blowing them, or making short bluffing charges. The second fusillade knocked down seven of them, but two got to their feet, and roaring their hurt and rage, bounded toward the youths.

Before they could reach their objective, they fell dead with several missiles in them.

Hadon was not among those who released his last bicone. He wanted to save it for an emergency. He did not think that this would be long in coming. Thirteen of the anthropoids had been killed or rendered *hors de combat*. This left seventeen with only eight projectiles still unslung. And even if all eight hit their targets, there would still be nine gorillas left. And, facing them, ten humans with only six-inch knives.

More gorillas, driven by another hail of stones from the trainers, advanced toward the youths. One suddenly broke into a charge that did not end after a few yards. Hadon called out, "Save your missiles! Taro, you alone use your sling!"

Taro's projectile disappeared within the wide-open mouth of the ape, which fell dead. Hadon then called out the names of those who had missiles left, one by one, and they released them. Eight more gorillas died or were so badly wounded that they could not get up. But nine of the beasts remained, and these were brave with hysteria.

Four died under the knives, though not before they had killed three youths and badly maimed three more. If they had attacked together, instead of singly, they could have wiped out the humans. But they did not think like men, and so they died as beasts.

Hadon, Taro, and the two other youths still on their feet proceeded to dig out missiles from the carcasses with their knives. Hadon had just removed one bicone when he heard, "Watch out!" He looked up to see another hairy, long-canined monster rushing at him and his companions scattering. Hadon dropped the lead missile, transferred his bloody knife to his left hand, removed from his belt the clean knife he'd taken from a dead man, placed its blade in his palm, and cast it. The gorilla quit roaring, began screaming, somersaulted, and slid to a stop on its back just before Hadon. The hilt of the knife stuck out from its huge paunch.

After that, the four youths used the retrieved missiles to slay the four remaining gorillas. Then, saluting the king and queen, they walked out. Attendants poured in to drag away the dead, carry out the wounded humans, and set up the field for the next ten youths and thirty gorillas.

The next day the funerals for those who'd died were held, and the day after that the youths faced hyenas. There were four starved hyenas to each slinger, and each slinger had four missiles and an ax. The hyenas were more dangerous than the gorillas. They were carnivores, used to hunting in packs, and had been fed human flesh for two weeks before being starved. Their jaws could crush a man's leg or arm as if they were made of linen, and they had an awe-inspiring tenacity. Of the ten youths in Hadon's group, five were killed or bitten so badly that it was eliminated from the Games.

The following day, more funerals were conducted. The next day, the contestants faced leopards. These were man-eaters who'd been trapped in the jungle hinterlands of Wentisuh. They had been starved for three days, and goat blood had been smeared on the contestants to arouse beasts that did not need arousing. Three of the big cats were released at a time against two slingers, each of whom had two missiles and a sword. Hadon was paired with Gobhu, who was an even better slinger than his tall companion. Hadon's first throw broke the hind leg of a big male, and this caused the other two, a male and a female, to charge Gobhu. The mulatto knocked the eye out of the female and sent her rolling over and over. But the male knocked

Gobhu down and tore his throat before Hadon's second missile broke some of its ribs. Hadon cut off its head with his sword, dispatched the stunned female in the same manner, and finally cornered the male with the broken hind leg. Though crippled badly, it charged, and Hadon half-severed its neck while it was in the air.

That night, he and Taro sat at a table talking in a barracks which had grown larger and emptier with death.

"I overheard a judge saying that he understood that Minruth was considering making the Games a yearly event," Hadon said.

"How could he do that?" Taro said. "How often does a chief priestess lack a husband?"

"Oh, it wouldn't have anything to do with that. He would hold the Games just for the amusement of the people, not to mention his own. The winners would get large sums of money. And glory."

Taro made a disgusted sound. There was silence for a while, and then Hadon said, "What I don't understand is how Minruth thinks he can institute such games. He won't be king after these are over."

"Maybe he thinks none of us will survive," Taro said.

"That wouldn't do any good. New Games would have to be held."

There was another silence, broken when Hadon said, "Once the kings ruled only nine years and then were sacrificed. But the first of the Klemsaasa to rule—his name was Minruth, too—abolished that custom. Do you suppose that Minruth intends to refuse to give up the throne?"

Taro was startled. "How could he do that? Kho Herself would destroy him! Nor would the people put up with it!"

"Kho didn't destroy the first Minruth," Hadon said. "And the people who rose against him were destroyed. Minruth controls the army and the navy, and while a part of the services would revolt, the other might not. Minruth favors Resu, and he has taken care to make sure that the officers and the soldiers who favor Resu are in key positions. I'm only nineteen years old, but I know that."

"But, if he did that, what about the winner of the Games? He would have gone through all this for nothing!"

"Less than nothing, if such a thing can be," Hadon said. "He would be slain by Minruth. You can be sure of that."

"Oh, that's all nonsense," Taro said. "He wouldn't dare!"

"Perhaps not. But why should that judge have heard that rumor? Who else but Minruth would originate it? He would put it out as a feeler, so he can judge the reaction of the people. One thing is sure, Minruth is exceedingly ambitious, not likely to surrender easily. He's old, fifty-six, and you'd think he'd want to do the decent thing. Retire full of honors, enjoy a leisurely life, and cherish his grandchildren. But no, he acts as if he will live forever, as if he's a randy young bull."

"You have to be wrong," Taro said.

"I hope so," Hadon replied.

5

The next-to-last game lasted two days. On the first day, fifteen contestants chosen by lot took their turn facing a bull buffalo the tips of whose horns had been fitted with sharp bronze spikes. The contestant was given a three-foot-long wand on the end of which was wet ocher paint. He went into the center of the arena and waited until the bull was released. From then on, his aim was to mark the exact center of the bull's forehead with ocher. And he must do it when the bull was facing him.

Once this was done to the satisfaction of the three judges, who sat in a box a safe distance from the bull, the contestant was free to go. All he had to do was to run to a low wall and dive over it before the bull got to him.

"Speed and agility," Hadon said to Taro. "That is what this takes. Plus courage. Hewako has the courage, I'll give the surly pig that. But he is heavy and slow. Faster than he looks, but still slow."

But Hewako did succeed, though not before being gashed lightly along one arm. And in the short dash to the wall, he seemed almost a blur, he ran so fast.

Taro laughed and said, "If that bull had been behind him during the races, he would have won all of them."

Taro was the last of the fifteen that day. Before going through the gate, he turned to Hadon and put his hand on his shoulder. He looked very pale.

"I had a dream last night," he said. "I was drinking blood from a bowl that you had filled."

Hadon felt a shock going through him. "All dreams are sent by the deities," he said. "But a dream does not always mean what it seems to say."

"Perhaps not," Taro said. "In any event, we two would have faced each other with the swords. One of us would have been pouring out blood for the other's ghost. Why did we not shake dice in Opar to see who went to the Games? One of us would have lost a chance to be the king, but he would never have been forced to take his dear friend's blood. We have loved each other too much even to think of that. Yet greed made us ignore that, greed and ambition. Why did we do that, Hadon? Why didn't we leave it to the throw of the dice? Whoever won could then have brought his friend to the palace to share in his good fortune."

Hadon choked up but managed after a struggle to speak.

"Kho must have blinded us. No doubt, for Her own good purposes."

The trumpet blared, and Taro said, "Why blame the gods and goddesses? Think often of me, Hadon, and do not forget to sacrifice now and then to me."

"You may have misinterpreted the dream!" Hadon cried desperately, but the gates had swung shut. Taro walked out into the center of the field stiffly, and when the bull, black, snorting fury, ran out from his gate, Taro did not move. The bull pawed the earth and then raced around for a minute. At last, downwind from Taro, it hastened bellowing toward him and then charged. Taro extended the stick toward him and marked the forehead, but he was slow, oh, so slow, far slower than swift Taro had ever moved when danger threatened.

Afterward, Hadon wondered if it had not been the dream itself that had made Taro so sluggish. Had dread Sisisken sent him that vision because she had marked him for death, knowing that the dream itself would ensure his end? And why had Sisisken wanted him? Why had she allowed him to survive the Games thus far and no farther?

Was it because her sister, Kho, wished to spare Hadon the agony of killing him?

He did not know, but he wept that night in the barracks. Yet, when he fell asleep, he felt a tiny spark of gladness falling through the dark grief. However much he sorrowed for Taro, he would not be responsible for killing his best friend. Kho had spared him that.

The next day Hadon performed a deed which brought the crowd, gasping and cheering, to its feet. As the bull charged, he ran toward it. Just before the lowered horns were to meet him, he gave a great leap up and forward, brought his feet up, stroked the black hairy forehead lightly with the end of the stick, and landed on the beast's back. His inertia, plus the bull's, rolled him forward, and he fell sprawling on the sand. But he was up, though slightly stunned, and running. Behind him he heard the bellowing and then the thundering of hooves. He dived over the wall, which shook as the bull rammed into it.

He rose and looked at the judges' box. They were standing up, both hands raised, the fingers outspread. He had marked the beast perfectly.

The cheering continued for a long time, and after a while Hadon understood what the crowd wanted. They were demanding of the queen that she dedicate this event to him, so that in future Games it should be called Hadon's Day.

Hadon felt a glow of exultation, tempered with sadness that Taro was not here to see him. Perhaps his ghost was, and Hadon would see to it that a bull was sacrificed to Taro tonight—though it would cut deeply into his personal money—and that Taro would be told about this while he drank the substance-giving blood.

And so, a day later, the final event began. There were only twenty of the original ninety left. The buffaloes had taken a toll exceeding that of the gorillas, hyenas, and leopards combined. At the ninth hour, the trumpets sounded, and the twenty, clad only in scarlet loincloths and carrying the broad and long *tenu* in one hand, marched out. They stopped before the box of Awineth and Minruth and saluted.

Awineth arose and tossed out across the heads of the mob below a thin golden crown. It sailed out into the arena, rolled, and stopped by the edge of the track. Hadon noted that the impact had twisted the soft gold. But the victor could easily bend it back when he placed it on his own head.

Awineth looked beautiful. She wore a long scarlet skirt, a necklace of red emeralds, and a scarlet flower in her black hair. And was her smile for him? Or was it for one of the others, say, the tall and handsome Wiqa?

If it were the latter, she was doomed to sorrow, because Hadon severed his right arm after ten minutes of furious fighting. Wiqa was very good, and if he had not lost some blood two days before when a horn sliced along his thigh, he might have been faster. But he was carried off, gray, dying, blood spouting from the stump.

Hadon stared after him and felt no exultation. He had killed his first man, a good man whom he had liked. That Wiqa had been trying to kill him made no difference in his feelings.

The contests were run off one at a time. At the end of the day, the twenty were down to eight. Of the losers, eight were slain and four had been so seriously injured that they could no longer hold the hilt of the sword with both hands.

The next day was occupied with the funerals, and a day of rest followed for the survivors. Hadon exercised lightly and reflected on the weaknesses and strengths he had observed among the others. Hewako and Damoken, a tall lithe youth from Minanlu, were the two greatest dangers. Both of these had made just enough points in the various contests to remain in the Games. But they were superb swordsmen, and that was what counted now. Nor were any of the others to be taken carelessly.

When the second day of sword fighting came, Hadon was matched, by lot, with Damoken. The battle was a long one, with both feeling the strength drain out of their arms and legs as they danced, parried, and sliced. At last a swift stroke of Hadon's, though partially blocked, cut off Damoken's ear and gashed his shoulder. Damoken stumbled backward, the sword dropping out of his hands. Hadon stepped forward and put his foot on the blade, and the referees hastened to take Damoken from the field.

"Do not weep," Hadon said. "It is better to be earless than to creep around palely and hope for blood to drink. I wish you a long happy life."

Damoken, holding a hand to his bloody head, replied, "When you become king, Hadon, remember me and make a place in your service for one who, under different circumstances, might have been your king."

Hadon bowed and picked up the sword and handed it to a referee.

The next contestants took their places, and Hadon went to the sidelines. He watched carefully as the others fought, noting especially Hewako's style.

When the sun was more than three-quarters across the sky, Hadon of Opar and Khosin of Towina fought, both for the second time that day. Five minutes after starting, Hadon, though bleeding from a gash on his left arm, was standing and Khosin lay dead.

Hewako of Opar and Hadar of Qethruth engaged in the final battle of the day. At the end of two minutes, Hewako gave his opponent's blade such a stroke that it fell from his nerveless hands. Hadar dived for it, and the edge of Hewako's sword severed his neck.

In the tumult cascading from the crowd, Hadon and Hewako were silent. They looked speculatively at each other. The day after tomorrow, one of them would surely be dead, and the other might be king of kings of Khokarsa. Which would it be for Hewako and Hadon? The arms of dread Sisisken or of warm and glorious Awineth?

6

For the final bout, a platform had been built close to the wall near which the queen and her father sat. It was fifteen feet high, only five feet below the top of the wall enclosing the field, five feet below and ten feet away from the royal box. Its surface was a square of closely joined mahogany planks, thirty by thirty feet. A circle with a diameter of twenty-four feet had been painted in white on it. Bisecting the circle was a white line. The area outside the circle was for the referee. His only duties were to start the contest and, thereafter, to lop off the head of either contestant if he stepped outside the circle during the fighting. He was also there to ensure that only the victor left the circle alive.

As the Flaming God reached his zenith, twelve trumpets blared. Awineth and Minruth sat down in their box on comfortable cushions and under a shady canopy. The trumpets blew again, and the crowd sat down on hard stone and in hot sunshine. At the third blast, Hewako and Hadon appeared from gates at opposite ends of the fields. They were naked, and each carried his sword upright before him. Behind each was a naked priestess who slowly banged a large drum while the youth proceeded to the platform. They met at the bottom of the broad mahogany steps that led up to the platform, bowed to the referee, bowed to each other, and then followed the referee up the steps. The priestesses stayed below, slowly beating the drums.

Within the circle, the two youths faced their rulers, Hewako on the left of the bisecting line, Hadon on the right. The trumpets blew again, the priestesses' drums stopped rolling, the two raised their blades above their heads with one hand and shouted, "Let Kho decide!"

"And Resu!" Minruth bellowed.

Those around the king gasped; Awineth jerked upright from her reclining position and said something to Minruth. He laughed and waved at the referee to continue.

The referee had been startled by Minruth's irregular interjection, but he recovered quickly. He stood just outside the circle at the end of the bisecting line, raised his sword high, and shouted, "Take the line!"

The two turned to face each other across the line.

"Cross ends!"

The two swords rose until they were at a forty-five-degree angle to their holders, and their square tips touched. Hadon stood straight, his green eyes staring into Hewako's brown eyes. His left hand held the end of the foot-long hilt in a pivot grip, his right hand was placed around the hilt just behind the circular guard.

The iron hilt was covered tightly with python hide. The carbonized-iron blade was five feet two inches long, two-edged, slightly curving on the lower edge, and square-ended. It was called Karken, or Tree of Death, and it had been made at great expense by the legendary smith, Dytabes of Miklemres, for Hadon's father. With it Kumin had slain fifty-seven warriors, of whom ten were *numatenu*, seven warrior-women of the Mikawuru, forty Klemqaba, and a lion.

"That one-legged worker of magic told me that he dreamed of Karken the night before he completed work on it, before he cooled its hot blade with snake's blood," Kumin had told his son. "Dytabes said that he saw a vision in which the holder of Karken was seated on a throne of ivory. And by him was the most beautiful woman Dytabes had ever seen, truly a goddess. And around him was a multitude praising him as the greatest swordsman of the world and as the savior of his people.

"But Dytabes could not see clearly the face of the man who held Karken. Evidently it was not I. I hope that it was you. In any event, take this sword, Hadon, and do nothing to disgrace it. As for that dream, do not think too much about it. Smiths are notorious drunks. Dytabes, though the greatest of smiths, was also the deepest of drinkers."

Hadon thought of his father's words, and then he heard the referee shout, "Begin and end!"

Iron clanged. Hewako had stepped over the line, right foot forward first, and had swung the blade toward Hadon's left shoulder. Hadon had also stepped forward, though only a half-step, and had parried successfully.

"Watch the eyes," his father had said many times. "They often tell what is coming next. The footwork is second in importance, but unless you know what the man is going to do, or what he thinks he means to do, footwork means nothing. Courage and strength are important also, but the sight and the footwork come first."

And Kumin also said, over and over, "Immediately after the defense, the counteroffense."

He had also said, "Do the unexpected, though not just for the sake of novelty. The unexpected must have a point, a goal in mind which the conventional, the expected, cannot reach."

Hewako reached back and raised his sword above his head. He had to retreat when doing this, because Hadon, swift as he was, would have swung his blade sidewise and cut deeply into his ribs. But by stepping back, Hewako prevented Hadon from doing this. Then Hewako planned to rush forward and bring his sword down straight ahead of him toward the crown of Hadon's head. Hadon would have to parry to keep his skull from being split. He dared not cut at Hewako then, even though Hewako was wide open. If he did wound Hewako, he would still take the full blow on his head. And he would be dead.

Or so Hewako thought. But as Hewako retreated, Hadon stepped forward. Instead of bringing his sword in a cutting motion, he thrust. And Hewako, who could have parried a cut, was caught wide open.

The thrust was not fatal, nor even badly wounding. The blunt end of Karken, though delivered with strength, could do no more than break the skin. But it drove into Hewako's throat at the base, just above the breastbone. Hewako's mouth opened wider; his eyes bulged; a hoarse pained sound came from the injured throat. And he failed in his surprise and agony to bring the blade down.

Hadon had moved back immediately after the thrust in case Hewako did complete the downward cut. Now Hewako, bleeding from the break just above the breastbone, his face red with anger, charged, bringing the edge down furiously.

Hadon moved one step forward and brought his blade up so that Hewako's struck it glancingly and went off to one side. And at the clang Hadon suddenly *knew* that Hewako was doomed to die. Something had leaped down the sword and had run up his arm and into his breast. Something told him that he could not lose this fight, that Hewako had only a few minutes of life left.

Nor was he the only one to know. Hewako had turned pale, and the sweat that polished his skin, the sweat which had looked so hot before, now looked cold. In fact, goose pimples had appeared all over Hewako's body. And the eyes had become shadowed.

Nevertheless, he fought bravely, and none among the crowd would have known what had passed between him and Hadon. They would have noted only that Hadon took the offensive, that he parried every stroke of Hewako's, that he thrice went in through Hewako's guard and inflicted deep gashes, one on the right ribs, one on the left ribs, and one on Hewako's right shoulder.

Suddenly Hewako stepped back three steps, raised the sword high above him, and shouting, ran at Hadon. Hadon stepped forward, brought up his blade, and caught Hewako's mighty swing against it, sent it off to one side, and once again thrust into the base of Hewako's throat. The squat bull-like man staggered back, his sword dropping from his grasp, and his hands caught at his throat. Hadon slid one foot forward and then placed it on Hewako's sword. The crowd roared, though there were many boos and catcalls among the cheering. Evidently many felt that there was something somehow unsporting about Hadon's use of the thrust. It was so seldom seen. The professionals looked with approval at Hadon, however, and they spoke quietly of his unorthodox technique. None of them admitted that they would have been caught off-guard by it, but it had been appropriately used in this contest. After all, Hewako was an amateur.

He would also soon be a dead amateur. He stood close to the edge of the circle, breathing heavily, sweating so that water pooled by his feet, one hand pressed on the bleeding wound at the base of his throat, his eyes sick.

Finally he said hoarsely, "So you have won, Hadon?"

"Yes," Hadon said. "And now I must kill you, as the rules decree. Do I have your forgiveness, Hewako?"

Hewako said faintly, "I see you, Hadon."

Hadon said, "What? *See* me?"

"Yes," Hewako said. "I see you and your future. Sisisken has opened my eyes, Hadon. I see you in a time far from now, though not so far that you will be an old man. For you will live past your youth, Hadon, but you will never be an old man. And your life will be troubled. And there will be many times when you will envy me, Hadon. And I see...I see..."

Hadon felt chilled, as if the ghost of Hewako had left his body and had passed by him. Yet Hewako still remained alive, though the crowd yelled at Hadon to strike, and the referee was gesturing at him to get it over with.

"What do you see?" Hadon said.

"Only shadows," Hewako said. "Shadows that you will see soon enough. But listen, Hadon. I see that you will never be the king of kings. Though you are victor today, you will never sit upon the throne of the ruler of Khokarsa. And I see you in a far-off land, Hadon, and a woman with yellow hair and the strangest violet eyes, and—"

"Strike, Hadon!" the referee yelled. "The king and queen are impatient; they have twice signaled that you should strike!"

"Do you forgive me, Hewako?" Hadon said.

"Never," Hewako said. "My blood be upon your head, Hadon. My ghost bring you bad luck and a grisly end, Hadon."

Hadon was horrified, and the referee cried out, "Those are not the words of a warrior, of a hero!"

Hewako smiled faintly and said, "What do I care?"

Hadon stepped forward and swung Karken sidewise, and Hewako's head fell off and rolled across the floor and almost went over the edge but was snatched by the hair at the last moment by the referee. His body toppled forward, the blood jetting from the neck and bathing Hadon from head to foot. Hadon closed his eyes and endured it, and when he opened his eyes, he thought he saw a flash of something small and dark leap from the corpse and drop over the edge of the platform. But it was surely a trick of his imagination. At least, he hoped it was.

And then the priestesses came up onto the platform with buckets of water to cleanse the platform and him and to utter the cleansing words.

7

The next day the final funeral ceremonies were held. Though Hadon did not like to sacrifice to Hewako, he had to. It was expected of him, but even more important, if he neglected to spill a bull's blood for Hewako to drink, he would be haunted forever by his ghost, and ill luck and an early death would be his fate. Hadon's own money was too little for him to buy the fine bull needed, but as the king-soon-to-be, he had no trouble getting credit.

In fact, there were many who were eager to give him the money, though it was evident that they expected favors after he had ascended the throne. He was besieged by people who wanted favors, who were crying out for a justice that he was in no position to give, or who just simply wanted to touch him because of the good luck it would give or because the touch might heal their diseases. He retreated to the barracks, though he could not get away from the clamor.

Officials came who were to prepare him for the days ahead. They told him how he must march to the palace tomorrow, what dress he must wear, and what traditional words he must say and what gestures he must make.

Mokomgu, the chamberlain of the queen, also told him what restraints would be placed on him for some years to come.

"If you will forgive me for saying so," Mokomgu said, "you are a youth of nineteen, and you have no experience in governing anything, let alone the mighty empire of Khokarsa. Fortunately, your wife has been trained in the duties of governing since she was five, and she of course has control of everything in government but military, naval, and engineering matters. But what do you know about the ins and outs, the complexities of the army, the navy, and the building of roads and forts and government buildings and temples to Resu?"

Hadon had to confess that he knew nothing of these matters.

"It will take you at least ten years to grasp all that is needed to regulate matters efficiently, and then there is, of course, politics. There are many power groups within the court, and you must understand what these want and why they want them, and you must make decisions, simple decisions based on complex reasons, all for the greatest good of the empire."

Hadon, numb with the responsibility and the awareness of his ignorance, merely nodded.

"Minruth can advise you, but he is under no obligation to do so," Mokomgu said. "However, he is not a man to endure idleness, and he no doubt will wish to give you the benefit of his wisdom and experience. You, on the other hand, do not have to accept his advice."

Mokomgu paused, smiled, and said, "You have an advantage at the start. You can read and write as well as any clerk, which is a blessing. We have had kings who were illiterate when they came to the throne, and they died only half-lettered. But we have investigated you, and we find that you, though poor and without funds to hire a teacher, taught yourself the syllabary and arithmetic. That is the mark of ambition and intelligence. Awineth was pleased when she heard that, and so were we. There were some who were not so pleased, since they would like to be at the elbow of a king who cannot read reports but must depend on those who can."

"Hewako could not read well," Hadon said. "What if he had won?"

"Awineth does not have to accept the winner," Mokomgu said. "That she did not announce your rejection after the final event means that she finds you pleasing. She likes you and thinks you are very handsome and have the makings of a great warrior, not to mention those of a husband."

"What does she mean by that?" Hadon said.

"Our intelligence service has questioned every woman known to have bedded you," Mokomgu said. "They all report that you are exceptionally virile. That is not necessary, of course, since the queen may take lovers if she wishes. But she admires you, and she is also pleased that you are good-natured."

Meaning weak-natured, Hadon thought. Awineth was used to having her way; his brief meeting with her had shown him that.

"And what else did your spies find out?" Hadon said. He was beginning to feel quite warm—hot, in fact.

"That you are a good conversationalist, drink quite moderately, are adaptable, a hard worker, responsible, though still given to youthful pranks at times, able to take punishment if it's deserved, in short, though only nineteen you have the makings of a fine man. And of a fine king. You are a great athlete, of course, but things are no longer as they were in the old days. Muscles and a strong wind are the least of qualifications for the throne.

"Awineth is also pleased that you are a devout worshiper of Kho, unlike, I might add, her own father. Though, of course, she was dubious at first about your relationship to Kwasin. But she was assured that you could not help it that you are first cousin to that ravisher of priestesses and murderer of temple guards. Besides, we ascertained that you did not like Kwasin. As who does?"

"Is there anything you don't know about me?" Hadon said.

"Very little," Mokomgu said.

Don't look so smug, Hadon thought. What I was does not assure what I shall be.

The next day, after a service in the great sacred oak grove high on Khowot's slope, Hadon was given a ritual bath by priestesses. He was anointed with sweet-smelling balsam oil and dressed in a bonnet of fish-eagle feathers, a kilt of fish-eagle feathers, and sandals of hide from a sacred hippopotamus. Since he was a member of the Ant People Totem, a stylized ant head was painted in red on his chest. He was then marched behind a silent band of musicians to an empty grave along the Road of Kho. Here he was shown his golden crown, placed at the bottom of the grave. He had to jump into the grave, pick it up, and climb out. During this, a priestess chanted, "Remember, though you are king, that all, kings and slaves, must come to this!"

Then, with the crown in one hand, he walked behind the band, which played loud martial music, while behind him came priests and priestesses, a guard of spear-carrying soldiers, the queen's chamberlain and his staff, and a crowd of the curious.

They marched along the road, the sides of which were massed with cheering and petal-throwing spectators. Hadon felt his numbness thawing out in the heat of exultation. At the great gates of the wall of the Inner City, he knocked with his crown, crying out to open in the name of the winner of the Games. The gates swung open, and he walked through and soon was ascending the broad and steep marble steps to the citadel. At its top he repeated the knocking and the demand to be let in, and the citadel gates swung open.

And presently he was in the enormous high-dome-ceilinged throne room and crying out the set words that Minruth should descend from the throne and allow him to sit upon it beside the high priestess and the queen of the two seas. However, Minruth was not expected to actually give up the throne then. His role was to acknowledge Hadon's right to the throne. Until the marriage ceremony took place three days from then, Hadon would not officially be the king.

Minruth, grinning as if he were delighted, answered, and it was then that Hadon realized that affairs were not proceeding automatically. He should have been warned by Awineth's look of fury and the set and pale faces of the courtiers.

"Gladly, O Hadon, would I step down from a place which imposes wearisome burdens and the glory of which is more lead than gold. And my daughter desires a young and handsome man, a vigorous youth, to rule with her and to pleasure her, as she has so often told me."

Here he looked venomously at Awineth, who glared at him.

"But what I, the king, wish, and what great Resu and Kho wish are often not the same. And we mortals must bow to the words of the deities.

"Now, as you no doubt have heard, Hadon, a man has recently come to us from the Wild Lands beyond the Saasares mountains. He is Hinokly, sole survivor of an expedition I sent some years ago to explore the shores of the great sea beyond the Wild Lands on the edge of the world. While you were displaying your heroic prowess in the Games, he came to us, to my daughter and me. And he told us of a harrowing journey, of men dead from disease, from lions and the great nose-horned beast, the *bok'ul"ikadeth*, from the great gray-tusked *qampo*, from drowning, and most of all from the arrows of the wild tribes. From arrows which our enemies may use but which Kho has forbidden us to use, much to the disadvantage of her people."

"Beware, Father," Awineth said. "You tread on dangerous ground!"

"I only tell the truth," Minruth said. "Be that as it may, the expedition did reach the mighty sea that rings the world in the north."

He paused and said loudly, "And on its shore they encountered the great god Sahhindar himself!"

Hadon felt awe invade his fury. Sahhindar, the Gray-Eyed God, the Archer God. Sahhindar, god of plants, of bronze, of time itself. Sahhindar, exiled god, disgraced son of Kho. And men had seen him!

"They not only saw him, they *talked* to him! They fell to their knees and worshiped him, but he bade them rise and be at ease. And he brought out of the trees nearby three people, mortals, who had been hidden there. One was a tall woman, beautiful beyond dreams, golden-haired and with eyes like a goddess, violet-colored eyes. At first our men thought that she must be Lahla herself, goddess of the moon, because Lahla is golden-haired and violet-eyed, if we can believe the priestesses. Is that not true, Hinokly, did she not look like Lahla?"

He spoke to a short thin man of about thirty-five who stood on the edge of the crowd.

"May I be struck down by Kho Herself if I am lying!" Hinokly said in a reedy voice.

The courtiers around him stepped back, but Hinokly stood calm.

"And did she not have a name which sounds much like Lahla?" Minruth said.

"She spoke a strange language, O King of Kings," Hinokly said. "The sounds of her tongue are weird. But to my ears her name was Lalila."

"Lalila," Minruth said. "*Moon of change* in our tongue, though she told them that in hers it meant something else. And she claimed that she was no goddess. But gods and goddesses have been known to lie when they come down among mortals. In any event, goddess or woman, she acknowledged Sahhindar to be her master. Is that not true, Hinokly?"

"That is true, O King of Kings."

"Then she is no goddess, Father," Awineth said. "No goddess would bow her head to a mere god."

Minruth, face contorted, said, "Things change! And I find it significant that this woman of divine beauty is the moon of change. Perhaps her name is an omen. In any event, this woman was accompanied by two others—her child, a daughter with the same golden hair and violet eyes as her mother, and a manling named Paga."

"Pardon, lord, it is Pag," Hinokly said.

"That's what I said, Paga," Minruth said.

Hinokly shrugged, and Hadon, fluent in several languages, understood. The Khokarsan language had no syllable ending in *-g*, and so the ordinary Khokarsan would pronounce the name according to the rules of his native tongue. There was no syllable such as *pa* either, open syllables beginning with *p* being confined to *pe*, *pi*, *poe*. But such a syllable was easy for a Khokarsan to pronounce.

"This Paga is a dwarf with one eye, the other having been knocked out with a rock thrown by some bitch-tempered woman," Minruth said, glancing at his daughter to catch her reaction. Awineth merely frowned.

"He carries with him a huge ax made of some iron that is far tougher than any we have. Paga says that it is iron from a falling star, and he fashioned it into an ax for a hero named Wi. This Wi is dead now, but he was the father of the child, whose name sounds like Abeth. And before he died he gave the ax to Paga and told him to keep it until he met a man who was great enough to receive it as a gift. But the ax is—"

"Get to the meat of the matter, Father," Awineth said harshly.

"We must not displease the high priestess of Kho," Minruth said, rolling his eyes. "Very well. Sahhindar himself ordered my men to take Lalila, the child Abeth, and Paga to this city. He ordered them, under pain of terrible punishment, to take good care of them and to see that they were received as honored guests. He could not come with them because he had business elsewhere, though he did not say what that business was. But he promised to come here someday to make sure that Lalila and the others were honored. When, he did not say. But what the gods promise, they perform."

"And what," Awineth said loudly, "about the ban of Kho! Would Sahhindar dare return to the land from which his great mother drove him?"

"Sahhindar said that he was not aware of such a ban," Minruth said, obviously pleased. "So perhaps the priestesses have not told us the truth."

Awineth said, "Beware, Father!"

Minruth said, "Or, more likely, they misunderstood the oracles. Or perhaps Kho, being a female, changed her mind. She has relented and would see her son walk again among the people to whom he gave such great gifts in the days of our ancient foremothers.

"But on the way back, evil befell the party. They were shot at by savages with arrows, the arrows which Kho has forbidden us, her chosen people, to use. Our men took to dugouts they found, but the savages killed many from the banks and then pursued them in boats. The boat with Lalila, the baby, and the manling overturned, and the last that the men in the other boat saw of them they were struggling in the water. And of the men who escaped, only Hinokly survived to bring us the news. Is that not true, Hinokly?"

"The Wild Lands are terrible, O King," Hinokly said.

"It is too bad that you must journey through them again," Minruth said. "But consider yourself fortunate. You should have been flayed alive for deserting the people whose safety was charged to you by Sahhindar. I am a merciful king, however, and after consultation with my daughter it was decided that you should guide the rescue expedition, since you alone know where Lalila is. Or was."

"I thank the king and the queen for their mercy," Hinokly said, though he did not look grateful.

Hadon's awe was being replaced by a mounting anger. He did not know exactly what the king had in mind, but he thought he could guess it in general. And he could not understand why Awineth seemed to be going along with her father.

"What does all this mean?" he cried. "Why has the ancient ceremony been interrupted for this tale, however wonderful it is?"

Minruth roared, "Until you sit on this throne, you will speak only when requested to do so!"

Awineth said, "In short, it means that our marriage must be delayed until after you bring back this woman and the ax from the Wild Lands. It is not my doing or my wish, Hadon. I would have you on this throne and in my bed as soon as possible. But even the high priestess must obey the voice of Kho."

Minruth smiled and said, "Yes, even the high priestess! An ancient custom may be disregarded when Kho says so!"

"If I may speak?" Hadon said, looking at Awineth.

"You may."

"Am I right in guessing that I have been chosen to lead this expedition?"

"You have quick wits, Hadon. You are right."

"And I am not to be your husband until I have returned with this woman, the ax, and I suppose, the child and the manling, since Sahhindar has ordered that they also be brought safely to Khokarsa?"

"That, to my sorrow, is true."

"But why have I been chosen? Surely you would not...?"

"Not I! It was my father who suggested that this be done, and I said no! But then he said that this was no mere matter of mortals, that the deities were involved. And so we journeyed up Khowot's slope to the Temple of Kho and there we spoke to the oracular priestess. 'What should we do?' we asked. 'What does Kho Herself wish in this business, if, indeed, She wishes anything?'

"And so we went into the cave where the priestess keeps her vigil, where the dangerous breath of the fires underground issues. And the priestess sat on her three-cornered stool and breathed the fumes, while my father and I, our faces covered with cloaks, sat in a corner on the cold hard stone. And presently the oracle spoke in a strange voice, and a light seemed to fill the cave. My father and I put our hands over our eyes, since whoever sees Kho in Her glory is blinded, and we listened trembling to Her voice. And She said that the greatest hero of the land must go out immediately to find the witch from the sea and the witch's daughter and the little one-eyed man and the ax. And the hero must not tarry to take his ease with any woman, nor marry nor transact any business. And the voice said that the woman and the ax might bring ill or good or both to the land, but she and the ax must be looked for.

"She said nothing about your returning, only that the hero must go at once on his quest. Nor did She say anything about Sahhindar."

Hadon was silent with awe for a moment, and then he spoke.

"And when was this, O Queen?"

"Last night, Hadon. While you slept with the golden crown of the victor in your bed, and no doubt dreamed of me, my father and I hurried up the slope of forbidding Khowot."

"But why am I the greatest hero of the land?" he said.

"That hardly needs answering," Minruth growled.

"But you, O King, are the victor of the previous Games, and you sit upon the throne, and you led your soldiers in the taking of the rebellious city of Sakawuru, and you defeated the Klemqaba so severely that they are now giving tribute at least on the coast—and you it was who slew the ravaging black leopard of Siwudawa with your bare hands. Surely you are the hero of whom the oracle spoke."

Minruth stared, and then he burst into laughter.

"Surely you are cunning, Hadon, and you will someday make a great king. If you pass through the Wild Lands without harm and fulfill Sahhindar's request, that is. No, Hadon, I am getting old, and my deeds were done a long time ago. And new bright deeds are what figure greatly in the minds of the people and the deities, not old stale deeds. You will find that out someday, Hadon. Perhaps. But do not try to talk your way out of this, as the fable says that the fox did out of the trap.

"The news about this is being printed now to be shipped out to every city of the empire. And the people of Khokarsa are being informed of this by the criers at this very moment."

"Then when do I leave?" Hadon said.

Awineth, tears running down her cheeks, arose. "This very moment, Hadon."

She came down the steps and held out her hand to him. "Kiss it, Hadon, and remember that you will have all of me when you return. I will grieve for you, but I must obey the voice of Kho, just as all mortals, even queens, must obey."

Hadon dropped to one knee and kissed the back of her hand. Then he arose and seized her soft white shoulders and pressed her warm breasts to his and kissed her upon the lips. There was a gasp and a murmur from the crowd and a strangled roar from Minruth. But she responded warmly, and then she freed herself, smiling, though the tears were still in her eyes.

"Any other man would have died on the spot, unless I had said he might take me in his arms," she said. "But I know that you are the man I love, and that you are worthy of me. So hasten hence and hasten back, Hadon. I will be waiting."

"The Voice said nothing about his coming back!" Minruth shouted, but Hadon turned and strode away. At that moment, he felt happy.

8

His buoyancy did not last long. By the time he had reached the docks, he was scowling and his face was red. He did not respond to the crowds who cheered him and threw petals at him or tried to break through the guards to touch him. He almost did not see or hear them. He was turned inward and backward to the room which held the throne and the woman out of whom he had been cheated.

He realized that his thoughts were blasphemous. Though Kho Herself had decreed that he should go out on this quest, he felt that he had been cheated. And there was nothing he could do about it. He was as powerless as the lowest of slaves, as the poorest of the poor, he, the winner of the Great Games, a hero!

Burning with the fire that freezes, numb with anger, he boarded the unireme waiting for him. He was scarcely aware of the people to whom he was introduced—the captain, the ship's priestess, and some of his fellow passengers. They must have been awed by his expression and his bearing, because they got away from him as swiftly as they could. And while he paced back and forth on the narrow foredeck, he was not approached by anyone.

The galley was pulled along swiftly by the oarsmen and headed northward and slightly eastward. It passed the fortress on the western tip of Mohasi island and soon was going through the broad strait between the naval-base island of Sigady and the two-pronged peninsula, the Python's Head, which projected from the mainland. The fortresses on each ran up their flags in salute to the ship which bore the hero of the Games. At another time, Hadon would have swelled with exultation. Now he felt that he was being mocked, though he had a residue of common sense which told him that this was not really so.

Then, as the hours passed and great Resu began his descent, the galley went northwestward along the cliffs of the western side of the Gulf of Gahete. When night fell, the ship was still deep in the narrow gulf. The air cooled, and with it Hadon. The stars shone brightly, and after a while Lahla, goddess of the moon, Kho's fairest daughter, showered her grace upon all who would appreciate it. She was so bright that Hadon could see smoke rising from Khowot, the Voice of Kho, a cone rising toward the sky. The smoke was a series of broken and strangely shaped clouds, illuminated by intermittent flashes of fire. He tried to read the shapes as if they were parts of a syllabary, but he could make nothing of them. Was Kho sending him a message which he was too unperceptive to understand?

After a while, the first mate approached him and asked him if he cared to dine with the captain and the priestess. Hadon, suddenly aware that he was hungry, said that he would be pleased.

The roof of the captain's cabin had been removed to let in the moonlight and the cooling air. The interior was bright with pine torches set in brackets on the bulkheads, and the odor of resin was so strong that Hadon almost could not smell the food. A table was set within the narrow cabin for six people and the ever-present unseen guest, dread Sisisken. Hadon stood by his oak chair while the priestess prayed to Kho and Piqabes, Kho's green-eyed daughter, to bless the food and those about to partake of it. Hadon sat down then and ate voraciously, as if he were gobbling up those he hated—Minruth and those vague forces that had brought him to this sorry position. But the hate disappeared in the savory okra soup, the tender juicy buffalo steak, the fillets of horned fish, the emmer bread, the black olives, the cabbage, the delicacy of fried termites, and the papyrus piths. And he indulged himself with one beaker of mead, made from the far-famed honey of the bees of the city of Qoqada. Afterward he sat at the table talking and chewing on a soft twig to cleanse his teeth.

Three of his tablemates, he found, were to accompany him on the expedition. Tadoku was his second-in-command. He was middle-sized, very lean, about forty, a *numatenu*, and a major in the Vth Army, which meant he was a native of Dythbeth. His body and face were scarred from a hundred fights, and his skull near the right temple was slightly indented where a stone from a Klemqaba sling had almost killed him. He was, Hadon judged, a tough and shrewd man. And, no doubt, he could give Hadon many points on the wielding of a *tenu*.

The second was Hinokly, whom he had seen and heard in the palace. Hinokly was to be his guide through the Wild Lands. Judging from his moroseness, he was not pleased with the task.

The third was the expedition's bard, Kebiwabes. He was about thirty and was dressed in the bard's white linen robe, which concealed somewhat a short slim body. His head was large, his hair a glossy brown, his nose snub, his mouth full and broad, his eyes large and russet-brown and merry. Near him, on a peg on the bulkhead, hung his seven-stringed lyre. It was made of boxwood, and the strings were from the small intestine of the sheep. One of the projecting upper ends was carved with the figure of the goddess of the moon, who was also the patroness of music and poetry. Kebiwabes also seemed to be under the influence of Besbesbes, goddess of bees and mead, judging by the many beakers he drank. As the evening progressed, his russet eyes became blood-red, and his voice thickened as if honey had been poured down his throat. And he became indiscreet, talking openly of things better said in privacy if they must be said.

"When we land in Mukha, Hadon, you will be given command of as sorry a body of soldiers as ever disgraced the army. Misfits, goldbrickers, troublemakers, loonies, thieves, and cowards. All, except for the *numatenu* here, Tadoku, men whom Minruth should have discharged or hanged long ago. Men whom he will be glad to get rid of. Men who will ensure that your expedition is a failure. Why the great soldier Tadoku was assigned to you, I do not know. Is there something of which I am not aware, Tadoku? Have you, like me, offended Minruth in some way?"

"I was chosen by Awineth herself and assigned over the protests of Minruth," Tadoku said.

"That's one good thing, perhaps the only good thing, to happen," the bard said. "Does Awineth know what kind of personnel poor Hadon here has to command?"

"I am not that much in her confidence," Tadoku said, glaring at him.

"Well, I was chosen as the bard for this lousy expedition because I composed and sang a satirical song about Minruth," Kebiwabes said. "Minruth did not dare to touch me, because bards are sacred. But he was able to honor me—honor!—by appointing me your bard. In effect, it's an exile from which, most likely, I will not return. But I don't care. I have always wanted to see the wonders of the Wild Lands. Perhaps they will inspire me to compose a great epic, *The Song of Hadon*, and my name will rank with those of the divine bards, Hala, she who composed *The Song of Gahete*, and Kwamim, she who composed *The Song of Kethna*. Then all will have to admit that a man can create music and poetry as well as a woman."

"Neither of those were drunks," Tadoku said.

Kebiwabes laughed and said, "Mead is the blood of Besbesbes, and if I take enough in, perhaps I will sweat out the effluvia of divinity. In any event, once we are deep into the Wild Lands, there will be no more mead. Willy-nilly, I must be sober. But then I will become drunk on moonlight, on the silver liquor which Lahla pours so freely."

He drank deeply, belched, and said, "If I live that long."

Hadon concealed his dismay. He spoke to Hinokly, who was languidly stirring a spoon in his cold soup.

"And you, Hinokly, do you take as dark a view?"

"Of all the good men who went out into the Wild Lands, I was the least fitted to survive," he said. "I am a scribe, small and weak and unused to hardships and terrors. The others were tall strong men of the stuff of heroes. Minruth himself picked them for the qualities those who go into the Wild Lands must have. Yet I alone did not die. I alone came back. So I will say only that we are in the hands of Kho. Success and failure and the names of those who will die and those who will not are already written in the rolls that no man may read."

"Which is to say that we can't know the future and must act as if the goddesses were on our side," Tadoku said briskly. "As for myself, I pray to Kho and to Resu, who, besides being god of the sun and of the rain, is also god of war."

The priestess said sharply, "And what about Bhukla, the goddess of war! War was originally her domain, and Resu usurped it. At least, he did so in the minds of some, but we priestesses know that Bhukla was the first, and the soldier who neglects her will find sorrow."

"I pray to her, of course, priestess, since she is now the goddess of the *tenu*," Tadoku said. "Every *numatenu* prays to her in the morning and before going to bed, and she presides when the swords of the *numatenu* are being made. But, as I was going to say, I rely not only on the gods and the goddesses. I trust in myself, in my hard-won skill with the sword.

"Tell me," he said, turning to Hadon, "what do you know of military service?"

"Not much," Hadon said, "which is why I am glad that you are my lieutenant. As a child, I used to hang around the parade grounds and watch the soldiers drill, and I learned something of procedure and discipline when I worked in the kitchens and as a water boy in the fort near Opar. And I learned some things from my father."

"Then you're not a raw recruit, and your task will be easier," Tadoku said. "You must have picked up much about the politicking and the passing of the buck which are, if not the backbone of the army, the ribs. And you must know that having good cooks is very important. Most laymen think only of the glory of the battle when they think of the army. But having good cooks and good doctors and an incorruptible but foxy supply sergeant are things that occupy an officer's mind more than leading men into fray."

"As I understand it," Kebiwabes said, "you are a poor man. Or were."

"And what is that to you?" Hadon said angrily.

"Much," the bard said. "I am interested in the character of the man who will be leading us into unknown dangers. I have observed that the rich are always corrupted, and the poor are corrupted too, though in a different way. Money and power change a man as surely as if the hands of terrible Khuklaqo, the Shapeless Shaper, had seized him. However, the rich man attempts to disguise it from himself—he becomes arrogant, and he acts as if dread Sisisken were not always around the corner. He becomes hard but not strong, brittle as a badly cast tool.

"On the other hand, poverty is a demon with an odor of its own. The rich stink of money, and the poor stink of its lack. The middle classes stink of both. But a poor man may rise above his poverty, whereas a rich man seldom, if ever, rises above his wealth."

"I don't think I understand you," Hadon said.

"It doesn't matter. You are young yet, but you have wits, and if you live long enough, you will understand. Though understanding, as usual, will have as its companion sorrow. Suffice it that I have faith in you. Lahla has given me the ability to hear a man's vibrations as if he were a lyre plucked by her fingers. In your case, the seven strings of the soul make a sweet music. But the song will not always be a merry one."

Kebiwabes arose and said, "I must go to sleep."

The priestess said, "I had hoped that you would sing for us."

"The sweet mead would come forth as sour music," he said. "Tomorrow I will sing for you. But not until evening. Good night, all."

Tadoku stared after the staggering bard and said, "There goes one of the misfits and troublemakers."

"But he seems to be more troubled within himself than by things outside him," the priestess said. "He has never been violent. He uses only his voice to express his discontent and to criticize the things amiss in this world."

"That kind is the worst kind of troublemaker," Tadoku said. "He speaks, and many act out his words."

"I rather like him," Hadon said. "Major, would you do me the honor of sword-exercising with me tomorrow?"

"Gladly," Tadoku said.

Hadon dreamed that night, not of the beautiful Awineth, as might have been expected, but of his mother. He kept running after her, and she, though standing with arms open to receive him, moved always backward and finally was lost in the shadows. He awoke sobbing and wondering if Sisisken had sent him a message that his mother was dead. After breakfast he wrote a long letter to his family. But the letter would have to be posted in Mukha, and it would be many a month—if ever—before it arrived in distant Opar.

Kebiwabes, up earlier than Hadon had expected, saw him writing the last paragraphs on the roll. He approached him as Hadon sealed the letter and said, "You can write? I am impressed. I myself have some facility with the syllabary, but I am afraid to become too literate."

Hadon was surprised. "Why is that?"

"Writing is the enemy of memory," Kebiwabes said. "Look at me. I am a bard who must memorize, and has memorized, thousands of lines. I carry the words of a hundred songs in my head. I began to learn these when I was three, and my lifelong labor of learning these has been hard. But I know them well; they are stamped onto my heart.

"If, however, I depended upon the written word, my heart would grow weak. I would soon find myself halting, searching for the line, and would have to go to a roll to find the lost words. I fear that when all become lettered, which is what the priestesses would like, bards will have as short a memory as everybody else."

"Perhaps," Hadon said. "But if the great Awines had not invented the syllabary, science and commerce would not have progressed so swiftly. And the empire of Khokarsa would not be so wide-flung."

"That might be just as well," the bard said. When he was questioned about the meaning of this, he did not reply but said, "Tadoku asked me to tell you that he will meet you at midmorning on the foredeck for an exercise. At the moment he is busy dictating to Hinokly letters to the palace. He seems upset by my words last night."

"You remember them?" Hadon said.

The bard laughed and said, "I am not always as drunk as I seem. He was disturbed because I knew more about the type of men he will command than he did. Apparently no one had told him."

"And how did you find out?" Hadon said.

"Next to the queen's bedchamber, the best place to find out secrets is the tavern. Especially if the palace servants do their drinking there."

"I have a lot to learn," Hadon said.

"Admitting that means that you can learn," Kebiwabes said.

At midmorning Tadoku entered the cabin and saluted Hadon. Hadon returned it with the right arm held out straight before him, the thumb and little finger touching tips, the three longest fingers spread out.

"Officially, you will not take command until we reach Mukha," Tadoku said. "But we might as well get accustomed to our roles before then. And if there is any advice I can give you, anything I can teach you, I am yours."

"Sit down," Hadon said. "First, I would like a frank answer. Do you, an experienced officer and a famed *numatenu*, resent serving under a green youth?"

"Under different circumstances, I might," Tadoku said. "But this is an unusual situation. Besides, you aren't a know-it-all. And, to be frank, if I serve you well, my career may be advanced. After all, you may be king someday."

"You say that as if you don't believe I'll ever sit on the throne."

"Our chances of survival are not high," Tadoku said cheerfully. "And if you will allow me to continue to be frank, if we should get back, our chances of survival may be even less."

Hadon was startled. He considered Tadoku's statement and then said, "You think that our king would dare to kill us?"

"It's a long voyage from Mukha to the island," Tadoku said. "And much can happen aboard a galley. Especially if it is manned by those faithful to Minruth."

"But we will be, or anyway should be, under the protection of Sahhindar."

"If there is a Gray-Eyed God in the Wild Lands and if Hinokly did see him," Tadoku said. "Hinokly may be telling the truth. On the other hand, he may have made up the story to save his neck. Or Minruth may have put him up to it to get rid of you."

Hadon had another mild shock. He said, "But the Voice of Kho? Surely She would not be deceived, nor would She deceive us?"

"She would not be deceived," Tadoku said. "But She may have said what She did in order to carry out plans of Her own. Besides, the oracular priestess always says something which may be interpreted in more than one way. Only after the event can mortals know what She truly meant."

Tadoku paused, and then, as if the words came hard, said, "Moreover, priests and priestesses are men and women, and men and women are corruptible."

Disbelief choked Hadon. He said, "You can't mean that Minruth might have bribed the oracle? The voice of the Voice of Kho? That couldn't be! Kho Herself would strike the woman dead!"

"Yes, but Kho may have allowed this so that She could carry out her plans, as I said before. However, I don't really believe that the priestess would lie for the sake of money. She would be too terrified. I just suggested that because one should consider all possibilities, no matter how farfetched they seem."

"You are cynical!" Hadon said.

"I have a sharp eye, and I have been close to the great ones of the empire for a long time," Tadoku said. "In any event, I have checked out the personnel of the vessel. It's a merchant ship, you know, basically a mail-carrier. That is odd. Why weren't you put on a naval vessel, since you're such a precious cargo? Why weren't we given a naval escort? What if a pirate ship were to attack us? It's true that pirates haven't been in the waters north of the island for two hundred years. But that doesn't mean that they might not appear again. And what if the pirate vessel were in the employ of Minruth?

"Not that I consider that likely. Such a thing would be too raw for anybody to digest, and the rage of Awineth, as everybody but you seems to know, is awful. Minruth would be the first to die, unless he ordered his troops into action at once. And then he would likely be defeated. On the other hand, Minruth is called the Mad for good reasons, and you cannot expect him always to act as a rational man would.

"However, assuming that he does use good sense, he will take no action until, or if, you return. In the meantime—which will be a long one—much can happen in Khokarsa."

Hadon, instead of being depressed, became angry. When he and Tadoku practiced with wooden swords, he attacked Tadoku as if he meant to kill him. But Tadoku gave him a beating that soon cooled him down, and the points Tadoku gained were thereafter much less. Finally, panting and sweating, the two ceased. A sailor emptied buckets of cool seawater over them, and they sat down to discuss the exercise.

"You have the makings of a great swordsman," Tadoku said. "You will be one in five years if you get enough experience. And if you live that long. Bhukla is fickle, and I have seen better men than myself go to her sister Sisisken. A man has an off-day, and a lesser swordsman kills him. Or he may have problems which he cannot thrust out of his mind during the fighting. Or something has happened to break his spirit, and he may unconsciously wish to die. Or chance, a foot slipping in blood, the sun in his eyes, a fly landing on his nose, weakening caused by the onslaught of a cold or an ill-digested meal—all these and much more may cause the death of even the greatest swordsman.

"However, the chief killers are booze and too much food and the loss of youth. You can do something about the first two, but over the last, no man has control. A man should know when to quit, when to hang up the iron *tenu* and wear only the honorary copper *tenu.* Pride may prevent him from doing this, and then Sisisken, who loathes pride and arrogance, will chop him down."

"And when will you hang up your *tenu*?" Hadon said.

Tadoku grinned and said, "I don't expect to find any great swordsmen, or any swordsmen at all, in fact, out in the Wild Lands. The savages have only stone or wooden weapons—the ax, the spear, and the club. And the sling and the bow, which are not to be sneered at, but swords wielded by the greatest are no good against arrows, so why worry about them? After we get back—if we get back—then I may start wearing the copper. In the meantime, I serve my queen."

They discussed the relative merits of the sword, the ax, and the club.

"At close range, the axman is at a disadvantage," Tadoku said. "But beware the skilled thrower of the ax. As for the club, if it is brassbound, it can be dangerous. However, the only club I would fear would be that in the hands of the monster Kwasin. I saw him once, when he was on his way to the Western Lands, just after he had been exiled. He is as tall as a giraffe and as strong as a gorilla, and when he is fighting, as berserk as a rhinoceros in rut. He is strangely quick for such a giant, and he seems to know all the tricks of a swordsman. But it is force he depends upon, force that only the heroes of old had. I doubt that even the giant hero Klamsweth could have stood up to him."

"I know," Hadon said. "Kwasin is my cousin."

"I'm well aware of that," Tadoku said testily. "I didn't want to bring it up, since I thought you might not like to talk about it. No relatives of his that I have so far met ever wanted to admit that they were related."

"I'm not fond of him," Hadon said. "But I feel no shame because of his crime. I didn't commit it, and besides, he's not of my totem."

"That's a sensible attitude," Tadoku said. "The more I know you, the less I resent serving under you."

"Ah, then you do resent me!" Hadon said.

Tadoku merely grinned.

9

The galley slowly rounded the curve that took the cone of Khowot out of sight. At midday it was free of the mouth of the Gulf of Gahete. As the cliffs dwindled, Khowot became visible again. At dusk it could still be seen, but it was sinking into the horizon. Clouds of smoke were still rising from it, great black masses, and Hadon wondered if it were about to erupt again. The last serious explosion had half-destroyed the city of Khokarsa two hundred and fifty years ago. It would be ironic if he completed his mission only to find that Awineth and Minruth had perished under gas, smoke, and lava.

Since the wind was from the northwest, the galley was unable to use its sails. It could beat against the wind only to a limited extent, and in this case it had to depend entirely upon the oars. Once again Hadon asked for permission to row at least twice a day. The captain reluctantly said yes. Tadoku was at first upset. It was not fitting that a hero should work side by side with common fellows. But on seeing that the rowers were very pleased because Hadon was working with them, he changed his mind.

"You're shrewder than I thought," he said to Hadon. "It is well to become popular with the lower classes. As long as you preserve your dignity, of course, and don't become a clown to please them. The rowers will boast about this in the ports, and the story will spread throughout the empire faster than mail can be delivered."

Hadon did not disillusion him. He had only wanted to keep in shape, but if others thought he was intelligent enough to have done this for a political motive, let them think so.

Days of hard rowing passed, and the city of Mukha rose from the round of the sea. At noon the galley pulled past the opening of the massive stone breakwaters and docked. Tadoku hurried into the city to warn the rulers that they were to make no fuss about the appearance of Hadon. The orders were that the expedition was to be organized as quickly as possible and marched off northward into the Wild Lands. But such was not to be. Hadon waited in the camp northwest of Mukha for a week before the first contingent of his force rowed into the harbor.

"Break your back hurrying so you can sit on your ass," Tadoku growled. "The old army motto."

At the end of another ten days (the Khokarsan week was ten days), the last shipload marched off to the shrilling of bagpipes, the throoming of bullroarers, and the clanging of bronze gongs. These were the Klemqaba assigned to the expedition, and Hadon's heart, already low, sank even further. The wild Klemqaba were recruited from the coast northwest of the Strait of Keth and from the even wilder tribes of the mountainous interior. They were short, broad fellows, half-neanderthaloid, half-human, tattooed in blue and green all over, wearing only codpieces of polished buffalo horn which projected in a semicomic, semisinister fashion. They carried small round shields and heavy bronze axes and slings of goat hide and pouches of stones for the slings. Their standard was a carved figure of Kho as the Goat-Headed Mother on the end of a long pole bearing on its length dried phalluses of famous enemies slain in combat. Their breaths stank of *s"okoko,*[2] *the water of life*, a liquor made in the high mountains, a harsh peaty-flavored drink which only they could down with ease.

"The best fighting men in the empire," Tadoku said. "Stronger than we are, and without fear, able to eat food which would kill us off, meat a week rotten, vegetables fit only for garbage, and they never complain as long as they're in action. But they're hell to discipline when there's no fighting. And the fact that they're entitled to bring their women along causes discontent among the other troops."

"I don't see why," Hadon murmured. The women were a squat, ugly lot, most of them stronger than the average human soldier, wild-haired, slack-breasted, clad in animal-skin loincloths, some pregnant, others nursing babies. Like the men, they were tattooed from head to foot.

"Why would a soldier, or anyone, desire such women?"

"After a long time without women of any kind, they begin to look good," Tadoku said.

"Couldn't we at least make those with babies stay behind?" Hadon said.

"If they have to make a choice they'll kill the babies," Tadoku said.

Tadoku started to add something but swore instead. He gestured at a group of twenty soldiers in the rear guard. These were bearded and tattooed red and black and carried kite-shaped shields, and their standard was the figurine of a bear-headed woman.

"Minruth is doing his best to screw us up!" Tadoku groaned. "You never, just simply never, put the Klemklakor with the Klemqaba!"

Hadon asked for an explanation and was told that not all the tribes of these people were of the Goat Totem. A few belonged to the ancient Bear Totem, and these were sworn enemies of the Klemqaba.

Hadon had never seen a bear, though he had seen drawings and statues of them. At one time the mountains north of the Kemu had been heavily populated by the small brown bear and the giant russet cave bear, huger than, as the saying went, a lion and a half. But there had been no validated reports of the russet bear for two centuries, and the brown bears had been hunted close to extinction. Nevertheless,

2 Khokarsan had two syllables for water. *-kem-* meant any relatively unconfined liquid or jellied mass, hence, *-kemu-*, literally, *water-great* or *sea*. *-s"o-* referred to liquids, jellies, or gases in containers.

their totems were still in existence. In fact, Kwasin was a member of the *Klakordeth* or Thunder Bear Totem. Which made him, though not a blood brother, since he was all-human, a spiritual brother of the hybrids.

"If you give an order to the two totems," Tadoku said, "make sure that an officer of one is not to transmit it directly to the other. The officer just won't do it."

"How can we maintain discipline then?"

"That's just one of the many problems this fouled-up outfit presents us with," Tadoku said.

Hadon looked thoughtful. During the week in camp, he had learned all he could about the army procedure, and he had considered carefully the welfare of the expedition. He had been given two hundred and fifty men and women, far too large a force. He desired only fifty. A larger body would cause very slow marching and be difficult to feed. When they were about halfway on their outward journey, they would run out of supplies, and from then on they'd have to depend on their hunters. He had a plan to weed out all but fifty before they got to the last outpost of civilization.

That night he had to settle five quarrels and numerous complaints. He stopped a brawl between the Klemqaba and the Klemklakor only by threatening to smash the *s"okoko* containers if peace was not restored at once. The officers retorted that, since they were mercenaries, they would quit if he carried out his threat. He told them that that was fine with him. They could return home in disgrace, and they would miss out on fighting the wild savages.

Tadoku turned pale when he heard Hadon, but he said nothing. Later, after the two totems had sworn not to fight among themselves for at least ten days, Tadoku commented.

"That was a narrow escape. If the totems had said to hell with you, we would have had a battle which would have cut us down to less than fifty. And I'm afraid that less than half of that would have been human. Though the humans are nothing to brag about."

"It worked," Hadon said. "Now, I want some officers and enlisted men to spread stories about the horrors waiting for us in the Wild Lands. I want the weak-livered ones among us to desert. Give the guards orders to ignore anyone they see sneaking away. Even if they're carrying stolen supplies. Be sure to pick good men as guards, because we don't want the guards deserting too, and leaving us wide open for attack."

Tadoku saluted and hurried off, though he evidently did not like this unconventional breach of discipline.

By the morning of the third day, Tadoku reported that thirty-five men had stolen away in the night. He was surprised, because he had thought that they would lose a hundred. None of the AWOL's were Klemqaba or Klemklakor, which was to be expected.

"The road ends tomorrow at the outpost," Hadon said. "We've been making only about ten miles a day because we have to match our pace with the oxen-drawn wagons. Also, we'll be stopping every two miles to mark our trail. Once we get to the rough country, we'll be reduced to about five miles a day, if that. We're going to lose the oxen, eventually; they can't survive long in the Wild Lands. So we're going to have another test. Announce tonight that the wagons will be abandoned. Slaughter the oxen for a feast, and tell everybody to drink everything except what they think they can carry. Move the Klemklakor about a half-mile away so they won't be fighting the Klemqaba. Station your best men around the camp, and if things get out of hand, they're to interfere only if I give the order."

"May I ask you what the object of this is?" Tadoku said.

"Tomorrow, before breakfast, I will tell them that they are not to eat until they get to the outpost fort. They must pack up and run for the fort. The first fifty only will be allowed to continue into the Wild Lands. The rest will either be sent back to the fort at Mukha or paid off."

"The Goat and Bear people won't stand for that," Tadoku said.

"If they want to argue with us, they'll have to catch us first," Hadon said. "And when we get to the fort, we'll have the garrison to back us up. I intend to eliminate as many problems as possible right now. It's going to be tough enough when we get to the Wild Lands."

"The women will abandon their babies," Tadoku said. "The hyenas, the jackals, and the vultures will be eating them before the sun has quartered the sky."

"Very well. We'll cheat a little. There are five babies. Pick seven of your best men, fellows you know are trustworthy, and hide them outside the camp. They can follow and pick up the babies, and the mothers can claim them later. Let's hope none of the mothers will be among the first fifty. Oh, yes, we have to have Hinokly and the bard and the doctor, so tell them to start marching at midnight. With that headstart, they should be all right."

"They march in the night?" Tadoku said. "This is leopard and lion country. They might not get to the fort."

"We need Hinokly as a guide and Kebiwabes for morale," Hadon said. "Very well. Pick six good men to escort them."

"I don't think I have that many," Tadoku said, and he groaned.

"Do the best you can," Hadon said.

There was an uproar when Tadoku announced Hadon's orders. Hadon immediately told them that he wanted only men and women who had the stuff of heroes on this expedition. Anybody who would confess that he didn't have it should step forward, and he would be sent back to the fort at Mukha. There would be no official penalties attached, though he could not control those who might jeer at them.

Not a single one of the Goat and Bear people moved. Ten of the humans shamefacedly crossed the line that a sergeant had drawn in the dirt.

"Very well," Hadon said. "Tonight the rest of you may feast and drink all you wish. But don't look to replenish your supply of liquor at the fort."

He dismissed them. The oxen were killed and the clay bottles and goatskin containers of beer, mead, and *s"okoko* were opened. Hadon retired to his tent, which he would use no more after that night. It would be left with all tents and burdensome baggage.

From now on all would be sleeping in their bags under the open skies. Tadoku was scandalized when he learned that all officers, including Hadon, would have to carry their own bags, armor, and weapons.

"It just isn't done! It puts us on a footing with the common soldier!"

"Except for a leather helmet and cuirass, I won't be wearing any armor," Hadon said. "Nor will anybody. We don't need bronze armor against the stone weapons of the savages, and we'll be much more mobile without them."

"But armor is expensive!"

"There's a cave up in the hills," Hadon said. "One of the scouts located it for me. The armor will be cached there, and we'll pick it up on the way back. If it's stolen, I'll pay for the loss. As king, I will be able to do that. Everyone will be given a receipt now, collectible in Khokarsa. Oh, by the way, what about the priestess for this expedition? Are we suppose to pick up one at the fort?"

"There is nothing about a priestess in our orders, as you well know," Tadoku said. "Either it's an oversight, which doesn't seem likely, or Minruth is sending us out without a spiritual guide."

"We'll get one at the fort anyway," Hadon said. "If they have only one, they can get another from Mukha."

"And suppose the priestess doesn't want to go with us?"

"I'll tell her we'll take a priest of Resu instead. If she's conscientious, she won't allow that."

"Then we will have a mutiny."

"Perhaps you and I and Hinokly and Kebiwabes and the doctor may be the only ones left," Hadon said, smiling. But he wondered if he was predicting accurately.

Hadon left his tent at midnight. Taps had been ignored, at his orders. He wanted the self-indulgent to eliminate themselves for the race in the morning, and apparently there were many doing just that. The shouting, singing, and laughing were almost as loud as they had been two hours ago, and eight men and one woman had been carried off bleeding and stunned to the medical tent, where the drunken doctor, Onomi, treated them. Hadon walked away from the camp toward the site of the Klemklakor. When the din had become low, he listened for noise from the Bear people. But all was silent. He smiled. They had chosen to quit drinking early and go to bed so they would be in shape tomorrow. Only a desire to beat out their hereditary enemies, the Goat people, could have induced them to refrain from gulping their beloved *s"okoko* to the last drop. And they must have a strong leader, otherwise they would never have been able to practice such self-discipline.

At dawn, the drums and trumpets of reveille got most of the camp to its feet, though here and there a sleeper snored heavily. Hadon gave them a little while to drink water and to eliminate, and then he lined them up across the broad plain.

"When the bugle blows, the race is on!" he cried out.

A few minutes later, he gave them the signal, and two hundred and five men and women, uttering savage cries or hoarse croaks, ran forward. Rather, some did. Most staggered or shambled.

Hadon took the lead and never gave it up. He swung along easily, trotting, and when he had covered the ten miles, felt that he could go another ten. The fort was a massive earthworks construction with several stone towers flying the flags of Khokarsa and of the Mukha queendom. The commander had not expected the force so soon, and there was a delay until he could be summoned from the little wooden temple in one corner of the court. He came cursing and red-faced. Hadon found out later that he and the priestess had been busy at something or other in the privacy of her quarters, and he resented being disturbed. But when he saw Hadon, he forced a smile and greeted him as enthusiastically as he could under the circumstances.

Hadon explained what had happened after he had recovered his breath. The colonel laughed and detailed soldiers to set up two posts and to mark the first fifty to arrive. Hadon talked with Hinokly, the bard, and the doctor, who had made an uneventful journey, though they had heard the roars of hunting lions nearby. After a while, the first ten straggled in, tough old Tadoku and three commissioned officers among them. These were, as Hadon had expected, human soldiers who had abstained from drinking. The Goat and Bear people were very powerful, but long-distance running was not their specialty. Their short legs and massive physiques handicapped them.

Nevertheless, the next group held about twenty of the Bear people and one Klemqaba sergeant. Two more humans walked in, and then a mixed group of humans and Bear and Goat people.

Hadon counted fifty, excluding himself, the bard, the scribe, and the doctor. He ordered the fort's soldiers out to line up along the road.

"Take their weapons away from them. They will be too tired to resist. Give them food and water after they've rested and send them back at once. Without their weapons. These will be shipped back after they've reported to the Mukha commander."

"I suggest that they be sent back under an armed escort," the colonel said. "Otherwise, they might just become outlaws, and we've enough problems with these."

"As you wish," Hadon said. "We need a priestess. Do you think yours would do us the favor of accompanying us?"

The colonel turned pale and said, "She wouldn't want to leave—"

"You," Hadon finished for him, grinning. "We'll see. Please conduct me to her so I may make my request."

On being introduced to the priestess, Phekly, Hadon could understand why the colonel did not want to lose her. She was a beautiful young woman with glossy black hair and large bright black eyes and a superb figure. And it became evident that she and the colonel were in love.

"I'd have to get authorization from the Mother at Mukha," she said. "That would delay you for many days. However, I have no intention of going with you into the Wild Lands unless the Mother orders me to do so. Which I doubt very much, since she is also my physical mother. I could appoint our priest of Resu as a temporary priestess of Kho—there is precedent for that—but unfortunately he is very sick with a fever. Besides, he is a drunkard and a coward."

"I bow to your wishes, priestess," Hadon said. "Even though they leave us without spiritual guidance and protection."

"You could wait until a priestess could come up from Mukha," she said.

"I have orders from the queen not to delay," he said.

He withdrew, leaving a troubled woman behind him—evidently her conscience was hurting her—and he went out of the fort again. Presently he saw a squat, powerful Klemqaba woman, holding her baby, trotting stubbornly toward him. The spiral tattoos on her forehead indicated that she was a priestess, and, seeing these, Hadon was struck with an idea. He didn't like it, but expediency overrode prejudice now.

"Is she the last?" Hadon asked Tadoku.

"Probably she's the last who will show," Tadoku said, checking the count with Hinokly.

"Appoint her as our priestess," Hadon said.

Tadoku and Hinokly gasped, and Tadoku said, "Sir?"

"I spoke clearly enough," Hadon said. "Yes, I know that no Klemqaba priestess has ever presided over rites attended by the Klemkho. But she is a priestess of Kho, and there is no written law that says she can't conduct rites for humans. Besides, she is tough, otherwise she would have given up long ago. And I like it that she did not abandon her baby. She has a strong character."

"The men won't like it, sir," Tadoku said.

"I don't ask them to like it," he said. "I doubt that they will insult her, even though she is a Klemqaba. But my orders are that any man who does so will be executed."

Kebiwabes, who had been standing nearby, said, "This is a queer expedition, Hadon. Sent out to find a god, and vicared by a Goat woman. But I have more confidence in its success than I had when I boarded the galley at Khokarsa. In my opinion, Hadon, you have the makings of a king. And in you I may have the makings of a great epic."

"Let us hope so," Hadon said. Hadon looked at Tadoku, who was talking to the woman, and he called for his second in command, a man from Qethruth named Mokwaten.

"Let everybody rest for an hour, then feed them. As soon as they have eaten, we will resume the march."

Mokwaten said nothing, of course, but the bard groaned and said, "That march last night wore me out."

"Be glad you didn't have to run today," Hadon said. "We stop at dusk, and you can get a long night's sleep then."

10

It took many days to pass the western flanks of the great Saasares mountains. Their slopes were covered with wild olive trees on the lower levels, oak higher up, and then fir and pine. Far off, whiteness glittered, ice and snow which did not melt even in summer.

"A thousand years ago, the tops of the mountains and the high valleys were filled with rivers of ice," the bard said. "But the climate has been getting drier and warmer, and the ice rivers have melted away."

"The ice rivers still exist in the great mountains along the shore of the world-ringing sea to the north," Hinokly said. "We did not go very high into the mountains there, but we went far enough to see those cold and brooding masses. Then we turned eastward and walked along the foothills until we came to a river fed by the melting snows of the mountains. We made dugouts and voyaged down that river to the Ringing Sea."

"And that is where you encountered Sahhindar?" Hadon said.

"Yes. But he said that we were mistaken about the sea being on the edge of the world. It is only another sea, and there are islands in it, and on the other side is more land. He said that there is no edge to the world. It is"—he hesitated—"round. Shaped like an olive."

"But that's crazy!" Tadoku said.

"I thought it improbable," Hinokly said. "However, I was not about to argue with a god."

"Tell me more of Sahhindar," Hadon said. "And this beautiful witch from the sea, this Lalila, and her child, and the one-eyed manling, and the great ax made from a fallen star."

"He is somewhat taller than you, Hadon, and has bigger bones, and is somewhat more muscular, though not much more. But I have seen him lift a boulder that four men could not lift, and I have seen him outrun a charging elephant. His body is scarred from the knife and the claw and the tusk. Perhaps he bears a hundred scars in, all. The most prominent is on his forehead, however, which he said was the result of his scalp being torn open by one of those half-men, the *nukaar*. He has large dark gray eyes, and—"

"Wait," Hadon said. "If he is a god, why does he not heal the scars? And can a god be wounded?"

"You may ask him if you ever meet him," Hinokly said. "I did not question him; I only answered him. And he has long straight black hair, and he wears only a loincloth of antelope hide and a belt with a leather scabbard holding a large iron knife. He carries on his back a quiver of arrows and a bow. The strong men could not bend that bow. The tips of the arrows, however, are of flint."

"Did he say he was indeed the son of Kho, Sahhindar?"

"We addressed him as such, and he did not correct us. But he carries the bow and he looks as Sahhindar is described to us by the priestesses and priests. And he has companions that only deities would have."

"You mean the violet-eyed woman and the others?"

"No, I mean the great lion, and the elephant on whose back he rode, and the monkey that sat on his shoulder. They obeyed him as if he were their mother, and I swear that he talked to them. The elephant stayed away from us, but the lion walked among us, and we were very nervous."

"Then he never said that he was a god?"

"Never. Actually, he did not talk much to us except to find out where we were from and where we were going, and to charge us to bring the woman and her party safely to Khokarsa and to treat them well. Oh, yes, he spoke our tongue, of course, but strangely. He said that it had changed somewhat since he had last been in Khokarsa."

Hadon felt his skin prickle. "If he was in Khokarsa that long ago, then he must truly be Sahhindar. But why did he not come back with you?"

"I wish he had, since we would not then have suffered such misfortunes. On the other hand, he terrified me when he was around, and I was glad when he left. Anyway, he said he had business elsewhere, and I did not ask him what it was. He was lifted by the elephant onto its back, and he rode off on it with the lion walking beside them and the monkey screeching between the elephant's ears.

"I cannot tell you much about him, but if we should find the woman, we should learn more from her. Apparently Sahhindar had brought her and the others across the Kemuqoqanqo, the Ringing Sea, from lands beyond, and he talked much to them. I did not get a chance to talk to her, because it was shortly after Sahhindar had left us that we were attacked by the savages. The rest you know."

Hadon knew the rest and was not comforted by it. Hinokly had made a map on the way north, but on the journey back he had lost all of his papyrus rolls. He was leading the expedition by memory now. That was not good, because they had a vast area to get lost in.

The days and nights passed, one much like the other. The savannas rolled away as far as the eye could see, waist-high tawny grass with short bushy trees here and there and an occasional waterhole or small lake around which grew taller trees. The animal life became more numerous and at length awesome in its number. There were times when the party had to halt and wait for hundreds of thousands, perhaps a million antelopes of many kinds as they ran before them, scared of something behind them and chasing the horizon in front of them. The earth shook and drummed, and dust rose high and then settled, streaking them with brown dirt. They saw many prides of *ruwodeth* (lion), lone or paired cheetahs, leopards, packs of the white-and-black hunting dogs, hyenas, jackals, herds of many *qampo* (elephants), the huge white *bok'ul"ikadeth* (rhinoceros), the tower-necked *c'ad"eneske* (giraffe), the *q"ok'odakwa* (ostrich), the *bom'odemu* (warthog), the *bog"ugu* (giant wild pig), and the terrible *baq"oq"u* (wild buffalo). There were many *akarwadamo* (monkeys) in the trees near the waterholes and the rain lakes and also the *akarwadamowu* (baboons). And everywhere there were birds.

There was no lack of meat, if it could be killed. But fifty-six people had to be fed, and hunters had to go out every other day. Individually, they were not very successful, so Hadon arranged for all to take part. Some would lie in ambush while others, jumping up and shouting and waving their spears, initiated a stampede. Then the ambushers would throw their spears or cast their stones from slings at the passing gazelle, antelope, or buffalo. Twice they also flushed out prides of lions which had been stalking the same prey, and one man was severely mauled. He died two days later, and they heaped stones over him and erected over the pile a wooden pole with a tiny figurine of Kho at its end. The priestess, Mumona, chanted the burial rites over him, and the throat of a hare was cut and its blood was poured over the cairn.

"An ill omen," Hinokly said. "The first man to die on our expedition was killed by a lion under the same circumstances. Let us hope that this expedition does not follow in the footsteps of the first."

"That is up to Kho," Hadon said. "Don't spread such talk among the men. They're frightened enough as it is."

Hadon was not scared, but he was worried. Even if the three people he was seeking were still alive, which was doubtful, how could they be found in this great wilderness? He could see his party years from now, reduced to a very few, getting old and weak, wandering here and there, knowing their quest was hopeless. Minruth would not wait for more than two years, if he waited that long. Even if Hadon did complete his mission, he might find that Minruth had talked his daughter into marrying him. Or perhaps Awineth, wearying, had decreed another Great Games and taken a husband.

On the thirtieth day after leaving the outpost, they saw their first savages. These consisted of a dozen men, women, and children, who fled as soon as they caught sight of the Khokarsans. They were short, slim, and dark-haired, wore skins around the loins, and were painted with red-and-black designs. The men were bearded. Some had bows, which made Hadon so curious that he almost sent some men out after the savages. He had seen bows only in drawings and sculpture, and he would have liked to try one. But even in the Wild Lands the taboo against bows held. It would be dangerous even to touch one.

The next day they saw the peaks of some mountains. Hinokly said that he recognized them; they were on the right path. They should go along the foothills of these, keeping northward, until they rounded them. After traveling eastward, they would come to a river that originated somewhere up in the mountains.

"That river eventually joins another which flows southward from the even greater mountains to the north. The two form a broad river which flows into the Ringing Sea. But it will be about three months before we get there. Having to gather plants, hunt animals, and heap trail-mark cairns will slow us down considerably, even though we are going faster because we're not handicapped by oxen."

Hadon stopped and said, "Something's happened! That scout is running as if a lion were after him!"

Hinokly looked in the direction in which Hadon's finger was pointing. Coming from the west was Nagota, one of the better scouts and hunters, a citizen of Bawaku. He was running with all his strength now, though not going swiftly, since he had obviously been running for some time. He almost fell when he got to Hadon, and it was a minute before he got breath enough to gasp out his message.

Hadon could see no cause for alarm. If any danger threatened, it had to be at least half a mile away. He had told Tadoku to draw the party up in a battle formation. They assembled in a center of spear and ax men with two wings of javelin and sling men. Kebiwabes, who had been singing, walked toward them with his lyre in hand. As a bard, he would not be taking part in any fighting unless the situation became desperate.

The scout said, "Sir, there's a giant out there, about a mile away by now, I suppose. He's running toward us, and about a half-mile behind him is an army of savages."

Hadon asked him a few questions and found out in detail what had happened. The scout had been on top of a hill about fifty feet high when he had seen the man on the horizon. He had waited until the man came closer, since one man did not represent an immediate threat. Then he had changed his mind. This man, this giant, rather, looked as if he could take on a whole corps. He was about seven feet high and as muscular as a gorilla. He wore a lionskin kilt, and he was bearded. The beard had made the scout think he was a savage, but when he saw the brass bands around the huge club he was carrying, he was not so sure.

Hadon swore and said, "As if I didn't have enough troubles!"

"What is the matter?" Tadoku said.

"My cousin, Kwasin, is coming! With a pack of savages on his heels!"

"But he was in the Western Lands!" Tadoku said. "What is he doing so far north?"

"We'll soon find out," Hadon said. "Or we will if we can fight off the savages. Scout, how many were there?"

"About fifty."

"And how are they armed?"

"They have no shields. They carry spears, knives, axes, bolas, and bows."

Hadon wondered what had brought so many of them together. Usually, according to Hinokly, their bands seldom numbered over a dozen. But occasionally they assembled for a big hunt or a tribal ceremony. Kwasin must have stumbled across them during one of these events.

Hadon ordered his force to run to a round hill topped by three trees a quarter of a mile away. They could make a better stand there. He waited, and presently he saw a tiny figure come from a clump of trees near a waterhole. Then he went to the hill, where Tadoku had arranged the men in two circles, one within the other.

Shortly thereafter, the first of the savages ran out from behind the trees. He was gaining on the giant, which was no wonder. Hadon thought that Kwasin must have had a long head start; otherwise, the heavy man could not have been so far ahead of his chasers. Hadon signaled, and two slingers raced toward him. He picked his leather cuirass and helmet from the ground, where he had set them, and donned them. The helmet was conical, with a neck guard and nose flap, and the cuirass was fitted with a leather apron to guard his genitals. He drew his *tenu* from the scabbard and slashed through the air to warm up his arms.

Kwasin came near enough to recognize Hadon, and his eyes opened even wider. He said nothing because he was out of breath; he puffed like a bull buffalo cornered by lions. Sweat matted his long hair and beard and coated him with a silvery shine. Hadon gestured at the hill, and Kwasin trotted on by him.

By then the first group of savages, about twelve, were a quarter of a mile away. They were tall, and their hair and beards were dyed scarlet, and their dark-white bodies were painted with red, black, and green swirls and X's, and slivers of bone were stuck through their septums.

The first group stopped then, and one of them turned and called out to those streaming behind them. There was a roar, and the rest ran up and lined up before the man who had spoken. Thirty of them carried quivers and short, thick wooden bows. They drew arrows from the quivers and fitted the shafts to the strings. However, they did not fire, since they were about 1,250 feet away and so out of range. But Hadon's slingers could cast their missiles over a fourth of a mile, and at his orders they each loosed, in rapid succession, four biconical lead missiles. Only after three of their men had fallen did the savages realize what was going on. Then, yelling, they charged, and Hadon and his two slingers ran back to the hill and up it. The spearmen opened their shields to let them in, and Hadon joined Kwasin, Tadoku, the bard, the priestess, the scribe, and the doctor. The savages, however, had retreated.

Tadoku ordered the outer ring of spearmen to kneel so the slingers behind them could have a clear field. Kebiwabes started to sing a war song while playing on his lyre, but Tadoku ordered him to cease. He wanted the officers' commands to be clearly heard. The baby started crying then, and the priestess shushed it by giving it the breast.

Kwasin was not breathing so heavily now. He grinned at Hadon and said, "Greetings, cousin! We meet unexpectedly and in strange circumstances in a strange place! What are you doing here?" His voice was deep and booming, a lion's.

"Explanations will have to wait until after we settle with the savages," Hadon said.

Kwasin took another drink of water from a clay canteen. Then he wiped his huge hairy hand over his lips, and his strong white teeth and black eyes glittered in a smile.

"I would not have run like a jackal," he roared, "even though they be fifty strong! But they have arrows! Now the situation is different! As soon as they have exhausted their supply of shafts, I will charge them. And you will be troubled no more!"

Except for Hadon, all stared. Hadon was accustomed to his bragging, if it was bragging. He wasn't sure that Kwasin could not do just what he said he could do.

One of the savages must have been carrying a drum, since a booming came from somewhere in the mob. The savages yelled and screamed and started dancing, with the exception of ten archers. These circled the hill and slowly started up it. A slinger, at Tadoku's order, loosed a missile at one of them. The man had time to duck, and he yelled a warning at the others. They retreated a few steps.

The pounding of the drum increased its tempo, and with a yell the savages quit dancing and began running toward the hill. They came in a disorganized mob, some of them tripping over others. In their lead was a tall fellow with a sunburst of yellow painted on his forehead and five ostrich feathers sticking out of his hair.

"That's their leader!" thundered Kwasin. "Here, you, give me your sling!" He tore a sling from the grasp of a startled man and squeezed his other hand. The slinger yelled with pain; Kwasin caught the falling bicone with his left hand.

Hadon almost struck Kwasin with his sword. "You don't give orders or interfere with discipline!" he shouted. "I am the commander, and if you stay here, you will obey me!"

Kwasin looked startled; then he grinned. "You, my cousin the stripling?" he said. "In command? Kho, how things have changed! Well, cousin, I owe you my life, so far, so I will obey you like a good soldier during this battle—if I like your orders. But grant me this one indulgence!"

Holding the two ends of the sling, he whirled it around and above his head and then loosed it with a *ha!* The missile sped true, so far that the slingers gave a low cry of amazement. The chief of the savages suddenly fell backward. The others stopped, piled up, and crowded around him; in a minute they cried out a mourning. They withdrew then, leaving the corpse on its back while their new leader took over.

This time, ten archers advanced while the rest, brandishing spears and axes, trailed behind them. Halfway up the hill, the archers stopped and aimed their bows. There was a twang, and the arrows flew upward. At the same time, the slingers, at Tadoku's orders, loosed their missiles.

The archers were at a disadvantage in having to shoot uphill. Most of the arrows went too high or too low, but one plunged through a shield of wood and leather and through an arm. Another struck a slinger through the throat. The archers retreated, dragging two corpses and two wounded with them. They went just far enough to be beyond effective range of the slingers. There was a roar, and the spearmen and axmen surged forward up the hill past the archers, who then followed them. These fired over the heads of their fellows, but the arrows went at too high an angle to hit the Khokarsans.

Kwasin suddenly gave a yell and leaped over the two rows of the kneelers, landed, and ran down the hill waving his huge club. Hadon gasped; that jump would have done credit to a lion. Then, seeing that those in the forefront of the enemy turned and ran into those behind them, Hadon shouted an order. The soldiers stood up and began to form into a wedge shape. Hadon waited impatiently until they had arranged themselves into a ragged V, and he gave the command to charge. He was at the head, as was his duty, his sword held in two hands. Ahead and below, Kwasin smashed into a knot of men, and they and he went over and were rolling in a tangle down the hill. But he was up again and swinging the club as if it were a wand, smashing spears out of the way, cracking skulls, shattering arms.

The savages broke and ran, and Hadon was the only one of his force besides Kwasin to spill their blood. He overtook a squat man pumping his short legs furiously and with a stroke sent his head rolling from his shoulders. The body continued running, blood spurting a foot high from its neck, and then it fell forward.

The savages ran until they were near the clump of trees. There they regained their wind and talked for some time. Hadon ordered his men to retreat to the top of the hill. The wounded would be treated while he decided what to do next. He had considered charging them while they were still disorganized, but he was afraid that his men might get carried away and break ranks in pursuit. If they did, they might get cut off.

Hinokly said, "I think that if we'd let them take their dead, they'd go away. They can't take many casualties; they need every able-bodied man for hunting, and the survivors won't like having to take care of the dead men's families. From what I know of these savages, they would just as soon go home with the corpses and brag to their women what great fighters they are and how they slaughtered us."

"What will they have to show their wives as trophies?" Tadoku said.

"We'll have to give them our dead, too. Part of them, anyway. If these are like the others I've seen, they'll want the heads and the prepuces."

"The ghosts of our dead would never forgive us!" Hadon said.

"Well, you can bury them and march off. But these savages will dig them up after we've left and take what they want," Hinokly said. "Of course, then the ghosts will be angry at the savages, not us."

Four of his men were dead and six wounded, three severely. The enemy had discharged about half of their arrows, but they still had enough left to inflict heavy casualties. However, they were undisciplined. If Hinokly was right, they would be glad to retreat with honor. On the other hand, they knew the country, and they might be able to arrange an ambush later on. Or they might dog them, trying to pick them off one by one. It would be better to smash them now and utterly discourage any thoughts of further attack. It would be worth it, even if he sustained more casualties.

Hadon went to Kwasin, who was sitting on the slope with the dead around him and blowing like a hippopotamus. He was terrible-looking, splashed with blood, though none of it seemed to be his own.

"Do you feel up to leading another charge?" Hadon said, knowing that his words would sting Kwasin.

"Up to it, cousin?" Kwasin rumbled. "I was just planning on charging them all by myself, as soon as I recovered my wind!"

"In which case you would bristle with arrows," Hadon said. And a good idea that is, he thought.

Kwasin heaved himself up and said, "I am ready. I will eat them up; my club will pound them into bread."

"It is better to let men see deeds than hear words," Hadon said. He called Tadoku to him. After a short consultation, Tadoku arranged the men into battle order. With ten slingers in each wing and twenty-four spearmen in the center, they advanced on the enemy. Hadon and Kwasin were about ten feet ahead of the spearmen.

The savages lined up two deep with the archers in the rear and the spear and ax men kneeling in the front. When his force was just out of arrow range, Hadon ordered the center to stop while the wings advanced. Some of the savages, becoming nervous, loosed ineffectual arrows. The slingers kept on coming, and then they stopped and cast their stones. Two savages fell, and the archers began firing. Three of his slingers fell, at which Hadon gave the order to charge. The slingers dropped their slings, unslung their little round shields, pulled out short, heavy leaf-shaped swords or axes, and ran yelling forward. A few more arrows whistled around the Khokarsans, but none struck.

Their chief shouted at them, apparently urging them to hold. But the sudden exhaustion of their arrows and the glinting of the sun on the bronze swords and spearheads seemed to unnerve them. Or perhaps it was the sight of the bloody giant Kwasin roaring and waving his club. Before he could get to them, they turned and ran. All, that is, except their chief. He ran desperately at Kwasin and hurled his spear, but Kwasin struck it aside in its flight and was on the chief. The chief pulled his flint knife from his leather belt, but he must have known that he had no chance. He seemed to stand as paralyzed as a sheep about to have its throat cut, and his head broke apart under the brassbound club. Hadon was disappointed. He had hoped that they would hold, and thus be so badly hurt that they would from then on leave his men alone.

From the speed with which they were retreating, however, it seemed that they intended to run forever.

Kwasin leaned on his club, panting, and then sat down on the grass in a puddle of blood, bone, and brains.

"I feel as if I could sleep and eat for a week!" he muttered.

Hadon gestured to Tadoku and told him to bring four slingers and four spearmen. Then he stood over Kwasin, his sword raised in both hands. He said, "Cousin, I must have your oath by Kho and Sisisken that you will obey me from now on as if you were the least of my men. This is a military organization, and no one may accompany us who does not acknowledge me as the chief. Either give your word or die! I will not let you go, since I know how vindictive you are! You would get revenge later!"

Kwasin's face became even redder, and he stared as if he could not believe what he was hearing. He started to get to his feet, but when Hadon raised the sword higher, Kwasin sank back.

"You would take off my head?"

"This sword has sheared through the neck of a lion," Hadon said. "And thick as your neck is, a lion's is thicker."

"This isn't fair!" Kwasin said. "You can see how tired I am! My muscles quiver as if they were jelly, and I am slow with fatigue! Another time, and I would knock your legs out from under you with my club and break your back with my bare hands!"

"This is not another time," Hadon said. "Give me your word now, or you will speak no more."

"My ghost would haunt you and bring you, too, down to the queendom of Sisisken," Kwasin said.

"I'll take that chance. Quickly now! Karken hungers for Kwasin."

"What?" Kwasin said.

"Karken, my father's sword."

Suddenly Kwasin lay flat on his back and laughed. It was weak laughter, because he was so tired. But it was evident that he thought the joke was on him and he was willing to laugh at himself. Hadon watched him warily, because Kwasin might be trying to gain an advantage. Kwasin sat back up and said, "You're the only man who ever stood up to me, Hadon, and lived to brag about it. And you wouldn't be doing that if you were not shrewd as a fox and know that I am too fatigued to lift my club. Very well, I swear by mighty Kho Herself that I will obey you until you die or until we get back to civilization. After that, my oath no longer holds."

"You heard him," Hadon said to Tadoku.

11

He lowered the sword and walked away. A moment later, he looked back. Kwasin, still sitting, was wiping off the club on the grass.

Hadon ordered the force to fill their canteens and water-bags from the water-hole and then to bathe in it. He cleaned off his sword and saw to the wounded, among whom were three savages.

That evening they buried the dead and cut the throats of two of the wounded savages, draining the blood into a leather helmet so that the ghosts might drink from it. In the morning one of the wounded soldiers had died, and he was buried and the surviving savage was sacrificed over his grave. That left two walking wounded and three whose recovery, if any, would take weeks. One was a Klemqaba whose sergeant obligingly put him out of his pain after being forgiven for shedding his blood. The remaining two, humans, were placed in litters made out of poles, and the expedition resumed its march.

Days passed with a feeling of smallness, isolation, and pointlessness growing larger each day. The mountains on the right, the unending savanna on the left, were the same. Mountains, trees, and lion-yellow grass were always there in the burning sun, and when the eyes were closed for sleep, they were still there behind the lids. Again and again, Hadon wondered what he would do when he reached the shores of the Ringing Sea. Which way to go, east or west, or turn southward? Where in this vast land could the three he sought be? For all he knew, he might pass by their bones and never see them. They could be hidden in the grass, behind a bush, in a hollow. Or they might be alive but only a few miles away, perhaps lying behind some bushes and afraid to call to them.

One of the wounded died one night, and for no reason that the doctor could determine. He had been well enough to walk and had even been joking when he lay down to sleep. And in the morning he was dead.

A hunter died of a snakebite; another, of an insect bite. A third just disappeared, and though Hadon sent out searchers, they could find no trace. One evening a Klemqaba and a Klemklakor quarreled. The latter was killed and the former was badly wounded. For one tense moment the Bear and the Goat people were about to fall on each other. Hadon shouted that he would massacre them all if any on either side used his weapon. This would have been a laughable threat, since the tattooed soldiers outnumbered the others. But Kwasin was looming behind Hadon and shaking his great club, and the chiefs of the two groups harshly ordered their men to lay down their arms. Hadon conducted a court-martial and found that the survivor had been the offender. Fortunately, he did not have to execute him. He died that night.

As for Kwasin, he was an endless irritant. His bragging and boasting got on Hadon's nerves, and though he obeyed Hadon's orders, he jeered at him. Hadon remonstrated with him for this, but Kwasin merely said, "I did not swear to keep my mouth shut."

Kwasin did have some interesting stories, however. After he had been sentenced to exile, he had been shipped to the city of Towina, which lies southwest of the island of Khokarsa on the shore of the Kemu. From there Kwasin had been escorted deep inland to the last outpost. He had wandered into the Western Lands, his club on his shoulder, stalking wonder and terror as if he were an ogre. At least, that was the way it was if he were to be believed.

"At first there were only the savannas, endless leagues over which great herds of antelopes and elephants roamed. And over which hundreds of prides of lions and packs of wild dogs and the lightning-streak cheetah hunted. I have a mighty body to feed, as you no doubt observed, and I would starve on meat that would make two men fat. How was I to kill the fleet and wary antelope, I, with my great body which can be so easily detected and with only a club and a knife to hunt with?

"And then I saw how the hyena and the jackal follow the lions and how these beasts, thought to be so cowardly, would dash in behind a lion, sometimes in front, snatch a piece of meat, and dash away. And I also observed packs of wild dogs worry a lion eating a carcass and sometimes drive him off. So I said to myself, very well, I will let the lion do the killing for me and then take his meat away from him. And so I did. I would walk up to the carcass and its killer, or its killers, since lions usually work in prides, and I would run them off. Or if they attacked, as they often did, I would stun them with my club or break their legs. Then I would cut off enough meat from the kill to last me several days and leave the rest for the lion. Or if I had killed a lion, I would eat him."

Hadon noticed Kebiwabes taking this in. Doubtless the bard was thinking of composing another epic, *The Song of the Wanderings of Kwasin*. Hadon felt jealous, though he also felt that jealousy was unworthy of him.

"Every once in a while, I would see a small group of blacks, and then I would stalk them and swoop in, smashing them, and would run off with a woman. I am as lusty as a sea otter or a hare, as you well know, Hadon, and where one man may be satisfied with one woman or indeed unable to satisfy one woman, I need a dozen. The black women are ugly and do not bathe often, but one must be philosophical and thank Kho for what is available."

"And did you then kill these women?" Hadon said.

"Only with a surfeit of love!" Kwasin said, and he guffawed. "No, I let them go, though few were able to rise and walk away at once. And some begged me in their tongue, which I did not understand, of course, but the expressions were eloquent, some, I say, were obviously begging me to keep them. No, I did not kill them. I wanted them to bear my sons and daughters, since the breed needs improving, and eventually, who knows, all the blacks of the Western Lands may be my descendants.

"By the way, I see you have only one woman with you, and she is an ugly Klemqaba. Where is the priestess?"

"She *is* the priestess," Hadon said. "Don't force yourself on her, or you may be doubly cursed by Kho. Besides which, I would regard that as a serious, that is, fatal, breach of discipline."

"And if I should humbly ask her?" Kwasin said, sneering.

"She may accept you as a husband. By now she is married to half the men and all the Goat and Bear people."

Kwasin haw-hawed and said, "Once I have been with her, she will divorce the others. Well, I am glad we are in the Wild Lands, where the savages are white and not so squat, and some of the women, under the stink and the dirt and the paint, may even be good-looking. But surely, Hadon, you are not married to this half-ape?"

"Of course not," Hadon said stiffly.

Kwasin laughed again and said, "To continue! Then I came to the jungles, where there were no lions to hunt for me. The leopardess is queen there, and it is not easy to find her in that thick tangle. I thought I would starve, but then I came across a great river—"

"The Bohikly?" Kebiwabes said. "The river discovered by the expedition of Nankar in six-eighty-five A.T.?"

Kwasin stared and said, "Do not presume on your sacred status as a bard and interrupt me, Kebiwabes. Only Hadon may do that, since I have sworn an oath of obedience. However, I do not mind intelligent questions. Anyway, I found thousands of crocodiles along that river, and so I took to dashing out of the jungle and overhauling them before they could get into the water and cracking their thick skulls with my club. They make good eating. Occasionally I found a tiny settlement of blacks along the river, though mostly in the northern regions. Apparently they haven't worked their way down to its mouth yet. Then I would ravage among them and ravish their women. Some of them I kept so they could teach me to find plant life, since I was weary of meat only.

"Eventually I came to the headwaters of the Bohikly and wandered westward. And then I was stopped by the Ringing Sea. I thought of making a dugout and venturing out westward, hoping to come to the edge of the world itself. But, I thought, what if the sea extends for a thousand miles? How could I survive? So I did not venture out. Besides, Kho might not wish a mortal, even such a mortal as I, to look over the edge into the abyss. Who knows what secrets She hides down there?"

Kwasin then had thought of roaming along the shore of the Ringing Sea and perhaps circumambulating it. He could not decide which way to start, north or south, so he sacrificed a red river hog to Kho and asked Her to choose his way. He waited, and after a while a white *kagaga* (raven) swooped over him and flew northward. And so he had set out in that direction, keeping to the shoreline.

"But after a year, I became convinced that I could walk forever and still I would not come to the place from which I started. Besides, I grew lonely. I saw only three settlements of blacks along the shore, and I lusted for women. I did take several of the women I abducted along with me, but one died of a fever and one I had to kill because she tried to knife me, and two escaped.

"Then I came to a great mountain range which ran northward and eastward along the beaches. I followed that, and behold, one day I saw across the sea a great rocky mountain.[3] The Ringing Sea was *not* a sea which ran around the edge of the world. There were other lands beyond that land."

"Or perhaps," Hinokly said, "the mountain was only an island in the Ringing Sea."

"I said I didn't like to be interrupted, scribe," Kwasin said. "So I considered crossing the waters to that rocky mountain, but the current is swift there, though the waters are narrow. I walked on, and after many months came to a place where the mountains cease—at least for a while. Here a great river ran into the sea—"

"Probably the river which we found," Hinokly said.

"Scribes have big tongues and thin skulls," Kwasin said, glaring. "Anyway, I had become weary of the sea, so I turned inland and made a dugout and paddled up the river. Now I was in the land of white savages, and the women were more pleasing, though they smelled as bad as the blacks. However, after I dunked them in the river and got them to comb out their hair and wash off the paint, they were acceptable. Some of them would have attracted attention in Khokarsa, they were so comely. And so I improved the stock along that river.

"Then I came to the mountains from which the river flowed, and I set out wandering the savannas southward. I thought that perhaps I might return to Khokarsa. Kho might have forgiven me by now. I had done enough penance for what was, after all, only a drunken prank."

"Raping a holy priestess of Kho and smashing the skulls of her guards was only a prank?" Hadon said.

"That priestess was a teasing bitch," Kwasin said. "She urged me on, and then, when I had bared myself, became terrified, though I suppose I shouldn't blame her for that. And I was only defending myself when I killed the guards. You have to admit that there were extenuating circumstances. Otherwise, why was I not castrated and flung to the hogs? Why was I punished with exile only, though Kho knows that was a horrible punishment?"

"You escaped execution because the oracle said that you should not be killed," Tadoku said. "No one except Kho knows why you were let off so easily after such a grave crime. But Her Voice must be obeyed."

3 Gibraltar.

"I thought I would go to an outpost or perhaps even Mukha itself and ask if my exile was over," Kwasin said. "After all, the oracle had said that I would not have to wander forever."

"Perhaps she meant by that that death would put an end to your exile," the scribe said. "The Voice of Kho speaks words that have more than one interpretation."

"But a club on the skull of a gabby scribe has only one interpretation," Kwasin said. "Do not arouse me, Hinokly."

And so the giant had walked around the mountains and then gone south. Then he had come across an assembly of the tribes in this area. They were, he supposed, holding some yearly religious rite. He did not know, but he did know that there were many good-looking women there. When he had his chance, he had seized one and run off with her. But the savages had tracked him, and he had to run.

"Only because they had arrows," he said. "Otherwise I would have scattered them as a lion scatters a herd of gazelles."

"Of course," Hadon said, and he laughed. Kwasin scowled and clutched his club.

"Can you retrace your route to the river that empties into the sea?" Hadon asked.

"With my eyes closed!" Kwasin bellowed.

"Good! Now we have two guides, you and Hinokly. Surely we cannot get lost now."

But they could. The mountains here were not one formidable range but many small ranges and isolated mountains and valleys. Hinokly confessed that he did not know where they were. Kwasin refused to confess, but it was evident that he was as confused as Hinokly. After they had wandered for three weeks, often backtracking, Hadon decided that they should go west until they were clear of the mountains. Then they would march north for a week before turning eastward. And in another three weeks, they came across their first river. Both Hinokly and Kwasin declared that this was the river up which they had come.

"There must be still another farther eastward," Hinokly said. "This stream and the other originate in these mountains and run parallel, I suppose, northeastward until they run into a larger river. That one must originate in the great range which runs inland along the Ringing Sea. The three rivers become one, which flows into the sea."

"Are we near to the place where you lost the witch, the baby, and the manling?" Hadon said.

"No, that was below the confluence of this river and the one from the northern mountains. It was somewhere between that confluence and the confluence of the river east of this."

They felled trees, chopped off the branches, shaped the exterior and interior into dugouts, and shaped planks into paddles. Each dugout could hold seven, a lucky number, and there were seven dugouts, some of them undermanned. Hadon put the giant Kwasin in a vessel with two others. This was designated the scout boat, since Kwasin wanted to lead them. Also, the sight of the monster might discourage the savages from attacking. They were vulnerable now, especially to arrows, because the river was lined with a broad and thick jungle. They encountered hippopotami and crocodiles, and elephants often came down to bathe and drink. Birds by the hundreds of thousands lived along or on the river, and the trees screeched and vibrated with monkeys. Now and then they glimpsed the small antelope which made the jungle its home, and the leopard which hunted them, monkeys, and river pigs. The slingers killed monkeys and birds, and the spearmen slew crocodiles, hippos, and pigs. For the first time since leaving the outpost, they had more than enough meat. The river also contained many kinds of fish, which gladdened the Khokarsans.

Unfortunately, the day before they arrived at the confluence, a wounded hippo upset a dugout, and he and two bulls had killed five men before anything could be done. One man was pulled out of the water; the other swam to a mudbank only to be seized by a monstrous crocodile and carried off into the river.

Afterward, the priestess cast her omen bones, and reading them, declared that they had offended the godling of the river. They sacrificed two pigs, a boar and a sow, which they had captured during a hunt, and the next day went smoothly. Near evening they came out onto the broad river that ran down to the sea.

Hinokly, sitting behind Hadon, said, "I last saw the three about twenty miles from here. But I won't be able to recognize the exact spot. There were no distinguishing landmarks around."

"In any case, they wouldn't be likely to stay there even if they survived," Hadon said. "But we'll explore the area around there. If they died, their bones might still be there."

The next day, what with traveling with the current and a steady paddling, they reached the place where Hinokly thought the attack had occurred. Hadon ordered the dugouts to put into a marshy spot that contained several small islands. They camped on one, huddling around fires the smoke of which was supposed to keep the mosquitoes off. But it didn't.

"Some of us got sick with swamp fever," Hinokly said. "Five died, and when the savages attacked, many were too weak to fight. You can expect to lose some men before we get to the sea. Fortunately, there are not many mosquitoes on the beaches."

"What do mosquitoes have to do with swamp fever?" Hadon said.

"In fifteen-thirty-nine A.T.," Hinokly said, "the priestess-doctor Heliqo observed that in areas where swamps and standing water were drained off, the mosquito population decreased. And the incidence of the fever dropped in proportion. Also, where there were no mosquitoes, there was no swamp fever. That was fifty years ago, and she was scoffed at then. But lately the doctors say that she was probably right."

"That's nice to know," Hadon said. "But in the meantime, about all we can do is pray to Qawo, our lady of healing, and M'agogobabi, the mosquito demon, that we be spared.

"Or," he added, "the next best thing is to get out of here and go where there are none of the little devils. I can't imagine those three staying here, and if they did, they are surely dead. The fever might not kill them, but they would be too weak to hunt, and the leopards would get them."

Despite this reasoning, he knew that they had to search the region. They started the next morning, wading through the marshes until they got to higher ground, walking a half-mile, and plunging back through the marsh to the river banks. As they went, they shouted the names of Lalila and Paga. Though the noise would attract the savages, they had to call out. Otherwise, the ones they sought might be very close and yet not know their saviors were nearby. Also, so much din might scare away both savages and the large predators. At least, Hadon hoped that it would.

By the end of the second day he knew that this method of search was hopeless and stupid. If they were alive, they would not stay here. They would either have gone back to the seashore or gone south toward Khokarsa. The best thing was to proceed to the sea first and find out what they could there. If there was no sign of them, they would go south again.

That morning, many of the party became sick. Hinokly and the doctor shook their heads and said, "Swamp fever."

Hadon moved them to the higher land, since there were too many sick men to paddle the boats on down the river. He found a place on top of a hill about sixty feet high that had a spring of good water. They settled down to battle out the chills, the fever, and the sweatings. He fell sick the third day and experienced once again the coldness, the heat, the sweatings, and the delirium that had several times afflicted him in his youth. The few left standing, including Kwasin, who claimed immunity from the demon, had to take care of the others and hunt for food. The priestess, Mumona, was also spared, and the chief burden of nursing fell on her. The doctor died the sixth day; several days later most of the humans and some of the Goat and Bear people were dead.

On the twelfth day Hadon felt well enough to take short walks around the camp. On the fourteenth, he went into the wilderness to set traps for hares. He also brought down a monkey with a stone from his sling, a welcome addition to the pot. When he returned, he was greeted with a loud cry from Mumona. Her baby had just died.

"She'll soon enough have another," Kwasin said unsympathetically. "Though no one will know who its father is."

Kwasin was angry at the priestess because she had refused to lie with him. Under other circumstances he might have brained her, since he could not see why she would reject a man who was not only the strongest man in the empire but the handsomest.

Hadon went to comfort her. He had grown fond of her during the sickness, and he admired her uncomplaining attitude and the skill with which she treated the men. She could not cure them, but she had eased their chills and fevers as best she knew how.

The expedition, only thirty strong now, paddled away from the place of death a few days later. Of the humans, only Hadon, Tadoku, Kwasin, the bard, the scribe, and a young private from Miklemres had survived, and most of these were weak.

They traveled uneventfully, getting stronger each day, until they reached the falls of which Hinokly had warned them. Here the river went through a narrow rocky valley and fell about sixty feet in thunder and steam. They got off the boats as soon as they heard the roar and portaged the dugouts, with much difficulty, down the steep slopes beside the cataract. A mile below, they camped for the night. The next morning, as they set out, three arrows shot from the dense brush nearby. And a Klemqaba was dead of a shaft through his neck.

Though burning to get revenge, Hadon gave the order to move to the center of the river out of range and go on. To have plunged into the jungle against an unknown number of enemies would have meant only the loss of more men.

Twelve days later they came out of one of the mouths of the river and gazed awe-struck at the Ringing Sea.

12

There were, Hadon found, about a hundred and fifty savages, mostly consisting of groups of a dozen to a score, living along a twenty-mile stretch of the shore. These might have the information he needed, and dead people could not give it. He ordered that his men should not attack unless attacked. Leaving the force, he walked alone into the nearest encampment. This was a dozen small cone-shaped huts of poles covered with hides. The people fled as he approached them, gathering on a little hill near the camp and shaking their spears at him. He walked boldly up to them, his hands held to indicate his desire for peace. Presently, one of the slim, dark, hawk-nosed men, holding his stone-tipped spear before him, walked slowly toward him. He jabbered away in a harsh tongue which Hadon did not, of course, understand. He stood his ground, continuing to make peaceful gestures, and then, slowly, held out a rosary of tiny emeralds, a gift to Hadon from the priestess at the outpost fort. It was an expensive gift, but he hoped that it would be worth it. Though the man would not take it, probably because he thought that it might contain an evil magic, his wife could not restrain herself. She came forward and gingerly took it and then put it around her neck.

It took several days before their suspicions melted and he could bring in the Klemqaba woman, the bard, and the scribe. Kebiwabes charmed them with his singing. The scribe drew some pictures for them, and Hadon passed out some copper coins. They had no idea of the meaning of money, but they found ways to use the coins as ornaments. Hadon, meanwhile, was learning the language. It had a number of back-of-the-mouth and throat sounds that he found difficult to master. But he had a throat that could change shape like mercury, and he was soon speaking it well enough so that the savages no longer broke up in merriment at his abominable pronunciation.

Hadon permitted his force to move in within half a mile a few days later. They had orders that they were not to molest the women on pain of instant death. Kwasin complained about this; he was all for spearing the men and using the women.

"You are worse than the savages," Hadon said. "No, I need these people. Perhaps they might be able to tell me something of the people we are seeking."

"And after you find out?" Kwasin said. "Then do we take the women? There is a little one with big eyes and conical breasts whom I cannot stop thinking about night and day."

Hadon spat to show his disgust and said, "That would be the basest treachery. No, you will not. If we find out that the men are not jealous of their wives, and if a woman says yes, then you may vent yourself. As for that woman you spoke of, I think she likes me but fears you."

Kwasin roared with frustration and banged the end of his club into the ground. Hadon, grinning, walked away. Nevertheless, he was worried that some of his men might try to sneak around and take the women into the bushes.

At the end of three weeks, Hadon felt qualified to ask about Lalila. He talked to the chief and found at once, to his delight, that these people knew of her. Moreover, they knew of Sahhindar.

"We first met them two winters ago," the chief said. "They came into the village, the violet-eyed yellow-haired woman, her child, the one-eyed manling, and he whom you call Sahhindar. My grandfather and his grandfather knew him, and they would have worshiped him as a god, since he lives unchanged through time, as a god lives. But he forbade any to worship him, saying that he was subject to death and was no true god. I had seen him when I was a child, and I remembered him. He stayed with us for a while, helping us to hunt and to fish, and telling us many wonderful tales. Then he and his people, who he said came from across the great water, moved on. They were going southward, he said.

"I thought that I might never see him again, since he usually appears only once or twice in a generation. But only four moons ago the woman, the child, and the manling reappeared. Sahhindar was not with them. The woman said that Sahhindar had entrusted them to a party of men from the far south, who also live on the shores of a great sea. They were attacked and separated from these men, and they found their way back to us. I asked them to stay with us, but they said that they would go after Sahhindar. He had gone along the coast toward the rising sun, and he may be anywhere in this world by now, for all anybody knows."

"Was he with a lion and a monkey and an…?" Hadon hesitated, at a loss for a word. He described an elephant as best he could, but the chief was confused. Apparently he knew of lions and monkeys, but he had neither seen nor heard of elephants.

"No, he was with none of these beasts," he said. "If he had been, I would have said so."

That night the Khokarsans and the savages feasted on two hippos, and the next day the visitors set out. The woman with the big eyes and conical breasts threw her arms around Hadon and cried. He regretted that he had to leave so soon, but he promised himself that if it were at all possible he would return this way. The band set out eastward, with two men keeping an eye on Kwasin. Hadon feared that the giant would try to sneak back to the savages, and so ruin all the goodwill that had been so patiently built up. There was little to keep Kwasin from deserting them, of course, but if he did, he would not be permitted to rejoin them. Kwasin showed no signs of doing so. The loneliness of his wanderings was still with him. He did not want to be where he would have no one to talk to.

"Kho is with us," Hadon said to Kebiwabes. "We should overtake them. The chief said that they will not turn southward for many, many days' journeys. There are vast and rugged mountain ranges between the shore and the inland savannas, and to reach the savannas they have to go around the mountains. We will march as swiftly as possible and overtake them before they get to the far end of the mountains."

"If Kho is willing," the bard said. "I weary of this wilderness. I would see fair Khokarsa gleaming white in the sun and go into its streets, crowded and noisy though they be. I would drink again in the taverns and in the halls of the noble, and sing songs that the people will love and my colleagues will find it hard to fault. And the women…ah, the women! Slim and fair-skinned and smelling sweetly of perfumes and speaking with soft voices of love."

"Yes, but if you had not come with us, you would not have the seeds of a great epic germinating in your heart," Hadon said. "That is, if you can make something out of what has happened. To me it has not been poetry, but vexation, hardship, solving trivial and important problems every hour of the day, sickness, wounds, and worries at night that keep me awake."

"That is the stuff of great poetry," Kebiwabes said. "The voice and the lyre change all that into glory and beauty. Men and women will weep with sorrow or exclaim with joy at my words and music, and you, the harassed, bone-tired, mosquito-bitten, worrying man will be transformed into the brave hero whose only cares are great issues and whose lusts become great loves. The song will not mention your dysenteries, your fever, the bags under your eyes from sleeplessness, the fleas you scratch, your uncertainties, nor the way you cursed once when you stumbled on a stone and hurt your big toe. And that skirmish with the savages will become a battle in which thousands participate and the faceless of the ranks are slaughtered by the heroes, and the heroes indulge in long-winded dialogues during the battle before they clash for glory.

"And yet, in a sense, what I sing will be as true as if it actually happened."

"Let us hope that you have the genius to work this transmutation," Hadon said.

"That is what worries me," the bard said, and he looked sorrowful. But a moment later he was grinning as he sang for the delight of all the bawdy song of Corporal Phallic.

Meanwhile, as they marched, Hinokly, the scribe, was making a map of the country. "Two previous expeditions have gone as far as the sea along approximately the same route we took," he said to Hadon. "But none have gone east along the coast from the river that empties into the Ringing Sea. We are the first Khokarsans to come this way."

Two months later, after encountering a few dozen small tribes who either fled inland or took to their boats, they had come to what seemed the end of this range of mountains. Ahead lay flat savannas. They had found no sign of Lalila and the others.

"We could go ahead," Hadon said during a conference with Tadoku and the scribe. "But I think that it is likely that the three went southward after the mountains ceased. If they did not find Sahhindar, they would decide to try again for Khokarsa. And if they did find the Gray-Eyed God, he would have directed them southward. Or perhaps he himself is guiding them southward."

Hinokly, who had been looking at the map, said, "I would guess that we are directly north of the city of Miklemres. I may be wrong, of course, but if we go south now, we should come to the Saasares massif. In either event, going west or east on the north side of the Saasares, we shall round it and come to Mukha or Qethruth. Or we might hit the pass through the Saasares. Of course, there may be other mountains between us and the Saasares, and if we go around these, we might get lost again."

"We have the stars and the sun and great Kho to guide us," Hadon said. "We will march south."

First he let the troops camp by the seashore for a few days so they could catch fish and swim and sleep. On the day before they were to leave, he went out by himself, climbing around the hills, meditating, fingering his rosary, now and then sitting down to gaze upon the beach and the great rolling sea, the waves of which were higher and heavier than those of his native seas. At midafternoon he sat down on top of a cubical hill of rock, leaned against an oak, and looked down toward the shore. Directly below, the beach ran to the sea. On his right a ridge of hills thrust like a stone finger into the waters. Below it huge boulders were scattered in the sea, which was shallow at that point. They formed a natural breakwater against which the waves flew apart in foam and spray or shot through the spaces between. Hadon watched the sea and the white birds that wheeled above it, dropping now and then to clutch a fish. The sun shone brightly; the breeze was mild and cooling; before he knew it, he was asleep.

Sometime later he jerked awake, his heart hammering. How foolish he had been! He was alone in dangerous country, and though he had seen no savages for a week, that did not mean that there were none. Also, there were antelope and gazelles in this area, and where they were, leopards were. He vaguely remembered a dream that had come as he struggled up from sleep, something to do with Awineth. Had she not spoken to him, warned him of something? Of what?

He shook his head, scanned the countryside around, but could see nothing but birds and a small foxlike creature with huge pointed ears slinking from one bush to another. And then he heard, faintly and far off, a barking that was not quite like a dog's. He rose and looked to his right, and presently he saw the round black heads of those flippered creatures which the Khokarsans had called sea dogs[4] when they first saw them on the shore of the Ringing Sea. These were putting out to sea to dive for fish, and they had come from behind the wall of boulders below the hills to his right.

He decided to go down to the boulder breakwater and spy upon these beasts. The natives at the village near the mouth of the river said that they were the companions

4 Seals.

and the guardians of their sea goddess. If a man could catch one and keep her from slipping out of her oily coat, he could learn the secrets of the sea and be forever free of hunger. Once, they said, in the far past a hero of their village had seized one, and she had left her skin behind, but he had swum after her and caught her, and she had turned into a beautiful sea woman. She had taken him down with her to her home at the bottom of the sea, where he lived forever, eating and making love. She was the daughter of the goddess, and she loved the mortal, and if a man could emulate that hero, he, too, could become immortal. But he must never again go on the beach, or he would suddenly become very old and very sad, because he would have lost all.

Hadon had no desire to live deep in the cold waters forever. He did hope that the sea dogs might shed their skins if they thought no man was around. He would then see the daughters of the goddess in their naked beauty. Or would he be so enchanted by the glory that he would forget Awineth and the throne, which after all were only temporal delights, and try to lay his hands upon one of them?

His own people had a story of the hero who saw Lahhindar, the Gray-Eyed Archer Goddess, as she bathed. He had been torn apart by her hyenas for the blasphemy. It was dangerous to spy upon goddesses.

Nevertheless, Hadon went down the hill and across the beach and presently was wading through the sea. He crouched low, bracing himself against the waves, and peered around the side of a boulder that was twice his height. At first he saw only the surging waters inside the ring of boulders and a sea dog sitting on top of a boulder near the center of the circle. Then he heard voices, and his blood seemed to run backward, and he grew faint. Was he indeed about to witness the dangerous beauty of goddesses unclothed?

He hesitated, but his curiosity was far too great for him to walk off as any discreet and wise man would.

He inched around the side of the boulder, keeping his chest close to it. Finally he had a clear view of the arena of water. To his right, on a narrow beach, was a little bearded man with a big head, and beside him was a naked child of about three. Her hair was yellow, and her skin was the whitest he had ever seen.

He knew then that he had found those so long sought. Or, at least, two of them. The Goddess had directed him to them; it must have been her voice, not Awineth's, he had heard in the dream.

But where was Lalila, the White Witch from the Sea, the Risen-from-the-Sea?

Suddenly the waters roiled before him, only a few feet away, and a woman burst from the green. She stood up, smiling, and her wet hair was long and yellow, her oval face was beautiful, more beautiful than that of any woman he had ever seen, and her eyes were large and of a strange color, like those of the violets that grew on the mountains above Opar.

Hadon gasped with more than the shock of recognition. Then he was trying to assure her that she was in no danger, because she was screaming, and those eyes were full of fear.

13

Hadon thought of trying to grab her so that he could tell her that he was no enemy. Instead, he let her go. He waded after her as she swam swiftly toward the manling and the child. The two were standing up now and shouting, and the manling was brandishing a long-handled iron ax that looked too heavy for him even to lift. Hadon held his hands out to show that he was peaceful. The woman, halfway toward her companions, stopped swimming and stood up, the sea just below the superb breasts. She was not smiling, but neither did she look fearful now. And when Hadon and she got onto the beach, she spoke to him in a heavily accented Khokarsan. The manling, though no longer shouting, held the ax ready if Hadon should make a threatening move.

"You frightened me," she said in a lovely voice. "But then I realized that you had to be a man from the inland sea, because of your leather helmet and armor and the great sword that you carry in the scabbard on your back. But how…?"

"It is a long story," Hadon said. "Let us sit down here, and I will tell you as much as I can before we go to my camp."

Lalila and Paga dressed themselves first. The manling put on a long kilt of gray fur, and the woman put on a short kilt and a poncho of the same material. Then she combed her dripping hair with a notched mussel shell. Hadon observed them closely during this dressing. How beautiful she was, how white-skinned! And she was tall, perhaps five feet six inches. She did indeed look like a goddess.

The manling was as Hinokly had described. His legs, though thick and powerful, were no longer than those of an eight-year-old child's. His torso was, however, that of an average-sized man. His shoulders and long arms were heavy with muscle, and his chest was deep and broad. His hair was brown, flecked with gray, a tumbled mass on top of a huge head. The right eye was filmed over, the result, according to Hinokly, of its striking a stone when his mother had thrown him into the bushes shortly after his birth. His nose was flat, his mouth full and broad, his face scarred. Despite its ugliness, it had a strange attractiveness. When he smiled, he became almost beautiful.

According to Hinokly, he had been born far to the north, in a land beyond the Ringing Sea, a land largely covered by moving rivers of ice. When his father, returning from a sea-dog hunt, had found out that he had been thrown away and left to die, he had gone looking for his bones. Weeks had passed since his mother had cast him away, yet the father found him alive and healthy except for the shattered eye and the scarred face. A wolf bitch had found him and suckled him. It was said that Paga sometimes went into the forest and talked to the wolves. It was also said that he sometimes became a wolf at night and ran with his mother and her pups. Hadon hoped that this was not true. Wereleopards, were-eagles, and werehyenas were burned alive in Khokarsa. Hadon had never seen a wolf, of course, but Hinokly had mentioned one as described to him by Lalila, and Hadon supposed that the fur these two wore was that of the wolf.

The two, now dressed, sat down. The child, reassured by her mother, paddled around in the sea close to them. Hadon told them his story as briefly as possible, stopping now and then to define a sentence unit they did not know. When he had finished, he said, "We would probably have missed you, but Kho Herself sent me to you. And Sahhindar? Have you seen him?"

"We have been looking for him," Lalila said. "When we left him to go with the men from the south, he said that he was making a pilgrimage far to the southwest, to the sea that runs on the extreme edge of the world beyond the mountains southwest of the city of Mikawuru. He was visiting again the place where he would be born in the far future. I did not understand his words, and he did not explain. He did say that he was not a god, that he could die, and that he had traveled backward in time but now had to travel forward, as all mortals do."

"I do not understand that," Hadon said. "But is it true that it was he who brought in plants which until then had not grown around the two seas and gave them to the Khoklem, and showed them—my ancestors—how to cultivate them, how to domesticate animals, and how to make bronze?"

"Yes, he did," Paga said in a voice as deep as Kwasin's. "It was also he who once came to Lalila's ancestors and showed them how to domesticate goats and sheep and how to weave and dye."

"But it was all in vain," Lalila said. "The man whom you call Sahhindar told me that he knew it would be in vain. My people are dead now, and their knowledge is lost and will not be regained for many thousands of years."

Lalila paused, looked strangely at Hadon, as if she might not say what was in her heart, and then said, "Just as his gifts to your ancestors were in vain."

Hadon felt a slight shock, and he said, "What does that mean?"

"I do not know," Lalila said. "But once he spoke idly of Khokarsa as if it had long been dead, buried, and forgotten. Except for the city of Opar. He said that it had been built long before he was born and that it was still standing when he was born. But it had been rebuilt many times.

"And he said also that he would teach the savages no more new things, that they must proceed at their own pace. Time would defeat him, no matter how many people he raised from savagery."

"Perhaps he may visit Khokarsa again, and then we will learn more," Hadon said. "In the meantime, we must proceed on our own. Let us walk back to the camp, which is several miles from here, and you can tell me your story."

Lalila called the child Abeth in, and she put on her a cloak of antelope skin that, Lalila said, Sahhindar had made for her. They walked along the beach silently for a while, the woman and Hadon matching their pace to the short legs of the child and the manling. Paga spoke first. He was, he said, born in a very small tribe of people so isolated that they thought they were the only people in the world. They lived by hunting and fishing, their chief prey being the sea dogs and an occasional stranded whale, a creature like a monster fish, but warm-blooded. Paga, cast out a second time, had been rescued by a man named Wi and had voluntarily become his slave. The tribe was dominated by a cruel giant who had slain Wi's daughter, and so Wi had challenged him for the chieftainship. Paga it was who had found a stone fallen from the sky, a stone made of iron and some other metal that was even harder than iron. He had crudely fashioned it into an ax for Wi, and Wi had slain the giant with it and become the chief.

"And then Wi's problems, instead of being solved, were greatly increased," Paga said. "Once he had been the slave of the chief. Then he became the slave of the people. And he had much trouble with his wife, who loved him but could not endure me, as most women cannot. And she was jealous because Wi loved me and would not drive me out into the wilderness again. She could not understand that Wi was both wise and good-hearted and that he loved me, not as a man loves a woman but as one who needed his protection and who, in turn, could counsel him wisely. He did not believe the people when they said that I was a worker of evil and that I took a wolf's shape at night.

"And then, one day, a dugout floated onto the shore, and Wi found in it a woman near death. This woman, Lalila. And the troubles he had had before he found her became trivial."

"True," Lalila said. "Though I am not a troublemaker in my heart, my presence seems to cause trouble. To make a long story short, Wi nursed me back to life and protected me. We fell in love, though for a long time Wi would not marry me because of a law he had originated, which restricted one wife to one man. And he did not have the heart—"

"The guts," Paga said.

"The heart to cast out his wife. In the end, the great river of ice whose front loomed over the village moved and wiped out most of the tribe. Some of us—Wi, Wi's son, Wi's wife, his brother, his brother's wife, Paga, and I—were left alive but afloat on a mountain of ice. It began to melt, and we had to get off it in our boat, which was only a small hollowed-out log. Wi, seeing that if he got in, his weight would sink the boat, shoved it out with the rest of us in it. The fog blew in then, and we could barely see Wi. But Paga dived into the cold sea and swam to the remnant of the ice mountain. If he had to die, he wanted to die with Wi. Besides, he could not see leaving Wi to die all alone. To die with your loved ones around you is bad, but to die alone is terrible.

"I did not know what to do. I loved Wi and wished to die with him. Life was not worth living without him. Or so, at least, I thought at the moment. But Wi's son was with me, and he needed a protector. Then I considered that he had his mother and Wi's brother and sister-in-law. And with one fewer, their chances of survival would be greater. So I swam to the ice mountain too.

"There we waited for the cold or the sea to take us, but presently the fog cleared. The others were not in sight, and we never saw them again. But there was land a mile or two away, and then we saw several uprooted trees drifting by. We swam to one, and Wi chopped off the branches on top and rolled it over and chopped off those on the other side. Using some branches as paddles, we got the log to the shore. We almost died doing it, because our legs were in the icy waters. But we did not die."

"And then," Paga said, "we wandered along the shore looking for the others. As Lalila says, we never saw them again. Finally we turned inland for Lalila's homeland. We found the lake over which her people lived in huts on piles. But the huts were empty, and the bones of their owners lay in the lake or along the shore. We did not know what had caused their deaths. We thought that a pestilence of some kind had struck many, and the others had fled. We waited for three moons for some to return, but they never did. Lalila's child by Wi was born. Then a band of tall yellow-haired men came, and we fled into the mountains. They pursued us until we were trapped in a cave, trapped by the bear in the cave and the men without. Wi slew the bear, a creature twice as large as a lion, but he was clawed badly across the back. Then he turned and fought the yellow-hairs while I thrust with a spear from behind him, between his legs. Seven men he slew with the ax before a spear went through his throat.

"All seemed over, but then came cries from the men still outside. Those within ran out, only to be felled by arrows that came so fast that it seemed three men were firing. The remaining yellow-hairs fled, and presently a tall man with black hair and gray eyes came out from behind a boulder. It was Sahhindar, who had visited the village again, seen our tracks, and followed us."

"We buried Wi, and with him my heart," Lalila said. "Then we told our story, and Sahhindar said that he would take us to a land where we could live in comfort, a land such as we had never dreamed of. When we encountered a Khokarsan expedition, Sahhindar entrusted us to their care. The rest you know."

"Not all of it," Hadon said. "When the expedition was attacked, how did you escape the savages after your boat overturned?"

"We swam to the opposite shore," Paga said, "though the weight of the ax almost drowned me. It was tied to my wrist, and I couldn't get the knot loose. But Lalila helped me support the ax. We carried it between us, each swimming with one hand. The child could swim almost at birth, and so we did not have to worry about her. By the time we reached shore, the river was alive with crocodiles attracted by the uproar. That was fortunate for us, since five savages had remained behind to go after us. But they did not dare attempt the river. And so we decided to go northward, in the direction they would not expect us to take. As I said, we also decided to seek out Sahhindar and tell him what had happened."

Hadon said, "I wonder why Sahhindar did not accompany you all the way to Khokarsa? Surely he knew that there were many dangers between the Ringing Sea and the Kemu?"

"I think that he was on a mission of his own when he rescued us," Paga said. "He deferred it to see us to safety. When we met the Khokarsans, he thought he could entrust us to them. He was eager to get going."

"Perhaps he would not have left us if he had known that I was bearing his child," Lalila said. "But then I did not know it myself. Of course, that did not matter in the end, since I lost it two moons after it was conceived."

"You carried the seed of a god in your womb?" Hadon said. He felt awe at the same time that, for some unknown reason, he felt sick. Or was the reason so hidden? Was it because he felt jealous?

"He says he is no god, but certainly he is as close to being a god as a mortal can get," she said. "However, I am not unique. He says that half the population of the lands north of the Ringing Sea and half the population of Khokarsa must be descended from him. After all, he has been roaming about for two thousand years."

"I myself can trace my descent to Sahhindar," Hadon said. "Though to tell the truth, I have often wondered if the genealogy was not just something that my ancestors made up. But apparently not."

"Lalila is also a descendant of Sahhindar, a great-granddaughter, I believe," Paga said. He chuckled and said, "In fact, Sahhindar once commented that he was a descendant of himself. Though what he meant by this, I do not know."

They came into sight of the camp then and were quickly challenged by a sentry. Hadon went through the ridiculous rigmarole of identifying himself, and escorted the three to his headquarters, a tiny hut made of poles covered by leafy branches. There he told Tadoku to summon all to be informed that the first phase of their mission was completed. He had no intention of looking also for Sahhindar. If Minruth demanded to know where he was, he would be given the general location. Let him send someone else to look for him.

14

Kwasin was the one who gave the most trouble, as was to be expected. All the males adored Lalila, but though they might wish to lie with her, they would not have dared suggest it by words or touch. Hadon had ordered that she was to be treated as a priestess even if she were a savage. The order was not necessary, since word spread quickly through the small camp that she was indeed a priestess of the moon. This was not true. However, her mother had been one and Lalila in due course would have succeeded her. Moreover, her name, which meant *moon of change* in Khokarsan, reinforced the belief that she was a holy one. And her titles, the White Witch from the Sea and the Risen-from-the-Sea, were enough to scare off even the randiest. The latter was also, by another coincidence, a title of Adeneth, goddess of sexual passion and of madness.

Kwasin was the only one not scared, of course. On first seeing her, he exclaimed with wonder, fell on his knees, seized her hand, and kissed it. Hadon watched him in alarm, because there was no telling what the giant would kiss next. He put his hand on the hilt of his sword, ready to draw it and lop off Kwasin's head if he should insult her. Kwasin rose to his feet and bellowed that he had never seen a woman so lovely or so radiant, that she was indeed like the goddess of the moon, fair and remote and holy. He would bash in the skull of anyone who dared even hint of violating her. Hadon hated him for that. To tell the truth—and he did so in his heart—he desired her mightily. And he suspected that Kwasin, if he managed to be alone with her, would not find her untouchable. At least, not as far as he was concerned.

And what of Awineth, the young and beautiful queen who was waiting for him by a throne that would be his? Ah, yes, what of dark-haired, dark-eyed, shapely Awineth? She was far off, pale and tenuous as a ghost seen at dawn. Which was not a very realistic attitude, Hadon told himself. She represented glory and power, and to give these up by giving her up was madness. Besides, Awineth would regard such an act as an unforgivable insult. She could reject him if she wished, but for him to reject her would probably result in…what? Exile? Or death on the spot? The latter, most probably.

It was truly insane to consider such a thing. Unthinkable. But he was thinking it, and so was mad. And knowing this, he still was happy. Why was he happy? Lalila had not given the slightest sign of any tender feeling toward him.

They had a long way to go, and who knew what might happen before they arrived at the border of the empire?

Kebiwabes, the bard, also seemed struck by the madness which the full moon or a beautiful woman sometimes sends. He began composing the *Song of the Moon of Change*, the *Pwamwotlalila*, and at the end of the second week of their journey southward sang it. It was not an epic, but a lyric modeled in the spirit and after the structure of the songs that the priestesses of the temples of the moon, the *Wootla*, the Voices of the Moon, sang at the beginning of the annual orgiastic rites in the ancient days. These rites had been suppressed for five centuries, though they were still practiced secretly in the countryside and in the mountain areas. Hadon, listening, felt arousal of spirit and flesh. Kwasin stripped and danced the ancient Dance of the Mating Bear, causing Lalila to turn away in embarrassment. Mad Kwasin danced on, his eyes glazed, seemingly unaware that she had walked away into the darkness.

Hadon followed her to apologize and found her and the manling standing by a great boulder in the moonlight.

"I could not stop him," he said. "To have interfered would be insulting the goddess of the moon, since her spirit has seized him."

"Do not apologize," she said. "My people have had similar dances, and I have witnessed them without being offended. But in this case the dance was not impersonal. It was obviously directed at me, and it made me very uncomfortable. I fear that monster; he has been touched by the moon; there is no telling what he may do when he is possessed. And from what you and the bard have told me, Kwasin is no respecter of chastity or holiness when he is seized."

"True," Hadon said, "but he knows that the next time he transgresses, he may die. If men do not strike him down, Kho may. And he also wishes to have his exile terminated, which will not happen if he offends her again. So, though he is possessed, he is still trying to control himself. I will give him that, and I am not one to give him much."

"He is also possessed of a stature and strength which all men should desire," Paga said. "But I do not. Both Kwasin and I are misshapelings. He has been given too much and I too little. But whereas the deities have made me small, have cut off my legs, they have given me an intelligence to compensate. Him they have given too much of the body and so have deprived him of his wits. I have a keen nose, Hadon, and I smell misfortune and evil sweating from that great body. Tell me, is it true that you lived with him for a while when you were both young?"

"That was my misfortune," Hadon said. "We both resided with our uncle in a cave high above the Sea of Opar for a few years. Kwasin had to have someone to bully, and since he dared not insult my uncle, who would have kicked him off the cliff into the sea, he bullied me. I am good-natured, and I put up with it for a while, trying to get him to be more agreeable, trying to get him to become a friend. Eventually I lost my temper and attacked him. It was humiliating, because he beat me severely and laughed at me while doing it. I am strong, but I am a weakling compared to Kwasin, as, indeed, all men are.

"My uncle did not say a word to Kwasin about this, but he did arrange a series of athletic contests for us with malice aforethought. Whoever lost would be beaten by him, and my uncle saw to it that the games were to Kwasin's disadvantage. We ran the quarter-mile and the half-mile, and though Kwasin, huge as he is, can keep pace with me for fifty yards, he lags far behind in the longer runs. So my uncle beat Kwasin severely when he lost. Kwasin was probably strong enough even then to strike my uncle down, but he was afraid of him. I think my uncle was the only man Kwasin ever feared. Perhaps because he was even madder.

"My uncle also had us exercise with wooden swords. Though I took some very hard, near-crippling blows, my skill overcame Kwasin's brute force, and I bruised and stunned him often. At last he caught on to what was happening and said he wanted no more of the races and the wooden swords. My uncle smiled and said that that was all right with him. But he might renew them if he thought it was wise. Kwasin ceased to bully me, except in subtle ways, and he has never forgiven me. He considers that I defeated him, a thing which he cannot forget. He must always have the upper hand, always be the dominant. Now I am his commander, and he hates me even more."

"Yet he sometimes jests with you, and even seems to like you," Lalila said.

"Kwasin is two people in one. He is one of those unfortunates whom Kho has given two souls. Too often, the evil soul is the ruling one."

The child, sitting nearby, complained that she was tired. Lalila took her to their little lean-to to sing her to sleep. Hadon listened to her voice, as silvery and as soft as the light of the moon, and he was consumed with a fire as hot as the sun's, as if the moon had summoned the sun to rise before its time.

Paga, watching him, said, "It seems the fate of some to be driven mad and of others to drive people mad. Lalila, unfortunately for her, is of the latter. She is not evil, but she brings evil. Or rather, she brings out the evil in people. Her beauty is a curse to her and to the men who desire her and to the women who are jealous of her. It is sad, because she desires only peace and joy; she has no wish for power over others."

"Then she should live in a cave far from all men," Hadon said.

"But she loves to be with people," Paga said. "And perhaps deep within her there is a desire to have power over men. Who knows?"

"Only the Goddess knows," Hadon said.

"I do not believe in gods or goddesses," Paga said. "They exist only in the minds of men and women who created them so they can blame someone outside themselves for the things they themselves bring down on their heads."

Paga, carrying the ax on his shoulder, waddled away while Hadon stared after him. But no thunder and lightning, no heavings of the earth followed. The moon shone serenely, the jackals yapped, the hyenas laughed, in the distance a lion roared. All was as before.

They continued southward. Ten days later they came to a river the headwaters of which were somewhere in the mountains to the northwest. Paga felled trees with his keen-edged iron ax, and they chopped off the branches with their bronze axes.

With fire and ax, they shaped the logs into dugouts and made planks for seats. These were fitted into grooves in the interior and secured with wooden pins. They put their supplies, armor, and weapons underneath the seats, and using paddles they had fashioned from long blocks of wood, they set out.

The current was swift here, and Hadon hoped that it would remain so for hundreds of miles. It was pleasant not to have to paddle hard, to allow the stream to do most of the work. Moreover, getting food was easy. The river was full of fish, and ducks and geese thronged its surface and the banks. The fish were easily caught on hooks, or speared, and the vast numbers of crocodiles and hippopotami ensured that they would not suffer for lack of meat, though the taking was dangerous. The jungle alongside the river harbored many types of antelope. Several types of berries and nuts and a variety of green cabbage provided plant food.

Moreover, Hadon had a chance to talk to Lalila, since she sat directly behind him. As the days drifted by, Awineth receded even more in his mind and heart and Lalila became ever more glowing. Sometimes he suffered from the sharp points of the trident of conscience, but he could not control the workings of his love for Lalila.

Hadon regarded the finding of the river as a good omen. On the tenth day of travel, however, he changed his mind. The muddy shore, which had sloped gradually from the river, suddenly became steep and rocky, and the narrowed river became stronger. As the hours passed, the stream sank deeper into the rock, and at noon the tops of the cliffs on both sides were twenty-five feet above them. The current was too swift to paddle back up the river. The sky, which had been bright, became black. A strong wind whooped above them, and a half-hour later rain fell. It was so thick that Hadon sometimes wondered if a river high in the sky had not fallen on them. He set Paga and Abeth to bailing with the leather helmets, while he, Lalila, and the two soldiers in the stern steered with their paddles.

Lightning cracked above them, fiercely illuminating the darkness and frightening them. The flashes showed them that they were now perhaps fifty feet below the tops of the cliffs. Hadon did not need the lightning to know that the water was becoming rougher. The river had become even more narrow, and they were beginning to encounter huge boulders.

Then they rounded a curve and were in the grip of rapids.

There was nothing to do but pray to Kho and the unknown river godling and to ride it out. Their boats were tossed up and down, turned around, the sides sometimes striking the perpendicular walls of the canyon. Once, during a flash, Hadon glanced back. He saw the third vessel behind him spin, its stern smashing into the side of a great rock near the wall. When he looked during the next flash, the boat and its occupants had disappeared in the foam. Lalila's face was white and strained. Paga looked pale too, but he grinned at Hadon, his large teeth like gold insets in a curved alabaster skull.

That was Hadon's last look behind. The rest of the transit, he was too busy trying to keep the boat straight, trying to steer it past the threatening rocks, shoving his paddle at times against the canyon wall to keep the boat from colliding.

No use. The dugout rode up, up, up a white-headed wave, leaned far to the left as it scraped against the wall, and turned over. He heard Lalila shriek as he pitched into the maelstrom. Something struck his shoulder heavily—either the boat or a rock—and his head came above the surface briefly. He went under again as if the river godling had seized him by the ankles. He scraped against stones, fought upward, heard a roar louder than that of the rapids, and was cast outward and down. Half in water, half in spray, he fell, struck solid water, was plunged deep, scraped again on the rocky bottom, fought upward, and suddenly was in relatively smooth water. But the current was still strong, and he had to fight hard to get to the shore.

He dragged himself up a gentle slope of grass-covered earth and sat panting. Then he saw Lalila and the child clinging to the bottom of an upturned dugout, and he swam out to help them. Lalila, gasping, said, "Get Abeth! I can make it!"

The child seemed in even less danger than her mother. She swam strongly to the shore, and Hadon, hearing a cry through the thunder of the cataract, turned. For a minute the large brown head of Paga was above the surface. Hadon dived toward it, and by accident or the grace of Kho, his hands touched Paga. He felt blindly around, touched him again, felt along his arm, felt the thong attached to the wrist and knew that at the other end was the reason why the manling had been dragged down. The ax. The wonder of it was that Paga had been able to swim up even once.

Hadon seized Paga's long hair and swam heavily upward. Reaching the surface, he pulled the manling on up. The current carried them past Lalila and the child, who were crawling out onto shore. Hadon, his one hand under Paga's chin, towed him in to land about fifty yards down. Paga's head kept going under, but he did not struggle against Hadon, and suddenly Hadon was able to stand up. He lifted Paga above the water and walked backward to the shore. There he placed the manling face-down, his one arm outstretched, the ax still in the water. Paga coughed and wheezed, and water ran from his mouth and nose, but he would live.

As suddenly as it had come, the rain left.

Several boats, upside down or rightside up, floated by. Tadoku, the scribe, and the bard swam by, and Hadon plunged into the water to help them. Tadoku made it by himself, but the scribe and the bard might not have gotten to safety without Hadon's aid. All three were battered, bruised, and bleeding.

Hadon waded out again, waist-deep, and grabbed the Klemqaba priestess and pulled her in. Some more dugouts floated by, one with the Klemqaba sergeant and a Klemklakor private clinging to it. Five more men succeeded in getting ashore; they said that their two boats had stayed unhurt until they had gone over the falls. Their fellows must have drowned after striking the bottom at the foot of the falls.

Hadon thought that that was to be expected. The cataract was about fifty feet high.

He dived in again and pulled a man ashore, but the fellow was dead. That one seemed to be the last they would see. The others were either whirling around in the turmoil below the falls or had been carried along under the surface past them. Of the fifty-six who had left the outpost above Mukha, only twelve were alive. Except for Paga's ax and the knives they wore in their scabbards, they were weaponless.

"I did not think that even the river godling could defeat Kwasin," the bard said. "Surely he could not have drowned. That is too commonplace a death for such a hero. If he is to die, it must be with the corpses of his enemies piled high around him, himself and his club bloody, and Sisisken hovering above him, waiting to take his ghost off to the garden reserved for the greatest of heroes."

Paga, who was now standing, though weakly, snorted with disbelief.

"He is, though a giant, only a man," he said, "and a river is no respecter of men."

He looked upward at Hadon and said, with a strange smile, "I am your slave now, Hadon. You have saved my life. Once Wi saved my life, and I became, as is the custom of our people, his property."

"You are not among your people now," Hadon said.

Paga spat and said, "That is true. Nor do my people exist anymore. I alone survive, I, Paga, the ugly one-eyed manling, the rejected. But I choose to observe the custom, Hadon, and I am yours. Though I hope that I bring you more luck than I brought Wi. However, I am also Lalila's, which might become embarrassing if I should have to choose between you two."

"If I had my way, she and I would become one," Hadon said.

The statement surprised him, but it seemed to surprise Lalila even more. She gasped and looked with an undecipherable expression at him.

"So that is the way it is," Paga said. "It is to be expected, however."

Lalila did not speak. Hadon, feeling foolish, turned away. At that moment the others shouted. Hadon looked toward where they were pointing and saw the massive dark head of Kwasin appear out of the boiling water and spray below the cataract. He swam slowly toward them, and when he stood up in the shallows, blood from a deep gash streamed from his side.

Kwasin paid it no attention. His face was twisted and black with fury. "I lost my club!" he roared. "My precious club! It fell from my hand when I was forced to cling to a rock! Then I dived for it, but the river was too strong even for such as I, and I was swept away! Where is the godling of the river? I would seize him and choke him until he gave it back to me!"

"Brave words," Paga said, sneering.

Kwasin stared at the manling and then said, "I may step on you and press you into the mud as if you were a loathsome lizard, ugly one. Do not anger me, for I am eager to kill someone. Someone must pay for my loss!"

Paga got to his feet and began untying the knot that bound the thong to his wrist.

"This was almost the death of me," he said. "It was the death of Wi. I do not think that those yellow-haired men would have chased us so eagerly if it had not been for the desire to get this ax, though perhaps they were equally eager to get Lalila. In any event, I am convinced that the Ax of Victory, as I sometimes call it, brings victory for a while to its owner, and then death."

He finished the untying and held the ax out to Kwasin.

"Here, giant, is a gift from a dwarf. Take it and use it well. Wi, some days before he died, told me that I should have it if he died. I told him I did not want it as my property. I would carry it only until I came across someone who deserved to wield it. You are that one, since I doubt that there is on earth a mightier. But I warn you. Its luck lasts only a short time."

Kwasin took the haft in his right hand and swung the ax.

"Ha, that is a mighty weapon! With it I could crush battalions!"

"And no doubt will," Paga said. "But he who loves killing must in the end be killed."

"What do I care for your savage superstitions!" Kwasin bellowed. "However, I thank you, manling, though you must not expect me to love you for it!"

"Gifts don't bring love to giver or taker, giant," Paga said. "Besides, I love Lalila and Abeth, and, I believe, Hadon. I don't have any more love to go around. As for your love, you love only yourself."

"Careful, manling, or you will become the first victim of your own gift!"

"The elephant trumpets when he sees a mouse," Paga said.

The ax was indeed a curious one, one which Hadon might have coveted if he had not been a swordsman. Its head was massive, so heavy that only a very strong man could use it effectively. It was crudely fashioned from a lump of iron and some other metal, but it had a sharp edge. The handle, according to Paga, had been made from the solid lower leg bone of some kind of antelope[5] that was found only in the northern part of the lands beyond the Ringing Sea. This beast was twice as big as an eland. It did not have horns but had some kind of bony growth from its head which spread out into many points. Paga had dug it out of a bog, where it had been so long that it had half-turned to stone. He had worked out a deep slot at one end for receipt of the neck of the ax, and he had bound it with strips from the hide of a creature something like the giant antelope but smaller.[6] After the haft and the ax had been lashed together with these, he had knotted the ends and poured the resin of heated amber over the lashings. The bone haft was also lashed with strips of hide. At the other end of the bone, which was as hard as elephant ivory, was a knob, the knuckle joint. Paga had rubbed this down to make a smooth sphere.

"Have you forgotten that you are wounded?" Hadon said to Kwasin.

Kwasin looked down in amazement at his side and said, "I must attend to it," and he hurried off to see what the Klemqaba woman could do for him.

They stayed the rest of the day below the rapids, fashioning spears for those who had lost them. They found some quartzlike rocks which Paga chipped for them into points, he being the only one who knew this art. Hadon watched him closely, since he might someday again be in a situation requiring the working of stone into weapons.

Finally he decided that watching wasn't enough. He asked Paga to teach him, and after painfully banging and bloodying his fingers, he managed to knock off a

5 The giant Irish elk.

6 The reindeer.

"mother," as Paga called it, a section of a rock from which he had to knock off the "daughters." These he ruined, but on his second round of attempts, he worked a spearhead that Paga said was satisfactory though not praiseworthy.

"But this knowledge may save your life someday," Paga said.

He did not sleep well that night, because of the pains in his side where he had struck the rocks of the rapids and because of a swelled thumb from the stone-working. When he finally did sleep, he dreamed that Awineth came to him, first reproaching him for unfaithfulness and then warning him of great danger. He awoke with all asleep around him except for two guards under trees nearby. A ghostly owl floated over them, making him wonder if it was an omen sent by Kho. But what good were omens if he did not know what they meant?

Nevertheless, he kept awakening the rest of the night, each time thinking that something dreadful had happened. Once he saw Lalila sit up and look at him. The moon was bright, and she was near enough so that he could see that same unreadable expression. For a moment he thought about talking to her, but she lay back down, and he drifted off again.

15

They rose stiffly at dawn. An hour's gathering in the jungle brought in enough berries and nuts to fill their bellies, and they set out again. They had not gone more than two miles when Hadon saw two dugouts caught against a fallen tree by the other shore. One was turned over; the other was upright. Unfortunately, there were crocodiles nearby. As the river was a quarter of a mile broad at this point, Hadon did not believe that it was wise to swim to the boats. Yet there might be weapons in them, secured under the seats. Also, he had a faint hope that one of them carried his sword.

"If we can get the boats, Kwasin can chop us another out of a tree, and we'll have swift transportation again," Hadon said. "So we'll create a diversion. We'll give the saurians some tempting food a little downstream."

That was easier said than done. They spread out into the jungle to hunt an animal whose carcass would be large enough to attract all the great reptiles. Lalila, the child, and Paga stayed behind, guarded by two soldiers.

Near dusk, hungry, tired, and frustrated, the hunters reassembled on the shore. No one had caught anything large, though two had stoned three monkeys. But there, drawn up on the mud, was a dugout with Paga grinning beside it.

Hadon asked Paga how he had done it, though he knew before the manling told his tale. He cursed himself for his lack of wits. Paga had walked upstream until he came to a place where there did not seem to be any crocodiles. He had swum across, walked back down, and with a branch managed to paddle one of the dugouts back. He had been carried downstream about a mile, but then he had walked back in the shallows, shoving the boat ahead of him.

Paga leaned into the boat and drew out something that brought a cry of joy from Hadon. It was Karken, his sword.

"I seem to be a dispenser of weapons," Paga said.

Kwasin said, "You are not as useless as your size would indicate, manling."

"The sea dog seems clumsy on the land, but in the ocean he is swift and graceful," Paga said. "My ocean is my intelligence, giant. You would drown there."

"If you had not given me this ax, little one, I would crack open your ocean."

"So much for gratitude," Paga said.

"Kwasin, put your ax and your arm to use and spare us your tongue," Hadon said. "Fashion some paddles, so we may cross to the other boat. And after that, chop down a tree so we may fashion out of it another dugout."

"The ax is getting dull," Kwasin said. "Nor am I a carpenter."

But he obeyed, and when Hadon and Tadoku paddled across, they heard behind them the lusty blows of his ax against the trunk of a tree.

Three days later they set out once again. This time Hadon determined that if they came to a canyon, they would retreat upstream at once and walk along its side. The river, however, wandered back and forth across a land only slightly higher than itself. Except for the flies in the day and the mosquitoes at night, their life was almost idyllic. Even the giant Kwasin lapsed into a decent human being for a while, though Hadon was afraid that the strain would eventually result in an explosion of temper. Kwasin had, however, talked the Klemqaba woman into marrying him, and this seemed to pacify him somewhat. Her other husbands were not happy about it. They complained that he had ruined her for them. Hadon paid them no attention. What the woman did with her mates was up to her, as long as it did not interfere with discipline.

At the end of fifteen days they came to a large lake alive with many thousands of ducks, geese, herons, cranes, pink flamingos, and a giant blue-and-black flamingo unknown to Khokarsa.

They paddled across the lake to the other side, searched along its shore, and concluded that it had no outlet. Reluctantly they abandoned their dugouts and set out on foot. And then, after weeks of walking through the lion-yellow grass, they saw the first peaks of a vast mountain range, some of which were snow-capped.

"According to my calculations, that should be the Saasares," Hinokly said. "If we can find the pass that leads to Miklemres, we can proceed south, and our journey is ended. If we can't, we'll have to go eastward until we can round their end and then go south to Qethruth."

"I never thought we'd get this far," Kebiwabes said. "How far have we gone, Hinokly?"

"It's a year and one month since we left Mukha," the scribe said. "If we find the pass, it shouldn't take more than two months to get to Miklemres. Less, if we can find the pass at once."

And in a year much can happen in Khokarsa, Hadon thought. Has Awineth given me up for dead and chosen another husband?

Unsurprisingly, he found himself hoping that she had. He would be free to ask Lalila if she would accept him as her mate. It was not easy to give up the desire for the throne, but she would be worth it. However, so far she had given no indication other than a warm friendliness that she was thinking favorably of him. He would have asked her how she felt long ago if he had not been the queen's affianced. What if Lalila said yes and when he got to Khokarsa he found that Awineth was still waiting for him? She might—no, *would*—have him and Lalila killed. Well, *he* would die, but surely Awineth would not dare touch one who was under the protection of Sahhindar.

When they came to the foothills, Mumona, the Klemqaba woman, drew out the carved goat's teeth from the pouch dangling from her belt. She chanted while whirling widdershins and then cast the teeth into the ashes of their campfire. After studying the pattern they formed, she announced that they should go west. After a few days' journey, they would come across the military outpost that guarded the entrance to the pass. And, sure enough, after walking for five days, they saw its walls and sentinel towers, built of oak logs.

The sentinels saw them long before they had toiled up the slope of the great hill to it, and the wanderers could hear drums and brazen trumpets far off. Presently a troop of soldiers, their bronze armor and spearheads bright in the sun, trotted toward them. Hadon explained to the officer who they were, and a runner was sent to speed the news to the commandant. Thus they entered with a fanfare of trumpets and were greeted warmly. They were bathed in warm water and animal-fat soap and anointed with olive oil. Hadon, Tadoku, Kwasin, the scribe, the bard, and the three from the far north were invited to eat with the commandant and the fort's priestess. The others were sent to the barracks to eat with the soldiers, but Hadon insisted that Mumona must sit with them.

"But she is a Klemqaba!" Major Bohami said.

"She is also our priestess," Hadon said. "Without her, we would have no spiritual guidance. And she has been of great help in taking care of the physical needs of my men. Without her, I myself might have died of swamp fever."

"What do you say, Mineqo?" the major said.

The fort's priestess was of ancient stock, as were many who came from the northern shores of the Kemu. She was tall, blond, blue-eyed, and beautiful despite a hawkish nose and thin lips. She wore a bonnet of the tail feathers of eagles, indicating that she was a priestess of W"uwos, goddess of the red-headed female eagle. Around her neck was a chain of eagle bones from which hung a tiny figure of W"uwos carved from an eagle's leg bone. Around her waist was a belt of eagle skin, and below that a kilt of skin covered with eagle feathers. On a stand near her was a giant eagless, chained, glaring at the party as if she would like to eat them. But she was not hungry; she was fed living hares and snakes.

"If she is a priestess and has done all that Hadon says, then she will sit with us," Mineqo said. "But if she eats disgustingly, as I understand the Klemqaba do, then she will leave."

"I have trained her not to blow her nose or relieve herself while eating with others," Hadon said.

The Klemqaba was summoned and sat quietly through the meal, saying nothing unless she was addressed, which was not often. The meal was delicious. Hadon forgot his usual abstinence and ate of tender partridge stuffed with emmer bread, sweet pomegranates, domestic buffalo steaks covered with hare gravy, *mowometh* berries (the sweetest thing in the world), okra soup in which duck giblets floated, and fried termite queens, a rare delicacy. He also indulged too much in the mead, which was cooled with ice brought down from the mountains. This was the first time in his life that he had experienced iced drinks, though if he became king he could have such every day.

Kwasin ate three times as much as the others, gobbling, smacking, and grunting, and when he finished, belched loudly. The priestess frowned and said, "Hadon, your bear-man has cruder manners than the Klemqaba."

Kwasin stared, his face becoming red, and said, "Priestess, if you were not a holy woman I would eat you too. You look good enough to eat."

"He has been out in the Wild Lands a long time," Hadon said hastily. "I am sure that he did not mean to offend you. Isn't that so, Kwasin?"

"I have been gone a long time," Kwasin said. "And I would not offend the first beautiful woman I've seen, Lalila excepted, since I began my wanderings so many years ago."

"Kwasin? Kwasin?" the priestess said. "Now, where have I heard that name before?"

"What?" Kwasin bellowed, spraying mead down his beard. "You haven't heard of Kwasin? Have you been in the sticks all your life?"

"I was born here," Mineqo said icily. "I have been to Miklemres twice, once for five years to attend the College of the Priestesses and once to attend the coronation of the high priestess of that city. But no, savage, I have never heard of you."

"I thought you knew," Major Bohami murmured.

She turned to him fiercely and said, "Knew what?"

"This is the giant that ravished the priestess of Kho in Dythbeth and killed her guards," he said weakly. "Instead of being castrated and flung to the pigs, he was exiled. The Voice of Kho Herself decreed that sentence."

"Why didn't you tell me?" she said.

"I was busy arranging for the comforts of Hadon and his people. And I thought you knew. It is not up to me to advise you on what to do."

"And you are the man whose child I carry," she said. "I hope it isn't as stupid as you!"

The major reddened but said nothing. Kwasin gulped down a beaker of mead, belched again, and said, "O Priestess, do not get angry. It is true that I was exiled, but the Voice of Kho also said that I would return someday. She did not say when, so I have come back to plead forgiveness from Her. I have suffered more than enough; my sin should be expiated by now."

The priestess rose from her chair and said, "That is for Kho to decide! But you have been forbidden to step inside this land, and this fort is in the boundary of the empire!"

She pointed a finger at the doorway and shouted, "Out!"

Kwasin heaved himself up and gripped the edge of the table with his massive fingers. "Out, you say? Out to where?"

"Out of this fort!" she cried. "You may sleep by the gate for all I care, like an outcast dog, but you will not stay in this land! Not until the Voice of Kho has been notified that you are knocking at the gate and not until She says—if indeed She will—that you may enter!"

For a moment Hadon thought that Kwasin intended to upset the table. He moved his chair back, at the same time whispering to Lalila and the child to get out of the way. Paga, he noticed, had already done so. But Kwasin, quivering, his eyes black lava, managed to control himself.

He said, "It is only because I do not wish to offend mighty Kho again that I do not ravage through this fort, slaying everyone. I will go, Priestess, but I won't hang around here like a jackal waiting for scraps. It will take months to get a message from the Voice of Kho, and I am impatient! I will go on into the land, and woe to him who dares to get in my way! I will go to the mountain of Kho myself and there throw myself on Her mercy!"

"If you attempt to enter without Her permission, you will be slain!" the priestess said.

"I'll take that chance," Kwasin said, and he turned and walked out. Hadon followed him in time to see him come out of his room with the great ax. Kwasin said, "Ho, cousin, do you mean to stop me?"

"Why should I?" Hadon said. "No, I am not trying to get in your way. But though you have offended me and been as troublesome as a fly up my nostril, I would not see you commit suicide. I beg you to do as the priestess says. Stay here until Kho bids you come or bids you depart."

"Kho is a woman and no doubt has changed Her mind about me by now," Kwasin said. "No, I am going to Her and demand that She say yes or no Herself. I'm not going to wait. As for my being killed before I get there, that is nonsense. I don't intend to march through the land where everyone will see me. I will steal through the country like a fox, steal a boat when I get to the Kemu, and sail to the island. And then I will go softly and at night up the mountain and face the oracle, the Voice."

"And if Kho is still adamant?"

"Then I just might ravish the oracle and knock the temple down with this ax," Kwasin said. "If I die, I will not do so meekly."

"Sometimes I think you mean it when you say fantastic things like that," Hadon said.

"Of course I do," Kwasin said. He strode out of the room, which suddenly became much larger.

Hadon returned to the dining room. Lalila said, "What does he mean to do?"

"He is indeed mad," Hadon said. "Kho has taken his senses away, and I am afraid that She will take his life soon."

"Perhaps he would be better off if She did," Paga said. "He is a miserable creature, full of arrogance and hate. But if such were to be struck down, this world would have only a few people left in it. Which would be a blessing."

"Let us not talk of him," Mineqo said. "Sit down, Lalila, my dear, and we shall talk of you. Before that elephantine buffoon interrupted us, you were telling me that you were a priestess of the moon among your own people."

"Not I," Lalila said. "My mother was. I would have been if my tribe had not perished."

"And what other goddesses do you worship?"

"Many. We also worship many gods. But the two greatest deities are the moon and the sun. They are twin sisters, daughters of the sky, who gave over her empire to them after the first humans were created by her."

"Ah!" Mineqo said. "Among us the sun is the god Resu, though in the ancient times Resu was Bikeda, a goddess. She is still worshiped as such in some of the rural and mountainous areas. Just so was Bhukla once the chief deity of war but was dislodged by Resu and became the goddess of the sword. All this came about because the Klemsaasa, the Eagle people, conquered Khokarsa when she was weakened by earthquake and plague. They strove to make Resu greater than Kho but did not succeed. But the priests of Resu have not given up the struggle, even though they tempt the wrath of Kho."

"I do not understand," Lalila said. "How can the deeds of mortals cause changes in the heavens?"

"That is a deep question, and the answer is deep. It was all explained to me when I was in the college, but it would take me an hour to explain to you. First, I would have to define the technical terms, and that might cause more confusion than ever. However, you may be enlightened when you get to the city of Khokarsa. Since you are a priestess of the moon, even though from an alien people, Awineth may decide that you can be initiated into the priestesshood."

"Sahhindar suggested that I might benefit if I did become a priestess," Lalila said.

"Sahhindar!" Mineqo said. "The Archer God came to *you* in a dream?"

"No dream," Lalila said. "Sahhindar talked with me and walked with me in the flesh, as a man, as real and solid as Hadon. It was he who sent Paga, Abeth, and me here. He put us under his protection."

"Is this true?" the priestess said, turning to Hadon and Hinokly.

"True, Mineqo," Hinokly said. "I was there when the Gray-Eyed God charged our expedition to return to Khokarsa and see that she was given both safety and respect there. Evidently you had not heard of this."

"But why didn't you tell me this before? I thought that your expedition was only a scientific survey team."

"There was too little time, O Priestess," Hinokly said.

Mineqo looked bewildered. "I do not understand this at all. Sahhindar was exiled by Kho because he disobeyed Her. The priests of Resu claim that Sahhindar is therefore the ally of Resu."

"He is no god, Mineqo," Lalila said, "though godlike. He told me himself that he is only a mortal. He says that he was a traveler in time, that he had been born in the future, over eleven thousand years from now, and that he traveled backward by use of a..."

She hesitated and then said, "We do not have a word for the thing which transported him. He used a word from his own language to name it...a...mashina, I believe he, said."

"And what is this...masina," Mineqo said, unable to utter the *-sh-* sound.

"Something like a boat which carries a device that pushes it through time, as a boat is pushed by wooden blades."

"Pardon, Priestess," Hadon said. "Lalila has never seen a boat with sails. A more apt analogy would be that time is like a wind which pushes the time boat's sails."

"But Sahhindar was the one who taught the Khoklem how to domesticate plants and animals, how to make bricks, how to make bronze, how to add and subtract and multiply," Mineqo said. "That was two thousand years ago. Do men live that long?"

"Sahhindar said that there are a few people of the far future who have an elixir which keeps them from aging," Hinokly said. "But I myself heard him disclaim his godhood."

"Do they know that at the palace?" Mineqo said.

"They do," Hinokly said. "I imagine that that revelation has caused a storm of controversy among the colleges."

"Such things are beyond me," Mineqo said. "I have lived too long in this isolated post to remember all the philosophy I was taught as a young girl. Let the colleges decide what this means. I will send all of you with an escort to the chief priestess at Miklemres, and she can decide what to do with you."

"That is *my* province!" Major Bohami said. "I am the military commander here, Mineqo, and I say who is to come and to go. At present, we are short-handed, and I cannot spare more than a couple of guides."

"I have heard you boast that you and five men could disperse any attack by the barbarians," Mineqo said. "And the last trouble we had with them was when I was a little girl. The Klemklakor are too few around here to be a danger, but what if they attack this party deep in the mountains? You know that they often try to ambush our supply trains."

It was evident that the major felt that he had to protest his sovereignty, yet wanted a way to agree with the priestess. He said, "Since you put it that way, I agree that there is sense in what you say. But I will issue the orders, and I do so only because our guests are so important. The wishes of the king and queen and of Sahhindar make it imperative that I give them all the protection that we can spare."

Hadon said, "We would like to leave shortly after dawn."

"That shall be done," Mineqo and Bohami said at the same time.

Bohami glared at her, and she spoke in a low voice, "You will sleep alone tonight, Bohami, unless you apologize."

"So be it," Bohami said. "I don't like your undercutting my authority. You should consult with me in private and leave the public issuing of orders to me."

Hadon was embarrassed and so bade them good night as quickly as he could.

16

The party, accompanied by twelve soldiers, climbed up the narrow cliff-girdling path. Toward noon they put on the thick mountain-leopard furs provided them. The snows hung above them, making them uneasy. The soldiers said that more than one patrol and supply train had been buried in avalanches. In fact, the fort was beginning to run short of goods from Miklemres because the last train had been wiped out. The avalanche may have been an accident or it may have been triggered by the wild tribes of the Bear Totem. These, the soldiers said, were the descendants of the mountaineers who had stayed behind when the Klemsaasa invaded Khokarsa with their rebellious Miklemres allies and conquered the devastated capital. Since the Klemklakor had been at war with the Mountain Eagle Totem then, they had not taken part. Escaped criminals and runaway slaves had added to their numbers during the one thousand and eleven years that had passed since the Klemsaasa had left the Saasares ranges. It was said that the Klemklakor were so numerous now that they needed only a leader to unite them to become a dangerous threat to the Miklemres queendom. So far, they were so busy fighting among themselves that the Khokarsans had been able to control them.

"Klemklakor is a generic term for them," Tadoku said. "Actually, though the Bear people are in the majority, there are a dozen totems in these mountains, most of them descended from refugees. But all are enemies of the Khokarsans. If we should have another Time of Troubles, they would sweep down on Miklemres like locusts. United, they would be a formidable enough force. Being heretics, they use the bow and arrow, and this makes them triply dangerous."

The trail wound down again. By the morning of the second day they were warm enough to shed their furs. Two days later they put them on again. On the fifth day they saw a bear only a quarter of a mile away. Hadon became excited because he had never seen this legendary creature in the flesh.

"If you think it is big, you should see a *klakoru*, a cave bear," Hinokly said. "Rumors have it that there are still a few in the highest ranges. Those who have seen them say that they are as big as elephants, though no doubt that is an exaggeration."

At noon of the seventh day they were proceeding down a trail halfway up the slope of a mountain. Suddenly the earth trembled and the mountain roared. They looked up and saw a dozen gigantic boulders bounding toward them, followed by a mass of smaller stones and snow. There was no place to run, though some did run. The rest, Hadon among them, jumped below the trail into a depression and flattened themselves out against the earth. Within a minute the first of the boulders soared over them, striking a few feet past them. Others followed them, rumbling and banging, one smashing a fleeing soldier, and then it became quiet, the only sound that of the boulders still leaping and rolling far below.

They got up cautiously while snow powder and dust fell on them. The mass behind the boulders had slid to a stop a few yards above the trail. Kho had protected them.

The incident, however, was not over. Far above were the yells of men in a desperate fight. Hadon saw tiny figures emerging from a stand of firs. They scattered in two directions along the slopes, and presently they had run into the trees to the north and the south. After a while a familiar figure emerged. It came slowly down the slope, skirted the loose mass directly above the party, and walked toward them on the trail. It was Kwasin, gigantic in bearskins, covered with blood, and carrying his bloody ax on his shoulder. One hand held two severed heads by their beards.

He flung the heads at the feet of Hadon and roared, "Behold the ambusher of the ambushers, cousin! I spied them long before they saw me, and I crept up on them. I wasn't in time to prevent their rolling down boulders at you, but shortly thereafter I launched my own avalanche! Myself! Though they were a score, I attacked them and slew half a dozen before they decided that I must be a werebear! Then I clothed myself in furs they no longer needed and cut off some trophies. You may thank me now, cousin, for saving your life, though if the beautiful Lalila had not been with you I might not have interfered!"

"In which case, Lalila may thank you, but I won't," Hadon said. "And what now?"

"I will go with you to Khokarsa and protect you!"

"After we reach Miklemres, it is you who will need the protection," Hadon said. "Are you depending upon my status as the king-to-be to get you to the capital safely?"

"You see through me!" Kwasin said, and he laughed.

"Then you will have to obey my orders again."

"So be it! But when we reach the capital, cousin, and Awineth compares you to me, she may change her mind and take me as her husband. How would you like that, little one?"

Better than you could guess, Hadon thought, but he did not reply.

Two months of slow up-and-down travel passed. Four times they were lucky enough to escape hunting or raiding bands of the Bear people. Their scouts saw the barbarians and warned the party in time to permit hiding or flight. And then, at noon one day, they came around a trail, and the plains of Miklemres spread out below. Their joy was quickly smothered, however, when they saw heavy smoke rising from two places along the river. The next day they cautiously approached the first site. Seeing no one living, they entered into the charred area. Many mutilated corpses lay in the ashes. The sergeant from the fort poked around and confirmed what they all knew.

"The Bear people. There must have been at least three hundred."

"There aren't many women and children," Hadon said.

"Oh, they took the women as wives, and the children will be adopted into the tribe and will grow up to be as bloodthirsty as their foster fathers."

He shook his head and said, "They are getting arrogant. The last time this happened, about ten years ago, we sent up large punitive expeditions which cleared the mountains for many miles roundabout. General D"otipoeth collected three thousand heads and brought in five hundred prisoners, men, women, and children, to be hanged along this road as a warning. At the last minute the chief priestess reprieved the children."

They proceeded quietly with scouts far ahead and that evening came to the ruins of the second village. There they found the same ruin and carnage. They went without incident through this country of grapevines, beehives, and emmer fields until they encountered the third village. This was as large as the first two together and was protected by a log fort containing three hundred soldiers. The commandant, Abisila, a tall gangling redhead, came out to greet them. Grimly he asked them to identify themselves. Hadon gave their names. The commandant looked even grimmer and said, "I thought so. There is no mistaking you and that bearded monster. Hadon of Opar and Kwasin of Dythbeth, I arrest you in the name of Minruth, king of kings!"

17

Resistance was useless. They were surrounded by fifty men pointing spears at them. Hadon finally said coolly, "And what is the charge?"

"That I do not know," Abisila said.

"But that is illegal!" the scribe said. "The law clearly states that when a man is arrested he must be informed also of the charge!"

"Haven't you heard?" Abisila said. "No, I suppose you haven't. There is a new law in the land!"

"Why?" Hadon said, but the commandant would not answer. He gestured at his men to take the weapons of the prisoners. Hadon withdrew his sword to hand it to Abisila but hesitated. Should he instead chop off the commandant's arm and try to break out? But if he did, he would quickly be run through. And—a stronger motive for surrendering peacefully—Lalila and the child might be harmed in the melee.

Kwasin, as usual, did not think of the consequences. He roared, and his ax flashed by Hadon and sheared off Abisila's arm. He turned then and leaped at the ring of spears, cut through or knocked aside a half-dozen spearheads, and in a few seconds had cut off two heads and an arm. There was shouting and confusion as the soldiers milled around, too closely packed to get at Kwasin and many not knowing what was happening. Kwasin picked up a headless corpse with his left hand and cast it at the outer ring and knocked down three men. Then, his ax flashing out to one side and shearing a spear, he had broken through.

For several seconds no one pursued. The second in command restored some order, and ten men ran after the giant, who had disappeared in the nearby village. The others surrounded Hadon's party with their spears again. Hadon handed the sword to the captain and said, "I warn you that the woman, her child, and the manling are under the protection of Sahhindar."

The captain turned even paler and stammered a question. Hadon explained as best he could, and the result was that Lalila and her two companions were taken to the quarters of the dead commandant. Tadoku, Hinokly, Kebiwabes, and Hadon were locked inside a large room behind bronze bars. Tadoku protested. He was told that though he was not under official arrest, he was to be treated as a prisoner until his case was judged at Khokarsa. The scribe declared that this was illegal, but the captain merely walked away.

And so, three weeks later, all except Kwasin were on a galley headed for the city of Khokarsa. Hadon, though chained, was allowed to walk the deck during the day. The captain and the priest were permitted to talk to him, and from them he learned much of the situation. Minruth, becoming impatient, had demanded that Awineth forget Hadon and marry him. She had refused, and her father had confined her in her apartments. The king's troops had then seized the city. Those military and naval units loyal to Awineth had been disarmed or slain. The Temple of Kho on the slopes of the volcano had been occupied and the priestesses there put in prison.

The men who did that must have been brave, Hadon thought. Even the most fanatical devotee of Resu would have feared the wrath of Kho. But Minruth had promised them great rewards. Power and wealth were more important than even fear of the deities to some men. Minruth had picked these to carry out this outrageous mission. He had not, however, dared to violate the oracular priestess, the Voice of Kho Herself.

There had been, of course, a mass uprising. The poor and many of the middle and upper classes had swarmed out to avenge the blasphemy. But the undisciplined mob did not stand a chance against catapults of liquid fire. The troops of Resu cast hundreds of bundles of the incendiary composition on the people in the jammed streets and burned them alive. The residential and commercial areas around the Inner City burned to the ground, killing thousands and leaving the heart of the city, except for the Inner City, in ashes.

The key centers of the other cities of the island had been simultaneously seized and the mobs there dealt with in a similar fashion. Only Dythbeth, always a thorn in the side of Khokarsa, had revolted successfully. Minruth's armed forces had been massacred. But Minruth had it blockaded now, and it was said that the citizens were eating rats and dogs to stay alive. They could not hold out for more than another week.

Part of the navy had stayed loyal to Awineth and Kho. After some strong fighting, those ships that could get away had fled to Towina, Bawaku, and Qethruth. These cities, like most in the empire, had seized the opportunity to declare independence. The empire was aflame with revolution. Minruth did not care. He would reconquer.

"Mighty Resu will defeat the mortals who persist in placing Kho above her natural master, Resu!" the priest cried.

Hadon felt like kicking the gaunt, blazing-eyed priest into the sea. The captain, though a follower of Resu, winced. Evidently he had not shed all fear of Kho. Nor was he accustomed to being without a priestess. A priest on a ship without a priestess was supposed to be bad luck. Piqabes, the green-eyed Our Lady of Kemu, did not favor such vessels.

The captain told Hadon of the rumblings and shakings of the earth below the city of Khokarsa and of the clouds of smoke and the sea of burning lava that had issued from the volcano.

"Awineth is said to have declared that Kho Herself was going to destroy the city," the captain said. "Many of us wet down our legs when we heard that rumor. But Minruth said that that was not so. Resu was locked in combat with Kho deep within the mountain, and he would eventually overthrow Her. Then She would take the lower throne and become his slave."

"And Minruth was right!" the priest blared. "Otherwise, why would the lava have destroyed the sacred grove and inundated the temple, knocking it down and burning all the priestesses within it? Would Kho, if She were all-powerful, have permitted this? No, Resu did it, and She was powerless to prevent it!"

"The grove and the temple are destroyed?" Hadon said. "Those ancient holy places?"

"Destroyed forever!" the priest shouted. "Minruth has promised that he will build a new temple there, dedicated to Resu!"

"And what of the oracular priestess? Was she killed by the lava?"

The priest gaped at Hadon and then said, as if it pained him, "She seems to have escaped into the wild lands back of the volcano. But Minruth's men are searching for her. When they find her, they will bring her back in chains! Once the populace sees her in Minruth's power, they will know that Resu is all-powerful!"

"If they find her," Hadon said, "I hope that this struggle does not cause Kho to destroy all the land and those within it."

"Resu will triumph, and things will be as they should have been long ago!" the priest said.

"What of Lalila?" Hadon said. "What does Minruth plan for her? After all, she is under the aegis of Sahhindar. The Gray-Eyed God said that he would avenge her if she were harmed in any way."

This last was not true, but Hadon did not mind lying if he could help Lalila.

"How would I know?" the priest said. "Minruth does not confide in me. When she stands before him, then she will be dealt with as justice requires."

Or as Minruth requires, Hadon thought. The dispenser of the law is the interpreter of the law.

The days and nights passed steadily but slowly. Once again Hadon, desiring to stay in shape, asked to be allowed to pull an oar. The captain was scandalized but after a brief argument gave his permission. Hadon wore handcuffs when he worked and was forbidden to speak to the other oarsmen. The captain wanted no subversive talk spread among the sailors.

At long last the northeast coast of the island rose from the horizon. The galley followed the coastline, which was flat farmland for many miles at first. Then a mountain range, the Saasawabeth, arose. Hadon overheard the captain and the priest talking of the guerrillas holed up in it and of the expedition against them. Apparently the seven mountain ranges of the island were the strongholds of thousands of Kho worshipers.

The Saasawabeth became farmland again, but in a few days they were opposite the Khosaasa. The galley left those behind, though not out of sight, and after a week they were entering the mouth of the Gulf of Gahete. Even from this distance the tip of Khowot could be seen. The smoke issuing from it had, however, been visible after passing the Saasawabeth. The galley pulled steadily down the gulf, the cliffs on its right, the high farmlands on its left. Smoke rose from many of the peasants' huts and barns, burned by the troops of Minruth.

Then mighty Khowot rose from the sea, and after two days its base was in sight. On the fifth day, the higher part of the Tower of Resu came into view. This, the priest said, was no longer dedicated to both Resu and Kho. In fact, he had heard rumors that Minruth intended to name it after himself. It was said that the king of kings was considering making a certain theory of the College of Priests a fact. This was that the king was, in essence, Resu himself, that a piece of the spirit of Resu inhabited the king's body and so made him holy. He would be the sun god incarnate, and hence worshiped as a god.

"He is indeed mad," Hadon said.

The priest glared at Hadon and said, "That blasphemy will be reported to Minruth!"

"That won't make my case any harder," Hadon said.

The spires and the towers of the city of Khokarsa lifted, though not as soon as Hadon had expected. This was because the city no longer glittered white. Smoke from the volcano had settled on it, and to this had been added layers of smoke from the burning buildings outside the Inner City.

"Thirty thousand people perished during the uprisings and the fires that followed," the priest said. "The scourge of Resu is terrible indeed! Minruth is said to have wept when he heard this, but later he became joyous. He said that it was the will of Resu and so was necessary. The hardhearted must be destroyed in a ritual of purification of the land. The spirit of blasphemy must be stamped flat forever."

"But all those innocents, the children?" Hadon said.

"The sins of the parents descend upon the children, and they must pay too!"

Hadon was too shocked by this insanity to reply.

The galley proceeded through waters that had once been crowded with seagoing merchant vessels and river boats and barges from inland cities and the rural areas. The stench of the charred corpses beneath the ruins struck them full force, choking them. Then the galley passed between the forts of Sigady and Klydon, and then the fort on the western tip of Mohasi island. The ship bore to the southwest and turned south into the entrance of the great canal. It eased gently in between two docks while drums beat. The prisoners were marched off to a customs house. The captain sent a runner with a letter enclosed in a silver box on the end of a golden staff. This would be delivered to the king of kings, who would read therein that the hero Hadon and his party were awaiting the king's disposal.

Hadon looked curiously at the Great Tower, which was indeed awe-inspiring. Its base was almost half a mile in diameter, and its staggered stories rose to almost five hundred feet. Yet it was only half-built. And it might be a long time before work was resumed on it. Twice before, its building had been halted for long periods during Times of Trouble. And during periods of comparative prosperity and peace, the enormous expense of its construction had taken a large, much-resented portion of tax money.

Two hours passed before the runner appeared at the head of a dog-trotting corps of palace guards. The prisoners were hustled out and marched off behind a blaring band to the citadel. Once again Hadon crossed over the moat and ascended the broad and steep steps to the acropolis, though this time it was from the western end. And he did not come as a conquering hero, victor of the Great Games, husband-to-be of the chief priestess and queen of queens.

They passed through huge bronze gates into the citadel and through broad streets lined by marble temples and government buildings. Some of these were round, or nine-sided, built in ancient times. Others were square, of the style that had come into being about three hundred years ago. The palace itself, the most ancient building, of massive granite blocks overlaid with marble blocks, was nine-sided. Hadon was grieved to see that the statues of Kho and Her daughters, upholding the roof of the great porch, had been defaced. Surely the hands of those who had committed this blasphemy would be withered.

A herald met them at the western doorway, and the prisoners were officially delivered to him. The interior palace guards replaced those who had conducted the prisoners, and two trumpeters replaced the band. They marched through broad stately halls lined with works of art from all over the empire. Then they were in the enormous throne room, glittering with gold, silver, diamonds, emeralds, turquoises, topazes, and rubies. They walked down a long aisle formed of silent courtiers, most of them men. The herald halted before the thrones, thumped the end of his staff on the many-colored mosaic floor of marble and inset diamonds, and cried out the greeting. This time it was Minruth he addressed first. His final phrase, "And remember that death comes to all!" was omitted. Instead the herald shouted, "Mighty Resu, in whom our king of kings is incarnate, rules over all!"

As if that were not shocking enough, Minruth's throne was now on the higher dais, and the fish-eagle which had once stood on the back of Awineth's throne was chained to Minruth's throne. Moreover, judging from its smaller size, it was a male. Minruth, heavily bearded, sat on the throne. This was another change Hadon had noticed among the soldiers and the courtiers. All were unshaven.

Awineth sat on her plain oak throne, clad in a garment that matrons wore after their breasts had begun to sag. From neck to foot, her superb figure was hidden in a voluminous linen robe. She seemed to have aged several years; her eyes were underscored with the blue-black of anxiety and sleepless nights. But her eyes were bright when she looked at Hadon.

There was a long silence afterward, broken only by the coughs of courtiers. Minruth gazed long at Hadon while he chewed his lower lip. Finally he smiled.

"I have heard much about you, Hadon of Opar, since you returned to our land! None of it good! You unlawfully conducted the exiled Kwasin into the land, and that requires the extreme penalty!"

This was a lie, but he who sits on the throne may twist the truth to suit himself. Hadon thought it useless to protest.

"Kwasin was, however, no longer an exile. The ban imposed by the wife of Resu no longer holds, and I would have welcomed the hero Kwasin if he had forsworn loyalty to Kho. But he broke free from arrest and murdered my soldiers while doing so! Thus, he will die after suitable torture!"

If you can catch him, Hadon thought.

Minruth paused, glared at Hadon, and then looked at Lalila. When he spoke, his voice was gentler.

"I have been informed about this woman, the Witch from the Sea, I believe she is called, among other things. If she is indeed a witch, she will be burned. It does not matter that she might be a good witch! There is no such thing now. All witches are evil, and magic is to be practiced by the priests of Resu alone!"

"Science, you mad fool," Hinokly said, so softly that Hadon could barely hear him. "There is no such thing as magic. Science!"

"But I have been told that her witchery consists only of her beauty, and she cannot be blamed for that! If my interrogators are convinced that she is truly not a practicer of magic, then she will be free and honored. I like what my eyes see, and what the king of kings likes, he takes to his heart. I may honor her by taking her as my wife. You may not know it, Hadon, but men may now have more than one wife."

Awineth stirred and said, "That is not according to our ancient law, Father. We are not barbarian Klemqaba. Nor is it lawful to have forced me to marry you."

"I did not ask you to speak!" Minruth said. "If you speak once more without my permission, you will be conducted to your apartments, and we will hold court without you!"

Awineth looked angry but did not reply.

"The ancient laws are repealed. The new laws rule the land," Minruth said. "Now, there are also the cases of the child and of the manling to be judged. The child would be burned with her mother if she were judged a witch, but I do not think that that will be the verdict."

Hadon felt a new shock. He had never heard of such a horrible thing. To burn children for the crimes of the mother was one more evil that would surely bring the wrath of Kho down on Minruth's head! The wonder was that he had not been struck down long ago. But Kho bides Her time.

"The child is as beautiful as her mother, and when the time comes, she may also become my wife."

Hadon ground his teeth and thought of hurling himself at Minruth. Minruth was as mad as a buck hare during mating season. He was fifty-seven now, and though it was said that he was still as virile as a young bull, he could not seriously assume that eleven years from now he could bed Abeth. Or could he?

"And then there is the hairy one-eyed manling. It has been reported that he is a werebeast, that he assumes at night the shape of an animal like a dog, an animal known only in the lands of the far north. Is this true, manling?"

Paga said, "It is true that I was suckled by a four-legged bitch, O King of Kings. The two-legged bitch who bore me cast me out into the bushes to die. She had no heart, but the beast who found me had one full of motherly love, though doubtless she would have eaten me if she had not just lost her cubs. The first milk I tasted was hers. She gave me the only love I have known, excepting that of the hero Wi and of Lalila and her child, though the god Sahhindar was kind to me, and Hadon does not reject me because I am a misshapen manling. I am not a werebeast, O King of Kings, though I am half-beast and proud of it. Often the beasts are more human than the humans. But when the moon is full, I am no more affected by it than you, and perhaps not as much."

"Big words from a little man," Minruth said. "I will not inquire into the meaning of that last statement, since you would lie about it anyway. And you bring up Sahhindar, the Gray-Eyed Archer God. He is a younger brother of mighty Resu and no lover of Kho. Like you, he was abandoned by his mother and raised by the half-apes of the woods. And it was he who gave man plants and taught him how to domesticate them and the beasts, and how to calculate, and how to make bronze. Even the priestesses admit that, though they say that he committed a divine crime by giving us these gifts before Kho had decreed that they should be given.

"It is said that the woman and her child and you have been placed under Sahhindar's protection. Is this indeed so, Lalila?"

"Indeed it is true," Lalila said. "Hinokly can vouch for that."

"But it is also true that Sahhindar has told you that he is no god, that he is only a man, though a strange one? Is this true, Lalila?"

"It is true," Lalila replied.

"Gods often lie to test mortals. But if he should come to this land, he will be interrogated. And if he is an impostor, he will suffer what all mortals must."

"But he is no impostor!" Paga said. "He does not claim to be a god!"

"Strike him with the butt of a spear!" Minruth yelled. "He must learn to unloosen his tongue only when I say he may!"

An officer took a spear from a soldier's hand, and Paga fell to the floor beneath the blow. He groaned once, clamped his teeth, and got to his feet shaking his head.

"The next time, it will be the point, not the butt!" Minruth said. "And now for the scribe, the bard, and Tadoku. They too accompanied Kwasin, and so share in the guilt of the murder of my soldiers. Major, take them with Hadon and the manling to the cells reserved for traitors."

"The queen and Kho forever!" Tadoku yelled.

Those were his last words, brave but foolish. Minruth screamed an order, and Tadoku died with three spears through him. Hadon swore that if he ever had the opportunity, he would see to it that Tadoku was buried under a hero's pylon with the sacrifice of the finest bulls. Then he was taken away while Awineth and Lalila wept. He was led with the others to a door that opened onto steps that wound down and down, down a long hall along which torches flared, down more winding stone steps, down another long hall, and down a final spiral staircase. The two upper halls were lined with cells packed with men and women, and sometimes with children. Hadon had heard that the rock beneath the citadel was as tunneled as an ant's nest, that its network of corridors and shafts was equaled only by that beneath the city of Opar. But whereas Opar's had been dug to remove gold, the citadel's was intended for the deposit of criminals. It was also a place of refuge for the tenants of the citadel if invaders should ever take the surface buildings.

They went along a hall carved from granite, past cells, most of which were empty, and halted before the last door at the end. A turnkey unlocked it while the thirty guards held their spears ready. That their escorts were so many indicated that the prisoners must be thought dangerous indeed. But when he saw a giant figure in the darkness at the rear of the room, he knew what generated the fear.

"Welcome, cousin!" a familiar voice boomed. "Come in and enjoy Kwasin's hospitality!"

18

The guards withdrew, and the only light was that which traveled weakly from torches at the far end of the hall.

Kwasin said, "You will be able to see better soon, though not much better. Forgive me if I do not as yet approach you, cousin. I am chained to the walls, chained with iron, not bronze. The first time I was put in a cell, in one on the floor above, I broke the bronze chains and killed four men before they beat me unconscious. I awoke here, locked in iron."

"When did they catch you?" Hadon said.

"They didn't. I got across the river after killing the ten men who ran after me, and I hid in the hills. But I was hungry, so I stole a calf from a peasant's yard. As ill luck would have it, the peasant's daughter attracted my attention. I carried both her and the calf off into the woods, and I satisfied myself with both of them. But the bitch took advantage of me when my back was turned and raised a great bump on my head with my own ax! When I awoke, I was bound, and soldiers were cursing and puffing as they carried me off down the hills. That may be the Ax of Victory, Paga, but it carries bad luck with it."

"Perhaps it does," Paga said. "But in this case, it was stupidity and lust, not an ax, that got you captured."

"Do not think that because I am chained I cannot get at you, manling. I have loosened the bolts from the walls, and I can walk to the door whenever I choose. Are the guards all gone?"

Hadon said, "As far as I can see."

There was a screech of metal pulling loose from stone. His chains clanking, Kwasin began walking about.

Hadon explored the chamber, his eyesight having become adjusted to the dim light, as Kwasin had said it would. It was cut out of granite to form a room thirty feet wide, sixty feet long, and about fifteen feet high. A faint breeze came from a hole in the ceiling.

"The air shaft is large enough to accommodate you, Hadon," Kwasin said. "But getting to it is another matter. Besides, I was told that about ten feet into it is a bronze grille that would stop you if you did get that far."

"We will see about that," Hadon said. He found a dozen old blankets smelling of mildew, a great vase of water, six clay cups, and six chamberpots. And that was all. Kwasin, questioned by Hadon, said that he had been fed only twice a day. During that time, the chamberpots were replaced with empty, though not always clean, pots, and the water supply was replenished.

"They will come with the second meal in a few hours or so," Kwasin said. "I'm not sure of the time, since I've lost all sense of it."

"We might as well see now if we can get one of us into the shaft," Hadon said. "If you will be the base, Kwasin, I will stand on your shoulders as the second story of the human tower. Then Kebiwabes, who is the next tallest, can climb up us."

"But even if I could do that," the bard said, "how do I get up into it? And what about the grille?"

"I will lift you up, throw you if I can, so you can brace against the walls of the shaft," Hadon said. "I want you to find out just what is above. Perhaps the guards were lying when they told Kwasin that there was a grille there."

"But I might fall!"

"Then you will die a day or two sooner. And be thankful, since you will escape the torture."

"I am a bard. My person is sacred."

"Is that why you are in jail?"

Kebiwabes groaned and said, "Very well. But I fear that the songs of a great artist will die before birth in this dismal cell."

"That is up to dread Sisisken," Hadon said. "She is mistress of the underworld, and surely she is unhappy with Minruth and the worshipers of Resu."

Kwasin braced himself below the hole. Hadon backed to the door and then ran forward. Using as a springboard the back of Paga, who was on all fours, he leaped up onto the shoulders of the giant. Kwasin clamped his hands around Hadon's ankles. Hadon wavered for a moment, then recovered his balance.

"Not so tight, Kwasin," he said. "You are cutting off the blood."

Paga and Hinokly lifted Kebiwabes as high as they could. He took hold of Hadon's waist and began to climb up Hadon's body. Twice Hadon almost fell with him, but he managed to keep his balance until Kabiwabes's legs were around his back. There the bard stuck, unable to go any higher.

"You will fall, Hadon, and I with you."

Kwasin rumbled, "Get on up, bard, or I'll smash your head against the wall."

Kebiwabes groaned and inched on up. With a convulsive effort, he pulled himself up, his legs dangling. Hadon toppled forward, and the two, Kebiwabes yelling, fell heavily on the stone floor.

Hadon got up and said angrily, "I told you to make no sudden moves! Are you hurt?"

"I thought my arm was broken. However, it is only skinned. But badly, badly."

Kwasin growled and seized Paga by the waist and hurled him straight up the shaft. Paga yelled, but he did not fall back. Hadon, looking upward, could barely distinguish him. The manling's back was against one wall and his feet against the other.

"Being small has its uses," Kwasin said. "Though perhaps I could throw even you, Hadon, as far." He guffawed and said, "Of course, if I missed, your head would break open."

Hadon said, "Paga, can you make it?"

"With much loss of skin," Paga said. "This rock is hard."

They waited for what seemed to be an interminable time. Then they heard Paga, apparently swearing in the language of his tribe.

Presently he was back at the mouth of the shaft. Kwasin gave the word, and Paga fell into the giant's arms.

"Ho, hairy baby, you are as bloody as if you had just been born! Did you indeed come from a stony womb?"

"No stonier than that of the woman who gave me birth," Paga said. "Let me down gently, elephant."

"Perhaps you would like to suckle?" Kwasin said, laughing as he forced the manling's head to his nipple. Paga bit, Kwasin yelled with agony, and Paga fell.

"Do you want to bring the guards?" Hadon said fiercely. "Are you hurt, Paga?"

"Not as much as the elephant," Paga said.

"If we did not need you, I would brain you against the wall!" Kwasin bellowed.

"The fault is yours, giant," Paga said. "You owe me an apology."

"I apologize to no one!"

"Quiet, for the sake of our lives," Hadon said. "Paga, what did you find?"

"The guards did not lie. There is a bronze grille about ten feet up the shaft. It is composed of four bars, melted into each other at the junctions. The bars are about half an inch thick. Their ends are in holes dug into the stone. I could bend the bars but could not get them loose from the holes."

"You are too huge to climb the shaft, Kwasin," Hadon said. "Even if we could get you within it. Do you think you could get me inside it?"

"Your legs are too long," Paga said. "You would be folded like a babe in its womb."

"My mother said I was a difficult birth," Hadon said. "Nevertheless, I got out. Kwasin, you must throw me hard enough so that almost my entire body will enter the shaft. Stand below to catch me if I fall."

"Of course I can do it!"

"I hope so," Hadon said. "If it were anyone but you, I would not even let you try it."

He told the giant how he wanted it done. Kwasin crouched, placed his hands palms-up under Hadon, who faced him. He lifted Hadon, who balanced himself, until his hands were even with his knees. Then Kwasin crouched a little, and said, "Here goes, cousin!" and straightened upward with a grunt. Hadon shot out at a slight angle from the perpendicular, drawing up his feet as he did so. He felt as if he had been propelled from a catapult. His shoulder rubbed along the wall, he fell back, but his legs, now against his chest, straightened out a little. And he was lodged in the shaft with his buttocks hanging out of the shaft.

"See, I told you!' Kwasin shouted.

"Quiet, monster, or our work will be undone," Paga said.

The ascent was painful and slow. It was necessary to brace his back against the wall and to shove himself upward a few inches with his legs. The skin quickly wore away from his back. Moreover, the walls were slippery in several places from Paga's blood. He gritted his teeth, and sweating and panting, got to the grille. It was as Paga had described it. He bent his head to look down the shaft and saw Kwasin, a lighter darkness in the darkness of the cell.

"I'm going to hang from the middle of the grille," he called down. "Perhaps I can weaken it by my weight alone. Then I will brace myself again and try to pull one end loose."

"If you fail, I will catch you," Kwasin said.

Hadon gripped the grille in the middle and let his legs go. The bars bent; suddenly they tore loose with a screech. Hadon yelled briefly but clamped his teeth. He had, however, drawn his legs up, and he shoved them out again. A few feet above the mouth of the shaft, he slid to a stop. His back felt as if it were covered with a thousand army ants.

He told Kwasin to get out of the way and worked the grille, which he held perpendicularly, past his body. He let it fall with a clang, and a moment later he dropped into Kwasin's arms.

"No nonsense," Hadon said. "Let me down."

"I have delivered twins," Kwasin said, obeying. "One, very short-legged and hairy; the other, very long-legged and bearing a gift of bronze. Both are ugly indeed."

"Hide the grille under the blankets," Hadon said.

"No, wait a moment," Kwasin said. He picked up the grille and began to bend it. After a few minutes he had a rod, which he swished above his head.

"Here is a weapon for you, Hadon, though a poor one. I will use the bolts at the end of my chains as a scythe."

"We need to know what is at the other end of the shaft," Hadon said. "Paga will go up again, since he is the shortest. But we will wait until after the meal. It wouldn't do for them to find one of their prisoners missing."

He had Hinokly wash his back with water from the vase. When the guards were heard coming, he and Paga sat with their backs against the wall. Kwasin reinserted the bolts in the holes and leaned against them. He complained to the guards about the small portions served. Their officer chuckled and said, "Weak prisoners make good prisoners."

Hadon noted that this time there were only ten spearmen. That "only" was a big "only," however.

Though there was not enough food to satisfy Kwasin, the others had plenty. Its quality was poor, consisting of cold okra soup, stale millet bread, and chunks of tough beef. But they ate with gusto, and Hinokly gave Kwasin a piece of his meat.

"We must keep you strong," he said.

"I wish the others were as thoughtful as you," Kwasin growled. "My belly is bounding toward my backbone like a leopard after an antelope."

"We'll wait an hour for the food to digest," Hadon said. "Then Paga goes up, if he's willing."

"I am not so sure my back can stand it."

"I'll go up this time," Hinokly said. "Though I am a skinny old man of thirty-six, I am wiry. But let's see if we can make a poncho from a blanket. That should help keep the skin from scraping off."

Using the end of one of the bronze bars of the grille, Hinokly tore out a hole from the blanket and slipped it over his head.

"The latest fashion in escapee wear," he said.

Once again Kwasin tossed a man through the hole. They sat down to wait, or paced back and forth in the gloom. Several times Hadon looked up the hole, but could see only a very faint light issuing from someplace far up. He lay down on a blanket after a while but could not sleep. Just as he was about to rise, he heard Hinokly's voice issuing hollowly from the shaft.

"I'm back. Catch me, Kwasin."

Hadon jumped up, and when Hinokly had been set on his feet by Kwasin, he said, "What did you find?"

"About another ten feet above the place where the grille was are two shafts that run horizontally. One is at right angles to the other. Both are big enough even for Kwasin to walk upright in. I went down the one to my right and came to another vertical shaft. This, I believe, admits air to the corridor outside our cell. There is a grille in it, but it is only a few inches below the lip of the shaft. You could probably tear it out, Hadon. I jumped over it and continued. I came to another shaft which ran at right angles to the one I was in. I went down it a little distance and passed over another shaft. This, I believe, leads to the cell across from ours. I continued down it and went past the place where the wall in the corridor below seems to end. I came across another vertical shaft and looked down into another cell. It was lit more brightly than ours, so I concluded it was near torches. I watched and listened for a while, but if the cell was occupied, the men in it were silent.

"Apparently that cell is in a corridor which does not connect to that outside our cell. I went on, feeling in the dark, because I could not see these shafts, of course, unless there was a source of light below. Then I came to the end. There was, however, another vertical shaft there. I listened and heard, from far below, the gurgling of water.

"I suppose that that shaft leads to the underground water supply. You know, don't you, that there is an underground water tunnel connecting the citadel to both gulfs? If the citadel were besieged, its defenders would not run out of water. Of course, the tunnel is probably guarded, especially now that Minruth fears attack from the worshipers of Kho. The tunnel is supposed to be a little-known secret, but anyone who has delved into the Great Temple archives, as I have, knows of it."

"Was there a ladder in the water shaft?" Hadon said.

"I felt for one, but if there is one, it starts below the reach of my hand. I then went back, retracing my route to where I had turned into this horizontal shaft. I was afraid of getting lost, and carefully memorized my right and left turns. I proceeded down the shaft, that is, I stayed in the same shaft that ended in the water shaft. Twice my foot came to the lips of vertical shafts, and I jumped over these. The light from below got stronger with each one, so I knew I was getting close to the end of the corridor which runs outside our cell. Moreover, two of the cells were occupied, and I noticed when we passed through our corridor that the two cells closest to the bottom of the staircase contained prisoners.

"But the shaft I was in must lead past the staircase. It ran straight for approximately half a mile. And there were a dozen horizontal shafts at right angles to it, each intersecting with a vertical shaft. Then I came to its end. I looked up the vertical shaft there and saw stars. But how could I get up it? It was possible to go down it, since I could lean out against the opposite wall, and then, bracing myself, work down it. But to go upward was impossible. I had no way of getting to a point where I could brace myself.

"I felt upward on the chance there was a ladder. I almost cried out! Above, on the wall nearest me, was a bronze bar! I gripped it with my hand turned inward, swung out, turned, gripped it with my other hand, and reached up and found another bar. I felt uneasy, of course, because I didn't know how long the bars had been set into the stone. They might be corroded, since the shafts are at least a thousand years old. However, it seemed reasonable that they would be replaced from time to time. This shaft must be one of the escape routes arranged for the royal family, in which case the ladder would be inspected from time to time."

"You are intolerably long-winded!" Kwasin said.

"He has to tell it step by step," Hadon said. "We all must know the route by heart before we go blundering around in the dark."

"And how am I to get up this shaft?" Kwasin said. "Do you plan to leave me here?"

"If we do, we'll come back with a rope," Hadon said. "I promise that if it is at all possible, we will get you out."

"On your honor as an Ant man and as my cousin?"

"Yes. Continue, Hinokly."

"I went up and up until I was sure that I was above the underground shafts. Moreover, the solid granite had become marble blocks. There was no mortar between them, but I could feel the divisions with my fingertips. I kept going on. Oh, yes, I heard water far below when I first came to the shaft, and the breeze was stronger and more humid. And at last I came to the opening and stuck my head out. The moon was out by then, so I could see, though not as well as I would have if it were not for the smoke from Khowot.

"I was on the roof and looking eastward. I hung out of the opening as far as I could and determined that the entrance was actually the mouth of one of the many carved heads that adorn the roof."

"But the palace is domed," Hadon said. "Isn't the dome too steep to allow climbing on it?"

"I would say so. What you mean is that if there are entrances to the shaft, they must be from the apartments of the royal family itself. So when I went back down the ladder, I felt on both sides of the ladder. And I found at one place hairline divisions outlining an oblong section in the wall—door-shaped, that is. Moreover, the ladder ceases to be continuous at the upper and lower parts of the hairlines. Obviously the rungs are attached to a panel of stone which slides or falls inward to give entrance. But I dared not thump it to test it for hollowness. Now, it seemed reasonable to me that there should be something in the shaft which would permit one in it to activate a mechanism that would cause the section to open. I could find none. So the section can be moved only from the other side. It is a one-way escape route."

"If we had a torch, we could examine it closely," Hadon said. "There may be something that you could not see in the dark."

"We now have torches," Hinokly said. "I'll tell you why in just a minute. I got to the bottom of the ladder, and I swung on the lowest rung back and forth and got my feet onto the lip of the shaft. When I was back in it, I felt downward. My arm could not reach a rung below, but I lowered myself over the edge, and sure enough, my feet touched a rung. So I went downward, down, down, at least two hundred feet, I estimate. When I came to the last rung, I lowered myself with my feet hanging. My toes touched wet stone, and then I was on a stone floor. I groped around. The shaft led downward for about twenty feet at a forty-five-degree angle to the horizontal. And then I was on what seemed a level stone floor that was very near a running stream. I went forward cautiously, but quickly stopped. My outstretched hand had encountered wood. I felt the object and determined it to be a boat. It was long and slim, and the walls were thin. It seemed built for speed. Inside it were seven paddles. But it was like no boat I have ever heard of. A wooden runner curved above it from prow to stern.

"I went past it for about ten feet and came to the water itself. Then I went back and searched on both sides of the boat. And I found seven other boats. Nearby, against the wall, were several large barrels. The tops had bronze handles, so I pulled the tops off and felt within. One contained torches, tinder, flint, and irons. One contained dried meat and hard bread. Another held infantrymen's swords. And the fourth held a long coil of rope."

"Did you bring any of the food back?" Kwasin said.

"Forget your belly," Hadon said. "Where are the torches?"

"I made three trips," Hinokly said. "There's food, a torch and igniting materials, and two swords on the floor of the shaft just above us. And the rope. That was very heavy, but I tied one end around my waist and pulled it along behind me."

"Even in sealed barrels the supplies would get wet in a short time," Hadon said. "They must be replenished from time to time. What is their condition?"

"Good," Hinokly said. "They must have been stocked recently."

"Well done indeed, Hinokly," Hadon said. "Now, there are two things we can do. We can go back up the shaft now, haul this hippopotamus up with the rope, and go to the boats. I would guess that if we went up the water tunnel to the right, we'd go northward and come out on the Gulf of Gahete. That will bring us close to the volcano, and we can escape up along the Road of Kho, around the volcano, and get to the wild lands back of it.

"The second thing is to wait until after breakfast. We'll be more rested then, and the guards won't check on us until about midafternoon when the second meal is brought in. Also, there should be more visibility in the day; the light from the shafts will be brighter. But for all we know, we may be taken out in the morning. So I say that we should leave now."

Hinokly groaned and said, "I am so tired, I don't think I can get back up the shaft. My muscles are quivering, and my back is raw. The blanket quickly wore out."

"Paga can go first and let the rope down. He can hold it while Kebiwabes and I go up. Then we'll haul you and Kwasin up. Provided that he isn't too big to squeeze through."

"Paga, throw down some food first," Kwasin said. "I'm starving."

"Food will add to your weight, elephant, and it might make you too swollen to pass through. Your paunch blows up like a cobra's hood when you eat."

"Get ready, you two," Hadon said. "Every minute will count. And—"

"Kho, what is that?" Kwasin bellowed.

Hadon heard a rumbling, and he felt slightly nauseated. For a few seconds he did not understand what was happening. He seemed to be standing on a bowl of jelly or a raft that was being tossed up and down.

Then he cried, "Earthquake!"

19

It lasted for only eight seconds, though it seemed much longer. They rose from the floor, feeling in the soles of their bare feet dying vibrations deep beneath them. Down the corridor cries for help came from the prisoners, and the panicky voices of guards echoed.

"Quick! Put the bolts back into the wall!" Hadon said to Kwasin.

Kwasin obeyed, none too soon. Running footsteps and a torchlight approached. Two guards stopped before the bars, looked within, and raced away. Kwasin pulled the bolts out, and Hadon told him to throw Paga up the shaft.

They waited impatiently until Paga called down for them to stand clear. The end of a thick rope made of cords of papyrus dropped onto the floor. Hadon tied it around his waist and was tossed upward. He caught like an olive pit in the throat of the shaft. Paga took up the slack and kept it tight while Hadon inched upward. On reaching the horizontal shaft, he felt around until he located a torch, a flint, a box of tinder, and irons. The torch was pine impregnated with fish fat. He struck sparks from the iron with the flint, and presently the tinder was flaming. He dropped some of it on the head of the torch, which soon was flaming and smoking. Paga untied the rope from Hadon's waist and let it down again. Hadon placed the torch on the floor and helped Paga draw up Hinokly and Kebiwabes.

Kwasin tied the end of the rope under his arms. All four above took hold of the rope, with Hadon and Paga at the edge of the shaft and the scribe and the bard pulling behind them. The giant's three hundred and ten pounds of flesh and thirty pounds of bronze gyves and chains came up slowly. Hadon called down to him to brace himself against the walls and thus ease the weight.

Kwasin said, "That is impossible! The skin on my shoulders is being pulled off; I'm being flayed alive! I can't brace myself!"

"Either the rope will break or our arms will come out of their sockets," Paga said.

"Pull!" Hadon said. "And whatever happens, don't let loose. If another—"

This time there was a crack as of a hippo-hide whip. Then a rumbling, louder than the first, and a shaking, more intense than the first. Kwasin's terror yowled up the shaft. Hadon shouted to the others not to let loose, and they held. In about twelve seconds the stone was quiet, except for a distant rumbling. Hadon ordered the resumption of the hauling. Kwasin, moaning with fright and with the pain of seared skin, moved slowly upward, like a bird being swallowed by a snake.

Hadon and Paga had to take frequent rests, and when they finally unplugged the shaft, they were exhausted.

"You could have been more gentle," Kwasin growled, inspecting the bloody skin on his shoulders.

"We could have left you stuck there, too," Paga said. "I don't think I can lift my arms."

They ate, though Hadon was impatient to get going. He kept looking down the shaft, dreading the appearance of a light. If the guards checked on them again, they would raise an alarm. On the other hand, they might be so panic-stricken that they could not be bothered to search for them. Especially, he thought, since no one would want to enter the shafts at a time when they might cave in.

"Mighty Resu is struggling with the Mother of All," Kebiwabes said. "We are ants under the feet of battling elephants. Let us hope that they do not destroy us during their struggle."

"We are fortunate," Hadon said. "The king's men will be too disorganized to worry about us."

"You call it fortunate to be buried alive?" Kwasin said.

"Quiet!" Hadon said. "I hear voices!"

He looked below and saw lights. A man shouted. The bronze door swung creaking inward, and then a guard was looking up the well. Hadon withdrew his head.

"Rested or not, we must go," he said. "They will have to go after ladders, but that might not take them long. Also, they may have other entrances we don't know about."

Hinokly, holding the torch, led the way. Hadon and Kebiwabes carried the swords; Paga, one end of the rope; Kwasin, the food, which he continued eating. When they were over the shaft leading down to the corridor, Hadon saw a number of guards run past it.

"Their commander is a cool one," he said. "He's sticking to his duty even if the city falls in on him."

He quit talking. The walls and floor were shaking again. But the shock was much less than the first two. After it ceased, they continued to the shaft up which the scribe had climbed. Here Hadon said, "You may go down if you wish and take a boat out at once. But I am going up."

"Why?" Kwasin said.

"He means to look for Lalila," Paga said. "I will go with you, Hadon."

"I will be looking for Awineth, too," Hadon said. "I am duty-bound to do so."

"But not love-bound?" Paga said.

"You are crazy!" Kwasin said. "You would venture into the beehive when there is plenty of honey outside? The world is full of beautiful women, cousin!"

"I don't expect you to understand," Hadon said. "There is nothing to keep you from leaving me."

Kwasin snorted and said, "Nothing except that people, if they heard about it, would say that I was a coward! Lead on, Hadon!"

Hadon tied the end of the rope around the bottom rung. When they came back they could slide down past the mouth of the horizontal shaft to the top rung of the lower ladder. He swung out and pulled himself up rung by rung until his feet were on the lowest rung. Then he climbed swiftly up. The odor of smoke came to him. Looking up, he saw that the stars were no longer visible. Behind him came Paga, and behind Paga came Hinokly, the end of the torch clamped between his teeth. Kwasin came last, with one end of the rope tied to his neck. Halfway up, Kwasin would coil the rope around a rung so that the guards would not see it dangling down the shaft if they came this way. On the way back, they would untie the rope at this end and drop it. Though Kwasin's wrists were connected with a heavy chain, its length enabled him to reach up for one rung while clinging to a lower one. The chains from the iron collar around his neck dragged below him, the bolts now and then catching on the rungs and causing him to swear.

When Hadon saw the oblong of hairlines in the rock, he had Hinokly pass up the torch to him. Hinokly was glad to get rid of it; he muttered that his jaw had been about to break. Hadon examined the face of the section for controls but could find none. He pulled out on the bars and pushed in on them. Nothing happened. They did not seem to be connected to a mechanism within. That, he told himself, was to be expected. The royal family would not wish to arrange it so that an enemy could figure out a way to get in.

Perhaps the wall was thin at this point. Should he thump on it with the hope of attracting someone inside? If it were Minruth's apartment, he would have them at his mercy. Guards might be stationed by the exit to ensure that no one left or entered without royal permission. In fact, Minruth would be sure to have guards here if this were Awineth's apartment, since she would know about it.

Far below, a bellow welled up. The walls quivered, and Hadon hung on with one hand, clutching the torch with the other. When the temblor ceased, he pulled at the bars to determine if they had been loosened, and he found them still firm.

Hadon told the others his conclusions. Paga said, "It is useless to stay here. The guards will soon be at the mouth of this shaft."

Hadon hesitated. Should he knock at the door?

Someone shouted from far below. Hadon looked down and saw torchlight and a soldier leaning out of the mouth of the vertical shaft to look upward.

There was still the exit from the head of the statue on the roof. They could climb down the steep dome with the aid of their rope. Perhaps they could go down that to another carved head, which might be the entrance to another shaft.

Hadon made up his mind. He passed the torch down to Paga, drew out the short leaf-shaped sword from his belt, and thumped its hilt end against the stone. It rang hollowly. He had not been mistaken in thinking that the section was a thin shield leading to rooms beyond.

But what if there wasn't anyone there?

He banged the hilt heavily, again and again.

Kwasin roared, "They're coming up! And I can't reach down! They'll cut my feet off!"

Hadon looked down. Two torches were being held out from the horizontal shaft to light up the lower rungs. Three guards were climbing up, with a fourth hanging on the lower rung. The soldiers wore bronze cuirasses and helmets and carried swords in scabbards. And they were coming swiftly.

Even if Kwasin could hold them off for a while, and that did not seem likely, they could soon be attacked from the secret exit. An intelligent officer would find out where the party was located in respect to the shaft and could send men to go through the exit. That is, he would if he knew about the exit. Perhaps he did not. Minruth and Awineth would not wish many to share their knowledge.

Hadon repeated the heavy thumping. Whether enemies or friends were within, someone should come. If an enemy, he might be taken. At least Hadon would have someone to fight. He wouldn't be clinging helplessly to a rung, waiting to be cut down and to fall to the hard stone far below.

"Pass the torch down to Kwasin," Hadon said to Paga. "He can drop it on the first soldier."

Paga did as ordered, and Hadon beat on the stone again. But the section did not move. There was still time to go up to the end of the shaft. He could fight a rear-guard action while the others slid down on the rope over the dome. But was there anyplace they could go to when they reached the end of the rope?

Hinokly said that there was a stone head about fifty feet below the one from which he had looked. The rope should be just long enough to reach it. They would have to leave the rope and climb over the top of the head and let themselves in from above. That is, they would if the head contained an entrance to a shaft.

"Let's go," Hadon said, and then he fell inward with a crash.

20

He was lucky. If a man with a weapon had been standing on the other side, he could have killed him while he sprawled astonished, half on the section, half on the floor. He was up quickly, however, and shouting, "Awineth!" She came to his arms, clinging to him and kissing him passionately while she wept.

Hadon pushed her away and said, "No time for that. What is the situation?"

She looked past him at Paga scrambling down the section. "There are others?" she said. "How did you get out?"

"No time for stories," he said. He was in a small room lit by a bronze lamp. The walls were unpainted, and a rack held swords and spears and axes. The door was open, showing him a much larger room with bright murals of pastoral scenes and a life-size, life-colored marble statue of Adeneth, the goddess of passion, in a corner. At the foot of a great bed a corpse sprawled. His armor showed that he was an officer.

"He was stationed in this room," she said. "There are two guards stationed outside the door of the room beyond my bedroom. He heard the noise you were making. After he had listened a moment, he unlocked the door, came out, locked the door, and started across the room. Meanwhile, I had taken a dagger from my jewel box. I called to him, and when he turned, I stabbed him in the throat. Then I opened the section, though I did not know whom to expect. But I prayed that Kho would intervene, that by some miracle it would be you."

"Where is Lalila?" Hadon said.

"Why do you care?" she said.

"It is my duty to keep her from harm," he said, hoping she would not ask why. "Quickly! Where is she?"

"In an apartment down at the end of the hall," she said. She looked at him strangely and said, "But my father spent the night with her."

"That is to be expected," Hadon said, though he felt sick. "I don't suppose he would still be with her?"

"With Khowot shaking the earth?"

Hadon moved into the great bedroom to make room for the others. Puffing and cursing, Kwasin climbed out, looked around him, saw the axes, and roared, "Paga, you are strong, though a manling! Cut my chains off with an ax!"

Hadon asked Awineth how the section was closed. She pointed to a large closet just off the little room. He entered and pulled down on a huge lever. The section, attached to chains at its end, rose quickly, presumably pulled by counterweights beyond the wall. There was a cry from the frustrated soldiers below, and then silence.

Kwasin lay face-down on the marble mosaic floor and stretched out his arms.

Paga said, "First your head and then the chain, Kwasin," but he brought down the edge of a warax on the chain that connected the wrists. It took five strokes before the link parted. Paga then chopped off the chains connected to the bolts.

Kwasin heaved up, bellowing, "At last I am free!" and seized the largest ax and sword from the rack. With an ax in his right hand and the *numatenu* sword in his left, he roared, "Now we will cut our way out of the palace!"

"Let's hope we don't have to," Hadon said. "And keep quiet! There are guards a few doors away!"

At that moment the palace cracked and shook again. Through the shafts which led to air vents on the dome, a roar came. It was followed by a number of thuds, as if heavy objects had struck the roof.

When the temblor ceased and the noise had stopped, Hadon said, "Where are Minruth's apartments?"

"Would you slay him?" Awineth said.

"If it is possible."

"Let me do it," she said. "Kho will forgive me for killing my own father."

"Where are his apartments?"

"They are on this floor in the northeast corner on the other side of the building. But he has ten men, all famed *numatenu*, stationed at all times at his door. Besides, he will be on the ground floor or out in the streets trying to calm his people."

"How many guard Lalila and the child?"

"Three, the last I saw."

"Do you know where my ax is?" Kwasin said.

"The ax and Hadon's sword are kept in my father's apartment."

"Such luck!" Kwasin bellowed.

"Ten men guard them," Hadon said. He went into the entrance room and took a *numatenu* sword. It wasn't Karken, the Tree of Death, but it would do.

Hadon told the others what to do. Awineth put the dagger in her belt and chose an infantryman's sword. Hadon said "You hang back, but if you see anybody in trouble, you may help him."

"I am not a man," she said, "but I have trained with the sword since I was a small child. Bhukla has had many sacrifices from me."

Hadon went into the next room, the others behind him. This was twice as large as the bedroom, being a hundred feet long and forty wide. In its center was a sunken marble bath ringed by statues of the beasts and heroes of the nine-year Great Cycle. Its gold-plated and jeweled door was at the far end, which was a good thing, since it had kept the guards from hearing the noise within. They passed through this, opened the door, and went into another large room. On the left as they stepped into it was the door which gave entrance to the corridor.

Hadon said, "Call to them, Awineth."

Awineth rapped on the door with a heavy golden knocker. A voice came through the thick oak bronze-bound door. "What is it, O Queen?"

"Your officer has had a fit, one probably brought on by the fear of the quake. The Divine One has seized him."

There was a moment of silence, then the soldier said, "Your pardon, O Queen. But we have orders from Minruth himself that no one is to open this door but Major Kethsuh."

"How can he do that when he is jerking and foaming at the mouth?" she said. "But I do not care, even if no one now guards me."

"Do they know of the shaft exit?" Hadon said.

"No."

"Then they won't be worried that you will escape."

The guard outside said, "One of us will summon an officer, O Queen, and he may decide what to do."

Hadon whispered to Awineth. She said, "Just a moment. I think that the major is reviving. I will see if he is capable of staying on duty."

"As you wish, O Queen."

Hadon was relieved. He did not want any more soldiers brought to this end of the palace.

"We won't be able to get any of them in here," he said. "So we'll go out after them."

He unbarred the door, waited a minute to assure himself that the others were in position, and then shoved the door outward. It struck one of the guards; the other was standing back a few paces, facing Hadon. He brought his spear up, but Hadon's sword sheared it and on the return stroke cut half through the man's neck. Paga fell on the soldier on the floor and stabbed him in the eye. Kwasin leaped over the two and charged down the long hall, the bard and the scribe behind him.

There were two soldiers before the door at the end of the hall. One ran, doubtless to get help; the other stood his ground. Kwasin bellowed and hurled the ax, and it rotated, its butt striking the fleeing soldier and knocking him down. Kwasin swerved after the fallen man, leaving Kebiwabes and Hinokly to deal with the lone sentinel. This man began shouting an alarm. The felled man got to his feet and picked up his spear, but Kwasin smashed it aside and split his bronze helmet and his skull. Hadon ran to help the scribe and the bard. Before he arrived, the scribe had cut through the spear and Kebiwabes had chopped down on the man's arm. The soldier staggered back against the door, then slumped down as Kebiwabes cut through his neck.

Hadon burst through the door, causing Lalila, sitting on a chair, to scream. Abeth came running through the door beyond, then halted to stare white-faced at Hadon. A moment later, both were weeping, laughing, and hugging him. Hadon freed himself, looked at her bruised face, and said, "No time for that. Come with me."

He halted. Awineth stood in the door, her large dark-gray eyes bright. "So this is the way it is?" she said.

"She has never said she loved me," Hadon replied.

Kwasin entered, saying, "Let us go after our weapons, Hadon."

"We have five men against ten," Hadon said. "All ten are professional swordsmen, and three of us are unskilled with the sword. The odds are too high against us. Besides, the men in the shaft will have told Minruth what has happened, and he will know at once where we are. We must get away before he sends more men up here."

Kwasin said nothing. He stuck his sword and the handle of his ax in his belt and lifted a long and massive oak table. Holding it vertically before him as if it were a shield, he walked through the door.

Hadon cursed and said, "My duty is to see that the women are gotten out of here. Yet I feel—"

"That you are deserting him?" Paga said. "No such thing. He is deserting us for his own mad reasons. You have no reason to feel that you are a coward, Hadon."

"I know," Hadon said. "But if we were at his side, perhaps..."

He stopped and then said, "Back to the room!"

"I wish that I could witness that battle," Kebiwabes said. "The last battle of the hero Kwasin! What a scene for my epic!"

"You would have to be alive to sing it," Paga said, "and you won't be if you stay here."

Hadon did not think that Kebiwabes would ever sing of anybody, but he thought it wise not to say so.

He led them back to Awineth's apartments, where they barred the doors behind them as they proceeded to the entrance room. Here he stationed the others behind him while Awineth pulled on the lever. The section could be released slowly or quickly. Awineth disengaged it so that it fell suddenly, and with a crash it hit the floor. A soldier who had been clinging to the rungs on the outside also fell in. Hadon cut his arm off and leaped up the slope of the wall to the entrance. The head of another man appeared. Hadon smote through the helmet and skull. The man fell straight down, dislodging two below him. They fell screaming past the torchlight below and into the darkness.

Cautiously Hadon stuck his head out. But there was no one above him.

Ten men were still on the rungs below. He carried the bloody body of the man he had first struck down and eased it over the side. It struck the top man, and three hurtled together down the shaft. The others began to climb down. Hadon went into the bedroom, seized a heavy chair, brought it back, and dropped it. Three men were knocked off. That left two desperately climbing back down. Paga and Kebiwabes brought in another chair and a heavy marble bust. Hadon dropped the bust, after which the chair was not needed.

"There are still men in the horizontal shaft," Hadon said. "How many I don't know. I will soon find out."

Hinokly entered the room, saying, "The king's men are beating on the door."

"If we pile heavy tables and some of those statues against the door, we can delay them," Hadon said. "And it would help if we could fire the room. Awineth, have you any flammable materials?"

Awineth did not answer for a moment, because the palace shook and rumbled. More objects struck the dome far above them. When the palace had quit shaking, Awineth said, "There is a charcoal fire always burning before the image of Great Kho in the chapel beyond the reception room. You can set the draperies on fire with that. And perhaps the furniture will catch fire."

Hadon went into the reception room, which was noisy with the crashings of a heavy object against the door. Then there was a pause, and he heard Kwasin's bellow.

"Let me in, you fools! It is I, Kwasin!"

Hadon hurried to draw the massive bar. Kwasin entered, looking disheveled and sweaty, but his expression was triumphant. He carried the Ax of Wi and Karken.

"Here, stripling!" he shouted. "Here is your sword, which you were too timid to go after!"

Hadon shot the bar and said, unbelievingly, "Ten *numatenu* slain, and in so short a time!"

Kwasin put his ax down and began to pile chairs, tables, and statues before the door. "Ten *numatenu*? Ten ghosts! They were all gone! Evidently Minruth had called them to his side. So I broke down the door with my table and went in for my ax. There were two swordsmen inside, making sure, I suppose, that no assassins sneaked into the apartments to surprise the king when he returned. I slew them and then hunted for my ax. I found it, and with it your sword, which I brought along for you, though I should have sent you after it. No thanks to you that we have our beloved weapons! But when I came back, I looked down the great staircase in the northeast corner, and I saw that a horde, an ant stream of men, was swarming up the steps. I ran into a room and dragged out four heavy tables and put them at the head of the stairs with a marble statue of some king or other. When they had rounded the last landing and were coming four abreast up the steps, I raised the oak table above my head and launched it at them. It crushed scores and knocked down many more.

"Then, as the survivors behind came over the table and the pile of corpses, I threw the second table at them. And when the next wave came, I crushed them with the third table. By then they had decided to retreat, but I dropped the statue on more and hastened their flight. I ran down to this room then, only to find that you had locked me out. I was breaking down the door with another table, and cursing you for your lack of foresight, when you opened the door."

"I thank you for the sword," Hadon said.

He helped the others tear down draperies and pile furniture, and he dumped the brazier of coals on several papyrus rolls. These blazed, presently the draperies were afire, and the wooden furniture began to smoke. A moment later, axes crashed against the door. They ran to the entrance room, where Hadon climbed out onto the first rung, with Kwasin behind him.

When he reached the sixth rung above the opening of the horizontal shaft, Hadon tied the end of the rope to the rung. He then untied the end attached to the bottom rung and hauled it up. Holding his sword in one hand, and the rope in the other, he launched himself down and out. The rope carried him in an arc which brought him within the opening. He released it and swooped in against five startled soldiers. His feet knocked down one torch carrier, and he fell heavily on his back. The pain of the impact on his raw back almost tore a scream from him. But he was up quickly and laying about the others before they could bring their swords into play. Two fell, and two retreated to spread out as far as the tunnel would allow them. Hadon whirled, kicked the torch carrier in the face, knocked him against the wall, and cut his head off. He whirled again, but he did not charge. In a moment Kwasin hurled in, fell forward on his face, cursing and skinning his knees, but he retained his hold on his ax. At sight of him the two soldiers fled.

Hadon and Kwasin picked up the two torches. When Paga came down the rope and was drawn in, Hadon handed him a torch. Kwasin held the other while they went after the soldiers. These had gone into the shaft leading to the shaft above the cell. The last one was just going down a ladder. Kwasin ran bellowing into it, dragged up the ladder as far as it would go, and banged it around. The soldier screamed as he fell.

Kwasin chopped off the ladder level with the floor. Hadon pulled the rest on up until its end hit the ceiling. Kwasin chopped three more lengths, after which the pieces were dropped down the shaft to discourage the soldiers from looking up it. Hadon said, referring to Paga and the others, "They must all be near the bottom of the lower ladder. Let's go."

On returning to the big shaft, they saw by the torchlight that Hinokly and Kebiwabes were still climbing down. The rest were at the foot of the ladder, looking anxiously upward. Hadon and Kwasin climbed down, the latter holding the end of the torch between his teeth. When they got to the bottom, Kwasin took the lead, and they followed him down a shaft running at an oblique angle. They came out into an immense tunnel fifty feet wide which ran straight into the darkness. They stood on an apron of stone holding, as Hinokly had described, a number of long slim boats and barrels of supplies. They broke open the barrels and put food and some extra weapons in the two boats. Seven boarded one; Kwasin took the other. The torches were inserted in sockets near the prow, and they shoved off into the dark stream and began paddling.

The stone walls were smooth for a while; then openings appeared, out of which sewage poured. They had just skirted one of the noxious cataracts when Paga said, "We are being followed."

Hadon looked back and saw four lights in the distance. He said, "Paddle faster. And be prepared for trouble ahead, too."

The shaft abruptly began to narrow, and its roof angled downward. Hadon had expected this, since there would be no other reason for the overhead runners. In a minute the wooden strips were scraping against the stone overhead, and the boat was pressed downward. They dug their paddles into the water and shoved, forcing the boats ahead, the wood grating against the stone. The water rose almost to the wales, making Hadon wonder if the boat was not overloaded.

Suddenly the tunnel enlarged, and they saw the opening about sixty feet ahead. It was lit by torches and by a light beyond them the nature of which they did not comprehend at once. As they paddled closer, they saw a fiery mass splash into the bay, and they smelled brimstone.

"Khowot explodes!" Kebiwabes said.

Hadon had anticipated guards here. There was a platform of stone about ten feet above the water level, and torches flared there. But the guards had deserted their post.

It was no wonder. As they emerged onto the choppy waters of the bay, they cried out. Another flaming object was falling from fire-lit skies, falling toward them.

21

There was no time to change course. Their fate was in the hands of Kho. The mass struck between the two boats with a roar and disappeared with a great wave and a cloud of steam. Hadon's boat reared up, up, so high and at such a steep angle that he thought surely it would fall back and turn over. But it suddenly leveled and plunged downward. A moment later they were paddling ahead again.

The volcano was spouting flame. A many-miles-broad sheet of bright red flowed down its side toward the city and the area to the northwest. Flames of sulfur filled the air, causing them to cough violently. Flames and smoke arose also from the buildings on the shore and up the hills. What Minruth had not burned, Khowot was now destroying.

Hadon gave the order to drive straight ahead. He had planned to go along the shore northeastward until they came to the entrance of the canal which ran down from the lower lake near the coliseum of the Great Games. But that was too close to the volcano. By the time they got there, the lava might be filling the upper part of the canal. It would be better to go much farther north, past that canal which ran straight to the bay from the larger upper lake. And perhaps, when they got there, they would find that they must continue their flight on the water. The buildings beyond the upper canal were burning here and there, though the whole area was not yet afire.

"At least, we can get lost in the confusion!" Hinokly called to Hadon.

Hadon hoped so. The bay was swarming with boats and ships, all heading toward Mohasi and Sigady islands. A naval galley passed them on their left, its gong master beating a tempo that indicated the depth of desperation and panic of those aboard.

Hadon glanced behind him again and saw three boats full of men paddling after them. Their bronze armor and helmets gleamed dully in the red light. An officer standing up in the prow of the lead boat was pointing at them and shouting. At least, his mouth was open and working. The rumblings and the explosions overrode everything, even the yelling and screamings of the panicky mob ashore.

"They're not going to quit their chase!" Hadon shouted back. "Faster! Faster!"

The waters were becoming increasingly choppy, no doubt agitated by the quakes. They were shipping water, and though Hadon hated to lose any paddlers, he ordered Kebiwabes to help Abeth bail with helmets.

Presently, with the chasers drawing nearer, they passed the mouth of the lower canal. People swam toward them, shouting for help. Behind them was a horde, heads bobbing in the waves, arms waving. On the shore was a mob rushing into the water. Behind them a wall of flame ravened.

Hadon directed the boat outward then, because he did not want to be slowed down while beating off the swimmers. If several managed to cling to the boat, they would pull it under. His heart ached for them, especially for the children he saw among them. But trying to save even one would cause all aboard to perish.

Ashes were filtering through the smoke now, ashes that burned and stank. Those on the boats became gray, as if they were ghosts, and the surface of the water was thick with gray. For several minutes the visibility was so limited that they could not see their pursuers. Hadon hoped that now they could elude them. But after five minutes, the ashes suddenly became less, and the first of their chasers, phantom-gray, solidified from the cloud. A moment later the second boat emerged. The third, however, seemed to be lost. Perhaps some of the swimmers had grabbed it and overturned it. In any event, the odds were now cut down.

It was a long pull under such conditions. By the time they reached the mouth of the upper canal, only Hadon and Paga had any strength left. Their boat slowed down while the pursuers continued at an unremitting, though slow pace.

The shore here was the closest point to the eastern end of Mohasi island, which accounted for the greater number of swimmers here. To try to put ashore would only bring the boats among them. Yet they could not paddle much longer.

Kwasin, who had been looking back frequently, suddenly turned his boat around and came at them. Hadon ordered his paddlers to steer away. Kwasin bellowed, "Lalila! I will stop the soldiers! When I come back alive, I claim you as my reward! I am doing this for you! You will be mine!"

Lalila tried to yell at him, but she was too tired. She said weakly, "I will never be yours."

Hadon shouted, "Kwasin! You may do what you wish, but Lalila is no cow to be bought and sold! She loathes you!"

Apparently Kwasin did not hear him. Smiling, he shouted back, "I am yours, Lalila! You will have the greatest man of the empire as your lover!"

"He is indeed mad!" Lalila said, and she groaned.

Hadon said, "He can't hold you to that, though I doubt that even he can overcome all those soldiers. He won't be back."

"Let him sacrifice himself," Paga said. "We must go on!"

They bent to their paddles, with Hadon looking behind him at every sixth stroke. When he saw Kwasin leap aboard the lead boat, he did not stop to see what would happen. Instead he dug in, and the boat continued northwest, toward the peninsula of Terisiwuketh. It terminated in two extensions which suggested the gaping jaws of a snake, hence its name of Python's Head. Hadon wanted to land near the base of the lower jaw and continue across it to the northern shore. From there they could go along the shore until they came to a part of the city that was comparatively free of fires. They would go inland and into the mountains north of Khowot.

Hadon's last sight of Kwasin was his smoke-and-ash-blurred figure swinging lustily with his ax while the boat sank under his weight and soldiers fell into the water.

Hadon's group stopped paddling while they laid about them with paddles and swords, beating back the screaming people trying to get onto their boat. Then they were free. Hadon changed his mind and ordered them to go straight north. Though the city ahead was flaming, he had decided to chance crossing the peninsula much farther to the east. His crew was too exhausted to make the base of the lower extension.

At last they inched onto the shore, Paga and Hadon the only ones able to lift their paddles. They scrambled ashore and got out of the way of a number of women, children, and men fighting for their boat. Hadon led them down a street of mean tenements, the white plaster overcoats of which were black with smoke. Once he looked behind him and saw dim figures. Were they the soldiers on the second boat?

As fast as they could go, which was only a swift walk, they proceeded down the street. When they came to intersections, they ran across to get by the heat striking at them. The fires had advanced within six blocks of their route and were coming swiftly.

They made it to the other shore of the peninsula, though they were now black, not gray, and their lungs seemed seared. They walked along the street that paralleled the shore until Hadon saw that an advance guard of the flame-storm was going to cut them off. He led them into water waist-deep, and they continued along the shore. They had to submerge now and then to coat themselves with water as insulation. The wind, built up by the roaring inferno, pushed them inward into the shore. They resisted successfully, but their pace was considerably slowed. Hadon took the child from Hinokly and told her to cling tightly to his back.

They had gone perhaps a mile when he thought it safe to venture ashore again. They staggered coughing along the street in a steady northeastward direction. Finally, when Awineth and Kebiwabes could not go another step, they halted. All except Hadon lay on the ground. He eased the child down and walked back a few blocks. Seeing no sign of the soldiers, he returned.

After a fit of coughing, he said, "We must go on. If we don't, we'll choke to death on the gases."

They struggled groaning to their feet and followed him. From time to time they waded into the water and soaked their kilts to hold over their noses. After another mile the gases became only a faint odor. The fires were advancing toward them, but at a slower rate. And then came blessed rain, though the wind howled around them and lightning flashed in the distance.

Soon they were past the walls of the Outer City and on a dirt road running by farmlands. Many of these had been burned to the ground by the soldiers of Minruth. Those citizens who would not renounce Kho or those suspected of falsely swearing renunciation had been slain, their houses and barns burned down, and their animals seized.

The houses that remained were dark and silent. Either their occupants had fled, fearing the volcano, or they were hiding trembling inside their walls, hoping that doom would pass by them. Kebiwabes suggested that they take refuge in a house and rest there. They could continue in the morning. Hadon said they would not stop until they had at least come to the bases of the mountains. When they came to a road running inland, he led them down that. At dawn they were trudging along, Hadon holding the sleeping child in his arms. After passing several farmhouses Hadon turned into a dirt road leading to a house set far back from the main road. It was a bad choice; two huge dogs rushed growling at him. He barely had enough time to place Abeth on the ground and draw his sword. One dog stopped; the other leaped at him. Hadon took off its head in midair and ran at the second dog. It ran away, but stopped when Hadon quit chasing it. A wooden shutter of the lower story of the log cabin swung out, and a dark face appeared.

Hadon said, "Call off your dog, or I'll kill it too. We don't mean you any harm. We are just refugees from the wrath of Kho who need food and rest. That is all we ask."

"Go away!" the farmer said. "Or my sons and I will kill you!"

Awineth stepped forward and said, "Would you turn your queen away!"

Hadon cursed under his breath and said softly, "You should not have done that, Awineth! Now the word will be out!"

The farmer scowled and said, "You look like a bunch of tramps to me. Do not try to fool me, woman. I may be a rube, but I am not stupid."

Hadon looked at the tall totem pole near the road. He said, "Kebiwabes, you are a member of the Green Parrot people. Appeal to this man to help one of his own totem."

The bard, filthy, naked, and shaking with fatigue and hunger, called out in a weak voice, "I ask for your hospitality in the name of our tutelary bird, farmer! And in the name of the law that requires that you give a wandering bard food and drink and a place under your roof!"

"When the deities quarrel among themselves, there is no law for mortals!" the farmer shouted. "Anyway, how do I know you are not lying?"

"I, your queen and high priestess, demand that you welcome us as guests!" Awineth said. "Do you want to call down the wrath of Kho on your heads?"

"Big talk!" the farmer said. "You are lying! Besides, even if you were queen, what are you doing here? Resu rules the land now, and you are the slave of Minruth! Perhaps, if I held you for him, he would reward me!"

"I was afraid of that," Hadon said. "Let's go on before they get the idea of holding you for money and glory."

"They would not dare touch me!" Awineth said. "I am the chief priestess! My person is sacred!"

"You're also worth a vast sum," Hadon said. "And the fact that you're a refugee shows that you have no power. To him, he'll be safe under the aegis of Resu and Minruth. Let's take one of his goats for food and go on."

"I will not be insulted!" Awineth cried.

"You can punish him when you're in a position to do so," Hadon said. "Face reality."

The door to the house swung open on its bronze hinges. The farmer and six men followed him out onto the bare earth. He was a short but powerful man of about fifty. Four youths who looked like they must be his sons ranged themselves beside him. The other two were tall thin men who were, Hadon supposed, his hired help. All were holding small round wooden shields covered with bullhide, and short heavy leaf-shaped swords.

The farmer said, "We call on you to surrender in the name of Resu and the king of kings!"

"You are seven men to four men and two women and a child," Hadon said. "But I am a *numatenu*, and I do not need these others to help me fight against only seven bumpkins."

That was a lie. Hadon had not been officially initiated into the *numatenu* class, but the name of *numatenu* must surely terrify these peasants.

There was only one way to find out. Hadon summoned a loud cry from a parched throat and strength from his weary muscles. He charged, holding the sword before him with both hands. The peasants stopped, their eyes wide, and the two servants fled toward the rear of the house. Why should they face what seemed to them a certain death for a family which had overworked and underfed them?

Whatever their original spirit, that of the father and sons was shaken by the desertion of their servants and by a man who looked as if he intended to rage among them as a leopard among sheep. They turned and fled into the house, or at least they tried to. The doorway was not wide enough for two to get through at once. They coagulated there in a shouting, clawing frenzy that would have been comical under other circumstances. Hadon could have cut off the heads of most of them if he had wished, but he was weary of bloodshed. He laughed and walked away, saying, "To the barn!"

There they took some freshly laid duck eggs and a kid on a leash and proceeded up the road. Awineth, raging, demanded that the house be burned down and the peasants slaughtered as they ran out.

"We shouldn't leave any witnesses!"

Hadon agreed with her on the latter point but did not say so. Though the farmer could tell the king's men which direction they had gone, they would be in the mountain forests by then, perhaps over the mountain.

With the frequent halts, they walked until noon. By a clear running mountain stream they slaughtered and cooked the kid and sucked out the contents of the eggs. They also stuffed themselves with berries Abeth had found on a bush nearby. All but Hadon then fell asleep.

An hour passed. Hadon fought heavy eyelids. The sun was hot, but the breeze was cool in the shade of the grove in which they were hiding. He was thinking of rousing Hinokly to replace him as the guard when he saw Lalila sit up. She yawned, looked gravely at him, and rose. She said, "Is it all right if I get a drink of water?"

"There's no one in sight," he said. "Go ahead."

She walked down the steep grass-covered hill to the brook flowing at its foot. He watched her while she drank and then washed off the dust and mud. Her long yellow hair and her shape were indeed beautiful, and she had a gentle yet strong soul to match their beauty, he thought. The bruises on her face angered him. Should he ask her about them, or did she prefer not to speak of them?

After a while she returned, her skin glowing, her large violet eyes wondrous. She sat down by him, saying, "I need much more sleep. But I don't think I can sleep. I am too troubled."

"What is it that troubles you?"

"Minruth disturbs me in my dreams."

"He will pay for that someday."

"That will not undo the horror or heal these bruises, though the marks will go away in time. But not the bruises inside."

"You cannot expect such a man to be gentle," he said. "He takes a woman as a bull takes a cow."

"He did not get much satisfaction. I did not fight, which I think he expected and perhaps hoped for. I lay as if I were dead. After he had spent his lust twice on me, he cursed me and said I was no better than a statue carved from soap. He would give me to one of his Klemqaba slaves. I said nothing, and that made him even angrier. It was then that he struck me three times on the face. I still did not cry out; I just looked at him as if he were the most vile creature on earth. Finally, swearing, he left me. I wanted to kill myself, not because of what he did but because of what he might yet do. But I could not leave Abeth motherless, and I would not kill her. Perhaps, no matter what, I might escape. Or perhaps Sahhindar might come to this land and rescue me."

"He is not here," Hadon said. "But I am."

She smiled and touched his hand. "I know. I also know that you are in love with me."

"And what about you?"

"Time will have to tell me."

"Then there is..."

He stopped and held his hand up in the air as if he would catch something. He rose, listening, scrambled up a tree, and then came quickly down.

"Soldiers! They have dogs with them! And the farmer's sons!"

They woke the others, explained the situation, and went on up the hill. This led to another even higher; beyond that were more hills, with the mountain waiting behind them. Their progress was slow and arduous. They were tired and had to push through heavy brush and thorny berry bushes. Nor could they see how close their pursuers were.

Finally, panting, bleeding from thorns, they came to the mountain itself. Before them was a very steep slope on which grass grew in patches and lone trees clung.

They toiled on up, with frequent looks behind them. After a while Hadon heard the dogs. Looking back he saw them burst out of a heavy patch of forest. After them came five men hanging onto their leashes, and thirty soldiers, the sun shining on bronze helmets and cuirasses and spear points. Behind them were the farmer's sons.

He turned back in time to see Lalila, crying out, fall back down a rocky slope, sliding in a cloud of dust as she grabbed for a hold she could not find.

He ran as swiftly as he could to her. Her face was twisted, and her hands were grasping her right ankle.

"I've sprained it!"

Hadon told the others to go on. He sheathed his sword, stooped, and hoisted her up. Carrying her in his arms, he climbed up, though his legs turned to water. When he reached a narrow rocky pass with high walls, he let her down. The others were waiting for him, their faces pale where their sweat had washed off the grime.

After he had caught his breath, he said, "You all go on ahead. I will help her walk."

He lifted her up but had not gone more than six steps when he knew that it was useless. She could travel only if carried, which meant that they could never keep ahead of their pursuers.

He let her down again and said, "There is only one thing to do."

"And what is that, Hadon?" Awineth said.

"This pass has room for no more than one person at a time. I will stand here, in the narrowest part, and hold them off as long as I can. The rest of you must get away as swiftly as you can. Hinokly, you carry the child."

Lalila cried out, which caused Abeth to run crying to her mother's arms.

Awineth said, "You will die here for Lalila?"

"For all of you," Hadon said. "I can hold them here long enough to give you a head start. Don't argue! They are getting closer every second. This must be done, and I am the only one who can do it."

"If you stay here with her," Awineth said, "you are deserting me. Your duty is to protect your queen and high priestess."

"That is exactly what I am doing," Hadon said. "They must be held up long enough for you to get far ahead of them."

"You can hold them off for a long while, perhaps," Paga said. "But some will eventually climb up the slopes outside the pass and come at you from behind."

"I know that," Hadon said.

"I order you to leave the woman, who will die in any event, and accompany me!" Awineth said.

"No," Hadon said. "She will not be left to die alone."

"You *do* love her!" Awineth cried.

"Yes."

Awineth screamed and jerked her dagger out of its sheath. She ran at Lalila, but Hadon caught her wrists and twisted, and Awineth, with a sharp cry, dropped the dagger.

"If she dies now, there is no reason for you to stay!" she shouted.

"Awineth," he said hoarsely, "if you had the sprained ankle, I would do the same for you."

"But I love you! You can't leave me for her!"

Hadon said, "Kebiwabes, take her away."

The bard picked up the dagger, put it back in its sheath, and drew her, weeping, away. Hadon took the child from Lalila's arms and gave her to Hinokly. Abeth, crying and struggling, was dragged away.

Hadon watched them until they had disappeared. Then he said, "I'll help you up to the narrow way. And we will both rest there until we can rest no more."

When he had eased her down behind a rock, he looked down the pass. Far below, the dogs bayed, and the men toiled upward.

"It will be a good fight," he said. "I can feel my strength flowing back. It is too bad, however, that Kebiwabes is not here to see this. He could fashion from it a fitting climax to his song. If he lives to sing it, that is. If he does, he will have to depend on his imagination. Which means that the fight will be even more glorious than it will be in reality."

"I hope that my child will be all right," Lalila said.

"Is she the only one you think of?"

"The main one. I am not eager to die, and I do not wish you to stay here with me, though I am grateful to you. But if you would kill me, so that those men will not be able to harm me, I would be even more grateful. Awineth is right. You should go with them. Then my child will have a protector."

"Paga will protect her, and Hinokly and Kebiwabes will help take care of her. They are all good men with good hearts."

"But you are sacrificing yourself in vain!" she said. "And you are giving up all chances of becoming the ruler of Khokarsa."

"Let's save our breath," he said. "I, at least, will need it."

He sat down by her side and picked up her hand. Presently she kissed him long and warmly, though the tears still ran.

"I think I could forget Wi," she said. "Oh, I don't mean that I'll ever *forget* him. But love is for the living."

Hadon broke into tears then. When he had wiped them away, he said, "I wish I could have heard those words while we were still in the Wild Lands. We would have had much time to love each other then. Perhaps, when we go down into the realm of Sisisken, we can love there. The priestesses say that some men and women are selected to go to a bright garden where they live happily, even if they are phantoms. Surely we will be chosen to go there. If there is such a place. Sometimes I have been guilty of doubts about what the priestesses say. Do we really have a life after death? Or do we just become dust, and that is our end except in the memories of those who won't forget us because they love us?"

"I do not know," she said.

He kissed her again and then arose.

Huge clouds of smoke still rose from Khowot. At its foot lay a blotch that was ruined Khokarsa. Nearby, a bird sang sweetly. A mouse ran out onto a shelf of rock from its hole and twittered at him.

They would be alive after he was gone. They would sing and twitter in the bright sun below the blue sky while he lay a bloody, unseeing, unhearing, unfeeling corpse.

But then, what would they know, if they lived to be a hundred, of love? Of his love for Lalila?

He leaned on his sword and waited.

Flight to Opar

Philip José Farmer

Dedicated to J. T. Edson, Honorable Admiral of the Texas Navy, Honorable Deputy Sheriff of Travis County, Texas, and Thurston County, Washington, and creator of the epical Dusty Fog, the Ysabel Kid, Mark Counter, Ole Devil Hardin, and Bunduki.

Foreword

Those unacquainted with *Hadon of Ancient Opar*, volume one of the Ancient Opar series, should refer to Map 1. This shows the two central African seas which existed circa 10,000 B.C. At that time the climate was much more humid (pluvial) than now. What are now the Chad Basin and the Congo Basin were covered with fresh water, bodies whose area equaled and perhaps surpassed that of the present-day Mediterranean. The Ice Age was dying, but large parts of the British Islands and northern Europe were covered with glaciers. The Mediterranean was from one to two hundred feet lower than its present level. The Sahara Desert of today was then vast grasslands, rivers and freshwater lakes, and was host to millions of elephants, antelopes, lions, crocodiles and many other beasts, some now extinct.

The map also shows the island of Khokarsa, which gave birth to the first civilization of Earth, and the largest cities which grew around the Great Water, the Kemu, and the Great Water of Opar, the Kemuwopar. The prehistory and history of the peoples of the two seas are outlined in the *Chronology of Khokarsa* in volume one.

The map is a modification of a map presented by Frank Brueckel and John Harwood in their article: *Heritage of the Flaming God, an Essay on the History of Opar and Its Relationship to Other Ancient Cultures*. This appeared in *The Burroughs Bulletin*, Vernell Coriell, publisher, House of Greystoke, 6657 Locust, Kansas City, Missouri 64131.[1]

This series basically derives from the Opar books of the Tarzan series, and the author wishes to thank Hulbert Burroughs again for the permission to write these tales.

There is a rumor that this series is based on the translation of some of the gold tablets described by Edgar Rice Burroughs in *The Return of Tarzan*. That speculation will have to be dealt with in an addendum to a later volume of this series.

---

1 Although scheduled for publication in *The Burroughs Bulletin* at the time this foreword first appeared in print, Brueckel and Harwood's article went unpublished until it appeared in the collection *Heritage of the Flaming God: Ancient Mysteries of La and Savage Opar*, eds. Alan Hanson and Michael Winger, Waziri Publications, 1999.

1

Hadon leaned on his sword and waited for death.

He looked down the mountain slope from the mouth of the inner pass. Once again he shook his head. If only Lalila had not twisted her ankle, they might not be in such a hopeless situation.

The slope leading to the pass was steep, requiring a hands-and-knees approach during the last fifty yards. For a hundred yards from the inner pass, cliffs at least a hundred feet high and sixty yards wide walled the approach. These formed a sort of outer entrance. The walls went rapidly inward from that point, like the edges of an arrowhead. The slope and the walls met at the point of the arrow. Hadon stood now in the narrow aperture. Here the path began from a rocky ledge about ten inches high. It ran at a slightly less than forty-five-degree angle to the horizontal for a hundred feet, the cliffs that caged it rapidly dwindling in height.

It came out on the top of the cliffs, where the ground was fairly level. Beyond it was the vast oak forest.

The distance between the cliffs in the inner pass was just enough for a man to wield a sword. He had an advantage in that anybody trying to fight him would have to stand up before he could gain the less steep incline. That warrior would not have a stable footing. Hadon, standing on the ledge, would have a relatively firm stance.

The cliffs extended their high verticality for five miles on either side, however, so the pursuers did not have to attempt a frontal attack. They could go along the base of the cliffs until they came to a climbable part. Then they could ascend it and come back along the top of the cliffs. But it would take them about eight or nine hours to do this. They could not progress more than half a mile an hour on the steep rough terrain.

The soldiers would have their pride. They could not allow one man to scare off forty. In either event, direct or circuitous attack, they would be giving Awineth, Abeth, Hinokly, Kebiwabes and Paga time to get many miles into the forest. They would not know about Lalila's injured ankle and so would assume that he was making a stand just to give the refugees plenty of time to get lost in the woods. It would not take them long to know, however, that they were up against the man who had won the Great Games, who had been taught by the greatest swordsman in the Empire of Khokarsa.

Down on the slope, about twenty minutes away, the soldiers climbed steadily. In the lead were five dogs, straining at their leashes, digging their paws into the sparsely grassed dirt, slipping now and then. Three were keen-nosed tracehounds, belling as they sniffed the smells of the pursued. Two were wardogs. They were descended from the wild dog of the plains, bred to the size of male leopards, without the endurance of their ancestors but with no fear of man. Part of their training was the attacking of armed slaves. If the slave killed the three dogs loosed at him, he was freed. This seldom happened.

Some distance below and behind the dogs and their handlers was the lone officer. He was a big man, wearing a conical bronze helmet sporting a long raven feather from its top. His sword, still in its leather sheath, was the long, slightly curving, blunt-ended weapon of the *numatenu*. The same kind that Hadon was leaning on, which meant that the officer would be his first antagonist. The code of the *numatenu* dictated this. The officer would be disgraced if he sent in lesser men to face another *numatenu*.

Still, things were not always what they had been in the old days. Now there were men wearing the *tenu* who had no right to do so, men who often went unchallenged. The moral codes were breaking down, along with much else in these times of trouble.

Behind the officer, in straggling disorder, were thirty soldiers. They wore round bronze helmets with leather earflaps and noseflaps, leather cuirasses and leather kilts. They carried small round bronze shields on their backs and held long bronze-tipped spears. They dug these into the ground to assist their climb. Short stabbing swords were in their leather scabbards. On their backs, under the shields, were leather bags of provisions.

Behind the soldiers were four peasants clad in kilts of papyrus fiber. They carried round wooden shields on their backs and short swords in sheaths at their broad leather belts. Their hunting spears were in their hands, and slings and bags of slingstones also hung from their belts.

They were close enough now for Hadon to recognize them. These were the sons of the farmer at whose house Hadon's party had stopped to get food. After a brief show of resistance, the peasants had fled. But Awineth, in a fury because they had refused hospitality, had indiscreetly told them who she was. They must have gone to the nearest army post to notify the commander. He had sent this small force after the daughter of Minruth, Emperor of Khokarsa. And after Hadon and the others too. Awineth, of course, would be brought back alive, but what were the orders concerning the others? Capture so they could be brought back for judgment by Minruth? The men would probably be tortured publicly and then executed. Minruth, who seemed to have a passion for Lalila, would keep her as a mistress. Perhaps. He might have her tortured and killed too. And he was insane enough to wreak his hatred on Abeth, Lalila's daughter.

The dog tenders were weaponless except for daggers and slings. That made nine slingers in all. These were the deadliest weapons he would face. He had no room to dodge a lead missile traveling at sixty miles an hour, but they would have trouble getting into the proper stance for action if he had his way.

Hadon turned to look up the steeply sloping pass at Lalila. She sat at its end, about two hundred feet away. The sun shone on her white skin and long golden hair. Her large violet eyes looked black at this distance. She was bent forward, massaging her left ankle. She tried to smile but failed.

He walked up to her and, as he neared, he was struck with a pang of longing and sorrow. She was so lovely, he was so much in love with her, and they both had to die so soon.

"I wish you would do it, Hadon," she said. She indicated the long narrow dagger lying on the dirt beside her. "I would rather you killed me now and made sure that I died. I'm not sure that I'll have the strength to drive the blade into my heart when the time comes. I don't want to fall into Minruth's hands. Yet…I keep thinking that perhaps I might escape later on. I don't want to die!"

Hadon said, "You may be sure that you'd never get away from him again."

"Then kill me now!" she said. "Why wait until the last possible moment?"

She bowed her head as if to invite him to bring the sword down on it.

Instead he dropped to one knee and kissed the top of her head. She shuddered on feeling his lips.

"We had so much to live for!" she murmured.

"We still do," he said after rising. "I've been a fool, Lalila. I was thinking of making a stand according to the dictates of tradition. One man in a pass, valiantly fighting, slaying until the warriors are piled before me, then dying when a spear drives past my arms, too weary to hold the sword up any more.

"But that's stupid. I can do other things, and I will do them. First, though, we'll get you away from here—not too far, since we don't have time. Come."

He raised her to her feet. She winced with the pain of the ankle but did not cry out. "It'd take too long for you to hobble there, even with me supporting you," he said. He put the sword in its sheath and picked her up in his arms. She started to ask him what he intended to do. He said, "Hush! I need my breath," and he hurried toward the forest. Coming to its edge, he halted a few seconds while he looked around. Then he plunged into the half-darkness under the great oaks, carrying her to the foot of a mottled white and brown giant.

The lowest branch was two feet above him. He lifted her up so that she could grasp it and then heaved her up. She stretched out on it face down, looking back at him.

"It may hurt you, but you'll have to do it anyway," he said. "Climb up as far as you can and conceal yourself in the foliage. I haven't got time to wait here and see how you do while you climb."

"But what are you going to do?"

"I'm going to kill as many as possible. Then I'm going to run, drawing them away from you and the others."

"You'll leave me here to…?"

"To starve, possibly. Or be eaten by leopards or bears or be taken by the outlaws," he said. "That's a chance to be taken, Lalila. It's better than waiting for a sure death here. I'll be back for you. Somehow, I'll get back to you. But if I shouldn't, then take the same path the others took. It'll lead you to the temple, and you'll be safe in the sanctuary there."

Lalila smiled then, though it was certainly not with joy. The probability that he would return was small. She could not walk the many, many miles through the forest, up and down mountains. She could easily get lost, and there were bears, leopards, hyenas and many other beasts of prey hereabouts. Even if she somehow did find her way to the temple at Karneth, she might find that the sanctuary was no longer sacred. The followers of King Minruth, worshipers of Resu, would probably violate the temple.

She did not voice her doubts. Instead she said, "Go quickly then, Hadon! I will pray to my gods, and your goddess, that we will see each other again! And soon!"

She reached down and he kissed her hand, then turned without a word.

2

Hadon ran down the ancient hard-beaten path between the oaks for about fifty yards. Then he cut to his right, paralleling the path, and returned to the exit of the pass. If the dogs did track him to the oak where he had left her, they would smell only him. The trackers would see only his prints. The ground was not soft enough to show that his feet had sunk into the earth too deeply for one person. The dogs would follow his tracks down the path and then, hopefully, back to the pass through the forest…if there were any dogs left by then, and there wouldn't be if he had his way.

There was nothing to stop the pursuers from just ignoring his tracks and following those of the refugees. He hoped that by the time they were through the pass they would be in a fury of vengeance, bent only on chasing him down and killing him.

He raced back to the pass. Instead of entering its narrow high walls, he went around its right side. He ran along it, going up a slope, and presently was standing on the edge of the cliffs. To his left was the wide mouth of the outer pass, a hundred feet below him.

He looked over the edge. The frantic barking of the dogs was loud now. The lead pair was only fifty yards from the mouth of the pass. But here the slope was even steeper and the going slower. He went back along the edge until he stood over the place where the narrow passage began.

He searched for rocks small enough to carry but large enough for the task he had in mind. By the time the lead dogs were several yards below the mouth of the slot, he had piled seven small boulders by the edge.

The officer had called to the dog handlers to stop, though he had trouble getting their attention. One of the tenders finally saw the officer's lips moving and spoke to the others who yelled at the tracehounds to keep quiet. This failing, they struck them with their hands. The animals yelped, but they obeyed.

The wardogs made no sound. They crouched low to the ground, their yellow eyes round, slaver dripping from long yellow teeth.

The officer gave a few orders, not quite loudly enough for Hadon to distinguish the words. The men kept looking up, but they were intent on the pass and so did not see his head further down the edge of the cliff. They would become aware of his location soon enough.

Two tenders suddenly released their dogs and spoke to their charges. These, breaking into a loud barking, bent like bows and then sped like arrows up the slope. Hadon waited. He could deal with them later. The dogs ran up the pass barking, while the men below listened carefully. As the clamor became fainter, they realized that no one was in the pass to oppose them. The officer smiled and said something to the other three handlers. These, still holding the leashes, urged their frenzied beasts ahead of them. Hadon rolled away so that no chance look would detect him. When a few yards from the edge of the cliff, he stood up. He picked up a boulder, heaved it above his head and walked to the edge. Just below him were the three dogs, in single file, each pulling hard on the leash held by its tender.

Hadon estimated their rate of progress, strained, holding the heavy rock, and then cast it out a few feet.

It fell true, driving in the bronze helmet of the man in the lead.

His dog burst loose, trailing the leash behind it. The other two men halted suddenly and looked upward. Their mouths were open and their faces were pale.

Hadon turned, picked up a smaller stone and hurled that down. The two men turned to run back down the pass, but the stone struck one on the shoulder, breaking it and knocking him flat on the ground. The survivor, crying shrilly, leaped out from the pass and rolled down the steep slope.

Hadon picked up another boulder, as large as the first, and moved to the edge of the cliffs. He looked over, saw that the rolling dog handler had knocked down the officer and two spearmen. All four were rolling out of control.

He gave a mighty heave, and the stone shot out, fell, hit the slope, bounded and shot into a group of four spearmen. One must have been killed by the impact; the others were hurled back down the mountain. One rolled into another man, knocking him off his feet.

The boulder, its rate of descent only a little slowed by striking the soldier, smashed into the legs of another spearman, knocked him down, rolled, leaped and slammed into the stomach of one of the farmer's sons. Then it continued on down the mountain. None of the men hit by the boulder got up or showed signs that they were able to do so.

Hadon, instead of running back for another boulder, returned to the point where he could not be seen by those below the pass. He dropped the sword, still in its sheath, over the edge. He let himself over the edge, clung to the rock a moment, then dropped. It was fifteen feet from the top to the bottom at this point, but he was six feet two inches tall, one of the tallest men in Khokarsa, and his arms were exceptionally long. He rolled without injury, rose and picked up the sword. After fastening the sheath to his belt, he ran down to the two fallen men. One was dead; the other was unconscious. He removed their slings and bags. Then he used the injured man's dagger to ensure that he would never be a danger to anyone again.

He unsheathed his sword, Karken, Tree of Death, and drove its blunt point into the thin hard earth. Within a few seconds, he had placed a biconical lead missile in its sling. He moved to the mouth of the pass.

The officer was on his feet by then, bringing the soldiers to order. He looked up while shouting and saw Hadon. Hadon grinned and began whirling the sling at the ends of its thongs in a horizontal circle over his head. The officer cried out, his face pale. Perhaps he was protesting against a *numatenu* using a sling against another, not at his being in peril. But Hadon believed that the officer had lost any right to individual combat when he had loosed the dogs. Besides, he had decided not to play the game according to the rules. It would be stupid to give up his life for the code if it meant Lalila and the others would not escape. His highest duty was to Awineth, the high priestess of great Kho, now a refugee from the blasphemer Minruth. And also to Lalila and her child.

The angle was a difficult one for a slinger. It was not easy to estimate the trajectory of the cone. There was a tendency for a slinger in his position to underestimate, to cast the missile too low. But Hadon had given hundreds of hours to practice with the sling and he had hunted successfully in the jungle around Opar.

He released the end of the thong as it came down and the cone sped true. It was a blur on its way, but suddenly it bounced from the officer's nose. The nose disappeared in a gout of blood; the man was hurled back down the mountain. He fell on his back and slid for sixty feet downward, finally stopping when the top of his head was caught on a projection of rock.

The slingers had their lead missiles in their thongs by then and were whirling them. He stepped back, out of sight. Some missiles shot upward past the lip of the cliff. Others struck against the rocks below him, knocking off chips.

In those few seconds of observation, Hadon had seen that the other two dogs had been dragged back down the slope. One dog was in sight now, out of the pass, baying as it sped after Hadon's scent. It would follow his track into the forest, then double back and eventually find him. Hadon had some time, however, before he had to deal with it.

Suddenly the pass was loud with belling and growling. Hadon took a quick look over the edge. It was as he had thought. The *rekokha* or sergeant now in command had loosed the other dogs. Now he was shouting at the men, and they scrambled up on all fours. The noncom evidently hoped that the dogs would keep Hadon busy while they got through the pass. The sergeant was a good thinker; Hadon would have to eliminate him as soon as possible.

Hadon whirled around, placed another missile and spun the sling. Four dogs shot out of the end of the pass, the two swifter tracehounds in the lead, the two wardogs close behind them. The stone struck the rear dog in the left rear leg, knocking him over. He got up, howling, his leg trailing, and tried to run after the others. He fell and could not get up again.

Hadon went to the edge of the pass, back from the edge of the cliff, however. In that glance, he had seen six slingers standing up, though with some difficulty, whirling their slings. They would throw at him if he showed himself.

Hadon pushed a boulder over the edge into the narrow pass. He dropped down after it, picked it up and staggered to the mouth of the slot. Easing it down to the ground, he waited, his sword in his hands.

Presently he heard a puffing. He crouched down. He held the sword above his head. Suddenly the hands of a man gripped the shelf of the entrance. The head of the sergeant followed. His eyes opened, his flushed skin whitened. He started to cry out, and his hands released their hold. The *tenu* whipped downward. The sergeant fell back, leaving his two hands on the rock, spouting blood briefly.

There were cries from below. Hadon stood up, heaved the boulder above his head, almost losing it because of its weight. He took one step forward and cast it outward. It hit a soldier who was on all fours, staring at the body of the sergeant just before him. It crushed in his helmet and then rolled over his body and continued down the slope. A man screamed and tried to roll out of the way, but the boulder ran over an arm.

Hadon ducked back as the slingers shot their lead at him. They struck the rocky walls above him, knocking off chips which cut his face and arms.

He ran back up the pass. It was not likely that the soldiers would be trying again very soon. He would have time to take care of the dogs. He hoped he would, anyway.

The animals were coming back. They burst out of the shadows of the oak forest just as he got to the exit. The tracehounds halted on seeing him. The wardog, growling, bounded toward him. Hadon dropped the sling. He waited and, as the wardog leaped toward his throat, swung the sword. The blade cut its head off, its impact driving the body to one side. He whirled and then stepped away, but the spouting blood covered his feet.

At that the tracehounds moved in. Though primarily bred for tracking, they had been trained to attack too. One sped in directly toward him, then stopped just out of reach of his sword. The other circled around behind to dash in and nip at his legs. Hadon shifted the *tenu* to his left hand, pulled out his knife and threw it. The tracehound dodged to one side, too late. The knife drove into its body just before the right rear leg.

Hadon whirled, shifting the *tenu* back to his right hand. The tracehound which had run in to bite his leg skidded to a halt. It bounced back and forth sidewise, baying. Hadon backed up, keeping his eyes on the beast. He shifted the sword to his left hand again, bent down, quickly pulled the knife out, wiped it on the grass and waited. The dog moved too quickly to be a reliable target for the knife.

After a few seconds, Hadon moved toward the dog. It retreated, keeping a distance of about thirty feet, moving back and forth, in and out. Hadon kept walking toward the cliff's edge. Suddenly the dog realized what was happening. It was twenty feet from being backed off the top of the cliff.

As it ran at an angle away from Hadon, Hadon ran toward it. It was no longer shifting around; now it ran in a straight line. Hadon threw the knife, and the blade sank into its neck.

A moment later he peeped cautiously over the edge. Most of the group was gathered about thirty feet below the pass. Two men were almost at its mouth. They were on all fours but gripping spears. Evidently they planned to rise simultaneously just short of the mouth and cast their spears if Hadon was waiting for them.

He ran to the dog, picked its body up and ran with it to the top of the pass. Just as the two soldiers rose to their feet, he threw the carcass down. It struck one and knocked him back down the slope, into the knot below him. The other looked startled and for a moment did not seem to know what happened.

Hadon looked around. There were no stones handy for throwing, no boulders to drop. He rolled quickly over the edge and dropped to the floor of the pass. The soldier saw him then and scrambled upward, crawling into the pass. He rose as Hadon ran toward him, raising the spear to throw. Hadon's knife flew, plunged to the hilt in the man's mouth, and the man fell backward.

His knife was gone, but the spear had fallen within his reach.

3

An hour had passed. Hadon crouched near the mouth, waiting. The soldiers had retreated to a distance of fifty yards down and about forty feet to one side of the pass. They were sitting down, talking among themselves. They seemed to be in disagreement. No wonder. Their dogs were dead, which meant they would have to do any tracking without their indispensable aid. Three of them were disabled, out of action. Eight were dead. That still left twenty-nine, but these could only get into the pass one at a time and their antagonist was better armed now than when the attack had started.

Hadon looked across the wide valley. To his right, far below, part of the road at the bottom was visible here and there among the trees. There were very tiny figures on it. Occasionally the sun flashed on a helmet, a spearpoint. Reinforcements were coming, with more dogs. It would take them until nightfall to get to the pass, but they would not wait for daylight, knowing that Hadon could slip away in the dark. Moreover, their main quarry, Awineth, would be getting further and further away.

They would light their torches and release the dogs. This time they would have too many dogs for him to handle; and they would storm the pass while he was occupied with them.

It seemed that the soldiers on the slope had not yet seen the men on the road. But they would. Then what would they do? Wait for the newcomers? Or continue the onslaught?

Far to the right, beyond the shoulder of the mountain across the valley, rose the Khowot, the Voice of Kho, the Great Goddess, Mother of All. Just past it was a dark splotch, all he could see of the city of Khokarsa. The Voice of Kho had discharged great quantities of lava and poisonous gases while he and Lalila and the others were fleeing Minruth's underground prison. It was fortunate for them that the earthquake preceding the eruption had opened the way for them, and the shaking of the earth had tumbled down buildings and panicked the city. Afterward, mighty Khowot had belched white-hot lava and huge chunks of stone and lava. In the chaos of the flight of the citizens, Hadon's group had managed to escape into the countryside.

Even then, Minruth's soldiers had been after them—and they might have caught up with them—but Kwasin, Hadon's herculean cousin, had leaped onto the boat full of soldiers. The last Hadon had seen of him, before the smoke veiled the battle, was Kwasin's tremendous ax rising and falling.

Hadon was grateful for Kwasin's sacrifice, though it had been motivated more by egotism than anything else. Kwasin thought he was the strongest man in the world—and probably was. But he hated Hadon, and he had promised to find them later and take Lalila away.

First, though, Kwasin would have to kill Hadon.

Fearsome as Kwasin was, he was going to have a battle he would never forget—if he survived. Kwasin was much larger and stronger, but he was not as quick as Hadon. Nor was he the equal of his cousin in swordsmanship. Yet that ax, that great ax made from a fallen star by Paga...it was so heavy that only a giant like Kwasin could wield it as if it were fashioned from papyrus.

Hadon thought back to the time when he had left Opar for the Great Games at Khokarsa. Who could have foreseen the chain of events which would lead him to this mountain pass? Only Kho Herself, and She had let drop only a few hints through the mouth of Her speaker, the oracular priestess in the cave near the top of the volcano.

Hadon had contested with the other ambitious athletic youths in the Lesser Games at Opar. Three had been chosen. Himself, his friend Taro and the surly, hateful Hewako. These and their substitutes had traveled on a galley through the Kemuwopar, the Southern Sea of Opar. They had gotten through the spooky Strait of Kethna and then had crossed the length of the Kemu, the Northern Sea, the Great Water.

Awineth, Queen of Khokarsa and high priestess, daughter of Minruth, wanted a husband, a king her own age. Minruth had asked her to marry him, but she had refused him. It was rumored that Awineth had taken her father to bed before making up her mind and had found him wanting. Hadon doubted the story because it was evident to all that daughter and father had long been hostile to each other. Another rumor had it that Awineth suspected her father of poisoning her mother. Hadon doubted this too, though Minruth was not called the Mad without good cause. But even he would not have dared to murder his wife, the high priestess, supreme vicar of Kho. Surely he would have feared the wrath of the Goddess too much. But then perhaps he *had* done it and, finding that lightning did not strike him, the earth did not open up beneath him, he had lost much of his dread of Her. It may have been that he dared to think of overthrowing Her, of making Resu, the Flaming God, the supreme deity. And with that the dominance of the kings in all matters, spiritual and temporal. And with that, a revolution in the role of the male in Khokarsa.

Minruth was not satisfied with being lord of the army and navy and in charge of the construction of roads and major buildings. He wanted to control the taxes, the postal system and the religious organizations. Above all, he wanted to finish the building of the Great Tower of Kho and Resu, that project begun five hundred years ago by King Klakor. The legend was that the king who completed it could ascend to the sky, to the blue palace of the Flaming God, and become immortal. It was half finished now, and Minruth was fifty-eight years old. He wanted to spend every cent possible, to draft an all-out construction. But the priestesses had been interfering for half a millennium, slowing its construction. Times of troubles had also blocked its progress. The priestesses claimed that the Empire would be ruined if all efforts were directed to the tower's completion. That was obviously true. Additionally obvious was the fact that the structure could not take much more weight. The tower would have to be abandoned unless someone could invent a new type of very light-weight brick. Minruth had offered a reward equivalent to the annual taxes of the city of Bawaku to anyone who would come up with the desired construction material.

Hadon had won the Great Games, though he had been grieved when his friend Taro was killed. The proud victor, he had marched to the palace expecting to be proclaimed the husband of Awineth and Emperor of Khokarsa. Instead he was given news that staggered and outraged him.

The Voice of Kho, the oracle in the cave high on the volcano, had said that his honors must be deferred. First he must lead an expedition into the far north, to the shores of the Ringing Sea. There he must locate and bring back three people from beyond the Ringing Sea. These had been brought to the southern shores of the Ringing Sea by Sahhindar. But the exiled god of bronze, plants and time had left them there, sending Hinokly, a member of a previous expedition, to Khokarsa with his orders.

Why? Only Kho Herself knew. Hadon had suspected in his fit of rage that Minruth had somehow contrived to bring about this unjust deferment. But, cooling off, he had realized that he had been guilty of blasphemous thoughts. No priestess of Kho would dare speak falsely. Not when the commands of Kho were involved. The retribution would be swift and awe-inspiring.

Hadon had reluctantly led the expedition northward, past the Saasares mountains and onto the vast savannas beyond. During the journey, he had run across his cousin Kwasin. The giant was fleeing from a tribe of wild men, and he had been saved only because Hadon's men fought the others off. Kwasin had been expelled from Khokarsa some years before because he had raped a priestess and killed some temple guards defending her. Ordinarily he would have been castrated and his body thrown to hogs.

But the Voice of Kho spoke, and his punishment was exile for an indeterminate time.

Kwasin accompanied them the rest of the way. The three strangers, Lalila, Paga and Abeth, had been located. Lalila claimed that Sahhindar had indeed brought them from across the Ringing Sea. For reasons known only to himself, he had then left them. They accompanied Hinokly's expedition back to Khokarsa, but savages had attacked them, killing all but the three and Hinokly. The three had been separated from him, so he had made his way back to his native land.

Lalila, however, said that Sahhindar had disclaimed deityship. He was, he said, only a man. But he did admit that he had lived over two thousand years. And he had been born, he said, in a far distant future. Somehow, sailing in "a ship of time," he had traveled back to a period two thousand years before the present. And it was indeed he who had made the civilization of Khokarsa possible.

On the return journey, Hadon had fallen in love with Lalila. He was not the only one. She seemed to project an aura which drew men to her as the scent of the female moth drew male moths. She was undeniably beautiful, but there were many women in Khokarsa as beautiful. Paga had said that she carried a curse. It maddened men and at the same time brought them to death.

Hadon had not cared. He was in ecstasy when Lalila told him she loved him. She was ready to forget her grief for Wi, her dead lover.

Arriving in Khokarsa, they were greeted with shocking news. Minruth had imprisoned Awineth in her apartment and declared himself supreme ruler. Hadon, with the men in his party, was taken prisoner and conducted to Khokarsa, the capital city of the Empire of Khokarsa. Kwasin had escaped, but he was later retaken.

During the earthquake preceding the eruption, Hadon, Kwasin and Paga had escaped, rescued Lalila, her daughter and Awineth, and fled into the mountains northeast of the city.

Awineth and the others might still get away. Lalila might also escape, though her chances of survival in these woods infested with outlaws and beasts were few. More likely she would starve to death.

Still, he had done much better than he had expected. Now he permitted himself to hope, both for himself and Lalila.

4

The sun was in its final quarter. By then Hadon had rolled a boulder from the edge of the forest to the edge of the cliff about forty feet outward from the inner pass. He pushed it over and watched while it bounded down the slope. The men below, hearing the crash as it struck the bottom of the cliff, looked up. They rolled to one side, hoping to be out of the way of the bounding death, or got to their feet and ran. Some lost their footing on the steepness and fell.

The big rock struck a projection and leaped up, striking a dog handler full in the chest. He shot backward, sliding on his back for at least a hundred feet, then lay still. The boulder, only slightly checked by the impact, rolled and jumped the rest of the way down the mountain, lurching across a meadow at its foot and stopping when it struck the trunk of a tree.

Hadon had hoped to kill more than one. He was not, however, too disappointed. His main purpose had been to assure the soldiers that he was still in the area. He wanted them to think that he intended to guard the pass until nightfall and perhaps after that.

He was successful. The men went back down the slope to the meadow. Here they talked for a while, looking up at the pass now and then. They were evidently going to wait until the reinforcements arrived.

No, he was wrong. Now they were moving along the meadow. As he watched, they began climbing, this time at an angle. The end of their path was about five miles away, where the cliffs dwindled. They planned to ascend the climbable heights there and come back along the cliff's edge. At the rate they were going it would take them at least nine hours. Hadon went to the forest. He walked up the fallen tree supported by the two oaks. He called softly, "Lalila!" but got no answer. He climbed to a branch just above the broad limb on which she lay. She was on her side, sleeping, but she opened her eyes when he called again.

He lowered himself from the branch, saying, "Don't be alarmed." He explained the situation to her.

"What do you plan to do now?" she asked. Her violet eyes were wide, showing the redness of the eyeballs. She looked haggard; when she moved her foot without thinking, pain shot across her face.

"We're going to leave," he said. "I'll carry you on my back for a while, then I'll support you while you hobble. Do you think you can make it?"

"I have to," she said, trying to smile. "There isn't any choice, is there? But you were going to leave me here...."

"I changed my mind because the situation has changed. I may have to abandon you again for a while, if they get too close. But the deeper I can get you into the woods, the less distance I'll have to travel to come back for you. Besides, there is the chance that we might lose them entirely. But..."

"But you'll still have to leave me," she said. "You can't let them follow the trail of the others."

"If they find it," he said. "We will have to trust to chance...and to Kho."

He helped her down from the tree, no easy task. When they were on the ground, he shifted to his chest the pack of provisions he'd taken from a corpse. He bent down and Lalila, biting her lip to keep from groaning, got onto his back. He rose, placed his hands under her legs and started walking. They were soon under the branches of the oaks spreading above the trail. Hadon made no effort to go swiftly, since he must not spend his strength. He had a long, long way to go. Besides, the events of yesterday and today had weakened him. He had not gotten much sleep, and he had used up enough muscular effort and nervous tension for four warriors.

He kept his eyes on the trail, noting that the tracks of Awineth's party were visible even to an untrained person. His own tracks were evident for a while; then they ceased. At this point he had gone off into the woods to double back. It had not been wasted time, though. It had led the dogs astray long enough for him to have time to handle them.

It was cool under the shade of the oaks. It was comparatively silent too, except for the croak of a nearby raven and the far-off chatter of some monkeys. After a while, he saw some of the oak-monkeys, creatures not much larger than the squirrels with whom they competed for nuts and berries. They were reddish except for faces outlined by a ruff of white hair. A small band followed him for a while, leaping from one oak to the next before losing interest. But he heard their cries for a long time.

From time to time, Hadon bent down and Lalila eased off his back. They would walk slowly while he held her and she hopped on one leg. When her good leg got too weak for her to proceed, they rested for about fifteen minutes. After that, she mounted him again.

The trail went steadily upward, though gently. By nightfall they were at the top of a saddleback with peaks on each side. Ahead, its snowy top illuminated by the setting sun, was a mountain twice as tall as the one on which they stood. The valley between was too dark for them to distinguish any features. They were surrounded by pines now; it was too cold for oaks here.

Lalila, sitting on wet leaves, shivered. "We'll freeze."

Hadon chewed on a piece of hard bread and even harder beef jerky. He swallowed and said, "It's not too cold to sleep. We'll get some rest until the moon comes up. That should be about two hours from now. Then we'll go on. Exercise will keep us warm."

"But you can't," she said. "You'll be too tired. Haven't we got a long head start on them? Couldn't we sleep until dawn at least?"

Before replying, he went to a nearby spring and scooped up some water in his hands. After drinking, he said, "It depends on whether they follow us in the dark or decide to wait until daybreak. Ordinarily, they wouldn't dare enter these woods now. It is said..."

He paused. She murmured, "It is said...?"

Hadon bit his lip. He hadn't wanted to scare her, but if he was silent she would be even more frightened.

"It is said that this forest is haunted by demons. And then there are the leopards and the hyenas. The tale about the demons may be an idle one, something people like to scare themselves with. I have heard many; while it's true that I've never seen a demon, yet I've heard stories from those who claim that they have...or knew people who claimed they had. But there is no doubt that the mountain forests of Khokarsa are inhabited by leopards, hyenas and bears. If we're moving, we're not likely to get attacked. But if we're sleeping, who knows."

He did not tell her about the *kokeklakaar*, the Long-Armed Killer of the Trees. This was said to be a hairy half-man creature which waited on a branch for the unwary traveler. When its prey passed below, it hung by one arm from a branch and reached down with the other and closed its crablike pincers around the neck of its victim. Snap! The pincers squeezed the breath out of the throat, cut through the flesh, half severing the head.

Then the thing threw the corpse up into the branches, clambered after it and settled down to sucking the blood through its trumpet-shaped mouth, formed of horn.

No, he would not tell her about that. She had enough to worry about.

"The men of Minruth may feel they are numerous enough so that even the demons will not dare attack them. If so, they'll light torches and follow the dogs. They can travel much more swiftly than we can. If they push themselves, they might be here by dawn. Or perhaps before then."

Hadon pointed out to her that the spring had become a small stream. It seemed to descend slantwise across the mountain, at least it did for as far as he had seen it in the light. Perhaps it became falls here and there later on. But they could proceed down it, allowing the water to wash out their tracks.

"Why didn't they"—referring to Awineth's party—"go down the stream too?" she said.

"I don't know. Perhaps they did further down."

"But won't the soldiers know that's what we did when our tracks disappear?"

"You're too logical," he said. "Of course they will. They'll send some men after us while the others follow the trail. But if we can lose those who'll be after us, I may be able to cache you some place. Then I'll come back and see what I can do."

The creek's water was very cold. They had not gone far before their feet were numb. Lalila did not comment on this until their feet slipped out from them and they sat down hard. Hadon, cursing, got up quickly. When he helped her up, she said, "I just can't feel anything below my knees."

"That's an advantage," he said. "You can't feel the pain of your injured ankle. You should be able to walk on it now."

It was true, but his own legs felt as stiff and dead as crutches. The loss of sensitivity made him unable to feel out the rocks and the holes in the bed of the stream. As a result, he fell now and then and was shocked by the ice-cold bath. He was shivering, sure that if he could see his skin, he would find it blue. Lalila's teeth were chattering, and he felt her body shaking when he supported her.

After an indeterminate, almost unendurable time, they came to a falls. It was too dark to tell how far it dropped. Not that that made any difference. They had to climb out and go through the woods where the slope was not too steep. Half of the time they slid on their rumps through the wet leaves and the mud. Bushes scratched them and stones cut their legs and buttocks.

The moon came out. It was not much help where they were because of the dense growth of trees. After a while they saw the water gleaming and returned to it. The stream allowed them passage for perhaps a mile, then became a cataract again. This was at the head of a deep but narrow gorge, compelling them to walk along its edges, though not too near. Once Hadon slipped on a patch of mud and both were nearly precipitated into the chasm. Lalila hurt her ankle again.

By the time they reached the valley, they saw clouds covering the stars to the west. Within fifteen minutes the moon was veiled, then shut out. A heavy rain battered at them a little while later. They took refuge under a tree, sitting with their backs against its trunk. Rain fell through the leaves and ran down the trunk against their back. It was cold, but not as cold as the mountain stream.

"If I had known that it would rain," Hadon said, "I would have gone on the trail. It's going to wash out all the footprints and the scent too."

"Then we won't be able to find Abeth!" Lalila cried.

"We can find the path and follow it. But if they had any sense, they will have gotten off it at the first place where they wouldn't leave tracks. Don't worry. If it's at all possible, we'll find them. If we run across a temple, the priestesses will help locate them for us. They know everything that's going on in these mountains."

He lifted her up, held her in his arms for a while as she clung to him. Then he broke the embrace and, speaking roughly to hide his own exhaustion and despair, said, "We don't want to go back to the trail yet. We'll cut through at an angle toward the gap we saw. The trail undoubtedly goes through it, but when we get to it, we'll see if we can't go higher somehow. And not leave any clues."

They reached the gap near dawn. It was about a hundred yards wide and walled with steep limestone. There were some ascendable places, however, and at the top of one was a ledge.

"We'll go up there and sleep, out of sight. The dogs won't be able to smell us if we're up there—I hope. And the rock won't leave much of a scent behind. It'll be gone by the time they get here, anyway." He silently added another *I hope.*

Normally they could have reached the ledge in fifteen minutes. Now they had to halt frequently to catch their breath, to still their gaspings and quiet the tremblings of their legs. Lalila had to ride on his back half the time. They pushed on and after a long while crawled up to the ledge. It was about fifteen feet long and ten deep.

"A cave!" Lalila said.

Hadon rose, drew his sword and advanced cautiously. When he was close, he could smell a fetid odor, the stink of hyenas, with which he had had extensive experience while on the expedition across the savannas north of Khokarsa. But no slinking, slope-backed, trap-jawed beasts rushed out at him. Peering within, he saw some crushed bones, hair and droppings. The latter were old.

He entered, still cautiously, until the ceiling sloped downward sharply. Getting down on his hands and knees, he looked into the darkness. More bones, and then what looked like rock.

Coming out, he said, "We can sleep here, but first…"

He looked out across the valley they had left. Tiny figures were crossing the bottom of the valley—a stream of figures. At a rough estimate, two hundred.

Lalila said, "I'm glad this ledge is on the sunward side. I don't think, though, I'll ever get warm again."

"They're coming," Hadon said.

She looked stricken. He hastily added, "But it'll be a long time before they get here. There's no use pushing on. We'd drop dead before we got to the bottom of the next valley. We'll sleep."

"And then what?"

"The dogs will make enough noise to wake us. Then, well, then, Lalila, I have to leave you. Just what I'll do after that, I don't know. Improvise. Pray to Kho to help Her devoted worshiper against the men of Resu."

He ate some more bread and jerky and insisted that she eat too. Then they lay down in the mouth of the cave in each other's arms. Hadon, feeling her naked breasts against his, was surprised by a stirring of desire. He had thought he was too tired to lift his head, let alone anything else. He told himself that this was no time to even think about such a thing.

And while he was thinking he fell asleep.

5

For some time he was vaguely aware that he was being disturbed. Suddenly he felt a hand tugging at his hair. He groaned "Go away!" then woke as he was slapped sharply. He sat up and looked at Lalila. "What…?"

The baying of dogs and the voices of men answered his question.

Grimacing with the pain of fatigue-rusted muscles, he rose. He crept out on all fours and peered over the edge of the ledge. Down below was a long procession, armored and armed soldiers. And at least forty dogs. Their clamor, if not enough to wake the dead, would quickly rouse the deadest of the tired.

Hadon withdrew his head. If one of those men should happen to glance up…

Lalila had crawled out to him. She started to look over the edge, but he pressed down on her shoulder.

"Wait until the last man has gone by."

He crawled back until he was out of sight from below. He rose, entered the cave and removed the provisions from the pack. He returned to Lalila and handed her her breakfast. While they ate and washed the food down with water from a ceramic canteen, he told her what she must do. It was simple: wait until he returned.

"I can endure being left here," she said. "But if you are not back in two days, I'll have only two choices, starve or kill myself. I can't climb down without your aid."

Hadon did not answer at once. He looked to the north. The valley there was much wider than the one they'd just left. Even higher mountains walled it in. Because of the shoulder of the mountain they were on, he could only see the eastern half of the valley. It was heavily wooded except for the terminus of a lake at the west. If there were any villages on the lake, they must be out of sight beyond the shoulder. Suppose there were villages there? Could he trust them to take care of Lalila? This was an area dominated by the worshipers of Kho, and there were supposed to be several temples somewhere in these mountains. She could take sanctuary in one of them, except that what was once a sacred place, inviolate, untouched by even the most evil of men, might no longer be so.

He said, "Perhaps you are right. I'll take you to the bottom, and then you'll have to take your chances. Somehow I have to get them off the track of Awineth and the others, although it's possible they might have already lost their trail. But they are so numerous, they can split up and send parties all over the valley. I really don't know what I'm going to do—whatever one man can do against so many. But you'll be in more danger there than here."

"I want my daughter back," she said. "I'll do whatever you say. I just thought I should point out what will happen if…if you don't come back."

He had been looking at the valley to his left while he talked. Now he started and said, "Look there!"

Lalila began to crawl to him, but he lifted her up. She looked where he was pointing. "More soldiers!"

"I don't think so," he said. "They don't seem to be wearing armor. They could be hunters. They might be traders; they're carrying big packs. They must know what they're doing, since the tracks of the soldiers must be plain. They're coming along very swiftly too. It's as if they're trying to catch up with them."

He paused. "This makes things different. I can't take you down after the soldiers are gone. These men would be too close behind us. They'd catch up with us."

Lalila said, "I'll do whatever you think is best, Hadon. I don't like to be stranded here, but I can take care of myself."

He permitted himself a quick look over the edge. The dwindling of noise sounded as if the soldiers had passed by. Yes, there went the rearguard with not a backward glance. He rose and said, "I don't like to leave you here, but there's no other way. And I have to get going at once. I must get into the forest before those men get here and see me."

"Very well," she said. "May you be back soon. With Abeth."

"Kho willing, I will be."

He leaned over and kissed her upturned lips. They were cracked and dry, but though she looked worn out and her mouth was arid, he felt desire stir again. He straightened up and, smiling, said, "You'll be able to rouse passion in men when you're on your deathbed."

"What?"

"I love you," he said, and he was gone.

Coming around the shoulder, he saw more of the valley. The end of the lake became large, oval-shaped. In its center was a small island, dominated by a building glittering white in the sun. It was round and topped by a dome. It would be made of limestone—it would be too difficult to ship marble in—and it would be a Temple of Kho or one of Her many daughters. Which meant that Awineth and the others would have headed for it.

That is, if they had gotten this far. It was possible that they were hiding in the valley behind him.

But the soldiers would have known that. They would have sent at least several small parties to hunt for them while the others continued. They had not done so, which meant that their commander knew of the temple, and that Awineth would know of it also. Like Hadon, the officer had calculated that the temple would be the refugees' goal.

Westward, the lake became a river, winding through the forest. He slipped into its safe shade and headed in as straight a line as possible for the nearest lake. There was some underbrush in the pines, but as he descended he entered the oaks. Their close-packed ranks and far-flung branches ensured that not much vegetation would grow beneath them. He walked swiftly, running now and then, working the stiffness and ache from his muscles. Though he was in rougher terrain than the soldiers, he was making better progress. The trail they were on wound to the northeast somewhat, then, he supposed, would cut back to the lake. Unless something happened, he would get to the lake first.

Twice he crossed creeks and stopped to drink. He finished the bread and jerky he'd brought along. It was not enough, but he did not have time to hunt. Besides, what could he catch with only a knife and *tenu*? The question was answered when, suddenly aware of his opportunity, he snatched out his knife and threw it at a monkey. This was a larger specimen than the small oak-monkey, and it had ventured to a low branch to scream at him. The knife caught it just as it turned to leap away and drove halfway through its side. It fell with a thump while its hundred packmates leaped around and hooted and screamed at him.

He stopped long enough to remove its head, tail, limbs and skin. Cutting out pieces of the flesh, chewing on them, he walked on. He would have preferred it cooked, but he had eaten raw meat as a boy in the jungles around Opar. He looked back once and saw several ravens settling down around the leavings. Perhaps the Raven-Goddess, M'adesin, would bless him for giving her charges food.

On the other hand, and here he almost lost his appetite, the monkey might be sacred to this forest. You never knew what the local taboos were until you asked around, and there was no one to ask.

"If I have sinned, O Goddess," Hadon said loudly, "forgive me! It was done out of need and ignorance. I needed sustenance to see me through this mission, which is to save the high vicar of Kho, to fight for Kho against Her enemies."

Actually he was far more concerned at this moment about his friends, Hinokly and Kebiwabes, and the manling Paga—so beloved by Lalila—and her daughter Abeth. There was no need to mention this, however.

Nor was there reason to comment that Awineth, though the chief agent of mighty Kho, was a bitch.

Hadon detoured to the creek to wash the blood from his face, hands and chest. He threw the rest of the carcass away and continued. He saw a number of deer browsing in the more open spaces between the oaks. Where deer were, there would be leopards. Of these he saw no sign, except for some pawprints in the mud near the creek.

Nightfall found him still far from the lake. He pushed on through the darkness, though he knew the absence of light would give him a tendency to circle. When the moon rose, he was still going, though more slowly than in the morning. His desire to lie down and go to sleep was counterbalanced by two motives. One, he had to get to the temple before the soldiers did. If their officers drove them, refusing to camp, then they would get there first. Second, he heard the roar of a leopard somewhere near. It would be hunting deer, but it might consider him for supper if it found him sleeping.

He murmured a prayer to Khukhaqo, Our Lady of the Leopard. But he could not help thinking that she could consider her first duty was to the leopard.

That thought hastened his pace. And then, after an hour or so—he wasn't sure of the time at all—he saw a light.

It was straight ahead and small, but within fifteen minutes it had gotten much larger. He was at the edge of the forest; the lake was before him, separated by a narrow dirt road and twenty feet of cut grass. The fire turned out to be three huge bonfires, all close together. They blazed in front of the white temple he had seen from the ledge. Shouts and screams traveled three-quarters of a mile over the stretch between the shore and the island, the voices of women mingled with the shrilling of trumpets, the beating of drums and the twanging of a harp. Now and then a bullroarer throomed.

The hair on the back of his neck seemed to rise; a chill raced over his neck and down his back.

The priestesses were holding one of their orgiastic rites. And he, as a man, was not even supposed to be looking at the fires and the tiny figures which danced before the flames. Any male passerby was obligated to avert his eyes and pass by swiftly. This road was probably forbidden to men at this time. The locals would be staying in their homes tonight and they would not venture out until dawn.

He looked down the road from behind a tree. About a hundred feet down, near the edge of the lake, a statue loomed. He could not make out its details; the light of the full moon and the glimmer from the fires did not furnish enough illumination.

Unable to repress his curiosity—pleading to himself that he had to investigate because of the urgency of his mission—he went along the edge of the forest toward it. Closer, he could see that it was about thirty feet high and was carved from wood. It represented a being which was half-woman, half-tree. Carved leaved branches crowned her head; her widespread arms were branches ending in gnarled fingers. Her breasts were huge; one suckled a squirrel. From holes here and there the heads of birds and animals protruded, civet cats, servals, deer, pigs, ravens, bustards, oak-monkeys and lemurs. The largest carving was that of a baby, extending halfway from the enormous vagina.

Hadon walked to the idol and made a closer inspection. The baby held an acorn in one hand, symbolizing, he supposed, the gifts of the goddess to the inhabitants of the oak forest.

The idol was of Karneth, deity of the oak. He did not know much about her, since there were no oaks around Opar. Though Opar was in the mountains, it was too far south and hence too hot for this tree to flourish.

So the temple was dedicated to Karneth, and the priestesses were conducting their secret ceremonies under the full moon.

Awineth and Abeth could be on that islet now. The male members of the group would be forbidden to touch the sacred soil of the isle. Where were they?

He looked up and down the shore. Nearby was a long wooden dock, but there were no boats tied to it. They had been taken to the islet to prevent any foolish—no, mad—males from using them to spy on the rites.

Hadon felt a chill again when he remembered tales of what happened to nosy men who had been caught where they had no business. They had lost more than their noses.

He sat down and considered the situation. If Awineth was on the island, she would have to attend the rites as the chief priestess. But Abeth, now that he thought about it, would not be there. Only adult women participated. She would be with the men. Since he could see no houses along the shore, it was reasonable to assume that the men had been sent, with the child, to the fishing village on the other lake.

That would be so if the group had actually arrived here. For all he knew, it had not.

He sighed and rose. There was only one way to find out. He must go the long way to the village. This road undoubtedly led to it, but it would take at least five hours to get there. And dawn would be here in two.

He was not about to swim to the island and ask Awineth. No excuse would be accepted for violating the sanctity of the temple.

At that moment he heard a noise to his right. He stepped out into the road and looked to the east. He groaned. A shadowy mass was moving along the road toward him. Faint voices reached him. As the dark bulk came closer, it separated into men. And dogs!

The dogs were silent, though, which meant they must be muzzled.

The soldiers had moved even faster than he had expected.

Now the moonlight flashed dully on spearheads.

Hadon froze into a half-crouch. The dogs would soon smell him. Their frantic whinings and growling would notify the men that someone was in the neighborhood. The muzzles would be taken off, the leashes unsnapped...and the dogs would be after him.

He was too tired to outrun them. Even if he was fresh, he did not have a good enough head start.

He groaned again. There was only one escape route—the lake.

There was no time to lose. Still crouching, he entered the water behind the dock. It was cold, though not nearly as cold as the mountain stream. It lay at the bottom of the valley and had been soaking in the heat of the summer sun. But not nearly enough, not nearly enough.

For a moment he contemplated caching the sword under the dock. It was heavy, and he needed all the buoyancy he could get. It would be foolish to insist on taking it and then be dragged under, drowned, just because he could not bear to part with it.

Very well, so it was foolish. He did not want to be without it when he got to the other shore. Who knew how soon he would desperately need it?

He began dog-paddling. He had to get far enough out so the soldiers would not see him. Using a fast stroke would disturb the water and possibly catch their eyes.

He went steadily, swimming at a northwest angle because the current would otherwise move him eastward toward its outlet. But his fatigue, plus the weight of the sword, slowed him down too much. He was being carried past the island.

Perhaps he was far enough away from the shore to swim now. He began using his arms to pull and his legs to propel. The moon shone whitely on the disturbed water, but perhaps the soldiers would think it was caused by fish leaping from the surface.

No. A shout carried over the water. He turned and treaded water to look at the shore. The men were on the edge and on the dock now, looking out at him, some pointing. They had spotted him. In this light and at this distance, however, they could not identify him. And even if they did, then what? He had a lead on them, and they would be just as tired. They had no boats, so they would have to shed their armor and all arms, except for daggers. That would take a few minutes, which would enable him to get even more distance between himself and them. They would never catch up.

Of course, they could send men around the lake to intercept him on the other side. He would still get there before they did.

Then despair seized him. He was not going to get to the other side. He was just too tired. His legs and arms felt like they were made of solid bronze, and he was breathing heavily. The sword was an arm reaching up from the bottom, trying to drag him down.

Though continuing to crab, heading to the northeast, he was actually going in a straight path to the island. After a few minutes he realized that this too had changed, that his course would take him past the island. That did have one advantage: if he could make it to the leeward side, he would find the current diminished.

He resumed dog-paddling, the water just below his nose, sometimes above. As a result, he was swept ever more swiftly past the island, but he had no alternative. To continue his stroking was to exhaust himself utterly.

Soon he was about twenty yards past the islet. Summoning the last of his strength, he made progress northward and then was on the east side. The current was noticeably weaker here; it became even weaker as he neared the land. Then, during one of his exploratory ventures, his foot touched bottom. He managed to keep on going for a few more feet and he could stand up, the surface just below his chin. He stood there for several minutes until his gaspings eased off into heavy breathings. Then he pushed forward until the water was to his knees.

He sat down, feeling the cold ooze close around his buttocks. He would rest here, then continue to the other side. Why swim? he thought. He would steal—borrow, rather—one of the boats docked on the west shore. He would not even have to commit blasphemy, since he was not setting foot on the island. He would stay offshore.

When he felt that he had strength enough, he rose and trudged through the water a few feet from the grassy edge. The music and the shouts, screams and chants were loud. He kept his head turned away. As long as he did not see the ritualists he was not spying on them, so Karneth and her worshipers would have no reason to be angry at him.

He was about a hundred yards from the dock when he looked across the lake. He froze. There were boats on it. Six. Long craft with at least ten men in each.

6

Now he could see that a line tracing back down their path led to a shadowy clump under some trees on the southeast corner of the lake. There had to be buildings and a dock there, probably used by fishermen who supplied the temple with their catches. The soldiers had found them after sighting him. Or perhaps they had noticed them on the way in. It made no difference. They were coming after him.

Or did they only suspect that he was a refugee, their main purpose the seizure of Awineth? Would they be invading the island even if he hadn't been seen?

They must be driven by powerful motives. No man would venture on this taboo soil unless he was in great fear or in great desire of reward. In this case, the soldiers would be compelled by both. Minruth would brook no obstacles, accept no excuse. He would execute anybody who pleaded religious sanctity—after some suitable torture, of course. And he would have offered an enormous sum for the capture of his daughter. Given this double incentive, the soldiers were ignoring their fears.

He still found it hard to believe that anyone would deliberately violate a sacred isle and temple.

Yet here they came.

What was worse, personally speaking, was that he would be seen when he found a boat and rowed away. And those longboats, paddled by ten men each, could catch up with him before he got halfway across the rest of the lake.

Gritting his teeth in frustration, he went under the shadow of a tree growing out over the water. He sat down, careful not to touch shore.

All was not lost—not yet.

The boats headed for the dock, passing within thirty feet of him. Each held eleven men, ten paddlers and an officer at the steering-sweep. The moon shone on strained faces. Though fatigue could account for part of their expressions, fear, Hadon was sure, made the other part. King Minruth proclaimed Resu the chief deity now and Kho his subordinate. But Minruth's men had been conditioned from infancy to worship Her as the Creator and the Replenisher of all things. That this island was not sacred to Her made no difference. Karneth was Her daughter. Besides, they were preparing to attack in the name of Resu and so were attacking Her.

Hadon wondered if these men had been ordered to man the boats or if they were volunteers. It was one thing to chase the high priestess and another actually to lay hands on her. The commander, if he was wise, had probably asked for volunteers. There were always some men who put greed above religion, and there were also men who had secret doubts about the reality of the deities.

Hadon watched them put up their paddles and allow the boats to ground gently on the beach. Then they climbed out and drew the craft up.

The commander, a tall man whose helmet bore three parrot feathers, walked to a tree which grew at the top of a stone staircase. He crouched by it, looking out from behind it at the spectacle.

Hadon looked also—he could not restrain his curiosity—and his eyes bugged. In front of the three fires was a weaving, dancing, leaping crowd of naked women. They ranged in age from twelve to a withered, shuffling crone who had to be at least eighty. Their faces were contorted, expressing savagery and ecstasy; black spittle ran down from their chins to their breasts. Their hair was unbound, flying every which way. Sweat polished their bodies, and they made frantic clawing gestures. They whirled and pranced and swung back and forth and forward and backward.

The musicians were naked also, the same dark saliva covering their mouths and breasts. One played a tortoiseshell harp of seven strings of goat-gut; three blew on brass trumpets; six beat on drums; nine twirled bullroarers over their heads.

The wind carried an acrid odor, which he supposed came from the stuff they were chewing. Some said this was laurel leaf, though others claimed it was ivy. Still others guessed it was something else. No man knew; they just speculated about this in guarded talk when women were not present.

Whatever it was, it was supposed to drive them into an insane frenzy, to enable them to see Karneth herself. It was also said that it gave them the power to detect male spies.

Thirty feet from the largest fire, the central one, was a cage of wooden slats. Inside it crouched a frightened male leopard. This, Hadon assumed, was to be the sacrificial beast. In the old days, over five hundred years ago, a man would have been in the cage, imprisoned until time for him to be torn apart by the nails and teeth of the worshipers. It was said that human males were still victims of such rites in outlying areas. Though the practice had been outlawed, not many had been executed as punishment for its infraction. Male police were forbidden to enter the site of the alleged crime, and investigating priestesses were likely to be lenient.

Except for the night's activities, no male animals were kept on such islands. But tonight, a male beast had been brought in, and would be ripped apart. The leopard would surely kill and injure some women, but they would be fearless, not caring about what happened to them in their frenzy.

The ceremony was going to be interrupted, which was, in a way, regrettable. As long as he was guilty of watching anyway, Hadon would have liked to have seen just how the leopard handled himself. How many would the cat take with him?

Hadon had expected the troops to spread out then, at a signal from their commander, to charge in on the women. But the officer apparently had different thoughts. He was still watching, waiting for something.

Suddenly Hadon knew what it was. Of course! Awineth was not present! There was no reason to attack if she was not there.

Where was she? Probably somewhere in the wilderness, perhaps in the fishing village, perhaps still in the valley beyond the western range. Or she might have continued with the others in the eastern mountains, but this did not seem likely. They would have left tracks, and the soldiers would have followed them.

The officer left the tree and went back to the beach.

Hadon looked back at the fires and saw why the man had acted. Awineth was now standing in front of the central fire, screaming so loudly it carried above the music and the cries of the others.

She was a wild but beautiful figure of medium stature, her hair long and jet black. Her face was striking and bold, her eyes large and dark gray but looking black at this distance. Her skin was white as milk. Her breasts were large but shapely and bore scarlet-painted nipples; her thick pubic hair was dyed green in honor of Karneth. Sweat filmed her; black spittle covered her face and breasts and thighs. Blood stained her hands, which meant that she had been making a preliminary sacrifice in the temple, attended only by the most select of the priestesses. The victim would be a raven, if what Hadon had heard was true.

Behind her were the high priestesses of the island, a young woman, a middle-aged woman with many birthmarks and an ancient, white-haired, wrinkled woman, her breasts hanging almost to her navel. Blood smeared her mouth; she must have drunk from the neck of the beheaded bird. Yes, she was holding the head in one claw.

The music stilled, the voices dying away as everybody turned toward Awineth. She continued her screaming chant, but Hadon, though he could distinguish the syllables, did not understand a word of it. She must be speaking in the secret ritual language, which his friend Hinokly had said was actually the language spoken when the hero Gahete landed on the then uninhabited island of Khokarsa.

Hadon moved closer to the soldiers, keeping within the shadows of the trees, floating, pulling himself along with handfuls of mud and weeds. He stopped when he was about forty feet away from the nearest spearman.

"We'll move in in ranks of six, running," the commander was saying. "We'll seize Awineth, and then you, Tahesa, and your squad will search the temple for the child. I don't think she'll be in there. It's not customary, as far as I know, to permit girl-children here. But she may have been locked in a room so she couldn't witness the rites. These women will attack you, so defend yourselves.

"After we've grabbed Awineth, we'll proceed to the temple itself and form a ring at the entrance while Tahesa looks for the little girl. I give you two minutes, Tahesa; it's not a big place. Then we move back to the boats."

Hadon, his ear close to the water, heard the man nearest him mutter, "I don't like it, Komseth."

Komseth said, "I don't either, but what the hell, we are under Resu's protection, aren't we? And what can naked, unarmed women do against us? Besides, look at the reward. We can retire, get out of this chicken army."

"It's still sacrilege," the first speaker said.

"Quiet back there!" the commander said. "Tahesa, get those men's names. No, never mind, they'd just deny it anyway. No time for that."

The soldiers stood up and waited for the order to charge. Hadon looked at the women. Awineth, wailing a chant, was walking to the cage. The women formed a circle around her, blocking her and the cage from view. The commander said, "Good! They won't even see us until we're on them."

Awineth had stopped chanting. There was silence except for the growls of the leopard, then a scream from Awineth and the women closed in on it, shouting, yelling.

The commander roared "Follow me!" He leaped forward, the soldiers at his heels, between the two oaks framing the top of the steps.

Hadon waited until the last six men had gone up the steps. He rose and ran to the beach—no way to work for Awineth and Kho unless he stepped on the soil, mighty Kho and Karneth forgive him—and seized the prow of the nearest longboat. It slid into the water, where he pushed it to set it adrift.

He ran back to the second boat and repeated the procedure.

Behind were screams, yells and the roar of the leopard, but he had no time to stand and stare.

By the time he had the sixth longboat into the lake, he was panting. The bedlam on the isle was frightening, but he did not once look away from his work. There were six rowboats to launch after the longboats and one to climb into. He pushed and hauled and, after what seemed a long time, he was rowing a boat around the island. When he got to the other side, behind the temple, he beached the craft.

Then he sat down to rest for a moment. For all he knew, the soldiers might have Awineth and be hustling her back to the beach. He hoped not. The longer the capture took, the more time the boats had to drift away.

From the noises, the soldiers were not having an easy time of it. Nor could they expect to. The women numbered about eighty, priestesses and women from the village in the western lake. They would be inflamed at this desecration. Their lack of weapons would not stop them from attacking the men. Crazed with the drug, they would launch themselves without fear of death. The men, though fighting for their lives, would still be inhibited. They couldn't overcome a lifetime of conditioning. Not at first, anyway. When they found themselves seriously threatened, then they would.

He rose and strode around the temple on a walk of flat round stones. Near the front, he peered around. There was no semblance of order among the soldiers now. They were milling around in the crowd, each man battling for himself. At least twenty of them lay on the earth in front of the bonfires. About the same number of women were dead. As Hadon watched, three men went down, each attacked by two or three clawing, biting, kicking females. A woman, eyes glazed, rose from one of them, holding in one hand the soldier's torn-out genitals. A trooper thrust a spear into her back and then he went down, his knees bending under as a screaming fury tackled him. He tried to pull his short sword, but a big beefy woman grabbed his ears, yanked his head against the ground and fastened her teeth on his nose. Both rolled out of sight.

The big cat, blood dripping from its mouth, was trying to get out of the melee. He ran through the swirl, was half flattened when a struggling couple fell on him, rolled away, got to his paws and was confronted by a man with a sword; the leopard crouched, leaped and fastened his jaws on the man's throat. The cat whirled away, reared up and swiped once with his paw. A woman crumpled, her breasts torn.

The leopard spurted through the human whirlpool, dodging, weaving, and then found the walk leading to the beach. He disappeared through the archway of the oaks. Undoubtedly he would swim across the lake and into the forest.

Hadon ventured further around the curve of the building. Now he could see Awineth before the entrance, struggling with two soldiers. Arranged in a semicircle in front of her were the commander, helmetless, wielding his *tenu*, and five spearmen. They were hacking and thrusting at about twenty women. A woman seized a spear shaft and fell backward, jerking its holder forward. Two women grabbed him and the three spun into the crowd. Then Tahesa charged out of the doorway, two men following. Abeth was not with them.

Tahesa shouted at the commander, who partially turned to speak to him. A woman grabbed the commander's ankles and pulled his feet from under him. He fell hard on his back, striking his head on the limestone. Tahesa sliced the woman's skull open, but another woman grabbed his sword arm and he disappeared.

At that the other men lost all courage. They ran along the temple away from Hadon—he was glad of that—pursued by a howling, screeching mob.

Awineth leaned against the entrance, her mouth hanging open, her breasts rising and falling quickly.

Hadon glanced at the scene by the fires. The surviving soldiers were fleeing, throwing their weapons down, intent only on getting to the boats. Few of them made it to the oaks, and those who did would find themselves stranded. They would have to swim to get away, and it was doubtful that, burdened with leather cuirasses and helmets, they would elude the women.

Hadon ran quickly along the front of the temple to Awineth. She looked up when he stood before her, her face twisted and, screaming, she attacked him. This was not unexpected, since to her he would be merely another male intruder. Even if she recognized him, she might have attacked him. The last time he'd seen her, she had been very angry with him because he had stayed behind to protect Lalila. In fact, she had tried to knife Lalila.

His fist buried itself in her diaphragm. She bent forward, vomiting black liquid all over him, and collapsed in his arms. Throwing her over his shoulder, he ran as fast as he could to the rear of the temple. There was some activity behind it, but at the other side. Hadon got to the boat without being observed and placed Awineth on its deck. He pushed the boat out, climbed in and began rowing. Just before dawn, he pulled into the narrow river feeding into the lake. The vegetation closed around them, blocking them from the view of the soldiers who had stayed on the mainland. Awineth had awakened, but she was too sick to do anything but moan and stare at him. Some time later, she had recovered enough to curse him.

He hadn't expected gratitude.

7

About three hours later, the boat left the river and entered the western lake. This was three miles wide. Judging from its shape as seen from the mountain the day before, its length was six or seven miles. The oak forest circled it; beyond that, higher up, grew the pines.

The sun shone on the square green sails of a number of fishing craft of different sizes. Here and there were boats propelled by paddlers, hauling seines behind them.

Hadon made for the island about a mile away, though he paused several times to answer the questions of the fisherfolk. They were almost pure Khoklem stock, descendants of those who had first peopled the great island of Khokarsa. They were short, snub-nosed, thick-lipped and straight of hair. Their skins were darker than those of the city-dwellers, who were mixtures of Khoklem and the later arrivals, the Klemsaasa. The men wore round wide-brimmed straw hats and loincloths; the women, conical brimless straw hats and loincloths. The children wore nothing. All were painted on the forehead with a blue stylized horned fish.

Hadon had some trouble making himself understood, since they spoke a dialect. Their vocabulary was different and they still retained some click-consonants which had dropped out of standard Khokarsan over a thousand years ago.

Awineth took over then. She understood them much better, though not wholly, since their tongue resembled the ritual language of the priestesses. When they learned that she was Queen Awineth, the high priestess, they broke into an uproar. They had known she was at the Isle of Karneth because, on reaching the eastern lake, Awineth had sent the rest of the party on. Now, learning about the events of last night, the villagers were troubled. Several boats set off at once after Awineth ordered them to get their women off the island. They were to bring back the priestesses also, if they still lived and if they did not refuse to desert their posts.

Hadon and Awineth transferred to a seine boat, which took them to an island village, about a hundred feet wide and a half-mile long, dotted here and there with huts on the shore. The stockaded village was on the northern shore. Drums on their boat had notified the people of their coming, and so a crowd awaited them on the docks. This was mainly composed of children, men and some women too old to attend the rites.

In their front, smiling, were Hinokly, Kebiwabes, Paga and the child Abeth. Their smiles faded, though, when they could not find Lalila.

Hadon jumped to the platform of the dock and embraced each one. Abeth, beautiful, golden-haired, violet-eyed, threw herself into his arms and cried for her mother.

Hadon shouted to make himself heard above the gabble.

"Lalila is safe! I had to leave her in the southern pass! We'll go get her as soon as I've had some rest!"

Awineth climbed out, assisted by the chief, and she spoke rapidly to him. He turned and yelled until he had everybody's attention. He spoke quickly and fiercely, pointing to the east. A man ran into the largest building, a longhouse built of pine and oak, covered with the carved heads of beasts, birds, fish and spirits of the lake and forest. A minute later the man appeared on top of the hall and began beating on a large drum. Those boats still on the lake began to make their way toward the island.

Awineth summoned Hadon to her.

"The rest of the soldiers should be on their way here. They won't have boats, but they have axes, and they can build rafts. These people are peaceful; they know little of organized warfare. I think it best that we keep on going. The valley beyond the next valley is large and well populated with devout worshipers of Kho. In fact, there is a college of priestesses there, where we can be safe. The pass into the valley is trapped; it can be closed at any time. We would be safe for a long time, and I can conduct my campaign from there."

"Are you asking me or telling me?" Hadon said.

"I want your advice. After all, you are a soldier. And you would have been my husband...if Kho had not dictated otherwise."

"Are you up to continuing?" he said. "You've been awake all night and must be terribly tired after the flight and the strenuous rites. As for me, I am too exhausted to walk, let alone run."

"If I can do it, you can," she said scornfully. "Besides, I was thinking of getting just far enough away so we can hole up some place and sleep. We don't want to be on this island when they come."

"We can't try for the main pass," he said. "For all we know, soldiers may have been sent there to hold it. Do the fishermen know of any other passes, ones which strangers would not be aware of?"

"The headman has told me there is one. It is difficult but it can be traversed. Some of his men will guide us."

"Then I think the other tribesmen should follow us, trampling our tracks to confuse the soldiers. When we get to a place where we won't be leaving tracks, a rocky place, for instance, they will go in a different direction, leading our pursuers astray."

"That is the kind of advice I want," she said. She looked into his eyes for a moment, then said, "I need you, Hadon. I want you to lead us, to guard your Queen and the chief agent of great Kho. So if you are thinking of going back to get that yellow-haired savage, that bitch Lalila, forget it."

"She can't walk!" Hadon said. "You know that! She will starve!"

"It's too good a death for her," Awineth said.

Hearing this, seeing her smile of triumph and hate, Hadon felt himself sway. A shock ran through him and for a moment everything became dimly red.

"Would you dare?" Awineth shrilled. He became aware that he had raised his fist, that Awineth had stepped back.

He breathed in deeply and lowered his hand. His voice shook as he said, "This is not the order of a great ruler. To condemn a woman who has done you no harm…"

"No harm!" she shouted. "No harm! She stole your love from me; she bewitched you! She is indeed the Witch-from-the-Sea, Hadon! She took your senses away, she turned you into a traitor! And you know what happens to traitors, Hadon! And you are not just a traitor to the Queen, Hadon! You are a blasphemer, an infidel! To turn against the one who speaks for Kho is to turn against Kho Herself!"

"I have not betrayed you," he said. "I have fought for you, helped you escape from Minruth! Would you be free today if it were not for me? If I had not stayed to fight at that pass, would you be free?"

"You stayed because of Lalila, not because of me!" she yelled.

"I stayed for both of you," he said. "Even if she had been able to walk, I would have stayed!"

"Yes, so you could delay them long enough for *her* to escape!"

The chief said something to her. She turned and spoke rapidly. Then she said to Hadon, "He wants to know if you are friend or enemy. He said that you can be killed now if I so order."

Hadon forced back the words choking his throat. He said, "What are your orders?"

"That we leave at once."

She began speaking to the chief again. Hadon walked away and sat down on the stoop of the longhouse. Abeth, frightened at the angry talk, ran to him. He put her on his knee and held her. She wept again. His three friends surrounded him.

Paga, the manling, spoke first.

"Do you really intend to leave Lalila there? To die?"

Hadon looked up. In a low voice, he said, "You are all my friends. I know you won't betray me. No, I do not intend to desert her. But now I must pretend to obey Awineth. If I do not, she will have me killed. When we get to the forest, I will leave at the first chance. But it is a hard thing to do, friends. It brings problems. How can I rejoin you if I have disobeyed Awineth and if I bring Lalila back with me? Awineth is capable of having both of us killed.

"So what do I do then? If Lalila and I do not rejoin you, she will never see Abeth again. She could not endure that; she has had sorrow enough."

Paga said, "First get Lalila. Then think of how to get Abeth away from Awineth. But do not forget that I want to be with Lalila and her daughter. I, too, would grieve if anything were to happen to either of them. But I would make sure that Awineth did not live. She would have little time to enjoy her revenge."

Kebiwabes and Hinokly were shocked. Though they did not love Awineth, they held her in great reverence. It was blasphemy to even think about harming the highest priestess.

Kebiwabes said, "There must be a way. You are too tired to think clearly now, Hadon. Once you have rested, you will find a way. It need not involve the killing of Awineth."

"Paga said that, not I," Hadon said. "Though, come to think of it..."

He fell silent. No use upsetting his friends even more.

Paga said, "When you leave, take Abeth and me along. Then you will not have to come back."

"Your legs are too short, Paga. And the child would also hinder me. I must get to Lalila as quickly as possible. She doesn't have much water or food, and there are leopards and hyenas against which she would be helpless."

"Take us with you for some distance then. Leave us where we will be hidden from Minruth's and Awineth's people alike. Then come back with Lalila."

"And where would you go then?" Hinokly asked.

"Far away."

"And spend the rest of your life running and hiding?"

"What else have Lalila, the child and I been doing for years?" Paga said angrily. "What is the great and glorious Queen of the mighty Empire of Khokarsa doing now? She is running and hiding. But I do not plan to live the rest of my days like a hare. No, I know of a place where we could go and be far from Minruth and Awineth and all the other plagues that make this *civilized* nation a pesthole."

Paga glared and looked around him. Hadon studied him. Though the manling stood no higher than Hadon's solar plexus, though he was a savage from the icy lands beyond the Ringing Sea, he was highly intelligent and resourceful. He was perhaps the shrewdest and most perceptive of the group.

He had a large head topped by a tangled mass of brown, gray-threaded hair. His shoulders were as broad as Hadon's; his arms were thickly muscled and long. His torso was thick, long and potbellied. If only his legs were not so short, he would have made an impressive figure of a man. A frightening one, perhaps. One eye was filmed, milky and ringed with thick scar tissue. His wild bushy beard fell almost to his scarred belly button. When he opened his mouth, he exposed extraordinarily thick teeth, beast-like.

His mother had cast him into the wild shortly after he was born. Something about him repelled her, though it may have been that she was sick, or that she had an ominous dream about him. In any event, he was hurled against a stone and he lost one eye when he struck it. His mother walked away and his father, though he searched for him, could not find him.

Paga claimed that he would have died, but a wolf-bitch had found him and brought him to her den. Instead of eating him, she had raised him with her cubs.

Hadon did not know if this was true, though he could see no reason for Paga to lie. There were stories throughout Khokarsa of babies who had been taken in by female beasts: bears, hyenas, wild dogs, lions. He had never met any of these—they were always in the far distant past or in a far-off land.

Whatever the truth of the story, Paga had been accepted back into his native tribe. There he had met Wi, who became his only friend. Paga had made an ax for Wi from a fallen star, a massive lump of nickel-iron. Wi had used the ax to kill a giant who had tyrannized over the tribe.

Paga had another friend too, Lalila. She had been found in a cave by Wi, who had taken her into his home, though he had a mate and a child. The women did not like her; they claimed that she was a witch from the sea and so should be put to death. She brought misfortune and evil with her.

Paga had hated all women because of what his mother had done to him. Lalila, however, treated him kindly and so won his love. He was ready to die for her, to die if she went out of his life.

Later, the glacier near the village of Wi had moved in and forced the people to flee. Lalila had been separated from Wi, but she swam through the icy cold waters to the iceberg on which Wi and Paga were stranded. Though this melted as it floated south, the three managed to get to land. From the shore they walked far inland to Lalila's native village. It was deserted; the inhabitants had died of plague or fled enemies.

There Lalila's child by Wi was born. Near there Wi was slain defending his woman and child, swinging his great ax until he had corpses piled up before him. All seemed lost then, but a stranger appeared, armed with a bow and arrow. He killed the savages and took the three under his protection. Lalila had then become with child by him, but she had a miscarriage.

The stranger took them south and, after much wandering, they were south of the Ringing Sea. They met the expedition of which Hinokly was a member. The Khokarsans thought the stranger was Sahhindar, the exiled god of bronze, plants and time, Resu's younger brother. Sahhindar, using his authority as the supposed god, ordered this expedition to take the three back to Khokarsa. He ordered that they be treated well since he would some day come to Khokarsa to make sure of their well-being.

So far the god Sahhindar had not reappeared, but deities often did not show themselves in their true persons, instead manifesting themselves in disguise.

"All right, Paga," Hadon said. "Where is this place?"

"The place you often spoke of when we were roaming the savannas," Paga said. "A place far to the south, at the extreme of the Southern Sea, up in the mountains. Your native city, Hadon. Opar."

8

Kebiwabes woke him with rough shakes on his shoulder. He lay for a moment without moving or speaking until the bard whispered fiercely, "Hadon, it's time! Hadon, for the sake of Kho, wake up!"

The sky was black, clouded with the promise of more rain. He turned his head and saw that the campfire had almost died out. A man, wrapped in a blanket, sat by it, his head bent low. Snores issued from him.

The others lay under the pines, blanketed, silent. No. There were some missing. Hinokly, Paga, Abeth.

"They are behind a tree," Kebiwabes said. "We let you sleep until we had everything packed. You need all the rest you can get."

Hadon got up and quickly bundled his blanket around his pack. Making sure that he had his weapons—he was so sleepy he wasn't thinking straight yet—he stumbled after the little bard. The three were waiting for him under the tree, as Kebiwabes had said. Hinokly held the child in his arms, but she was awake. Her eyes were huge holes in a dim whiteness. Before they walked softly and slowly away, he turned for one last look. Awineth was a dark shape under a tree, surrounded by four villagers. The sentinel and two more made seven. All of them were hunters, not fishermen, skilled in providing meat from the forest for the village, familiar with the mountains. They would be good trackers. Hadon, however, was betting that Awineth would not waste time sending them after him. She would rant and rave for a while and talk of what she would do to him when he was caught. But she would know that she was in danger as long as she stayed in this valley.

Though he would be handicapped by them, he had decided to take his friends and the child along. He could not take the chance that Awineth, in her rage, might kill them all. For all he knew, she might be planning on doing just that anyway. Once she had used them to assist her on the perilous way to the stronghold, she could get rid of them. She hated Hadon; Abeth was the child of the woman she hated most, so she would be murdered. And Awineth would take satisfaction in having disposed of Hadon's friends, who had witnessed her humiliation.

They moved along softly in the darkness, bumping into trees or bushes now and then. The trail they had followed up was narrow and winding, felt more than seen. Two hours later, they were partway down the slope. The sun rose and they went more swiftly. At noon they stopped to eat the food in their packs.

Hadon said, "We can't cut straight across the valley. We'll have to go around the edges, up on the slope. From this point, we leave the trail. The underbrush will slow us down even more."

Having eaten, he climbed a tall pine. He was near the top when he saw smoke rising from the lake. He looked around the entire valley carefully, then descended.

"The village is on fire. The soldiers must have taken it."

"And probably slaughtered the fishermen," Kebiwabes said.

"If so, that will mean fewer men will be out hunting for us," Paga said cheerfully. "Those fisherfolk may be peaceful, but they would have fought."

"We are in another Time of Troubles," Hinokly the scribe said. "There will be thousands of such fires before this is over. Minruth will not find it easy to force the people of Kho to admit that She is inferior to Resu. Besides, there are many cities which would like to be independent. They will seize this opportunity to do so."

"Let us hope that She does not get disgusted with us all and destroy the world," Kebiwabes said. "She did that once, long ago, before the Khoklem came to the Kemu. She was softhearted, however, and spared one man and a woman. She may not be so merciful the next time."

"Was it a flood that drowned all but one couple?" Paga asked.

"Yes, how did you know?" the bard said.

"My tribe had a similar story," Paga said. "Only it was not Kho but our god, the Sleeper, who sent the waters to rid the earth of the pernicious race. He too allowed one couple to live. The man built a huge raft and put on it all of the animals of the earth. Some raft, when you consider how many beasts, birds and insects there are! I have seen enough to crowd a raft as big as this mountain if it were flattened out—even if only two of each kind were on it. And I know there must be many more kinds of creatures than I have seen. It would take a raft six times the size of this mountain just to hold them. And a raft twenty times that big to hold the food needed to feed them until the waters subsided.

"And then what? Would not the trees and the grasses be drowned? What would grow for the plant-eaters to eat? And would not the meat-eaters destroy them before they starved?

"For that matter, where did the waters come from? And where did they go?"

Hinokly smiled. Kebiwabes and Hadon were shocked. Then Kebiwabes said, "All things are possible to Kho."

"According to my people it was not Kho but the Sleeper who sent the flood. Does your deity look like an elephant, a hairy elephant, and sleep in a vast block of ice?"

"Kho takes many forms," Kebiwabes said.

"I think the Sleeper was an elephant, bigger and hairier than your southern beast," Paga said. "It fell to its death into the ice and so was kept from decaying. And the ice moved slowly down a valley and out into the sea, carrying this dead beast. And my tribe, the ignorant fools, took it to be a god."[2]

"You think, then, that the priests and priestesses are lying to us?" Hadon said.

"First they lied to themselves."

Hinokly said, "It would be wise, Paga, not to voice those thoughts. The priestesses are tolerant. They do not mind non-Khokarsans worshiping others than Kho. They say that these really do worship Her because Kho is everywhere and is, in fact, every deity. The minor deities are only Her varying manifestations. But the godless are exiled; if they try to reenter the land they are killed.

"The priests of Resu maintain that all who do not worship Kho and Resu should be slain. So far their views have not become law, but if Minruth wins he will impose the will of the priests on the people."

There was silence for a long while as they followed a new trail. They went down the slope of the western range, heading for the southwest corner of the valley. Once they stopped as they heard the pig-like grunting of bears somewhere near. Hadon went ahead, spotted a female and her two cubs in a hollow and gestured to the others to follow him. The mother, a large reddish brown fat beast, stood up on her hind legs to sniff the air. She dropped down after a moment and went back to eating berries.

At dusk they were in the oak forest. A fire was too likely to be seen, so they ate a cold meal. Hadon found enough large flat branches among three trees for them to lie on, and they tied themselves to them for a night's sleep. It was broken occasionally by the cough of a leopard, the grunting of a herd of pigs, the scream of an animal caught by a predator, the uproar of a pack of disturbed monkeys. They rose at dawn, ate a hurried breakfast and traveled under the mighty branches. Their progress was swifter now because of the relative scarcity of underbrush. On the other hand, they were more exposed to view.

At the end of half a mile, Hadon stopped, his hand held up. The others halted behind him.

"What is it?" Kebiwabes said in a low voice.

"Men. Coming this way. Get down in that hollow behind that tree."

As they crowded together, Paga said, "Do they have dogs?"

Hadon said, "No, I don't think so. We'd hear them. Abeth, do not say anything no matter what happens. Hinokly, if she opens her mouth, put your hand over it."

"I won't say anything," Abeth said, "I'm not scared." But her pale skin and wide eyes showed that she was just trying to be brave.

"Get down," Hadon said. "Lie absolutely quiet until they have passed."

He pressed into the earth, his ear against the ground. The bard's body, close against him, trembled. Paga, on the other side, was as steady as a rock. Presently the thud of footsteps came faintly through the earth. The men were passing only ten feet from them. They were silent, moving at a swift walk. The odor of long-unwashed

2 The full story is told in H. Rider Haggard's *Allan and the Ice-Gods.*

bodies drifted to his nose. Someone spit loudly and was shushed. Hadon wondered who they were. The two men he'd seen in the lead were unarmored and carried large packs. They certainly were not soldiers.

Then he remembered the men he'd seen in the valley from the ledge on which he'd left Lalila.

But if they were traders, as he guessed, why were they sneaking through the forest? Why so far from the village? Was it because they had witnessed its destruction? No, they wouldn't be this far off the track. They would either have returned to the lowlands or gone through the next pass to the valley beyond.

Could they be volunteers for the army of Awineth? Had word passed down from the priestesses of Kho to gather in the mountains at the temple two valleys away?

It did not seem likely. Not unless there were long-range plans for just such a situation, calling for the temple to be Awineth's headquarters.

His guess was that these men were outlaws who had taken their loot down to the coast to sell. They had found civil war and, since there were too many soldiers around, they had turned tail.

Or perhaps these were criminals of the city of Khokarsa who had found the lowlands too hot for them and had decided to take refuge in the mountains—after they'd picked up some loot to bring with them.

The last of the band passed by. Hadon warned the others to keep still. He crawled out of the hollow and looked around the trunk. At least ten were still visible; the others had passed around the corner of the trail. The first two were carrying a crude pole stretcher.

On it lay a woman. A shaft of sunlight fell on long golden hair.

"Lalila!"

9

"What did you say?" Paga whispered from below.

Hadon turned a pale face, but he said nothing. Not until the last man had gone around the corner did he speak to them.

"Abeth, don't cry out. Promise?"

She shook her head, Khokarsan for yes. He said, "Maybe you'd better hold her mouth anyway, Hinokly. They have Lalila!"

The scribe was just in time to stop the child from crying out. She struggled against him, then suddenly stopped and began weeping.

The others came out of the hole. Paga growled, "Who are they? What would they want with her?"

"What would any men want with her?" the bard said. "Though I may be doing them an injustice."

"The only thing we can do right now is follow them," Hadon said. "They may be all right. But if I show myself to them, I might find out that they are evil. And then it would be too late. There must be at least thirty-five of them, if they're the same fellows I counted two days ago. Far too many for us to handle if they're hostile."

Abeth got on Hinokly's back and Paga carried the scribe's pack. The five set out with Hadon about fifty yards in the lead. He kept the back of the last man in view, staying far enough behind and off to one side so that if the rearguard should look back, he would not be seen. After a while, he had left his companions way behind. The burdened scribe and the short-legged manling could not match his pace, and Kebiwabes had been ordered to stay with them.

After an hour, the caravan stopped to rest. Lalila sat up then and accepted a drink of water from a clay jug. She was pale, gaunt and stony-faced. A tall skinny man, heavily bearded, said something to her. She turned her face away while he and his fellows grinned. But they did not laugh. Apparently they had orders to keep the noise down.

Several conferred with the tall man, most likely the leader, then fresh carriers lifted the stretcher and they renewed the march. By then the others had caught up with Hadon.

"I don't think they're friendly," Hadon said. "Lalila doesn't seem to be at ease. They must be outlaws."

The party now cut across the forest to the west, leaving the marked trail. Hadon had no trouble following them, though they were not in sight. After half a mile of increasingly thick undergrowth, he came to another path. This was a hidden trail, starting abruptly from an oak, apparently not used very often. A person not skilled in detecting marks might not have noticed it.

He did not know whether to continue on it or go back to his group. Deciding that Paga was woodsman enough to see the turnoff, he went on.

After a quarter of a mile, the outlaws again stopped to rest. Hadon went back on the trail to make sure that his band had not missed it. Seeing them just coming out from the woods, he gestured for them to follow his tracks.

The oaks thinned out, pines replacing them. The trail zigzagged back and forth on ever-rougher and steeper ground. He topped a promontory and was looking down into a little bowl-shaped valley. Beyond it, the mountain continued another five hundred feet. Several hundred feet below the apex was an opening in rock, obviously a cave. Several men sat before it, sharpening iron swords. Seeing this, he knew that they were criminals, though he had by then convinced himself they could be nothing else. Some of their swords were those of the *numatenu*, which meant they had stolen them or killed their owners.

Goats browsed in the little valley. Five men sprawled near them, drinking from a goatskin bag under a tree. These jumped up as the caravan filed out from the pines. They ran grinning and shouting toward them.

Hadon lay down to watch. Lalila was carried toward the cave while the men at its mouth entered it. They soon emerged, followed by a dozen more. Lalila was taken into the cave. Her stretcher-bearers came out quickly to join in the drinking and talking. Everybody seemed to be very happy, judging from their laughter.

Paga and the others joined him. Kebiwabes said, "They must not get a chance to have a woman often. Yet they aren't raping her. Why not? The gang that brought her here may have done it already, but those others...they wouldn't wait."

"Lalila is easily identifiable," Hadon said. "Minruth must have put out the word that he wants her and will give a large reward for her capture—unharmed. What I don't understand is why they didn't take her back to Khokarsa."

Paga hissed with excitement and grabbed Hadon's wrist. He pointed with his other hand. "There's the reason!"

Hadon followed the direction of his finger. A woman had stepped out of the cave into the sunshine. She stood as if reveling in the heat and light. The tall skinny man shouted at her. Two men hurried toward her and she stepped back into the darkness.

"Awineth!" Hadon said.

10

It was not difficult to imagine what had happened. Part of the outlaw band had been returning from the next valley and had intercepted Awineth's party as they came through the pass. Her guides had probably been killed, as they were worthless for ransom purposes. She would have announced her identity, hoping that this might cow them into releasing her. She had probably promised them a big sum if they conducted her to the temple.

Instead they had brought her back here to get their chief's decision on her disposal. He, realizing what a treasure he had, would take her back to the city. There he and his fellows would be pardoned and would become rich citizens. Their cave now held a double prize.

"Who said crime doesn't pay?" Hinokly snarled.

"They'll rest tonight," Hadon said. "Then their leader will send messengers to the capital to notify Minruth that they have the two women. They'll negotiate for all they can get, then they'll arrange to bring the women in. That's why they brought Lalila here. And why they haven't raped her. The King wouldn't want the spoiled meat of filthy outlaws."

"Then we have time to do something," Paga said. "How many men are there?"

"About fifty-five," Hadon said. "But they won't all be around at the same time. A gang that size eats a lot of food. They'll have to send out a number of hunters. We'll just lie low here until nightfall."

Shortly after dusk the men, all drunk, retired into the cave. Two of them piled a great heap of brush over the opening and went through a passageway left in it. They reached out with hooks and dragged in more brush to conceal even that. The covering was thick, but not enough to hide all the light from a fire inside the cave.

"There must be another opening somewhere in there," Hadon said. "Otherwise there'd be no ventilation."

He left after a brief argument with Paga, who wanted to accompany him. He went slowly down the slope and skirted the grove where the goats were kept. They bleated at him. He paid them no attention, knowing that the noise the outlaws were making would drown out the beasts. He made for the side of the cave and climbed up on top of the projection. His nose led him to the smoke issuing from a vent, a natural crack in the rock.

Upwind of it, he placed his ear close to it and was gratified when he was able to distinguish some voices. These were from speakers who stood near the fire. Other voices were mumbles or slurs, though advanced drunkenness could account for the latter. He got the impression that the cave was large, extending deep into the mountain. It had to be to hold so many comfortably.

What seemed hours passed while he tried to eavesdrop. There was so much shouting and singing now that he could not even clearly hear the conversation of those who stood almost directly below the vent. Suddenly all voices but one were stilled. That, he presumed from the words, was the chief's.

"Yes, by Kho, I will have her and only I! I haven't had a woman for three weeks! The last was that stinking fat fisherwoman I caught in the forest and I smelled of fish for a week afterward!"

"You still do!" someone shouted. Laughter bellowed, then died.

"You have heard what the Queen said. The King isn't concerned about her chastity. All he wants is a healthy body he can torture. He isn't going to make her his concubine; he could care less. Ain't that right, Your Majesty?"

"That is right," Awineth's voice came faintly.

"So, if Her Majesty don't care, and His Majesty don't either, why can't I have her?"

"Damn it," a man said, "if you can have her, then why can't we all?"

"You can...tomorrow! Tonight she's all mine! By the breasts of Adeneth, look at her! Have you ever seen such a beauty? What'll she look like when you horny goats get through with her? She'll be ruined! No, she's mine first...all night, haw, haw!"

"What're we supposed to do?" the same protester asked. "Play with ourselves while you're thumping her? What the hell, Tenlem, what kind of share-one-share-all is this? You promised..."

"Shut up, Seqo!" Tenlem roared. "Shut up or I'll slit your throat! What I say goes! You all agreed to that! So I say I'm taking this woman out and enjoying myself! I'm entitled! If it wasn't for me, you'd all be hanging upside down in some marketplace bleeding to death from your severed genitals! How many times have I saved you dullwits? How many times have I scouted a fat prospect for you and arranged it so we could take it with only the loss of a few! How many times, I say!"

"Go ahead!" Seqo yelled. "But while you're out there, cheating us out of our rightful enjoyment—share-one-share-all, you said, you liar—maybe we'll be enjoying ourselves with this here woman!"

Silence again. Then a roar, a clash of metal and a scream.

Tenlem, panting a little, spoke loudly. "Any more of you want to die? If so, speak up now!"

Awineth said something, but she was too far away for Hadon to make out her words.

"No, Your Majesty, they won't touch you! They're not going to throw away a hundred thousand *nasuhno* and their pardons! They're drunk as swine, but they won't touch you!"

Awineth's words, now louder, became clear.

"If they should even try, Kho would blast them!"

"Yeah! Kho would hit them with lightning, haw, haw! Your father don't seem to be bothered about Her anger! He ain't been struck with lightning, has he? Come on, violet-eyes! I'm going to show you what a real man is!"

Hadon felt a storm of passion, an almost overwhelming desire to attack Tenlem as he came out of the cave. But he gripped the rock and held on to it and his feelings, trembling. Mingled with his kill-lust was hatred for Awineth. She had urged the chief to assault Lalila, not to save herself, but to get revenge.

Panting, he crawled from the vent to the edge of the rock just above the entrance. He flattened out as a torch flared below him. Two men were carrying Lalila out. Tenlem was holding the torch, walking in front of them. Lalila was not struggling; she lay limp as if she had fainted. He did not think she had; she was too tough for that.

When the party was halfway down the slope, headed for the grove, Hadon slid off the rounded wall of the cave. He walked swiftly through the darkness, lit faintly by the distant torch. It would not do to stumble over something and make a noise.

Instead of following them directly, he curved to the left. The goats were moving back and forth at the ends of their long tethers, bleating. The men would attribute the uneasiness of the animals to their own presence.

He stepped behind a tree. Tenlem had driven the point of the torch into the earth. Now he was sticking the point of his dagger into the ground beside the torch. Evidently, he was making sure that Lalila would be some distance from the weapon. He removed his kilt and loincloth and stood looking down at her.

She lay on her back, naked, unmoving, silent.

The two men stood by the torch and grinned at Tenlem.

Tenlem turned his head and roared, "Get back to the cave, you two hyenas!"

"Aw, come on!" one of them said. "At least let us watch!"

"Ain't you guys got any decency?" Tenlem said and he bellowed laughter. "Get back to the cave. And be sure to pile the brush back over the entrance. You want them soldiers to see the light?"

They turned away reluctantly. "Get going!" Tenlem said. He let himself down on Lalila. She erupted, grabbing his nose with one hand and his genitals with the other. He yelled with pain, and the others wheeled back. Tenlem struck her hard on the side of her face with his open hand. Her hands fell away while Tenlem yelled at her, "You want me to soften you up first? Or do you want to make me happy?"

Lalila did not reply. The others walked about forty feet away and hid behind a tree. They giggled and poked each other in the ribs.

Hadon ran out, circling widely, and came up behind them out of the dark. He brought the edge of his sword from the left against the neck of the man on his left, whirled and cut from the right into the other man's neck. Their necks half severed, they fell.

Hadon stepped out from behind the tree. Tenlem, still shouting, was half crouched above Lalila. His hands gripped her shoulders, pinning her to the ground. She writhed soundlessly while he yelled at her to keep struggling since it made him even more excited. Suddenly the yell ascended into a scream. Lalila had brought her knee up hard between his legs.

Tenlem rolled away, doubled up, holding himself again. Lalila got to all fours, her face distorted with the pain from her ankle and with rage. She scuttled toward the dagger standing upright by the torch. Tenlem did not see her; he was too concerned with his own pain. She grabbed both the weapon and the torch and, holding one in each hand, scrambled back to the outlaw.

Hadon moved slowly toward them, his sword held ready.

Tenlem saw her then and somehow got to his knees, facing her. He yelled at her to drop the dagger or he would tear her to pieces. Ignoring him, she continued to crawl until she was several feet from him. She got to her knees and thrust the flaming end of the torch at him as he started to get to his feet. It drove into his mouth and, squalling with agony, holding his face now, he went backward.

Lalila got down on all fours again and went after him. Tenlem called to the two men for help. Lalila got to her knees once more and stopped his cry with the end of the torch in his mouth. He rolled over and over, screaming, toward her. When he rammed into her, he almost knocked her over. She struck him on the head with the torch, then she drove the dagger to the hilt between his ribs.

Hadon ran up to her. Tenlem was on his side, jerking, his eyes glazing.

She sat up, staring at him, her mouth working. He knelt down and took her in his arms, and both wept. Finally she said, "How did you…? Never mind. You're here! Where are the others? Where's Abeth?"

"Nearby," he said. "Listen, I'm going to leave you here for a few minutes. I will bring them down here. We can't run; we can't go fast enough because of your ankle."

"It's better now," she said. "But I still can't walk very far."

"I know. So we have to keep them from following us."

"How can you do that? There are so many."

"Never mind. I'll be back."

It took twenty minutes for the round trip. Abeth ran crying to her mother. Paga stroked the top of Lalila's head, Hinokly and Kebiwabes smiled, though tightly. Hadon had told them on the way back what they must do.

Leaving the child and Lalila in the grove, the men climbed the slope to the cave. Hadon carried the torch. At the entrance, he handed it to Kebiwabes. "Don't set the brush on fire until we have blocked this completely."

"But what about Awineth?" the bard said. "She'll die too."

"I can't figure out a way to get her out!" Hadon said, snarling. "Besides, the bitch should die!"

"She is the Queen!" the bard said. "And the highest priestess of Kho! The Goddess will not take this lightly! Also, if she dies, who will be the rallying point for Her against Minruth?"

"If it's at all possible, I'll get her out of there," Hadon said. "But the others die!"

They went to work with Paga's ax and the swords taken from the two Hadon had killed. Though their chopping was loud, the noise would not penetrate into the cave. The brush already piled outside it helped deaden the sound. The walls were thick too, and the mob within was creating a bedlam. In an hour a huge mound of brush was over the opening. Another pile lay by it in reserve. Much of the vegetation was green, but interspersed in it were dry sticks and branches.

The lack of ventilation presently sent the smoke swirling out from the fire inside the cave. Hadon heard several men approaching down the short corridor which formed the entrance to the large chambers. He snatched the torch from the bard and ignited a number of dry sticks and leaves. There was a shout from within and men started to tear at the barricade.

Hadon waited. If any did burst through, they would be blinded for a moment, helpless against his sword and the weapons of the others.

This did not happen. The dry wood caught quickly; the green, less quickly, but emitting choking fumes.

As the blaze increased, screams and shouts came from inside. Smoke poured out of the vent. Apparently no one had yet thought of stopping it up and so cutting off the draft. Hadon hoped that by the time they did, they would be too overcome to do anything about it.

Men lunged at the brush, trying to bull through. The flames drove them away for a moment. In a few seconds, some of the more hysterical were back, tearing at the barricade with their bare hands, screaming as they were burned, begging for mercy. The fire became a roaring blast and the men retreated. Their coughing mingled with the crackle and whoosh of the flames.

Hadon went up to the vent. He could not look down through it because of the smoke, but he placed his ear close to the edge. He could hear violent racking coughs and a sound as if stones were being thrust up the hole. He rose and drove his spear down it. It hit something solid; someone screamed. He drew the bloodied point out.

Hinokly climbed up to him. The light from the fire at the entrance showed a strained face.

"I understand your hatred of Awineth," he said. "And I would agree with what you are doing—if she were not the Queen. But she is. For the sake of our land, for its people, you should not kill her."

"I have been thinking of that too," Hadon said. "It may be too late now, though. However, we'll see what we can do. I hope we won't regret it."

Paga objected violently. The others told him that he was not native-born; he did not understand how deeply they felt about their Queen, high priestess and chief goddess.

"If you do save her, you'll get no gratitude," Paga said.

"Perhaps not," Hadon said, beginning to knock away the burned and burning branches. It was hot work. By the time they had dragged everything out with the points of their swords and spears, they were blistered, burned and coughing. They stood back for a minute to let the smoke thin out, drinking water from their clay canteens and pouring it over their heads. No sounds came from the cave. They ran in, trying to breathe as little as possible. The torches stuck into the holes in the rock walls were out, their oxygen cut off by the smoke. The fire below the vent was still smoldering. Bodies lay on the floor of the first chamber. The light from Hadon's torch showed him more bodies in the second room. The third was jammed with people who had fled into it because the smoke was less dense here. All were either dead or unconscious. Awineth was leaning against the back wall. She was slumped forward but kept from falling by a man lying across her legs.

Hadon felt the pulse along her neck. "She's still alive." He coughed, then said, "I'll take her outside. Paga, Hinokly, see if anyone else is alive. If they are, kill them."

"Here's one," Paga said. He brought his ax down on the man's skull. "Ah!"

"I found another," the scribe said. He drove his spear into a throat.

Hadon picked up the woman and, coughing, carried her into the open. The three men came out a moment later. The manling said, "One of them sat up. So maybe she is not too near death."

Awineth began coughing. Her eyes opened and she stared at them from a blackened face.

"You'll be all right after a while," Hadon said. He knelt, propped her up and poured water into her mouth. She coughed it out, but he persisted and finally she was able to swallow some. In a hoarse voice, she said, "You came after me?"

"Obviously," he said. "Lie down and rest now."

A long time later, she said, "What happened to your woman?"

"She's all right."

He told her what had happened. A strange expression passed over her. Whether it was disappointment or remorse, he could not tell. He doubted that it was the latter.

Crouching down by her, speaking softly so the others would not hear, he said, "Listen carefully, Awineth. You owe your life to me and me only. If I had gone away, leaving you in the hands of those men, you would have been given to your father. If I had just let the fire keep on burning, you would be dead.

"You owe me the greatest debt possible. You can repay it by giving me your word that you will not harm any of us from this time on."

"My lungs burn," she said. Then, after a silence during which her face twisted with hard thoughts, "And what if I do not give my word?"

"I won't kill you, though I should. We will leave you here. You can make your own way to the temple. But the soldiers are looking for you now and there will be more, many more, joining them. You can bet on that. Perhaps Kebiwabes and Hinokly will stay with you. I don't know; they have little love for you as a person, though much for you as the Queen. Perhaps they might get you through. Neither, however, is a woodsman or a good swordsman."

"You and that woman have hurt me very much," she said.

"Not intentionally. The good I've done far outweighs any involuntary injury to you. Also, you will need every warrior you can get for your struggle with Minruth. I am well-known, since I'm the winner of the Great Games. And I have proved my worth as a warrior. Men will be proud to serve under me, serving you."

She stared at him for a while, chewing her lip.

"Very well. I will give my word."

"You will swear by Kho Herself?"

"I will. I do. But it would please me, if after this is over, you would go to Opar and take that bitch and her cub, and that one-eyed manling, with you. I do not like the sight of any of you. I can, however, endure it until we have won."

"I want your word, not your love," Hadon said.

11

The valley at Kloepeth was twenty miles long and fifteen miles wide. Unlike those between it and the Gulf of Gahete, it was heavily populated. It held a large lake and a river and many farms. Its people were relatively more sophisticated too, since it had access at the northwest end to the sea. A pass there led down to the Kemu, and a road had been built to a port there, Notamimkhu. The sea-end of the pass was so strongly fortified, however, that no army could hope to invade through it.

The southern pass was narrow, mountains bulging on both sides of it. Long ago, the priestesses had had a defense system built above the trail.

A month after Hadon and his group entered through it, the pass was closed. An army of two thousand men had attempted to march through it; a thousand got away alive. The avalanches, triggered by the men of Kloepeth, buried the others.

It was a heavy blow to Minruth, who could ill afford the loss. Though his armies had retaken Mineqo and Asema, and Awamuka was on the verge of surrendering, Dythbeth still held out. Qoqada had been bypassed, an army left around it to starve the citizens out. But Kunesu, Oliwa and Saqaba had won a battle against the Sixth Army, its survivors running back to Asema.

Still, Minruth had devastated a hundred villages and lesser cities, burning them out and slaughtering their citizens. Thousands of refugees had crowded into the rebellious cities, straining their facilities and food supplies. Disease had broken out in these areas, sending thousands down to the dark house of dread Sisisken.

Most important at the moment, the King's navy held the sea around the island of Khokarsa. In two pitched battles, it had sunk the fleet of Dythbeth and the combined fleet of the three cities of the southeast.

The people of the capital had moved back in when it seemed that the volcano, Khowot, had subsided. They began the work of rebuilding the houses destroyed by the rock bombs and the lava flow. The shipyards were constructing a fleet of thirty triremes, sixty biremes and several hundred smaller craft. Men were being trained to sail these. The demand for labor was so high that Minruth had stopped the building on the Great Tower. It was said that he had flown into a rage when notified that he would have to do this, and he had cut out the tongue of the officer who gave him the news.

Awineth had established her headquarters in the temple at Kloepeth. She was busy night and day, reading the letters sent her through the secret postal system of the priestesses, interviewing spies from all over. These came to her in a steady stream, though Minruth's ships had set up a blockade of Notamimkhu. The fleet had tried to run the Scylla and Charybdis of the cliffs leading in to the port. After three ships had been burned by giant, oil-soaked flaming missiles shot by catapults high above, the fleet had turned tail.

Word came that Kwasin, Hadon's cousin, had escaped to the city of Dythbeth. And he was now its king!

Awineth had called him and told him the news. Hadon said, "How could he do that?"

"King Roteka was killed while fighting on the walls. His wife Weth married Kwasin the next day."

"Knowing him, I'm not surprised," Hadon said. "Well, his being there will hearten the Dythbethans. Whatever else he is, he is a mighty warrior. Like a hero of old."

"When giants walked the earth," Awineth said sarcastically. She addressed the general of the Ninth Army, located in Kunesu. He had arrived a week before to report to her.

"Keruphe, what do you think of that? Would it be better for me to go to Dythbeth or to your city?"

The general, a short, bald-headed, bull-like man of ruddy complexion, frowned with thought. "The southeast area is well entrenched and in no immediate danger. Minruth knows this, so he is concentrating on Dythbeth, which has always been a hotbed of sedition. He is intent on conquering it before he moves on to the next biggest threat. In fact, he has sworn to kill every creature in it, man, woman and child, dog, cat and mouse. My intelligence tells me that for that purpose he has pulled out two armies, one from Minanlu and one from Qoqada.

"Though Dythbeth is in grave danger, it is not a hopeless case. If you were there to hearten the people with Kwasin leading the defense, Dythbeth might hold out. Kwasin is a legend, you know, everybody has heard of his exploits.

"While Minruth is engaged at Dythbeth, our armies could break through the light forces holding Mineqo. From there we could attack Asema. If we could take that, we would control the entrance to the Gulf of Lupoeth. Minruth's navy would still have it blockaded, but that would not prevent us from controlling everything up the Gulf from Asema almost to the capital. That would cut off supplies and food to the capital. It would also threaten it. Minruth might have to draw troops from the siege of Dythbeth to make sure we didn't attack Khokarsa.

"On the other hand, if Dythbeth fell while you were in it, the loss would be grievous. We cannot get along without you, Your Majesty. If you died, the faithful would believe that Resu was stronger than Kho."

"I won't," Awineth said. She looked around the long oblong table. "Is there agreement on this, that I go to Dythbeth?"

The priestesses and officers shook their heads. It was the only thing to do, since she had obviously made up her mind.

She rose. "Very well, I'll leave soon. Just when I won't say now. I know that you are faithful, that you are closemouthed, but Minruth may have his spies here. I want to leave suddenly, in the dead of night, without fanfare. That way, I will be in Dythbeth before my father's spies can get word to him.

"In the meantime, General, we'll coordinate a detailed campaign. I like what you propose; I think it is the best plan."

The officers rose, bowed and withdrew. The twelve *numatenu* composing Awineth's day-shift bodyguard—among them Hadon—remained. Awineth, still seated, called him to her.

"It will take at least two months to get everything prepared before I go to Dythbeth," she said. "There is no hurry as far as Dythbeth is concerned, since it should be able to hold out for six months or more. My father has tried three times to storm its walls and each time has been repelled with heavy losses." Awineth smiled and said, "That means you have two months to be with your bride."

Hadon kept his face emotionless, though he felt angry.

"Then you are rejecting my petition to take her and the child and Paga along with us?"

"Yes. They will only be burdens. I'll be traveling in a small, fast ship; space is at a premium. Moreover, Dythbeth has enough useless mouths to feed. Besides, why should you want to take them away from here, where they are safe, to a place where they will be in grave danger?"

"My wife says she wants to be with me, wherever I am."

Awineth's smile showed that she knew he was furious and was enjoying it.

"I think you're both being selfish," she said. "Neither of you are considering the well-being of the Empire. I understand why you don't want to be parted, but this is war and we must all make sacrifices."

"It will be as the Queen wishes," Hadon said stonily.

"We may be gone for a year," she said. "Perhaps two years. Only Kho knows how long it will be before we are victorious. In the meantime, you should be happy knowing that Lalila is safe here. And"—she paused, still smiling—"your baby."

Hadon started. "What?"

"Yes. A messenger told me this morning that your wife is pregnant. Lalila went to the temple to determine if she was conceiving. She was immediately given the necessary ritual and was found to be with child."

Hadon had known about her condition, but he had not been aware that Lalila intended to be tested. This was done through means which only the priestesses knew, though he had heard that it involved the sacrifice of a hare.

"Suguqateth tells me that she had a dream two nights ago about the baby," Awineth said. "That is why she summoned Lalila to the temple this morning. Apparently, if her dream is not false, your child is destined for great things. But it will be necessary for Lalila to visit the oracle before we can learn details of her glorious future."

"Her?"

"Suguqateth dreamed of a female baby. Of course," Awineth continued, "the child may not be yours. My father raped her shortly before you rescued her, though I suppose it is unnecessary to remind you of that. And if she had been a few minutes late in slaying that outlaw chief, there might be even more doubt about the paternity."

Hadon mastered his desire to hit her in the face. He said, "There are not many in this land who can be sure who their father is. It does not matter."

"It is a good thing that Lalila had a child before she married you," Awineth said. "Otherwise she would have followed the ancient custom."

She referred to the holy prostitutes. All women, if they were unpregnant at the time of their first marriage, and had never delivered before, went to a temple to be a holy prostitute for a month. Conception as a result of this attendance was supposed to be of divine origin. Theoretically, a god inhabited the body of the fertilizing male during the intercourse. The god was held to be the father of the child. It was a great honor to the family.

Though the ancients had believed in this literally, it was known now that the male sperm was responsible for conception. But the millennia-old custom held, and the facts were ignored. The ministers of Kho claimed that this made no difference. The god still possessed the body of the man and hence the sperm was metaphysically his, though it was physically that of the human father.

The priests of Resu, the Flaming God, held that this was a false doctrine. If Minruth triumphed this custom was likely to be suppressed, the first step in making women subordinate to men. In fact Minruth had already repealed a number of customs and laws in the capital city regarding the equality—some said the superiority—of women. To do this, it had been necessary to execute a number of resisting women and men as an example.

The main resistance to this new order was in the rural districts. Farmers and fisherfolk were very conservative, stubborn in opposing change. They were especially hardheaded when it came to their religion. The city-dwellers were more flexible, though even they had vigorously opposed the King and the priests until a number of protesters had been publicly hanged.

"The oracle will speak for Kho tomorrow evening," Awineth said. "Suguqateth and I will be there. And so will you. The oracle has asked that you attend, which means that you, of course, will not refuse her invitation."

"I would like to be there," Hadon said.

He was pensive the rest of the day. As a result, he made a bad showing during the exercise with wooden swords in the afternoon. Despite his youth, he was the best swordsman in the Queen's bodyguard, which was composed of veterans of many years of experience. But he could not concentrate properly and so lost on points to men he had always bested before.

Awineth, watching the display, smiled each time he was beaten.

12

The Temple of Kho was on a high hill to the north of the town. It was surrounded by giant oaks, some of which were said to be a thousand years old. The building was round and domed, composed of massive marble blocks transported through the mountain pass over eight hundred years ago. Hadon and Lalila passed through a nine-sided entrance into a chamber whose walls were decorated with murals. These were painted in cool blues and light reds and depicted stages in the creation of the world by Kho. A massive bronze tripod sat in the center; the bell-shaped bronze object on top of it emitted clouds of burning incense through holes in its sides.

Hadon glanced through a round doorway to his right and glimpsed the room of the divine whores. It was separated into small rooms by light wooden walls, painted scarlet and blue. In its center was a great round pillar around which the women waited. Several men were talking to them, among them Paga and Kebiwabes. The manling, happening to look his way, grinned and waved. He took the hand of a blonde who was almost twice as tall as he and led her toward a room.

The next room had a ceiling twice as high as the first. A nine-legged altar-stand squatted in its middle. The third held a twelve-legged stand; its ceiling was three times as high as the first. Here Awineth and the head priestess of the temple waited for them. Near them lounged the Queen's nighttime bodyguard.

Suguqateth beckoned them to follow her. The next chamber was the holiest, vast, oval-shaped. Its floor was paved with white tiles and a spiral of varicolored mosaics. The spiral began at the center of the floor and was composed of a line of twelve-sided pieces. On each was painted a tiny scene depicting a great historical event. The spiral went in tight curves, around and around, the outer part almost touching the walls on three sides. It ended just before the base on which stood the statue of Kho. Its termination was a still-unpainted square.

The blank piece bothered many people. Why were there not more pieces to be painted? What did this mean? Surely the history of Khokarsa did not have only one more great event to be portrayed?

Hadon was curious and uneasy about that too, but he asked no questions; the priestesses never divulged such information.

The main object of attention in this chamber was a towering statue of Kho. This had a core of marble over which carved elephant ivory had been fitted. Her crown was of gold, each of its twelve points bearing silver shields inset with many large diamonds. Her eyes were painted solid blue. She was nude and held in her right hand a cornucopia stuffed with sheaves of millet. Her left hand held a sickle, an instrument used for reaping or, as among the original dwellers of this valley, also for war.

Except for the three women and Hadon, the great room was empty. They stood for a moment, making the ancient sign of obeisance, while silence settled around them. The torches placed high above their heads, ringing the room, guttered. Shadows danced along the wall and someone in white peered from around the base of the idol.

The chief priestess said, "We will take off our clothes. When one appears before the voice of Kho, one should be as when one is born."

They shed their garments, leaving them on the floor behind them. Suguqateth led them across the floor. The white-clad figure came from around the base, carrying a three-legged stool of oak. She set it down in front of the statue and removed her robe. She was a very old woman, white-haired and wrinkled. Her pupils were enormously dilated and her breath stank of something acrid.

Hadon noticed then that there was a hole in the floor just in front of the stool. As the old woman climbed onto the tall stool, smoke began to rise from the hole. It was bluish and thin at first, but as the hag, her eyes closed, began to chant, it became denser. It rose toward a hole hidden in the shadows of the domed ceiling, its tentacles swirling out, enveloping all. Hadon coughed as he breathed in a heavy, sweetish odor, one he had never smelled before.

The woman, swaying, chanted in the old ritual tongue. Hadon moved closer to Lalila; the priestess motioned him to return to his original place. She took Lalila's hand and led her to within three paces of the oracle priestess. Then she took three steps backward, stopping by Awineth.

The smoke continued to pour out. The shadows seemed to thicken, to ooze out from the base of the walls. Suddenly Hadon felt cold. The air, though it had been cool when he entered, was now freezing. He shivered and his teeth chattered. Awineth looked back at him with an annoyed expression. He clenched his teeth, but he could not keep from shaking.

Now the shadows were in fact advancing. They crept closer, at the same time building up toward the torches. Presently they were halfway toward the ceiling. They covered the torches with roiling veils, never extinguishing them but making them faint and faraway.

Suddenly he gasped and his heart, which had been beating hard before, began racing. The Goddess Kho had moved!

No, it was only his imagination. The statue was as still as stone; it had not stepped toward him.

He could not be sure. Things out of the corners of his eyes were distorted, lengthened. When he turned his head to look directly, they resumed the appearance of normality.

He leaped, uttering a strangled cry, as the sickle swooped over his head. It was a blur, casting a swift shadow, come and gone. But he had heard the hiss as it cut through the air.

Yet Kho had not moved.

Or had She? The blank azure eyes seemed to become liquid, as if alive. Tiny golden flashes swam through them, then lined up into three concentric circles. They began rotating, slowly at first, then more swiftly, whirling and whirling, then expanding into solid golden orbs, burning like stars.

His legs quivered and his belly contracted. His genitals drew up. The floor felt like ice to his feet; a cold wind was blowing down his back.

He fell to his knees, crying, "Great Kho! Spare me!"

The women paid no attention to him; their eyes were locked on the oracle.

She was screaming now, spittle flying from her mouth, her eyes wide, her scrawny arms stretched out to each side of her, then flapping as if she were a vulture.

Abruptly she pitched forward, landing with a thud on the floor.

The smoke thinned out; a moment later it was no longer rising from the floor. The shadows retreated and the cold evaporated. Hadon, shaking, got to his feet. The women had not yet moved, though the hag was obviously in need of attention. Blood was running from her nostrils and mouth.

Presently the chief priestess advanced and knelt down by the old woman. She felt her pulse and looked into an eye. Then she rose, saying loudly, "The oracle is dead! She was unable to bear the presence of the Goddess any longer!"

Awineth, pale beneath her dark pigment, turned wide, dark eyes toward Hadon. "Great Kho has indeed laid a heavy burden on your unborn daughter," she said. "A heavy burden, yet one that is glorious!"

Lalila turned then. She was almost blue-white; her eyes had gained dark rings in a few minutes. "What did she say?" she cried.

Suguqateth said, "Your child will become a great priestess! Or else she will have a short and terrible life! She will be the savior of a city and founder of a dynasty that will continue for twelve thousand years! Or she will die when young after the most miserable of existences!"

Awineth said, "It depends upon whether or not she is born in the city of your ancestors, Hadon. If she enters the world there, in Opar, then she is indeed blessed! But if she does not, then she will suffer greatly and go early to the dark house of dread Sisisken!"

Lalila gave a short, sharp cry and collapsed to her knees, weeping.

Hadon was too stunned to say a word. Besides, what use would it be to protest? Kho Herself had spoken.

Lalila raised her head, tears falling on her breasts.

"What else did she prophesy?"

"Much else. But we are forbidden to tell you or anyone else. Kho's secrets will be kept locked in the hearts of myself and the high priestess."

"Then," Hadon said slowly, "Lalila must go to Opar."

"That is up to the Witch-from-the-Sea," Suguqateth said. "No one can force her to go. But if she loves her child..."

"Will Hadon be allowed to go with me?" Lalila cried.

"No!" Awineth shouted. "He must stay here or wherever I go! He is my bodyguard, sworn to accompany me wherever I travel, sworn to fight for me until Minruth is dead and I am seated on the throne in the palace of Khokarsa!"

Hadon said nothing. Awineth smiled.

He was in utter despair and would have continued to be so had not a strange thing happened. Suguqateth, the head priestess, had nodded. And she had smiled encouragingly at him. She was secretly saying no to Awineth, though just what that negation implied he did not know.

13

As usual, Paga was skeptical.

"The future cannot be foretold," he said. "If it can be, then it is as fixed as the past, which means that all to come is already here, in effect. It also means that you and I, everybody, all of us, have no choice in what we do. We just think we act freely. But in reality we are helpless to act otherwise than as the deities decree. We are like the puppets in those shows you have described, Hadon. Dolls pulled by strings.

"That is, we are if the future is indeed fixed. But I for one do not believe so. If I did, I would kill myself."

Hinokly said, "But you couldn't commit suicide unless the deities had willed that you should do so."

Paga's good eye flashed and the long graying hair on his face parted to reveal strong blocky teeth.

"A good point, scribe, and an unarguable one. So let us be practical and drop this useless speculation about prophesies and fixed futures. What do we intend to do? Or perhaps I should say, what do we *think* we intend to do? Whatever the truth, we act *as if* we have free will."

They were seated around a large round table of polished oak within a smoky wing of the largest tavern in town. Screens of pine, painted with scenes illustrating stories about Besbesbes, the bee-goddess, were set around the table giving them semi-privacy. The bellowing and laughter and shouting from the tables around made it impossible for anyone to eavesdrop.

Within the circle of the screens were Hadon, Kebiwabes, Hinokly, Paga and Lalila. The child Abeth was home, guarded by a temple retainer sent by the head priestess, Suguqateth.

Lalila sipped at locally brewed sweet mead, then said, "It does not matter whether the prophecy is a true one or one which Awineth arranged. I for one believe that it was indeed the Goddess speaking. If the rest of you had been there, you would believe so too. Even Paga, who believes nothing unless he can see it—and sometimes not then—would have been convinced.

"But whatever the truth, it is evident that Awineth does not want me to stay here. She would like me to make the trip to Opar as soon as possible. Indeed, if I am to get there before the child is born, I should leave at once."

"That is a long enough and dangerous enough trip in the best of times," Hadon said. "Now..."

Lalila placed her hand on his. "I would not worry if you were my guide. But that is just it, you're not. Awineth is determined to keep you with her. I don't think it is because she hopes to take you as her lover once I am out of the way. She hates you too much for that. No, she is spiteful and wants to separate us. Her vow keeps her from harming us directly, but it does not stop her from indirect action. She can deny that she is hurting us in any way, is doing the contrary, in fact. Getting me out of the way, sending me to Opar, is for the sake of the unborn child."

"I will be with you and Abeth, wherever you go," the hairy manling said.

"Unless the Queen requires my services," Hinokly the scribe said, "I'll accompany you as far as Rebha, Lalila. I have a brother there who will take me in, and I can get work there. Rebha is probably the safest place in the Empire."

"I'll stay with Hadon," Kebiwabes said. "I must stay with him to the end."

Hadon laughed and said, "Let us hope that the end is not soon."

Kebiwabes smiled but said nothing. During his wanderings over the northern savannas he had decided that Hadon was to be the hero of an epic poem which he would compose. This was titled *Pwamwothadon, The Song of Hadon*. Parts of it had been completed. The bard, accompanying himself with his stringed tortoise-shell harp, had sung these passages in marketplaces, taverns and the chambers of chief priestesses. It covered events from Hadon's departure from Opar for the Great Games in Khokarsa to his stand at the inner pass against the soldiers of Minruth.

Kebiwabes discreetly refrained from singing the latest part. This concerned Hadon's rescue of Awineth and the vow Hadon forced from her. Though the persons of bards were supposed to be sacred, they were not always immune from retaliation. No one, no matter how highly placed, dared exact public revenge, but things could happen to a bard who had insulted someone high. He or she could have an accident or just disappear, never to be seen again. That the Goddess would punish the murderer was no consolation to the murdered.

"There is no need for us to decide who shall go with whom," Paga said, "if Hadon also goes to Opar."

"How can I do that?" Hadon said. "I have sworn to guard the life of Awineth until she is safe on her throne in the palace of Khokarsa."

"But she swore she would not harm us," Lalila said. "Now she is making sure that we are parted and that I have to undertake a very dangerous journey to Opar. She has broken her vow, which means that you cannot be held to yours."

"But you just said that you believed Kho Herself spoke through the oracle. So Awineth is in no way responsible for your going to Opar."

Lalila said, "No, she is not. But she is responsible for your staying here. If the Goddess wants me to get to Opar so that our child may have a long and glorious life, surely She will want the father to be with us. Especially since the father is a hero and so is needed to see us through the dangers. And so Awineth is resisting the orders of the Goddess."

Hadon smiled and said, "I don't know who is better at rationalizing, you or Awineth."

"Rationalization is any woman's other name," Paga said. "Look, you two, Hadon says that Suguqateth indicated that Awineth was not going to get her own way. You don't know why she would go against the Queen, even secretly. But you say she did signify that she intended to do so. If this is true, why haven't you heard from Suguqateth? It's been three days now!"

"I don't know," Hadon said. "But the priestesses seldom do anything prematurely. She will let us know when she feels it is time to act."

Hinokly said, "She had better do so soon. I heard that Awineth leaves this valley within the week and goes to Dythbeth."

"What?" Hadon said. "You heard that? Where? From whom, Great Kho's teats! That is supposed to be a staff secret, known only to... Never mind—I shouldn't even be talking about it. But if you have heard this, who else knows? Who told you?"

"The maid who changes the sheets in my bedchamber," the scribe said. "I talked her into a little extra duty, you might say, and while we were talking afterward, she said that she had overheard a butler tell her supervisor that the royal party would be leaving within ten days."

Hadon slammed his fist on the table, shaking the mugs so hard that some mead slopped onto the wood.

"Don't repeat that to anyone outside this group, Hinokly! The rest of you, keep this to yourself! Do you realize what would happen if Awineth found out how loose-mouthed someone on her staff is? Everybody would be subject to intensive questioning. By intensive, I mean torture! She'd go right through you, Hinokly, the maid, the butler, the supervisor and on to the source of the leak. And none of us here would be safe, since we'd heard about this from you. I would be, I suppose, if I told Awineth about it. But she'd take the opportunity to lock you up, Lalila. She couldn't hurt you, since you obviously aren't involved in disseminating the information. She would, however, keep you incommunicado so you couldn't pass it on. I wouldn't get to see you at all. We'd leave and you'd be released then, sent to Opar."

Lalila had turned pale. The others didn't look too healthy either, not even in the reddish light.

"But if I don't report this I'm disloyal, failing in my duty," Hadon said. "But how can I? You'll all be in grave peril then, and I surely will not see Lalila again!"

He groaned.

"It's not an unsolvable dilemma," Lalila said, stroking his arm. "Send her an anonymous note warning her. But don't tell her the source of your information. That way you fulfill your duty and yet avoid hurting the innocent people."

"Innocent people?" Hadon asked. "Who knows who is or is not guilty? There may be no one guilty on the staff. Awineth herself might have let slip a word to her maids-in-waiting, one of whom might have let slip a few words to her lover. But you can be sure Minruth has his spies here. If they find out that Awineth is leaving the valley, they'll be watching for her. And once she's on the way, accompanied by a relatively small guard, she's open to attack."

"So write anonymously to her that she has to change her plans, that she must not let anyone know about the change until the last moment," Hinokly said.

"Easier said than done," Hadon said. "Just how do I get the note to Awineth? Any messenger will be detained and the identity of the note-sender forced from him, you can bet on that."

"Write the note," Lalila said, "and I will see that it gets into the temple mail system. Suguqateth has asked me to see her tomorrow morning. I do not know why, though I suspect she will tell me what she means to do about you and me, Hadon. In any event, I will drop the note into the offering basket outside the hall of the holy whores."

"It's too bad I have to resort to such indirect ways. It would be nice to be able to go straight to Awineth and tell her she's in danger."

"You're old enough by now to know how the world works," Hinokly said.

"Yes, I am, and I do," Hadon said. "But that doesn't keep me from complaining about it now and then."

"Heroes don't complain," the bard said, but he laughed.

"Heroes exist only in songs and stories," Hadon said. He shoved back his wooden chair and rose. "Heroes are men who happen to deal, more or less adequately, with heroic events. And who are also lucky enough to catch the attention of a singer or a teller of tales. For every sung hero there are a hundred unsung. Anyway, I am tired of this talk of heroes!"

The next day he felt much better. He had written the note and given it to Lalila, who took Abeth with her to the temple while Hadon put on the dress uniform of the Queen's *numatenu* guard. He wore a tall, three-sided scarlet hat, rounded on top, sporting a red fish-eagle's feather. Around his neck was a rosary with one hundred and forty-four blue electrum beads, each nine-sided. Over his shoulders was a short blue shawl of woven papyrus fibers, from the edges of which dangled twenty-four leather tassels, each knotted thrice. These stood for the largest cities in the Khokarsan Empire.

On his shaved chest was painted a stylized head of a red ant, indicating Hadon's totem and incidentally his birthplace, since this totem was found only in Opar.

A broad belt of leopardskin held up his striped kilts of honey badger fur. The belt also supported a rhinoskin sheath for a throwing knife on his right side. On his left was a wooden holder into which was thrust his *numatenu* sword. The slot admitted the blade only to its widest part. This resulted in half of the long, slightly tapering, blunt-edged sword projecting above the holder. Thus Hadon, like all the Queen's uniformed *numatenu*, had to support the upper part by holding the hilt with his left hand. He didn't mind. Only the *numatenu* bore their weapons in this manner; it was an honor.

Hadon had inherited the sword from his father. Kumin had been a *numatenu* who had hired out to the rulers of Opar, though he himself had been born in

Dythbeth. Kumin had married Pheneth, daughter of a mining foreman. Pheneth had seven children, but only three reached maturity. Her first child had been by Resu, the Flaming God, conceived in Resu's house during the month when Pheneth dedicated her body to the god's temple. This child had died of a fever.

When Hadon was seven his father lost an arm in a battle with pirates in the vast underground complex beneath the city. His king had also died then and a new king, Gamori, had been chosen and wedded by the widow, Phebha. Kumin had contemplated—and rejected—suicide, the usual course taken by crippled *numatenu*. Instead he accepted a job as a sweeper of floors in the Temple of Golden Kho of Opar.

Hadon's childhood from then on had been penurious. And he had had to endure many humiliations because of the change in his social stature. But his father had taught him to be proud, to endure much for the sake of a worthy goal. His Uncle Phimeth, probably the greatest swordsman in the Empire in his youth, had taught him all he knew about the *tenu*.

Hadon was given his father's sword on winning the Lesser Games in Opar. Though no longer technically a *numatenu*, Kumin had the right to give his weapon to whomever he thought deserved it. Hadon, though he could use the sword by right of inheritance, was not technically a *numatenu*; according to custom, he had a certain time after getting the sword to establish his right to it. If he earned it, then he was to be initiated into the rather loosely organized guild of *numatenu*. He had earned the right at least a dozen times over and so had gone through the rites shortly after entering this valley.

He had expected to be made captain of the guard. After all, if he had not been cheated, he would have been Awineth's husband and thus ruler of all Khokarsa. The least she could have done was make him head of her personal bodyguard. But no, he was given the lieutenancy, immediately under Captain Nowiten, a thirty-five-year-old veteran.

Under other circumstances Hadon would have been grieved and offended. Now he had only two great concerns: to get Lalila to Opar, and make sure that he went with her.

Pondering just how he could accomplish this without breaking his word, he wandered around the town of Akwaphi, first past the Temple of Resu, a large square building of granite topped by phallic minarets at each corner.

Four priests stood talking on the columned porch. Their heads were shaved except for roaches of hair from the forehead to the nape of the neck, brushes kept stiff and upright by eagle grease. They had sported full beards and mustaches in accordance with Minruth's decree, defying ancient tradition, but when the news of Awineth's imprisonment had reached this valley, the priests hurriedly reverted to their shaved state. In addition, they had renounced Minruth's doctrine of the domination of the Flaming God. Whether this step was taken from true orthodoxy or a desire to survive was not known. Whatever the motive, the priests had saved their lives. If they had stood by Minruth, they would have been torn to pieces by the wrathful worshipers of Kho. The temple might have been taken apart and the idol of Resu shattered or else moved into Kho's temple to be placed at Her feet.

These acts of desecration would have resulted in guilt among the responsible and horror among the nonparticipants. No matter how high passions rose in this matter, Resu was a god. He had been placed on an equal footing with his mother in theological theory, though in practice most worshipers placed Kho first. Yet he was a deity, and to lay violent hands on his vicars, idols and houses of worship was blasphemy. The priestesses said this was permissible, that Resu himself had repudiated those of his worshipers who tried to displace his mother. Those who had committed blasphemy in their wrath still felt uneasy. They expected retribution at any moment.

When divine vengeance did not come after a long period of waiting, the blasphemer had one of two reactions. One was that the priestesses were right: Resu had turned his back on his own people because they had tried to raise him above his mother. But another reaction was the feeling that perhaps Resu was dead—if indeed he had ever lived. And if he had not existed, then what about Kho?

Very few people dared voice such thoughts and they were never uttered publicly, of course.

The priests stood closely together, their flowing robes lifting and falling in the breeze. Their right hands, the ritually pure hands, worked their rosaries while they gestured with their lefts. They stopped talking for a moment as Hadon, passing, saluted. He wondered what they were discussing. Grave matters of theology? The difficulty in getting enough rations in this now overcrowded valley? Or, as many suspected, were they spies transmitting information on Awineth's movements?

If the latter was true, it was not his concern. It was up to Awineth's counterintelligence to determine such matters.

14

Hadon strolled through the marketplace, a broad square formed by various government buildings, the Temple of Takomim, goddess of trade, thieves and the left-handed, the Temple of Besbesbes, goddess of bees and mead, and a gymnasium. In the center of the square was a fountain, a broad shallow bowl of limestone with a statue on a pedestal in its middle. This was of bronze and represented the local river godling, Akwaphi, in the act of making the headwaters of the river. The local belief was that women who had failed to get pregnant as divine prostitutes might become fertile if they drank from the godling's spout. This had also resulted in males shying away from the source of water.

Hadon was thirsty, but instead of drinking from the fountain basin, he purchased a cup of hot hibiscus-steeped water. While sipping it, he looked around at the scene which never failed to interest him. It was noisy and colorful, alive with traders, merchants, townspeople, farmers and hunters. Adding to the clamor were ducks quacking in cages, pigs grunting in pens, domesticated buffalo mooing, obese food-dogs yapping in wickerwork baskets, collared and leashed monkeys chattering on stands, ravens and parrots croaking or screeching, hunting dogs—for sale—barking, a baby leopard in a cage squalling. There were small open booths everywhere, arranged in no pattern, and merchants hawked their wares from these. Fresh and dried fish, dressed carcasses of pigs, sides and legs of beef, unplucked ducks and game fowl hanging by their necks, fresh or hard-boiled duck eggs, loaves of acorn-nut bread, cartloads of millet grain, jugs and barrels of mead, kegs of honey, high-priced hogsheads of wine and beer imported just before the blockade; dried hibiscus leaves and medicines and charms for curing acne, decaying teeth, cataracts, smallpox scars, impotency, piles, glaucoma, obesity, anemia, fevers, worms, amnesia, insomnia, backache, anxiety, bed-wetting, constipation, diarrhea, bad breath, strabismus, stuttering, stammering, shyness, tumors, malaria, colds, the itch, lice, crabs, deafness and the many others in the long, long list of things plaguing humankind even in 10,000 B.C.—giving some people even then a chance to make a profit.

The square was unpaved. Though water was sprinkled on the earth several times a day, it was not enough to prevent the dust from rising. It rose and fell, coating those who hung around all day. Their sweat lined their faces with clean stripes. At the end of the day, the stink of unwashed bodies, human urine, animal dung, bird droppings, spilled and breathed-out mead, wine, beer, decaying meat, fowl and fish, all created a medley of repugnant odors. Nobody knew they were repellent, however. They had been used to them all their lives, just as they were used to the thousands of flies circling, buzzing, crawling on meat, excrement and faces.

Hadon finished the hibiscus-tea and passed on, loitering, idly examining merchandise, eavesdropping, passing the time while waiting for Lalila's interview with the head priestess to end. His attention was finally held by a man who had entered the market a few minutes before. He was about six feet three inches high, a stature which would attract Hadon at any time. Hadon was six foot two, which had made him the tallest man in Opar. On arriving at the capital of Khokarsa, he had been somewhat upset to find that he was not also the tallest man in the Empire. Even so, those who could look down at him were few.

The stranger had walked out from a side street with a bold, long-stepping stride. He held his head high and proudly, resembling an eagle in the manner with which he turned it from side to side. His hair was long, straight and very black. It fell over his forehead in bangs, chopped off several inches above the eyebrows. His large eyes were widely spaced and, when Hadon was near enough, he perceived they were dark gray. They looked strange and unsettling, as if they saw everything before them quite distinctly and analytically, yet also saw things which were not there.

The face was handsome, though not regularly proportioned. The nose was short but straight, the upper lip short, the chin square and deeply cleft. His physique was big-boned and muscular, but suggestive of the leopard rather than the lion.

His only clothing was a loincloth of antelope hide, which made Hadon think that he must be a mountain-dweller, since these folk wore very little during the summer. On the other hand, the hill people wore skins obtained from local animals, and there were no antelopes in this area.

His only weapon was a large long-handled knife in a leather belt.

The soles of his bare feet were calloused at least half an inch thick.

The stranger sauntered around, occasionally meeting Hadon's glance. Hadon did not wish to appear too interested, so he looked away at once. Others were looking at the stranger. His height attracted notice, but the fact that he was a newcomer was enough to cause curious stares and muttered asides. Everybody was spy-conscious, especially since the Queen had offered high rewards for such information.

The stranger moved around, stopping to sip some hibiscus-tea, munching on some nuts, watching a puppet show. Then he chose a shady place under the roof of a hare-seller's booth and squatted. He stayed there so long, motionless except for brushing the flies off his face, that Hadon began to lose interest. The fellow, though striking in appearance, was probably just a hunter. He'd come down to look at the sights and perhaps take in some of the cosmopolitan attractions. He did not seem to have much money; the few coins he'd spent had come from a small flat bag attached to his belt. If he needed women, however, he didn't have to have money. A man of his physique and good looks would be grabbed by the divine whores. His only difficulty might be in getting out of the chamber.

Hadon was chuckling at this thought when he saw five hillmen walk up to the stranger. These wore caps of honey badger fur with the heads still attached, badgerskin vests and loincloths, and cross-gaitered boots of foxskin. The stylized head of the honey badger was painted on their bare chests and foreheads. They carried leather sacks on their backs and long spears, bronze-tipped, in their hands. Short swords and knives hung in sheaths from their belts.

Hadon drifted closer, drawn more by curiosity than anything. The stranger had not risen; he looked up at his questioners from under heavy lids and smiled faintly. Hadon stopped when he was close enough to hear them. He could also smell the smoke impregnating the badger skins, the long-unwashed armpits and crotches, the rancid badger fat on their hair and the sweetish odor of mead on their breaths.

"We was kinda curious, stranger," one of the men was saying. "We ain't never seen a hunter like you in these parts, if you are a hunter."

"I'm a hunter," the stranger said in a deep slow voice.

"Not from these parts, you ain't," the first speaker said. He swayed and blinked bloodshot eyes. "I know every accent in this valley, all through these here mountains, in fact. No one speaks funny like you do."

"Too bad," the stranger said. "However, my business is not yours."

"Is that so?" another hunter said. "Right now, anybody's business is everybody's business. Minruth's got spies everywhere, and Awineth's people are keeping an eye out for them. Did you report to the commander of the garrison?"

"I didn't know I was supposed to," the stranger said. "I'll do just that. When I feel like it."

He looked at Hadon and said, "*Numatenu*, Son of the Red Ant, citizen of Opar. Perhaps you can tell me if what these badger-men say is true? Am I required to report my visit to the local post?"

"The first time you come here, yes," Hadon said. "Apparently you haven't been here before."

The first speaker, a tall, heavily built man with brown, gray-flecked hair, hunkered down. He leaned forward to look at the knife at the stranger's side. "Say! That ain't bronze! That's iron! By Renamam'a, it's iron but not like any iron I ever saw!"

Hadon saw that about half an inch of shiny gray blade stuck up from the sheath.

"Would that be steel, stranger?" he asked. "My own sword is made of carbonized iron, but I have seen a sword made of carbonized iron mixed with nickel and tempered to a great hardness, holding an edge such as no metal ever had before. Kwasin, my cousin—you may have heard of him—has an ax which is made of the hardest iron I've ever seen. It came from a falling star, though, and so must be the metal used by the deities."

"That would be the ax of Wi, fashioned by a one-eyed hairy manling named Pag," the stranger said. "How did it fall into the hands of this Kwasin?"

Hadon was too amazed to answer. This stranger was no hunter from the hills, ignorant of affairs outside this valley. Moreover, he was no native speaker of Khokarsan, forced by the phonetic structure of the language to add *-a* to Pag. But how would this fellow know that Pag was the true name of the manling?

Hadon, speechless for the moment, stared at the stranger. Meanwhile, the big hillman rose to his feet swiftly, almost losing his balance, and reached out to grab the stranger by the wrist. But he missed as the gray-eyed man stepped back.

"Listen," the hillman said. "How'd you ever get a knife like that? You ain't no rich man or *numatenu.* You musta stole it!"

"The knife was my father's," the gray-eyed man said. "However, I don't have to account to you or any man."

He stared around him. The hillmen had gathered in front of him in a semi-circle. His retreat was cut off by the booth.

Hadon stepped away, saying, "He's right. His only duty is to report to the post-commander. He doesn't have to answer any questions from you."

"Yeah?" the big hunter asked. "And if we let him go how do we know he's going to report? What's to keep him from just walking out of town, back to his spy-post in the hills?"

"You've accused me of being a thief and a spy," the stranger said quietly.

"Yeah? Well, so what?"

Another hillman, lean, one-eyed, snaggle-toothed, broken-nosed, said, "Better give us your knife, totemless. You do that and we'll forget your insults."

The gray eyes widened but he did not reply. Hadon saw now what they meant to do. They were not concerned about his being a spy; they coveted the knife. And they intended to get it if they had to kill for it. After all, he was unknown, hence a suspect. He wore no totem mark to bring his fellows to his defense.

Hadon said, "This man is under no obligation to give you his knife. You have no authority here. So back off. I'll take him to the post myself."

"He's a spy and a thief!" the big hunter bellowed. "Surrender that there knife, bootless! Or by the Great Badger herself, we'll take it from you!"

Two of the men turned toward Hadon, gripping their spears in ready position. "Now you just go on and mind your own business, *numatenu*," one said. "We'll take care of this here dirty spy."

"Thank you for trying to protect me," the stranger said to Hadon. "But you can avoid trouble and bloodshed if you'll just allow me to handle this."

The man certainly spoke a strange Khokarsan, his manner and language belying his savage appearance. He sounded very much like a well-educated upper-class person.

"I don't allow mangy acorn-knockers to order me around," Hadon said. He still did not draw his sword, since he hoped to scare the hillmen away. Once he had removed the blade from its sheath, he was committed to use it.

"Acorn-knockers!" the nearest man bellowed, his eyes wide, his face red. "Why, you big-city popinjay, I'll show you who's an acorn-knocker!"

He lunged with his spear. Hadon whipped out his blade just as the man finished his sentence. It sheared off the bronze spear's leaf-shaped point, came around and severed the man's left hand. Hadon whirled then, bringing up the blade at the end of the cycle, repeating the first stroke, removing the head from the shaft of the spear of another back woodsman. This man dropped the shaft and hightailed it through the market, screaming for help.

All this had taken perhaps six seconds. Now three of the hillmen lay on the dirt, dead. The throats of two were slashed; the third had a bloody wound in his solar plexus. The stranger wiped his knife on the vest of the biggest man and stuck it into its sheath. He straightened up then and brushed his bangs away in an angry gesture. Hadon glimpsed a thin scar which started just above the left eye, ran across the top of the head and ended above the right ear.

"This whole affair was stupid," he said. "I tried to avoid it, but they insisted."

"There shouldn't be much trouble," Hadon said. "They were the aggressors; I'll testify to that. Some of their totem might decide to get blood revenge, though. These hill people are old-fashioned, you know. There is no doubt they were trying to rob you, however, so their kin might take that into consideration."

"The knife was just an excuse," the stranger said. "They knew that I saw them commit a crime two days ago, in the mountains north of here. I was coming down the trail when I heard some cries. I took to the bush and crept up unobserved on these men. They had cut the throat of a farmer and his two children and were raping the wife. Or trying to. They were all so drunk that none could manage it. So they cut her throat too, and staggered away with their pitiful loot.

"I came out of the woods to check the dead and one of the killers happened to turn around and see me. I walked away, but they did not try to trail me. I came here and we met again. You saw what happened."

Hadon looked across the marketplace at the northwest corner. Officers, led by the surviving hunter, were swarming out of the constabulary building. The man was shouting and pointing at Hadon and the stranger. After a brief conference, the constables walked swiftly toward them, the hillman trotting ahead of them, turning his head now and then to shout back at them.

Hadon thought that the hillman either had an excess of confidence or else he was too drunk to care for the consequences. He knew that the stranger had witnessed the murders, so why was he bringing in the police? Did he think that his accusations of espionage would cloud the issue, discredit anything the stranger might say?

He might have been correct but, in his intoxication, he had forgotten that Hadon could testify against him. And if he thought the constables would also arrest Hadon, he was very mistaken.

Hadon started to tell the stranger this, but the man smiled and said, "I am no spy. But I can't afford to be questioned."

He was gone. Hadon stared at him in astonishment. He had never seen a man run so swiftly yet so easily. He looked like he was loafing, saving energy for an emergency.

"He went that way!" the hillman shouted. The constables started to follow him but were called back by Hadon. He explained what had happened; as a result, the hillman was arrested and taken off to jail.

The chief constable was deferential but firm.

"We can't hold the man unless you charge him with unprovoked assault," he said. "After all, we have only the stranger's report of the murder, if it was a murder. It may have just been a feud killing, in which case the respective totems will take care of the matter. Unless the stranger appears as a witness, we can do nothing. And you must admit it's suspicious that he fled."

"Not necessarily," Hadon said. "There is so much hysteria about spies that he may have felt he wouldn't be safe no matter how innocent he was. As for the hillman, I do charge him with unprovoked assault with intention to kill."

"It's his word against yours," the constable said. "So the trial'll be a mere formality. Do you want him executed, beaten or sold into slavery?"

"I surrender my prerogative to the judge," Hadon said. "I suggest, however, that if he's enslaved he not be sold to an individual. He's too dangerous for that. He should go into a government chain gang."

"I'll give your recommendation to the judge," the constable said. He saluted and then gave instructions for the disposal of the corpses.

Hadon left the marketplace, arriving at the Temple of Kho a few minutes before Lalila walked out from it. She looked haggard, as if she had been through an ordeal. On seeing Hadon she smiled, then she looked wide-eyed. Hadon looked down and saw dried blood on his legs, almost hidden under the cluster of flies.

"I overlooked that," he said. As they walked to their apartment he told her about the incident in the marketplace.

She stopped, her hand on her breast. "Sahhindar!" she said.

"What?" he said, shock running through him, followed by a feeling of unreality. "You can't mean…?"

"Who else is six feet three and has black hair cut in bangs, hiding such a scar, and has gray eyes and speaks archaic Khokarsan? Who else has such a knife, a knife of such hard keen metal?

"But what is he doing here? Is he checking up on us, Abeth, Paga and myself? He said he would."

"I have seen a god," Hadon half whispered. "A god in the flesh."

"He said that he was no god, that he was as vulnerable to death by accident or homicide as any of us," Lalila said. "It is just that he ages very slowly. I didn't understand most of what he told me; he comes from a different world."

"Whatever the truth," Hadon said, "he doesn't concern us unless he makes us his business. And it's up to him to let us know that. What did Suguqateth tell you?"

Lalila looked around her and lowered her voice, though no one seemed to be interested in them.

"She said first that we must not tell anyone else what I am going to tell you. Kho would not like it. Second, when we were with the old oracle, Awineth did not tell us all that the old woman said. Suguqateth heard everything, of course, but she had been ordered by Awineth to keep silent. Suguqateth feels that Awineth is wrong, however; she has no right to suppress Kho's words when they were addressed to us. Awineth, she feels, is putting her personal feelings above the dictates of the Goddess. And so Suguqateth feels she is justified in revealing all of Kho's words."

"Which were?" Hadon said.

"I must leave for Opar as soon as possible. And you must accompany me there. Only thus will our unborn child achieve long life and greatness."

15

At one hour to midnight, the party left the Inn of the Red Parrot. The sky was clouded; the only lights were a few distant torches carried by the night patrols. All were cloaked and hooded and carried weapons and bags of provisions—all except Abeth, who rode sleeping on Hinokly's back. Their guide was a priestess, muffled in a black cloak.

By dawn they were in the mountains northwest of the town. They continued up, reaching the narrow precipitous pass at noon. This led them down into a little valley and up another steep and even higher mountain.

Near dusk of the next day, they climbed onto a plateau. By the setting sun they saw the Kemu, the Great Water.

"We need rest, but we cannot stop," the priestess said. "Awineth will have an army out looking for you. Doubtless she has sent troops through the pass at Notamimkhu. They'll be searching along the shores east and west of the pass. The port at Notamimkhu is blockaded, but that doesn't stop us from using small ships elsewhere."

She led them to the edge of the plateau and gestured at something below. About four hundred feet down, at the foot of the cliff, the sea rose and fell sullenly in the moonlit darkness. Something gleamed whitely in it, a ship riding at anchor about a quarter mile out.

The priestess blew on a bone whistle shaped like a parrot-headed fish. From a cave nearby came six men carrying ropes, blocks and heavy wooden tripods. They set up the equipment, and in a short time Hadon was being lowered in a sling at the end of a rope.

A ledge jutted from the cliff several feet above the surface of the sea. Hadon landed on this, got out of the sling, yanked twice on the rope and watched the sling climb back up. Within fifteen minutes all of the party, including the priestess, were on the ledge. She lit a storm-lantern and waved it back and forth. Presently the dim bulk of a rowboat could be distinguished putting out from the white sailship.

Hadon, Abeth, Lalila, Paga, Hinokly and Kebiwabes were on the ship in two trips. They were hustled belowdecks at once, and the anchor was pulled up. The ship began moving out toward the sea, slowly at first, then heeling suddenly under a breeze.

Morning found them crowded and cramped together, with the ship rolling more than at first. The hatch was opened and daylight flooded in. At the top of the ladder was a young fellow, freckled, blue-eyed, red-haired. He wore a vest of brown sea otter, a rosary of wooden beads, each carved with the face of Piqabes, goddess of the sea, and a codpiece formed from the head of a fish-eagle. His chest bore the blue outline of the deep-sea gruntfish.

"Captain Ruseth at your service!" he said merrily. "Come on out! Breakfast, such as it is, will be served soon!"

Ruseth did not look old enough to be a captain, though Hadon reminded himself that the title was not necessarily a grand one. A commander of a two-man ship would be the captain. His mission was an important one, however, even if he was young, so he had to be very competent. Suguqateth would not have trusted him otherwise.

They came out yawning, scratching, farting and blinking. The sun was up in a cloudless sky. The sea was heavier, coming in great broad rolls. To the south, just visible, were the tops of the mountains along the northwest coast of the island of Khokarsa. There were no other ships in sight. No other living creatures, indeed, except some of the omnipresent *datoekem*, large white birds with hooked black beaks.

There was a good breeze, coming from the northwest. The ship was sailing almost straight east. The swinging yardarm was let out to the right by ropes so the wind struck it at an angle, causing the ship to heel over at an angle uncomfortable for the landlubbers. Ruseth and his four sailors seemed at ease.

One of the seamen brought buckets filled with hard biscuits made from emmer wheat, hard-boiled duck eggs, beef jerky, olives and wine. Hadon took his over the sloping deck to Ruseth, who had taken over the rudder. "I am no sailor," he said, "but we seem to be moving along more swiftly than any ship I've ever seen."

"Isn't she a beauty!" Ruseth cried. "I designed and built her myself. And I invented that triangular sail; I call it the fore-and-aft, as contrasted with the old square sail."

"It looks weird, I must admit," Hadon said. "Just how is it superior to the square sail?"

"It enables us to sail against the wind!" Ruseth said, grinning proudly.

"Against?"

Hadon stepped back from the redhead. "That smacks of—"

"Magic? Evil magic? Nonsense, my friend! Do you think for one moment that the vicars of great Kho would be my patrons if I were using evil forces? No way!" And he proceeded to explain tacking into the wind with a rotatable yardarm.

Hadon listened, then said, "Amazing. It seems so simple when you describe it. I wonder why no one ever thought of it before?"

Ruseth looked angry, then he laughed. "That was probably said to the man who first thought of making fire. Or to the man who first made mead.

"I conceived this when I was sixteen, living in a little fishing village off the northwest corner of the island. The idea came to me one night in a dream, so I can't take credit for it. Piqabes herself undoubtedly sent it, though I had been thinking about sails and sailing for a long time. Anyway, I dreamed of the fore-and-aft sail and worked on some small models in my spare time. Not much of that, you know, for a fisherlad. Then I made a small ship of my own—took me a year to do that. And months to learn how to sail the craft.

"The villagers were interested; they admitted I could sail faster than they could, but they said the old ways were good enough for them. I thought I had a fortune in this, so I went to the capital to get a hearing from the Naval Department. It took me three months to get it—I had to work nights at an inn as a waiter. Daytimes I sat in an outer office cooling my heels until an admiral deigned to see me.

"I showed him how my invention worked, with models and sketches. I invited him to come for a trial run in my little ship.

"Here was something revolutionary. It would change the whole history of ships, make sailing much faster and easier. So guess what?"

"I think I can guess," Hadon said. "I've had some experience with the military mind."

"I was thrown out! And told not to come back! That admiral, a heavy-drinking old duck, said I was crazy. In the first place the rig wouldn't work the way I said it would. And in the second place, its principle was against nature, it was blasphemous.

"I was angry, scared too, because I didn't want the admiral siccing the priests of Resu on me. I thought about going home and maybe forgetting the whole thing. Instead I went to the Temple of Piqabes on a little island near the mouth of the Gulf of Gahete. I showed the head priestess there what I had shown the naval bureaucrat. I told her how much more swiftly my ship could carry the temple mail. She liked the idea and, to make a long story short, here I am, sailing a ship built by the Temple of Kho, in the service of Awineth, taking you to a far-off city of the Southern Sea, the Kemuwopar. Think of it! I've never even been to the mainland north of here!"

Hinokly had been standing nearby. He said, "Then this ship can outrun and outsail anything on the seas?"

"No doubt about it!" Ruseth said. "The *Wind-Spirit* can show her heels to any craft on the two seas!"

"And if the wind fails how will she get away from a galley?"

"She won't," Ruseth said. "The only thing to do then is pray to Piqabes to raise a wind."

Hadon talked for a long time with the little redhead. Ruseth said they would proceed east along the north coast of the island but stay about ten to fifteen miles out to sea. Most of the patrolling by Minruth's navy was done very close to shore. Once the island of Khokarsa was behind them, they would sail southeasterly along the coast of the mainland toward the city of Qethruth.

"Under ordinary conditions, I would head directly southwest toward the pile-city of Rebha," Ruseth said. "But the ship is overloaded now. We don't have enough food to last us until Rebha, so we'll stop off at a village about four hundred miles upcoast from Qethruth. I've never been there, of course, but the priestess gave me directions and also a letter of introduction to the priestess at Karkoom. We'll reprovision and then cut south for Rebha."

Hadon asked what they would do if the village was blockaded. Ruseth laughed and said, "You don't know much about naval realities, do you, my tall friend? Minruth's forces are spread thin enough as they are. He doesn't have ships to blockade every little village along the coast or even on Khokarsa itself. I doubt that he even has a bireme at Qethruth."

"What about Rebha?"

"You were on Awineth's staff," Ruseth said. "What did you hear about Rebha?"

"Nothing," Hadon said. "No courier ships arrived from Rebha. It's a long way, and ships are always disappearing."

"Yes," Ruseth said. "I would guess that the navy does have some big ships stationed at Rebha. It's a very important reprovisioning and refitting port, if it can be called a port. It also controls the southern part of the Kemu and, in a sense, the Strait of Keth."

Days and nights passed without incident. The weather was generally good, though there were rains and an occasional squall. They saw ships now and then, but always at a distance. Most of them seemed to be merchant galleys or fishing ships hauling their dried cargo from the waters off the mainland to the islands.

"There are rumors that piracy is flourishing again in these parts," Ruseth said. "It's only to be expected, of course. Minruth's navy is too occupied with the war to go chasing pirates. We don't need to worry. No pirate could catch us."

"Unless there's a calm," Hinokly said.

Ruseth laughed, but he did look worried afterward.

Conditions were crowded. The cabin became too hot and odorous when they all slept in it. Whenever the weather and the seas permitted, Hadon, the scribe and the bard slept on deck. After a week, Hadon became impatient and irritable. It was impossible to lie with Lalila because of the lack of privacy; they were not Gokako, the apish slaves of Opar who coupled publicly and often en masse. Besides, there was not much to do on board a small vessel. Hadon did dissipate some of the boredom by learning all he could about sailing. Before a week was up, he was relieving the sailors in their duties.

Hadon took the rudder every day for two hours. He was nervous at first and made some bad mistakes in tacking or beating. Ruseth was at hand to take over if anything went wrong, and nothing disastrous happened.

"You're a good fair-weather sailor now," Ruseth said. "We'll find out what you are when we get a bad storm, though I pray Piqabes spares us that."

Hadon insisted that the others also learn as much as possible about the ship. For one thing, it kept them from being bored. For another, it ensured that they would not be handicapped or helpless if anything should happen to the sailors. "Also," Hadon said, "in the future we might have to handle a ship like this by ourselves. We might even have to steal a ship and take it into the deep seas."

Because of this, Hadon also had Ruseth teach him all he could about navigation.

"The sun by day and the stars at night," Ruseth said. "Unfortunately, the Kemu is often clouded and there is much rain, though I've been told that the climate is drier and hotter than it used to be. Either way, you can't depend very often on the stars to guide you. But the lodestone compass is fairly dependable. My grandfather says that it's not so dependable in the Kemuwopar, the Sea of Opar. He claims there are too many mountains with too much iron ore along the shores."

"I doubt that," Hinokly said. And the two were off into another argument.

To make the time pass more pleasantly, Kebiwabes sang. While plucking on his tortoiseshell lyre, he recited love songs, sea chanties, ballads, mourning songs, prayers and the epics: *The Song of Gahete, The Song of Rimasweth, The Song of Kethna.* He also tried out on them passages and sections from his work in progress: *The Song of the Wanderings of Hadon of Opar.*

The subject of this enjoyed hearing his adventures recast into poetry. Much of it was exaggerated or distorted or sometimes it was even a downright lie. But he did not object. Poetry was about the spirit, not the surface, of reality. Nor did he mind at all hearing himself described in glowing terms as a hero. Modesty was not a virtue in Khokarsa.

After two weeks, they began seeing more ships. Most were fishing vessels from the coastal towns and villages, but the number of merchant galleys rose in proportion. Though the rebellion had cut down maritime trade considerably, there were still many men who would brave pirates and blockaders to make a profit.

Karkoom was a village of about five hundred in population, a cluster of huts and longhouses on stilts behind a stockade. It was at the end of a rather narrow harbor formed by two rocky peninsulas. Ruseth took the ship in cautiously, ready to run if any naval vessels were at anchor there. There was just enough room in the passage for him to wheel tightly about, though not much space for tacking or beating against the wind.

They breathed relief when they saw that the four large vessels were merchantmen. Two were from Qethruth, one from Miklemres, one from Siwudawa.

Ruseth took the ship in and tied up at a dock. Leaving two of the crew to guard the ship, Ruseth and the rest visited the local Temple of Kho. They were well received after Ruseth had handed in his letter of introduction. The head priestess, Siha, gave orders that the vessel be provisioned. She then held a small private feast for them where she heard the news from Khokarsa and passed on the news and rumors she had received in the last few months.

For the first time in a long time, Hadon and Lalila slept together—and on a bed that did not rise and fall, roll and yaw. The next day they left at noon, after, of course, a ritual blessing by the priestess.

Several priests from the Temple of Resu were also there; they seemed friendly enough. The villagers, like the citizens of Qethruth, had declared neutrality, but Hadon did not trust them. For all he knew, the priests could have sent a ship out with the news that the refugees were here. On the other hand, to whom would they take the information?

By the time the news got to Khokarsa, it would be too late for Minruth to do anything about it. There might be a naval vessel stationed somewhere near the coast, but that wouldn't make any difference. No ship was going to catch up with the *Wind-Spirit.*

It was possible, however, that a message would be sent to Rebha. The priests could guess, or could find out through espionage, that Hadon was taking Lalila there.

If this was so, there was nothing he could do about it. He shrugged. He would consider the possibility when they got to their destination.

16

Rebha rose slowly out of the southern horizon. Ruseth was delighted because he'd had to spend only two days circling the area before he found the city. During this time they passed many ships, which meant that Rebha had to be in the neighborhood. Ruseth hailed a number of them, but they were in the same situation. Some of them, convinced that the captain of this strange-looking vessel might be a magician who would know the way, had attempted to follow them. But large heavy ships depending on oars could not even keep the *Wind-Spirit* in sight.

"Many ships must miss Rebha," Hadon said to Ruseth.

"No," the redhead said. "Their captains have been on this route so often that they have developed an extra sense. They feel something tingle when they are in the area; they know almost to the minute when it's time to slow down and start casting about. Besides, a captain who keeps a close watch on his knottage and his compass, on the sun and the stars when they're visible, isn't going to be off course much."

An hour later, he shouted. The others came running to the tiller, which he was still handling. "See that smoke to the northwest?" he asked. "That's from the top of the tower in the center of the pile. Unless, of course," he added, "it's a ship on fire."

It was not. Late the next day they saw the upper part of the structure, called the Tower of Diheteth. This was of cedar and had been built a hundred years ago by the admiral who was its regent. Its top, five hundred feet high, was floored with stone. A large fire was kept burning there so that ships could observe its smoke or light. On a clear day the top of the smoke cloud could be seen from over a hundred and twenty miles away, provided the wind was not so strong it dissipated the smoke too quickly. On a clear night, the fire on top of the tower was visible for over twenty-six miles.

The traffic at this point was increasing: uniremes, biremes, triremes and sailing craft were on every side, though separated by hundreds of yards. Hadon was amazed at their number. Rebha had to be large to handle all these craft.

Indeed it was large, Ruseth assured him. It stood on top of a submerged island into which thousands of wooden and stone piles had been driven or built. The sea-bottom was twenty-five to fifty feet below the surface of the island, and the city rose on piles thirty to fifty feet above the island—not counting the signal tower. The piles had been sunk into the ooze overlaying the limestone surface of the broad plateau. The city was roughly circular with a diameter of two miles. The estimated population, permanent and transient, was about forty thousand.

Hadon was eager to see this fabled city on stilts. He had heard much about it on the voyage from Opar to the Great Games, but the galley taking him had bypassed it, going directly from the Strait of Kethna to the island of Khokarsa.

Ruseth refused to enter it during the day, circling it instead, waiting for nightfall. When dusk came, Ruseth headed the *Wind-Spirit* for the setting sun, a red coal in the dark smoke. Presently the stars came out and with them the small bright flare on top of the Tower of Diheteth. It increased in size and brilliance, rising like a star as they neared.

When they were within a mile of the vast dark pile, shot with tiny lights here and there, he hauled the mainsail down. By this time the stink from the city, carried by the wind, was powerful.

Hinokly, who had been to Rebha once to visit his brother, explained the reason for the odor.

"All garbage, refuse and excrement is dumped into the sea beneath. Most of it is slowly carried out by the current, but much is caught by the piles and the floating docks. You saw the garbage floating in the sea when we were passing southeast of Rebha. We were miles away, yet it was thick."

"Yes," Hadon said, as he helped Hinokly with one edge of the sail. "I also saw the sea crocodiles, the gruntfish, the birds and the sea otters. There must be thousands around here, living off the garbage and the excrement."

Hinokly added, "There are so many birds that Rebha is half white with their droppings. Under the city, the crocodiles and the otters make life very dangerous for anyone who happens to fall into the water, or ventures too close to the edge of the docks. Every now and then, according to my brother, a massive hunt is organized to clear the predators out. They kill a lot of crocodiles and gruntfish, though not so many otters. These are too smart; they swim out and away as soon as they get wind of the hunt. No ships can catch up with them.

"So Rebha has a big crocodile feast—they're good eating—and for a while it's comparatively safe to walk on the under docks. That is, the sea crocodiles are scarce then, though the two-legged crocodiles are not. Rebha has a serious crime problem, but what city doesn't?"

The wind died suddenly and the sea subsided into long flat rollers. As the ship slid forward on its own momentum, the crew stepped down the mast. Then they hauled out long heavy paddles and began the work of getting the vessel under the bottom of the city. It moved slowly under the bulk overhead, passing between two massive pylons bearing huge white numbers. Though it was dark, there was enough light from distant torches and large fires in braziers to see a hundred feet ahead. They steered by docks at which lay huge merchant galleys, small private galleys, fishing boats and even rowboats. Some two hundred yards in, torches flared around a building by a long dock. They were too far away to distinguish the words painted above the structure, but Hinokly said that the building housed customs inspectors and marines.

They headed away from it, passing behind a series of great monoliths and vessels in docks. Several times they bumped against a ship or grated along a dock, but their slow passage prevented any loud noise or damage. Occasionally they heard a deep grunting, like that of swine, or a slurping noise. These were made by the monstrous deep-sea fish that fed here. Hadon dimly saw one by the distant light of a cluster of torches. Its flat oily back was wide enough for three men to stand abreast; its length would have taxed him to long-jump across it. Tendrils of thick knobby flesh sprouted from above its eyes. Its mouth was shaped like two shovels, one above the other.

A few minutes later Ruseth stopped paddling. In a low voice he said, *"Kwa-kemu-kawuru-wu."*

Something moved a few feet away in the water to Hadon's right. Foam shone dirty white in the dimness as an object as long as their ship slid by. Hadon had an impression of knobbed eyes and a ridged back and a long tail, but that could be his imagination, since he knew it was a great sea crocodile. Then it was gone.

They resumed their paddling, feeling that at any moment rows of teeth set in iron-strong jaws might clamp on the blades of their paddles and tear them out of their hands. It had happened before, if Hinokly's stories were true.

They were forced to veer from their desired path by a brightly lit galley. Armed men moved over its decks, and from its depths came grunting and squealing and the stench of pigs.

"Livestock has to be guarded until it can be hauled up to the first level," Hinokly said. "There are human thieves, though these are not the greatest threat. The sea otters will get into a ship and suck the blood from cattle and pigs, then eat them. They won't attack a man unless cornered, but then they are as dangerous as a leopard. Maybe more so, since they are bigger than leopards. I saw a sea otter fight a leopard once—this was at a party given by my employer in Khokarsa—and the otter killed the leopard. It died two days later, though, of its wounds."

Something creaked above them. Hadon looked up and saw a faint oblong appear in the darkness about fifty feet above. Something splashed into the water, just missing the vessel, throwing a spray against his side. The oblong disappeared.

Hinokly said, "Somebody dumped their garbage."

"Paddle faster," Ruseth said. "The noise and the odor will bring the beasts."

They hastened to obey. Hadon thought it time to ask a question: "How do you know where you're going in this dark maze?"

"The head priestess gave me a map and also verbal instructions," Ruseth said. "I was to take the ship in through the fortieth and forty-first piles from the southwest corner along the south side. We were then to shift one row of piles to the west every twelve piles. After reaching the tenth row, we were to proceed past twenty piles to a dock on which are three burning torches," he continued. "That one ahead. We couldn't take a straight path in because we had to avoid certain well-patrolled docks and water lanes."

The ship bumped slightly on its starboard against the edge of a slip and then bumped harder against the end. A face appeared in the window of a shack. A moment later three robed and hooded figures came out. One quickly doused the torches in the water. Another said, "What word, strangers?"

Ruseth said, "That Word spoken in the Beginning..."

"By great Kho Herself," the priestess answered. "Come into the shack."

They crowded in. The woman closed the wooden shutters, putting them all in darkness. A moment later a spark flew from flint against iron, fell into a basin full of oil, and the oil burned. By its dim, bluely flickering flame, the woman ignited a candle, then three more. She placed a metal cover over the basin, extinguishing the fire, but not before the smoke had set them to coughing.

Her hood was thrown back, revealing the face of a woman in middle-age. "You have papers?"

Ruseth took a roll of papyrus paper from a leather bag slung over his shoulder. She broke the seal and spread it out on a table to read it by the candle's light. Her eyes widened, and she looked up now and then to stare at the newcomers. Finally she took a bronze-tipped bone pen, dipped it into a bottle of ink and wrote a note at the bottom of the last page. She signed it with a flourish, sanded the ink, pressed it, rolled the paper up and affixed a seal to it. She handed it to Ruseth.

"So you are Hadon," she said. "The man who should have been Emperor, consort of our high priestess, if the Voice of Kho had not decreed otherwise. And you," she said, staring at Lalila, "are the Witch-from-the-Sea. Suguqateth tells me that you carry one in your belly who is destined for great things—if she is born in the treasure city of Opar. We will see what we can do to get you there."

Hadon had read her signature. He said, "Karsuh, you seem to have been waiting for us. Apparently the news about us has raced ahead of us, though we were in the swiftest ship on the two seas."

"No, Hadon," she said, "we were not waiting for anyone in particular. A watch is always kept here; this is a station in the secret message-transient system. It is true, however, that we have heard something about you. Four days ago a swift naval galley docked here. Admiral Poedy received a message from Minruth. It warned the admiral that Awineth, Hadon and others could possibly be on the way to Rebha. There was no positive data to this effect. It was just that the authorities at Rebha should be on the lookout for you. Minruth thought you might try to flee Khokarsa if Awineth's forces suffered defeat. There was no description of your ship, Ruseth, which is fortunate. But that does not mean there won't be."

"If we could get provisioned tonight, we could leave before dawn," Hadon said.

"That won't be possible," Karsuh said. "We can get a certain amount of food into the ship tonight. But there is so much patrol activity now that a large amount being moved at one time would be certain to attract attention. It will take several days. You see, Admiral Poedy fears—and rightly—that there are many people loyal to Awineth in Rebha. These don't include most of the great merchants who live on Rebha, and Poedy is certain that the majority of his officers are faithful to Minruth. It is the lower classes, the fisherfolk, the sailors, the laborers, the smugglers of Rebha whom he mistrusts. So he keeps patrols busy at all hours, especially at night. That is why we have to move slowly and circumspectly.

"In fact, if he should discover that the Temple of Piqabes is aiding Hadon and Lalila, he would arrest every priestess in the city. He is looking for an excuse, though he realizes the dangers. Perhaps he even hopes for an uprising, since that would give him a chance to clean out the slums. We know through our spies that he has marked at least three thousand men and women for death, people whom he suspects of criminal activity or subversion. Rightly, I might add."

"How long will the restocking take?" Ruseth said.

"From what you've told me of your lack of supplies, about three nights," Karsuh said. "In the meantime, we must hide your ship. Even with the mast stepped down, its lines are obviously unfamiliar. An inspector would know at once that it had entered illegally. If such a vessel had come in through proper channels, he would have heard about it, you may be sure of that."

"I must know where you're taking the ship," Hadon said, "in case we have to leave suddenly; we'd be in a bad situation if we didn't even know where the ship was."

"It'll be in an enclosed dock ten piles west and thirty north of this pile," the priestess said. "My men will take it there. Come, let's get out of here."

The woman leading, holding a fish-oil lantern, they walked along the dock until they came to the bottom of a wooden staircase which wound upward into the darkness. They climbed swiftly, pausing on three landings to catch their breaths. At the top, they found themselves in a narrow street. Here, above the city, the sky was cloudless except for a half-veiled moon. On both sides rose unpainted wooden houses three stories high. The windows on the street level were shuttered: the doors looked solid and were fitted with massive bronze locks. The windows on the upper stories were open. The far corner of the street was dimly lit and, when they arrived there, they saw two giant torches burning on stanchions before the door of a large building. As they passed it they heard sounds of revelry from within. Over the doorway was a large board on which was painted the head of a beach baboon. This marked the hall where sailors of this totem could stay and where Rebha citizens of the same totem gathered for social events.

The priestess led them on, up a flight of steps alongside a ramp to a higher level. Hadon tried to memorize the route, but the darkness and the many turnings and climbings and descents confused him. He wondered at the absence of people at this early hour. Karsuh told him that there was a curfew.

"Poedy imposed it two months ago, ostensibly to prevent any more rioting. It also makes it easier to control criminal activities. Anyone caught out after dusk is automatically convicted, except for provable emergencies, of course."

She stopped. "Oh, oh!"

A light had suddenly illuminated the corner of the street about a hundred yards down. It swiftly became stronger.

"The patrol!"

17

She turned and ran by them, and they hastened after her. Kebiwabes, who was carrying the sleeping Abeth, began to fall behind. Hadon took the child from him. The party fled back up the steps until it came to the previous junction. There they turned to the north and walked swiftly until Karsuh halted.

"This is the Street of the Overturned Hives," she said.

She rapped on the door of a run-down structure, giving three quick beats with her fist, then six, then nine. She waited and presently somebody on the other side of the door rapped twelve times. Karsuh struck the door three times.

Just then lights flared strongly at the junction. Several men, their bronze helmets, cuirasses and spearpoints gleaming in torchlight, stepped into the open. A few seconds later lights appeared at the other end of the street, and a second patrol appeared in the junction there. The party was caught between the two.

Chains rattled behind the door. Karsuh said, "For our sakes, lovers of Kho, open quickly."

A chain banged; a bolt was withdrawn; wood squealed against wood as if a bar had been fitted into too tight arms. A patrolman shouted, his cry echoed by the group at the other junction. At the same time both patrols began running toward the group in front of the door.

It swung open suddenly. The priestess's lamp showed a man clad only in a kilt, clutching a short sword, blinking. Behind him was a narrow hall with walls of peeling paint and a stairway halfway down it.

"Karsuh!" the man said. He stepped back, and the refugees poured in.

"The patrol!" Karsuh said. "They're after us! Lock the door!"

The man quickly obeyed, though he had just shot the bronze bolt when men hammered on the other side.

"Open in the name of the Emperor Minruth and his vicar, Admiral Poedy!"

"There's little time for explanation!" Karsuh said to the man. "These people are important! This is Hadon of Opar; you know of him. This woman and her child are under the protection of Kho Herself."

The door shook under hard buffetings. Suddenly a spearpoint rammed an inch through the wood. Lights appeared in the hallway and at the top of the stairway. Men, women and children looked out from the doors and the steps.

"Gahoruphi," the priestess continued, "you'll have to move everybody out of here. The soldiers will call in help and seize everyone. Poedy is looking for a chance to make an example of those who resist him. It'll be the crocodiles for all of you, even the children!"

"I know," Gahoruphi said. He turned and shouted at the people who were now filling the hall. Hadon wondered where they had all come from; they must have been stacked in their rooms.

A fat naked woman nursing an infant gestured at the priestess, who told the others to follow her. They single-filed down the hall between armed men and up the creaking stairway. The blows on the door were getting louder and more frequent. Hadon looked back down the steps. The head of an ax crashed through the wood. It was withdrawn, and Gahoruphi stabbed his spear through the hole. A man cried out. Gahoruphi withdrew his spear and shouted, "First blood!"

Lalila said to the priestess, "Won't they be massacred?"

"Some will be killed," Karsuh said. "But the rest will follow us through secret ways to the temple."

Abeth, who had been silent with terror since being so savagely awakened, now began to cry. Lalila took her and comforted her.

On the hallway of the second story, others poured out of the rooms. The reek of unwashed bodies filled the air, and shouts and questions dinned around them. The priestess stopped to tell them to follow her. Hadon, however, grabbed her by the arm.

"Why should we run?" he said. "There are still only a few soldiers outside. Why can't we kill them before they call more and then dump their bodies into the sea?"

There was a crash from below as the door fell in. The clang of blades and the cries of injured men arose.

"I will take the woman and the child to the temple!" Karsuh said. She called to the fat woman, whose baby was bawling loudly. "Hinqa! You stay here until Hadon is forced to run, then lead him to the temple."

Lalila gave a despairing look at Hadon, as if she did not expect to see him again. Then she hurried away down the hall and up another flight of steps. Presumably she would go to the roof and across it to wherever the priestess led her.

The manling Paga hesitated for a moment. He was evidently torn between his desire to fight by Hadon's side and his desire to make sure that Lalila was safe. Hadon pointed his sword at Lalila, saying, "She will need a man to guard her, Paga, if I should fall."

The scribe and the bard looked longingly after Lalila. They wanted to get away from the bloodshed to come, but they were not cowards and so would do their duty.

Hadon rammed his way down the stairs through the crowd. Kebiwabes and Hinokly followed him. The hall was jammed with men trying to get at the soldiers, who had advanced only a few feet into the house. Hadon, seeing that the situation made it impossible for him to help, retreated. He fought his way back through the screaming women and children to the second floor. There he went to the window overlooking the street and opened its wooden shutters. Below were about two dozen soldiers. Two were blowing bronze whistles to call in more patrols.

By now the windows all along the streets, as far as he could see, were lit. Heads protruded from them, and there were even citizens out on the street, some with lamps, some with torches. All carried swords, axes or knives.

Hadon went into the nearest apartment, two rooms with blankets on the floor for beds, and rushed through them to stop at the window and look down. The street just below him was unoccupied. The soldiers were all crowding around the door or hammering at the shutters on the windows with spears and axes.

Kebiwabes, Hinokly, Ruseth and his four sailors entered a moment later. Hadon said, "Follow me!" and he let himself out of the window. After dangling for a moment at arm's length, he dropped. He brushed against the side of the house, shoved with his hands, propelled himself a little away. His long legs, bent, took the impact easily. And then he had his *tenu*, Karken, Tree of Death, out of its scabbard. Its edge cut into the back of a soldier, then into another, and another. The head of a fourth fell on the planks; the arm of a fifth thumped into it.

A spearman turned then, his mouth opening to cry alarm, his weapon turning toward Hadon. Karken severed the head of the weapon from the shaft and the head of the man from the trunk. Ruseth joined him then, picking up a spear from a fallen man and driving it into the throat of a man just turning around.

Men came running from doorways up and down the streets, emboldened by this attack on the patrol. Within two minutes it was all over for the two dozen soldiers.

But their whistles had called in more patrolmen. From a distance came shouts and shrill replying whistles, and the light of many torches lit the tops of houses some streets away. It was at this moment, as the mob that had spilled out of the houses into the street suddenly became quiet, that the wind struck the city of Rebha.

One moment all was stillness, as if a sack had been jammed down over everyone. The noise of the approaching patrolmen was still distant. The next moment the wind whistled over the houses and down the streets, and the flames of the torches leaned away from the wind. The sweat on their bodies cooled them, evaporating suddenly.

To the north, lightning still flickered. Dark, angry-looking shapes, evil faces, were revealed in the twisting blazes. These hastened toward the city.

The fat woman, Hinqa, holding the baby with one arm, snatched a torch from the hand of a man near her. Screaming, causing the baby to start screaming again, she whipped the torch over her head. All turned to look at her.

"Kho has sent us a wind!" she cried. "Let's use it as She intends!"

Hadon stared at her, wondering what she meant, what she intended to do. He was not the only one. Those near her shrank from her, scared of her wild-eyed look, her obvious possession. The Goddess seemed to have taken her over; her eyes seemed to blaze like the distant lightning.

"Burn down the city!" she cried. "Burn! Burn! Burn! Destroy the worshipers of Resu and the subjects of Minruth the Tyrant! Let the faithful of the Flaming God burn in flames!"

Her torch soared in an arc which ended inside a second-story window. That it had found sustenance was evident a moment later. Flames broke the darkness of the window and quickly spread through the room.

"Yes! Let it burn!" a man shouted. He threw his torch through the window of a house across the street.

"Burn! Burn! For Kho's sake, burn!"

Hadon was appalled. They seemed to have all gone crazy at once, as if the wind had indeed blown divine madness on them. If they burned the city down, where would they run to? They would either have to flee in ships, of which there were not nearly enough, or jump into the sea. And there they would drown or be devoured by the crocodiles, the otters, the gruntfish.

"Stop it! Stop it!" he yelled. No one heard him except the bard, the scribe and Ruseth. They looked as pale as he felt, gathered together as if they were the only islet of sanity in a sea of craziness.

Now everybody was throwing torches through the windows. The wind whipped the flames as if they were galley slaves, urging them to work faster.

Now the patrolmen were running, drawn by the flames and the mob. The mob threw itself on the patrolmen, overwhelming them, tearing them to pieces with their nails or hacking them to bits.

In the distance, upwind, the shrilling of many whistles floated down. Drums beat somewhere, and then a great bell began to clang. This was soon followed by the clamor of many bells. It seemed that the city was vibrating in wood and air, shivering everywhere from strokes of bronze.

Hinokly shouted in Hadon's ear, "They're mad, mad! They *will* burn the city down, the fools! Unless the authorities can put the fire out! But these people aren't going to let the firemen get close enough to do that! What's the matter with them?"

"I don't know!" Hadon said. "We have to find Lalila! We have to get back to the ship as soon as possible!"

He motioned to the others to follow him. With some difficulty he got through the ever-increasing crowd to the house. It was empty inside, but flames and clouds of smoke filled the second-story hallway. The whole house would be on fire within a few minutes.

With the others behind him, he ascended the stairs to the third story and up a ladder to the roof. This was flat enough to allow them to walk along its sloping surface. The roof of the neighboring house was accessible; a long step and they were on it. A trapdoor lay open there—was it the one Lalila and the priestess had gone through?

Smoke began curling from the trapdoor. Several seconds later, flame tongued from it.

"The roof behind it," Hadon shouted, and he led them across the roof, which was hot on their bare feet, to the next roof. This belonged to a house along the next street over. At that moment he wondered what had happened to Ruseth's four crewmen. Never mind. They would have to save themselves.

He looked over the edge of the roof. This street was also filled with a maniacal mob, and torches were being applied to houses and furniture. The wind was driving these fires southward; some sparks and small burning pieces of wood were being carried across the street to the houses on the other side. These were already burning, but this transmission of flame indicated how quickly the whole city would soon be on fire.

There were many lights out at sea. Hadon supposed these were naval vessels sent out to stand by. From the rapid rise and fall of the torches and lamps, the sea was very choppy.

"We have to get down before we're cut off!" Kebiwabes shouted. Hadon nodded, and they raised a trapdoor and went quickly to the ground floor. They made it just in time, emerging into the street with scorched clothing and singed hair.

Much of the mob had left by this time, apparently having gone to join a battle several streets away. From the clash of blades and the screams of wounded and dying, Hadon supposed that several hundred must be engaged there.

Seeing the entrance to a public stairway, he ran to it. There were some people on it with the same idea. He followed them down the turnings until he was on a dock. The wind blew the flames of the torches set in brackets on a shack wall; if it got much stronger, the torches would be extinguished. By their guttering light men, women and children were climbing into boats or ships or already pulling away. The sea was heavy here, long and rolling, broken somewhat by the massive piles. Several of the vessels were carried, despite their crews' efforts, against the sides of the piles. The side of one was smashed and it began to sink.

"Not everybody is a maniac," Hinokly said. "Soon everyone, crazed or not, will be down here, striving to get away from the inferno."

Hadon did not reply. He pulled a woman from the water onto the dock and while she sat gasping, he asked, "Where is the Temple of Kho?"

"My husband was killed," she said, moaning.

Hadon shook her by a shoulder. "Where is the Temple of Kho?"

"I don't care."

"If you don't tell me, I'll let you stay here and die!"

"I don't care," she said, and she began keening.

Kebiwabes said, "The street above us is on fire. It'll be coming down the stairway next. This dry wood."

Screams came down from above, from those trapped by the flames. The fires they had originated were turning on them.

"We'll swim to that dock over there," Hadon said. "There are ships there, and nobody is on the dock."

"There they come," Ruseth said, pointing at the steps where a dozen people were scrambling down.

Hadon put his sword in its sheath and dived into the water. He came up in a large swell with stinking garbage and turds. A huge round-sided, flat-backed form rose before him, grunted and then sank. He swam over it, feeling panic for a second as his foot struck something soft and greasy.

It was twenty yards to the next dock. Hadon climbed up and then helped Ruseth and the others up to it. By then six craft had been seized, three rowboats and three small fishing boats. A longboat with a single mast was the only one left, and a dozen people were running toward it. Hadon roared and dashed up to them, grabbing them from behind and hurling them into the water. Six went in before the others realized what was happening. They turned with knives and swords in hand. Ruseth joined him, and the two advanced against the six men and women. They did not try to close with him; the fact that he wielded a *tenu* discouraged them. Suddenly Hadon halted and said, "There is no need for bloodshed. I want this boat just long enough to get to the Temple of Kho. You can come with us and, after we get there, you can go on with the boat. In fact, it'll be better that way for all. We need you to help us paddle the boat there, and you need us."

Kebiwabes and Hinokly ranged themselves by Hadon's side. This additional force, as much as the logic of Hadon's argument, convinced the six that cooperation was best. They all got in and pushed the boat away from the dock as more people ran screaming out onto it. Some leaped into the water in a vain attempt to get aboard. All but one made it back to the dock; this man screamed and threw his hands up in the air and disappeared as if something had pulled him under—which no doubt was what had happened.

With ten paddlers, the boat moved along swiftly enough. There were several tense moments when a swell lifted it against a pillar, but they were able to avoid collision by shoving their paddles against it. A section of the street floor above fell in once, the flaming wood hissing and splashing water into the boat. Sparks and hot fragments fell on the paddlers, causing them to cry out in pain or fright, but none was seriously burned.

Their guide, paddling in the lead on the right, turned now and then to order a change of direction. Within ten minutes they seemed to be past the area of fire. At least the light cast by the flames lessened, and there was no odor of smoke. But there was much activity overhead everywhere, people shouting, bells ringing, occasionally a heavy thudding as of many men running. The number of people running in panic down the stairways and seizing vessels steadily increased. Evidently they were taking no chances. If the city did go up in flames, they would not be there to be burned.

At last the man gestured to his right and made a peculiar sign with his hand. Hadon said, "What's that mean?"

Ruseth said, "It means we dock there," pointing to a series of parallel platforms, rising and falling with the swells.

The longboat came in on the crest of a swell between two platforms; the people on the right grabbed the free ends of ropes tied to posts. With some difficulty, Hadon and his group got out onto the dock and clung to the rope railing. Those in the longboat shoved against the dock or dug in their paddles, and the boat moved out from between the platforms.

The ends of the center platform extended outside and past the stairway, sliding up and down as the swells rose and fell. An ingenious mechanism of bronze worked back and forth, up and down, to permit the platform dock to move vertically without being disconnected or bumping into the stairway. The metal arms and joints squeaked, however, as if they needed oil.

Hadon leading, they got to the stairway. There was light furnished by torches on the platforms, but it diminished as they climbed up. By the time they were at street level, they could see only dimly. They came out of the staircase into a dark room. Hadon told the others to stand still while he groped around for a doorway. Presently he found one. Its latch moved easily upward, and he stepped through into another dark room. He immediately felt something light across his face, chest and legs. Whatever the things were, they moved easily at first, then began to resist. Little bells tinkled in the room. Suddenly a door at the opposite end was thrown open. Light streamed in. Men armed with swords poured in. More light fell, this time from a trapdoor in the ceiling. Men looked down at him from behind their spears.

18

The bells had given their warning when Hadon pulled the strings attached to them. He stood still but he cried, "I am Hadon, husband of Lalila, the woman who came here only a short time ago! Karsuh brought her here with the child!"

An officer said "I know." He gave an order and the strings fell to the floor. After checking out the rest of the party—evidently Karsuh had described them—he led them into the next room. They climbed another high spiraling staircase to emerge into a large chamber. This was made of marble and was decorated with murals and statuettes of ivory and gold set in niches. They followed the officer through a series of splendid rooms and ascended another staircase to the third story. They walked down a hallway and then went up another staircase for seven stories inside a tower, as they saw when they got to the top. Lalila, Abeth, Karsuh and a number of others were in the open-sided chamber. They were looking down at a city rapidly being consumed. The flames had spread to new areas, and fires had started in many places remote from the main blaze. These had evidently been ignited by people infected with the same hysteria and self-destructive mania which had seized those in the Street of the Overturned Hives.

Much could be seen from this height. The flames lit up firemen and volunteers pulling buckets of water up through openings in the streets, soldiers battling rioters and looters, people cramming avenues, running into soldiers intent on getting to the flames to extinguish them, refugees piling up on top of each other, screaming and clawing outside the entrances to the stairways.

Here and there, buildings folded into themselves and into the flames, sometimes collapsing through the bottom level and leaving empty smoking spaces.

Hadon took a quick look, then put his arm around Lalila's waist and kissed her. She gave a startled cry—she had not seen him arrive—and then buried her face against his chest.

"Wherever I go," she said, "wherever I go, death, misery, hate, destruction."

"That's only because there is death, misery, hate and destruction everywhere," Hadon said. "You are not under a curse. No more than anybody else."

She started to say something, but the outcry of those around them drowned her words. They looked out to see the cause of the uproar. Fire had broken out in the buildings around the base of the great tower in the center of the city. Whether it had been deliberately started by someone or if the wind had carried sparks and burning pieces to the houses, no one knew. Nor did it matter. The flames were raging now, lighting up the houses and the streets, which were jammed. At the rate the fire was traveling—flames were licking at the first story—the tower would soon be past saving.

Karsuh turned away from the scene. The lights from the fires and the torches set along the railing made her face glisten. It was a copper mask of grief.

"Rebha will soon be aflame from one end to the other," she said. "Kho must have sent this wind; Kho has driven the people out of their minds. Together, wind and madness will burn ancient Rebha to the sea. Nothing, not even the piles, will be left."

"Then we must get away," Hadon said. "Will you lead us to our ship, *Wind-Spirit*? You can go with us, of course."

Karsuh shouted at her guards, who surrounded the entire party. They went down the stairway quickly enough; the temple seemed to be empty except for those who had gathered at the top of the watch tower. Hadon carried Abeth this time. The child clung to him, her face pressed into his neck. She did not cry out or even whisper; she was too frightened. Whatever her internal feelings, outwardly she was as still as if dead.

When they reached the staircase below the street level, Karsuh cried out, "The boats are all gone!"

The men ahead of Hadon roared and began running down the steps. He turned and thrust Abeth at Hinokly and raced after the guards. Their quarry was a rowboat just leaving the dock. Six persons were in it, three men, two women and a boy of about twelve. They were all bent to their task, which was to get the boat away before it was boarded by others. On the dock, rolling back and forth, were the bodies of a dozen people, some temple guards, some thieves. The latter must have swum over from docks under nearby streets after every craft on those docks was seized. Some must have drowned in the attempt; others had been killed fighting for the boats. And now the last boat was being rowed away.

The guards were brave. They leaped without hesitation out after the boat. One landed on the stern and sprawled forward. Before he could rise, he was struck on the neck with the edge of a paddle. Another guard fell into the sea and grabbed the edge of the stern. He started to pull himself up but was hit on the top of the helmet by an oar. He still managed to cling on, then lost his grip as the oar broke the bones of his fingers.

The boat lost some headway, however, when its rowers stopped to beat off the guards. Three of them, though they had fallen short of the craft, were now swimming toward it. Though their bronze helmets and cuirasses weighed them down, they managed to keep their noses above water. What they intended to do when they reached the boat was something they probably had not considered. They were obeying the orders of the priestess, and that was all they had to think about for the moment.

Hadon stopped at the foot of the steps, then stepped to one side to allow the others to pass by. Three of the rowers were still using their oars; the others were standing up, or attempting to, holding their oars to bring down on the swimming guards. One of the rowers was the young boy and he was not very effective.

There was a distance of about thirty feet now from the dock. Too far for him to jump even if he had been able to make a good run.

He reached out and grabbed Ruseth. "We have to get that boat," he said. "Otherwise we'll burn to death—or drown ourselves to keep from burning. How good a swimmer are you?"

"You're asking a fisherlad from Bhabhobes?" Ruseth replied.

"We'll swim out and then dive under and come out ahead of them," Hadon said. "I'll climb up on the left side of the bow—"

"The port," Ruseth said.

"To hell with that," Hadon said. "The left side. You take the right—"

"The starboard," Ruseth said, grinning. Hadon did not know whether to hit him or pat him. The little redhead certainly had guts. To jest at a time like this!

"We have to come up, out and on very swiftly," Hadon said. "Let's go!"

Shouting, he rammed his way through the crowd, knocking people down and some into the water. He poised at the edge as Ruseth arranged himself by his side. As the dock rose to the top of a swell, he leaped out. He stayed under the surface of the water, striking out with all his strength, letting his heavy sword drag him down a little. The current tended to sweep him to the right, but then it was doing the same to the rowboat.

When he could not hold his breath any longer, and his arms and legs seemed filled with lead pellets, he came up, ahead of the boat by ten feet. He could see the rowers frantically working against the torchlight from the docks. He hoped they would not be able to see him in the darkness ahead.

A head emerged a few feet from his—Ruseth. The sailor turned and his teeth gleamed. Hadon gestured at the boat, which was approaching rapidly. He dived again and came up as the boat started to slide down a swell. He reached up and grabbed the wood of the prow just ahead of the nose. With a heave that cracked the muscles in his back—or was it the timbers of the boat?—he was up on the edge, his belly pressing down on it. A moment later, Ruseth's head appeared on the other side, rising, then falling forward as Ruseth also fell on his belly. He held his knife between his teeth.

The two closest rowers were the boy and a woman. The boy was on the left, only a few feet from Hadon. He and the woman must have heard them or felt their weight on the prow. Yelling, they rose to their feet and turned, using their oars as weapons. Hadon, scraping his belly raw, pulled himself over the edge. Ruseth did the same; they collided. The boat pitched, and the woman and the boy lurched back down again on the bench, their oars still up in the air. The boy was not strong enough to keep his up; it went back over his shoulder. The woman raised hers and got halfway up from the bench, intending to bring the oar down on Ruseth.

By then the two men had scrambled up, hampering each other, but still working effectively enough. Hadon kicked the boy in the face; Ruseth stabbed the woman in the neck. Behind them the other four quit rowing and rose to bring their oars into play. The boat swung sideways and then slid down a swell. For a moment the four were diverted by the need to keep their footing. Hadon ignored this, though he could have been hurled out by any too violent a pitch, and advanced. By then he had his sword out. Within twenty seconds, he had cleared the boat.

Ruseth threw the woman, who was wounded in the neck, and the unconscious boy into the sea. The boy, apparently shocked into consciousness, began swimming toward the dock. Hadon did not think he would make it, but he wished him luck. He had nothing against him. In fact, if there had been room, he would have let him stay aboard. But his own came first, Lalila and the child, then Paga, because he loved Lalila and she loved him, then his friends.

Getting the boat back was not difficult, since it had not progressed far. It came in so fast, sliding down a swell and then up it, that its side ground against the dock. Some people on the edge of the dock had been too hasty in trying to get to the boat. They were crushed between the hull and the platform. Fortunately, Lalila and the others had not been on the edge. They had been pushed back by those who were now drowning or screaming with pain and horror.

While Ruseth grabbed a rope to keep the boat from drifting away, Hadon whirled the sword above his head. Those on the edge of the dock shrank back. The priestess Karsuh, shouting commands and threats, aided by her surviving guards, got the others away from the dock. Lalila, Abeth and Paga, the scribe and the bard clambered in. Hadon told the priestess to get in too. There was room for her.

She said, "No. I stay here. It is my duty to pray for salvation for my poor people."

Hadon saluted her, admiring her devotion but doubting her good sense. He gave the order and the others shoved off. As they pulled away, they saw more people descending, their press so great that some were spilled over the sides of the stairway. Smoke belched down after them, and then trickles of fire ran along the tar in the joinings of the planks.

Karsuh tried to get through the crowd to the stairway. She was swept to one side and into the water. If she had been on the near side, Hadon would have made an effort to get her into the boat. But she was quickly lost from view on the other side of the dock.

Hadon took an oar and began rowing with the others. They headed at an angle for the outer waters, beyond the area covered by the pile-city. Because of the heavy seas, it was impossible to cut straight west, the shortest route to safety, or at least a lessening of the present danger. The only practical route was to go straight between the piles in the direction of the current. That way they would avoid being carried sideways into piles. Even so, they had to go around a number of floating docks, which caused them to come perilously close to the massive columns from time to time.

When near the docks they were also threatened by hundreds of refugees who leaped into the sea and swam after the boat. Hadon had to keep urging his crew to row and pay no attention to the people trying to grab the oars and the sides of the craft. Though desperate, the swimmers were not strong enough to retain their holds on the oars. Their hands slipped away and they fell back. A few did manage to seize the edge of the stern. Only then would Hadon allow Hinokly and Paga, the rearmost, to stop rowing for a moment and stab the hands of the would-be boarders.

Finally they pulled out from under the cover of Rebha. Here the sea was even heavier, unbroken by the great piles. They needed rest, but Hadon made them press on.

"They're still swimming out," he said. "We can slow down after a while, when we're beyond the range of even the strongest swimmers."

By then the entire city seemed to be on fire. The flames rose high everywhere, outlining the crazy staggered levels of the buildings, the tower of the Temple of Kho and the Tower of Diheteth. The light showed hundreds of tiny dark figures along the edges of the outermost streets, milling around, then leaping, sometimes singly, sometimes by the dozens. The wind carried the screams even above the roar of the flames and the crash of falling walls and sections of foundation. Then the great Tower of Diheteth, wrapped in a red and orange winding sheet, toppled. Its collapse drowned out all other sounds. It struck the buildings below, sending a spray of flaming fragments high into the air, broke through the foundation and, carrying with it many of the surrounding structures, smashed into the sea. Though much of it was extinguished, a huge part was still burning. This bumped into pillars and docks, setting several aflame, and was lost in the general holocaust. By then wide areas of the city were falling into the sea. The smaller Tower of Kho slid gracefully through the foundation, retaining its vertical position until its base plunged hissing into the waters.

The rowers continued working, though they were numbed with awe. Within two hours, a mighty city of forty thousand people, an old city, the work of many hands and minds, through many generations, a unique place, erected in the desert of the sea, had been destroyed.

Hadon had had doubts about the rationality of human beings before this. From now on, he would never believe that people acted according to the dictates of reason. Perhaps they did most of the time. But behind, or below, that mask of logic was anarchy, unreason, emotion.

He exempted himself from this indictment, of course.

19

The storm struck a few minutes after the Tower of Kho fell. The survivors would connect the two later in cause and effect, and the story would spread throughout the two seas that it was Kho Herself who had started the fires and then sent the storm to uproot even the piles and scatter the debris of Rebha across the Kemu. Where once it had risen fifty feet above the waters, where its tower could be seen for twenty-six miles away, where the smoke from the tower could be seen a hundred and twenty miles away, now there was nothing to show that anything but the sea had ever rolled over this place.

At this moment, those in the rowboat were concerned only for themselves. The first blow of the storm front almost overturned them. They recovered and, while Lalila and Abeth bailed with crocodile-leather buckets, the men bent their backs to keep the boat in a straight line with the waves. If it was allowed to slide at an angle down the mighty waves, it might—undoubtedly would—go under or roll over and not come up again. At least not with its occupants still in it.

A trireme came up then, and somehow they managed to transfer to it, climbing up rope ladders, hanging on to other ropes thrown down to them. Abeth clung tightly to Hadon's neck, her legs wrapped around his torso, while he was half lifted to the deck. An especially heavy sea buried the deck a moment later. He heard a cry and, when he had shaken the water from his eyes, looked around. A moment ago Hinokly had been beside Hadon. Now he was gone. There was no time to reflect on his fate or feel sorrow for him. He had come through many adventures, survived much while others had died. And then, after all that, he too had gone down to dread Sisisken's house.

Clinging to ropes stretched along the decks, they followed an officer. Twice, heavy seas almost tore them loose. They half fell down a ladder into a hold jammed with refugees picked up before the storm burst. The hatch was closed and the people were left in darkness and terror, where the stench of vomit fought with that of fear. The child Abeth whimpered now and then; Lalila soothed her, but her voice betrayed her own suppressed panic. Hadon sat by them, holding one arm around Lalila. Paga and Kebiwabes pressed close to his back; Ruseth huddled in front of him. After what seemed hours, and might have been, Hadon spoke to Ruseth.

"How long can such a ship stand up to a storm like this?"

"There is no way of predicting," Ruseth said. "We can only hope that Piqabes has no plans for taking us to her bosom."

A minute later everyone in the hold was hurled forward, forming a heap six feet high against the bulkhead. A rending of timbers sounded even above their cries. Something struck the hatch cover, splintering it, and water poured in. Hadon fought to his feet and pulled Lalila, who was clinging to Abeth, out of the writhing, kicking, yelling mass. He held her up as he dragged her and the child to the foot of the ladder. Just as they reached it, the deck canted far to one side, pitching them backward against the far bulkhead. Fortunately for them, their impact was softened by the bodies of others.

They scrambled up to try for the ladder again. Once more the deck tilted, this time precipitating them forward against the ladder. Again they were spared immediate contact with hard wood. Those who had been trying to get up the ladder involuntarily acted as shields. Nevertheless, even the reduced effect of collision was enough to hurt Hadon and Lalila. Abeth was lucky; she suffered very little injury.

Those who were able to got up the ladder by pushing or pulling others out of the way. Presently all except the badly injured and Hadon's party were out of the hold. Hadon had restrained his comrades from joining the panic-stricken flight. He had yelled at them to wait, even punching the bard in the belly to keep him from the ladder. Then, with the way cleared, he said, "We can go now."

Hadon leading, they climbed up the steep steps. By then they could see things better; dawn had just come. The sky was still blackish gray, but the wind had died down as if Piqabes had issued a fiat. The waves were rollers again, no longer the high sharp cliffs which had sent the ship bucking and plunging.

In fact the ship, though leaning to one side now, did not seem to be moving much. Its rise and fall were very slight, and its forward progress seemed to be nil.

Hadon gave a cry. The others, crowding up after him, exclaimed also. They were on the forward section of the vessel, a fortunate circumstance for them. The aft part was gone. It had broken off and disappeared into the sea.

Hadon went down the leaning deck to the railing. He looked over the side at the shattered stumps of oars projecting from the three tiers below. Bodies hung out of the ports, but others, injured or whole men, were climbing out of the ports down to a surface under the wreck.

Hadon felt a sense of unreality. What had the ship struck? What was holding it up?

"It looks like logs, hundreds of tree trunks, thousands perhaps," he murmured.

"That's what they are," Ruseth said. "We have struck one of the colossal rafts of the K'ud"em'o, people of the Sea Otter totem who dwell on the coast below the city of Bawaku."

Bawaku, Hadon knew, was an important port city on the western coast of the Kemu. It too was in revolt against Minruth.

There was more life aboard the ship now. The sailors had recovered from the shock of the collision and were untying themselves from the ropes on the decks or coming up out of the hatches. An officer was shouting at some seamen to cut the rigging loose from the mast, which had snapped off and fallen across the foredeck. Several bodies lay beneath it.

"What does he think he's doing?" Ruseth said. "This ship isn't ever going to sail again."

Hadon looked around, then said, "The officer is a *datoepoegu*, a lieutenant. He's the only officer I see. The others must have been on the aft section or injured belowdecks."

"There are many hurt men," Lalila said, referring to the cries and calls for help from below.

Hadon pointed across the logs. "Here come some people. These must be the K'ud"em'o."

About fifty men and women with some children and dogs were advancing across the surface of the immense raft, their dark features indicating basic Khoklem stock: snub noses, thick lips, straight dark hair. Their chests were painted with red stylized heads of sea otters. Their long hair was gathered into seven pigtails, caught around the roots in bright blue beaded bands. The teeth of the men were filed to sharp points. They wore otterskin codpieces secured by narrow strips of skin around the hips and thighs. Aside from these and metal bracelets, anklets and rosaries, they were naked.

The women wore little triangular aprons of skin held by strings around the hips. Their cheeks were heavily rouged; their lips were painted with some bluish substance; large rings of bronze or gold dangled from their noses. All carried tridents or short stabbing swords. They did not, however, act belligerent or defensive; they just seemed curious.

By this time the lieutenant had realized he was the only officer aboard. He called the men away from the useless task of freeing the mast and set them to attending to the wounded, as he should have done at first.

Hadon threw a rope over the side of the vessel and let himself down. The ship had broken through the waist-high wall of small logs along the edge of the raft and thus admitted the sea. Water was ankle-deep here, mainly because the weight of the ship was causing this part of the raft to sink a little below the surface.

Hadon advanced through the water past the ship for twenty yards, then halted where the logs were just surface-wet. The raft people slowed down, talking among themselves. Their dogs, large skinny, mangy brutes, ran barking toward him. He waited, his right hand held up in the universal sign of peace. The beasts stopped only a few inches from him, and one nosed his calf from behind. He did not flinch; he waited, as still as a tree. A man wearing the only hat in the crowd, a high wide-brimmed cylinder with three long white feathers projecting from the top, came up to him. He was very broad, huge-paunched, slit-eyed, and stank of fish. Hadon supposed his grin was friendly, though the filed teeth made it look sinister.

Introductions were made. The man was Qasin, the chief of the Red Sea Otter clan. His name meant Black Heart, though this did not necessarily imply anything derogatory about his character. He certainly seemed generous enough. He offered to take the injured off and have them carried to a "sick persons' area." At least this was the interpretation Hadon made of the man's pronunciation. Qasin spoke Trade Khokarsan, the lingo understood in most large seaports and used by the polyglot crews of merchant and naval ships. His pronunciation of certain consonants and vowels made it difficult to understand him.

Hadon was able to make him understand that he had no authority over the ship or its crew. He and his friends were just passengers, picked up after the destruction of Rebha.

At this Qasin's eyes widened, and he asked Hadon to explain. The chief gave a shout then, and the others ran up to him. He jabbered away at them in a language which did not sound in the least like any Khokarsan Hadon had ever heard. In fact it resembled the language of the Klemqaba, the primitive peoples who lived far south of Bawaku.

Partway through the speech, the crowd began to rejoice, singing, dancing, whirling around and around, hugging and kissing. When the chief was finished speaking to his people, he turned to Hadon.

"We do not exult because all those people have been killed," he said. "Though doubtless they must have done something to deserve it, otherwise Piqabes would not have sent such a death among them. But we are happy because this means that Rebha is no longer a peril to us. Too many times our rafts have drifted into it, and the commander of Rebha has fined us heavily for the damage and the deaths our rafts caused. Yet we cannot be blamed for that, since Piqabes sends the currents which take our rafts sometimes into the piles of Rebha.

"Other times, though we do not come within dangerous proximity of Rebha, yet we come too close to it according to the laws of Rebha. Then the commander sends his marines to our rafts, and we are fined for breaking the laws. And the profits made from our hard voyage are taken away from us. These marines also take our women aside, presumably for questioning, and then rape them. If we dare complain, we are fined for making trouble, for lying!

"We have no love for Rebha and especially none for its navy. But Piqabes has revenged us. All honor to the Goddess of the Two Seas!"

Qasin uttered what sounded like a string of orders to his people. Meanwhile others had joined them, coming from up and down the raft. At least three hundred were finally gathered there. When their chief had finished, they swarmed up the ropes of the canted vessel. The *datoepoegu* tried to stop them, but they ignored him. When he drew his sword and threatened them, he was struck from behind with the flat of an ax. His unconscious body was dragged along the deck and thrown into the sea from the broken end of the galley. Hadon thought he was surely dead, but the officer broke surface a minute later, sputtering and choking. He managed to swim to the raft, where Hadon gave him a helping hand aboard.

After he had recovered enough to sit up and speak, the officer said, "I must have your name! I want you to be a witness when the time comes to put these savages on trial! You saw how they made an unauthorized boarding of one of His Majesty's ships and how they attacked *me*, one of his commissioned officers!"

"If I were you, I'd keep silent about my intentions," Hadon said. He turned and waded away.

He helped Lalila and Abeth down off the ship. By then most of the living sailors and refugees were off. Those who could walk were pressed into service to carry their more injured companions. Litters were taken from the ship's stores or quickly made from planks torn from the vessel. As soon as the sailors were marched away, under guard, the dismantling of the galley started. Hammers, saws and crowbars of bronze ripped up planks; ropes were coiled and carried off; the stores were emptied. In an astonishingly short time, the ship had disappeared. Its wood and metal fittings were transported inland—if such a term could be used for what was after all only a huge raft. The stores and ropes were carried toward a small village at the western end.

The dead from the ship had been laid out, side by side. Their clothes and rings and weapons were removed and taken away somewhere. The lieutenant was by then up on his feet and protesting vigorously. No one paid him any attention, which was a kindness, relatively speaking. The officer kept demanding that Hadon help him get the ship back. Hadon told him to leave them alone. Couldn't he see that he was completely at the mercy of the raft people? If the K'ud"em'o wished, they could kill him and throw his body into the sea. If he persisted, Hadon said, he would be endangering his whole crew. Should the Red Sea Otters find it necessary to slay him, then they would have to kill all the witnesses—which also meant that Hadon and his group could be in grave danger, even though they were not naval personnel.

In fact, Hadon said, glaring at the officer, if he did not cease his useless, indeed dangerous, meddling, Hadon himself might shove him back into the sea. He wasn't particularly concerned about the possibility of the lieutenant's sudden demise, but he did not want to get involved in repercussions.

"You are a traitor!"

"I am no follower of the blasphemer and traitor, King Minruth," Hadon said, sneering. He put his hand on the hilt of his sword. Should he behead this stupid fellow and avoid trouble in the future? Not to mention earning the gratitude of the raft people?

"You are a rebel, a denier of the primacy of Resu!" the officer said.

"Since I am in my right mind, of course I am," Hadon said. "As for who is the rebel and who is not, there is no question. You are the rebel and the traitor, and no doubt loathsome Sisisken, great Kho's eldest daughter, has marked you as an early guest in her house."

The officer turned pale. Hadon walked away, going toward a priestess who was administering final rites to the dead. She chanted the song of the dead while daubing the forehead of each corpse with black, blue and red clay, arranging the spots to form the corners of a triangle. Her nubile attendant, whose face and breasts were painted in alternating circles of black and white, swung a censer of burning pine needles over the face of each corpse after the priestess daubed it. Nine times the censer swung while the attendant shouted the name of the victim. Where she had not been able to learn the name from the survivors because of too mutilated features, she gave the name of the first man created by Kho, Qawi.

The chief, Qasin, stood for a while watching his wife and Queen, the head priestess, work among the dead. Then he nodded, and six muscular men began to throw the bodies into the sea. After the eighth corpse sank, the greasy back of a gruntfish appeared, and the ninth corpse was swallowed by cavernous jaws.

"Piqabes wastes nothing," Qasin said, making the ancient sign used now only among old people and primitives. "The fish eat our dead, and we eat the fish."

20

While they followed the chief to the central village, Hadon told the story of his group. He had hesitated at first about revealing their identities, but the attitude of the K'ud"em'o seemed to make it safe. Besides, Hadon felt this would assure the K'ud"em'o that they were not with the sailors.

The chief was astonished. He had had no news since the raft had been launched from the homeland coast five months ago, and news from Khokarsa reached there three months late.

Qasin listened carefully, though interrupting frequently with exclamations of horror or rage. It was not, however, the political changes which upset him, since his tribe's loyalty to the concept of empire was rather tenuous; it was the religious upheaval which drove him into a frenzy.

They came to the central part of the raft which, Hadon learned, was a mile and a half long and half a mile wide at its broadest. Here stood fifty beehive-shaped huts made of bamboo poles and mahogany shingles. They stood on stilts, the ends of which were driven into holes drilled into the logs. Each housed about ten people and several dogs. In bad weather, they also held goats and the pet monkeys and parrots.

The center hut was the largest. This was the shrine of green-eyed Piqabes, goddess of the sea. Standing before its entrance was a great block of mahogany wood with a stairway of twelve steps cut on each side. On top of this was set an immense upright oblong of granite. A hole had been cut through its upper part, and its interior had been chiseled into a spiral arrangement.

"The stone of C'ak'oguq"o," the chief said, seeing Hadon's questioning expression. "She is our goddess of healing, though you may call her Qawo if you wish. The stone sits before her temple in our chief village," Qasin continued. "That is, until we have put together our raft and placed our supplies and trading goods on it. Then it is carried with much ceremony to the raft and placed here, before the Temple of Piqabes."

Hadon was amazed at the chief's story. Every two years an enormous number of valuable trees were cut in the highlands of the K'ud"em'o country. These were floated down the main river, through a number of rapids and over many cataracts. Eventually they were brought to the mouth of the river and into a bay protected by a great breakwater of earth built by the tribe. The mouth of the river was at a shallow level at this time, since the tribe had diverted the main flow through an ancient channel.

The logs were arranged in the quiet area behind the breakwater into a raft three times as long as wide. Great vines held two-thirds of the logs together. The rest were secured by bridges of wood, fitted with underpins driven into holes bored in the logs. After the raft was completed, houses erected on it and the supplies, animals and people moved onto it, the breakwater was destroyed. This was comparatively easy, since the action of the sea had been slowly tearing it down anyway. The river was rediverted into the main channel, which moved the raft seaward and helped crumble the earthen breakwater.

The river's pressure slowly pushed the raft out into the Kemu. Here the sea current caught it and ponderously shoved the giant assemblage of logs toward the southeast.

The raft people lived on their floating wooden island for six months while it moved toward Wethna. Their main food was the fish they caught, but they drank goat milk and ate goat meat; their storehouses provided nuts and berries, okra for soup and emmer wheat and millet flour to bake bread. They also drank wine and the harsh peaty liquor, *s"okoko*, purchased from the Klemqaba to the south. They kept enough to sell at Wethna after watering it down five to one. The K'ud"em'o were not cheating the Wethnans by this dilution; only the Klemqaba could drink the fiery liquid straight and live to brag of it.

In addition, the raft tribe sold its logs for a great profit, since mahogany and the other valuable trees did not grow on the Wethnan side of the coast. They also sold or bartered artifacts, carved good-luck godlets, whistles of eagle bone, phallic jadeite statues of their aboriginal deities, fascinating to the Wethnans because of their unfamiliarity. And aphrodisiac and contraceptive powders, fertility charms, bracelets to ward off the evil eye and diseases, ceremonial dildos fringed with the feathers of a kingfisher found only in the K'ud"em'o country.

"Surely you don't end your voyage, at the harbor of Wethna?" Hadon said. "The current could not bring you right to its doorstep every time."

"It doesn't," Qasin said. "The rafts usually end up about fifty to seventy miles either way from Wethna. Then arrangements are made with the merchants of the city to transport the logs and goods on the coastal road. We pay for that, of course."

Once everything was sold, the tribe built a number of small ships and rowed back to their mainland. The largest carried the stone of their goddess of healing.

"Have you ever lost it in a storm or an accident?" Hadon asked.

"Never. We have been doing this for three hundred years and, though we have been in some terrible storms, always the raft with the stone gets through safely. There is a prophecy among my people, however, that if the stone should be lost, then the two seas will dry up."

Having arrived home after a two-month return trip, going against the current and the wind, the voyagers summoned those left behind. From the coast and the hills the tribesmen came down to rejoice with the rafters. The festival ran until all the money was spent, sometimes taking two months or more. During this occasion, all feasted and drank for free. Burials were conducted in drunken hilarity. Marriage ceremonies were held and infants, some of whom had waited for three years, were given their public names.

"Nothing of any real importance is done except during the festival of the homecoming," Qasin said. "Until then, the dead are placed in the open on top of a hill. When the festival is to start, their bones are collected, washed and wrapped in palm leaves and brought down to the coast for burial. No one can be married until this time, though of course couples live together and have children. Nor can one be divorced until the festival, though people do separate meanwhile. Nor can property change hands or accused lawbreakers be judged until then."

"If, as you say, the judge, the prosecutor, the defendant and his protector are all drunk, then you must have some grave miscarriages of justice," Hadon commented.

"No more than when all are sober," the chief said.

"But isn't it unjust to jail a man for two years while he awaits trial?"

"We don't jail the accused until time for the festival," Qasin said, "unless he is an obvious public menace, in which case we kill him. If he has fled to the hills, then he is automatically assumed to be guilty."

Qasin mounted a platform and ordered a large bronze bell rung. This summoned people from the little settlements at the four corners of the raft. When all were assembled, the chief gave them the news of the terrible schism which had plunged the Empire into a bloody time. There was an uproar which lasted for half an hour. The chief then restored order by having the bell clanged again.

The injured seamen and refugees, bandaged and smeared with healing salves, limped or were carried in. The priestess chanted over them, and then, one by one, they went through the hole in the stone. If they could not crawl through by themselves, they were dragged through. After each had been slid like the end of a thread through the eye of a needle, he was examined by two doctors, a priestess and priest, who felt the bodies and heads of the injured. They then made signs to twenty young men who stood nearby. The men took some off to a nearby group of huts to convalesce. Others they removed on litters to a hut set some distance westward of the central village.

Hadon asked the reason for the segregation.

"You see the spirals on the inside of the hole in the stone?" Qasin asked. "These are magical markings which collect the currents that pass through the body of the earth and the sea. They focus them, amplify them, build them up. The field of force is healing, and anybody who passes through it is healed of whatever ails them. Or, if healthy, then one becomes supercharged with the currents of goodness."

"Goodness?" Hadon asked.

"Yes," the chief answered. "To be good is to be healthy and vice versa. A man may be evil and yet seem to have perfect health, but he is not really healthy."

"What happens to those who were put in that hut to the west?"

"They are too far gone to benefit from the healing field in the hole," Qasin said. "They will be knocked on the head with specially blessed clubs—we don't want their ghosts haunting this raft—and then thrown into the sea."

"But—but—they may survive!" Hadon said.

"No, they won't," Qasin said. "The vicars of C'ak'oguq"o are sensitive to the aura which her stone lips radiate. They can feel the lack of the vital force; they shudder at the cold of dread Sisisken's hand on the flesh of the unfortunate. It is true that the sick might live for some time. But why drag out their pain and misery? Besides, we don't have a surplus of food aboard; we really can't afford to feed all these sailors. So…"

A few moments later the injured men were dragged out and their skulls shattered with stone axes. The lieutenant ran up to the slaughter and protested loudly. The chief made a sign with one hand and a young man swung his ax down on the head of the officer.

"We don't like people who interfere with our traditions," the chief said.

"I personally have always believed that a stranger should honor the customs of the people he finds himself among," Hadon said. But he felt sick when he turned away. Later he told himself that the killing of the officer was the best thing that could have happened. Now he could never report that the long-sought Hadon of Opar and the Witch-from-the-Sea were in Wethna.

This thought made him wonder about the fate of the sailors who had been spared. He asked Qasin about them.

"They will be questioned," Qasin said. "Those who are loyal to Kho, but who had to conceal their true feelings because they were in Minruth's service, will be allowed to step off the raft when we get to the coast. Those who would lift the Flaming God above his natural rank, who would degrade the White Goddess, Mother of All, will not be with us when we sight the shores of Wethna."

Further questioning disclosed that the raft carried no small ships which Hadon and his party could take for a faster voyage to the coast.

"You will have to remain here for the next two months," Qasin said. "Unless some ship comes near enough for us to hail and so put you aboard. That is not very likely to happen."

"Lalila is two months pregnant now," Hadon said. "She will be four months along when we get to Wethna. And it is a long and dangerous way to Opar from there. Ordinarily I would not worry about the time, since a galley or a swift sailing ship could get us there in two months. But there are pirates abroad now, and there is no Empire to maintain law. Every city is setting itself up to be independent, and many of the small towns and villages are eager to break away from the rule of the cities. We won't know what to expect whenever we put in to a port. Besides, from what I have heard, Minruth did leave enough ships and men to shut off the Strait of Keth, which means we'll have to go overland to Kethna. The peninsula is a wild, rough, dangerous area, mountainous, full of four- and two-legged predators. Five months is really not much time to get from Wethna to Opar under these conditions."

"True," Qasin said. "But why worry? You can do nothing until you get to Wethna. Meanwhile, enjoy yourself. Come to my hut. I will open a jug of *s"okoko* for us, and you will soon forget your troubles. Let us drift with the raft and enjoy life."

He grinned at Hadon with triangular teeth. He doubtless meant to show friendliness, but the smile still looked sinister.

21

Seventy days later, all of Hadon's party except for Ruseth left Wethna on a merchant sailing ship. Ruseth stayed behind, intending to embark the next day as deckhand on a merchant galley. Since his ship was lost, he considered that he was no longer under orders to take Lalila to Opar. He would return to Khokarsa and try to interest Awineth in building a fleet of fore-and-aft sailing ships. He would say nothing to her, of course, about his part in getting Hadon and Lalila off the island.

"I'll go to Dythbeth," Ruseth had said. "Or I'll try to get into the city. By now it may have fallen. If Awineth is alive and uncaptured, I'll find her and talk her into building a new navy. If she is in a position to do so…well, never mind. I'll see what I can do when I get there. If I get there. The Wethnans say there are so many pirates now that the navy can no longer keep order on thc high seas."

Hadon wished him luck, but he did not think Ruseth had much likelihood of success.

For that matter, his own chances were none too good. Neither of the two routes open was easy or free from perils. The regular way into the Sea of Opar was through the Strait of Keth. But this, according to Wethnan reports, was blockaded at its northern end. There were six triremes, four biremes and a number of smaller naval ships at anchor there. In addition, at least two hundred marines were stationed on the top of the cliffs forming the entrance to the strait. Minruth had ordered this fleet to remain on guard there, even though he needed them very much at Khokarsa.

Minruth knew well how ambitious the ruler of Kethna was. The kings of this city had always been overly independent, often arrogant, because they held the southern end of the strait. No ship could leave the Kemuwopar to carry its trade goods from Opar into the Kemu unless the Kethnan fleet permitted it to do so. And in times of troubles, the Kethnan fleets had ventured out into the Kemu and ravaged Khokarsan shipping and navies. A Kethnan expedition had in fact once raided the shores of Khokarsa itself and come very close to capturing the Emperor.

There was no communication from Kethna at the moment, but the authorities in Wethna expected the Kethnan fleet to come through the strait some day and attack the Khokarsan fleet. After all, the Kethnans had a much larger fleet available, and they could send an overland expedition against the marines holding the cliff exit.

Indeed, the main subject of conversation in the marketplace and on the docks was why Kethna had not already attacked. Some people speculated that Kethna had more immediate projects, such as defending itself against the pirates of Mikawuru. No one knew what the true situation was, since all communication had been cut off; of course this did not keep people from reporting all sorts of wild tales as the truth. It never had and never would.

Hadon considered going along the coast westward until they reached a small village about thirty miles east of the strait. Here they could disembark and proceed over the mountains of the peninsula to the Sea of Opar. They could make their way along the precipitous shore to the city of Kethna. And there, hopefully, they could buy passage on a merchant ship to Opar. Or else they could purchase a small sailing ship. Or, if they had no money, steal a vessel.

The main trouble with this plan was that the journey through the mountains, though relatively short, was known to be very dangerous. Of the two trails available, both were difficult to traverse and beset with wild beasts and outlaws. It was even said that a mountain-loving type of Nukaar, the hairy apemen of the trees, dwelt in that area. Much was said about this land, none of it good.

Another route would be directly south of Wethna. This too would be over mountains, and the passage through these would take about five times longer than the former route. Having crossed, however, the party would be much closer to Opar. They would, theoretically, come out close to the city of Wentisuh. From there they could take a ship or even a coastal boat to the port which served the inland city of Opar. After much asking about it in the bazaar and on the docks, however, Hadon decided against the second route. It was so dangerous that nobody knew of anyone who had ever used it successfully.

Paga suggested a third alternative.

"Why not take a small vessel into the strait under cover of night? If there is no moon, and the ship is little enough, we could slip by the big vessels. They won't be anchoring against the cliffs or across the mouth of the strait, you may be sure of that."

"No," Hadon said. "But the strait is very narrow; it's only about eighty feet wide at the mouth. The cliffs on both sides reach a height of two hundred feet there, though the mountains immediately beyond them tower several thousand feet. If there are marines stationed on both sides, they can observe anything that passes through on the waters below. They will most assuredly have torches or lamps floating on buoys in the mouth of the strait, and these will enable the marines to see at night too. They will undoubtedly also have large rocks ready to be cast down on a ship, and flaming oil and Kho only knows what else. They will be able to summon the blockading ships by bell or signal fire or some means, who knows?

"Besides, there is nothing to prevent them from stretching a net across the mouth."

"Could we slip past the guards on either side above?" Lalila said. "Then walk along the top of the cliffs to the other end of the strait?"

"No," Hadon said. "The cliffs become sheer mountains. There are some plateaus further along, but I wouldn't know how to get to them. Besides, the wild Klemqaba roam those parts."

While he was deciding what to do, Hadon took a job as bodyguard for a rich Wethnan merchant. Kebiwabes picked up some money by singing in the streets and in the taverns. Paga apprenticed himself to a blacksmith. Though he did not earn much, he did learn a lot about the skill of working iron. This went on for thirty-five days, at the end of which there was enough money to buy passage to the village of Phetapoeth. There was not nearly enough, however, to buy a small ship for their purposes.

"It will take three more months just to save enough to buy a very small fishing skiff," Hadon said. "Lalila has about four months left before the baby comes. I doubt that we could get to Opar in a month's time—not with the troubled situation. But if we took passage on a ship to Phetapoeth now, we couldn't leave the village after we got there. There are no jobs there. So..."

"So we steal a ship!" Lalila said. "Or we go to Phetapoeth and then go over the mountains!"

"I think," Hadon said slowly, "that we will try to go through the strait after all. It is dangerous, but the least dangerous way."

"And if we can't get through, then we can try the mountain passes above Phetapoeth?" Lalila asked.

She looked anxious, and rightly so, since such a trip would make strong men look forward to it with anything but joy. For a pregnant woman and a little child to venture there with only a bard, a manling and Hadon—swordsman though he was—was madness, or not far from it.

Hadon felt angry. Somehow he had failed her, yet what else could he do? He was not one of the heroes of ancient times, Nakadeth, for instance, who could steal a pair of magical shoes from an evil spider and walk across the skies upside down, thus going over instead of around those very mountains.

Lalila, looking intently at him, said, "Do not be angry, Hadon. You cannot help it that you are only human."

He was astonished, not for the first time, at her ability to read his thoughts. Sometimes he wondered if she was indeed a witch from the sea. The idea made him proud that such a woman would love him, yet, at the same time, it made him feel uneasy too, thinking of certain undesirable thoughts he'd had. For instance, if Lalila could read his thoughts when he saw the beautiful wife of the merchant for whom he was working, what would she do?

Come to think of it, she always had a rather peculiar smile at these times.

"What's the matter now, Hadon?" Lalila said.

"Oh!" he said, staring. "Nothing. I was just trying to envision the strait as I saw it some years ago."

She had that same peculiar smile.

He went to the docks that night after his shift. He inquired around, found a dockmaster and asked him about passage to Phetapoeth.

"Why would you want to take your woman and child to that Kho-forsaken place?" the dockmaster asked. "There's no work for a *numatenu* there. Besides, too many ships have disappeared on their way there. There are pirates along that route, honored swordsman. They lurk in every little bay and cove, ready to dash out and intercept any ship that looks like easy prey."

Hadon hesitated. His first impulse had been to tell the man that he was sticking his nose up the ape's ass.[3] He checked himself, however, because he did not want to anger the fellow. If he became suspicious of Hadon, he could notify the authorities and they could—no, would—arrest him for questioning. As in all countries, the spy-hunting fever was raging. Wethna was theoretically neutral, having declared for neither Awineth nor Minruth. This placed Wethna in a delicate situation, since whoever triumphed might decide to punish Wethna for not having taken a definite stand. In fact, Hadon thought, this would inevitably occur. The city fathers and mothers should have gone one way or the other, even if they had had to resort to tossing a coin.

The reasoning for Wethna's neutrality was the hope that the winner would be grateful to them for not fighting on the side of the enemy. Hadon considered this very unrealistic. Kings and queens always regarded the person who was not for them as against them. And history had verified that retaliation for less than wholehearted backing was a terrible thing. Entire cities had been leveled and their population, man, woman and beast, had been slaughtered because of lukewarm loyalty.

This was not, however, Hadon's concern. Even if it was he would have forgotten it because of a sudden and much more immediate worry. Five days before the group was to leave on a merchant galley, plague struck Wethna.

No one knew who brought the disease into Wethna, but most supposed that some sailors were responsible. It did not matter. What did was that this particular plague, called the sweating sickness, spread with frightening swiftness. And it killed with even more terrifying speed.

Kebiwabes was the first of the group to hear of it. He hurried home from a tavern at which he had been singing. He was bursting to tell the news, which was that several dozen people on the docks had been laid low with the disease. He found Hadon in its grip.

It ran its course in the usual three days. First Hadon was seized with an unaccountable sense of dread, a sense of overpowering but nameless doom. About fifteen minutes later he began shivering violently. He felt as if he had suddenly been plunged into the icy waters of a mountain lake. Then he became dizzy, suffered an agonizing headache and great pain in his neck, shoulders, arms and legs. He was unable to lift even his head.

3 A literal translation of a widespread Khokarsan phrase. This is based on an old folk tale which is too repulsive even for the standards of modern American publishing. However, like most old jokes, it originated in the Old Stone Age and is found, in one form or another, in all countries.

Three hours later he felt like he was on fire and began the profuse sweating which lasted for a day and a night. The perspiring stopped suddenly, but it was followed by more headache, intense thirst, a rapid beating of the heart and then delirium.

At the end of its course, Hadon was free of the plague's symptoms but was forced to stay in bed for four days because of extreme weakness. He was unattended by any doctor during this whole time. Though the bard and Lalila took turns looking for a physician while Hadon was nursed by one or the other, they could not get one. The doctors were either too busy to come or were themselves sick or dead. His friends could only nurse him and hope for the best. Lalila and Paga took turns squeezing water from a rag over his feverish body and lifting his head so he could drink great quantities of water.

The noise of the streets outside, the chatter and yelling of nearby pedestrians and the not too distant sounds of the marketplace, had died. Except for the tramping of feet and muffled booming of a drum as patrols passed, or the cry of the corpse-collectors to bring out the dead, all was quiet. Now and then a man or a woman screamed or a child cried.

A day after Hadon's sickness passed, Kebiwabes was seized with the irresistible sensation of impending death. Lalila and Paga now had two patients to take care of, though Hadon was no longer a constant concern.

The bard did not die during the first day, which meant he would probably survive.

Lalila and Paga had to take turns going out after water and food. The bazaar was closed, the sellers having fled to their homes or out into the country. But there was food to be had if one had enough money. A few merchants had set up a market on the docks, guarded by soldiers who would admit only those who could show their money. Once Lalila was robbed on her way home by a hungry trio. She was knocked down and her basket was grabbed and run off with. She made two trips that day, taking Paga with her the second time. She did not like to leave the convalescent and the sick one without any care, but if they did not get food, they would die anyway.

Sometimes, when the wind shifted, they could smell the odor of bodies burning in the great charnel pit outside the west wall. Then the giant bronze bells in the temples of Kho and Resu would toll sadly.

Lalila and Paga waited to be struck, thinking it inevitable. But neither was felled, and the child also escaped the malady. Abeth did become ill four weeks later, though with a sickness which resembled typhus.

The sweating disease raged through the city, slaying ten thousand out of a population of fifty thousand. At least a third of the city fled into the country as soon as the disease gained momentum. They took it with them, of course, and it spread through the rural areas. Eighty thousand farmers, fishermen, woodcutters and artisans died. The whole land of Wethna lay under a pall of stinking smoke from corpse-fires.

Among the victims was the beautiful wife of the rich merchant. He had stayed in the city, gathering the profits from his food supplies. She went to their villa up in the hills and was killed, not by the sweating sickness, but from snakebite. She encountered a cobra while strolling in her garden one evening.

In seven weeks the sickness had passed through the land and was gone. The survivors came out of hiding and began to put the nation together again.

Abeth's sickness passed, leaving her thin and listless. Not until almost two months after they had arrived at Wethna was the child fit for travel.

Hadon had gone back to work for the merchant since they needed money desperately. His position as bodyguard enabled him to overhear many of the details of his employer's business. He learned about a small fishing boat which the merchant had purchased at a low sum from the widow of a man who'd died of the plague. After looking it over, Hadon decided it was just the size he needed. He bought it at a fair price and still had money saved to rerig the boat. The men he hired to do the work evidently thought he was crazy. What was the yard attached to near the bottom of the mast and running lengthwise? What was the purpose of this? And why was he cutting a perfectly good sail diagonally, so that he now had two useless triangular sails?

Hadon smiled and said he was trying an experiment. He did not tell the truth because of what Ruseth had said about people's reactions to his own ship. He did not want to be suspected of sorcery and subjected to a court of inquiry.

One morning, an hour after midnight, he and the others took the boat out of the harbor. By dawn they were out of sight of the city. Hadon did not worry about being pursued. Who could care that he left? His employer would just shrug his shoulders and count himself lucky that he did not have to pay him for the last week—until he found that Hadon had charged his account for the provisions. The two sums balanced each other, so Hadon figured he had not done anything dishonest.

They reached the strait in five days. Before then, though, they knew something had happened there. They saw the wreck of a beached trireme, and two miles further on they came across a number of corpses floating over a wide area. Hadon took the vessel up boldly in daylight to the very mouth. There was no sign of a fleet until he got close to the entrance of the strait. The stern of a bireme jutted up from the water, almost blocking off the passage of Hadon's craft. He could not understand what was keeping the ship from sinking, since the depth here was about four hundred feet.

He had the sails dropped, and they rowed slowly past the wreck and the western wall. The sun was directly overhead at this time, enabling them to see for some distance down into the water. Hadon whistled and Kebiwabes swore. The galley was held up by a score of other ships, piled one on top of each other.

"There must have been a hell of a battle here," Hadon said. "But who tried to get out? The Kethnans?"

"More than likely," the bard said. "They must have tried to run the gauntlet of the marines on the cliffs. And some must have made it, otherwise Minruth's fleet would still be here. They must have closed with the blockaders then, and in the battle everybody was sunk."

That seemed the only logical explanation, though it could have been pirates who came through the strait, not Kethnans. Who it was did not matter; the way was clear. The marines stationed above had either deserted their posts or been killed by the invading fleet. Maybe a Khokarsan ship or two had survived the battle and taken the marines home, since one ship could not maintain the blockade.

The strait was still going to be closed to any vessel larger than a small fishing boat for some time. Eventually the current would move the wrecks on out into the deeper waters, or else the Kethnans would clear the top wrecks. Meanwhile, Hadon and his crew, not even excepting Lalila, who was far gone in pregnancy, rowed the boat through the fifty dark, silent miles of the winding strait. Because of their short-handedness they made slow progress, having to sleep at night. It took them over a week to get their vessel through, during which they worried about pirates or Kethnans. They were done for if they encountered another craft of any size. It would be impossible to flee.

But no one else was in the strait and, on the tenth day, they came out against the current from the darkness and the silence. Like Keth, the ancient hero who first entered the Southern Sea, they were dazzled by the brightness of the equatorial sun.

Hadon said, "Lalila! I was afraid our child would not be born in Opar. But now we have a good chance to make it on time. If Kho is with us, we shall be in my native city a week before your term is up."

Lalila smiled, though she looked tired, wan and anxious. Paga, forever the pessimist, growled, "Babies do not always come on schedule, Hadon."

22

Kebiwabes said that their journey from Khokarsa to Wethna had enough material for two epics. The voyage from Wethna to Opar had enough adventures to make three epics, and it wasn't even finished. Hadon, in a typical statement, replied that all bards exaggerated enormously, though their experiences since the flight from the capital of Khokarsa could easily make one epic, if the bard was long-winded enough.

"And I suppose," Kebiwabes said, "that you would compress all of the adventures into a lyric, into nine or twenty-seven lines?"

"That would be the ultimate in poetry," Hadon said. Then, seeing that the bard looked hurt, he added, "Don't pay any attention to what I say now, Kebiwabes. I am tired and hungry and anxious, since Lalila is so swelled that she seems about to burst like an overloaded wine sack. And I am taking my frustration and fear out on you."

"Not to mention that you have no taste," Kebiwabes said. He walked to the other end of the boat, which wasn't very far, and looked out ahead. His back expressed his anger.

What the bard had said was not really too exaggerated. There had been many times when Hadon thought they would all be dead within a minute. But somehow, with mighty Kho giving them invisible yet evident help, they had come through.

There had been other times when no danger pressed close, yet they felt imperiled. Just three days before, at dusk, their boat was passing close to a desolate marshy region, swamps which stretched inland for miles, then abruptly ended at sheer mountains. The only protuberance between the sea and the mountains was a hilly mass about a mile inward. Hadon was telling them that this was supposed to be the site of an ancient city.

"It was founded by Bessem, the exiled son of Keth. He quarreled with his father and then killed his brother in a rage, so he was forced to flee. Keth did not go after him—he was an old man then, almost sixty—but he proclaimed that if Bessem came back, he was to be slain instantly, without trial. So Bessem traveled south along this coast and stopped when he got here. This was not a marsh at that time, but a lowland which sloped gently to the mountains. And here Bessem built a city of red stone quarried from the mountains. It was called, of course, Mibessem, the city of Bessem.

"All went well. Many people came from Kethna and Sakawuru and from the Northern Sea, the Kemu, to live in the city of giant stone blocks. This was when the Sea of Opar was almost unknown and Mikethna was itself only a small colony. In fact it was about the same time that the priestess Lupoeth led an expedition into the hinterland and found the place which would later become Opar, city of treasures.

"Though the city of Mibessem prospered, however, there were at the same time unsettling stories told of something which lived in the mountains beyond the city. It was said to play a reed flute, its music driving men mad and enchanting women so they followed the player into the mountain forests and were never seen again. Misshapen creatures would be seen at dusk, near the limits of the farmlands around the city, and these, though they seemed bestial, resembled some of the women who had wandered away.

"It was said that Bessem, in an ill-advised moment, had chosen to build his city in the land of a demon. And it was said that this demon was in fact the chief of demons, the leader of those nameless creatures whom mighty Kho scourged from the Kemu so that Her people might settle there. The demons who were not killed or buried so deeply underground that they would not be able to dig their way back until the crack of doom—these demons fled into the land along the Southern Sea.

"And so now the nameless demon was angry because his refuge had been invaded. Yet he was under the ancient restraint imposed by great Kho on his kind. He could not lay a hand or a paw or a tentacle on a human being in anger. What the Mother of All had failed to do, however, was to prohibit the nameless ones from using other methods. Moreover, a demon could touch, or even embrace, a human if it did not do it in anger or with intent to harm. And so the flutist of the shadows, the distorted one, the nameless one who breathes at night outside windows, this thing played his reed flute. And men went crazy and women followed him into the burrow near the mountains. And there they laid strangely with it and conceived and bore hideous children.

"Now Bessem was a hero of old, you understand, a mighty man whose like the two seas have not seen for centuries. So he armed himself with a spear that two strong men today could not pick up, and he strode into the wilderness to find the nameless thing and destroy it. But he did not come back, and the flute played again in the fields outside the city. Sailors told about this in Kethna and the ports of the Kemu.

"And so one day the Empress of Khokarsa sent a ship to Mibessem to determine if the stories she had heard were indeed true. If they were, a priestess was to rid the land of the demon. The ship took a year to get to Kethna because of storms and troubles with pirates. There the captain was told that he was too late. A Kethnan merchantman putting into the port of Mibessem at dusk had heard weird blood-chilling music from a reed flute. It was heard miles over the still sea, long before the lookout could see the red city. In fact he never did see it, since he had mistaken the dark hill where it once stood. Or perhaps he saw its outer shell, the earth piled up over it by the nameless demon. No one knows, because no one has ever dared enter the swamp and dig into the hill.

"And so the ship neared the shore, which was no longer a fine sand beach but a swamp. The gentle slope had subsided into a perfect flatness, and crocodiles and hippopotamuses swam among the palm trees and the other trees growing on little islets.

"Where were the people? No one knew, but it was feared they had met some terrible fate and were lying under the waters of the swamp. Or perhaps under the earth that something evil and irresistible had thrown over the once-proud towers and massive walls of Mibessem.

"In any event, the crew of the ship did not stay long. The fluting became louder and louder, and they heard a splash as of mighty feet in the swamp. The trees bent as though something gigantic was brushing against them. Even the priestess became frightened, and the captain shouted at his rowers to get the galley out of there. They did escape whatever was walking in the swamp, but they did not outrun the noise of the flute until they had put many miles between them and the former land of Mibessem."

Hadon stopped. The only sound was the wind whistling through the rigging and the splash of water against the bow. And then, sending utter terror into them, there came from the shore the music of a flute.

Abeth screamed. Kebiwabes swore and turned pale beneath his sunbronze. Lalila's large violet eyes became even larger. Paga grabbed some shrouds and clung to them while he stared inland, his eyes huge and the nostrils of his flat nose distended. Hadon gripped the tiller as if it were the only real thing in the world. All else seemed wavy, slightly distorted, impalpable. Until that moment he had been enjoying the story, scaring himself and the others. Paga, of course, had looked skeptical and he had several times snorted disbelief. But evidently he had been more impressed than he had let on.

The sun disappeared below the horizon of the sea. Darkness fell swiftly. The shrilling notes became louder.

Hadon came out of his freeze and gave orders, quietly, so that the player in the swamps, whatever it was, would not hear him. He moved the tiller until the boat swung southwest. The boom traveled around, restrained by ropes in the hands of Paga and Kebiwabes. Hadon kept her steady, not coming around to beat back until the music had disappeared for an hour.

After a while Paga asked, "What do you suppose it was? Some fisherboy playing his flute?"

Hadon replied, "There are no fisherfolk, no villages, in this area. No one would dare live here."

"Maybe some fishing boat was driven into the swamp by a storm," Paga said. "Maybe it was wrecked. One of the survivors, perhaps the only one, used his flute to attract our attention."

"He could have done that better by shouting," Hadon said. "Do you want us to go back there to look for him?"

Paga did not reply. The others said nothing, but they would not have kept silent, it was evident, if Hadon had put the boat about. He had no intention of doing that.

The subject was not brought up again. It seemed best to everyone that they talk no more about the unknown flutist.

23

The pillar of smoke they saw all day was not from the port of Opar, Nangukar. That place had already been burned down and the ashes cooled by the rain. This smoke was from a pyre of pirate corpses. Eighty Mikawuru had been slain during the pirate raid. The attackers had been beaten off but had managed to rescue twenty of their dead. They had sailed off, leaving sixty of their fellows and a town in flames. The pirate corpses were being consumed by flames now, which meant their souls would flit through the clouds until Kho decided they had suffered enough as phantom nomads, driven by the winds. Then their ghosts would be sent down into the earth to awful Sisisken's dark house.

As Hadon swung his boat to the beach—all the quays were destroyed—he was stunned. All the buildings around the fort were burned. The huts and houses, the long halls, the warehouses, the stores and taverns, everything was in ashes. The two great wooden gates of the fort had been torn off, and some of the wooden buildings inside the walls had been leveled by fire.

Rebuilding had already started. The place was a buzz and yell of labor, with wagons full of newly cut lumber or bamboo, drawn by oxen, everywhere. Hammers and saws pounded and screeched.

Hadon anchored the boat about a hundred yards offshore. A longboat paddled by four men put out from the beach toward the newly arrived craft. Hadon bargained with the owner and presently all were being ferried to shore. Here a customs officer started to question them, then stopped as he recognized Hadon.

"How did you get here all the way from Khokarsa!" he cried.

"Kho Herself, through Her Voice, ordered me to return to my native city," Hadon said. "It was to fulfill a prophecy and so, though the way was long and dangerous, we are here."

The officer did not ask him what the prophecy was. He would have been indiscreet to probe into matters involving the Goddess.

"If things had gone a little differently," the officer said, "you might have arrived just in time to fall into the hands of the pirates. They were having their own way, storming the fort and breaking into the central keep. Fortunately about three hundred men had been ordered from Opar to reinforce the port just in case something like this happened. We caught the Mikawuru from the rear, and the garrison sallied out and attacked them from the front. They fought their way out and got to their ships, but their casualties were very heavy. We captured forty, most of whom were wounded."

Hadon did not ask what would happen to the captives. He knew that their chiefs would be tortured to get information about plans for future attacks. Torture of pirate leaders was a custom, based on the principle that it exacted vengeance. After all possible information was obtained, the chiefs would be beheaded and the able rank and file sent off as slaves to the mines in the hills above Opar. The badly wounded, the crippled, would be beheaded.

"You are the latest to get here from Khokarsa," the officer said. "We are hungry for news."

Hadon tried to tell him that he knew very little outside of rumors. He had been too isolated and so could not say truthfully what had happened. This made no difference. The people wanted to hear everything, fact, surmise, rumor, obvious untruth. The party was hustled in through the gateway and to the temple, where Hadon saw the head priestess, Klyhy, for the first time in years. She was still as beautiful as the night he and she had lain together, the night before Hadon was to embark for the Great Games at the city of Khokarsa. She had put on some weight, and her large shapely breasts had sagged a little, but the great gray eyes, the thick dark eyebrows, the long narrow nose, the full lips, the rounded chin, these formed one of the most beautiful and sensual faces Hadon had ever seen.

She smiled at Hadon and rose from her diamond-encrusted chair. She wore a tall thin crown of gold set with nine emeralds on the scalloped edges, a rosary of emeralds and rubies and an ankle-length skirt of white cloth. Her belt was of gold links adorned with tiny rubies. Her bare breasts were painted in concentric circles, red, white and blue, the nipples forming the red centers. She held in her right hand a long staff of oak wood, imported from Khokarsa. Its upper end held the carved representation of Kho as a steatopygic hippopotamus-headed woman.

"Thrice welcome, Hadon of Opar!" she cried. "He who should be Emperor by all rights but whom Kho decreed should not hold that rank! And thrice welcome, Lalila from beyond the Ringing Sea, the Witch-from-the-Sea! Welcome also to your daughter, of whom we have heard much, and to the unborn child, of whom much will be heard. Welcome also to the little man, though he claims to be an enemy of our sex, and to Kebiwabes, the bard who would be great!"

Hadon was not surprised at this greeting. The intelligence system of the priestesses was exceedingly good, and thus it was to be expected that Klyhy would have learned much about his party and his mission. There was probably very little he could tell her that was new, except for their adventures at Rebha and afterward.

Chairs were brought in by initiate priestesses and the party sat down. Abeth was taken off with the children of the temple. Food, mead and wine were offered and eagerly accepted. Klyhy questioned Hadon until, by the time he had eaten and drunk his fill, his tale was told. Silence fell for a while, broken only by belches from the guests, politely indicating that they found the food excellent.

Finally Klyhy said, "I have already sent a messenger to Opar to inform the Queen that you and Lalila are here. The messenger will reserve the news for the ear of the Queen alone. And I have also ordered Kaheli"—the customs officer who had talked to Hadon—"to tell no one that you are here."

Hadon, alarmed, said, "Why is that?"

"King Gamori has found out that you are—were—on the way here. He has many spies, not all of whom are priests of Resu. You see, Hadon, the schism which has rent the Empire in the Kemus is also working here. Gamori is a very ambitious man, like Minruth, and he too would like to elevate the Flaming God above the Great Mother—not for religious reasons but for ambition's sake. But we also have our spies and we know some of what passes between Gamori and the lesser priests of Resu. We know that Gamori loathes being subordinate to his wife. At the moment, indeed, Gamori and our high priestess, Queen Phebha, are no longer living together. They have parted after years of an unhappy marriage, quarreling on policy and the relative status of king and queen, of man and woman. Gamori is now living in the Temple of Resu, and he has not bedded Phebha for a year. He only appears with her at state functions.

"Also, as you are well aware, Gamori has never liked your father, Kumin. This stems from that fight in the tunnels against the outlaws when the old king, Phebha's first husband, was killed. Before your father lost an arm in that battle, he had, according to Gamori, tried to kill him. Your father claims that it was an accident, that the poor light and the heat of combat caused him to mistake Gamori for an outlaw. This is reasonable. Why should Kumin try to kill one of his comrades? Gamori claimed that he and your father had quarreled bitterly about something—what doesn't matter now—and that Kumin was trying to slay him because of this.

"Whatever the truth, Gamori then married Phebha and became King and high priest, in a position to persecute your father. It was only Phebha's protection which kept your father from being charged with attempted murder."

"I know that too well," Hadon said. "My father had to take a job inside the Temple of Kho, from which he seldom ventured because of fear that Gamori's men would murder him. My father, once one of the greatest *numatenu* of the Empire, was reduced to sweeping the temple floors for a living. Not that he was not grateful to Phebha for the work. If it hadn't been for her, we all would have starved to death. Gamori was very upset that I was one of the three youths to win the honor of representing Opar in the Great Games. He hates my whole family because of his old grudge against my father."

"Which is why Gamori must not know you are here," Klyhy said. "You see, there is another reason why Gamori would not want you to get to Opar alive or, once there, to take sanctuary in the Temple of Kho. Through his spies he has heard of Lalila, this Witch-from-the-Sea. He knows that great things are expected of her child. Rumors—unfounded of course, but still potent—rumors are that the child will be the sole ruler of Opar, that there will be no more kings here. This is ridiculous, but Gamori is frightened. Unreasoning beast that he is, he does not see that the child could be no possible danger to him; he will be dead before she attains her majority.

"On the other hand, the rumors may be correct in a sense. If Gamori attempts to harm her, he is liable to precipitate the very danger he fears. He will cause a confrontation which might have been avoided."

"What are we supposed to do?" Hadon said.

"You will stay here until nightfall. Then all of you will be escorted out of here, as inconspicuously as possible. You will be smuggled into Opar and thence to the Temple of Kho. Once inside the temple, you will be safe. Not even Gamori would dare violate its holiness."

"At one time I would have said that was a safe thing to bet on," Hadon said. "But Minruth has violated many of the temples, not to mention the priestesses. Nothing is safe from blasphemy or profanement nowadays."

"You may be right," Klyhy said. "But you can't stay here. According to the Voice of Kho, Lalila must bear her child in the temple. From her appearance, I would say that she has very little time to get there."

She picked up a little bronze gong from a recess in the arm of the chair and struck it with a tiny bronze hammer, the head of which was fashioned like a leopard's. At the third stroke a curtain at the far entrance parted. A boy of about four years of age was ushered into the chamber by a middle-aged priestess. He ran toward Klyhy crying, "Mommy! Mommy!"

She picked him up and kissed him, then turned smiling to Hadon.

"This is the fruit of our love, Hadon," she said. "He is our son, Kohr."

24

It took three days to travel up the river from the sea to the cataract. Hadon's party was in a longboat paddled by ten strong soldiers. Klyhy rode in the lead boat with the little boy. Sometimes she asked Abeth to get into her boat so the two children could play together. And sometimes she had Hadon sit by her side in the prow so they could talk. Several times, Lalila sat with her.

Lalila had been as surprised at the presentation of Kohr as Hadon. She had not, however, been jealous, knowing there was no reason for her to be. Klyhy had no designs on Hadon, nor any desire to take him away from Lalila. She had merely taken Hadon as a lover for several nights, not using sterility herbs during that time. She had wanted a child by a man who might win the Great Games. Klyhy had had many lovers before Hadon and many since and would have many more still.

"A dream convinced me that Hadon should be the father," she told Lalila. "Bhukla, the ancient goddess of war before Resu usurped her functions, appeared to me. She said I should lie with Hadon and conceive by him. I didn't need any orders for the first act, though I was happy to have divine sanction. As for the second, I felt that it was time I had a child anyway."

"And now," Lalila said, "what about Kohr? Does he stay with you or go with Hadon?"

Klyhy looked astonished. Then she said, "Oh, yes, I forgot! You would not be familiar with all our customs. If I should decide to get married soon, Kohr would stay with me and my husband. I don't plan to do that so, at the age of five, he will go to live with his father half of the year. You will be his mother-substitute during that period. If I should die, then Kohr becomes Hadon's full-time child. And yours."

The evening of the fourth day, they camped at the foot of the great falls. Here were a number of other people, members of trading caravans from Opar on their way to the port. At the advice of Klyhy, Hadon stayed in his tent as much as possible. If he was recognized, one of the priests of Resu might turn around and hasten back to Opar with the news.

Hadon, sitting in the tent, saw at least ten people he had known well in Opar. Others he remembered as being citizens of that city. Since he had lived all his life in Opar until a few years ago, he was a familiar figure there. After all, Opar had a permanent population of only thirty thousand. Since he had won the Lesser Games, he was familiar to all.

His tent was not struck until after the caravans had left downriver, then the party proceeded up the road cut along the face of the cliff. At noon they had reached the top and from there walked over the jungle path until they reached a docking area. Here were longboats left by the travelers they had met below the falls. They took two of the smallest and the soldiers bent their backs again. It was hard work because they rowed against the current all the way. They took three days, passing along bush-covered banks, occasionally coming to muddy flats where crocodiles gaped and bellowed or slid oozily into the brown river. At night they camped at walled places, sitting by large fires, hearing the coughs of leopards. They all stank abominably, having smeared themselves with hog fat to deter the multitudes of mosquitoes.

Four times they passed fleets of longboats laden with goods, heading for the port. Hadon ducked down when this happened, hoping the wide-brimmed hat he wore would keep his face hidden.

"Now that the Strait of Keth is closed, where are the goods going?" Hadon asked Klyhy.

"There are still Kethna, Wentisuh and Sakawuru," she said. "Though the pirates of Mikawuru are on the rampage, commerce still goes on. Moreover, a new settlement has been founded south of the Kemuwopar. Kartenkloe. It's purely a mining community so far; there is much copper and some gold down there. But it is the gateway to the savannas beyond the mountains, where great herds of elephants roam. The ivory trade is expected to become enormous, and Kartenkloe will handle everything passing through. It is ruled by Opar, and so Opar will get most of the profits. Some of those goods you saw are headed for Kartenkloe."

Hadon looked at the boy. Kohr was certainly his son: he had the same curly red-bronze hair, the same high and narrow forehead, slightly swelling at the corners. His ears were small and close to his head and somewhat pointed at the tips. His eyebrows were thick, almost joined. His nose was straight and not overlong, though he was too young for development of a long nose. His upper lip was short, his lips were full but not thick, and his chin was clefted.

His legs were long in relation to his torso and his arms seemed very long. He would have his father's stride and reach.

His eyes, however, were his mother's, large and dark gray.

"A beautiful child," Klyhy said, catching Hadon's look. "I love him very much. But I fear I will not be his mother very long."

"What do you mean?" Hadon said. She was an exceptionally merry person, always smiling and laughing. But now she looked grave.

"Shortly before you came to the port, I had a dream. I was in a dark place deep under the ground, wandering through a tunnel of some sort. And something terrible was chasing me. It caught me. Then I woke up, trembling, crying."

"But you were not slain in the dream?"

"No. But I had a feeling of unavoidable doom."

She smiled and said, "Now that you are here to take care of him, I am not worried. As for what may happen to me, well, no one lives forever. And I am getting fat, my breasts are starting to sag; I look in the mirror and see a face that can still attract lovers but in another ten years will turn them away. I have lived a good life, much better than most people have. And if I should die at this moment, I would be unhappy only because my son would grieve for me."

"If everybody had your attitude," Hadon said, "this world might not be such a miserable place."

"There wouldn't be any wars," she said. "Or so many going mad."

When Hadon had made his trip downriver, it had taken four days to reach the cataracts and three to get to the port from the falls. Going against the current, it took four to get to the falls and five and a half to Opar. An hour after high noon, the longboats rounded a curve of the river. The stream, which had been a quarter of a mile wide, suddenly widened out to a lake a mile and a half across. To their right was a narrow strip of flatland beyond which the cliffs rose abruptly. Past the cliffs were towering peaks. On the left, a mile away, was Opar. Opar, city of fabulous treasures, gold and jewels, gold-sheeted towers, minarets and domes, high massive walls of granite. Opar, his native city.

Tears filled his eyes. He felt a hurt in his breast; a sob burst loose from him. Lalila, seeing him so moved, put her arm around his waist and pulled his face down to kiss his cheek.

The longboats remained in the center of the stream until they had put half a mile behind them. Then they headed at an angle to their former course toward the city. There was much traffic here, fishing boats, skiffs and longboats carrying the produce of farms along the western shore north of Opar. This valley was long and relatively narrow, extending for fifteen miles until it terminated in a great falls to the north.

The western shore was flatter and broader than the eastern, but then the foothills began and after them the mighty peaks, tall as those to the east.

A mile directly due east of the city was an islet, the only one in the lake. Trees ringed its circumference; its inner part was dominated by a white domed temple. The islet was tenanted by only three people, priestesses who served the shrine of Lupoeth. The islet was the first place the explorer-priestess Lupoeth had stepped in the valley. It was there that she had met the first inhabitants of the valley, the primitive Gokako. And it was there that she had asked one what the name of the place was. And he, replying in his own language, had said "*Opar*," meaning, "I don't understand you." Lupoeth had named this valley Opar, mistakenly thinking that was its native name. Later, the settlement had also been named Opar.

The islet was also where the priestess had died at the advanced age of seventy. She had been deified, a temple erected to her. The Isle of Lupoeth, like that of the goddess Karneth, was taboo to males.

The boats glided through the paths of others and passed the wooden shacks and longhouses built outside the city walls. These extended for half a mile westward and a quarter of a mile inland. They were the homes of the Gokako slaves and freemen, and the human supervisors, foremen and soldiers who kept them in order. There were also large warehouses fronting on the wooden quays. Above the northern walls was a similar wooden city, but this housed the poorer classes, all freemen and human.

Hadon tied the strings of his hat under his jaw. The wind was blowing strongly today, and it would not do to have the hat sail off and reveal his hair and face. To further the concealment, he had tied a black patch over his left eye. His *numatenu* sword was wrapped in a blanket. He carried it over his shoulder along with a flat box of some trade goods. He was to trail behind Klyhy as if he were her servant.

The longboats tied up at a wooden quay belonging to the Temple of Kho. The priestess waited until they were ready to leave and then strode boldly along the street outside the wall. A soldier opened a parasol of bamboo and ran up to hold it over her; another beat a small drum; a third played a reed flute. Klyhy would have preferred to go quietly but, since many would recognize her, she thought it best to go in accustomed style. Otherwise people might have wondered why she was trying to be so unnoticeable.

The outer wall was fifty feet in height and composed of cyclopean granite blocks veined with pink quartz. Midway in the eastern wall was a gateway, wide enough for twenty men shoulder to shoulder to march through. The two gates were of massive bronze, ten feet thick, bearing scenes from Oparian history in high-relief. The gates had only been closed three times since being put up eight hundred years ago. They had been dashed to the ground three times, however, each time by an earthquake. The city itself had been rebuilt thrice and doubtless would be built many times again.

The travelers passed through the marketplace, which stretched along the riverfront for half a mile. This was much like any other market-bazaar in the Empire except for the presence of so many Gokako. These hairy people—short, squat, thick-necked, massively chested, slant-browed—were once numerous, but were now found only in this valley, though it was said that wild ones were to be found elsewhere in the Southern Sea.

On both sides of the gateway were spearmen. Each contingent numbered thirty: those on the left were the King's; the others, the Queen's.

Klyhy did not check her pace but proceeded as if she were on open and honest business. Which, indeed, Hadon thought, she would be if Gamori could be trusted. The officers of the guards saluted her; she blessed them and went on. The party went past the outer wall, twenty feet thick, and came to the inner wall. This was equally high but was topped with alternating small round towers and pointed granite monoliths. The towers held sentries; the monoliths memorialized the heroes and heroines of Opar. There should be two set up in his honor, Hadon thought, since he had won both the Lesser and the Great Games. They would be further down the line, however, out of view.

The inner gateway was also open, its ponderous bronze gates swung aside. They walked out onto the broad Avenue of the Deities-as-Birds. This was one hundred and fifty feet wide, much of it occupied by another market. Here many of the animals and birds on sale were to be sacrificed in the Temple of Kho across the street.

Klyhy led them through the stalls, pens and sheds past the noisy beasts, birds and noisier merchants and customers. Her goal was the gigantic nonagonal doorway in the temple, a massive granite-blocked pile capped with a gargantuan onion-shaped dome, covered with sheets of gold. On both sides of the doorway were three rows of granite monoliths, twelve in a row. Each was twice as tall as Hadon, and each was carved at the upper end into the shape of a bird. The attributes of the birds, all modeled on real ones, had been exaggerated and distorted. The heads were larger or smaller than normal, the beaks more curved or even twisted, the eyes numbered from one to nine, the feathers were too long or too broad, the claws enormous or sometimes nonexistent.

Though they seemed to have been carved by a demented person, they became intelligible after a close look. All represented birds turning into human beings, stages of various metamorphoses.

Hadon had been nervous and sweating ever since they had left the boat. Now, only twenty feet away from the doorway to the temple, he began to breathe easier. His mouth was still dry, but he could drink from the fountain that jetted just within the entrance.

And then he heard a call: "Hadon! Hadon!"

He turned and saw an old friend, Sembes, a childhood playmate and competitor at the Lesser Games. He had been eliminated during the wrestling matches by Hadon, but he had not been angry. When Hadon left for Khokarsa, in fact, Sembes had given him a gift and his good wishes.

But things might have changed now. Or Sembes might be under orders; he would be a good officer and do his duty, even if he was reluctant to obey.

Hadon was forewarned by Sembes' uniform, which was that of a lieutenant of the guard of the Temple of Resu, the Flaming God.

Sembes should have been smiling on seeing a friend who had been absent for years, but perhaps he was in a slight case of shock. Certainly his voice had been tight, as if he was under a great strain.

Behind him was a squad, twelve spearmen.

He strode toward Hadon, holding out his hand. His face seemed to break, then reform, then break again. His eyes looked narrow and bright and they shifted from Hadon to Klyhy to the rest of the party and back to Hadon.

"Listen, Hadon! I just happened to be patrolling this area and behold! I see you! I thought you were in Khokarsa!"

Behind Hadon, Lalila murmured, "Beware, Hadon! He is lying! He stinks of fear!"

Klyhy had stopped. Now she hissed like a snake and said, "Lalila is right! Someone saw you at the dock, Hadon, and sped to the King! His spies are everywhere!"

"Greetings, my old friend!" Hadon said. He eased the burden from his shoulder and put his hand within the blanket on its top. His fingers closed around the hilt of Karken, a piece of elephant ivory carved with ridges for better gripping.

Sembes stopped and said, "What happened to your eye, Hadon?"

Hadon said, "I have been resting it," and he ripped off the patch. To Klyhy, he said softly, "Get the others into the temple."

Sembes put his hand on the hilt of his sword, a heavy weapon of expensive carbonized iron formed from welded strips. It had the same leaf shape as the enlisted men's but was about a foot longer.

"So you know!" Sembes said, his eyebrows going up. "Well, I am indeed sorry, Hadon, but I have orders. You are under arrest for suspicion of treason!"

Hadon waited a moment before replying. Lalila, holding Abeth's and Kohr's hands, hurried behind him toward the doorway. Sembes' eyes shifted to her for a minute, but evidently he had no instructions concerning her. Paga was rolling after her, scowling, his hand on the hilt of his short sword. Kebiwabes hesitated, then said, "Officer, I am a bard and so my person is sacred." He added, "Inviolate in the eyes of great Kho and of all humankind."

"Stand aside then," Sembes said. Sweat rolled from him. He wiped it from his eyes with the back of his arm and then yanked his sword from its sheath. This was a signal for the soldiers to spread out into a semicircle, their spears leveled toward Hadon.

Kebiwabes, behind Hadon now, whispered, "I just said that to gain time, Hadon. I will fight by your side."

"Thanks," Hadon said in a low voice. "But get into the temple as quickly as you can. I don't want you in the way."

The bard gasped, then muttered something insulting. Hadon had no time to explain. He pulled his *tenu* from the pack and stepped forward.

At the same time Klyhy also advanced. She held up her staff and cried, "Hold! This man is under the protection of Phebha and hence mighty Kho Herself! He is the husband of a woman who has been smiled upon by Kho and who has been spoken for by Her Voice! Touch either and you will suffer the wrath of the Goddess!"

Sembes sweated even more heavily. The spearmen were all pale.

Hadon looked around. The screech and shout and chatter of the marketplace had died down. Most of the sellers and buyers were staring silently at them; the only noise was from the animals.

Sembes said, "I have my orders, Priestess, and they come from the King, the highest priest of Resu himself. Unless they are countermanded by an agent of the King, or by the Queen in person, I must do my duty. You understand that, of course."

"I understand that you are ignoring all I have told you!" she shouted. "Must I repeat it?"

Hadon looked to his left again. Lalila and the children were now inside the temple. Paga was standing in the entrance, glaring at them. He seemed uncertain, as if he could not make up his mind to stay and protect Lalila or come back out to help Hadon.

Hadon said, "Run as if Kopoethken herself were after your manhood, Kebiwabes! I can't hold them off any longer! Now go!"

With a shout, he stepped forward once more, holding Karken's hilt with both hands, the right palm cupping its end, the left gripping it above the ball of the right hand. Sembes yelled and advanced, his right foot forward, his torso leaning out to form a straight line with his left leg. Hadon's blade knocked his to one side and the keen edge slid along Sembes' jugular vein. Hadon stepped back while Sembes, his neck spouting blood, fell. Sembes was not the swordsman Hadon was, but he was the victim of the system. Only *numatenu* used the long blunt-ended, slightly curved weapon. Though this was obviously superior to the shorter stabbing blade in individual combat, its use was forbidden to military and naval personnel all over the Empire—except in Mikawuru, but the pirates had no sense of decency. It was true that Sembes, even if he had been armed with a *tenu*, would have lost anyway, but it would not have been in such a short time, and his spearmen might have moved in to drive Hadon off.

Now, before the spearmen could change their stance, lift their shafts to throw them, Hadon was off and away. The doorway was twenty paces away, and he was the swiftest runner in the Empire. Even so, he could not take the chance that spears might be flying before he reached the sanctuary. Within the last six feet he launched himself out, holding the *tenu* up with one hand, and slid on the pavement facedown. He burned his chest and knees and toes, but he shot inside the shadows of the chamber.

Paga had thrown himself to one side just in time to keep from being knocked down. Three spears came close, one hitting the side of the doorway, one flying over Hadon and transfixing a porter, one bouncing off the cement and sliding along to come to rest beside Hadon.

He was up and on his feet, bounding to one side. Though he was theoretically safe from further attack, he did not trust the spearmen to be cool enough to remember that.

Hadon got to his feet again. Paga, who seemed to be nothing but a beard with feet tumbled in a corner, struggled up. The unlucky porter lay on his back, the shaft projecting from his chest; he coughed blood and kicked a few times before dying.

Lalila and the two children were gone, supposedly into the next chamber.

Klyhy entered then. It was evident that she was shocked.

"You certainly did not try to talk your way out of that," she said. "I really expected to cow them, to get you in without bloodshed."

"I have a feeling for such situations," he said. "Talk was only going to delay the inevitable. Besides, I know Sembes—knew him. He was a fine fellow, a stickler for proper procedure, for legality—and he was in the service of the King. He would have been put off only so long. The first step I took toward the temple would have been my last; I would have gotten his sword in my back. I had to surprise him and his men. Too bad too—I liked Sembes. But there's no time to grieve for him now. That will come later."

If ever, he added mentally. Events had been going too fast lately for such things as sorrow or regret. And he felt the tempo would become even more demanding and swift in the near future.

The chamber he was in had not changed any since he had last seen it—not surprising, since it had not changed a whit in five hundred years. Its floor was of concrete—not the original, of course—and its walls were of granite covered with a thick plaster. This had been painted with murals of scenes from the religion and history of Opar. Most of them were set in the jungle, depicted in poisonous greens and bloody reds. Here and there, between the murals, were the carved figures of men and beasts. Oblong tablets of gold were fixed to the walls between the murals. These bore hieroglyphs, relics of the days before the hero Awines' syllabary had been adopted. It was an ancient place, like all the chambers and holy places of the temple. Time seemed to brood somberly over it, radiating a thick gray aura through the chatter of the crowds that filled it night and day. Time sat heavily here, soaking the granite walls and the artifacts, and seemed to have paid rent for eternity. It was said that the temple would abide for ten thousand years, that mighty Kho Herself had promised this to the builder, the priestess Lupoeth. It was indeed the only building in Opar which had not fallen during the three great earthquakes, though extensive repair had been necessary.

Hadon's reverie was brief. An uproar outside brought him back to the doorway. For a moment he could not determine what was happening. A mob was swirling just outside the entrance, screeching, yelling, crying. Then an opening in the wall of bodies revealed a spearman being beaten to death by the outraged crowd.

It was all over in a few minutes as whistles shrilled up and down the street. The mob came to its senses, realized the King's men were coming and scattered. They left behind them twelve purplish and bloody corpses.

25

Presently the street was emptied of civilians. Its only occupants were the beasts and birds abandoned by their frightened owners and about fifty soldiers. Hadon was glad to see an equal number of the Queen's soldiers arrive several minutes later. Otherwise, he would have felt compelled to retreat deep within the temple. Theoretically at least, he was safe a foot within the doorway, but he felt that in practice the overexcited King's men might violate the sanctuary. Now, faced by the Queen's men, they would not dare.

Klyhy had sent a novitiate after the Queen. She had then administered the last rites over the unfortunate porter. That finished, she went outside. She was saluted by the commanders of both forces, whom she took aside to discuss the situation.

While they were talking heatedly, Phebha appeared. She was a tall gaunt woman of about fifty. She had been beautiful as a young woman, her breasts full and upright, softly rounded in body, long-legged, her features striking despite a rather long nose. Now, wasting for some years with a fever of mysterious origin despite the prayers of her subjects, she was a hag. But she was still impressive and she could be frightening when she wished.

She wore a leopardess-skin kilt secured to her waist by a short girdle of interlocked gold rings embossed with diamonds. Her long black hair was tied in a Psyche knot and confined with a cap made of many oval and circular gold pieces. From each side of it strings of oval gold coins dangled to her waist. Her arms and legs were covered with many massive, jewel-encrusted gold bands. A long jeweled dagger was stuck through a gold ring attached to her girdle, and in her right hand she held a long thin wand of oak in the end of which was set an enormous diamond.

As she strode through the chamber, followed by a horde of priestesses, counselors and attendants, male and female, she greeted Hadon. Then she was in the street and loudly demanding to know what was happening.

Hadon was about to follow her when he heard his name. He turned at the sound of the familiar voice and hastened to embrace his father. Kumin put his one good arm around the shoulders of his son and wept. When he had mastered himself, he said, "I am weeping not only because you have returned after a long absence, my son, I weep because your mother is dead!"

"When?"

"Three days ago, son. She went to bed complaining of pain in her lower abdomen. She woke me sometime before dawn saying she was in intense pain, though I could tell that by looking at her in candlelight. She should have wakened me long before, though I doubt it would have done much good. I went for a doctor, but before she could come your mother gave a great scream and a few minutes later she died in great agony.

"The doctors performed an autopsy, since it was necessary to determine if she had died from poison or witchcraft or because great Kho had willed it. The doctors reported that some organ in her had been diseased for some time and had burst, loosing its poisons into her body.

"Your brother and his family were called down from the hills—he began working as a mining engineer there after you left—and she was buried at noon of the next day."

Hadon nodded. "I will sacrifice a fine cow over her grave," Hadon said, "when I get a chance." Then he wept with his father. Soon Lalila shook his shoulder and he looked up.

"The pains have started," she said.

Hadon rose, wiping his eyes. From outside came Phebha's strident voice. She was denouncing the King's men for having violated sanctuary, even though it was an accident. They had slain a temple porter, and Kho would not easily forgive that.

The colonel of the King's men shouted that the soldiers who had done the deed were dead, that they had paid. Anyway, it was an accident, as she admitted, and therefore was no profanation. She replied that she was not used to being argued with, but sacrilege was done, accidental or intended. The colonel started to say something, but she cried that he should keep silent. Then brass trumpets blared and drums beat and people cried out. "The King! The King!"

Hadon called to a middle-aged priestess at the back of the crowd inside the doorway. "Darbha!"

She turned and said "Yes?" and then, recognizing him, smiled and cried, "Hadon!"

"My wife Lalila is having labor pains," he said. "She should be taken to the Chamber of the Moon."

Darbha had a difficult time tearing herself away from the events in the street. Hadon said loudly, "She is Lalila! Do you know of the prophecy about her child?"

Darbha replied, "Yes, we know. We heard yesterday."

She forced her way through the crowd and spoke to Klyhy, who was standing just outside the door. Klyhy reluctantly left her post but, when she observed Lalila, she went into action very quickly. She called three priestesses to her side and issued orders that they should take Lalila to the chamber prepared for her.

Hadon kissed Lalila and said, "It will be all right."

"I wish it would be!" she cried. "But I fear that something terrible is going to happen here, Hadon! Very soon!"

"There is nothing you can do about it if it is so," he said. Coldness passed over his skin and dug into the back of his neck, but he acted as if her words were of no moment. "You must go with Klyhy. All will be well. We are in the temple now and, according to the oracle, our child will have a long and glorious life if she is born within these walls."

Klyhy spoke to a fourth priestess. "At the first chance you get, speak to Phebha. Tell her that Lalila is here and will soon be giving birth."

Klyhy and the others formed around Lalila and, while one began a slow chant, they hurried her off. Hadon turned back to the doorway. He would not be admitted into the Chamber of the Moon, so he could do nothing to comfort her.

His father looked puzzled. Evidently the priestesses had not told him anything about the prophecy. Hadon started to explain, but a flourish of trumpets and drums interrupted him. He said, "Later, Father, when there is time," and made his way through the crowd to the doorway.

The King had appeared with about a hundred more soldiers. He and his wife faced each other in the space between their two forces. They were almost nose to nose, in fact, shouting at each other. Gamori was a thickly built man, hawk-nosed, blue-jawed, hairy and dark, but with much gray in his black hair. His tresses fell below his shoulders, concealing the fact that he had long ago lost his right ear. It had been severed during the fight in which Kumin had lost his arm.

Phebha, as if tired of arguing and aware that she was in danger of completely losing her dignity, abruptly stopped speaking. She turned and walked toward the doorway while Gamori yelled after her. He ordered her to come back, but she, Queen and high priestess—therefore of higher rank—paid him no attention.

His face almost purple, Gamori whirled, seized a spear and yanked it from the hands of the nearest soldier. A cry of horror went up from the crowd, including many of his own men. Hadon yelled at her to beware and darted out toward her, his sword unsheathed. At the same time, the officer of the Queen's forces ran forward to defend her. Gamori snarled at him—Hadon could see his expression but could not hear his words—and thrust the spear into the officer's face. The blade drove into his mouth; the man dropped his sword and clutched the shaft, then fell backward. At this a roar went up from the Queen's men and they charged. Hadon grabbed Phebha around the waist and half carried her to the doorway, keeping his right side between her and the soldiers of the King. Gamori could have stabbed him in the back then but, his own back turned, he was running toward the safety of his men's spears. Then spears flew on both sides and the two forces had collided, were mixing, were swirling, were fighting savagely.

Hadon released Phebha inside the room. She raged mightily for several minutes then, as if water had been thrown in her face, became calm. "My men will die; they are outnumbered," she said. She summoned a trumpeter, who at her orders loudly blew the call for retreat. In a moment many of the Queen's men broke loose from the melee. About twenty made it into the chamber; the others stayed behind as corpses.

Phebha gave another order and a portcullis was dropped over the huge entrance. A solid iron door followed this, blocking off Gamori's men even if they had been willing to enter the temple.

"It's open war from this moment on!" Phebha shouted. "We will act at once!" She glared around, saw Klyhy coming to her and asked, "What is it?"

"The woman of Hadon, the Witch-from-the-Sea," Klyhy said. "She has been taken to the Chamber of the Moon. But her labor pains have stopped. They were false."

"Keep her there anyway," the high priestess said. "The prophecy will be fulfilled." She looked at Hadon. "Welcome home, tall one! Though it is a sad and grisly homecoming! Not unexpected, however! Well, Gamori has revealed his true ambition, which I knew all along. One who would exalt the Flaming God above the Mother of All. And one who would, not incidentally, exalt himself above the Queen. You see, Hadon, his agents have heard about the prophecy too, and Gamori fears the child. He also fears that you, though deprived of your emperor's throne, may wish to claim his as king. And he is afraid, justly so, that I might try to depose him and make you king."

"I? King?" Hadon asked.

"You won the Great Games," she said, "and so you should be king. You are a true worshiper of Kho and so should replace that miserable hyena Gamori. And then there is the prophecy. If your child is to attain the glories promised her, she must be protected. How better can she be protected than if her father is king? And her mother queen?"

"My Queen—" Hadon began.

"I am sick and do not have long to live," Phebha went on. "If I should die, soon, Gamori and the worshipers of Resu will have a great advantage. Klyhy is a capable woman, a strong one, but she needs a good man to lead her forces. You are the man. You can't marry her, since you are the husband of the violet-eyed woman from beyond the Ringing Sea of whom there is a prophecy. And you are the father of the child to be born. So I will proclaim you the new king, to take Gamori's throne by the dictates of mighty Kho. And your wife will become the new queen. Do not worry about Klyhy. She expects this and is glad. She has no ambitions to be high priestess and queen."

"That is true," Klyhy said. She had appeared by Hadon's side a moment before. "But there is a big difference between proclaiming Hadon and Lalila as rulers of Opar and actually being able to seat them on the throne. Gamori stands in the way."

Phebha looked around and said, "There are too many here to discuss affairs of state." She beckoned to a priestess and said, "Hala, take care of the girl Abeth and the boy Kohr, and see to the comfort of Hadon's men. Kumin, you come with us."

Phebha conducted them through many rooms. All were splendid, some offering even more magnificence and beauty than could be found in the palace of the Empress of Khokarsa. One room contained seven towering pillars of gold, and another was floored with a single sheet of gold said to be three feet thick.

Opar was rich indeed, but the pride of her citizens was tempered with the awareness that she was the object of envy and greed. She was safe when the Empire was strong, but now that civil war weakened it, Opar was vulnerable to attack. The raid by the Mikawuru pirates had only been a probe, designed to test the defenses. And suddenly Opar was herself being rent with war among her own citizens.

They ascended three flights of granite staircases and went down a long hall of polished mica into Phebha's apartments. These were luxurious indeed, but she took them through to a small room that was almost bare and bade them sit down at a plain wooden table. While wine and food were being brought in, she outlined her plan of attack. Hadon was amazed. Apparently she had been expecting this situation for a long time.

Before she could finish, however, she was forced to sit down in a chair. Her cheeks were red, her eyes feverish, her breathing heavy. The pendulous breasts rose and fell swiftly.

"It's the fever," she said, though no explanation was needed. "There is no way to overcome it. I have a strong will, but I cannot make my flesh ignore the fire that weakens it. But you, Hadon, and you, Klyhy, you know what to do. As for you, Kumin, you know the way. You have not forgotten the ancient tunnels, the old traps. You can lead your son to the battle."

"More than that!" Kumin said. "I may have only one arm, and I may have spent many years in sweeping floors and dusting statues, but I am a *numatenu*! I can wield a sword with only one hand and I can give a good account of myself!"

Phebha closed her eyes, smiled and said, "Good! You will do that."

Kumin looked excited. He was two inches shorter than his son, but at six feet he was still a tall man in Opar. His hair was gray, though when he was Hadon's age it had been as black as the wing of Kagaga the raven. He had picked up some fat and a paunch, but he was still massively built and he looked very strong. Indeed, having been forced to use one arm for twenty years, he had developed extraordinary strength in it.

"I gave my sword Karken to my son, but that does not mean I cannot swing another!"

"Then you must do it tonight, Hadon," Phebha said. "Pick out several other men; Klyhy will tell you the names of the best. And may Kho give you the stealth and the courage to rid us of this hyena Gamori."

A knock sounded on the door. A servant opened it, and a priestess entered. She bent down and whispered into Phebha's ear, looking up now and then at Hadon and Kumin, then she walked out. Phebha was silent for a minute.

"I have some bad news," she finally said. "Kumin, your son Methsuh has been captured by Gamori's men. He is being held just outside the Door of the Nine. My husband, the swine, has sent word that he wants to talk to you, Hadon."

Kumin swore. Hadon said, "What would he want with…?" He stopped, frowning, and said, "I suppose he wants a trade. If I deliver myself to him, he will release Methsuh unharmed."

"I imagine that is exactly what he will propose," Phebha said. "But you cannot do that, Hadon, even if you wish to. Lalila needs you; your unborn child will need you; Opar needs you. I am sorry for Methsuh, but you cannot sacrifice yourself for your brother."

"Let us go down and hear what Gamori has to say first," Kumin said. He looked pale but determined.

Phebha directed servants to bring in a litter. She was placed in it and carried after Hadon and his father. On the way, Hadon asked about his sister.

"Dedar is married now," Kumin said. "She went with her husband Nanquth—you remember him—to the new settlement of Kartenkloe. That was a year ago. I've heard from her six times. She's happy, though she says it's a hard life. She's pregnant, so I am happy. She is about to give me another grandchild, though Kho knows if I'll ever get to see it."

"You will live to see many more grandchildren, Father," Hadon said.

Again the crowd in front of the doorway had to be cleared so Phebha, Hadon and the others could look outside. The solid iron door had been pulled up; the portcullis was still down. After she had exchanged the litter for a chair, the Queen said, "Draw up the portcullis."

Men picked up her chair and carried her in it to the very doorway. Hadon did not think this was wise, since it made her very vulnerable, but evidently she believed that not even Gamori would dare attack her.

The marketplace was filled with about a thousand of the King's men, Hadon estimated, all in formation. By peering around the doorway, he could see down the street past the masses of bronze-armored, bronze-armed men. On both sides was a mob of citizens. Facing them were three ranks of spearmen. The citizens were not particularly noisy, but there were some shouts now and then soaring out from the sullen murmur.

They would tend to make Gamori discreet, Hadon thought. He would not want to enrage them by threatening the high priestess herself.

On the other hand, Gamori might be rash enough to force a showdown. He might believe that a massacre of the citizens in the street would cow the rest of the population. And he could be right.

Trumpets blew. The troops on the right opened, and six soldiers and a prisoner came through the narrow avenue.

Hadon cried "Methsuh!" and heard the name echoed despairingly by his father.

Methsuh, looking much like Hadon, his hands behind him, his face bloody and puffed, was thrown down on the pavement. Gamori gestured and the trumpets and drums were loud. The crowd became silent. Gamori roared, "A trade, Phebha! A trade! One traitor for another!"

Her voice was clear but weak. "What is this, Gamori? Who is a traitor? *You* are the only one *I* see!"

"Not I!" Gamori bellowed. "I am not conducting warfare against you, wife! I am only asserting the right of Resu to primacy, the order of things as they should be!

But I am not here to debate with you! I want that traitor, Hadon! Our Emperor has informed me that he should be arrested and sent back to Khokarsa!"

"There is no legal Emperor!" Phebha said. "Our Empress, High Priestess Awineth, has declared Minruth a traitor and blasphemer and profaner! So, Gamori, you have no legal basis for your claim! In fact, by pressing the rebel Minruth's claim, you proclaim for all to hear that *you* are a rebel and a blasphemer and a profaner! And so great Kho frowns on you, Gamori! And She frowns on all who support you! Death and destruction will visit those on whom Kho frowns!"

"Silence, you mangy lying bitch!" Gamori bellowed. His face was very red, but the faces of the soldiers near him were pale. "I am not here to discuss religion or politics or indeed anything except an exchange of traitors. I want Hadon! And if he refuses to surrender himself, or if you refuse to throw him out of the temple, then I will execute his brother! Now! Before his eyes and yours! And before the eyes of the deities! Methsuh's blood will be on Hadon's hands, on your hands!"

"You do not order the high priestess of Kho to be silent, nor do you insult her—and thus Kho—without retaliation!" Phebha said. Her voice was louder now, her anger having overcome her weakness for a moment.

Kumin, standing by Hadon, groaned. He said, "Great Kho, do not do this to me! I have lost my wife only two days ago, and now I will lose one or the other of my only sons!"

Methsuh was on his knees only twenty feet from the doorway. Two officers stood with drawn swords behind him. Gamori was to one side and about ten feet behind them. The nearest ranks of spearmen were about thirty feet from each side of the doorway.

Hadon wondered if the spacing had been arranged to tempt him to dash out and try to rescue his brother. Probably.

There was silence for a moment. Gamori, still red-faced, his lips open and his teeth clamped together, paced back and forth. Then he shouted, "Well, Hadon! I will not wait long!"

"You will, of course, do no such thing," Phebha said to Hadon. "It would be a brave and noble deed if you gave your life for your brother's. Also, an extremely stupid and selfish deed. The fate of Opar and the course of true religion in Opar depend on you. No one else can rally the worshipers of Kho as you can. You are a hero, winner of the Great Games—"

"I know all that!" Hadon said loudly, daring in his anger and grief to interrupt her. "I know that Gamori does not really expect me to sacrifice myself for Methsuh! What profit would there be in that except for Gamori and the cause of Resu?"

Kumin said, "It is cruelty which inspires Gamori to do this. He cannot violate sanctuary, so he is killing Methsuh to hurt us! He hopes that one of us will not be able to endure witnessing Methsuh's death and so will run out to save him!"

"You will not do that!" Phebha said sharply.

Kumin shouted, tore Karken from Hadon's hand and was out of the doorway before Hadon could grab him. Hadon started after him then, but a soldier by the

Queen's chair thrust his spear between his legs and Hadon sprawled out of the doorway. Spears were instantly hurled toward him. He rolled back into the doorway. Two spears passed over him, one so close its shaft banged against his ribs. A third struck the pavement just in front of him, its tip digging into the cement. He scrambled to the protection of the wall beyond the doorway, and no more spears were thrown.

He bounded back three seconds later, determined to see what was happening even if it meant dodging more missiles. He saw the two officers who had been guarding Methsuh lying on the street, their throats gashed. Methsuh was on his side, but struggling to get up. Gamori was defending himself with his sword against Kumin's bloody weapon. Though Kumin had only one arm, he was using Karken as if he held its hilt with two hands. And then the inevitable occurred. Spears thunked into Kumin from both sides and from behind. He staggered and fell, though still swinging at Gamori.

The King stepped up and brought his sword down against Kumin's neck. Blood spouted, washing Gamori's feet, and Gamori leaned down and picked up the head by the hair and held it aloft, crying exultantly.

Hadon, shouting, seized a spear from a soldier and cast it at Gamori.

It flew almost true, catching Gamori in the shoulder. He dropped the head and fell into the pool of blood, clutching at the shaft.

A soldier thrust his spear through Methsuh. Other soldiers, forgetting in their rage and excitement that they were committing sacrilege, threw their spears at the doorway. Several just missed Phebha and Hadon; one struck a priestess in the stomach. A second later the portcullis dropped and the door was slammed shut.

Observers in the windows of the upper stories of the temple reported later that Gamori was carried away at once. The spear did not seem to have inflicted a fatal wound, unless infection set in. But Gamori had given an order before he left, and it was carried out with ruthlessness: the civilian witnesses were massacred, though a number escaped. And civil war began in earnest throughout Opar.

26

Phebha said, "I have just come from the Chamber of the Moon. Lalila's labor pangs have started again. She is now an ordained priestess, and I have ordered that the news be spread that she will be our new queen. And that you will be the new king."

"How can you do that?" Hadon said. "No public criers will venture into the street. They would be killed."

"We have our ways," she said. "Lalila will have to learn them; she has much to learn, in fact. I will teach her what I can before I die. After that, Klyhy and Hala and the others will teach her."

"It is too soon to talk about that," Hadon said. "First we have to get rid of Gamori."

"Which shall be done before the night is over, Kho willing," she said. "In two hours it will be midnight. I have sacrificed a cock and found the omens good, if somewhat ambiguous. But aren't they always? Midnight is the best time to start. Klyhy will be your guide, since your father is no longer available."

Hadon tried not to think of Kumin or his brother. There was no time for grief now. There was only time for thoughts of vengeance.

He walked to the window and looked out. It was a cloudy night, when the city would normally have been dark except for the torches of patrols. But now the flames from the burning tenements of the freemen to the north and the slaves' quarters to the south and some large buildings in the city itself lit up the night. The clouds were red, reflecting the fires below. Here and there torches bobbed, looking at this distance like fireflies. Most of the fighting had died down for the night, if the reports were to be believed. The majority of the population had fled the city itself, avoiding being ground between the Queen's men and the King's. Many civilians, however, had either joined one side or the other or had plunged into looting. The wooden areas outside the walls were destined to burn completely. No one was trying to quench the flames; all fire fighting was confined inside the walls.

Since most of the city was built of massive stone, the fires there were limited. Much furniture had been carried out to the streets and set up as barricades, however, and these had been torched. Hangings and furniture in many buildings had also been heaped and set on fire in order to create diversions.

Gamori had surrounded the vast temple, leaving about a hundred men at each entrance. Then he had started the citywide slaughter which had sent the civilians into a panic. The stream of refugees had kept the Queen's men from fighting through to the temple for a long time. They could make no headway against the mass headed for the riverfront and the jungle behind the city.

Gamori had been taken to his quarters in the Temple of Resu and treated there. According to Phebha's spies, he had not left his apartment, but he was conducting operations through his general, Likapoeth. If the report could be believed, Gamori would be on his feet by late tomorrow morning. Meanwhile, Likapoeth had twice stormed the Door of the Nine, battering it with heavy bronze rams. At the same time soldiers had tried to get into the windows of the second stories. Flaming oil had been poured on them; the ladders, pushed aside or out, had fallen with their shrieking burdens. The rams had failed to beat in the double barrier of portcullis and door, and oil from the windows above had discouraged the attackers.

Then the portcullis and door had been opened, and Hadon had led a sally outside. This had resulted in his forces being driven back with heavy losses. He had suffered several minor wounds and once almost been captured.

Later, a force of about three hundred of the Queen's men had fought their way through to the doorway. Hadon had again led his men out to help them, and two hundred of the reinforcements had gotten into the temple.

Phebha had sent messengers to the port to order at least half the troops there, six hundred men, to come to Opar. But it would be several days before the messenger could get there, even if he traveled night and day. And it would take heavily armed men four days to get to Opar with forced paddling. Moreover, Gamori was sure to have the river watched, so there was no guarantee that the messengers would get through.

There were about five hundred soldiers inside the temple now. Unfortunately at least half of them were casualties. After eating the soup from the great kettles in the kitchen, two hundred and fifty had gotten very sick. Within an hour, almost a hundred had died in agony. The others had survived, but they were too sick to be of any use. Phebha started an investigation within half an hour after the first dozen became ill. By then the culprits, two chief cooks, had disappeared. Ropes dangling from third-story windows revealed their escape route.

"Gamori is not as stupid as I had thought him, though he is even more vile," Phebha said. "Well, he has hit us hard. But if you succeed tonight, Gamori and all his ambitions will go up in his funeral pyre."

Hadon was shocked. "You are going to burn him?"

"Why not? He deserves the fate of a traitor and blasphemer. Would you have me give him a hero's burial and erect a pylon over him just because he once sat on a throne and was my husband?"

"It's just that it's seldom done," he said.

"If you are to be a good king, you will do many things that are seldom done."

"I have been learning to do such things," Hadon said.

He excused himself and went to his apartment. Abeth and Kohr were asleep in an inner chamber, watched by an elderly priestess. She looked up as Hadon stuck his head into the room. She smiled and made a sign that all was well with the children. He went to his own bed but was unable to sleep at all. After tossing and turning, he rose and drank several cups of hibiscus-tea. Then he paced. After a long, long time the water clock indicated it was time to leave.

Klyhy met him outside the door of Phebha's quarters. "She is asleep," she said. "There is no need to wake her; we know what to do."

Klyhy's slave was carrying a large jar of some black stuff. She opened it, and Hadon and Klyhy stripped and smeared themselves with the ointment. Then they dressed, though there was not much to that. Each wore a tight black loincloth, antelope-skin moccasins and a belt holding several sheaths and metal hooks. Pouches dangled from some of the hooks. A loop in Hadon's belt held a curious T-shaped device of iron. During this time four men, all also covered with black ointment, entered. They carried coils of rope over their shoulders, and their sheaths held knives and short-handled axes. Pouches hanging from the hooks held lead double-coned missiles. Their leather slings were secured through loops on their belts.

Hadon had met these four that afternoon. He had gone over the diagrams with them and Klyhy until all could redraw them from memory. Like the other men, Hadon had sworn an oath never to reveal what he had learned from the diagrams. He had also sworn not to allow himself to fall alive into the hands of the enemy.

Fully accoutred, Hadon and Klyhy led the others down the hall, past a sentry around the corner and down a small side hall. At its end Klyhy drew a large iron key from a pouch and unlocked a small iron door. Inside the room, she groped around until she found torches in brackets. Using a flint and iron and some tinder, she got a tiny fire going and then dumped the tinder on the oil-soaked torch. Two others also lit torches.

The room was ostensibly used for storage. The priestess went around behind a pile of wooden boxes, the others following. There was a space between the pile and a single large box set against the stone wall. The wall itself was composed of stone blocks, each a three-foot square. Klyhy opened the lid of the box, revealing that it was half filled with rolls of papyrus. Klyhy told them to remove these, which they did. On the bottom was an ingot of lead weighing about forty pounds. They lifted that out and a plate of bronze rose a few inches from the bottom.

"The lead block holds the plate down," she said. "Lift it and the plate comes up, and counterweights behind the wall start to work. Quickly! Into the opening!"

A section of the wall had swung open and out. The others quickly moved through it into a tunnel beyond. Hadon, at her orders, pushed up on a huge wooden lever within the opening. Klyhy replaced the weight, threw in the papyrus rolls, closed the box lid and went through the opening. Hadon took the pressure off the lever and the stone section pivoted back.

"Only the Queen has the key to the storage room," Klyhy said. "Only she and two priestesses at any one time know the secret of this room. Now you men know because this is an extreme emergency. But Kho will blast you if you should talk about it. If we can use it to get at our enemies, they can use it to get at us."

The tunnel was about ten feet wide and eight feet high. It was well ventilated, though the source of the air was not visible. The torch flames bent toward the far end of the tunnel. Klyhy went first, turning to the left. There was no need for them to know where the right passage led, so they had not been told. The left was a lower, narrower passage. It ran for about a hundred yards, turning often, apparently going between the walls of rooms and corridors. Occasionally there were niches in the walls, some of which held skulls.

"They are supposed to belong to the slaves who built these secret passages," she said. "I doubt that, though, since they would be seven hundred years old, and I think a skull would rot in that time. The walls are thick, but they are damp. Personally, I think they're the relics of enemies of the high priestesses of the past few generations. But if that's true, where are the skeletons?"

Those who could answer her questions were also dead.

The men made a sign to ward off evil spirits as they passed each skull.

Occupied with his own thoughts about the skulls, Hadon trailed Klyhy. All of a sudden he bumped into her, causing her to gasp and then curse.

"You clumsy hulk!" she said. "Watch where you're going! You, almost knocked me down that!"

She pointed at the open well just below her feet.

Hadon said nothing. She was right. He should have been paying more attention. If he did not forget everything except the work at hand, he was likely to forget everything for all time.

The torchlight struck water far down. It also showed a bronze ladder affixed to the stone. Klyhy lowered herself over the edge and went down it swiftly. A man called Wemqardo held her torch out so she could see all the way to the bottom. Reaching it, she swung around the ladder and disappeared into an opening. Wemqardo lowered the torch to her at the end of a rope and then went down himself. Within a few minutes all six were inside another tunnel. This one curved rapidly to the left, taking them for a quarter of a mile in a path like a snake's. On coming to what seemed the end of the passage, the priestess pushed against one side of the wall close to the corner. It pivoted ponderously, requiring Hadon's weight to move it. The bronze pins squeaked loudly, causing Klyhy to curse.

Cold, wet air struck them. They advanced through the opening onto a curving piece of granite which held a boat just large enough to accommodate six adults uncomfortably. Though small, the boat took up almost all the room on the projection. A river, dark and greasy, lapped a few inches below the surface of the stone. Hadon lifted his torch to get a better view. The other side was at least three hundred feet away. The ceiling and walls formed an arch which glittered in the light; there were many veins of quartz in the granite. The highest part of the ceiling was about thirty feet above the water, though its height would vary further along.

Wemqardo said, "I have heard of this river deep under the city. It is said that the Cold Snake dwells at its bottom in the thick mud, and when—"

"Quiet, fool!" Klyhy demanded. "Would you scare everybody to death!"

Wemqardo said nothing more, but he had started a series of thoughts in the minds of the others. Hadon thought of creepy tales he had heard when a child, horrifying stories of the demons of the rock, of the things, half-gorilla, half-worm, which were supposed to haunt these tunnels. It was said that the slaves who dug for gold in these deeps often unaccountably disappeared. Or their fellows saw them being dragged away by things dark and misshapen.... It was good not to think about such monsters, but how did you *not* think about something?

They got the boat into the water and themselves into the boat, though they came close to overturning it. They drove it downstream with the short-handled paddles stored in the craft. Brackets on the prow and stern held torches; the third had been extinguished. Their flickering light revealed niches carved into the walls, each of which held a skull. It also showed, now and then, a sudden boiling of the water when a paddle dipped in. Hadon, in a low voice, asked Klyhy what caused this phenomenon.

"It's a small fish which infests these waters," she said. "They're blind and colorless and only about four inches long. But they have a big head and many sharp teeth and they occur in great numbers. So it won't do to fall into the river. You'd be stripped of flesh within ten minutes."

"Why didn't you tell us about them earlier?" Hadon said somewhat angrily.

"You have enough to worry about."

Hadon lifted his paddle and held it in the torchlight for a moment. The wooden blade was pitted in many places.

"If there are so many of them, how do they get enough to eat in this sterile environment?" he asked. "Are there many other kinds of fish here? What do these eat?"

"There are some other types of fish," she said, "though not many. Not enough to account for the swarms of those devilfish."

"Then what do they eat?"

"I wish I knew," she replied. "Though perhaps it is better for my peace of mind that I do not."

Hadon wished he had not been so curious.

After passing two aprons of stone, presumably opening to pivoted sections also, she told them to head for the third. They got onto the tiny dock without mishap, and she and Hadon pushed open the section. This, like the last one, squeaked loudly. The boat had to be left on the apron, since it was a little too large to get through the opening. Hadon did not like this. What if the King's men patrolled this area—as the priestess said they sometimes did—and saw the boat? They might take it with them, leaving Hadon and his group stranded.

"They don't come around very often," she said. "And since Gamori needs all the men he can get for the fighting, I doubt he'll spare any for this area. Besides, the

King's men don't know anything about the secret passages. They might suspect we have them, but they don't know where they are."

"Won't they think it peculiar when they find a boat all by itself, up against a wall?"

"I suppose so," she said. "Occasionally a boat does disappear, and we figure that a patrol found it and took it along with them, although a rising of the river could account for it. Whatever the reason for the disappearances, the King's men seem never to have pushed on the wall sections. They might have thought the boats were being used by demons of the rock or some other things even more unpleasant. I don't think the patrols like to linger down here."

"One more thing to worry about," Wemqardo muttered.

Hadon, in turn, would have worried about Wemqardo, but he had been assured by Phebha that the man was a very dependable veteran. Wemqardo might grumble and appear apprehensive, but when the time for action came he would be very active indeed.

They proceeded down a narrow tunnel so low that Hadon had to duck down a little. Then the ceiling suddenly became quite high. After three hundred feet, Klyhy halted. Hadon expected her to push on the wall section ending the passage, but she held her torch high. Looking up, he saw a square opening about three feet across the ceiling. She handed her torch to him, removed and uncoiled the rope from her shoulder. Its end held a three-pronged grapple of iron. She tossed it up through the hole three times before it caught. After pulling on it to make sure it was secure, she braced her feet against the wall and hauled herself up to the opening.

Hadon's torch showed that the rope had caught on the rung of a bronze ladder set into the stone. Klyhy was now climbing on up it.

He followed her with the torch. Within five minutes, all were climbing up the rungs after the priestess. At the top they went along a tunnel so narrow they went single file and so low they had to crouch or crawl. Reaching the end of this, they descended another bronze ladder, at least fifty feet down, then they took a tunnel which led directly below the river.

Klyhy stopped again after more winding. She pointed to a sign carved in the rock on her right, about five feet above the floor. It was a simple, single vertical line crossed by two horizontal lines near its top.

"It means a trap," she said, though they had all been instructed in the use of the secret signs by Phebha.

She walked up to the oblong stone set in the floor just beyond the sign. It was five feet across, an easy standing jump. She leaped across and went on down to make room for the others. They hopped across, taking care to land at least a foot beyond the crack.

"The last time I was here—the last time anyone was here—was six years ago," Klyhy said. "I opened the trapdoor at the orders of my superior—she's dead now—to check it. There were two skeletons down at the bottom which had not been there before, according to my superior. You see, the stone does not give way immediately.

There is a delay which allows several people to get on the stone before it drops. Apparently at least two of the King's soldiers had found this passage. Their armor identified them. But they had fallen in, and if anyone else was with them, they decided not to explore any further."

"What keeps the King from setting traps too?" Wemqardo said.

"Nothing at all," she said, not very cheerfully.

Wemqardo grunted. Klyhy turned and led them for about fifty yards in a straight line. Then she cast her grapple again, and after a while they were going along another horizontal passage. Once she stopped to point out another incised sign, a horizontal line just below a circle. A foot from it was a recess carved into the rock. This was large enough to admit a big man's hand. She put her fingers within it, gripping the raised edge.

"Pull hard on this stone and it comes out, causing the ceiling blocks for a hundred feet that way"—she pointed ahead—"to fall in. Don't forget that."

"Has this device been tested?" Wemqardo said.

"Well, no," she said. "At least not as far as I know. It was built Kho only knows how many years—perhaps centuries—ago."

"Then it may not work," Wemqardo said.

"Just hope you don't have to use it," she said. "Or, if you do, that it does work. There are about two dozen such devices in this complex. If you're pursued, keep your eye out for this sign. The recess grip will be near it."

"Just my luck not to have a torch," Wemqardo said.

"Talking about bad luck brings bad luck," one of the other men commented.

"Quiet now," Hadon ordered. "We're getting near the shaft to the roof of the temple, aren't we?"

"Yes," Klyhy agreed.

A minute later they came to another seeming end to the tunnel. Klyhy worked this device to swing it on its pivot. The group went through to an extension of the tunnel with a hole in the floor about six feet ahead. Above the hole was a shaft going upward and holding a bronze ladder. The hole went down, Hadon found out when he leaned over it, about thirty feet.

"The underground river," Klyhy explained. "It was the King's men who sank this shaft," she went on, "old King Madymeth, Gamori's great-great-grandfather. He wanted an escape route to the river in case of revolt or invasion. He did not inform his wife about it, but she found out, of course, and had the necessary shafts and tunnels carved to come out here. Thus the vicars of Kho have long had a secret passage into the Temple of Resu, though it has never been used until now. The original bronze ladder was also set there by Madymeth. About fifty years ago an earthquake tumbled part of it down into the river, and the present one was set into the stone."

"I hope the men who did it were good artisans," Wemqardo whispered.

"We'll find out," Hadon said. He leaped out across the hole and caught one bar with his two hands while a foot scraped down the wall and then against a rung.

The bronze seemed to give a little, but that was probably only his imagination. He climbed up until there was room for the next jumper. Klyhy grabbed a rung, but her foot slipped and she dangled, swearing, no doubt sweating, for a moment until she had found a foothold.

A torch was tossed to Hadon, who knotted his rope around it and carried it up that way, out to one side so the torch would not drip on those below. When he reached the sign—incised there how many decades or centuries ago?—he stopped. He drew the torch up and tied it two rungs above his head.

The last man had tied the second torch to the ladder at the level of the tunnel. Now they had light from above and below and were unencumbered. Far up, a pale oval indicated the top of the shaft. The light came from the reflection of fires against the clouds.

The sign was an inverted arrow on a horizontal line, the character of the syllabary which meant, among other things, sun, sungod, eagle. In this case it indicated the entrance to the apartment of the chief vicar of Resu, the Flaming God.

According to Phebha, the wall here was very thin. It was in fact a stone plate, a shell. It would operate like a drawbridge, its upper part describing an arc inward toward the floor. Originally it was operable only from the interior of the apartment. Madymeth had not wanted anyone coming *in* from the shaft, of course. It was accessible from the roof, however, which was why there were always twelve guards at the top of the shaft.

Madymeth had not reckoned, of course, with the silent and enduring cunning of the high priestesses, who knew there might be a showdown some day between Resu and Kho. The priestesses had cut and drilled and scraped passageways through the solid granite, taking perhaps fifty years or more, and at last attained their objective.

The final stage had involved drilling a hole in the stone near the plate, giving access to the equipment which lowered the wall section. Now Hadon removed from his belt the long instrument of iron curiously fashioned centuries before. It had been waiting for its single occasion of service all this time. It would not be used again.

He inserted the swelling end of the iron device into the hole and then pushed in two-thirds of the stem. The capped end slid smoothly over the nine-sided end of a crank. Then, making sure that it was on securely, he twisted the T-shaped handle. Nine times he turned it completely, grimacing at the squeals issuing from the hole.

Something bellowed from above. He was so startled that he almost lost his hold on the rung. He jerked his head back, looking upward. The faint light from the clouds was gone now, replaced by bright torchlight. And then a section of the light fell off and was hurtling down toward them.

Fortunately the flaming torch only came close. If it had been on target, he would have had to let loose and drop, which he certainly could not do, or else let it strike him.

Klyhy cried out in horrified protest. Wemqardo swore and said, "I knew it! I knew it!" The others voiced their terror in their own fashions, but Hadon could not distinguish what was said. Nor was he concerned about that. How had they been found?

Surely those on guard had not seen the torchlights? The shaft was too far up, and there would be too much glare from the great fires and reflections from the clouds.

Perhaps somebody long ago had detected the additions of the Queen's men to the wall-opening mechanism and, instead of removing them, had attached an alarm to them. Thus, when Hadon had turned the crank, he had triggered a notice to the King's men that someone was out in the shaft.

Whatever had caused the alerting of the sentinels, it was too late to get into the apartment. In fact, there would be no getting into it in any event. The wall section was not responding, was not beginning to move down inward as it was supposed to do.

In fact, and here he began to feel more than just a little alarm, the top of the wall was coming outward!

Hadon just had time to note that his idea was correct: the mechanism had been found long ago. The wall was fixed now so that it would open out to the shaft. And anyone clinging to the ladder would be hanging upside down from it unless he could get to the rungs immediately below.

Hadon yelled at Klyhy to get down, but she was already on her way, dropping after the others, who fortunately had not frozen with fear. His hands were on the rung just below the bottom of the wall section when it fell outward, its upper part banging to a stop against the far side of the shaft.

At least the section would act as a shield, Hadon thought frenziedly. It would prevent the guards at the top of the shaft and in the apartment from dropping things on them. The damn fools in the apartment wouldn't be able to pursue them. Didn't they realize their own trap would stop them from getting out into the shaft?

Yes, they had considered that. They weren't such damn fools. The wall section continued to lower itself with a screech, flattening straight toward Hadon along the length of the ladder.

27

Since the wall would not miss him, it forced him to take the only action possible. He released his grip on the rung and jumped back, falling down the shaft, holding himself upright as long as he could.

Above him, men shrieked as the wall section struck them.

Everything outside him was a blur and he was frozen internally, not even wondering what had happened to Klyhy, nor why she was silent.

Then he was past the area of light of the torch on the lowest rung. He was in darkness and falling, falling, though still upright. Perhaps the water at the bottom of the shaft would be deep enough so that he might survive the impact if he entered it feetfirst.

Then he was out of the shaft—a very brief sensation of suddenly expanding space around him, a coolness—and he hit the river.

The force of the blow was enough to stun him a little, though he had entered it cleanly, presenting a minimum of surface. He went down, down, slowing. His toes were suddenly in cold ooze. His knees had bent and for a few seconds he was crouching on the bottom like the godling of the river, that often described but seldom seen monster. He too squats at the bottom and looks upward, waiting for victims, usually a young girl, squats huge and misshapen, breathing water slowly, waiting, waiting, patient as only immortals can be patient.

With such thoughts, Hadon rose to the surface. The current had carried him away from the shaft, or at least he supposed it had. He could see nothing and he could feel only the cold water and a far more numbing terror. He was not thinking of the godling of the river now, but of the little blind fish with the big heads and teeth. He expected to feel something rip out a piece of flesh at any moment, then a hundred jaws fastening onto him, then—his outflung hand struck something—flesh—and he almost cried out.

Though he had pushed himself away from it, he swam back and ran his hands over it. It was the corpse of a man. The head was split open. A coil of rope was still over its shoulders. One of his men.

There was little sound except for the lap of water against the walls and some gurglings here and there. Hadon swam toward his right and within a minute felt cold stone. He dogpaddled then, feeling the stone now and then, hoping that he would bump into one of the projections leading to a passage. So far, there was nothing except rather smooth stone. He did not really have any strong expectation of finding a projection: the passages must be very limited in number and restricted to a certain area. For all he knew, he was past that area. After a while he would be past the city above, borne only Kho and the deities and demons of the dark underground knew where. He would become too tired to swim and would sink. Or the ceiling would get lower and lower until it dived beneath the surface, taking him with it. Or the blind little fish…

The scream was so unexpected, so close, so shrill with utter terror, that it almost stopped his heart.

He knew, however, that it had to be Klyhy.

"Help! Help! Oh, Kho, help me! They're eating me alive!"

Hadon treaded water, turning, straining his ears to determine her direction.

He shouted, "Klyhy! It's Hadon! Where are you!"

The screams and his shout bounced off the walls of the tunnel and reverberated. He could not tell where she was, though he thought she was to his left.

"Oh, Kho!" Klyhy screamed. "Help me! I'm being torn apart!"

Hadon swam toward the voice. She stopped screaming for a moment. He heard a thrashing and swam toward that, sure now that he knew approximately where she was. And then something touched his right leg. A second later a number of somethings were biting into his calf, fastening down on his toes, on his Achilles tendon. At first there was no pain, only numbness. Then fire struck in a dozen places.

His left hand struck soft flesh. Klyhy screamed in his ear. His right hand struck the wall, slid along it, stopped against a shelf of stone perhaps five inches thick. His fingers locked around it; the fingers of his other hand seized Klyhy's shoulder. In her agony she tore away from his grip, but his fingers clenched around her long hair.

Yelling at her to quit fighting him, he pulled her close to him. She struck at his face; fingernails tore at his eyes and nose. And now his left leg was being attacked. Pain shot through it. And then more pain, this time in his buttocks, then a tearing and plucking at his loincloth.

It was this last attack that gave him superhuman strength. He pulled himself up on the apron with one hand, afraid to let go of Klyhy with the other. While the upper part of his body was on the apron, his legs and groin area still undergoing attack, he pulled Klyhy on to the little tongue of stone. He struck her in the shoulder with his fist, felt to her face and struck her jaw. She collapsed, screaming no more.

He pulled himself completely up on the stone, gibbering in a frenzy of loathing and fear, and hacked the fish off his legs with the edges of his palms. The teeth came loose reluctantly, taking more flesh with them. He bent down then and dragged Klyhy further along the apron and repeated the dislodging process. Some of the writhing greasy things were knocked off easily; others clung, forcing him to grab them by their heads and rip them off, causing Klyhy to scream. And though he could not see the blood, he could feel it.

He turned then and groped around the apron, hoping to find a boat on it. There was none, so he felt around the wall, traced the thin line of partition with a finger and pushed on one side of the section. It swung slowly, groaning, requiring a great effort from him. Apparently this section had not been used for a long, long time.

The air inside was musty and heavy and surprisingly dry, but cooler and wetter air from the river quickly replaced it. He felt along the wall to his left, raising and lowering his hand. When he found a large recess, he stopped. His fingers detected several torches—rather dry—some flints, irons and a box. The latter contained some tinder, also surprisingly dry. Within a few minutes he had the torch lit; he had never been so glad to see light in his life.

His legs and buttocks were bleeding, though fortunately the wounds were not deep. They were painful enough, however.

He went out to the apron and stood aghast for a moment. Klyhy's body was a bloody ruin. Chunks of flesh had been torn out everywhere, and it was a wonder that she could live after having lost so much blood.

He lifted her and carried her into the tunnel. When he put her down, he saw that she had lost several toes and a nipple, and the bones of a little finger were bare.

She moaned and looked at him with glazed eyes. "I hurt, Hadon!"

"I know, Klyhy," he said. "But you are not dead yet. You will live."

He removed her loincloth and his, wrung them out and tied them around her worst wounds. But the blood continued to run.

"Oh, great Kho, I hurt!" she said, moaning. Then, looking down at herself, she asked, "Why should I live? Like this? Who would ever want to lie with me again?"

"There's more to living than lying with lovers," he said. "Besides, the wounds will heal."

"You're a liar," she said in an even weaker voice. "Hadon..."

He bent down so he could place an ear close to her lips.

"Take care of Kohr. Tell him..."

"Yes?"

"I hurt, only..."

"What is it?" he said.

"I don't feel pain now. It's getting dark..."

She mumbled something, and with a sigh she had gone.

Hadon muttered the ritual words and made the necessary signs; he promised Kho and Sisisken to sacrifice a fine bull and a fine cock to them for the sake of Klyhy. He also promised her ghost that she would be honored as a heroine of Opar. He would erect a pointed monolith over her body after it had been suitably buried, and he would see to it that one of the gold tablets in the Temple of Kho bore her name and her deeds. Her tablet would be next to his.

At that moment he became aware of a very faint light coming from down the river. He rose painfully, noting almost unconsciously that his wounds had mostly stopped bleeding now; only a few still trickled. He stuck the torch in the recess, so its light would not shine directly out through the mouth of the tunnel. Then he pushed the wall section until only an inch-wide gap remained between the wall and the side of the section. Putting his eye to this, he looked up the river. A longboat had just come into view.

It held about thirty men. Four torches, two at the prow, two at the stern, lit up the bronze helmets and cuirasses of the paddlers and the two officers. There were no spears in sight, but these, he supposed, were placed on the deck.

He shut the section and removed the torch. He took Klyhy's dagger and stuck it through his belt. He was entirely on his own now, intent only on escape. His mission had failed, and the King's men were out looking for him. Not exactly for him, since they would not know the identity of the invaders—nor would they know if any had survived the fall—but search parties were out, looking. The men in the longboat would see the blood on the apron and would stop to investigate. They would push on the wall section and in a short time would be on his trail.

For all he knew, other men would be coming along the tunnels ahead of him. They would have the advantage, since presumably some of them would know these passages or at least have diagrams of them. He didn't have the slightest idea where any of them led.

Hadon walked for several hundred feet until he came to what seemed to be the end of the passage. After passing the torch slowly along the wall to check for warning signs, he pushed the section open. It gave to a round room which was the bottom of a vertical shaft. A series of bronze rungs set into the stone enabled him to climb for about fifty feet upward. The shaft ended in the center of a horizontal tunnel. Hadon hesitated, not knowing which direction to take. Suddenly he heard a noise behind him. He looked down the shaft and saw men below. Ten were coming up the rungs, while others were crowding into the round room. Those on the rungs were making slow progress, since the lead man was holding a torch in one hand. He was forced to hook his right wrist over a rung instead of seizing it firmly.

Hadon thought it best to slow them down as much as possible. He went down the tunnel to his right—the clean or good-luck side—until he came to a bend. He placed the torch on its side and returned, guided by the light of the torches in the shaft. He lay down by the lip of the shaft and waited. Presently the light grew very bright and he could smell a strong resinous odor. The face of the lead man appeared.

Hadon ripped the torch from the man's hand. He flung it behind him and seized the man's throat. His dagger's point went through the man's eye, into his brain. The man ceased his cries.

Hadon dropped the dagger and grabbed the man's neck with his other hand. He pulled the body over the lip and into the tunnel. Below, men shouted. They did not know what was happening, but the cries of the lead man had alarmed them. Hadon removed the sword-belt of the corpse and strapped it around his waist. Then he took the helmet and the cuirass off, and leaned over the lip with the helmet in one hand and the heavy cuirass in the other. The man now on top looked up and cried out. His face was only five feet below Hadon, who hurled the bronze cuirass into it.

The man gave a choked cry and fell back, missing those on the rungs. But his body struck the crowd at the bottom, hurling most of them to the floor.

Hadon threw the helmet into the face of the next man, also causing him to fall and injure or kill more.

Hadon lifted the corpse above his head with both hands, the effort causing some of his wounds to start bleeding again. He hurled the body down. It struck the first man and dislodged him, both falling on the man just below; the three fell, two screaming. Four more men were knocked down, all crashing into the heap of dead and disabled on the bottom.

That still left two men on the rungs. Besides, despite the groaning tangle on the bottom, more soldiers were coming out from the tunnel into the shaft. Hadon counted eight. So he had immobilized all but ten of the thirty. Not bad for one man, he thought.

The survivors were either fools or very brave or both. They were coming up the rungs after him, ignoring the calls for help from the bloody mess on the bottom.

Hadon decided the climbers were stupid. They were in a helpless position if he stayed where he was, and he would be crazy to leave now. Once they were on the level, he would be outnumbered.

Hadon waited by the lip. After a while he heard the heavy breathing of the first man. He sat up then and when the bronze helmet slowly appeared—the man was cautious—he brought the sword's edge down on top of the helmet. Not, however, hard enough to split it or knock the soldier unconscious. The man cried out but clung to the rungs. Hadon stood up and leaned down, unloosening the chin strap and removing the man's helmet. The soldier stared at him with crossed eyes. Hadon grabbed the long hair and yanked the fellow on up. As he came over the edge, Hadon brought his knee up under the man's chin. The fellow sprawled out senseless.

Leaning over the edge, Hadon hurled the helmet into the upturned face of the next man, who was climbing up swiftly and desperately. The force of the blow broke the man's nose, but he did not let go of the rungs.

Hadon removed the sword and dagger from the man on the floor beside him. He rolled the groaning man over the edge. There were two cries, one from the falling man, who had just regained sufficient consciousness to realize what was happening; the other was from the man beneath the body. His grip broken, he fell with the other on top of him, and three others were scraped off.

Which left three.

These men became very wise very suddenly and retreated. Hadon did not want anybody able to follow him, however. He hurled a sword down and it went point first, striking the lead man on top of his helmet. He fell with a scream into the man below him, and both smashed into the heap at the bottom of the shaft. The sole survivor went down swiftly, too swiftly in his panic. He lost his hold and fell twenty-five feet on his side. Hadon thought he had been killed but, no, he was up on his feet and climbing over the tangled bodies.

Hadon threw a dagger at him. It missed, sinking instead into the neck of a man lying facedown on top of several bodies. The soldier got through the doorway and, though Hadon waited for five minutes, he did not show his face again.

Hadon speculated about going back down the ladder and killing the man. But that would accomplish nothing. The man was trapped there, since he could not handle the heavy longboat by himself. He would not dare to come back up the shaft again for a long, long time. He would want to make sure that Hadon had left the area.

Which was just what Hadon was doing. He walked away, holding a torch, a dagger and a sword in their sheaths. There was no doubt now which one of the two tunnels to take. Down the one to his right was a faint light, a murmur of voices. And then a blood-stopping sound, a sudden outburst of barking! Dogs!

28

Hadon walked or trotted for what must have been hours. He went down and up and along, confused and thirsty. Once he came out onto another apron by the river, where he drank deeply. But there was no boat so he retraced his steps until he found another branch and went down it. Several times he heard the barking of dogs and the shouts of men, but he got away each time. At least he put a lot of distance between them and himself. Though the hounds had his scent, they could not climb the shafts. They had to be lowered or raised by ropes, so his pursuers lost much time at these places.

They would surely catch up with him in the end, unless he could find a way out of this three-dimensional labyrinth.

He went down a shaft about thirty feet deep which ended in the ceiling of a tunnel. He dropped from the bottom rung to the stone floor. Five feet away was a seeming dead end, a wall composed of granite slabs, ten inches wide and six inches high, set in concrete. He went to it and pushed on both ends but it resisted his hardest shoves. Either the bronze pivot mechanism was not operating or else it was truly what it looked like.

Ten feet the other way was a shaft. He went to it and looked down. His torchlight glittered on water, either the river or a well. A faint red light glowed at the top of the shaft—the open air. The great fires outside the city were reflecting from the clouds, providing a flickering light up there, a dim tawny oval.

But there were no rungs in the sides of the shaft. And the walls sloped slightly in from this point up.

The tunnel continued fifteen feet away at the other side of the well. He could not figure out why there was no bridge here. Did the carvers of the passage intend the wayfarer to jump the gap? Or had there once been a wooden bridge here, now rotten? Or a winch for a well?

He did not know what the situation had been. He did know what it was now.

He heard far-off barking and returned to the shaft he'd come down on. Torches flared at its head and several faces looked down at him. Frantic barking drowned out their cries, though their open mouths made it evident they were announcing his presence.

Hadon stepped quickly back out of sight. He turned and, holding the torch to one side, retreated to the wall of masonry. There he crouched, then ran as swiftly as he could; on reaching the lip of the well, he leaped.

He landed easily enough and with inches to spare on the other side. Fifteen feet was not much of a long jump for him. His pursuers were going to be stopped for a while, though. He doubted that the dogs would dare the jump. And the soldiers would have to shed their heavy bronze helmets and cuirasses before they made the attempt. As it was, only the most daring and agile would attempt it.

For a moment he thought about waiting on the other side of the gap to knock the jumpers back down the well. But the idea, though attractive, was not workable. The soldiers could throw spears at him, or sling missiles he couldn't dodge. No, he could only hurry on, hoping that the leap over the abyss would make them hesitate for a while.

The tunnel across the well was about fifteen feet wide. This side of it was narrower, only seven feet wide. He went along it for about a hundred feet, coming to a flight of steps cut into the stone and leading downward. The bottom landing was about twenty feet below, from which the tunnel continued. A few minutes later he came to a heavy wooden door secured by two enormous bars.

He shot the bars and opened the door. Its iron hinges screamed. Hoping there was no one on the other side to be warned by the noise, he passed through the entrance. He was in a large room, about sixty feet long, thirty wide and fifty high. It was empty except for three ingots of gold. Hadon thought this must once have been a storeroom, emptied except for the three ingots. Or perhaps it was being refilled and the three ingots were the first to be placed here.

That did not matter. What did was that near the door, on the sweating stone wall, was an incised sign, the same Klyhy had pointed out, a horizontal line just below a circle. Near it was the carved recess with the handgrip.

Hadon went across the chamber to the other side. There was another door here, but this was unbolted. Just outside the doorway, another sign and recess with handgrip were revealed in the torchlight.

Past the door the tunnel ran straight as a sword for as far as he could see.

Hadon went back to the chamber, trying to figure out the peculiar placing of the bars on the doors.

Why bar the doors at all?

Was it to keep someone else from coming this way?

Hadon had a hunch that the long straight tunnel led to a place outside the city walls. And since there were outlaws, runaway slaves, wild Gokako and even Nukaar, the hairy halfmen of the woods, out there, the doors might be barred against them.

Well, he would find out what this meant later on. Or perhaps he would not. It was of no immediate importance.

He looked through the door he had entered by. A light shone far down the tunnel, so somebody had made the jump—more probably somebodies, from the speed at which the light was advancing. One or two men would not proceed so boldly. Not when they knew he might be waiting in ambush.

Hadon ran back to the other door. He stopped just past it and put his fingers inside the recessed grip. He leaned back and pulled with all his strength. The stone section slid groaning out, then suddenly it was free and he had to stagger backward to keep from falling. Then he was running, while behind him the ceiling, which was made of bricks and cement for about thirty feet, fell in. The crash was loud, booming down the tunnel, echoing. There was no dust, since the moisture was too heavy on the stones for that.

He heard or saw nothing of pursuit after that. Even if the bricks had not filled the tunnel completely, they would have given pause to the King's men. They would wonder how many more such traps lay ahead of them. But Hadon did not think the passage would be cleared for some time. The mechanism of the ancient priestesses had worked quite well.

At the end of about thirty minutes he came to a narrow flight of steps. He went up this spiral, coming suddenly into a cleft just wide enough for his shoulders between two granite walls. The clouds shone redly above him. The steps had disappeared, replaced by a steep incline of polished granite. He went up it to find himself in the open air. He was standing on top of a huge boulder.

Below him was a tiny round temple of marble, shining whitely in the light of a big fire. It was more of a shrine than a temple, consisting of a circle of white marble pillars with a conical gold-plated roof. The floor was a mosaic of varicolored stones with a great statue in its center. Just in front of the statue was a fire, burning in a vast bronze box.

Hadon had been confused at first. Now he knew where he was. He was on the Isle of Lupoeth. There, a mile west across the lake, was the city of Opar. Its towers and domes and walls shone in the fires still blazing on both sides of it.

The tunnel had gone under the river beneath the city and led to this islet—this islet sacred to the demigoddess Lupoeth and forbidden to the human male. He had committed sacrilege, though unknowingly.

The deed could not be hidden from Kho, he knew. But perhaps, since he had come here while in Her service and he had not known what he was doing, he might be forgiven. If he could get away before the three priestesses discovered him, he might be able to get through this without harmful consequences. Since he could cover the whole islet with one sweep of his eyes, and since he could not see the three women, he knew they would be in their tiny quarters right below him, in the hollowed-out part of the boulder. One would be awake, since the fire had to be tended at all times.

He went down the back of the boulder, which was like a small cliff here. The river lapped the foot of the great rock, so he had to wade around the vertical shore. Once he slipped into some deep water and swam around until his feet touched bottom again. He rounded the whole body of land in five minutes, failing to find a boat.

The three priestesses had their food and firewood brought to them, probably by water, since the tunnel would be used only for emergencies or secret messages.

There was only one thing to do. He would have to swim the river to get back to Opar. But the current was strong in its middle, and he was exhausted from the emotional and physical stresses of the day and night.

He might make it to the shore, but he would be far past Opar when he got there.

On the other hand, he thought, why not swim to the eastern, the near, shore? There would be fishermen or hunters along the strip of land between the river and the eastern cliffs. They would have boats, and he would just borrow one.

That was the sensible thing to do.

Hadon sat in water up to his waist and rested a moment. The temple looked eerie in this strange light from the clouds and the fire within the bronze box. The giant figure of Lupoeth, three times life-size, towered in the midst of the marble pillars. It was in the stiff, graceless style of the ancients, of marble painted with flesh tones and hair and eye colors. As was still common in those days, the body from the waist down was theriomorphic, in this case a crocodile's hindquarters. Her breasts were huge and rounded, each marked with the stylized head of a crocodile, Lupoeth's totem. Her eyes were painted blue. Her hair was long and black, crowned by a triple tier of gold set with diamonds. In her right hand she held an immense spear of gold.

Through the pillars Hadon could see the dark opening carved into the foot of the boulder. Where was the priestess who tended the sacred fire?

This question was answered suddenly and startlingly. A white figure rose from behind a small boulder to his right. It advanced toward him, becoming somewhat more distinct as it neared the light from the fire in the bronze box. It was not a ghost, as he had thought for a moment when he had first seen it. It was a woman in a white robe with a hood.

Apparently the light was strong enough to distinguish Hadon. The priestess stopped at the edge of the solid rock shore and stood still, looking at him for a long time. Finally, nervous from the prolonged inspection and the silence, he said, "Guardian of the Temple of Lupoeth! I am Hadon, son of Pheneth and Kumin the *numatenu*, and I am the victor of the Lesser Games of Opar and the Great Games of Khokarsa. I am a refugee..."

The woman threw her hood back, revealing a middle-aged face. She said, "I know you, Hadon. Do you not remember Neqokla, keeper of the Chamber of the Moon for many years? I used to give you sweets now and then and a hug and a kiss too. I expected great things of you, Hadon, though I also predicted that you would get into much trouble."

"Neqokla!" Hadon said joyfully. "Now I remember! You were sent here about twelve years ago! I have not seen you since! And yes, I cherish the memories of your kind deeds and words. You were very good to a small boy who was only the son of poor parents."

"How did you get there?" she said. Then, "Of course, you came up through the tunnel to the river! I thought I felt a shaking of the earth some time ago, but I had been dozing off and I told myself that I had dreamed it. Or Lupoeth was making the earth shake to wake me up and remind me of my duty."

"The quivering of the earth was caused by the collapse of part of the tunnel outside the great chamber which contains three gold ingots," Hadon said. "I set off the trap to escape from the King's men. I did not know the tunnel led here. I committed sacrilege unknowingly."

"We only know what happened in the city up to late yesterday evening," Neqokla said. "The supply-boat captain gave us the news, saying he might not be able to return in the scheduled two days. We watched the fires for a long while and made some sacrifices to Lupoeth, asking her to guard the city she founded and aid the people of Kho in their battle against the heretics.

"As for the sacrilege, I am sure that some slight penance will satisfy Lupoeth. You are here in the service of Kho, her mother, Mother of All."

"In that case," Hadon said, "may I come ashore?"

"You may," she said, "but you may also have to take to the river again."

She pointed past him. He turned and saw an assemblage of torches moving out from the city toward the island.

Neqokla said, "They are coming this way. Those torches are fixed to a longboat manned by the King's soldiers. They must have guessed you would be here."

"How could they?" Hadon asked. Then, "I suppose the men blocked by the trapfall returned to the King to report. He must have determined from the location of the trapfall that it was under the river—then he would have also figured out that the tunnel was used by the priestesses to get to and from this islet. I have betrayed you!"

"It couldn't be helped," Neqokla said. "I'll rouse the others and we'll hear your story quickly so we can plan what to do."

She hastened toward the round doorway carved at the base of the immense boulder. Their voices must have awakened the two women, however, since they appeared in their ghostly white robes before she had reached the temple. She beckoned to them and they came swiftly. One was old, white-haired and bent-backed, crippled with arthritis. This was the chief, Awikloe. The other, Kemneth, was about twenty-five, a pretty girl who had been with Hadon at the temple school.

Neqokla explained quickly all she knew and Hadon filled in the missing data. Kemneth and Neqokla brought a great wooden chair from the quarters for the old woman. The chair was some twenty feet in front of the fire, which Neqokla replenished with fuel.

"Gamori is a desperate and a hard man," Awikloe said. "He has already sinned greatly by violating sanctuary and attacking and killing priestesses and worshipers of Kho. He will not hesitate to violate another taboo and set foot on this island. He may even plan to kill us, though that would be going far even for him. As for his men, they must be as conscienceless and greedy as he, otherwise he would never have gotten them into the boat."

"Pardon, Awikloe," Hadon said. "But you sound as if you think Gamori himself will be on that boat."

"I think he will be," she said, flexing her gnarled hands. "He will want to make sure you are killed; he will want to witness your death himself. Besides, his men, no matter how hard they may be, would be reluctant to touch taboo soil unless they were led by the King himself. But we shall see whether or not I am right."

"If I am not here, then they will have no excuse to come ashore," Hadon said. "I can swim to the eastern shore."

"After what you have been through?" Awikloe said. "Be truthful, Hadon. Could you swim half a mile in your exhausted condition?"

"I might," Hadon said.

"And more likely you would not be able to," she said. "Anyway, this is too good a situation to abandon. This business could be settled once and for all. If you kill Gamori, the rebellion would fall apart."

"And how can I do that when he has a boatful of men?" Hadon said. "Providing, of course, that he is on the boat."

"That is up to you," she said. "From what I have heard, you have been tricky enough. You are a man of many turns, equal to every occasion of danger, improvising where needful, eluding death where others would have been caught."

"Even the king of foxes was caught in the duckhouse," Hadon said.

"Don't quote proverbs to me, young man."

"If I stand here boldly defying him, his men will cast spears at me until I am a human porcupine, bristling with quills," Hadon said. "No, I must not be seen at first, at least not recognized."

Hadon asked some questions and then explained what might be done. The three agreed to do as he proposed. They did not think it had a high chance of success, but it was better than nothing.

And so it was that Gamori and his men saw an impressive sight when they neared the islet of the Temple of Lupoeth. The fire was blazing high, its light illuminating the giant statue from below, causing highlights and deep shadows. Lupoeth looked grim and terrible, harshness forming around the eyes and mouth. The aged priestess sat huddled in her chair, her back to the fire, her hooded face in darkness. The middle-aged priestess stood by the great bronze box, ready to throw more fuel on the flames. She too was shrouded in white. The young priestess stood at the right of the old woman, but she had removed all her clothing and gashed her breasts and arms and legs with a small sharp knife. Her unbound hair moved without a wind. Presently, as the prow of the boat ground gently against the rocky shore, Gamori saw why the hair seemed to have a life of its own: a small flat head with a darting split tongue raised from the mass, its head turned toward Gamori.

"By the venom of this snake, I summon death!" the naked young woman cried out. "By *my* blood I summon *yours*!"

There was a murmur among the men, thirty paddlers, a steersman and an officer who stood behind Gamori at the prow. The paddlers had put their blades on the deck and had unsheathed their swords or gripped their spears. Gamori held an officer's stabbing sword in his left hand. He was helmeted and cuirassed and wore a long scarlet cloak, a scarlet kilt to which the feathers of the kingfisher were sewn and sandals of hippopotamus hide. A thick white bandage was around his arm, covering the wound inflicted by Hadon's spear. Since he was left-handed, he could still handle the sword effectively.

"Do not come ashore!" the old priestess said in a high quivering voice. "This is sacred soil, Gamori, and all males are forbidden to touch it!"

Something was wrong with the tableau, but Gamori could not grasp just what it was. Then the officer, a colonel, tugged at his cloak and said in a low voice, "Your Majesty! The golden spear of Lupoeth is missing!"

Gamori looked up past the white figure on the chair and through the pillars and he felt a sudden shock. It was true! The great golden spear was gone! The hand of the idol was still bent, but it held only air.

"Where is it?" he said, looking wildly around the island. The fire lit up the white pillars and the white shrouds of the two priestesses and the white, darkly stained figure of the young priestess. It burnished the statue of Lupoeth, who seemed to be glaring at him, and the towering face of the gigantic boulder, said to have fallen from heaven shortly before Lupoeth and her expedition came to this river valley.

The chief priestess cried, "The spear of the goddess is with me, Gamori! The goddess has delivered it to me, her vicar, to use against the first man who violates this isle, who soils it, who mocks Lupoeth and mighty Kho! You have committed enough crimes against the Goddess, against your wife and Queen, the high priestess, Gamori! You will soon pay for these! But do not add to your heinous deeds by touching an area which the deities have forbidden you. Go away, Gamori, before the angry spear of Lupoeth exacts vengeance!"

The men in the boat murmured again. The officer shouted at them to be quiet, but his voice lacked authority.

Gamori, however, though he must have been just as frightened, could not back down. To show fear now after having attacked the Temple of Kho and slain priestesses, having slaughtered a quarter of the population in the name of the Flaming God and the superior rights of the King—to back down would weaken his cause, even fatally. It would not take much to reverse the flow of victory. Though he had driven his men to commit sacrilege, he had not eradicated all anxieties from them. Deep down, though they lusted after the treasures and the power promised them, they were still fearful of the Goddess. This unease had driven them to hysteria, a frenzied attack on all they had been taught to revere and honor since childhood. It was this hysteria which had caused them to slay where there had been no need to slay, to profane beyond their orders.

For Gamori to show the slightest weakness now was to weaken his believers too. They would wonder why Gamori had not trespassed when his greatest enemy, Hadon, was within his grasp. Hadon was somewhere on this tiny place, probably hiding in the carved-out chambers inside the boulder. And their wonder would lead to a great loss of confidence in him. If he hesitated now, perhaps he was having second thoughts. Perhaps he really believed, under his pretense, that Resu was not supreme, that Kho was the greatest of the deities.

Gamori's face was haggard in the firelight, deeply scored with fatigue, worry and dread. But he was not going to back down. He turned to his men and shouted, "I am going ashore! All of you follow me and search every inch of the island! And if the priestesses oppose you, slay them!"

He let himself down over the high prow, assisted by the officer. The river came to his waist at this point, but he held his sword up with his left hand, his right trailing in the water. He put his head down like a bull and thrust against the river. Soon he was standing on the shore, water running from his cloak and kilt.

The aged woman in the chair seemed to grow taller and straighter. She shrilled, "You have delivered yourself to the house of dread Sisisken! Do not follow him, you soldiers who are traitors to your Queen and your Goddess! You may yet escape the wrath of Lupoeth! Take yourselves and this boat away now! Report to Phebha and beg for mercy, saying that Awikloe sent you."

The colonel, who had been about to leap down from the boat, paused.

Gamori turned to the boat and yelled, "Obey me!"

The colonel did not move. Some of the soldiers had stood up, but now they sat down.

"They wait to see what you will do, Gamori!" the crone said, a definite jeer in her voice.

Gamori whirled, snarling, and said, "I will kill you, you wrinkled old bag! And then they will see that your Lupoeth is powerless to protect her own chief priestess! And if that is not enough, I will slay the other two!"

The young priestess gashed herself again on her arms and thighs, shouting, "*My* blood summons *your* blood, Gamori!" The snake slid out from her hair and down her neck, coiling itself around her bloody shoulder.

Gamori walked swiftly toward the chief priestess, his sword raised.

The priestess near the bronze box threw a bundle of split sticks on it and then cast a handful of green powder over the flames. A green cloud whooshed out and upward, covering her for the moment, then expanding to veil the old woman on the chair. The men in the boat gasped or moaned, and Gamori stopped.

The green cloud quickly thinned, revealing Awikloe standing straight and tall, magically tall, behind the chair. In her right hand she held the mighty golden spear, holding it above her head, though no man could have lifted that weight of gold in one hand.

"Behold!" she cried. "Lupoeth has given me stature and strength to slay her enemy and the Queen's enemy and my enemy!"

It may be that Gamori, who was much nearer than the men in the boat, saw the features under the hood. He may also have considered that the spear was not made of solid gold after all.

Whatever he thought, he had no chance to express it.

The spear went back and up as the priestess readied for the cast, then it flew to its target.

Gamori gave a cry and turned, but the point drove into his neck and through his windpipe. Choking, clutching the heavy shaft dragging on the ground, he staggered backward. The old priestess went around the chair and sat down, seeming to shrink back to her normal small size.

Gamori fell backward into the water, which covered his face. The golden spear disappeared under the surface, holding his body down, keeping it from moving with the current.

The priestesses were as still as the idol. They said nothing, nor did anything more need to be said. The colonel gave a sign and the soldiers seized their paddles and backed the boat out and around. They sped for the city of Opar, lurid in the flames.

Not until the boat was halfway to the city did the priestess arise from her chair. Then the robe was removed, revealing the grinning face and tall body of Hadon. The old woman came hobbling out from the round doorway. Hadon went to the body, drew the huge weapon out and threw it on the ground. Then he pulled the King's corpse ashore, because it would have to be shown to the people of Opar to convince them that he was really dead.

Neqokla, using a blanket to cover the fire at the correct intervals, had sent signals to the watcher in the dome of the Temple of Kho. A longboat put out an hour later, returning with Hadon at dawn. He was greeted at the quay by Phebha, who conducted the rituals cleansing him of the guilt of regicide and of profanement of the Isle of Lupoeth. After this, surrounded by soldiers who kept off the cheering crowd, he was led to the temple, through the temple to the room where Lalila lay in bed.

Though she looked pale and haggard, she smiled on seeing him. He kissed her, then took into his arms the tiny blanketed form. He lifted the flap from over the face and saw the most beautiful newborn baby he had ever seen. Wide blue eyes stared at him, focusing with an ability infants that age just never had.

Phebha, sitting in her chair behind him, said, "Hadon, behold your daughter! La of Opar!"

The Song of Kwasin

Philip José Farmer

and

Christopher Paul Carey

Dedicated to the immortal spirit and works of EDGAR RICE BURROUGHS and H. RIDER HAGGARD.

Map 4: Dythbeth and Surrounding Region

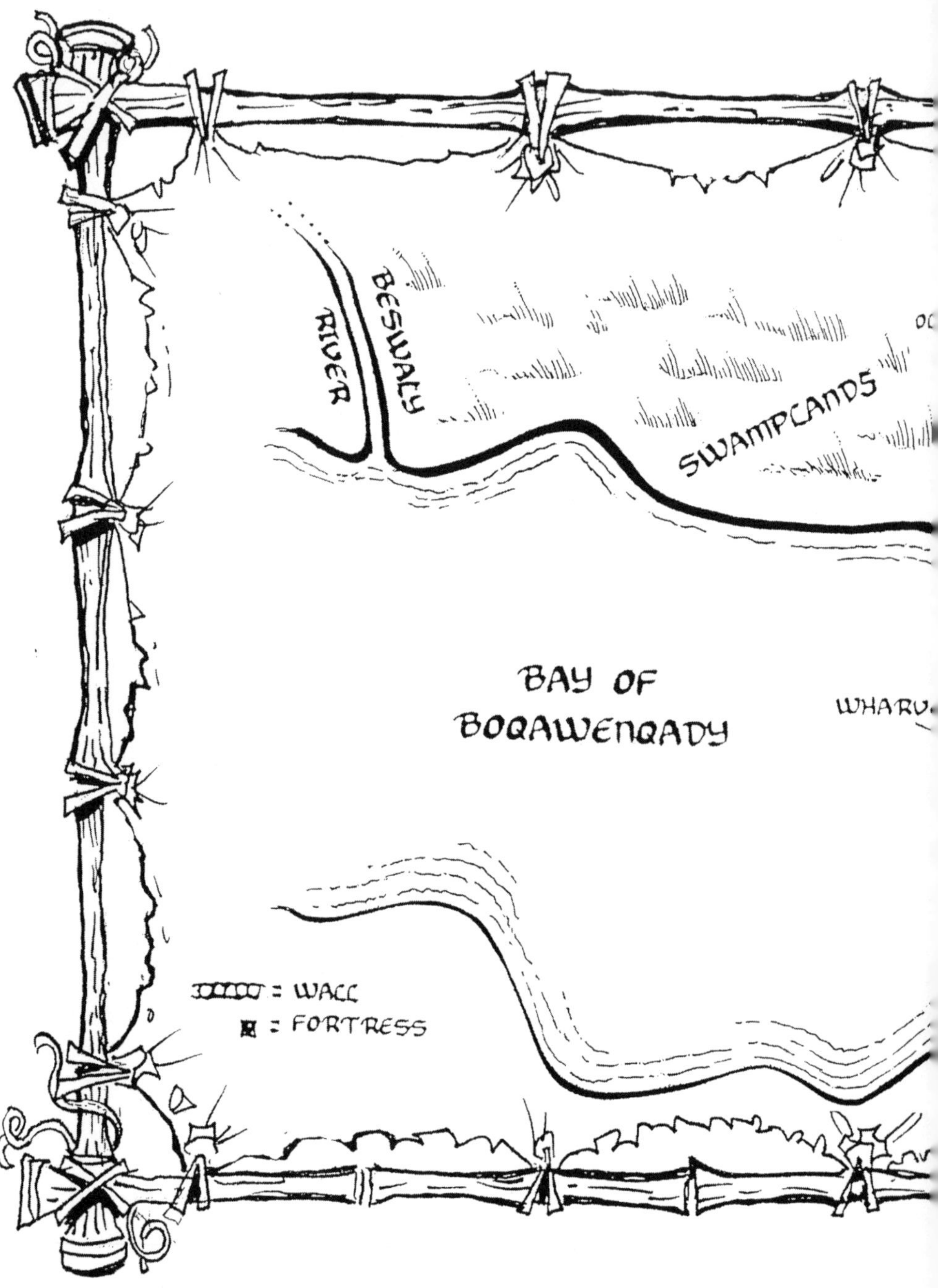

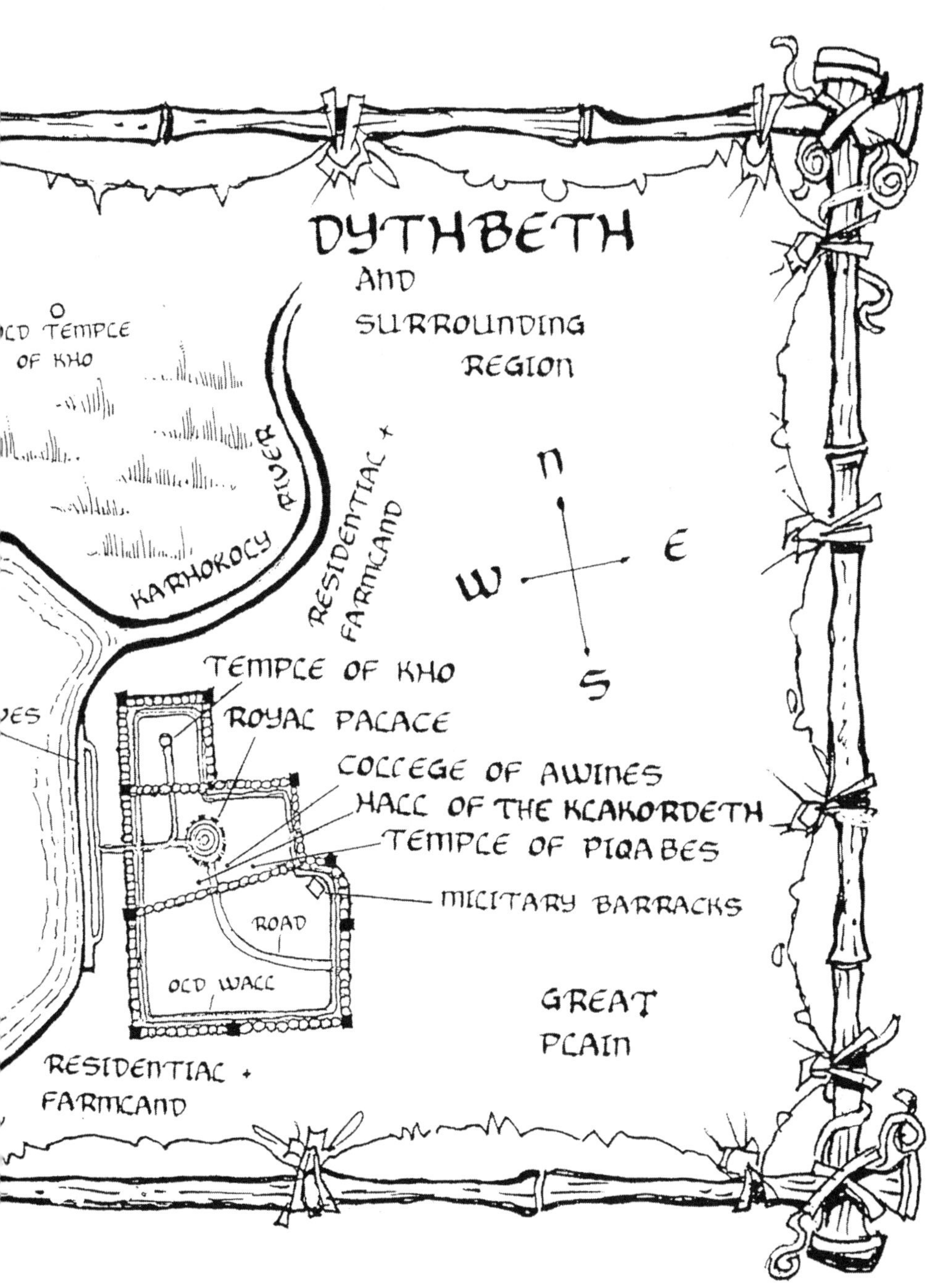
DYTHBETH
AND
SURROUNDING
REGION
LD TEMPLE
OF KHO
KARHOKOLY RIVER
RESIDENTIAL +
FARMLAND
N
W
E
S
TEMPLE OF KHO
ROYAL PALACE
COLLEGE OF AWINES
HALL OF THE KLAKORDETH
TEMPLE OF PIQABES
MILITARY BARRACKS
ROAD
OLD WALL
GREAT
PLAIN
RESIDENTIAL +
FARMLAND

1

The strongest man in the world came puffing over the top of the hill and met a god.

The being whom he saw leaning against an oak tree never claimed to be a god. Nor did Kwasin know that he was one when he first saw him.

Later, he thought that a third person, an observer objective because he'd never before seen either of them, might have guessed that it was Kwasin, not the other, who had the strongest claim to divinity.

There was Kwasin, seven feet tall and muscled like a bull, like an elephant, like a gorilla, like the long-dead heroes of old. A dragon of a man, his bones thick and with mighty muscles attached. Like no other man living and like few men of past ages. He had a thick growth of curly black hair and a long curly black beard which did not hide the extreme handsomeness of his face. Sweat made his body shine, that body which was the envy of men and the desire of women. He wore only a lion-skin kilt, and he carried only a huge ax. It was one which no ordinary man could wield and few extraordinary.

The man leaning against the oak was fully a head shorter than Kwasin. Though well-muscled and thick-boned, the stranger was built more after the fashion of Kwasin's cousin Hadon, with corded thews, narrow hips, and long arms and legs. Like Hadon, the man might be quite an athlete, but he would make no match for Kwasin, who outweighed him by a hundred pounds of bone and muscle.

Despite death being close at his heels, Kwasin stopped in his tracks and regarded the stranger. The man's arms were folded across his chest and his ruggedly handsome face—beardless, in opposition to the tradition imposed by King Minruth's followers—was smirking. Almost, it seemed to Kwasin, as if the fellow had been waiting for him.

By Wenqath's ass! Kwasin cast a cautious look down the valley behind him. He had no time for delay; a group of Minruth's soldiers followed right behind him. They had spotted him three miles back as he crossed a stream and dashed across a field for a thickly wooded forest. Normally, Kwasin's great stride would have allowed him to easily outpace his pursuers; but he was winded from his swim across the Gulf of Gahete, not to mention his escape from Minruth's prison and his battle on the water as Hadon and his companions fled. If Kwasin had been rested, he might not have run to begin with but rather turned and charged, his great Ax of Victory swinging. He had seen twelve men. In his adventures in the Wild Lands he had faced many more single-handedly and lived to brag about it. But these men were not ill-equipped primitives; they were armed with slings and accompanied by three wardogs. He had hoped to elude them in the forested hills outside the city of Khokarsa, but so far he had been unable to find a tributary of the stream he had passed and thus get the dogs off his scent. He could hear their barking coming from over the next hill.

"That ax of yours. Where did you get it?"

Kwasin looked at the stranger, who still lolled casually against the tree. Something about the man woke bees in Kwasin's stomach. Moments later he understood why he felt this way.

"I'd like nothing more than to discuss the virtues of this most faithful of women," Kwasin said, panting, and he swung his ax in a mighty arc sure to give any mortal enemy pause. "But the hounds are at bay, and if you don't get out of my way, my loving bride may yet turn fickle and leap out of my hands at you."

The stranger seemed unfazed by Kwasin's bravado. He no longer even looked at Kwasin, but now seemed intent on studying an insect crawling up a long grass stem at his feet.

Kwasin started up the hill toward the stranger, but when the man spoke again, surprise froze him.

"If I find that harm has come to Lalila, her child, or the manling Pag," the stranger said, "I will hunt you down and kill you." Then the man threw back his head and, shaking a black mane of hair, sniffed the air like a lion scenting its prey. "Though the wind tells me you may already be doomed," he added, his keen eyes again returning to Kwasin.

"How do you...?" Then the cloud of befuddlement cleared as if Resu, the Flaming God, shone forth his brilliant glory inside Kwasin's skull.

So this, then, must be the man said by many to be Sahhindar, the Gray-Eyed Archer God! The Son of Kho in the flesh! Or so the scribe Hinokly had claimed when he told the story of how his expedition encountered Kho's exiled son in the hinterlands beyond the empire. Sahhindar, protector of the golden-haired, violet-eyed beauty Lalila, the *moon of change*, and her daughter Abeth, and the dwarf Paga, who had given Kwasin his mighty ax, and whose name the god pronounced strangely. If not for them, Kwasin would never have ended his exile and returned to Khokarsa, at least not yet.

No, Kwasin thought, he would not now be standing upon this hill outside the capital if his cousin Hadon had not won the Great Games of Klakor, and if the oracle had not then sent him off on a fool's quest to the Wild Lands to bring back the woman, her daughter, and the manling, who were said to be under Sahhindar's guardianship. But the oracle of Khokarsa had decreed that only upon accomplishing this task would Hadon be granted the king's crown that should have been his right as victor of the Great Games. And it was during his fated expedition to the

Wild Lands that Hadon had run into Kwasin, serving out the sentence of exile that had been imposed upon him for ravishing a priestess of Kho. Kwasin had counted himself blessed by the Goddess and sworn an oath to obey his cousin until they got back to civilization, hoping that Hadon, with his expedition's goal achieved, would then assume the throne and pardon his exile.

That had not happened. Instead the journeyers returned from their adventures to find that King Minruth and his priests had revolted and overthrown the natural ascendancy of the Goddess and the rule of Her priestesses. War and chaos reigned in Khokarsa.

Now that Kwasin was here, at the empire's hub, he was released from his irksome contract with Hadon. Free, he thought, if not for the soldiers at his heels, the priestesses who wanted him exiled, and the god who stood mockingly before him.

"Sahhindar!" Kwasin bellowed. "If indeed you are the Son of Kho, then we are brothers! Both exiled by the Great Mother to spend our days wandering the Wild Lands. But an exile's dishonor need not be our fate. Let us turn and seek Kho's forgiveness by slaughtering Her enemies!" Kwasin waved his ax back toward the adjoining hill. The dogs' barking was much louder now and at any moment the soldiers might charge over the hill's crest.

Cool gray eyes regarded Kwasin. "Not my fight," the god said; then he turned and scrambled up the oak tree like a monkey. "If you run into Lalila or Pag," Sahhindar shouted down at Kwasin through the leaves, "tell them to head south, far south, as quickly as the wind will take them. There is not much time left." The leafy foliage swished in the god's wake and Sahhindar was gone.

Kwasin turned around just in time to see the first soldier sprint over the nearby hilltop. The soldier fought to hold the reins of a monstrous dog, its mane thick and bristling, and fangs so large Kwasin could see them even at a distance of two hundred yards. Several more soldiers followed over the lip of the hill, two of them also led by the large, wolflike dogs. But Kwasin did not take long to look at them. Quickly he slipped behind the same oaken trunk against which Sahhindar had leaned.

He waited. No longer would he run. He was not like his cousin Hadon, who had turned and fled as he, Kwasin, leaped into the nearest boat of Minruth's soldiers and stood alone against those who would have killed Hadon and his friends. No, Kwasin had stayed behind then, like any red-blooded man would have, to give the beauteous Lalila a chance at survival. As he had done then, Kwasin promised himself that one day, if the woman lived, he would look into those violet eyes again and that in them he would see Lalila's burning desire for him. He grinned at the thought. Then he corded the leather thong of his ax around his wrist and hand, stepped from behind the tree, and charged.

Down the hill he went, roaring like a mad lion, his mighty ax swinging above his head.

The three wardogs at the front of the group of soldiers strained against their handlers' reins. The men and dogs had already passed the bottom of the adjoining hill and were halfway up the hill down which Kwasin madly ran. Too close now to use their sling-stones effectively.

The plumed iron helmet of a captain in the Sixth Army of Khokarsa appeared behind the dogs. The handlers, amid much snapping of their charges, managed to steer the dogs off to the sides. The officer raced forward. Though Kwasin could not hear the man's words over the dogs' hellacious barking, he could see the officer cursing at the handlers as he passed them and moved into the lead. The man pulled a square-ended iron sword from its scabbard as he pumped furiously with his legs. A *numatenu*. Though Kwasin did not belong to the order of the *tenu*, the fool officer undoubtedly saw it as a matter of honor that he confront the giant before his soldiers did. To kill Kwasin, exiled ravisher of Kho's priestess, would certainly bring the fellow much fame. The man was so sure of himself he did not even carry a round wooden shield like his fellows.

Now the war dogs and handlers broke even farther to his left and right. No doubt they meant to outflank Kwasin while the officer took him on. Kwasin had just enough time to take this in. Then they were upon him. Or he upon them.

Kwasin's ax crashed against the officer's swinging blade, ripped it from the man's grasp. The man did not even have time to look surprised before Kwasin, bellowing with laughter, kicked him in the face with the thickly callused sole of his bare foot. Blood spurted from the man's crushed nose and teeth and he fell backward down the hill. They did not make *numatenu* like they used to.

Kwasin whirled, expecting the dogs to be upon him. Then he saw why they were not. Two more men with plumed helmets stood to either side of him on the sloping hill, their long, slightly curving iron swords drawn. Minruth had sent not one, but three *numatenu* after him. Kwasin's reputation had grown large indeed.

In the time it took him to observe this, Kwasin did not pause. Already his ax whistled at the man to his right. At the same time as the ax smashed a hole in the soldier's wooden shield, Kwasin spun toward the man on his left and with his bare foot kicked off against the advancing man's raised shield. The *numatenu* stumbled backward but did not lose his feet.

Kwasin turned back to the man with the damaged shield. He clung to the useless thing for a moment, but seeing the giant before him raise his enormous ax, the man cast the shield at Kwasin's face and retreated several steps. Kwasin raised his free arm to block the hurtled shield, which upon impact pivoted on his forearm and whacked hard against the bridge of his nose. Warm blood gushed from his nostrils onto his lips and bearded chin. Kwasin howled out his rage and whirled about with his ax.

The massive head of the weapon caught against the edge of the other man's shield and tore it from him. Under the momentum of the blow, the officer fell back and to the side, pummeling into one of the dogs behind him. This was too much for the blood-frenzied descendant of the wild dog of the plains. Barking and snarling, the dog leaped ahead and pulled its handler helplessly forward. Then the beast was on the fallen *numatenu*, its large, clawed feet scraping furiously at the man's lacquered breastplate as it tore open his throat with its teeth.

Even over the yelping and growling of the dogs Kwasin heard the heavy footsteps coming from behind. Knowing he did not have time to again raise and swing his heavy ax, he jumped forward, landing on his stomach close to, but not touching, the dog that had just dethroated the other *numatenu*. Then he rolled to one side and hurtled himself downhill through the gap between two of the surrounding soldiers. By the time he got back to his feet, he was grinning. The *numatenu* who had charged him had come too near the ravenous wardog, which—infuriated because it had not caught Kwasin before he rolled away—had locked its monstrous jaws upon the soldier's leather-kilted upper thigh. The man was down on both knees. Then a moment later, facedown, dead.

Kwasin's delight evaporated quickly. Now situated downslope from the soldiers, he faced a severe disadvantage. In addition to the fact that the high ground now made it much easier for his opponents to attack him, the soldiers could unleash their sling-stones on him; and though pleased to have eliminated three *numatenu* so easily, he had hoped to take down at least five or six men and one of the dogs while he still held the high ground.

No. He had not incapacitated all of the *numatenu*. The first man he had engaged in his charge down the hill was up again, shouting orders at his men. Blood spewed from the gap in the man's front teeth, but he did not seem to notice. Perhaps here was a real *numatenu* after all.

Under the officer's orders, the two handlers on Kwasin's upper-right flank sicced their dogs on him, coiling out the dogs' long leashes. Why the man did not order his slingers to take down their enemy, Kwasin did not know. Perhaps the idiot officer hoped for the beasts to bring down Kwasin so the man could then deliver the fatal blow to the legendary exile personally.

That did not matter now. His current situation was bad enough. The leopard-sized beasts bolted down the hill, and at less than half a dozen yards away the lead dog launched itself into the air at Kwasin.

Kwasin dropped to his knees and simultaneously heaved up his ax before him in a quick underhand swing that only he could have been powerful enough to accomplish. It hit the canine squarely beneath its jaw, cleaving in two the beast's head. Kwasin did not see what happened to the dog's corpse after that, as its two companions hurtled onto him from above.

He toppled back beneath the blow of their bodies, his ax arm carried backward over his head. One dog's jaws clamped his right thigh, and his left shoulder seared with pain under the other's teeth. While this happened he was sliding headfirst on his back down the wet, grassy hill, all the while trying to maintain a hold on his massive weapon which preceded him down the slope. The slick, resin-covered shaft that made it possible for Kwasin to wield the ax with lightning speed now threatened to cause him to loose his hold. He sought to get a grip on the knobby protuberance at the bottom of the haft, but a sharp rock on the hillside struck his hand. The ax flew out of his grasp, though the leather thong attached to it yanked hard against his wrist.

But the pain in his wrist was nothing compared to the fire in his leg and shoulder. As he writhed under his attackers, a thick doggy odor sought to smother him and he gagged. For a moment he thought he saw Sisisken's dread face, but then the visage of the goddess of the underworld vanished in the dark well of his anger. He was a hero—more of one than his spoiled cousin Hadon—and he refused to die under the fangs of the hyena's cousins.

Finally Kwasin and the mass of canine fangs and fur hit a shallow gulley in the hill and their wild slide stopped. Kwasin roared. He twisted his hips toward the dog biting his thigh and crossed his free leg over the beast's torso, sliding down along its body as he squirmed uphill, so that the dog's fangs could not emasculate him. But if the beast wriggled free, it would. Still, he had to do something, and as he clamped the dog with his legs, he reached for the other beast—its teeth sunk deeply into his shoulder's flesh—and grabbed it by the throat beneath its powerful jaw. He squeezed both dogs, the one with his hand, the other with his legs.

The dog between his legs squealed. Kwasin heard ribs breaking beneath the corded thews of his thighs, but he was forced to let go the canine when the other dog arched its neck and snapped out a fleshy chunk of his forearm.

With his free arm, Kwasin yanked and swung upward with all his strength against the ax's leather thong. He had not known if could do it, but he managed to tug the thong hard enough to send the bony ball on the end of the ax haft into his fingertips. He jerked the ball toward him, released it, and grasped the haft firmly.

A crimson haze swathed his vision, whether of blood or anger he did not know or care. In the haze, he saw the ax gleam as if lightning incarnate—or was it just the strong Khokarsan sunlight glinting off the weapon's metallic head? Whatever the case, it seemed as if the Ax of Victory moved of its own accord, arcing first in one direction, and then another. Using the impetus of the ax's swing to aid him, he jumped to his feet and found both dogs dead—laid low by his wild and brutal outburst. One of the canines' heads was rent in two, the other's chest gaping open, its vital organs spilling onto the ground in a deluge of blood.

Still Kwasin's anger raged. He charged up the hill, the turf tearing out from beneath his feet. A sling-stone whirred past his right temple, and then a second ricocheted off the iron head of his ax, which he had just raised to face-level as he ran. Though fury still held him, he grinned fiercely, recalling Paga's claim that the ax was cursed. Perhaps it had cursed the ugly manling, but right now Kwasin would not have traded it for all the women he had ever bedded.

He made for the five soldiers clustered around the surviving *numatenu*. Four other men stood several paces uphill to Kwasin's right. Whistling slings swirled at their sides, but he didn't believe the men would let loose their missiles for fear of hitting their fellows, whom Kwasin now engaged head-on.

Three soldiers' heads exploded under one terrific swoop of Kwasin's ax. A violent arc of blood, hair, brains, and skull fragments flew through the air and sprayed across the grassy incline. The remaining officer, who had recovered his *tenu*, swung his blade at Kwasin. Vulnerable because his own swing had carried the tremendous weight of the iron ax to the end of its arc, Kwasin stepped downhill, forcing the *numatenu* to advance. The man sliced his blade at him but Kwasin was out of reach, his ax already swaying back like a murderous pendulum.

Kwasin jumped forward with the ax's momentum. He landed on his knees, which burned as they slid across the wild grasses. He came to a stop with his ax buried deep in the swordsman's side.

Out of the corner of an eye Kwasin saw the dull sheen of metal reflecting sunlight. He rolled in the opposite direction, and a short sword cut the air within an inch of his neck. Now on his side, Kwasin kicked out at his opponent's leg and hit the soldier squarely on the kneecap. The man buckled forward with a throaty yell. Kwasin raised his ax and smashed it through his fallen foe's helmet as if it were but an eggshell.

Then Kwasin was up, heaving the dead soldier's body before him as a shield and barreling toward the slingers. Hot blood coursed through him in the frenzy of battle and he barely took note of the ax's tremendous weight as it dangled from the antelope-hide thong around his wrist. The corpse he held up in front of him—or was the man yet alive?—jarred as sling-stones impacted it. One of the projectiles tore through the flesh of the man's underarm and grazed Kwasin's shoulder where the dog had bitten him. He growled like an enraged lion through his clenched teeth.

Two of the slingers broke before Kwasin could reach them. Though he could not see them over his human shield, the two remaining slingers had to be directly in front of him. Then one of the men appeared over the corpse just before Kwasin rammed him.

Upon collision, Kwasin dropped the dead man and dug his uninjured shoulder under the chin of the soldier into whom he barreled. He fell with all his weight on the slinger. Wind whoofed from Kwasin's lungs. He rolled away from the soldier and onto his feet, gasping for air. The man on the ground did not move, but another man was running away. Kwasin slipped his ax's thong from around his wrist and, pivoting on one foot, swirled his whole body with the ax extended at arm's length. Just before he completed his circle, he released the ax. It arced shallowly upward, then down. The fleeing soldier fell beneath it.

The two remaining soldiers dashed for the hill's tree-covered top. One soldier lagged behind the other, appearing encumbered by his armor and the heavy iron *tenu* he had lifted from the corpse of one of the officers. The fleeing man must have been truly frightened. And stupid. If the other soldier witnessed his action and reported it to his superiors, the man, if apprehended, would be executed for thieving from a member of the noble swordsman class.

Grinning darkly, Kwasin picked up a sling and missile from the dead soldier at his feet and placed the stone in the leather pocket of the sling. Swiftly but calmly, he wrapped one end of the sling's strap around a finger and slipped the other knotted end between his thumb and forefinger. Then he held the sling to his side and with a motion of his wrist and forearm began whirling it parallel to his body. He released the free end of the sling on the fifth whirl. The stone missile shot off in a shallow arc.

When the man fell, Kwasin threw back his head and whooped with laughter.

Then he saw the remaining soldier disappear into the tree line as if fleeing the ugly face of Kopoethken herself. His voice still shaking with laughter, Kwasin shouted, "Go! Spread far and wide the name of Kwasin of Dythbeth, who has returned from his exile to slay the feeble *numatenu* of Minruth the Mad and turn the innards of his soldiers to soup!"

But with the words dying on his lips, Kwasin looked about at the dead that lay scattered across the hillside. As he surveyed the aftermath of his fury, a sudden emptiness replaced the joy he had experienced but a moment before, and he considered how easily he might have been one of the corpses. He had seen much death in his lonely wanderings in the Wild Lands. No living being could hold off personal oblivion, the ultimate writing off of self. Even the priestesses of Kho, with all their prayers, blessings, and ancient wisdom, could not avoid it or prevent it for another; nor could the great Kwasin, who possessed more stamina and strength than any other, ever hope to vanquish the terrifying void of *nothingness* that even now lay in wait for him in dread Sisisken's hollow dominion.

Kwasin left behind the hillside's bloody testament and climbed the next rise, yet the pall of his gloomy soliloquy hung over him. He thought of the oracle who had pronounced his exile, and of the priestess who had caused it.

Suddenly, as if Great Kho had granted him a vision, he knew where his wanderings would take him next; though maybe, he mused, his soul had secretly known where it had intended to carry him all along. Why else had he not traveled northward to learn the fate of Hadon and his companions and instead had swum westward across the Gulf of Gahete and set off over the hills in the direction of his native Dythbeth?

The thought—whether a gift from the Goddess or a quirk of his weary soul—raised up the dark veil that had hung over him, and his spirits lifted. He would return home, after eight long years of adventures and sufferings in the Wild Lands. Home, where he would somehow find a way to exonerate himself from the crimes of his past. Once again, he would be a free man.

Of course, he expected the priestess there would have something to say about that.

2

Two weeks later—having endured a journey over land, sea, and river that included as many adventures as it did hardships—Kwasin stared down from his mountain perch at the cyclopean harbor city of Dythbeth, its gilt-trimmed, white granite domes gleaming brightly in the distance beneath the strong noonday sun of the island of Khokarsa. A sparkling river stretched beneath him, the Karhokoly, its two tributaries snaking down to the marshlands that surrounded the old temple of Kho at Dythbeth and emptying into the long and narrow Bay of Boqawenqady. He breathed in deeply the minty fragrance of the thick fir and pine forest that edged the rocky overhang on which he stood. For a moment, he smiled.

The sweet smell of the trees triggered memories of his happy youth exploring the mountains outlying his birth city while under the supervision of his godfather. The husband of his mother's best friend, Pwamkhu had acted more like an older brother to Kwasin than a dutiful grownup. Together the two had engaged in much good-natured deviltry, often finding creative ways to bait Kwasin's peers into fights with the already large, athletic boy or taking joy in enraging shop owners with clandestine visits in the dead of night to egg their market stalls.

Those happy times had been in the years before Kwasin's mother, Wimake, had died. After that sorrowful event, the ten-year-old Kwasin had left Pwamkhu behind, having been sent off to the eastern shores of the southern sea to live with his uncle Phimeth in the dark caves of his cliff-side home. Though at first eager to experience an exotic new land and thrilled to learn the ways of the *tenu* from a legendary swordmaster, Kwasin's optimism quickly evaporated under his uncle's disapproving glare, and longing for his native Dythbeth soon gnawed at the boy's heart.

Phimeth turned out to be a strict and joyless man, at least as far as his ill-behaved nephew was concerned. The young Kwasin was a temple child. His mother, having failed to become pregnant at the time of her marriage to Toekha, a prominent merchant, had conceived Kwasin while serving as a divine prostitute in the temple of a god. Thus Kwasin's father was, religiously speaking, Khukhaken, the Leopard God, divine consort of Khukhaqo and the patron goddess of Dythbeth; and since Toekha had died in a skirmish with bandits before Wimake gave birth to her only son, Kwasin had known no earthly father figure besides the boisterous Pwamkhu.

Phimeth, a bachelor, did not like children, and the innately wild and rebellious Kwasin—made more unruly in the absence of his mother—did not make his newfound task of childrearing any easier. Phimeth had tried to instill discipline in his adolescent charge, but Kwasin resisted and was often disobedient, though he dared not step too far out of line for fear of his uncle's harsh punishments. Still, Kwasin attempted to bridge the gap between them and begged to be trained as a *numatenu*. Phimeth stubbornly refused and told Kwasin he was not mature enough. Though Kwasin fumed, he could do nothing. The will of the old *numatenu* was as iron as his square-ended weapon of trade. When, a few years later, Kwasin's cousin Hadon came to stay with them in the caves, the relationship between Kwasin and his uncle worsened. Phimeth suddenly announced that it was time to begin training with the *tenu*, and it was immediately clear to Kwasin that his uncle favored Hadon, the spry, long-armed son of Kumin. Kwasin's anger and resentment had blackened.

Kwasin heaved a deep sigh. Even Sahhindar, the god of Time, could not travel to the past now that Kho had banished him for his insolence, so why should he, Kwasin, be bothered by times gone by? The trivialities of the past could not touch him, especially now that Phimeth was dead, and probably Hadon as well; and though the oracular priestess at Dythbeth had condemned Kwasin to wander the Wild Lands beyond the empire's borders, she had declared that one day, when Kho decreed it, he would be permitted to return. Now, Kwasin believed, he had paid his debt to the past, had even stood up against the enemies of Kho by smiting down the insolent soldiers of Minruth. The Goddess and Her priestesses would surely forgive him his past transgressions—even if that two-faced bitch priestess who had accused him of defiling her sacred person was in truth the one who had transgressed.

His plan was to traverse the passes through the mountains and follow the river southeast. Then he would slip unnoticed into the city and, under cloak of night, enter the chambers of Weth, now high priestess and queen of Dythbeth—the very woman who had falsely accused him of ravishing her. Well, perhaps he had intended to ravish her, but her loving moans had begged him to do it, and who was he to disobey a priestess of Kho? Besides, he had not gone through with it. Weth had become frightened upon seeing his naked manhood, or perhaps it was the furious fire of lust burning in his eyes that had unsettled her. Whatever the case, she had screamed and her guards had entered and set upon him before ascertaining the situation. Kwasin had only killed them in self-defense. He knew the woman carried in her heart the truth of what occurred that night, and now that the Voice of Kho at Khokarsa was in hiding from Minruth's forces, Weth remained his best hope to clear his name. The endless wanderings of his exile wore at him, and if he had to endure even one more day in the Goddess-forsaken Wild Lands, he would go mad—madder than he already was, he thought, grinning.

The distant sound of men shouting, accompanied by a dull thudding that might have been weapons clashing, awoke Kwasin from his reverie. He stepped back from the rocky overhang, cupped a hand to an ear, and listened.

When passing south of Awamuka's farmlands, Kwasin had spied a large, well-organized assemblage marching out of the north. He had sneaked close enough to determine the group was a contingent of Minruth's Sixth Army, numbering perhaps five thousand strong. To avoid them, Kwasin had detoured far to the west and entered the landward region of the tall coastal mountain range about forty miles due northwest of Dythbeth, only to run headlong into a group of soldiers occupying a small mountain village of bear worshipers to the north. This had resulted in one of Kwasin's stranger adventures, in which, with some help from the local priestess and sloth of trained bears, he had assailed the village and managed to rally the villagers to rise up against their oppressors.[1] But Kwasin had been lucky; if he had not succeeded in fully routing the soldiers and they had been able to quickly summon reinforcements, things would have ended up much differently. Now, in the southern reaches of the Saasamaro, Kwasin feared the shouting from beyond the ridge might be evidence of a much larger contingent of Minruth's troops moving through the region.

Then again, it might be nothing more than bandits attacking a trader's party. Years of experience in the Wild Lands, however, had convinced Kwasin that it was better to know one's surroundings than to be surprised by the unknown. Lack of curiosity squashed the dungbeetle.

He jogged up the forested incline, angling toward the source of the disturbance. Upon nearing the ridge, he slowed and advanced with caution. Crouching, he peered over the summit and down at the situation below.

Outside of a wooden-walled fort at the base of the pass, a group of soldiers flying the leopard standard of the Fifth Army at Dythbeth had taken a defensive position against a much larger body of soldiers. Or two larger bodies. The attackers streamed into the pass from both the main road and an adjoining pass to the southeast. These soldiers carried the rising sun standard of Khokarsa's Sixth Army.

Minruth's mad ambitions had at last reached faraway Dythbeth.

The sight made Kwasin livid. Although Dythbeth had forsaken him and its oracle had condemned him to exile, the thought of Minruth and his power-hungry priests overturning the rightful rule of the Goddess outraged him. For all of his bravado, Kwasin could not escape the bowel-aching fear of Kho that had been instilled in him during his youth. The Great Mother, in Her anger at Minruth's blasphemy, would be sure to send pestilence and famine across the land, or worse, destroy the land altogether. Had not the sacred volcano Khowot, the Voice of Kho, belched its black smoke and fiery lava in the days following Minruth's revolt? Even a week ago, as Kwasin had passed south of Awamuka, the anger of the Goddess had rumbled the earth and a great cleft had appeared in the grassy plain before his astonished eyes.

Kwasin ducked behind the ridge and jogged eastward along it. When he felt he had gone far enough that the soldiers in the pass could not see him, he again peered

1 For a full recounting of this adventure, see the novella "Kwasin and the Bear God" by Philip José Farmer and Christopher Paul Carey in *The Worlds of Philip José Farmer 2: Of Dust and Soul* (Meteor House, 2011).

over the ridge. Since he saw no soldiers in the pass or forest below, he bounded downward, weaving through the trees. He did not stop when he got to the pass, but rather continued on across it and up the next ridge. The rise here was rock strewn and less thickly wooded, and Kwasin made his way to the mountain's opposite side, fearing the Sixth Army might have positioned scouts to follow along its rear.

He now headed west, back toward the fighting. The battle cries and wailings of the wounded grew louder. Kwasin stopped when he reached the southeastern cross-pass down which one arm of the Sixth Army had marched. Minruth's soldiers no longer occupied the area, though Kwasin could see the rearguard moving down the main pass.

Though he risked a scout seeing him, Kwasin ran down into the cross-pass and up its opposite side, so that he now darted behind boulders and the occasional tree on the steep and uneven mountainside above the clash of the two armies. The larger mass of Minruth's army had pinned the soldiers from Dythbeth up against the walls of their fort. Still the Dythbethans fought on, refusing to retreat into the fort, although the enemy seemed an unending river before them. Despite Kwasin's status as an exile, no small amount of pride swelled in his breast at the heroic display, though the plight of the Dythbethans seemed all but futile. By sheer numbers, Minruth's legions held the upper hand and Kho only knew the short span of time before the Fifth Army would be crushed and their fort taken.

But Kwasin cared little for odds when the mad fury of battle seized him. He spied his target and said a brief prayer to Khukhaken, whose spirit was still said to inhabit these mountains over fifteen hundred years after the hero Dythbeth had cleared the area of the Leopard God's four-footed children. Then Kwasin pumped his mighty legs and ran farther up the mountainside.

Midway into his ascent, he heard a shout. He looked up. A man's silhouette loomed above on the craggy summit. Then Kwasin saw three bronze-helmeted men with spears emerge from behind a boulder about two hundred yards to his right. Though he had thought he could run no faster, Kwasin leaned forward and increased his speed, now also using his hands to help propel himself up the steep incline. He reached his target ahead of the spearmen who now ran at breakneck speed toward him.

Kwasin stood before an immense boulder resting on a shallow projection of dirt and stone. The giant rock might have been pitched there during one of Kho's recent upheavals of the land.

The spearmen had only closed half the distance between Kwasin and their original position. Kwasin glanced up at the summit. The man, having come only partway down the mountainside, hovered half a dozen yards above Kwasin, his short sword drawn. Fortunately, he did not bear a spear. He made furtive glances toward the men on Kwasin's right. The fellow, shieldless like the spearmen, wore a conical helmet sprouting the black raven feather of a *rekokha*, or sergeant. He was apparently waiting for his men to close on their target before advancing on Kwasin himself. By now Minruth would have sent word out to his troops to be on the lookout for the ax-bearing giant who had escaped his prison and killed dozens of the faithful soldiers of Resu. The *rekokha* must have known that he faced the legendary Kwasin of Dythbeth, returned from his exile in the Wild Lands.

Kwasin grinned. Khukhaken must have heard his prayer. The officer's cowardice gave Kwasin just enough time to execute his plan.

He dropped his ax onto the shallow ledge and, groaning like a dying demon, leaned into the huge boulder and pushed off against the slope with his feet. The rock did not move. One of the men, now on his left as he faced the pass below, slipped on the treacherous incline and slid on his belly some ways down the mountainside. His companion did not pause to help his fallen comrade and was now almost within a spear's throw of Kwasin.

Kwasin looked back at the officer above him. The man had closed the distance between them, apparently bolstered by his proximity to the other soldier.

Roaring, Kwasin heaved again. His spine crackled under the force of his action. Then, at last, the great boulder gave out before him and he pitched forward in the rock's sudden absence. Something sharp grazed his back as he landed chest-first on the grit of the ledge and his torso slid halfway off the shelf. A spear. Below he saw the boulder rolling violently down the mountainside, following a trajectory that would land it in the midst of the Sixth Army's rearguard.

Without waiting to see if the boulder would hit its target, Kwasin swung around on the narrow ledge and pulled himself up just as the man with the short sword jumped from above, his blade stabbing downward. Kwasin canted hard to his left and kicked at the sword's flat side near its hilt. The blade dropped from the soldier's hand, and Kwasin, now on his side, kicked again, this time at the man's ankle. The soldier crumpled.

Kwasin got to his feet. The man who had launched the spear that grazed Kwasin's back booted recklessly along the sharp mountainside only paces away, his short sword drawn. Kwasin reached down and, groaning, lifted up the body of the stunned *rekokha*, who shouted in surprise and probably also pain from his injured ankle. The other soldier, seeing his superior raised high above the head of the giant, skidded to a halt. The man's face stretched long with fear just before Kwasin hurtled the body of the officer at him. Both soldiers went tumbling down the sheer mountainside, a tangle of arms and legs. Kwasin smiled broadly when he saw the soldier who had earlier slid partway down the rocky incline turn tail and head down the mountain.

Chaos reigned below, at least for Minruth's troops. The boulder now lay at rest in the center of the pass, having left behind a trail of corpses in its wake. The giant rock had hit the rearguard squarely, creating havoc among the slingers and spearmen. Those missed by the boulder ceased launching their deadly rain of missiles over the heads of their fellows in the mad rush to get out of the way. The men immediately in front of the rearguard, panicking, ran forward, creating a stampede that left many soldiers fallen and crushed beneath a human tide.

This would have also spelled disaster for the Dythbethans, who easily could have been crushed against the wall of their fortress if not for the quick thinking of their leader. Kwasin could see the man now, his *tenu* drawn, his king's crown gleaming golden in the sunlight, leading one flank of his men northward along the wall of the fortress. The other flank, apparently under the king's rapid orders, headed south along the wall. Meanwhile, the Khokarsan soldiers, attempting to escape the stampede that surged behind them, continued to charge forward.

Kwasin shouted his approval when the Dythbethan king signaled for his men to reverse course and converge on both sides of the Khokarsan phalanx. Now bottled between two flanks of their enemy, the panic-frenzied soldiers of Minruth fell before the swords and spears of the Dythbethan king's men.

Weth had chosen her husband well; though, of course, the king's fortune had depended solely on Kwasin's actions. And, Kwasin thought, I would have made her a better lover.

"But then," he said aloud, laughing, "what mortal man, king or otherwise, can compare to me?"

Kwasin recovered his ax and headed down toward the battle.

3

By the time Kwasin stepped into the pass, the bulk of the Sixth Army was in retreat, their advance guard dead or dying. The Dythbethans shouted taunts and insults at the fleeing soldiers while the victorious king got to the business of reining in his men to scavenge the bodies of the fallen for precious armor and weaponry. The accoutrements of war, always valuable commodities, would become even more crucial to the Dythbethans now that trade was cut off from the capital and the other cities over which Minruth held his sway. The latter would be many, at least according to the rumors Kwasin had heard while imprisoned in Minruth's dungeons. Still, other whisperings among his former guards told of thousands of Kho's worshipers who had formed a resistance in the mountains across the island. Of all the cities on Khokarsa, only proud Dythbeth stood any chance of holding out against Minruth's blasphemous new order.

When Kwasin approached, many of the soldiers stood up from their task of foraging among the dead. The jaws of the men gaped wide at the giant warrior, who might have been a hero stepping out of an epic of ancient times. Kwasin watched with amusement as the soldiers dropped their loot and backed slowly away as he passed. Murmurs of "Defiler of the Great Mother!" and "Traitor to Kho!" shot between the men. They must not have seen his exploits on the mountainside above and how he had saved them from certain defeat. Or if they had, they did not care. To them he was a blasphemer, excommunicated by the oracle for his sacrilege against the high priestess of Dythbeth. Only a pronouncement from the city's oracle, endorsed by Queen Weth, would change their minds.

One man, however, did not step out of Kwasin's way but instead navigated through the carnage, making straight for the giant. Ankle-length priestly robes hung from the gaunt frame of the long-faced man, and a stiff roach of greased hair, running from the nape of the neck to the forehead, stuck up on his otherwise shaven head. In disobedience to Minruth's decree that all priests grow beards, the man sported a clean-shaven face, though on his forehead he had painted in yellow ochre an inverted arrow on a horizontal line, the character in the syllabary that represented Resu, the sungod. He stopped about twenty paces from Kwasin and made the sign of Kho, touching his forehead with his three longest fingers, then circling the fingers out and over his loins before returning them to his forehead.

"Are you all cowards?" The man shouted his question at the soldiers. "In the name of Kho and Resu, take custody of this man! He is the criminal Kwasin, exiled from the land by the oracle!"

At the priest's words, the soldiers stopped backing away and yet did not advance. The face of the priest reddened and his fist shook at the men.

"Where are the valiant warriors of Dythbeth? Detain this man or I'll have your hides skinned and used as drapes in the temple of Resu!"

Kwasin, hefting his ax onto a shoulder, narrowed his eyes and stopped within arm's reach of the priest.

"Priest of Resu," Kwasin rumbled, "you speak of Kho from one side of your mouth but from the other cry forth the name of Resu. Can you blame the men of Dythbeth for hesitating to carry out your orders in this Time of Troubles, when an outlaw has saved them from Minruth's treacherous army and the words of the priests are as mutable as the face of the Shapeless Shaper?"

The priest's lips pruned as if he had just taken a bite of rotten pomegranate. "You? *You* saved them?"

"Lo!" Kwasin swept a mightily thewed arm to indicate the great boulder lying in the midst of the dead on the field of battle. "You think this rock fell from the sky? The oracle who banished me from the empire said one day I would return, and so I have, in the hour of my people's greatest need."

Slowly, and with caution written clearly on their faces, a number of soldiers crept closer until they crowded round Kwasin and the priest. The soldiers' attitude, Kwasin noted, was not threatening, and though some of the men carried the swords, spears, and slings they had looted from the dead, none of them presented the weapons menacingly. Instead, the eyes of the fighting men of Dythbeth seemed to sparkle with growing awe and admiration.

The priest's hands shook and his already reddened face grew darker. "Though a priest of Resu," he said, "I, Taphiru, have not forsaken Kho as many of my brethren have so foolishly done." As the man spoke, he looked up into the eyes of the giant before him, but his words projected loudly so that Kwasin knew the real audience was the group of soldiers about them.

"Yes, I remember you well, Kwasin the Troublemaker, from the days of your rabblerousing youth. Always causing grief, ever the bully. And always in the company of that…what was that lout's name? Ah, yes, that good for nothing ass, Pwamkhu. He bragged he was such a great warrior until one day that tiny little daughter of Besbesbes buzzed his way and stung him in the ass." Taphiru pealed with laughter. "Why, he just puffed up like a toad and died!"

All too keenly did Kwasin recall the story of Pwamkhu's death, and indeed, what a shameful end it had been for the hero of his childhood. After leaving Dythbeth to live in the caves with his uncle, Kwasin had never seen his godfather again. Years later, when Kwasin returned to his native city, he had visited

Pwamkhu's grave, with its pitiful marker consisting of a mere brick instead of a grand pylon and a hero's tomb; and on that sorry grave Kwasin had sworn never to let live any creature that dishonored the memory of the one man who had befriended him in his youth.

For a moment it seemed to Kwasin that the fury inside him would erupt like wrathful Khowot. Then he did explode, though in laughter, not rage.

"I will not fall into your trap, priest!" Kwasin's cavernous voice boomed. "Though it is easy enough to see how the fork-tongued followers of Resu convinced so many to join their wicked cause...and how they yet seek to divide the allies of the Goddess." Then Kwasin's eyes narrowed slightly. "By the way, where is the army's priestess? Surely the king has not gone into battle with only a priest to guide him?"

"The priestess Waneth has taken ill," Taphiru said, and Kwasin thought he saw a slight curl of satisfaction upon the man's lips. "Her attendants nurse her inside the fort."

Kwasin suspected the man had poisoned Waneth so that he could broaden his sway over the army, but he said nothing of his surmise. Instead, he put a hand to his forehead and staggered about the men, feigning a swoon. "I too feel ill," he moaned. "Summon the doctor! Now! Lest the plague vapors carried on this priest's putrid breath lay the whole army to waste!"

The soldiers standing about hooted at Kwasin's buffoonery and the priest's red-faced outrage. Taphiru seemed about to launch himself on Kwasin despite their disparity in size when a measured voice rang out from behind the man.

"What goes on here?"

The group of soldiers parted and a stocky, long-bearded man of about fifty, wearing battle-worn armor and a golden crown in the place of an iron helmet, stepped forward. Kwasin had never met King Roteka in person, although he had seen the old soldier about Dythbeth in the years before the man's marriage to Weth and his subsequent sovereignty. In his youth, Roteka had earned a generalship under Minruth when he turned back a much larger force of barbarians that had crossed the Saasares and threatened the coastal city of Mukha. The man seemed to wear his armor more comfortably than his crown, and Kwasin took an immediate liking to him.

When Taphiru, his voice quavering with outrage, explained that the infamous exile—and undoubtedly a spy for Minruth—stood before them, and that the king's soldiers had better do their duty and arrest Kwasin, King Roteka pulled at his graying beard and nodded.

"No," he said, "this man has opened the way for victory. Did you not see him, Taphiru, high on the mountain fighting our enemy? Like a thunder-god he hurled this great stone from the mountain and made Minruth's pawns scatter so that we might rout them. And a messenger has just arrived this morning from Q"okwoqo to the north, bringing news of how Kwasin freed the village from the sun worshipers' tyranny."

"But this is the man who defiled the high priestess, your wife!" Taphiru exclaimed in disbelief.

Roteka regarded the priest, and Kwasin thought the king's eyes carried a look of shrewd suspicion. Then the king took hold of Taphiru's arm and whispered something in the priest's ear. Taphiru did not speak after that, though his temples pulsed with what seemed suppressed rage.

"I know well who this man is," the king said, "and the heinous crimes for which he has been sentenced." Roteka stared fiercely up at Kwasin, then looked away. "But I remember too that the oracle didn't order him killed outright for his transgressions. I can only trust in the Goddess that the Voice of Kho knew what she was doing when she spared him castration and death. For that reason, and for the good of the people, I must put my personal feelings aside, as well as those of the queen... at least for the moment. Another Time of Troubles is upon us, and Dythbeth is in dire need of its own troublemaker. I won't so hastily dispose of a man who, by his recent actions, has demonstrated his capacity to leave our enemy reeling."

Then King Roteka, clearly uncomfortable and not hiding his disgust, lifted his gaze to meet Kwasin's. "Will you not join the men of Dythbeth in the struggle against the blasphemers? I could use your brawn almost as much as your reputation. In payment for your conscription, when we return within the city gates I shall petition the queen to consult the oracle on your behalf. It has been many years since you departed in exile and old Wasemquth may have changed her mind. But if she has not, you must agree to obey the oracle's pronouncement, no matter if that order be your immediate execution or the proclamation of your freedom."

Kwasin did not need any convincing. Even if he hadn't desired the old king's help in clearing his name, he knew accepting Roteka's offer still benefited him. Minruth had put a price on his head. Unless Kwasin gave up and returned to the Wild Lands, he would not be able to rest until someone defeated Minruth and returned suzerainty to Kho and her priestesses. He had to take the risk that the oracle would revoke his sentence. And besides, Kwasin thought, who better to break Minruth's neck than himself?

And so he who was loath to bow before any man dropped to a knee and, laying his great ax on the ground before him, swore his allegiance to the King of Dythbeth. For now, he thought, at least while Minruth yet lived.

When Kwasin arose, the surrounding troops broke out in a throaty cheer, apparently overjoyed to have the frightful, ax-wielding colossus fighting on their side and not against them. Kwasin, his spirits lifting, hefted up his ax and stood grim and terrible before them.

"Enough!" Roteka said before the cheer had yet quieted. "The enemy is in retreat and we must rout them out while the piss still wets their kilts. You, Kwasin, will fight by my side where I can keep an eye on you." The king turned to the priest. "And you, Taphiru, will return to the fort where your slick words won't confound the decisions of war."

The priest hesitated a moment, his brow creased with fury; then, still fuming, he obeyed his king and left for the fort while Kwasin set off with Roteka, a thousand strong surging behind them as they marched up the pass.

At the cross-pass they again engaged Minruth's troops, and throughout the day many men fell beneath the giant Kwasin's ax and the long *tenu* of King Roteka. At times it seemed as if the Dythbethans would inflict enough damage to again send the Khokarsans running. Then, late in the day, a courier arrived.

The man brought intelligence that a large enemy contingent moved along the vast plain to the south of Qoqada. The soldiers garrisoned at Dythbeth numbered too few to repel the new wave of invaders, and if Roteka and his men remained holed up in the mountains, the city would be taken.

King Roteka ordered an immediate pullback, ceding the mountain fort and the surrounding terrain to the enemy. The twenty-mile march back to Dythbeth would take two and a half days for the large contingent, and as they moved through the passes to the grasslands, they would be vulnerable to attack. Fortunately, as Roteka's troops pulled out, the Sixth Army made no move to pursue them. The fatigued and severely battered enemy seemed content to occupy the fort and lick their wounds.

On the trip out of the mountains, Kwasin spoke with the king and learned the reason for the presence of the Dythbethan troops in the high passes. "I received a plea of help," Roteka said, "from a group of guerillas fighting in the mountains. These were refugees from Awamuka whose allegiance stands with Kho. There are still some of them up here, though when we arrived we found many mutilated corpses strung up by the enemy. My intelligence had brought me word that Qoqada and Minanlu were in revolt. I thought that would buy me time, and so I left my best general, Hahinqo, in charge at Dythbeth and took half of my troops to the mountains to reclaim some of my old glory. I wanted to bloody the nose of Minruth the Mad, but I've been a fool—I should have stayed in Dythbeth!"

When, two days later, the Fifth Army bridged the ford of the Karhokoly, Kwasin could already see a dark mass moving across the great plain toward the city. The king ordered his men to cut a beeline across the plain and intercept the invaders. Soon, however, it became evident that if Roteka did not take his men directly to the city, the enemy would reach it first. Roteka had his lieutenants issue orders for the drivers to abandon their oxen and wagons and to hike it as fast as they could on foot. They arrived none too soon. As the bloody red eye of Resu cast its sickly light upon the city's proud towers and high granite walls, the two armies clashed on the great plain before Dythbeth.

The warring did not go well for King Roteka's already combat-weary forces. The battle consisted of a series of advances and retreats, and after each lull the Dythbethans found themselves pushed farther back. By early evening they were forced to retreat across the plain to the city. There they entered the eastern gate and took up position atop the city's fortified walls, launching spears and sling-stones and catapulting vessels of flaming oil down upon the invaders.

On fought Kwasin, bolstering the exhausted troops of Dythbeth with his crude taunts at the enemy and his unending vigor. When the Sixth Army's supply train brought hastily constructed wooden ladders across the plain and propped them up against the walls, Kwasin was the first among the defenders to jump upon one, scale down it, and meet the ascending soldiers halfway, his blood-covered ax swinging.

The soldiers below began to climb back toward the ground. Apparently they recognized the man on the ladder as the terrible giant who had single-handedly slain so many of them during the battle on the plain. Kwasin, seeing the men descend, clambered upward as quickly as he could. By the time he reached the ladder's top, the men below had already begun to swing the ladder back from the wall.

The gap between Kwasin and the wall widened to almost two yards. He hurled his ax to the battlement. Now three yards from the wall, the ladder stood almost vertical. He footed his way, handless, to the top rung and, just as the ladder was about to swing out from under his feet, launched himself into the air.

Kwasin hit the wall hard, narrowly managing to wrap his arms over the wall's upper edge. His legs flailed in the air, and for a moment he thought his prodigious strength would fail him. Then a hand reached out of the void of night. Kwasin grasped it, heaved himself onto the wall, and looked into the grimly smiling face of King Roteka.

"Like a hero of old!" he said to Kwasin. "I had my doubts about you, but no more. The day has darkened with men's blood, but because of you I still hold out hope."

Kwasin grasped arms with the old king and grinned. "Do not worry, O King! In the morning Resu will once again look down upon a free and gallant Dythbeth!"

The king seemed about to speak, but suddenly his body jolted and fell forward into Kwasin's arms. Blood spurted from Roteka's mouth and down his regal beard, and a long spear stuck out from his back.

Kwasin lowered the king's body to the wall, looking for a sign of life, but the man was already dead.

He cursed. Squinting into the darkness, Kwasin scanned for any evidence that an enemy soldier might have somehow surmounted the wall unnoticed. Right now the defenders of Dythbeth had moved along the wall to the south, battling more of the ladder-climbing enemy. No other soldiers remained in the vicinity.

Then Kwasin saw something: a dark form moving among the shadows of the inner wall.

A burning bottle of oil hurled out of the night and exploded in flames along the wall top. For just a second, the fiery blaze illuminated the fleer, the only person who could have held a position to cast the spear into King Roteka's back—Taphiru, the high priest of Resu.

4

Kwasin had no time to pursue the treacherous priest. The enemy, climbing off their ladders, swarmed en masse onto the wall.

He rose from the king's lifeless form. Then, raising his ax before him, Kwasin charged in among the men of Dythbeth in their attempt to beat back the attackers.

The Dythbethans rallied around Kwasin, and the first wave of Minruth's troops to come over the wall fell beneath their fury. When Kwasin smote down four men with a single swoop of his ax and then heaved two of the enemy ladders—heavily laden with climbers—to the ground, the men looked to the giant as if a god stood among them in the flesh. At least for the moment, the attack on the walls had been repelled.

Then a shout of despair rang out in the night.

"Kho help us! The king is dead!"

A member of the king's guard had found Roteka's body. Kwasin wondered why Roteka's guard had been absent when their king had needed them most. Of course, they might have been separated from him in the confusion of the Khokarsan assault, or else the king had ordered them to assist in repelling the attackers. But another thought made Kwasin's blood turn as frigid as the ice flows north of the Ringing Sea: the guard might have abandoned Roteka on purpose and been involved in a conspiracy to assassinate him.

The soldiers stood dumbstruck at the news—even Hahinqo, Roteka's general—and muted cries of anguish spread along the wall. Kwasin, fearing the men's discipline was on the verge of snapping, stepped forward and stood among the soldiers.

"Men of Dythbeth!" he shouted. "They have slain our king, whose dying wish was to protect the city and put an end to the foul stench that is Minruth's reign! Don't tarry over the king's broken and empty shell, but leave it where it lies and let the Goddess take care of his spirit! Now follow me and, Kho willing, together we shall wipe the followers of Resu from the land in the name of King Roteka!"

As if the men were a tuning fork and Kwasin's words the hammer that struck them, the Dythbethan troops bellowed forth a harsh cheer and surged about him. Ignoring General Hahinqo—who, red-faced, shouted at his men to come to order—Kwasin ran along the wall and then down the stairway that led between Dythbeth's inner and outer walls.

Already cries of "Kwasin! Kwasin!" filled the night as the soldiers charged behind him. When he had reached the bottom of the stairs, he found the city gate groaning open upon its enormous wooden hinges. Whoever was in charge of the gate had calculated that, rather than following the proper chain of command, it was better to let the giant and the men who followed him through the gate. Either that or the commander in charge recognized that Kwasin and his mad band of followers might be the city's last hope and had ordered the gate to be opened.

In the end it did not matter. Whoever had let Kwasin and his men through had made the correct decision. Taken by surprise at the force and ferocity of the Dythbethan tide pouring from the gate, Minruth's troops fell into disarray. The fighting continued with its wearying cycle of advances and retreats well into the early hours of the morning, when at last the men of Khokarsa found they could no longer hold their ground against the fury-driven Dythbethans, who, enraged at the death of their king, fought with all the fierce spirit of Khukhaqo, the Leopard Goddess. The Sixth Army retreated across the plain, their losses heavy.

The army of Dythbeth, though victorious, had also lost many men. Those among the living who were not too exhausted to walk scoured the plain along the city's eastern wall, putting to death the lame and seriously wounded. Many women would be weeping for their lost lovers with the next coming of Resu over the great plain.

Kwasin, bone-tired and covered in sweat, grime, and blood, much of the latter his own, dragged himself from the field of battle. He had not forgotten Taphiru's treachery; but rather than report the man's crime to the army commander, he wanted to deal with the priest himself. Besides, if he reported the crime to the authorities, there would be an official inquiry, and in the meantime he feared mob justice might rob him of the personal vengeance he desired.

He approached the towering city gate, its bronze exterior streaked with flickerings of orange from the burning torches of the men outside. A sentry, looking nervous, stood before the huge doors, which had been cracked open to allow soldiers to reenter the city with their wounded and scavenged war loot. When Kwasin arrived at the gate, the sentry blocked his way and asked him to identify himself, though the man's face looked ashen with uncertainty.

In no mood to be challenged by the soldier after the grueling day and night of combat, Kwasin said, "If you don't know who I am, then you have no business guarding the gate." As he spoke, he grabbed the man's spear, yanked it roughly from his hands, and tossed it to the ground.

Suddenly a group of twelve men—looking too fresh to have engaged in the recent battle—ran out of the gate and surrounded Kwasin. Their polished bronze helmets gleamed under the torches, and they pointed cleanly oiled spearpoints at him. A wiry, tough-looking man of about forty led the group.

"Kwasin!" he said. "Exile of the empire, and violator of the holy Temple of Kho! By order of the Queen of Dythbeth, I place you under arrest!"

Kwasin groaned. Then, wearily, he shook his head. "Fortunately for you I am too exhausted to argue," he said. "I will go with you peacefully. But I have urgent news for Queen Weth concerning the death of her husband. Before you imprison the man who led the charge that saved your worthless hides, grant me an audience with the queen."

He expected his request to be ignored, but the commander of the guard sighed in apparent relief and said, "You will see her now, but not because of any leniency on my part. The queen has ordered that you be brought to the palace immediately. Surrender your weapon and come with us."

Reluctantly, Kwasin complied. He groaned again, however, when he handed over the ax to one of the guardsmen, who seemed awed to hold the weapon, with its enormous head of exceptionally heavy iron. Or perhaps it was the legendary giant who awed the man. Right now Kwasin did not care.

When another guardsman made to place chains on his wrists, Kwasin said, "You may try, little man, but I will wring your neck first, and then that of your commander, before anyone can stop me." Kwasin glowered at the blanching man, and the commander of the queen's guard pressed his lips tightly together as if weighing the words of the giant before him.

Then Kwasin shook with laughter. "Don't look so sickly, commander. I swear to you on my honor as a Bear man that I won't harm the queen and will do as she bids. We are all allies against Minruth, are we not?"

The commander, from whose belt dangled a bone-carven fetish of the Bear Totem, stood silent. Then, somewhat to Kwasin's surprise, he ordered his man to stand down. Totemic glue had proven stronger than royal decree.

Kwasin and his escort passed through the giant doorways of the outer wall, and a moment later through the gate of the older inner wall. The latter rose not quite as tall as its companion, white plaster covering its granite foundation. While the stone of the outer fortification was barefaced, sculpted effigies of various animals and deities decorated the tops of its turrets. These included leopards, serpents, trumpeting elephants, Lahhindar pulling back her divine bow, and Kho as the Goat-Headed Mother, Her horns aimed menacingly at approachers to the city. Even though Dythbeth had for many hundreds of years sworn allegiance to the empire, the fierce and intimidating sculptures looming upon the city's walls bore witness to its long history of stubborn independence.

They followed the wide, stone-block road that curved round the massive military barracks on one side and a commercial and residential district on the other. The latter was made up of white plastered adobe buildings that stood two to four stories in height, divided by a crisscross of narrow streets and back alleys, many of which hosted bazaars and markets in the daylight hours. Torches and oil lamps burned in both sections of the city; the army still had much post-battle work to do and the concerned citizens undoubtedly could not sleep through the night's excitement. Overall, three main double-fortified enclosures, each decreasing in size with its relative age, outlined Dythbeth. The section through which Kwasin and his guards passed, the newest and largest, was built to provide support for the Fifth Army, with homes and shops densely distributed throughout the enclosed area.

Soon they came to the towering bronze gate that led to the city's center. At seeing the queen's guard, the sentries ordered the great doors swung open, and Kwasin and the guardsmen passed inside. This sector housed the royal palace and governmental buildings, and was also home to the many temples dedicated to various goddesses and gods. On their right, the temple of Piqabes, the green-eyed daughter of Kho and goddess of the sea—one of the most important deities in this port city—jutted proudly into the sky, taller than any other building except the palace and the Temple of Kho. They passed the College of Awines, the native genius of Dythbeth who a thousand years before invented the syllabary that was used across the empire, as well as conceived for the first time algebra, the science of linguistics, knowledge of the circulation of blood, the invention of the catapult, wooden blocks for printing, the water clock, the magnifying glass, and a solar calendar, among many other inventions, theories, and formulations.

And there was the temple of Khukhaken, where Kwasin's mother, Wimake, had conceived him while serving as a divine prostitute. Beside a great marble-hewn statue of the Leopard God, a priestess stood counting the jewels of her rosary, offering prayers of thanks to the returning soldiers who passed wearily by. Kwasin leered at her. He had not had a woman since the priestess at Q"okwoqo, and though he had thought himself utterly fatigued, lust stirred in his loins. Upon seeing Kwasin the woman stopped fingering her rosary and, glaring at him, muttered something beneath her breath. Recalling the reason for his long exile, Kwasin grimaced and looked away.

Kwasin's stomach growled as the aroma of stewed buffalo meat wafted his way from the hall of the Klakordeth, or Thunder Bear Totem. He had not eaten since early last morning, and that had only been a paltry meal of millet bread and *mowometh* berries, accompanied by one small spoonful of honey cultivated by the bee farmers of Qoqada, dished out to him by a stingy army cook. Hunger tempted him to ask the head of the guard if they could stop to eat an early breakfast with their totem brothers, but again Kwasin pushed desire from his mind and remained silent.

Leaving behind the temples, totem halls, colleges, taverns, and shops, they walked over the drawbridge that crossed the moat and led within the palace citadel. The dome-shaped palatial hall was ancient. Its original foundation was said to have been laid in the days when the hero Dythbeth settled the region. The building itself, however, had been built much later, when the science of architecture had advanced enough to allow for the lofty arches and the massive columns that supported the cavernous rotunda of the palace.

They climbed the palace's shallow marble steps, numbering one hundred and seventeen to honor the syllabary of Awines, and passed beyond the tall golden doorways and into a side room where buckets of warm, perfumed water were thrown over Kwasin to purify him and wash away the muck of sweat and battle. Here the palatial attendants allowed him to drink briefly from a tall cask of cool water, and though they offered him no food, he was provided with a new loincloth and a kilt of fine lion skin. From there his guards escorted him into an antechamber outside the grand rotunda, where he was forced to stand at attention in front of the royal doors for half an hour while waiting for the queen to beckon him. When, after that period, Kwasin asked that he be allowed to relieve his bladder, the attendant in charge refused. He changed his mind, however, when Kwasin threatened to empty himself on the queen's doors. Accompanied by six guardsmen, Kwasin was permitted to enter an adjoining room, a spacious and elaborately decorated lavatory meant for visiting dignitaries. He returned to the antechamber under the chief attendant's scornful eye just as the brass gong rang out to announce that the queen was ready to condescend to his presence.

The tall doors opened and a herald cried out, "Behold, priestess of Kho and of Her daughter, the moon, Queen Weth of the queendom of Dythbeth! Behold, Kwasin the Exiled!"

Kwasin smirked somewhat pridefully at his epithet and sauntered into the hall. Six guardsmen carrying bronze-tipped spears followed him on either side, their weapons angled toward him.

In his boyhood years in Dythbeth, and after his subsequent return as an adult following his almost eight-year stay with Phimeth, Kwasin rarely had occasion to visit the royal palace; and he had never been within the throne room's jewel-encrusted and gold-lined walls. Though not one to be impressed by such grand displays of opulence, even the seven-foot-tall Kwasin found himself feeling diminutive beneath the chamber's immense, high-vaulted dome, whose colorful mosaic artwork illustrated exotic scenes of the Khokarsan and local pantheon.

If the great rotunda and lavish affluence of the palace did not quite take away Kwasin's breath, the sight of Queen Weth on her throne did. Indeed, he thought, the high priestess of Dythbeth shone with more dazzling brilliance than all of the diamonds, rubies, and emeralds embedded in the walls of her throne room. And again, though he had thought himself too tired, Kwasin grew hot with lust. Then the queen locked a frozen gaze upon him and he felt as if Kho Herself saw through to his soul.

Still, he could not help but take in Weth's shapely hips wrapped in their leopardess-skin kilt, the smooth bronze skin above a narrow girdle of jewel-encrusted golden rings, the full and large-nippled breasts, and her long, glossy black hair tied up in a Psyche knot. Though dark half-moons of fatigue hung beneath her bloodshot eyes, the woman seemed not to have aged at all in the intervening nine years since he had last seen her. In fact, she looked more beautiful than he remembered.

He stopped before the throne. General Hahinqo stood to the queen's left, eyeing Kwasin coolly; on the queen's right stood a stooping, prune-faced priestess. The king's chair, its platform slightly lower than the queen's and its decorations not quite as elaborate, remained empty.

Kwasin bowed his head and examined the mosaic-tiled floor, not out of respect for the queen, but so that she might not see the desire in his eyes. Normally he cared little how anyone, be it royalty or savage heathen, might perceive him; but he could not risk offending the priestess this time. Besides, her husband had just been killed, and even if Kwasin were fortunate enough to discover that time had softened Weth's ire at him, the queen's mood was certain to be black.

He was not wrong.

The queen rose from her throne, her eyes cold flames, and said, "How comes it that Kwasin, desecrator of Kho's temple, exiled by the oracular priestess to the hinterlands beyond the empire, dare show his face in the queendom of Dythbeth and expects to live?"

Kwasin looked up and spoke in a rumbling voice made even more cavernous under the throne room's great dome.

"My wanderings in the Wild Lands have taken me to many wondrous and astonishing places, and I have stood upon the shores of the Ringing Sea and witnessed the very edge of the world," he said with his usual bombast; "but never have I seen a more welcoming sight than the proud homeland of my birth." He looked askance at the spearpoints aimed at him and smiled wryly. Then he bent to one knee before the queen and spread his arms wide as if in supplication. "Nor have I ever looked upon a woman as fair and virtuous as Kho's priestess at Dythbeth!"

"Rise, you honey-tongued fool!" Weth cried.

Kwasin felt cold bronze spear-tips press against his shoulders. He got to his feet.

"You are a giant like out of myth," Weth said in a shrill voice. "But your mind is very small if you think your fawning compliments will erase your crimes against the Goddess. And do you think the queen does not watch over her city and know all the evil that you do here?" Then she looked to the herald and cried, "Bring in the priest!"

Kwasin stood as still as one of the cold granite pillars that circled the hall as the royal guards escorted Taphiru, high priest of Resu, into the chamber. When Taphiru stood beside the queen, facing Kwasin with his narrowed, snake-gray eyes, Weth said, "Tell us what you have witnessed, vicar."

Taphiru played his part well. As he spoke, his face grew red and his hands shook with feigned outrage. "I saw the exile, the defiler of Kho's temple, slinking in the shadows along the outer wall. While the king fought gloriously against our enemy, this traitorous monster Kwasin crept up from behind, and before I could shout a warning, cast a spear into the back of King Roteka! He is the king's murderer!"

Gasps and murmurs came from the courtiers, and the queen's eyes flashed with fury.

"How do you speak now, Kwasin?" the queen asked. "With words dripping of sweetness?"

Silence settled across the hall. Then Kwasin's booming laughter shook the chamber.

"Yes, O Priestess, the king's murderer does stand before you," he said. "Indeed, while many brave men died defending Dythbeth against Minruth's blasphemous followers, this fork-tongued priest slithered into the shadows like a frightened snake." He looked to Hahinqo. "Any of the men who fought with me on the walls will testify to that. They cannot all have been bought with the coins of the priests."

Hahinqo's expression remained stony.

"Just what are you insinuating?" Weth asked, and Kwasin saw doubt cross her face.

"Why should I kill King Roteka, who promised to have you consult the oracle on my behalf?"

Weth looked to Hahinqo.

"It is true," the general said. "The king made such a promise."

"Kwasin is a necromancer!" the priest cried. "He has learned the dark ways of the outlanders during his exile. His enchanted words twisted the mind of the king!"

"And yet they do not twist mine," Weth said. A shrewd look came over her, and she addressed Kwasin.

"How would Taphiru benefit from the murder of my husband?"

"Perhaps he sees himself as king once Dythbeth's priests revolt, as the priests of Khokarsa did under Minruth." Then he added, "Though I would certainly make a better king for her highness than this gutless priest."

Again the room filled with gasps, and Weth's long nails dug into the flesh of her palms. Then her hands relaxed and she summoned Hahinqo to ascend the royal platform, where the two whispered for close to a minute. When Hahinqo had resumed his position at the foot of the dais, the queen said, "After your terrible crimes, the oracle spared you, Kwasin, from the death you so rightly deserved, and instead she condemned you to exile. But even as she cast you from the empire, the oracle decreed that one day you would return, whether to be executed or forgiven she did not say. General Hahinqo tells me that the city would have fallen without your mad charge, and so, until I have time to consult with the oracular priestess, I am forced to interpret the oracle's words as meaning that the Goddess, in Her unending generosity, has forgiven your transgressions against Her...and against me. The oracle foresaw that Dythbeth would one day need your great strength—no matter the severity of your past crimes or the unbounded stupidity of your loutish behavior."

"This is not Kho's justice!" Taphiru howled. "I saw him murder the king!"

"Silence, priest! Do not interrupt me!"

Two of the queen's guard moved away from Kwasin and stood beside Taphiru. Kwasin could not hold back his amusement and he haw-hawed loudly.

"Restrain yourself, Kwasin," the queen said, "or I may change my mind about how to interpret the oracle's words." Weth stepped down from her throne to the empty chair of King Roteka and placed her hand upon its arm. Wetness filled her reddened eyes; then her face hardened.

"You speak of the just Kho, Taphiru, even while across the land your fellow priests betray the Goddess and conspire to place Resu above Her. Yes, Kho is certainly just...and so She will replace one exile with another."

The queen motioned to her guard. Taphiru shouted in protest as the men took him by either arm and dragged him across the chamber toward the great doors.

"I am a faithful servant of Kho!" the priest yelled as he fought to free himself from the grip of the men. "The wrath of Resu will be on your head if you do this!"

"Did I not tell you he was fork-tongued?" Kwasin said.

"Throw the priest outside the walls," Weth ordered her guards, "and let Minruth's troops do with him as they will." She turned to Hahinqo. "General, I've kept you long enough."

Hahinqo followed behind the men. The golden doors swung open and then closed. Taphiru's muted cries grew distant.

Weth ordered the men on either side of Kwasin to leave the chamber, then stepped down from King Roteka's chair and spoke low so that only Kwasin could hear.

"Years ago you almost cost me the queenship! But we were young, only eighteen, and we both know the truth of that night. Your mad lust frightened me! I should have known better than to let you into my chambers—I'd had my intelligence check you out, so I knew about your fits. But in the folly of youth, I thought you'd be different with me! So, yes, Kho is fair, as is Her priestess." Weth's eyes narrowed. "You, Kwasin, ravisher of priestesses, scourge of women everywhere, are about to be tamed."

Before Kwasin could speak, Weth turned from him and addressed the old woman who stood by the throne.

"Gather the priestesses and tell them to prepare for a wedding in the morning. And clean up this rank-smelling giant of the wilderness! We are at war and the people will need to respect their new king!"

Then the queen strode from the throne room with the old priestess shuffling behind, leaving Kwasin to stand alone in the hall, for once in his life utterly speechless.

5

Preparations for the marriage of Kwasin and Queen Weth proceeded rapidly. Royal attendants ushered Kwasin to a luxurious sleeping quarters within the palace, with a large mahogany-framed bed piled high with soft, thick furs and fine linens. Kwasin felt he had just closed his eyes when a bronze gong sounded and three attendants lined up in the doorway to assist their soon-to-be king with his morning toilet.

Still exhausted from his long exertions and hurting from his many small wounds of battle, Kwasin threw off his coverings and raged against the men, who skittered off down the royal passageway, their faces pale and fear stricken. Though he returned to his bed and tried again to woo sleep, it would not come. His mind whirled with the events of the past few weeks, conjuring up visions of his escape from Minruth's prisons, his confrontation with the treacherous priest, the murder of the king, and the astounding pardon of his crimes by the beautiful Weth. The faces of the men he had killed in battle also flittered before his mind's eye, as if their ghosts sought to avenge themselves upon him by depriving him of sleep. When he opened his eyes and once again saw the frightened attendants lining up in the doorway, Kwasin cursed and got out of bed, stretching with a yawning moan that almost sent his royal attendants fleeing for a second time.

The men led him through a series of passageways and down a short flight of steps before they arrived at a spacious room with bright mosaics tiling the floor, walls, and ceiling, and a great pool of steaming water inlaid in its center. Kwasin took off his kilt and loincloth—which in his fatigue he had slept in—and climbed into the perfumed, salted, and almost scalding water. He hadn't taken a hot bath since the years before his exile, and the heat and minerals soothed his throbbing aches and sores. If this were a king's life, he thought, the annoyance of having royal attendants might be worth it after all.

His bliss did not last long. The chief attendant, bearing the determined yet hopeless look of a man committing suicide, strode up to the edge of the bath holding a large wooden bucket. "I do this by order of the queen!" he cried. Then he cast the bucket's contents of ice-cold water overtop of Kwasin, turned on his heel, and ran from the chamber. Again, Kwasin raged. He jumped out of the bath and ran after the man; but his feet, made slick from the bathwater, slipped out from under him and he landed hard on his rear. He roared with fury, but by the time he got to his feet, his anger had turned into howling laughter at the thought of the fleeing attendant's sick-faced expression. A moment later the man poked his head through the doorway, a hopeful half-smile turning his lips at the transformation of his lord's anger, then emerged fully and signaled the other two attendants to come dry off Kwasin with soft linen towels. Kwasin grabbed a towel from one of the men and brusquely ordered them away. Soon a fourth man appeared bearing a bowl of hot water and an iron razor. When the chief attendant dipped the razor into the water and made to shave off his lord's long, thick, and still dripping beard, Kwasin grabbed the man's wrist.

"It must be done, your majesty-to-be," the man said. "It is the queen's decree. Her new king cannot look like a follower of Resu."

"King Roteka wore a beard," Kwasin said, "and yet the queen did not shear off his manhood."

"With all due respect, O King-in-Waiting, but you are not King Roteka, and..." The man hesitated, either too embarrassed or too frightened to go on.

Kwasin squeezed the man's wrist until he continued. "...and there are those within the palace and in the army who question your loyalties. You have been in exile for many years, and in that time your reputation has spread across the empire. Though your sentence has been suspended, the guilt of your crime still stands. The oracle is never wrong."

Kwasin cursed and let go the man's wrist. The doubt among the troops might be due to his sullied reputation. Then again, it could be that Taphiru's priests had spread lies about Kwasin to foster sedition among the ranks.

"Shave off my beard," Kwasin said finally, "but if you so much as nick me I shall cut out your tongue with that razor!"

Once the remainder of his beard lay in wet clumps on the tiled floor, the men led him into another room where he found a doctor waiting who proceeded to rub healing ointments into his wounds and bandage them. Then the attendants fitted Kwasin with a loincloth, a kilt of fine lion skin, and calf-high antelope-skin moccasins, after which they escorted him to another room with a table on which sat a cask of water, a plate of sautéed termites mixed with assorted greens, and three large baskets filled with pomegranates, sweet *mowometh* berries, millet bread, and hard-boiled duck eggs. Kwasin devoured almost all of the food before yet another gong rang out. An attendant brought him some minty leaves to chew on and freshen his breath and then Kwasin was led down several more passageways and up a flight of steps.

They entered a waiting chamber outside the throne room. Here the attendants made him remove his clothing and three priestesses entered to chant prayers of ablution and to brush consecrated papyrus reeds against his naked skin. Two more priestesses entered, bearing earthenware pots containing ochre paint. With a stiff reed brush, one of the women painted the stylized symbol of the Thunder Bear Totem in yellow upon his chest, while the other decorated him in red with assorted geometrical designs. When they were done, another priestess instructed him that, unless prompted, he was not to speak during either the procession to the Temple of Kho or the wedding ceremony. Then she made him memorize his vows, which he did not understand because they were in the secret ritual language of the priestesses. When Kwasin asked what the words meant, he was told, "It is the vow all men must take who assume the queendom's highest office: 'I serve at the disposition of Kho. Death comes to all, even the greatest of kings.'" The woman ended Kwasin's instruction by showing him the particular manner in which he should kneel when ordered, on one knee with his forehead touching the ground and his arms extended palms upward.

A herald cried out to announce that Kwasin should enter the throne room. The doors swung open and Kwasin strode into the great high-domed chamber, where he stood waiting with his back to the empty throne. A moment later the herald called out again, this time to announce the queen's arrival. Weth entered from her private waiting room and stood beside Kwasin. She was naked except for a jewel-studded, golden-sheathed dagger belted around her waist by many interlocking gold rings and a circlet of gold with a single large emerald in its center crowning her head and holding back her long and sleek dark hair. Black and green painted spirals of various sizes decorated her face and body, representing her sisterhood among the priestesses of Kho. Kwasin thought her stunning and smiled widely upon seeing her, but Weth met him with a stony expression and looked away.

With the blaring of bronze trumpets and the throoming of bullroarers, the procession began. Followed by a long line of priestesses, priests, heralds, courtiers, and musicians—and surrounded on all sides by the queen's guard—they passed from the throne room into the spacious foyer, with its murals of the kings of Dythbeth acting out their many great deeds of heroism. Someday, Kwasin thought, he would be there among them; but then he recalled the ritual words the priestess had made him memorize, and his pride at being king faded. When it came time for his image to be painted upon the palace walls, he would most likely be dead, extinguished, a specter living his hollow afterlife in dread Sisisken's dark house. Once a year, if he were lucky, the people of Dythbeth would sacrifice a bull to him, as well as to the other fallen kings of the queendom, so that his spirit might quench its thirst on the beast's blood.

All the more reason to take from this life what one could, he thought, and as a king, he could take plenty. Beginning with Minruth's head.

They walked down the many shallow marble steps that led from the palace and turned north onto the temple road. Before long they passed through the looming bronze gates into the oldest, smallest, and holiest section of the city.

Spectators thronged along either side of the stone-block road. Some cheered their queen, but a general confusion seemed to mark the crowd. By now, the citizens of Dythbeth would be waking up to the news of King Roteka's death and of the exiled Kwasin's return. He heard a scattering of men throughout the crowd cheer out his name. These must have been soldiers who had accompanied him on his mad charge onto the great plain. No insults were volleyed at the infamous outcast—probably out of respect for the queen, and perhaps for fear of her heavily armed guard—but Kwasin could see many dark and doubtful looks cast his way as he passed.

They approached the Temple of Kho—the very building where Kwasin, drunk and full of lust, had wooed Weth and then killed the temple guards who had come upon hearing her screams. A well-tended and carefully landscaped garden of sculpted trees and shrubbery stretched along the slight rise that led to the temple's entrance. Here the road ended and a narrow stone path snaked ahead, flanked at its outset by two impressively tall oaks. The building itself was round, dome-shaped, and constructed of great blocks of white, red-veined marble. The temple had been built close to fifteen hundred years ago in response to a rapid growth in population that had made it inconvenient for the multitude of worshipers to travel from the city to the original temple of Kho, which now languished in disrepair in the marshlands between the forks of the Karhokoly.

Kwasin and Weth entered the temple's nine-sided entrance, accompanied by the priestesses and the queen's guard, with the remainder of the procession expected to wait patiently outside until the newly married couple exited the temple. They passed through three rooms, each larger and with higher ceilings than the last, before passing into the vast, oval-shaped, and most sacred temple chamber. Many colorful mosaic tiles were set into the floor of the large room, forming in their entirety a great spiral representing the chain of time since the creation of the world by Kho. Kwasin had seen such artwork upon the floors in other temples dedicated to the Great Mother, and as with those, a single tile remained unpainted where one of the spiral's arms reached out to touch a great marble statue of Kho, looming with terrifying beauty in the chamber's center. What the blank tile meant, no one but the priestesses knew, but it disturbed Kwasin. Was Time itself destined to meet the same fate as every man and woman who had ever lived? Now he lamented that he had not asked Sahhindar, the god of Time, at their chance meeting.

A priestess, whose shapely figure and shining blonde hair made up for a nose that was a trifle too long and narrow, presided over the ceremony. Even as he prepared to say his vows to Weth, Kwasin knew he would not be able to resist this priestess were she to ask him to bed her. He also knew, however, that he must be careful. Though kings were permitted to take lovers, they did so at the grace of the queen; and if Weth's cold look meant anything, she would extend little grace to her future husband.

The ceremony itself was simple. Kwasin and Weth stood before the presiding priestess, who announced herself as Nelahnes, chief keeper of the temple for the queen. While Nelahnes began uttering a long incantation in the ritual language of Kho's holy order, twelve other priestesses circled about them in a slow gait, carrying small bowls of burning incense. The priestesses stopped walking when Nelahnes bade Kwasin to kneel. He did as the priestess in the temple had instructed him earlier, touching his head to the floor with his arms extended before him, palms facing upward.

Then he heard the unmistakable sound of a knife drawn from its sheath, and a moment later felt the cold, sharp point of a blade press into the soft flesh on the nape of his neck. Kwasin tensed. Was the wedding but a ploy to lure him to this vulnerable position, so that Weth herself might have the pleasure of killing him? What if Weth had been lying when she said the oracle had yet to be consulted regarding his fate? The old and wizened Voice of Kho might have decreed that Kwasin, his exile ended, should be executed by the woman whom he had wronged.

A long silence followed, with the blade's icy point still digging into the back of Kwasin's neck. Then he remembered the words he had been told to memorize—that death came to even the greatest of kings—and he spoke aloud the strange vow, acknowledging his subservience to Kho and the mortality of kings. Nelahnes spoke again in the ritual language and the knife lifted from his neck. The woman stepped forward and placed a golden crown upon his head. Cautiously, he rose.

Nelahnes uttered a final pronouncement, again in words he could not understand, and the ceremony was over. The priestesses escorted Kwasin and Weth to the temple's entrance, where a herald cried out, "Behold, priestess of Kho and of Her daughter the moon, Queen Weth of Dythbeth! Behold, brother of the Klakordeth, son of Khukhaken, the Leopard God, King Kwasin of Dythbeth!"

The crowd waiting at the end of the temple path cheered and whistled, and again trumpets blared and bullroarers throomed. The dark faces he had seen earlier seemed to have disappeared.

The queen and her new king reveled before the crowd's adulations for only a moment. Then Weth took Kwasin by the hand and led him back into the temple.

At first he thought she might bring him into one of the many rooms off the entry chamber so that they could consummate their marriage. Weth, however, pulled him aside and said, "I have not married you for love, my husband, but because the queendom needs you. King Roteka was much adored by all of our people but especially by the men in his military. His death has dealt a severe, possibly fatal, blow to their morale. But your deeds last night have brought hope to many, and the priestesses have already begun to spread rumors that your reappearance in our time of need has been foretold by Kho." Weth laughed darkly. "Your murderous reputation is being played up as well. The priestesses are spreading the story that you have vowed to make amends for your past crimes by defeating Minruth's armies. The people see you as a giant and unstoppable mankiller, and in a time of war, that is exactly the type of king they want to lead them. As do I."

"Is it true?" Kwasin asked. "Did the oracle foretell my coming at this time? And where is the oracular priestess? I did not see her during the ceremonies."

"For her own mysterious reasons, Wasemquth has taken up vigil in the old temple of Kho, and truth be told, not all of her prescience with regard to your doings is known even to me. But the story has its own truth. You have indeed appeared at a time fortuitous for Dythbeth and for yourself. Still, you must visit the oracle and receive her blessing if you are to remain king. General Hahinqo has already been informed that he must provide you safe passage."

Weth eyed Kwasin sharply for a moment, then continued. "But before beseeching the oracle, you must review the troops and assert your authority as their commander. Though you are a mighty warrior, your insubordinate action last night could just as well have failed, and I don't expect you know anything about how to lead men. But don't worry. Hahinqo is really the one in charge, and unless I command otherwise, you must from now on obey him in all things. Even now he waits for you at the barracks."

Kwasin's face grew hot with anger as the queen turned her back on him and made to leave. Then she stopped and again faced him.

"I will watch you closely, Kwasin," she said, "and if I see that reason has finally entered your apish mind, I may grant you small favors. But if you do not control your failings, know that there are consequences, even for kings. Remember well the blade I set upon your neck this day."

6

Kwasin felt like tearing the temple apart, but instead he quelled his anger, accepted the adornments brought to him by a priestess—a leather kilt, lacquered cuirass, and bronze helmet trimmed with gold to replace his golden crown—and put them on. He found his own personal guard waiting for him outside the temple, but his black mood left him feeling less than flattered by their presence. In fact, he longed to be alone, stalking the Wild Lands with no one to bother him—hunting on his own, raiding on his own, thinking on his own. And most importantly, free from the humiliating manipulations of his new wife and queen.

He shouted at the stunned guardsmen as he strode down the path from the temple. "Follow at my heels like yapping dogs for all I care, but keep out of my way! Remember what I did to the guards at this temple nine years ago!" He did not look back, but he could hear the clap and scuffle of the guardsmen's feet on the stone path as they tried to keep up with his great strides.

Soon a tall, pale-faced man of about twenty-five appeared at Kwasin's side, his bright green eyes twinkling in the morning sun from beneath thick brows and mop of black hair. The gangly fellow wore a long white robe and carried under his arm a seven-stringed boxwood lyre. At six feet tall, the newcomer managed to keep pace with his giant king, though his pale face was quickly gaining color under his exertions. Kwasin looked blackly at the man, who grinned back as if to taunt his king.

"Either you're a fool who wishes an early end to his life," Kwasin said, "or you're a drunken bard who will get the same."

"The latter," the man said in a singsong voice. "Though I'm not drunk. Hung over, maybe. And I mean to live a long life. The name's Bhako, and I've been assigned to you as Royal Bard."

Kwasin growled. "At least your name isn't Kebiwabes."

"You mean Hadon's bard? Of course, you do! You came back from the Wild Lands as a member of the same expedition."

"How do you know that?"

"It's my job," Bhako said. "You know, to ask around, learn of your noble deeds so that I might put them to verse. Is it true that in your adventures you encountered a tribe of barbarians, where you lingered long enough to know you had made all of its women heavy with child? And that this tribe, with the exception of some justifiably resentful husbands, worshiped you as a god?"

Despite his dark mood, Kwasin laughed. "Yes," he said, not altogether lying. "With women more fair than any in Khokarsa. I bedded them all. Their heathen priests said they would train my sons by their women to become great warriors, who will one day storm out of the west and lay waste to the empire in honor of their great father." Maybe someday his travels would indeed give birth to legends among the savages about the giant foreigner who came among them with his brassbound club, wooing their women and entertaining their men with tall tales of his divinity—but he wondered if any sons that might seek him out would want to kill him rather than honor him.

"You don't seem intimidated, bard, to inconvenience your new king with your hot wind."

"Again, it's my job." Bhako was panting now. "And after hearing so many puffed-up songs of glory during my apprenticeship to the bards' guild, I no longer believe in being intimidated. All men, even great ones, have flaws, and the greater the flaw, the more poignant the ballad I can write." When Kwasin looked at him through narrowed eyes and with nostrils flaring, Bhako added, "But I do respect your authority, O King."

Kwasin came to the end of the temple path, but just before he passed onto the wide, stone-block palace road, Bhako leaped ahead into the throngs who stood waiting for a glimpse of their new sovereign. "Make way!" he shouted. "King Kwasin comes!"

The sea of onlookers, oohing and aahing, scrambled to get out of the way, though many reached out so they might be blessed by the touch of their king. Kwasin pushed them away with the back of his hand like so many bothersome insects.

"Keep back from the king!" Bhako exclaimed. "He has matters of war on his mind and cannot be disturbed." Many in the swarming multitude, however, ignored the bard's words. Kwasin quickly became irritated, though he had an idea. In the meantime he ironed his will and shouldered his way through the fawning touchers.

Kwasin headed for the palace rather than following the road around the moat that would eventually lead to the military barracks. A few minutes later, after entering the palace and yelling at the guards there, he once again possessed his great ax. He left via the south palace road and made his way toward the barracks. This time, however, Bhako did not need to part the crowds; Kwasin did that by himself by rolling the imposing ax before him in wide arcs. The onlookers quickly got out of the way, though Kwasin heard several men shout his name in encouraging tones. As during the morning's procession, the cheers must have come from soldiers who had fought alongside him on the previous night.

With the king's guard still trailing behind like obedient dogs, Kwasin made his way to the southern section of the city. He proceeded east down a street that paralleled the wall until he arrived at the barracks to find General Hahinqo waiting outside.

The short, ruddy-faced man saluted his new king. Then he scowled and said, "As your chief of command, O King, I must recommend that your guardsmen be allowed to do their duty and protect you. The king's guard is the army's elite. If the troops see that their superiors are not respected, dissention will surely follow in the ranks."

"And I am your superior, general!" Kwasin said. "Do not forget that!" He had had enough of Weth controlling him and was not about to let this man do so as well.

Again Hahinqo saluted, his lips pressed together into two whitish lines.

"The queen controls the city's bureaucrats," Kwasin said, "but the king its military. And if you had the proper respect for your king, you'd know his guard is not the general's guard. Now report!"

General Hahinqo's face reddened, though his voice maintained a quiet dignity. "May we speak where the men cannot hear us?" he asked. Kwasin nodded for his guard to move off, then followed Hahinqo from the barracks and across the courtyard, where they walked along the city's inner wall. The bard followed behind at a discreet distance.

"The army is in a poor state," Hahinqo said. "Already we are faced with severe supply shortages—food, drink, weapons, good armor. In stemming off last night's siege, we lost many spears, javelins, and leaden missiles. And the farmers from the countryside have come within the city walls for fear of Minruth's army, so we are sustaining ourselves on our stores. Perhaps equally as important, many of the men are, despite your inspiring presence, severely distressed at King Roteka's death. And frankly, if I may say so—and I must, because if I didn't I'd make you a poor general—many in the army are distrustful of you as their king. According to my feelers, rumors have already begun to circulate that you are a worshiper of Resu. They say you intend to overthrow the queen and place Resu over Kho."

"I have always worshiped the Goddess! Did the men not see me mock the priest Taphiru?" Kwasin let out a deep sigh of frustration. He had no patience for politics. "What do you recommend, general?" he asked at last.

"I have already sent spies into the ranks to root out the rumormongers, who will then discreetly disappear. Further, Bhako here has spent the morning balladeering among the men about what you have told him of your amazing feats of heroism in the Western Lands."

"But I have told him nothing!" Kwasin stopped walking along the wall and turned to glare at the bard.

"We of the sacred order can tell much from a hero's mere presence," Bhako said, grinning. "You might say we read the syllabary of silence. Truth is for the Goddess and dread Sisisken to decide! The bard merely uses his skills to interpret for us mortals. But the blood of gods runs deep in your veins, O King, and your giant presence conveys that you are a man of great deeds! Were you not fathered in the temple of Khukhaken? And indeed, it is said you can trace your lineage back to Sahhindar himself!"

"Do not remind the men of the king's relation to the Archer God," Hahinqo said. "The priests of Resu have spread word that even now Sahhindar returns from his exile to ally himself with his brother, the sungod. Then he will chain up Kho until She acknowledges Resu as Her master." Hahinqo shuddered, as did the bard.

"Sahhindar has already returned," Kwasin said. "I saw him in the foothills near Khokarsa."

"What?" said Hahinqo.

"Though he did not carry his bow, and he seemed more monkey than god."

"Then how did you know it was Sahhindar?" the bard asked.

"He knew of the woman Lalila, the *moon of change*, and her companions, the same people who claimed to be under his protection. And of my ax as well."

Hahinqo looked gravely at Kwasin. "Have you informed the priestesses? They must know immediately about this matter."

"I have been king for only minutes and just arrived in Dythbeth last night! It hardly seemed important, what with the fighting on the walls and King Roteka's death! Now on with your report!"

Hahinqo looked like he wanted to question Kwasin further about the matter, but the man took a deep breath and continued as they resumed their walk along the wall. "The Sixth Army is holding position two miles east on the great plain. They have set up camp there, although I don't expect them to bunker down for long. Word has come that Minruth's troops have abandoned the fort in the Saasamaro and are moving down the foothills. And though the armies of Minanlu still fight the Khokarsans, my intelligence reports that the situation there is worsening. If Minanlu falls, or if Minruth decides to pull his troops from there to reinforce those from Qoqada, we shall have a battle here at Dythbeth such as no one—goddess, god, or mortal—has ever heard tell."

"Let them come!" Kwasin cried. "That is a battle worth fighting!"

Hahinqo sighed wearily. "And that's not all. Two-thirds of Dythbeth's navy, along with the combined fleet of Asema, Minanlu, and Kaarquth, have been sunk in two pitched battles off the western coast of the island. The survivors of our fleet only escaped the second engagement by hightailing it into the bay, where our ships remain blockaded. Already rumors are spreading across the island that our entire fleet has been sunk. Admiral Poedy, who leads Minruth's navy, is said to be diverting more ships to the western coast, where he undoubtedly hopes to finish off our fleet. Admiral Nemusaketh wants to run the blockade, but he's doubtful of success. The last battle on the water expended much of the *s"okendon*[2] his navy needs to make its fire bombs and missiles."

Kwasin growled. "The men who fought at my side last night seemed high-spirited enough. Perhaps it is not the men who have a morale problem, but their general. Do you have any good news?"

---

2 The Khokarsan equivalent of Greek fire, invented by the native Dythbethan genius Awines by the year 11,118 B.C. (482 A.T.). Probably a liquid hydrocarbon used in conjunction with grease, oil, sulfur, and natural saltpeter. The breakdown of the Khokarsan word is *-s"o-* (referring to liquids, jellies, or gases in containers), *-ken-* (meaning *death*), and *-don-* (meaning *red*); in other words, "red death water."

"Intelligence from the other side of the island is spotty at best. By last report, the southeastern cities are in revolt. Minruth has stretched his forces thin. His obsession with building the Great Tower continues despite the war, and much treasure and manpower is yet being devoted to its completion. It is said that in the bowels of the Tower he houses a great and terrifying serpent, a creature brought in from the hinterlands at such enormous expense it nearly caused one of the king's generals to turn against him. But Minruth is ruthless. He executed the general after accusing him of being a spy for the priestesses and replaced him with an ambitious underling. But even more cruel is Phoeken, Minruth's supreme general, though the man is a genius. In the initial revolt, Phoeken rounded up all of Saqaba's farmers and drove them before his troops toward the city. Though the number of Phoeken's troops was minimal, he managed to fool the Saqabans into thinking he had a great horde at his command and the city surrendered. Then, when Phoeken led the attack on Oliwa, he cunningly gathered together a number of monkeys, and after dousing them with—"

Kwasin stopped walking and looked threateningly at Hahinqo. "I said good news!"

The general, clearly uncomfortable at being so berated by his king, combed back invisible hair from his bald pate. "Truthfully, there is not much, your highness." Then the man's expression of discomfort lessened, though not by much. "But a rumor—and I emphasize, this is a rumor, it's not coming from my couriers—has recently arrived from the east that Queen Awineth, Kho's high vicar, is alive and fostering the resistance in the valley at Kloepeth, in the mountains north of Khowot. This would be good news indeed, but I have not been able to confirm it. Just in case it is true, however, I've sent a courier to Kloepeth with word of our situation here."

If the rumor was true, then Hadon had probably succeeded in escaping Minruth's soldiers and both he and the fair Lalila might still be alive. Kwasin cared little about Hadon's fate, but he smiled as he recalled the woman's exotically violet eyes and the attractive curve of her lithe form. What a consort she would make him! Then his exuberance faded as the implication of Hahinqo's words sank in. If Awineth's resistance managed to overthrow Minruth, Hadon—if he still lived—would be named king of kings. Kwasin, as king of Dythbeth, would be obligated to bow down to and serve his cousin; and that, he resolved, would never happen, even if he had to declare Dythbeth an independent city-state at odds with the empire.

Still glaring at Hahinqo, Kwasin said, "If this is the best you can offer me, general, then I will take it and do with it what you apparently cannot! Summon together the men, and separate from the ranks those who accompanied me on last night's charge. The latter men will be given ranking above all the others, including the officers, and the best among them will serve as my personal terror guard."

Hahinqo gasped. "But, my king! That can't be done! The commissioned officers will be outraged, and who knows, they could desert and join the enemy. And besides, most of the lot that followed your charge was made up of the lowest of the low. They know nothing about how to lead men!"

"You will assemble the army, general," Kwasin growled.

Upon seeing Kwasin's face darken, Hahinqo said no more.

Within an hour, Kwasin, in the full regalia of war, stood outside the city's eastern gate before the assembled fighting men of Dythbeth. Numbering more than twenty thousand, row upon row of soldiers—spearmen, javelin-throwers, slingers, and infantry—stretched thickly before the wall. The war drums boomed deep and heavy beneath Kho's blue bowl. Kwasin, standing fully a head above the tallest warrior, strode back and forth before the ranks, his great ax resting on his shoulder. The soldiers who had made up the previous night's mad charge to save the city stood front and center. Kwasin grinned terribly at them as he paced, and they in turn cried out the name of King Kwasin until almost all of the soldiers in the great horde before him joined in the fury-fevered chant.

"I am not like any king you have ever served!" Kwasin said to Hahinqo, who stood at attention before the ranks. "I shall be like the giant leopard that in ancient times ravaged this land and terrorized the people! And these men, the proud soldiers of Dythbeth, will be my death-bringing children!"

General Hahinqo said nothing, but he did not look pleased. Neither did the commissioned officers who now stood in their lower station behind the king's new elite. The officers looked confused and angry, but even more they looked frightened by the frenzied shouts of the men around them. Kwasin, by his mere presence, had stoked the wild flame of Dythbethan independence and lit afire the men's fury. Kwasin doubted even the lies of Taphiru's priests would be enough to dampen the men's hearts. For a moment he feared that even he might be unable to control the raging mass of flesh before him.

Then, as the drums boomed and the men thundered, Kwasin looked high upon Dythbeth's wall and saw something sparkle golden with the sun's reflected light. Even without being able to discern in the distance the identity of the person looking down at him, he instinctively knew it must be Queen Weth.

Kwasin lifted his ax on high, causing the men to thunder even louder. Then he lowered his weapon and again addressed Hahinqo.

"I have given the queen what she wants," Kwasin said over the tumult; "an army that will follow me to the ends of the earth. Now tell her to stay out of matters of war, or I will hand her your faithful head on a platter. You work for me now."

7

On the night before he was to visit the oracle, Kwasin dreamed of his dead mother. Wimake appeared floating before him in the black void, her face moon-pale, as it had been when she had given the ten-year-old Kwasin her last tear-filled smile. In her dying moments, Wimake had meant to reassure her son, to fix him with that loving gaze that only a mother can give, so that he should feel no guilt at his unintentional role in her death. In the dream vision, however, the eyes of Kwasin's ghost mother did not beam at him reassuringly, but rather penetrated his soul with a white-hot intensity that woke him from his sleep and left his heart galloping out of control. Kwasin sat up in his sweat-drenched bed coverings, gasping for breath that would not come.

Though the daylight hours remained distant, he rang the brass bell that summoned his chief attendant, who scurried in a few moments later, rubbing sleep from his swollen lids and reddened eyes. Kwasin had the man bring him a hare, a dagger, and a bowl; and there, on the cold stone floor before his bed, he sacrificed the animal to his mother and drained its blood into the bowl. After the attendant had cleaned up the animal's remains and promised to have the bowl and its contents set upon the altar in the Temple of Kho, Kwasin returned to his bed of soft furs and linens. There he lay awake until Resu's red-orange glare regarded him through the tall and narrow arch of the room's window. Finally he fell asleep, only to be awakened an hour later by his chief attendant, who informed him that General Hahinqo waited outside with the men who were to escort the king to the old temple of Kho.

This time Kwasin did not mind being awakened. He tired of the dream visions that had haunted him since his return from the Wild Lands. Perhaps the oracle would tell him to what diety he needed to sacrifice and then the nocturnal apparitions would at last leave him in peace.

After a quick breakfast, Kwasin met Hahinqo at the foot of the palace steps. The escort—consisting of twelve of the king's terror guard, handpicked by Kwasin—stood at attention around a royal cart along with eight brawny bearers.

Kwasin swore and said, "I am not a toothless old woman! I don't need my food chewed by another before I can swallow it, and I certainly won't be carried about as if I am too feeble to walk!" He ordered the bearers to take away the cart and never to let it or them come within the king's sight again.

A moment later Bhako came scampering along the palace road. "Good morning, O King!" he exclaimed. "Your faithful servant is here with good cheer and song for your journey."

"I don't need a bard cluttering my thoughts before I see the oracle," Kwasin said.

"I am sorry, O King," said Bhako, "but I have orders to accompany you. I am to deliver the oracular priestess a communiqué from Queen Weth herself."

"Why doesn't she send a priestess?"

"I don't know, my king, but you may ask the queen if you like. However, if you do, we'll have to wait until this afternoon to depart, as her highness is currently conducting special rites in the Temple of Kho that may not be interrupted."

Bhako looked smugly at his king, and Hahinqo bounced on his heels, clearly amused.

"So be it!" Kwasin said at last. "But the swamps around the temple are deep, and the chirping of the frogs and insects so loud that I'll hardly notice if my expedition's bard happens to sink into the mud and drown." Then, with one last glare at Hahinqo, Kwasin strode off with the bard and his terror guard down the royal road and toward the city's western gate.

The towering bronze doors swung open before them and they passed through the gate, turning north along the wharves, which—though bustling at this time of morning—seemed less busy than Kwasin could ever remember them having been. The strained, wearied expressions of the fishermen hauling their feeble catches along the road confirmed the report he had received from Hahinqo: the bay was being fished out. Now that the Sixth Army's expeditions had successfully raided the silos of the local farmers, the only new foodstuffs entering the city came out of the bay. The food shortage was only one of the many problems Kwasin needed to deal with immediately upon his return from visiting the oracle. If need be, he would garrison each farmhouse and its silos, though that would not replace the grains that had already been stolen or destroyed by the enemy.

Farther out in the bay he saw floating on the still waters the pitiful remnants of what had once been Dythbeth's shining navy. In the center of the bay rose Admiral Nemusaketh's tall galley, the last surviving trireme in the fleet. Around it some forty-five biremes, uniremes, and an assortment of smaller craft lay at anchor. Their sails were furled and their oars drawn up, waiting for their king to once again send them out into battle against King Minruth's much vaster and better supplied fleet. That fleet now choked the mouth of the bay, cutting off Dythbeth and her increasingly hungry citizens from any supplies that might be bartered or begged from the rebelling cities of the mainland coast. Admiral Nemusaketh desperately wanted to break the blockade, not out of any expectation that his ships could destroy Minruth's fleet but instead hoping to get a vessel through to Mukha, the mainland city whose fleet was rumored to have sunk the triremes of two of Minruth's best admirals. Like General Hahinqo, Nemusaketh badly wanted to foster an alliance with Mukha's King Qanaketh.

Before long, Kwasin and his escort came to the end of the wharf road. Here he cursed and covered his nose at the stench carried to him from the barrels of excrement that lay in immense piles just north of the city wall. Normally the barrels would have been transported out to the farms to be used as fertilizer, but even at this distance Kwasin could see the fields were empty of their workers.

Kwasin led his men up the dirt road that passed through the once thriving residential farming district to the north. They walked by many white plastered adobe buildings, all of them deserted, until the silence began to wear on his nerves. After eight years of exile and excruciating loneliness, he had thought himself used to the absence of his kind; but the forlorn desolation of the farmlands seemed to echo the hollowness that so often plagued him now, and his thoughts grew darker as they walked on.

Just as he thought he could take the ghost houses no longer, the farmlands fell behind the party and the banks of the Karhokoly stretched before them. Here Kwasin smiled wickedly as he spied what the others did not: a dark form hiding in the shade of a large rock about a half-mile upstream on the opposite bank. Kwasin ordered his men to lie low in the grasses while he took off his armor and helmet and set his ax behind the bole of a sprawling khaya tree. Then, alone, he crawled down the bank and slipped into the frigid ice-melt of the Saasamaro mountains. The water here ran rough and fast, and swimming up-current made a difficult task even for Kwasin's powerful muscles. But Suhkwaneth, goddess of the scales, must have been with him, for the bad in this instance was equally weighed with the good. The rush of the water babbling over the river's many outcroppings served to cover the splashings caused by his efforts, so that the man on the bank remained oblivious when a heavily thewed arm reached out of the water and throttled him.

Before the man could scream, Kwasin clapped a giant hand over his victim's mouth and dragged him ashore. Then he shook the man like a dog does a caught rat.

"Are there any more of you? Answer me!" Kwasin removed his hand and the man shrieked in terror.

"Be quiet if you want to live!" Kwasin rapped his knuckles hard against his captive's brow. The man's eyes crossed for a moment and grew dull. Then Kwasin again shook his captive, until the man's eyes again widened with fright.

"I'm not your enemy!" the man pleaded between choked sobs. "Please leave me be!"

Kwasin scowled. "Your trappings reveal you're a sergeant in the Sixth Army."

"I'm a deserter! My name is Mimseth. I've had enough of war and wish to go back home to Wentisuh to see my wife and family. May Siwudawa poke out my eyes and eat my tongue if I am lying!"

Kwasin regarded the man's shield, which lay on the ground in the shadow of the great rock. It looked as if the man had used his knife to whittle away at the insignia on the face of the shield, perhaps in an effort to disguise the army division to which he was assigned. The man's voice did betray Siwudawan inflections and his reverence for the parrot-headed god seemed genuine.

Kwasin growled, and once again he shook the man. "You will go to Wentisuh!" he said. "But if I find out you have lied to me, I will kill you and then seek out your entire family. Go!" He lifted Mimseth to his feet and gave him a kick in the buttocks to set him on his way. The man ran off toward the northeast like a terrified hare.

Kwasin shook his head. He did not know why he had let the man go, and felt angry at himself that he had. For all he knew the fellow was a liar, a spy sent to reconnoiter the area, and he would return to the enemy to report the whereabouts of the King of Dythbeth. Though he did not really believe the man had lied, in war it was best to trust no one.

He signaled his men to retrieve his belongings and wade across the river. When the soldiers joined Kwasin on the other side, they asked him about the man and he told them it was but a frightened farmer. A squat, muscular sergeant named Rowaku looked at Kwasin askance but did not otherwise outwardly question his assertion. Still, Kwasin resolved to keep his eye on the man. He could not risk Rowaku spreading doubts among the men about the king's allegiances.

The sweltering sun dried Kwasin and his company as they marched northward through a region tangled with thick, prickly undergrowth. Soon, however, the ground grew soggy as they entered the marshlands that stretched between the forks of the Karhokoly. The water through which they waded quickly transformed from clear and relatively clean into a thick, dark soup that carried the rank stench of stagnant water and rotting vegetation. Though the water was in many places only ankle- or knee-deep, the soft quaggy ground beneath the surface often fell off without warning and submerged the men to their necks in the foul-smelling morass.

As a youth, Kwasin had heard tales of Konabasi, a demon rumored to inhabit the area, who lurked beneath the waters waiting for a stray boar or foolish human to wander into the marshes and become lost. Then, it was said, the swamp demon would wrap his long and powerful tongue around the ankle of his prey and pull the man or beast down into the dark mud. There, beneath the lurching slime, he devoured the spirit of his victim, afterward leaving the living but soulless body to rise up and float for all eternity in the swampy waters. The men of the king's escort appeared to have heard the stories as well, but Kwasin mocked their fearful faces and jittery whisperings.

"Are the men of Dythbeth such cowards?" he asked. "I have visited hundreds of villages in my long exile and heard many spectacular folktales, none of them true on the surface. Your soul-eating swamp beast is merely an old wives' tale, concocted to keep children from becoming lost in the marshes."

The whisperings of the men ceased after Kwasin's chiding, but their faces remained fearful.

As they trudged onward, Kwasin regretted he had not permitted the bearers to accompany the expedition so that he might rest in the dry comfort of the royal box while his men carried him through cold and stinking slop. In many places, however, the depth of the water made thoughts of such transport a mere fantasy. How the ancient, stoop-shouldered oracular priestess had traversed the marshlands that lay between Dythbeth and the old temple, Kwasin could not imagine. The interweaving trees and vegetation, and the long stretches where the water receded to slurping, ankle-deep mud, would have also made travel by boat impossible.

By midafternoon the blue sky that had peeked between the gnarled branches of the dark trees disappeared behind a veil of gray clouds, causing the spirits of Kwasin and his men to fall even further into gloom. Then, suddenly, a man cried out, splashing in panic as he attempted to make his way as quickly as possible through the waist-deep water and back the way they had come.

Kwasin grabbed the man as he passed.

"Speak, Komwi! What have you seen?"

"The living dead, my lord! Floating in the waters, just as the stories tell!" Komwi's voice quavered on the brink of hysteria. The other men, even the normally cheerful and fearless Bhako, also seemed ready to break for home.

"Run away, all of you!" Kwasin yelled. "But by nightfall you still will be only halfway home and will have to spend the night in the ghost-haunted swamp!"

He released Komwi. The man did not flee, though his face looked as ashen as the clouds above.

The men remained a good distance behind as Kwasin waded through the slimy waters to check out what had so unnerved the soldier. He returned to them a few moments later and said, "You have seen nothing but a waterlogged stump, Komwi, floating like a bloated fish below the surface."

Komwi sighed with relief but still looked somewhat uncertain.

Moving ahead, Kwasin made sure to steer clear of the area where Komwi had cried out, shouting scornfully that he would not have the other men imagining the rotting stump to be a monster or demon. Silently, however, Kwasin prayed to the Goddess that She might see them safely through the marsh and to the temple before nightfall. What he could not tell the men was that Komwi had seen no log in the depths. Indeed it had looked like a man, floating beneath the surface, its ghastly face pruned and lifeless but with blackened skin that bore no sign of decay. Kwasin shivered as the clammy waters suddenly seemed even more frigid, and he tried to quicken his pace through the waters.

Just as daylight began to fade and Kwasin began to fear that he and his men would indeed have to spend the night in the seemingly endless swamp, a narrow and winding platform of compacted dirt and stone rose up out of the muck. With exclamations of relief, the men climbed to the top of the platform, which seemed to be a road, ancient and long abandoned. Perhaps once it had run all the way from the old temple and across the river to Dythbeth, when the great city had been nothing more than a fledgling village. Now the road's southern stretch had collapsed and been sucked into the swamp's dreary sludge, though the northern way wound through the trees and into the distance. Kwasin could not imagine why the ancients had placed the temple of Kho in the inhospitable wetlands, though he intended to ask the priestess when he arrived.

For more than a mile they followed the old road, which snaked its dizzying way through the marshes and maintained an even height about fifteen feet above the surface of the swamp. The sky dimmed and Kwasin could see little of the road ahead, though the land on either side looked drier and the trees not quite as dense. Then, almost immediately, the land angled sharply upward. Here the road ended and the trees disappeared completely. At the top of an immense hill, a temple appeared before them, its white marble dome glowing surreally in the moonlight that shone through the soft blanket of clouds.

The soldiers, cold and exhausted, ran up the hillside in an undisciplined mass, overwhelmed with joy to find at last Kho's welcoming sanctuary. With his rumbling voice, Kwasin yelled at the men to stop and form a line behind him. When they turned around and saw Kwasin's giant form standing in the moonlight, his ax raised threateningly above his head, the men quickly complied. Grumbling that he should have listened to Hahinqo and chosen other men for his guard, Kwasin climbed the hill. When he reached the top, he found a priestess standing in the temple's doorway.

"Priestess!" Kwasin said, and he lay down his ax and knelt before the woman to allay any fears she might have at his unexpected appearance. "I have traveled far to consult the oracle and ask her if—"

"The oracle already knows your questions, Kwasin of Dythbeth," the priestess said sharply, "and she is not pleased you have failed to heed your mother's ghost."

Kwasin's skin prickled like gooseflesh.

8

The priestess led Kwasin and his men into the temple. In a side room off the entry chamber blazed a great hearth before which the journeyers took off their foul-smelling and soaked clothing. A very young and strikingly beautiful priestess brought each of the men a linen towel. She stayed a safe distance away from Kwasin and set down his towel on a stool instead of handing it to him as she had done with the others. Though Kwasin smiled at her as she passed to exit the room, the woman shrank back from him, her dark eyes wide with horror. Kwasin shrugged. It seemed that everywhere he went, his reputation preceded him.

The chief priestess of the temple, whose name was Qenwath, returned bearing a large basket of fruit, which Kwasin and his companions ravenously devoured. A short while later the young woman whom Kwasin had frightened entered lugging a great pot of steaming stew. Although the contents of the pot only smelled of garlic and wild turnips and did not appear to contain any meat, Kwasin's mouth watered nonetheless and his stomach growled loudly. As the stew was dished out to them in bowls much too shallow for his liking, Kwasin questioned the chief priestess about how she had managed to obtain such food in the inhospitable swamp.

Qenwath said that she and her young initiate Awamethna were the only inhabitants of the old temple besides the oracular priestess. Together they tended a small garden and fruit orchard in a clearing just north of the temple, which proved sufficient for their needs. They would not, however, be able to feed Kwasin and his men for any lengthy period, and the two women had only gathered such a large amount of fruit because the oracular priestess had warned them of Kwasin's coming.

Again Kwasin's skin crawled, as it had when upon his arrival the priestess had mentioned the oracle's awareness of his dream visions. Though old Wasemquth had spared Kwasin by exiling him when his crimes deemed that he should have been castrated and his body flung to the hogs, he still felt no love for her. While it was conceivable, though extremely improbable, that the oracle had received word of his coming from the network of priestesses, no earthly means existed for her knowledge of his mother's recent appearances in his dreams. The thought of the old crone, who knew things that no mortal should, unnerved him. The only thing that frightened him more was terrible Kho Herself.

Though famished, Kwasin suddenly realized he had allowed his bowl of stew to go cold. Dismissing his thoughts of the oracle, he downed the bowl's contents with his usual gusto and went back for seconds, thirds, and fourths. Still his enormous appetite left him hungering and he asked Awamethna for some more fruit. When she told him no more remained, he nearly threw his bowl against the wall. However, he stopped himself. He knew he must behave in the temple or the oracle might decide to renew his exile or commit him to an even worse fate. Forcing a smile, he proclaimed loudly that what he had eaten would do for now but that in the morning he would hunt down a deer, or at the very least a hare, and devour it raw—bones, hair, and all.

Qenwath regarded Kwasin coldly and sent the wide-eyed Awamethna away on some errand. Then the temple's priestess led him into a room that held a basin of hot water with which he could wash himself. When he was done, Qenwath came with his still damp but now clean kilt and told him to wait with the other men until the oracle summoned him.

Kwasin returned to the chamber, where he found his companions slumbering in their towels around the warmth of the great hearth. He kicked the bard, who had been sleeping with his arms wrapped around the neck of his instrument, the lyre having survived the wetness of the swamp within a waxed and airtight leather satchel Bhako had devised for their journey. Grumbling, the bard slid over to afford his king some room, and Kwasin, his back propped against the fire-warmed stone wall, quickly found himself nodding in sleep.

When the priestess awoke him, the fire had burned nearly to its embers. Groggily, he arose and reached for his ax.

"Leave your weapon behind," Qenwath said.

Kwasin nodded to indicate the Khokarsan denial. "Where I go, the ax goes," he said. "And besides, the voice of the Voice of Kho at Khokarsa commanded Queen Awineth herself to find the greatest hero in the land to retrieve the ax from the Wild Lands. I am that hero, and surely Dythbeth's oracular priestess will want to see my ax."

Qenwath frowned. "The Queen chose the hero Hadon, the winner of the Great Games, to bring back the ax, along with the three said to be under the protection of Sahhindar. The network of the priestesses tells me that it was Hadon who found the weapon you now hold."

"But it was I who brought back the ax," Kwasin said in a rumbling voice that roused the men sleeping at his feet. "My weakling cousin would never have succeeded in his quest if not for me, and I would be foolish to tell lies in the temple of the oracle, who sees and knows all."

Qenwath glared at him and said, "There is a reason, O King of Dythbeth, that you are known throughout the land as the ill-fated Kwasin. Now come. The oracle waits."

He followed the woman through two prayer rooms and into a vast, oval-shaped chamber with torches guttered high along the walls. Like its counterpart in the temple at Dythbeth, the same mosaic collage representing the chain of time since the creation of the world by Kho spiraled from the center of the chamber's floor.

Kneeling on the brightly tiled floor before an imposing marble-and-ivory statue of the Great Mother crouched a white-shrouded figure. The being before Kwasin seemed to be painting the single blank tile at the end of one of the mosaic's spiral arms.

Kwasin shivered. Though the figure's back was to him, it must be Wasemquth, the oracular priestess, and with a brush and paint she was completing the artwork on the tile that many said would one day illustrate the last great event in Khokarsan history. What could it mean? The tile had remained blank for centuries.

He tried to peer over and around the oracle, but could not quite manage to see the image she painted. Qenwath nudged him and whispered that they should take off their clothes. He did so, but he could not keep his eyes off the oracular priestess and her fear-invoking task.

"Priestess, we have come," Qenwath announced.

The old woman before them said nothing but continued on with her painting. About a minute later she rose and hobbled, stoop-shouldered, behind the base of the towering statue of Kho. Kwasin looked at the tile, and though it remained only half painted, he could see on it the image of what looked like the Great Tower of Kho and Resu at Khokarsa. He stepped forward for a better look, but Qenwath held out an arm and pushed him back. Then the oracle returned carrying a three-legged oaken stool, which she positioned in front of the area where previously she had knelt, thus again obscuring the newly painted tile from view.

"Leave us, Qenwath," the old woman said. "Warrior, leave your ax against the wall and come forward."

Qenwath looked as if she wanted to object, but after making sure that Kwasin had propped his ax against the wall, she left the chamber.

Kwasin stepped forward until he towered above the oracle on her stool.

"Kneel, warrior, so that I may look into your eyes."

Kwasin obeyed, and when he did he noticed a narrow crevice in the tiled floor before the oracle's chair. From this hole rose thin wisps of bluish smoke, the aroma of which was heavy and sweet. The only time he had previously smelled its like was in the temple of Kho at Dythbeth when old Wasemquth had sentenced him to exile.

The oracle smiled, revealing dark-stained teeth and several gaps where those which had rotted had obviously been pulled. "The oracle would much rather reside in the temple at Dythbeth," the woman said, "but the quaking and shifting of the earth has extinguished the holy vapors there. Here the fires of Kho yet smolder, at least for now."

Kwasin said nothing but it unsettled him that the oracle had answered the question he had been pondering. Wasemquth leaned forward and inhaled deeply the rising fumes. Her mysterious smile also unnerved him.

"Why, O Oracle, have I been permitted to speak with you directly?" Kwasin asked finally, for it was customary to have a priestess translate the oracle's holy utterances. Out of respect, Kwasin tried to speak in low tones but found that his deep voice resounded like rolling thunder within the cavernous chamber. A dizziness had seized him, however, so he was not sure—perhaps he only thundered in his own mind. His eyes had begun to tear from the smoke, and he felt queasy as the room seemed to contract to the size of a needle's eye and then expand into infinity.

When Wasemquth laughed it was with the sound of a gargantuan web being plucked by the legs of some monstrous and hideously insane spider. "You have long wondered," she said, "why Great Kho spared you from a sentence of death and instead sent you off into exile. I say to you, sometimes those who must accomplish great deeds need be forged in the fires of trial and denial. What have you denied yourself, warrior?" Again the woman made her hair-raising cackle, and Kwasin had no idea how to respond. Then the oracle continued.

"It is said by some that you are cursed with two souls. One that rages and is possessed by death's spirit and produces only sorrow and destruction. The other that rejoices with great humor and love of adventure."

Indeed, Hadon had volleyed such a taunt at him on more than one occasion, and Kwasin had always retorted by saying it was better to possess two souls than the half-soul with which Hadon had been born. His cousin's jibe, however, now took on an air of truth, coming as it did from the lips of the oracle. Had Hadon somehow actually caught a glimpse of his soul? Or souls?

"Is it true?" Kwasin whispered, fighting off a tremor of fear that sought to shake through his great frame. Cold sweat dripped from his forehead and onto his cheeks.

"Two souls may be forged together by fire," the oracle said, and now her eyes glazed as if the sacred trance had at last fully seized her. "Look up and know how a soul is divided!"

Kwasin lifted his gaze to the statue of Kho, whose blank marble eyes seemed to look down on him in judgment. Then something long and thick and dark moved beneath the crook of Kho's arm. He gasped and his heart raced as two tiny eyes glimmered redly in the torchlight. With a slow, malevolent grace, a cowled and thick-bodied serpent slithered from behind the statue and down its front.

"Do not move!" The oracle's shrill voice stopped Kwasin as he rose to back away from the snake. "Kneel or Kho will strike you dead! But do so slowly if you wish to live."

He almost found it impossible to obey. Though he held no fear of snakes besides the usual caution, this one was different, for he had seen it many years before. But no, he thought, his eyes must deceive him—it could not be the same snake, but instead must be one of its kin. Still, fear constricted his throat and his heart hammered a chaotic rhythm against his ribs.

The oracle peered up at him with her watery, red-veined eyes as the snake glided along the floor and caressed her ankles. Kwasin resumed his kneeling position but readied himself to jump up at the slightest indication of the snake's interest in him.

"Ask yourself, O Black-Hearted One, why you have allowed this one to divide your soul." The old woman bent forward. The snake coiled itself around one of Wasemquth's spindly arms and slid into her lap like an obedient pet.

Kwasin found himself unable to speak. He had never told anyone the story of how one day, when ten years old, he had brought home a long, black serpent such as the one the oracle now held before him in her lap. On that long-gone day, the young Kwasin's plaything had shot into a hole in the wall of his mother's house, and almost as quickly as it had gone from sight, the snake had vanished from the boy's mind. Kwasin had left home to spend the remainder of the day stealing fruit from the local shopkeepers, and when he returned, it was to inhale the delightful aroma of his mother's cooking drifting from the kitchen. A few moments later Kwasin's mother screamed, and his blood ran cold as he recalled his escaped pet. He ran into the kitchen to find his mother prone on the floor, the snake coiled and ready to strike. He grabbed a heavy mallet used to soften meat and with a single blow crushed the serpent's head, immediately killing the creature, for even at that young age Kwasin's muscles were immensely strong. But looking at his mother's face, he saw he was too late. Already a paleness had seized her, and she cradled her arm where she had been struck. With a kitchen knife he cut open her wound and sucked the venom from it as Pwamkhu had once taught him; but still his mother moaned softly and shivered, saying nothing. Kwasin, tears streaming down his cheeks, confessed to his mother how he had let the snake into the house and that it was his fault the creature had struck her. Wimake had shushed her son and, too weak to speak, looked at him with her kind, forgiving eyes and then passed quietly into dread Sisisken's shadowy domain.

Wasemquth grinned malevolently at Kwasin, stroking a hand along the snake's sleek, black body. As if drunk on Kho's sacred breath, the woman bobbed her head back and forth, and spittle ran down her chin in periodic gushes. Kwasin began to think the woman would never come out of her mind-numbing trance when, after a long period of silence, she looked to the far wall against which Kwasin's ax lay propped and said, "The serpent and the ax will be your undoing or your succor, and so shall it be for all the land."

The woman rose to her feet, and the snake that had been in her lap slid down her leg and onto the floor. Old Wasemquth got up from her stool and followed her familiar as it glided across the tiles. Then both woman and snake disappeared behind the base of the great statue.

Kwasin was about to rise and leave the chamber, which now seemed to spin dizzyingly, when the oracle returned bearing a large double-handled amphora made of fine black clay. The front side bore in somewhat crude bas-relief an image of what appeared to be Sahhindar, his bow pulled wide, launching a forbidden arrow into the side of a fleeing antelope. Wasemquth sat down upon her three-legged stool and passed the vase to Kwasin from her shaky grip.

"Drink, warrior!" Wasemquth hissed.

Kwasin lifted the vase to his lips and swallowed a mouthful of what tasted like mead or extremely sweet millet beer. When he pruned his face at the bitter almond and faintly charcoal aftertaste, the oracle motioned for him to down more of the liquid. After three additional mouthfuls he felt sick to his stomach and passed the amphora back to the woman.

Kwasin looked at her questioningly.

"I grow tired," she said, rising. "One day another may yet initiate you into these mysteries, but if that day comes and you dare forsake the Goddess, you will endure much suffering and pass even more to your descendants. Go now!" Then Wasemquth turned away from Kwasin and hobbled past the statue of Kho and into the darkness.

"Oracle!" Kwasin cried after her. "Our business is not complete! I must at least know if I am free to lead Dythbeth against her enemies. Has my exile indeed been ended?"

Wasemquth stopped in the shadows and turned. The light from the torches caught her eyes, which glared back at him demon-like.

"You are free to lead the city of Khukhaqo," she said, "but never shall your guilt be lifted. Never."

The oracle turned and disappeared around the statue. A moment later Qenwath appeared at Kwasin's side. After Kwasin had risen and retrieved his clothing and ax, she led him from the chamber and asked him what he had learned of his fate.

"All is well!" Kwasin boomed with all the inflated ego he could feign. "I have been forgiven!"

Qenwath looked at him sidewise, but said nothing.

Beneath his stony exterior, Kwasin felt his two souls tremble.

9

For three days Kwasin lay ill in the old temple of Kho while Qenwath and her apprentice administered to him. No matter the great pile of blankets with which they covered him nor the roaring hearth that burned in the chamber where he slept, Kwasin shivered with a coldness that ached to the marrow. He told himself he must have picked up the sickness from the journey through the fetid swamp, but deep in his heart he feared the oracle's words had stricken him down. Either that or the illness came from the queer liquid she had made him drink, which burned in his stomach long after he had consumed it.

One night Kwasin awoke and in his delirium thought he saw the oracle's terrible black serpent slithering along the chamber's high ceiling. He cried out for the temple priestess, but when she did not come, Kwasin swallowed his pride and summoned the bard to sit at his side and strum his lyre to drive away the nightmares. Bhako, happy to at last be of service to his habitually ungrateful king, took out his instrument and hummed a soft and tuneful ballad about the courtship of the heroine-priestess Lupoeth. Within minutes, Kwasin fell into a dreamless sleep.

That evening, Kwasin awoke to a terrible thirst and found himself hot and sweating out his fever. He finished off two great bowls of water and again fell asleep, only to awaken in the morning with a ravenous hunger and feeling surprisingly rejuvenated. He devoured the food brought to him and announced that it was time for him and his party to return to Dythbeth.

At first Qenwath objected and said he should remain at the temple to rest for another day. Then she said, "Perhaps it is just as well. While you slept, your men have eaten so much fruit from our small orchard that I fear we will not be able to survive the season with what is left to us."

And so Kwasin, the bard, and the king's guard left behind the temple and its oracle—both of which Kwasin wanted very much to forget—and entered the dreary swamp on their way back to the city. This time, however, they proceeded with instructions from Qenwath to follow a secret path that wound through the wetlands to the north and thus avoid the swamp's deepest and most treacherous regions. When he learned of the route, Kwasin swore. He wondered if Queen Weth had known of the path all along but had withheld the information so that he and his men would be forced to wade almost directionless through the wretched and nearly impassible quagmire. It would be like the woman to torture him so, he thought.

In any case, his spirits lifted when he and his company managed to pass through the swamp without incident. By midafternoon, they emerged on the eastern edge of the marshlands just south of the confluence of the Karhokoly and Beswaly rivers, thankful to see the dry and open plain before them. Here they waded across the Karhokoly and marched south along its eastern bank, stopping only to kill and feast upon an antelope that had been watering at the river.

Not long after they had again set out, a great cloud of black smoke arose from behind the river's curve. Fearing the worst, Kwasin ordered his men to quicken their pace while he jogged ahead.

Soon it became clear that Dythbeth's walls indeed lay under siege. He could see fiery spheres—tiny from this distance, although he knew the missiles to be the size of small boulders—fly up from behind the city walls, only to land on the great plain, where black and gray smoke billowed skyward. Since he saw no missiles catapulted in the direction of the city, he surmised that Dythbeth still held out.

Kwasin ran ahead of the others until he could at last make out the field of battle. He stopped for a moment and tried to take it in. A dark mass of soldiers swarmed across the great plain, surrounding the city's northern and eastern walls, and perhaps the southern as well, though he could not see it from his position. In the midst of the troops, harnessed oxen drew forward many large-wheeled catapults. Hahinqo had positioned his own troops in a great mass along the city walls, though their ranks looked feebly thin compared to the vast hordes of the Sixth Army. Indeed, Kwasin had never before seen such a staggeringly large gathering of men.

Bhako, panting heavily, jogged up to Kwasin's side. "Minruth's troops have been reinforced," he said. "Either Minanlu has been taken or our mad emperor has abandoned his efforts there and come after a prize more sweet. That is, your head."

"I must get through to the men," Kwasin said, gazing out at a vast phalanx of perhaps ten thousand enemy soldiers that stood between him and Hahinqo's troops.

"You are an imposing presence, O King," Bhako said, "but to rush madly into that fray would be suicide. It would be better if the king lived to fight another day. Queen Awineth is said to be leading a resistance in the eastern mountains. Perhaps if we joined with—"

"Flee if you wish, bard!" Kwasin growled. "I need no cowards at my side!"

And then Kwasin was off, running as fast as his long legs would carry him along the banks of the Karhokoly. If he could not cross the plain to rejoin his troops, then he would find another way.

When he neared the shallows where he and his men had forded the river on their journey to the old temple, he climbed a low rise and saw in the distance the rearguard of the Sixth Army's northern flank moving along the plain. Quickly, he ran back to the river and slid down its bank into the cold waters. He waded through the shallows for about a quarter-mile before he noticed abandoned on the bank an old fisherman's boat. He pulled the craft into the river and boarded it. Soon the river deepened and he paddled with the strong current for a half-mile until the river widened as it neared the opening of the Bay of Boqawenqady.

He fought against the strong urge to continue on into the bay to meet up with Dythbeth's navy. He did not know, however, if the fleet still lay at anchor in the bay or if Admiral Poedy, the commander of Minruth's navy, had staged an attack against the fleet to coincide with the Sixth Army's land assault. He might enter the bay only to find it occupied by Poedy's vessels.

He guided his craft toward the eastern bank, a steep ridge that traced the waterline and made it impossible for him to know what lay beyond it. In his previous scouting he had witnessed a flank of enemy troops not far from the area. He had no idea how he would pass through this thick contingent of Minruth's soldiers and enter the city, but from what he had seen, the enemy here was spread thinner than to the east. Perhaps chance would open a way—and if not chance, then his ax.

After fighting the river's current, which sought to carry him toward the mouth of the bay, he ran the boat up against the steeply angled eastern bank. Since no footing existed on which he could draw up the boat and anchor it, he hurled himself from the craft and dug his fingers deep into the weeds that grew on the nearly vertical incline. The weeds, however, were not deep or strong enough to support his great weight and that of the ax strapped on his back. Almost immediately, the roots ripped out of the soft dirt and Kwasin plunged into the river. Sputtering and cursing, he scrambled on hands and knees up the sloping and sludge-covered river bottom, which continued to slip out from under him the more he struggled. When he finally made it out of the water and managed to prop himself up in a semi-standing position hugging the bank, he saw out of the corner of an eye his boat drifting sluggishly downstream. He hoped it would not alert the Sixth Army to his presence.

He looked up. The top of the bank ended about a foot higher than he could extend his hands. Carefully, so that he would not lose his balance and fall back into the river, he reached back and unbuckled the strap which fastened the ax to his back. As the ax slid free, he caught its handle, though the weapon's heaviness nearly caused him to lose his footing. Slowly, he lifted the ax alongside his body and then above his head. Then he tried to lodge the bottom edge of the ax's sharp head into the ridge above. Several times the ax head cut through the soft dirt, which rained down in Kwasin's face. Blinded by the dirt, he continued to gouge the ridge to the left and right until at last the ax caught on a rock. He pulled down on the ax handle to make sure the rock would not come free. Hoping it would hold his weight and that of the ax, Kwasin released the hand that he had dug into the weeds along the bank and, gripping with both hands, hung suspended from the handle. Trying not to groan too loudly, he used his mighty biceps to pull himself up. He hooked one elbow, then another, over the riverbank's rim, swung a leg up over the edge, and rolled onto solid and level ground.

As Kwasin stood up, something whizzed by his head and thudded in the grass ahead. He turned quickly and saw on the opposite side of the river five soldiers emerging from the swamp's wooded edge. Each man was whirling a sling parallel to his body in synchronized motion with his fellows.

The invisible object that nearly hit him in the face had been a sling-stone.

Kwasin felt the blood drain from his limbs. Behind him stretched a broad field that offered no protection from the deadly projectiles, and the weeds along the riverbank were too thin to hide in. For a moment he considered setting off across the field to get as much distance as he could between himself and the slingers. Then he noticed something strange. More men, how many he could not say because of the denseness of the trees and overgrowth, hid in the forest behind the five visible slingers. He knew from his previous scouting upriver that the Sixth Army amassed openly in great numbers nearby. Why would these soldiers be hiding in the woods unless...unless they were not members of Minruth's army.

Kwasin dropped his ax to the ground and raised both hands over his head. The five men continued to whirl their slings. Kwasin began to fear he would be cut down without mercy when a plume-helmeted officer appeared on the forest's edge. The slingers put down their weapons and now gestured violently with their arms. Apparently they wanted Kwasin to get out of sight so he would not reveal their position to any enemy scouts that might be in the vicinity.

The only thing Kwasin could do to comply besides jumping into the river was to crouch low to the ground. He did this, but when the soldiers indicated that he should cross the river to them, he nodded deeply to indicate "No." Again, the slingers began whirling their leather thongs. Growling, Kwasin gestured profanely to the men across the river, then began removing his heavy leather-and-bronze cuirass. The slingers stopped. They shouted to him to lay down his weapons. Kwasin grimaced but did as they ordered. It pained him to leave behind the ax but there was nothing he could do; if he held onto it, the soldiers would use their slings on him. He stripped down to his loincloth but then, at the last moment, decided to take his chances and leave on the antelope-hide belt that supported his short sword and its leather scabbard. Then Kwasin leaped into the cold waters of the Karhokoly.

When he pulled himself up on the opposite bank—thankfully of shallower slope than its companion—he found the soldiers had retreated back into the forest. Kwasin joined them there and stood before the fuming officer, surrounded by many soldiers in the shadows of the thick wood. Though the officer dressed in a common soldier's cuirass, the feathers that fanned from his helmet indicated a rank of high commander in the army. Like the other soldiers, he looked ragged and filthy.

"I am King Kwasin of Dythbeth. Who are you and do you bring aid to the servants of the Goddess?"

The officer scowled and said, "Kwasin? The madman who defiled a holy temple of Kho?"

"The same," Kwasin said. "And now King of Dythbeth."

The officer looked incredulous. "What of King Roteka?" he asked.

"He died fighting on the walls," Kwasin said. "Queen Weth is now my wife and I command the Fifth Army."

The man's eyes narrowed. "What brings the King of Dythbeth alone to the swamplands?"

Kwasin explained his journey to the oracle and that his companions were but a short distance to the east along the Karhokoly.

"Even if you truly are king," the officer replied after hearing Kwasin's story, "you are a fool. If the enemy has seen you, he is now on the alert. Were you stupid enough to think you could attack the enemy alone?"

Kwasin remained silent but his mood blackened.

"You haven't yet explained who you are," Kwasin said finally, "though by your ill-kept appearance I'd guess you might be from Mukha. All the women I encountered from there while on my way to the Western Lands were as ugly and foul-smelling as the Klemqaba."

A number of soldiers stepped forward out of the shadows, their hands on the hilts of their swords. The officer, however, reined in his men with an irritated look.

"I am Wahesa of Mukha," the officer said, "high general of King Qanaketh's army. But I suspect you know that. You are not as thick-headed as your reputation allows, though you are certainly as boorish. But I have no time to waste on your hot air. My army has landed on the western shore of the island, just south of the Saasamaro. From there we marched overland to the Beswaly River and crossed into the swamplands, traveling east along the bay. At a much slower rate than I had hoped, I might add. My scouts have informed me about the present attack on Dythbeth. Have you any news on that front?"

Kwasin told Wahesa what he had seen of the enemy positions and the defensive catapult volley by the citizens of Dythbeth. "I don't believe the walls have been breached," he said. "And though the Dythbethan line is weak compared to the numbers opposing it, each of my men is worth at least two or three of these Khokarsan amateurs."

The general wiped a hand across his dirty forehead, looking tired. "Then perhaps we aren't needed here," he said, "and I should turn my troops around."

Kwasin was about to reply when the soldiers standing on his right stirred. They parted and a number of Mukhan soldiers came from the rear, herding ahead of them Bhako and the rest of the expedition that had escorted Kwasin to the old temple of Kho. Bhako smiled widely when he saw his king, but the smile did not last. He held up the leather satchel which held his instrument and exclaimed, "The heavy-handed louts broke my lyre! Now how am I to chronicle the great doings of my king?"

Ignoring the bard and turning back to Wahesa, Kwasin said, "What's your plan, general? We may have begun our acquaintance on the bad foot of Suhkwaneth, but let me assure you I welcome what assistance you may offer my people against the enemies of Kho."

While Kwasin spoke, a woman came out of the trees and stood next to Wahesa. She resembled in dress and physical type the tribespeople Kwasin had encountered in the Western Lands. About her neck, arms, and ankles she wore many circlets of gold and ivory. A long and richly colored sash wrapped around her waist and upper torso in place of the kilt customarily worn by Khokarsan women, but her black hair was drawn in a Psyche knot like that of a priestess of Kho. She was the tallest woman Kwasin had ever seen. Taller, in fact, than Wahesa, who himself was only an inch shorter than Hadon, one of the tallest men in the empire, Kwasin himself being the tallest. The woman's chestnut eyes held fast on Kwasin as she whispered something in Wahesa's ear. Wahesa in turn whispered back to her.

Kwasin felt lust stir up inside him as he drank in the woman's exotic beauty, but he restrained himself and looked away. She and Wahesa were obviously lovers. Not that this would have stopped Kwasin from making advances on the woman under normal circumstances; but he needed Wahesa's help, if not his respect, in opposing Minruth's vastly larger forces. He could not let his longings put the delicate alliance between Mukha and Dythbeth in jeopardy.

"While you whisper sweet words to your lover," Kwasin said, yawning, "I am going to fetch my ax." But when he made to leave, the soldiers closed in around him.

Kwasin reached for his short sword and had already drawn it halfway from its sheath when the woman said in a heavy accent, "You may be Dythbeth's king as you claim, but you will obey my husband for now if you want his help."

Grimacing, Kwasin slid his sword back into its bronze scabbard. The general motioned his soldiers to stand down and ordered a private to retrieve Kwasin's ax from the opposite side of the river.

"Daka is also the expedition's priestess," Wahesa said. "While you travel with us, you would do well to obey her orders as well as mine."

Kwasin's eyebrow raised but he said nothing. It was not uncommon for a commander to become involved with his priestess. Still, while a priestess outranked her male counterparts in every area of government except those that dealt with the army, the navy, and engineering matters, she had no place giving orders in a military context. He wondered what unusual pull Daka had upon her husband.

Suddenly a courier, puffing, his face drenched with sweat, elbowed his way forward through the soldiers surrounding them. He saluted his general, then stood aside. When Wahesa told him to report, the man said, "Captain Gawethmi asks that you come at once. A large contingent of Phoeken's troops is on the march just south of the river."

Wahesa grinned, then cast a measured look at Kwasin. "Time to see if the legends about you are true."

10

As the Mukhan army resumed its march along the edge of the swamp, Kwasin questioned General Wahesa further about the strategy of his campaign. What he learned both encouraged and disgusted him.

Wahesa told him that just before war broke out across the empire, Minruth had harbored a large contingent of troops at the port of Mukha. When Minruth launched his revolution in Khokarsa, his forces at Mukha struck like lightning and seized the royal palace. King Qanaketh and all his family found themselves under house arrest before they could even mount a resistance. Unwilling to see his family slaughtered, Qanaketh announced his allegiance to Minruth and offered his assistance in the revolt. Secretly, however, Qanaketh sent word to General Wahesa, who had been abroad negotiating a treaty with tribes in the west. Afraid a direct attack on Mukha would precipitate the execution of the royal family, the king ordered Wahesa to announce he had gone renegade while Qanaketh himself pretended outrage. Instead of bringing his troops to Mukha, Wahesa was to take them to Towina, which still remained faithful to the Goddess. Or at least it did at the time, Wahcsa said. Now he was unsure. His last report informed him that the priests of Towina had begun to challenge the high priestess there with accusations of scandal, surely a precursor to all-out rebellion. Such outbreaks were flaring up in all the queendoms of the empire. In any case, following King Qanaketh's secret orders, Wahesa was to regroup his forces in Towina and launch an attack on the island of Khokarsa herself. News had arrived of King Roteka's valiant fight against Minruth and that Dythbeth was being eyed as a possible last stand for the forces loyal to the Goddess on the island. Wahesa and his men were to go there and aid Dythbeth in its fight to extinguish the ambitions of the priests. Like any good soldier, Wahesa had obeyed, although he admitted his shame at his king's seemingly two-faced actions. Still, Wahesa was a realist. He knew politics guided all wars and his king had only acted for the good of his people.

"And his own self-serving head," Kwasin said with disgust. "Kho will not forgive his blasphemy."

Wahesa looked at Kwasin keenly and said, "The snake who speaks ill of another risks knotting his own forked tongue."

Kwasin felt hot blood rush to his face. He would not suffer any more of the man's insults, alliances be damned! With murderous thoughts on his mind, Kwasin moved toward Wahesa, but suddenly he found himself tripping over Bhako, who had been fiddling with his damaged instrument as the group trudged through the swamp.

"Get out of my way, bard!" Kwasin shouted, and with a shove he sent Bhako flying. Then Kwasin stopped and watched the bard pull himself up from the stinking sludgewater.

"Forgive me, O King," Bhako said, picking up his now thoroughly soaked lyre. "I didn't see you, so absorbed was I in my own troubles."

Kwasin considered knocking down the bard again, but then it dawned on him that Bhako's clumsiness had seemed all too calculated. Perhaps the bard was not the fool he appeared. In any case, though still somewhat rankled, Kwasin found his welling anger had subsided. The general for his part seemed to act as if nothing had transpired between them. Kwasin breathed a prayer of thanks to Kho. He had come within a hair's breadth of attacking the commander of Dythbeth's only ally. He would have to be more careful in the future.

When the travelers came to a place where the river narrowed, the general ordered his troops to halt. He whispered instructions to his *datoepoegu*, or lieutenant, a man named Kaminsuh, who took off into the swamp. A short while later, men came forward out of the woods carrying many wide, flat-bottomed boats. Using heavy ropes, the men connected the boats together sidewise on the rocky riverbank and, drawing the craft into the river, tied them to some trees growing near the water's edge. Meanwhile, other men waded out into the cold waters and climbed onto the opposite bank, where they secured the other end of the chain of boats to a pair of sturdy oaks. Next, the men went back into the forest and emerged lugging long and narrow cedar beams, which were placed lengthwise across the river and then bound together with rope. In this way Wahesa's men had in a very short time constructed a crude but nonetheless effective pontoon bridge. Within minutes, soldiers were crossing the river and assembling in formation on the opposite side.

"Now you know why it took us so long to cross the swamp," Wahesa said, standing before the rapidly growing contingent on the southern bank of the Karhokoly.

Recalling his own difficult journey through the swamp to the oracle, Kwasin said nothing; but quietly he marveled at both the stamina and organizational efficiency of Wahesa's army. The Mukhans would make great allies indeed.

A stream of soldiers that seemed as if it would go on without end continued to march out of the boggy wood and across the pontoon. When a substantial grouping had assembled on the riverbank, Lieutenant Kaminsuh ordered his men forward in battle formation while the new arrivals took up position behind. At the moment a grouping of low hills prevented a direct view of the plain, thus obscuring the actions of the Mukhan army from Phoeken's hordes. Still, Kwasin wondered if enemy scouts along the river might have already reported to their commanders the location and actions of the Mukhan troops. He did not relish the thought that Phoeken would be waiting for them.

Captain Gawethmi, however, arrived to report that Phoeken's troops seemed, at least for the moment, oblivious to the Mukhans' presence. Though Wahesa had not yet heard from the courier he had sent to Dythbeth to coordinate a joint attack, the news prompted him to act quickly. He ordered Kwasin to take charge of an advance battalion that would strike Phoeken's regiment head-on from the north. Meanwhile, Wahesa and Kaminsuh were to circle ahead with their own men and attack Phoeken's eastern and western flanks. "I can't rely on the hope that my courier got through to General Hahinqo," Wahesa told Kwasin. "I need you to cause as much hell as possible so that Phoeken will be unable to organize his men against the flank attacks. Do you understand?"

Kwasin unslung the ax from the harness on his back and grinned widely. "You don't need to worry, general." He caressed the ax's handle. "Causing hell is my specialty."

At Wahesa's command, Kwasin went to his men. Here he found Gawethmi waiting. The man was to serve as Kwasin's second-in-command.

The captain issued instructions to his troops while Kwasin donned his war gear. This consisted of a conical bronze helmet with neck and nose guards and a heavy leather apron to protect his genitals and upper legs. Kwasin almost refused the leather leggings brought to him by a sergeant, as he did not wish to be encumbered in battle by the hot and stiff coverings. In the end, however, he relented; he had seen too many one-legged soldiers begging in the streets of Dythbeth. Kwasin already wore a leather cuirass affixed with a bronze breastplate molded roughly into the shape of a leopard's head, and a leather kilt to shield his upper legs. In addition to the ax he carried in his hands, a short, though heavy iron sword and an iron dagger hung in scabbards attached to a thick belt that circled his waist. A round brassbound wooden shield completed his armament.

Now fully clad for battle, Kwasin took the lead as Gawethmi sent the wedge-shaped formation marching forward up the wide hill that stretched along the river. When they neared the top, Gawethmi ordered the men to stand just below the hilltop and remain quiet. Together, Kwasin and Gawethmi lay on their bellies at the top of the hill and looked out across the plain. About a mile to the south an enormous dark mass was moving westward. Kwasin nearly cried out in surprise as a large group of men emerged from behind a knoll and passed directly before them less than fifty feet away at the bottom of the hill.

In long rows of twenty men abreast, the soldiers marched west along the uneven hills that skirted the Karhokoly. Near the front of the marchers, the party's commanding officers filed ahead. One man stood out from the rest, though the warriors who walked on either side of him were extraordinary in their own right. This man, however, was obviously the commander of the group. While his leather cuirass and kilt looked battle worn, a fine golden-hilted *tenu* hung from his belt, and a fan of fish-eagle feathers sprouted from the top of the man's bronze, gold-inlaid helmet, which gleamed brilliantly in the harsh glare of the Khokarsan sun. Though Kwasin had never before seen the man, he knew it must be General Phoeken himself.

Kwasin also recognized two of the large men who strode alongside the general, though he had not seen them before either. Still, their faces gave them away, as they were identical except for a gouged cheek that marred the features of one of the men. It could only be the hero-twins Bhaqeth and Klaqeth. Klaqeth would be the one with the disfigured face, a token from his most renowned exploit.

At the time of Kwasin's exile, the fame of the twins was spreading throughout the empire like a wildfire across the savannas. The two claimed to have entered a valley to the east of Sakawuru where they had battled and slain a creature they called a *ko'bok'ul"ikadeth*, a giant three-horned, armor-cowled rhinoceros with skin as thick as iron and a temper as black as a starless and moonless night. Though the brothers brought back with them three enormous tusks to prove their claim, an expedition sent back to the valley by Minruth had found no trace of the daunting creature. Many began to question the brothers' account, but popular belief still held up their reputation as heroic monster-killers. Kwasin did not doubt the twins' story. Stranger beasts stalked the shadowy jungles around the two great inland seas. After all, he himself had once heard the terrifying cry of the *r"ok'og'a* while camping with his uncle along the shores of the southern sea—a hair-raising shriek that haunted him to this day. And if the dragon of the Kemus was real, why not an oversized, armor-plated, three-horned rhinoceros?

He eyed the hero-twins and the three other hulking warriors who surrounded Phoeken. Surely the tattooed one with the earring and the hook-ended broadsword was the hero Miwanes of Sakawuru. And the large, dark-skinned brute with the claw-raked face must be Toesem, the lion fighter of Towina. The third would be Kadyth the Silent, recognizable by the bright red scar across his larynx where a barbarian king had cut him before dying under Kadyth's ax. Minruth's greatest warriors—heroes all. And though none met Kwasin in terms of brawn or towering height, any one of them would have made a fearsome opponent; together, they might best a small army.

A bronze helmet, a cuirass affixed with a bronze breastplate, and a heavy leather kilt and leggings adorned each of the heroes. Each man except Miwanes, armed only with his ax, wore a *tenu*. Kwasin wondered if the warriors truly belonged to the brotherhood of swordsmen or if Minruth, following his mad reformations, had so adorned his champions in defiance of tradition.

"My scouts did not reveal this party, O King," Gawethmi whispered. "They must have been hiding in the hills when—"

But Kwasin did not want to hear the man's excuses, nor did he want to let the valuable target slip by while Gawethmi took the time to signal his men. Further, he feared that the Mukhans would make too much noise as they charged up and over the hill, thus alerting the enemy and allowing Phoeken to escape. He would have to trust, however, that the Mukhans would follow his lead. If they did not, what he did next would be an act of suicide.

Kwasin left the still speaking Gawethmi and barreled down the hill alone toward General Phoeken.

At the bottom of the hill, Kwasin leaped among the spearmen who marched along the party's flank. He let loose his wild energy, which had been pent up since his recovery from the illness that afflicted him in the temple. His ax swung out and cleaved clean through the bronze helmets of two marchers. The men fell, their skulls gashed open, before they even knew an enemy was among them.

Kwasin surged through the men toward his goal, his swinging ax clearing an opening before him as the startled soldiers retreated from his fury. Behind him, he heard a mighty uproar. The Mukhans had not abandoned him. They were charging as one down the hillside.

The tall form of the hero-twin Klaqeth appeared out of the confusion of men. Kwasin swung at him but the man parried with a spear he had grabbed out of the hands of a soldier. The spear shaft splintered like a dried twig. Klaqeth hurled himself backward, landing hard on his buttocks but unharmed by Kwasin's ax.

Not for long. Kwasin raised his great weapon above the man, who unsuccessfully tried to dig his heels in the soft and yielding dirt in a frantic attempt to stand up. Then Kwasin lost his own balance as the force of many bodies hurled into him from behind. The weight of the falling ax carried him forward and he landed chest-first on the ground, air heaving from his great lungs. He had somehow missed Klaqeth, who had mysteriously disappeared.

Feeling both helpless and foolish—like a mighty but doomed elephant he once saw downed by pygmy hunters during his exile—Kwasin rolled onto his side as many feet trampled or jumped over him. Then, noticing he had still somehow managed to hold onto the ax, he yelled at the stampeding men to get out of his way and cut his weapon at their legs. They were his own men, but their trampling would kill him if he did not act.

The charging men made clear. Kwasin got to his feet, groaning at the pain in his ribs from injuries yet unhealed from his previous battles. Before him, not fifteen feet away, stood Captain Gawethmi. His shield and helmet lay next to him on the ground and the man cradled the bloody stump of his right arm beneath an armpit. Towering behind Gawethmi, whose face shone as pale as the moon's, stood the hero-twin Klaqeth.

Kwasin shouted and ran forward, but too late. Klaqeth drove his sword through the back of Gawethmi's neck, then leaped over the collapsing body and advanced on Kwasin.

By the grace of the Goddess, Kwasin looked over his shoulder and saw Bhaqeth running at him from the rear. Kwasin crouched low and swung his ax at the advancing man, who fell back to escape the blow that would have cut him down at the knees. Then Kwasin allowed the weight of the ax to spin him back around at Klaqeth. Klaqeth jumped back. Kwasin, completing his rotation, found himself again confronting the other brother. The men were like hyenas, Kwasin thought, one retreating while the other advanced in a cowardly but deadly cycle. Doubtless they had slain the fearsome *ko'bok'ul"ikadeth* in the same manner.

A terrible din assaulted Kwasin's ears and all about him a tangle of soldiers surged forward. Then he was being pushed along by his own troops. Klaqeth and Bhaqeth were forced to run with him to escape from being trampled to death by the advancing Mukhan line. He no longer saw Miwanes, Toesem, or Kadyth. Perhaps they had retreated to protect Phoeken.

A cacophonous mix of shrill and throaty screams, accompanied by a heavy thudding and the sharp cracking and splintering of wood, filled Kwasin's ears. Soldiers ahead of Kwasin slammed into one another, thrusting spears and hacking swords against their enemies' shields. The splintering sound was that of many spears breaking, and doubtless many bones. The odor of blood, urine, and excrement caught on the hot wind.

The forward momentum stopped. He heard a whistling and looked up to see a blur of leaden missiles crisscrossing overhead. Both forces had unleashed their slingers, though the predominant number belonged to the Mukhans. So far Phoeken's men had been unsuccessful in their attempt to regroup after the initial assault. Now they would have a harder time as the Mukhan javelin throwers momentarily darkened the bright sky with their weapons.

Kwasin had little time to take it in. Now that the troops' forward motion had stopped, Bhaqeth was fighting through the men toward Kwasin. He turned and saw Klaqeth doing the same.

Shoving his own soldiers out of the way, Kwasin ran forward and took on Klaqeth. Kwasin slid the ax's thong from around his wrist and, with a mighty heave, launched the ax at the man. Letting go of the ax in the midst of battle carried much risk, as he might never recover it. But he could not hope to defeat the brothers by playing it safe.

The ax smacked hard against Klaqeth's shield and tore it from the man's grasp. Kwasin drew a dagger from his belt, swung it back behind an ear, and flung it at Klaqeth. The man raised his *tenu* and threw himself to one side in a reflexive attempt to escape Kwasin's throw.

Too late. The dagger plunged through the Klaqeth's scarred cheek and impaled itself between his jaws. Klaqeth fell backward, dead.

Just behind Kwasin, a man howled. Kwasin whirled and drew his short sword barely in time to deflect Bhaqeth's descending *tenu*. The blade hit with such force that even Kwasin's mighty muscles could not prevent him from being forced to a knee. A demon rage seemed to possess the surviving twin now that his brother had been slain. Kwasin parried blow after blow, regaining his feet but falling back as Bhaqeth lunged with his longer, square-ended sword.

Stepping back, Kwasin nearly tripped over Klaqeth's corpse. Still blocking Bhaqeth's repeated blows, he bent down, gripped a giant hand around Klaqeth's limp neck, and drew up the dead man before him as a shield. Bhaqeth's blade, which had been swinging out toward Kwasin, pulled back to avoid slashing his brother's corpse. Kwasin grinned devilishly. Taking advantage of Bhaqeth's hesitation, he hurled himself forward and slammed a foot against the surviving twin's shield. Again, a risky move. If Bhaqeth had not been so unnerved by the unconventional use of his brother's corpse, he would have been able to chop off Kwasin's leg at the knee. Instead, stepping backward from the momentum of Kwasin's kick, Bhaqeth lost his footing and fell to the ground.

Kwasin stood over Bhaqeth. Then, with all his weight, he pressed a foot down on the shield that rested on the man's chest. Bhaqeth groaned under the great pressure, his eyes bulging with terror as the end of Kwasin's short sword stabbed down at his head. The man turned away and the blade impaled his cheek. It reminded Kwasin of the way he had skewered the other brother with his dagger. He smiled at the epic symmetry, and at the fact he had finished what the legendary three-horned rhino could not.

Now the soldiers about Kwasin surged backward as the enemy reversed the gains made by the Mukhans' initial charge. Kwasin shouted hoarsely and shouldered his way forward against the tide. He needed to recover his ax before he lost his bearings in the mad rush of men.

Then he saw the ax on the ground before him, just as a large hand reached out of the chaos and wrapped itself around the weapon's haft. Kwasin looked into the face of Kadyth the Silent and swore. Kadyth must have lost his own ax in the melee. The man, greed twinkling in his eyes, took aim at Kwasin and swung back the ax.

Out of sheer reflex, Kwasin grabbed a man running by him and heaved the fellow at Kadyth. Fortunately the man was a Khokarsan soldier, although Kwasin had not checked beforehand—it could just as well have been an ally. Kadyth's ax sliced through the man's leather armor. With a cry, the man collapsed. Before Kadyth could recover from his swing, Kwasin lunged forward and chopped with his sword. Kadyth screamed as the blade cut through the heavy leather kilt covering his thigh, but he did not fall or let go of the ax. Instead, unable to swing the massive weapon back without again giving Kwasin the opportunity to attack with his sword, he thrust forward the ax. The blunt top of the ax's head drove into Kwasin's chest, and though he wore a cuirass, the terrific blow heaved the breath from his lungs. His breastbone and ribs seared with pain as he fell backward and to the ground. His vision filled with sparkling stars, through which he saw his own giant ax descending upon him. He willed his muscles to respond, to no avail. At last, the hollow oblivion of death had come.

Then, suddenly, his vision cleared. Kwasin saw the ax that had been falling toward him drop from Kadyth's hand and land harmlessly on the ground. Kwasin dropped the sword he had forgotten he still held and grabbed the ax, rolling out of the way just in time to prevent Kadyth's body from falling on top of him.

Kwasin vaulted to his feet to find himself looking into the dark and ugly face of Miwanes of Sakawuru. Blood rivered down the pirate warrior's hook-ended broadsword and onto the downtrodden grass, a testament to the gruesome work he had just finished on Kadyth.

"Why kill him?" Kwasin shouted, advancing toward Miwanes. "Are you an ally of Kho?"

Miwanes' laugh croaked like the caw of a dry-throated raven. "Haven't you heard?" he said. "Minruth has promised the kingship of Dythbeth to the man who brings him your head!"

Miwanes' sword whistled through the air at Kwasin, who deflected the blow with his ax. Somehow Miwanes managed to hold onto his blade, although his scarred face winced with pain at Kwasin's blow. Seizing on the man's discomfort and the opening caused by the lowering of his sword, Kwasin slammed frontally into his opponent, grabbing Miwanes' bronze nose guard and roughly heaving off his helmet. The two men fell backward into the grass.

Miwanes dropped his sword, which was useless at this proximity, then drew a dagger from a sheath on his belt and tried to stab it into Kwasin's throat. Kwasin grabbed Miwanes' wrist before the man could complete his motion and thrust the ax at the man's unhelmeted temple. Though Kwasin had little room to swing his ax at such close quarters, the heavy iron head still carried enough force to crush in Miwanes' skull.

Kwasin rose from the body of his dead opponent and scanned the chaos of battle around him. Somewhere amid the fighting, Toesem, the lion fighter of Towina, would be looking for him. But then, on the ground beyond the fallen body of Kadyth the Silent, he saw the bloodied corpse of the man he sought. Miwanes, in his greed for the king's reward, had already done Kwasin's work for him.

"So much for Minruth's great heroes," Kwasin muttered. Then he turned and rejoined the fighting.

11

By morning the tides began to turn in favor of the Dythbethans and their new allies. Phoeken's troops already stood demoralized by their losses in the face of General Wahesa's reinforcements. Then, shortly after dawn, yet another army appeared on the southern horizon. Kwasin immediately sought out General Wahesa in his tent, where he had been planning his next moves.

When Kwasin entered the tent he found a tall tribesman standing before Wahesa, his wife, and a captain of the army. The general, his eyes beaming as with satisfaction, looked up at Kwasin and said, "Just as your city entreated Mukha for support, I too have fostered an alliance." Wahesa eyed his wife as if pleased with her. "The army that approaches is under Mukhan command," he said at Kwasin's questioning look, "though Wan"so tribesmen make up nearly a third of the force."

Kwasin's eyes grew wide. He had never heard of anyone making an alliance with the west-coast or northern tribes.

"Times are changing," Wahesa said, "but so obsessed are we with this Time of Troubles, we fail to take notice. You may have heard reports lately that some of the more distant outposts have been engaged in skirmishes with the pygmies. As the seasons grow warmer, their tribes are growing in number. And as they hunger for new and fertile lands, they, along with the natives hitherto restricted to isolated regions in the west and northwest, have begun to encroach on the outskirts of the empire."

Kwasin had not heard these reports, but then he had returned to the island only months ago. He had encountered several tribes during his travels through the Western Lands, but he had found most of the territory he passed through stark and uninhabited. That Wahesa could gather together enough of the tribesmen to organize a working army surprised him.

General Wahesa went on to explain that the tribes from which he had recruited were under the suzerainty of Daka's father, King Mahedana of the Wan"so. Suddenly Kwasin understood the great pull Daka had over Wahesa and why the general had accepted an outlander as his army's priestess. Their marriage had been political. Wahesa would gain reinforcements for his invasion of Khokarsa, while Daka achieved for her father's confederation the lucrative support of the mighty

Khokarsan empire—that is, should Wahesa be victorious in his campaign against Minruth. Not to mention the fact that Daka was now a revered initiate of the Temple of Kho, a position rarely granted to foreigners.

Kwasin regarded Wahesa. The man was a keen politician, perhaps too keen. He would have to watch out for him. Kwasin knew that his own marriage had been one of convenience and that Weth held little love for him. The queen of Dythbeth was as shrewd as Wahesa. When the time came for the two to meet, they might conspire, and then things would go very badly for Kwasin.

The next few days passed by in a whirlwind of activity. Phoeken and his troops retreated to the west of the great plain, but Wahesa and General Hahinqo did not want to give the enemy a chance to rest and regroup. The second Mukhan contingent was ordered to swing to the west and cut off Phoeken's retreat. Then the combined forces of the Dythbethan and Mukhan armies were to draw the enemy to the north, in the hope of forcing the Khokarsans up against the banks of the Karhokoly. However, things did not go exactly as planned. Some of the Wan"so warriors accompanying the Mukhans could not understand the ancient ban on the bow and arrow enforced throughout the empire. Consequently, several of the Wan"so smuggled the Goddess-forbidden weapons aboard the galleys that had landed their people on the southern shores of the Kemsilemu, or Great Claw Peninsula. Somehow the Wan"so had concealed their bows and arrows from their Mukhan commanders on the trip overland to Dythbeth. Now that the Wan"so had encountered the enemy, they hungered to use the prohibited weapons.

A great argument ensued between the Mukhan commanders and the Wan"so, the result of which was that a handful of the more forceful agitators were executed. When it seemed that an all-out insurrection was brewing, the Wan"so officers serving as liaisons between the tribesmen and their Mukhan commanders turned to someone their men would listen to. This was Daka, who told the assembled tribesmen that those who disobeyed the prohibition would be cursed by their own gods and goddesses, as well as the Great Mother goddess of the Khokarsan people. Further, all ancestors of the disobedient would also be cursed. Almost immediately, the prohibited bows and arrows were turned over. The Wan"so regarded their King Mahedana as a god, and therefore Daka, his daughter, as a goddess. They believed every word she uttered, or at least believed in the reality of her threat, for often the deities had their own hidden reasons to mislead mortals. Thus the Wan"so's fear of divine wrath settled an argument that had begun over the Khokarsans' fear of their own Goddess' prohibition. Kwasin believed in Kho's wrath himself, but he did see the irony in the outcome.

In the time it took for the situation to be resolved, Phoeken brought his men to the north and, after successfully breaking through the forces stationed on the southern bank of the Karhokoly, crossed the river. Undoubtedly he hoped to regroup and relaunch his campaign from the northern hills. But General Hahinqo, as supreme commander of the forces of the Goddess at Dythbeth, still wanted to take the battle to Phoeken. Thus he ordered Wahesa to take his men and draw the Khokarsans up into the mountains. Hahinqo arranged for several of his own officers to accompany General Wahesa and his troops, believing that the Dythbethans, being familiar with the terrain, would aid the Mukhans in bringing devastating losses to the enemy. Kwasin was to join the mountain campaign, as Hahinqo also believed the fearsome presence of Dythbeth's giant king would inspire the Mukhans and dishearten their adversaries. Meanwhile, Hahinqo would try to bring order out of the chaos that was Dythbeth. Though many fields had been torched by the enemy, perhaps somewhere among the abandoned farmsteads a few crops had survived that could be scavenged for the city's increasingly famished inhabitants. And the opening caused by diverting the enemy would allow Queen Weth to send out more couriers seeking help from the mainland cities. Not that she expected them to send assistance; the war between Kho and Resu had enveloped the whole empire, leaving the mainland forces loyal to the Goddess with enough problems of their own.

The fighting in the mountain passes stretched on for weeks as Kwasin and the men under his command picked off Phoeken's soldiers one by one. The rugged slopes and the deep ravines of the Saasamaro made for good guerilla warfare, and Kwasin felt invigorated by the clean, fragrant air of his boyhood haunts.

Often Kwasin took off on his own, taking pleasure in finding devious ways to torment and otherwise lower the morale of the enemy. One of these occasions went so far as to make the Khokarsan commanders scream in high dudgeon for the head of Dythbeth's king, while many soldiers undoubtedly lay awake at night sweating in fear of the mad giant.

Kwasin had set out one morning to scout a large enemy encampment that had recently been set up only two miles northeast of the Dythbethan fort situated at the opening of the main pass—much too close for Kwasin's comfort. Attempting to avoid detection, Kwasin skirted the wall of a treacherous gorge as he made his way toward the encampment.

As he proceeded along the gorge, the morning sun peeked over the lower lip of a crevasse and cast its blood-red glare in his eyes. He looked away for a moment, but when he looked up again a sight met him that might have been a vision from angry Resu himself. Or perhaps, he thought a moment later, the vision came from the Goddess, and She had only brought Kwasin to this precise spot so that he could see the weakness of the Flaming God that had been revealed in his arrogant gaze. Surely Kho, in Her recent upheavals of the land, had created the peculiar formation of rock and dirt that stood silhouetted against the rising sun's blinding radiance. Whatever the case, it gave Kwasin an idea.

He surveyed the distance he would have to traverse up the steep side of the gorge for his plan to work. For a moment he considered returning to the fort to get help. But he knew that if anyone could carry out his plan, it would be him. Besides, accomplishing the task on his own would only aggrandize his already legendary status.

Cautiously, he ascended the mountainside and passed along its summit so that he could look down on the rock formation from above. Yes, that would do, he thought. Even more cautiously than he had climbed up, he descended into the saddle between the two great mountains and headed for the enemy encampment.

When he reached the northern mouth of the gorge, he was forced to scale a sharp rise of terrain littered with fir and pine trees. Some of the trees had been uprooted by the recent quakes, while others only half uprooted crisscrossed one another, angling out of the reddish soil in chaotic patterns. Kwasin looked for the easiest route through the labyrinth but did not find one; the entire slope seemed a treacherous tangle of Great Kho's wrath.

He shrugged. If the way would be difficult for him, it would be even harder for dozens of armored soldiers.

Finally, another valley appeared over the rim. A small lake rested on the valley's northern edge, and a great military encampment, consisting of a half-dozen large tents and many smaller ones, lay upon the lake's nearer shore. The soldiers were already up, drilling under the supervision of a *rekokha* on the flat terrain in front of the tents.

His timing could not have been better. He took a shallow drink from a sea-otter-skin flask slung over his shoulder, then rested for a moment to recover his breath from the climb up the tree-knotted slope.

While he was resting, Kwasin heard a rustling in the trees behind him and to his left. A man burst out of a copse of half-fallen firs and bolted for the pass into the adjoining valley. Kwasin took off after the man.

By the time the soldier—obviously a scout sent to monitor the valley pass—reached the crest of the slope, Kwasin was already upon him. The man died under a single mighty blow from Kwasin's ax.

Shouts now arose from below. The camp's inhabitants had witnessed the murder of their comrade. Kwasin lifted up the body of the slain soldier and held it high so that the men in the camp could see it. Then he cast the corpse down the slope before him.

A captain, holding his feathered helmet in his hands, came out of one of the tents and followed the collective gaze of the soldiers.

Kwasin stood on the top of the slope and held up his ax. He wanted the officer below to know that it was the giant king of Dythbeth who taunted him.

The captain raised an arm in Kwasin's direction. The *rekokha* who had been drilling his men turned toward the captain as if listening to orders. Then the sergeant turned back to his men and gestured rapidly for them to move out.

Still Kwasin waited. The longer he stood there, the more likely the officer in charge of the camp would send additional men to the ridge. The captain wouldn't believe a lone man would be foolish enough to take on his whole contingent and would think an entire army must lie in wait over the ridge in the bordering valley.

Kwasin grinned as his hopes were realized and what must have been more than a hundred soldiers peeled from the larger body of men and headed toward the pass. Something whirred by Kwasin's head and his smile faded. He had gauged the soldiers too far away for their sling-stones to reach him, but now he saw one man below so skilled with the sling he could have competed in the Great Games of Klakor. The fellow was reloading his sling. Kwasin dropped below the ridge and as fast as he could began making his way through the interwoven mass of trees.

When he made it to the bottom of the tangled slope, he stopped and took out his own sling. The barking of dogs, muted somewhat by the thick foliage, carried through the trees. The soldiers were already descending upon him.

He began whirling his sling. A patch of moving color appeared between two trunks. He estimated the speed and direction of the pursuer, and a brief moment later the soldier appeared again. Already Kwasin had released his sling-stone. He failed to see the soldier fall because once more the man passed behind the trees, but he heard a soft cry and the thud of a body hitting the ground.

Once more he downed a soldier in this way, but that was all he had time for. He wanted to motivate the bloodlust in the men so they would follow him, but he hoped he had not waited too long. As he bolted into the gorge, Kwasin turned to see several soldiers nearing the bottom of the slope, pulled along by the tethers of their yapping and slathering canines. The many fallen tree trunks caused the men to proceed slowly, though not slow enough for Kwasin.

His great lungs heaved like a bellows as he pumped his legs across the basin of the rock-strewn gorge. Again he looked behind. The larger body of the soldiers pursuing him had left the forest and now charged across the roughly flat ground between the two immense mountains. Kwasin veered to his left and skirted a shelf of rock that soared almost vertically for several hundred feet. Suddenly, the shelf forked to the left and he turned with it, crossing behind the mountainside and out of view of the soldiers.

Kwasin looked up. An enormous projection of rock cantilevered from the mountainside and blocked out the sky above him. Above it, he knew, another similar though slightly larger projection jutted out of the mountain. Though the soldiers would be upon him soon, he slowed his pace. The great mass of stone and earth above unnerved him; he did not want his pounding footfalls to cause his plan to end in disaster—at least not for him.

At last the sky's blue vault again appeared overhead and Kwasin thanked the Goddess. Here a wedge-shaped channel creased the steep mountainside. Kwasin crawled across the gravelly debris that led into the channel and began ascending the natural trail.

The dogs' barking and the gritty crunch of men's feet as they ran across the canyon floor echoed oddly from the overhanging stone. As he passed above the second and higher projection of rock on his left, Kwasin felt a hard blow to his back that almost caused him to lose his footing. He looked below and saw a man reloading his sling. It was the same fellow who'd made the long throw when Kwasin had stood upon the ridge over the camp. The soldier had hit his target true, but the massive iron head of the ax slung across Kwasin's back had deflected the deadly projectile.

Kwasin stopped his ascent and picked up a large rock. Leaning with his back against the inclined channel, he thrust forward the rock and watched it swing out into the air, plummeting in its arc toward the slinger. Though the rock did not hit him, the man retreated from the mountainside toward the center of the gorge. As he did so, he looked up and to his left. Then the man began shouting and waving his arms, not at Kwasin, but in the direction of the immense overhang of rock.

Kwasin cursed. The slinger's new perspective had alerted him to Kwasin's intent and the man was now attempting to warn his fellows to stay clear of the trap. Kwasin had hoped to ascend another seventy-five feet and then traverse a narrow ledge to his destination. Now he would be forced to go another way.

He climbed out of the channel. He would have to cross the face of the sheer stone wall that separated him from the top of the mammoth protuberance of rock on his left. At a reckless pace, he began shimmying across the rock face, trying not to look down from the dizzying height. The few handholds and footholds available seemed achingly far apart. Kwasin was only able to reach them because of the length of his great frame, and because of the wildly desperate leaps he took to make some of them.

A lead projectile cone splintered the stone next to Kwasin's head and embedded itself in the cliff face. Warm blood mixed with sweat beaded down his cheeks where the stone fragments ricocheting from the missile's impact had penetrated his skin. He did not stop his climb but continued bellying across the rock, his pace uninterrupted. There was nothing he could do now to stop the man except make it to the overhang quickly.

His mind emptied of all but the thought of making the next foot- or handhold. Time seemed to disappear along with self, interrupted occasionally by the chinking impact of a lead projectile on either side of him. Then, suddenly, his trancelike state vanished and he stepped onto solid ground—but not too solid, he hoped. He sprinted across the ledge, making sure not to tread too heavily. When he found the spot he was looking for he did not stop at it but headed farther up the sloping mountainside above the overhang. Then, gauging he had reached a safe enough distance, he picked up the largest rock he could find and hurled it below. When nothing happened, he picked up another rock and threw it, and then another and another.

His target was a weak fissure where the great protuberance of rock joined the mountain. He had been sure he would be able to jar loose the narrow channel of rock that served to mortar the massive outcropping to the mountainside. A small landslide should be all it would take. But though he hurled rock after rock, no slide came. Then, as doubt began to wear away at the wisdom of his plan, the rocks below finally gave. The earth rumbled and cracked louder than any thunder Kwasin had ever heard and the mountain beneath his feet shook violently. Kwasin fell on his buttocks, flailing his arms back in an attempt to stop his slide. By the time he finally did so, he found himself cradling an arm around a sharply projecting rock thirty feet below where he had been standing. The two massive projections of the mountainside were now gone and he looked through the dust-billowing air at the bottom of the gorge. When the air did not immediately clear, he struck out on the dangerous climb back up the mountain, which was now littered with debris triggered by the double avalanche. Arriving at the summit, he looked down to see a handful of tiny figures on the edge of the new mountain of gargantuan stone blocks formed by the landslide. The slinger had been too late. He, along with the majority of his fellows, had been unable to get far enough from the overhang before Kwasin triggered its fall. Kwasin had killed a hundred or more men, but he hoped by the time the rumors of the day's events had spread far, the number would be exaggerated to the thousands.

He did not return to the fort that day. Instead, he made for Wahesa's camp in the eastern mountains, knowing the general would want intelligence of the great blow against the enemy. Doubtless, Wahesa would want to strike the encampment while its soldiers still reeled from their losses.

Darkness had fallen in the mountains by the time Kwasin wandered into the camp. Above, fair Lahla the Moon was swinging her satisfied grin across the star-speckled firmament, but when Kwasin sought out General Wahesa, he found a scene that was anything but tranquil. A terrific shouting was erupting from within Wahesa's tent. Kwasin recognized the voices as those of the general and his wife. The two were having a lovers' spat, or perhaps they argued about war strategy. Kwasin could not tell because the two carried out their shouting match in the strange tongue of Daka's people.

Weary from his travels and the events of the day, Kwasin turned away from the general's tent and returned to the night guard, asking where he could sleep for the night. An officer on the edge of camp was awakened and ordered to give up his tent to Dythbeth's king. The man grumbled at first but quickly grew quiet, making a hasty evacuation from his tent when he saw the seven-foot-tall Kwasin looming above him in the moonlight. Kwasin fell asleep inside the tent listening to Wahesa and his woman presumably cursing one another in Wan"so.

Kwasin started awake in the dead of night in the middle of a dream about the oracle at Dythbeth. The old crone had been trying to tell him something, but when she spoke, her words came out like a garbled sob. Kwasin stretched out on his dry grass bedding and tried to shake off what seemed to him an ill omen.

Suddenly, he sat upright and listened. For a moment he heard nothing.

But now there it was again.

He shuddered when he realized the sound echoed the eerie sobbing of the oracle in his dream. Had the oracle passed from the living since Kwasin had last seen her and now her ghost came to his tent to warn him of something? Unable to rid himself the notion, he silently unsheathed his dagger and slipped outside through the folds of his tent.

Lahla still swung above but she had climbed past her zenith, her grin turned to a scowl. At first Kwasin saw nothing out of the ordinary, but then he noticed a shimmering of moonlight in a cluster of bushes just outside of camp. With a quietness that belied his hulking form, Kwasin slunk toward the bushes as if a ghost himself. As he neared his destination, he made out a tall, dark form in the shadows before him. Swiftly he sprang at the figure, which he throttled roughly under a mighty biceps. His dagger's point pressed into the figure's soft abdomen, but he recoiled when he heard a feminine cry. He quickly whirled the figure around and in the moonlight looked down into Daka's frightened, tear-filled eyes.

"Forgive me, priestess!" Kwasin cried, releasing the woman. "I had thought you a trespasser in the night!"

Daka's jewel-harnessed breast rose and fell rapidly, and at first Kwasin believed her expression revealed fear. Then she was pressing her warm lips upon his in a passionate kiss and running her hands over his arms, shoulders, and chest.

For a moment, Kwasin thought of Wahesa, and also of Weth, and of the terrible complications that would arise should either learn of this infidelity. But his concern did not last long.

Kwasin seized up the woman in his arms and carried her back to his tent.

12

Kwasin brushed past the guards, trumpeters, and throoming bullroarers into the palatial throne room of Dythbeth. Something was wrong. The palace guards had given their king, arriving home after his long absence, too much trouble for his liking. Instead of being greeted as a returning champion, Kwasin had been made to wait in the throne room's antechamber while the herald announced his presence. When finally he entered the spacious hall and saw who sat upon the queen's oaken throne, he should have been joyful; but something told him his problems had just grown much worse.

"Behold, priestess of Kho and of her daughter, the moon, the king of shining Dythbeth!" a herald cried out.

Minruth's daughter Awineth slouched against the high seatback of Queen Weth's throne as if weighed down with great fatigue. The raven-haired woman smiled blandly at Kwasin, looking pale and worn, though even her gaunt form and the dark circles that hung beneath her large, dark gray eyes could not conceal her ravishing beauty. Beside the empress, though at a lower station, sat Weth, her expression unreadable. Her chair, smaller and less ornate than Awineth's, rested above another chair, this one empty. It was Kwasin's throne, lowered to its customary position beneath the highest-ranking initiates of the Goddess in the city. Knowing the convention failed to alleviate Kwasin's sense of dread at the loss of power it implied.

He approached the royal dais and knelt with head bowed and hands outstretched in obeisance.

"Rise, Kwasin, and tell me your story," Awineth said.

Kwasin stood up but he made note of the woman's lack of etiquette. By failing to address him as king, she both humiliated him and lorded her authority. But Kwasin could do nothing. Though a bitch, she was also the Empress of Khokarsa and chief priestess of Kho.

In as few words as possible he recounted the results of the northern campaign. The enemy had suffered heavy losses, he told her. However, when Phoeken realized even his genius mind couldn't outwit an enemy so at home on the mountainous terrain, he had ultimately withdrawn his troops to the east. In fact, General Wahesa's intelligence supported the notion that Phoeken had personally abandoned the campaign much earlier and gone to Qoqada. There he had presumably taken over as direct commander of the ongoing siege against the bee city.

"Had the coward not been so eager to show me his backside," Kwasin said, "I would have brought back his ugly head for my empress."

Awineth did not look impressed, although she said, "Your wearisome bluster aside, you have done well to hold up the morale of Kho's children against my father's general." Then Awineth's expression darkened and her voice chilled. "But, as you say, you were not really fighting him these past weeks. While his army kept Dythbeth's forces occupied in the Saasamaro, he left and turned his attentions elsewhere. A soldier as cunning as Phoeken is not stupid enough to be baited if it does not somehow serve his own plans. The men he lost while you holed up his army were a calculated sacrifice. While you played soldier in the mountains and lost sight of the bigger picture, Phoeken was pulling my father's armies from the east to repress the rebellions in Awamuka, Qoqada, Minanlu, and Kaarquth. With sly promises of amnesty and forgiveness, Phoeken persuaded a number of the more craven inhabitants of those cities to lower their defenses. Now each of the cities has fallen. Only Dythbeth remains to stand against my father and his blasphemous followers."

The news left Kwasin mute. If he had been played for a fool, then so had Hahinqo and Wahesa; but as king of Dythbeth, Kwasin would take the full brunt of responsibility for any errors in strategy. He could dismiss Hahinqo and have him executed, but that would do nothing to lessen Kwasin's blame in the eyes of his people and the empress.

"What of the resistance in the mountains above Khokarsa?"

Awineth took a deep breath. "The great shrine at Kloepeth has also been taken. My father has subverted the lawful authority of the priestesses there and placed them under the rule of the priests."

The courtiers about the royal dais gasped as one. Minruth's actions were of the deepest sacrilege, a direct insult to Great Kho Herself.

"Do not underestimate my father's madness," Awineth continued. "It's said that those priestesses who resisted have been exiled to the northern shore. Popular rumor has it, however, that the ships that carried them were lost in a storm, along with all crew and passengers. But my intelligence has uncovered an even darker truth: the captives were not lost at sea but rather murdered en route and their bodies weighted and dropped into the Kemu. I was lucky to escape when I did, though Kho knows, the journey I undertook for the Goddess was terrible in itself." Awineth remained silent before Kwasin and the shocked courtiers. Then she said, "My father has crossed a very dangerous line, one which threatens the fate of the entire empire. I have received word from the new oracle at Khokarsa, who remains in hiding in the mountains above the capital, that she has been blessed with a vision from the Goddess. Kho warns Her children that the war between the priests and the priestesses threatens to break apart the very foundations of the world. That is why the great earthquake struck the island and why the earth's upheavals become more frequent."

Seeing Kwasin grow somber at the news, Awineth laughed haughtily. "You fashioned yourself a returning hero, didn't you? But now you find you are merely a child playing a game you can barely comprehend. Alas, if I had been here I could have advised you. Strategy is a grand mosaic, *King* Kwasin—concentrate on one tile and you miss the larger work."

Kwasin's face grew hot. Awineth's words came dangerously close to openly defying his authority. Military matters fell exclusively under the domain of the king, and although Awineth, as empress, outranked him, custom held that even the high priestess of Kho only advised, not dictated, the actions of any city's army and navy. Awineth's deriding tone, however, said otherwise, and Kwasin felt his authority dwindling with each word that passed from Awineth's lips. Were she not Kho's holy vicar, he would not have stood for it. Still, he had to say something to assert his power; but when he opened his mouth to speak, he received a cold and warning glare from Weth.

Minruth's daughter followed the gaze and said, "Your wife the queen has told me of your visit with the sacred oracle of Dythbeth. Since the oracle is reluctant to leave the old temple, I have summoned her priestess and sent back another to take her place. Qenwath has told me of Wasemquth's vision about you. Of the great serpent that divides your soul and holds your destiny...and the fate of all the land." Awineth leaned forward on her throne, and now keen excitement seemed to erase some of the tiredness from her gray eyes. "But Queen Weth has also told me something else, a thing that may be of great significance given the oracle's prophecy. It is said that Sahhindar, the brother of Resu himself, has appeared upon the island! And you, O Kwasin, by your very confession, have seen the Archer God in the flesh!"

When the courtiers had finished with their whisperings, Kwasin said, "It is true, O Queen, that in the hills outside the capital I encountered a man who met the description of Sahhindar. But what has that to do with the oracle's prophecy?"

"That is yet to be determined," Awineth said coldly. "Everyone knows that Sahhindar, like you, was exiled for displeasing the Mother of All, and that similarity is enough to cast doubt upon you, O Kwasin."

"Doubt!" Kwasin howled, laughing. "Do you think I conspire with the Archer God against Kho and all Her—"

Awineth cut off his words with an angry wave. "Say no more! Does the King of Dythbeth think to dispute the words of Kho's high priestess?" Awineth's eyes flashed with outrage, and for a moment Kwasin believed she would order the guards to attack him. But then her eyes softened, although the haughtiness remained in them. "I need you, Kwasin," she said. "I don't deny it. The people of Dythbeth will require much inspiration in the days ahead, and you have proven yourself a worthy warrior if not so much of a keen strategist. Don't worry, I will help you with the latter. For now, what you need to know is that my father has ordered his generals to let the mainland cities go and regroup their forces here. He wants to clean out any remaining opposition on the island before setting out to retake the mainland cities. Dythbeth has been a thorn in the empire's side for far too long, so my father seeks to aggrandize his armies by recruiting from among the wild mountain men beyond the northern coast. With promises of women and loot, he is also luring the wild Klemqaba from the southwestern mountains along the Kemu. He intends to raze your city once and for all and give the spoils to the half-men."

Kwasin felt incensed at the prospect of proud Dythbeth pillaged by the half-neanderthaloids, but even more so at Awineth's condescension. But Awineth had said she needed him…though he suspected that once he led Dythbeth to victory, she would find a way to absolve herself from her debt to him. The thought pushed to the surface his deepest concern, and he could no longer hold back the question that had burned within him since laying eyes upon the woman in the great hall.

"What has become of my cousin Hadon?" he asked, not sure he wanted an answer. "Has he too flown into Dythbeth's welcoming arms?" As winner of the Great Games, Hadon was betrothed to Awineth and should have been at her side. While Minruth's blasphemy had naturally removed his authority in the eyes of the priestesses, Hadon's claim to the throne remained valid. But then, perhaps Hadon had died helping Awineth and the others escape from Khokarsa. He could only hope.

Awineth's pale face reddened. "Hadon is a traitor," she spat. "He has flown to his backwater city, along with his filthy Witch-from-the-Sea and her companions. Should you run across them in your travels, you are to execute them on sight or feel the wrath of Kho!"

Awineth might have said more but suddenly a commotion arose from beyond the chamber's entryway. The great doors swung open and a herald called out in a hasty lapse of court protocol, "Holy priestess, General Wahesa of Mukha!"

The general strode so swiftly past the doors that the trumpeters and bullroarers had no time to sound their instruments. Anger stormed upon Wahesa's stern features, and behind him through the doors Kwasin could see many Mukhan soldiers standing with spears drawn at the vastly outnumbered palace guards.

Both Awineth and Weth rose halfway from their seats, clearly shocked and angered at Wahesa's ill-mannered entry, and, as Kwasin turned to face the new audient, he heard the women's startled gasps.

Wahesa, his face flushed with anger, had drawn his *tenu*. Its blade pointed directly at Kwasin.

13

Awineth now stood up fully from her throne and leveled a finger at Wahesa. "General, explain this violation of the queen's court!"

Wahesa's head ticked as he apparently struggled to find words lost in the raging seas of his anger. Finally, looking up at Kwasin with an expression of intense hatred, he said, "I have just received word from the temple. The priestesses have performed the proper rituals and found my wife to be with child!"

"Then you should be celebrating, general," Awineth said, her voice heavy with indignation, "instead of violating my private council and attacking my guards."

Before Wahesa could reply, Kwasin folded his arms over his great chest and threw his head back in laughter.

"I do not deny bedding your woman!" he said. "But don't fault me because your priestess frowns upon your lack of skill in the art of lovemaking!" And with those words Kwasin reached out a mighty paw, grabbed the blunt end of Wahesa's *tenu*, and plucked the sword right out of the man's grasp as easily if he were pulling up a stem of dried grass to clean his teeth. Kwasin cast the *tenu* to the tiled floor and said, "Don't feel too badly, general—it makes you no less of a man that Daka desires me. You should be honored. Not only am I the greatest lover in the land, but I am also a king. Besides, I don't want either your woman or the child, so what is your quarrel with me?"

"Silence!"

Kwasin turned to regard Weth, who had vacated her throne and now stood at the foot of the dais. The queen's clenched fists trembled, her eyes consumed with passionate rage.

"Not only are the actions of both of you an outrage to me," Weth said icily, "but you have also both affronted the graces of Kho's high vicar." She turned to glare at Kwasin. "Your shameful behavior reminds me of Minruth and his squabbling priests. We are in the midst of a civil war!"

Wahesa placed a hand upon the hilt of his short sword. "A war which cannot be won without the armies of Mukha," he said.

The Queen of Dythbeth looked at the general as if she wanted to draw the ceremonial dagger that hung on her hip and use it to flay the man alive. But instead she heaved a deep sigh and said, "How do you know, general, that my husband is the father of the child Daka carries?"

"The priestess in the Temple of Kho told me I cannot be the father," Wahesa replied. "And I have seen the way Daka looks at Kwasin. Once again the man has violated a priestess of Kho—the blasphemer should never have been allowed back from his exile!"

"A priestess cannot be violated if she takes a lover willingly," Weth said, "even if she is married to another." She narrowed her eyes at Kwasin. "I shall speak with Daka and determine—"

"And before that I will have Kwasin's head!" Wahesa cried, drawing his short sword and advancing on Kwasin.

Still smirking, Kwasin reached for his own sword. He left it sheathed, however, when many courtiers began running up the steps of the dais, inexplicably ignoring the fight about to break out between their king and the general of Mukha.

Kwasin turned to face the dais. Awineth lay in a heap on the floor beneath her throne. Many priestesses converged around her, one of them placing Awineth's head in her lap and whispering quiet words to her queen. Another priestess rushed from a side room carrying a ceramic urn and a swath of white cloth. She broke through the circle of women and knelt at Awineth's side, moistened the cloth with water from the urn, and began stroking the cloth across Awineth's forehead. A moment later Awineth's eyes fluttered open and she regarded the faces around her as if they were strangers and she had no idea of her whereabouts.

The woman who had brought the cloth, whom Kwasin recognized as a priestess of medicine, asked for the throne room to be cleared, but Awineth sat up and lazily shook her head. With a croaking voice she insisted that the audience remain, and after the priestesses lifted her back onto her throne, she exclaimed, albeit weakly, "I have been granted a vision from the Goddess!"

Astonished gasps filled the chamber. Kwasin, though not one of the gaspers, felt an icy chill run down his spine at the thought of Kho's spirit manifesting itself in his presence. Wahesa, he noticed, had sheathed his sword and was looking worriedly toward the throne. It seemed his anger had passed with Awineth's swoon.

Awineth waited as shock of her pronouncement settled in among the chamber's occupants. After a lengthy period of silence, she said, "Kho is angry at the bickering of Her children. She warns that Her worshipers will destroy themselves if they do not forget their petty disagreements and come together for the good of the Goddess and the land. Kho decrees that it is especially important for the matter of the unborn child to be settled as She wills, or terrible strife will fall upon Her people. The child is destined to become a tremendous force in the unfolding of the future, one who will sway events of great magnitude. It is the judgment of Kho that the child will be raised by the king and queen of Dythbeth. The honor of Wahesa has not been sullied, for it was the Goddess Herself who ordained the adultery. To prove his fealty to the Goddess, however, King Kwasin must guard against future infidelities. If he fails in this regard, he and his future kin will surely tempt Great Kho's wrath."

Then the empress rose from her throne, her frame slouching with apparent fatigue. "The matter is settled," she said. "The Goddess has spoken and I will hear no more of it." Then, shooing off her attendants, Awineth descended the dais to make her way from the chamber. As she passed Kwasin, she stopped briefly and in a low, scornful tone whispered, "If you do not keep out of trouble, I will have another vision, this one decreeing your immediate execution." With one last glare at Kwasin, she exited the chamber with her attendants in tow.

14

Kwasin staggered down the wide marble steps of his totem hall, feeling as if the Shapeless Shaper had snatched his soul and stretched its ghostly form until it oozed like a thick, spectre-laden syrup from his throbbing skull. He had spent the afternoon deep in his cups among his fellow Bear people, participating in an array of wild rituals as he and his totem brothers celebrated their recent victories against Minruth and the profaners of Kho. But that had not been Kwasin's only reason for imbibing the many great pitchers of mead and millet and sorghum beer offered him. While he held little trust in Awineth's vision and her interpretation of the oracle's vague words, deep in his heart doubt assailed him. Had he truly failed the Goddess by indulging in his loveplay with Daka? Had he thereby jeopardized not only the fate of the land, but also the outcome of Kho's great struggle against Her impudent son, Resu? Because of Kwasin's lustful indiscretion, Wahesa had almost pulled his troops from battle, an action that would have surely spelled doom for Dythbeth and all the worshipers of Kho on the island. Only Awineth's swooning vision, whether a sly ruse or a true warning from Kho, had prevented disaster.

No, he had not come to celebrate what in all likelihood was merely a fleeting victory for Dythbeth. Rather he had entered the hall of the Klakordeth to forget himself in an orgy of drinking. By the time he departed the hall, however, he found the alcohol had only deepened his feelings of remorse.

Too drunk to successfully descend even the broad, shallow steps of the hall, Kwasin lowered his great frame to his haunches and sat halfway down the steps, head and heart beating drums of pain.

"Those who try to avoid destiny through drink often forge a worse one!"

The voice that rang out from behind clanged in Kwasin's inebriated head like many large bronze gongs. As the voice echoed against the insides of his skull, he thought it sounded vaguely familiar. Then, when he placed it, he groaned and cradled his head deeper into his chest.

"Go away, bard," Kwasin's deep voice rumbled, "or I'll call my Bear brothers to take you inside and make you perform the Dance of the Castrated Baboon!"

A moment later Bhako was sitting on the steps beside Kwasin. "I merely read aloud one of the inscriptions carved into the stone archway above the College of

Awines," Bhako said, pointing to the grand structure opposite the sea of pedestrians, "surely the wisest son our city has ever spawned. And how he was treated! Exiled to Bawaku because the syllabary he invented was considered sacrilegious—but how times have changed! Now he is revered in the city that once spurned him and the syllabary is taught in every temple. Even you can read at least a little of it. No doubt you have taken notice and reflected many times upon the irony of that particular inscription. After all, the archway faces the hall of the Klakordeth, as well as the Temple of Khukhaken, both home to many great drinkers. And, according to my research as royal bard, two of your most frequent haunts before your exile."

Kwasin considered tossing the bard down the steps but even the thought of lifting a hand made his stomach lurch with sickness. Finally, when his belly settled somewhat and no longer felt as if it might erupt like holy Khowot, he managed to say, "I take no advice from a man who died trying to fly."

"It is said that Awines never drank beer or wine," Bhako said, "but was rather drunk on wisdom. If I might humbly offer some of the latter…"

Kwasin dragged up his head and glared darkly at the bard. The man's voice was all too cheerful, and Kwasin decided that, if he must, he would risk being sick for a chance to throttle the loudmouthed troubadour. Bhako, however, was already getting up to leave.

"Then I'll say nothing," Bhako said in apparent surrender. The bard headed down the steps, but upon reaching the street, he turned and called up quietly, "Except that it will do no good for the citizens' morale to see their king hung over. If he must be in public, he should at least go to the temple of the Great Mother, where the congregators might think their king reels with divine rather than worldly spirits."

Bhako's white robes became lost in the sea of pedestrians thronging the busy avenue.

For a great while Kwasin sat on the steps, at first occupying his beer-sodden mind with ways he might torment the bard the next time they met. But then Kwasin cursed. Bhako, though an annoying fool, was right. Kwasin knew his indiscretions had caused enough trouble already and he did not want to further undermine the effort of the Goddess by having his people doubt his competency as king. It would do no harm to go to the temple and make an offering. Besides, he didn't feel like returning to the palace and dealing with Weth and the empress.

His mind made up, he swayed upright on wobbly legs. Immediately Kwasin's guards, who had been standing farther up the steps under the awning of the totem hall, came to their king and surrounded him. His head still throbbing from drink, Kwasin tottered off toward the temple.

When at last he stood before the garden that nestled in front of the Temple of Kho, he knew he had made the right decision. The walk along the temple road had helped invigorate his alcohol-numbed limbs and already the fog of his mind was lifting. A priestess who emerged from the garden path smiled when she saw her king but, smelling alcohol on his breath, she blanched. Doubtless she recalled Kwasin's drunken visit to the temple nine years ago. Nevertheless, after calling back down the path for two of her initiates to accompany her, the woman bade Kwasin to follow, taking him down a narrow trail off the main pathway that ended at an artesian well. Here Kwasin was permitted to drink—which he did, deeply—after which he was asked to take off his clothes. The priestesses then blessed him with libations of the painfully frigid well water, which left Kwasin shivering despite the oppressive mugginess of the overcast summer day. He was then led back to the main path and from there to the steps of the great domed temple itself.

Kwasin climbed the steps and entered the building's nine-sided entrance, passing through the outer chamber, with its pale red-and-blue toned murals depicting the creation of the world by Kho. He tried to ignore the occasional giggle or passionate murmurings that arose from an adjoining room where the holy prostitutes entertained their patrons. His business here was not that of carnal pleasure, after all, but rather to ask forgiveness for the trouble his great lust had caused in the first place.

He left behind the outer chamber and entered the next room. Here he knelt before a broad-based altar crouched on nine ornately gilded iron legs. The lack of food offerings startled him. Prayer beads and other religious trinkets had replaced the usual offerings of fruits, berries, and bowls of cow, goat, sheep, and hare blood. Despite the trinkets, the altar's welcoming base lay mostly bare. The priestess who accompanied him, noting his concern, remarked, "Food becomes scarce even among the rich. If the king does not wish to spare his supper, a precious belonging will suffice."

Kwasin nodded. "It is wrong," he said, "to deprive Kho of Her proper offerings. Summon one of my guards to bring back a bowl of fresh bull's blood from the palace to place upon the altar." The woman raised her brows as if unaware any cattle still lived in the city, then departed on her mission.

Things were getting more desperate than he'd realized. Now he wondered forlornly if his Bear brothers would be left without drink, having squandered the last of their dwindling supply of alcohol upon their insatiable king. Phoeken's soldiers still ranged the countryside outside the city and, according to Awineth, treaties were being made that would pull troops from across the empire to once again lay siege to Dythbeth. Kwasin's patrols had found little to salvage from the burned and pillaged farmlands, and the bay had already been fished out to support the pitiful remnants of Dythbeth's navy. The arrival of Wahesa's armies only made an already grave situation much worse.

Kwasin prostrated himself and prayed. He had always been able to take care of himself, even against the worst of odds. But now he was responsible for an entire city and, by the grace of Kho, the empire itself. Though he knew how to inspire men to face their deaths, he now admitted he had little knowledge about how to govern and protect them in the long term. Perhaps Awineth had come along at just the right time. Though a manipulative she-demon, she was shrewd, and because of her experience in her father's court, she might know enough of politics to steer the unwieldy population and keep it from revolt. And as long as she felt his presence inspired the allies of the Goddess, she would put up with him. But as soon as she felt differently, then—

He started as he looked up from his prostrations. He had thought himself alone in the room, but now in a dark corner he saw a pair of eyes glimmer with the flicker of the torchlight.

"Come out of the shadows and show yourself!" Kwasin's words echoed queerly from the walls of the stone room.

Suddenly a woman emerged from the darkness. It was Nelahnes, keeper of the temple and the priestess who had presided over Kwasin and Weth's marriage ceremony. The shapeliness of the woman's nearly naked form made Kwasin's heart beat faster and he leered at the priestess, temporarily forgetting the great problems that assailed him.

"I am impressed," Nelahnes said, running a hand suggestively over the girdle of gold circlets that adorned her otherwise bare thigh. "Is the mighty King Kwasin humbler than I have been led to believe?"

"O priestess, your breathtaking beauty does indeed make me humble!"

Kwasin's heart fluttered like the wings of a bee ready to pollinate. It had been too long. His many attempts to get Weth into bed since their marriage had failed. It was no wonder he had fallen victim of Daka's passions, and could Kho really begrudge his needs? Had not the Goddess Herself imbued Kwasin with the lust of the stag?

He could not mistake the woman's longing gaze, and neither could he mistake the flames of lust that consumed him. Suddenly he found himself being led by the priestess back through the first chamber and into one of side rooms reserved for the divine whores. Once inside, Nelahnes kissed him wetly upon the lips, and then she was pushing him gently away so she could slip out of her girdle. Languidly, she stretched out upon the room's well-cushioned divan and, moaning softly, beckoned Kwasin to join her.

Kwasin did not need the invitation. Even his hangover could not take away the impulses that now possessed him, and he lay down upon the divan, nearly smothering the woman with his passionate embrace. Unlike Weth those many years ago, Nelahnes did not resist Kwasin's advances but only pulled him closer, whispering her amorous enthusiasm heavily in his ear.

Just as Kwasin began to lose himself in their lovemaking, he thought he heard something in the chamber behind him. By Adeneth's great breasts! he thought, unable to dismiss the feeble though persistently nagging voice which was all that remained of a conscience otherwise buried by lust. Though he tried, he could not shake the feeling that an angry Queen Weth stood behind him, her dagger falling toward his unfaithful back.

He turned around just in time to see a soldier running at him with his spear. Kwasin rolled out of the divan, one naked foot kicking out sidewise to deflect the oncoming spear, the other aimed at the soldier's kneecap. Though Kwasin, now on the floor, did not see what happened next, he later reconstructed it from the three sounds that followed: a sharp cracking, a man's throaty cry, and a woman's husky scream. The cracking was the soldier's kneecap snapping under Kwasin's blow. The man then reeled forward toward the divan, crying out in pain, his spear still extended before him. The woman screaming was Nelahnes reacting to the spear that had just impaled her abdomen.

Kwasin leaped up and, pulling the soldier from the moaning woman, hurled him against a wall. The man, trying to recover, drew his iron sword as he pulled himself up on one leg. Kwasin now recognized his opponent as Rowaku, the same sergeant who seemed suspicious of Kwasin's allegiances during the journey to the old temple in the swamps. Before the man could even hobble a single step, Kwasin pulled the spear from Nelahnes' body and ran the weapon's long, two-edged blade deep into Rowaku's chest. Blood spurted from the man's mouth as he collapsed and, in the room's dim torchlight, sprayed Kwasin's naked frame with dark crimson.

On the divan, Nelahnes was gasping and bubbling her last breaths. She had rolled onto her side. Blood streamed down one corner of her mouth, and she cradled her knees to her chest. Kwasin knelt beside her and grabbed the woman by the back of the neck, forcing her to look into his eyes.

"You lured me here to assassinate me!"

Nelahnes said nothing. Her eyes screamed with silent horror.

Kwasin drew close and whispered in the woman's ear. "You're not dead yet," he said. "A gut wound is bad enough, but I can make your last precious moments much more painful. Speak, priestess!"

Nelahnes sputtered, coughing, but a moment later she managed to talk, though with some difficulty. "Fortune brought you to me…or so I thought. Rowaku was to kill you before he escorted you back to the palace. Then you came to the temple and…knowing your reputation…I…I figured I would provide more than ample distraction for Rowaku to complete his mission." Now Nelahnes' teeth glistened with blood and smile. "Taphiru and I were to share the throne," she continued, her voice rasping heavily. "You have spoiled my half of our plans, but my lover will still rule Dythbeth." She laughed, coughing up more blood. "Minruth has promised it to him…assassins…many…paid off several in high places…and already his arrogant daughter Awineth…and your wife…" The woman's lids fluttered for a moment and then her eyes glazed with death.

Kwasin grew cold. He rose and ran from the death-scented room, retrieving his clothes and sword from where they had been laid out for him just outside the entryway to the first chamber. As he hastily donned his kilt, the priestess came up the temple steps bearing the bowl of bull's blood he had requested for the altar. The woman looked in horror at the blood smearing Kwasin's body and gasped, her trembling hands threatening to drop her burden. She must have thought history repeated itself and he had again raped a priestess and slain the temple guards. He could have tried to explain, but he could spare no time. The lives of the queen and the empress were in danger, if the two had not been assassinated already. He leaped down the steps past the priestess, whom he heard cry out for help a few moments later. Apparently she had discovered the body of her superior, Nelahnes. He would have much to sort out later, but just now he needed to get to the palace.

His guards, minus the man he had killed, were waiting for him on the street as he bolted from the garden path. He shouted at them to follow in haste and without question if they valued the lives of their queen and empress. Still, he did not trust the men. Where one traitor could be planted, so could another, especially when someone as prestigious as the keeper of Kho's sacred temple was party to the conspiracy.

All too long seemed the temple road as Kwasin ran along it in the direction of the palace, but finally he was crossing the moat and sprinting up the palace steps. As he passed inside, he volleyed orders at the royal guards to lock down the palace and to seek out and protect Queen Weth and the empress. The guards jumped as one to carry out their tasks, though Kwasin could not but wonder if one or possibly even all of the men could be in on the plot. Perhaps he should not have warned the guards at all but rather acted as if nothing out of the ordinary were underway. Too late for that. But then again, if the men were part of the coup, wouldn't they have attacked the king when he approached? He shook the questions from his mind and concentrated on finding Awineth and Weth as quickly as possible.

He entered the throne room and found it empty, then passed into the queen's antechamber, startling three priestesses who cried out at seeing Kwasin's blood-streaked countenance.

"Where is your queen?" Kwasin growled.

"She is in her chambers and not to be disturbed." The priestess who spoke moved in front of the passageway leading to the queen's quarters. "The queen has commanded it!" the woman added when Kwasin advanced toward her.

Kwasin's face must have blackened at her words, for the woman shrank before him, although she did not move from her position blocking the doorway.

"The queen is in danger! I don't care about—"

A woman screamed somewhere down the corridor. The priestess before him dropped a hand to the dagger on her hip, and now Kwasin understood why the customary guards were not stationed outside the queen's antechamber. The three priestesses were part of the conspiracy.

With a shout of rage, Kwasin shoved the woman out of his way and dashed down the corridor toward Weth's chamber. He turned at the end of the hallway and entered the room, his rage turning to anguish at the sight that met him.

Weth's unmoving form lay sprawled in the room's center, her white robe now darkened with red. An expanding puddle of blood pooled across the bright, mosaic-tiled flooring. Kwasin knelt beside his wife but dread Sisisken had already taken her spirit. He kissed her dead lips, swearing to holy Kho that he would make her murderer pay.

Whoever had killed her must have done so only moments before. He scanned the room for an exit other than the corridor from which he had entered. He saw nothing until his eyes alighted on a stone block in the wall directly adjoining a large wooden wardrobe. The large block, though identical with its companions, was set slightly ajar. Further, the murals painted on the plastered wall above it looked a shade brighter than those adorning the rest of the chamber, as if someone had recently moved the wardrobe from the spot.

He knelt by the block of stone and ran his fingers along its exposed edges until he found a groove that permitted a fingerhold. Kwasin pulled with his fingertips and the large rectangular stone facing swung out easily on oiled hinges, revealing the dark maw of a sharply descending tunnel. He knew of the complex maze of passageways that snaked beneath the palace, utilized by the priests and priestesses for their secretive purposes, though he had not yet had time to explore those accessible to the king. Quickly, he grabbed a torch from a wall sconce and descended into the pitch-black abyss.

After making several dizzying turns in the seemingly unending labyrinth, Kwasin began to doubt the wisdom of his actions. He cursed, realizing he had lost his way in the dark warrens when Awineth needed him most. Then, just as he determined he would try to retrace his steps back to Weth's chamber, he noticed a faint glow from a side tunnel ahead. Kwasin tossed his torch down the tunnel behind him, not wanting to alert anyone ahead of his presence, and padded forward toward the light.

The side tunnel narrowed, forcing Kwasin to turn his massive shoulders and proceed sideways. Now the floor angled sharply as the tunnel rose back toward the lower levels of the palace. At a reckless pace, Kwasin shuffled up the steep incline, once falling on his stomach, the skin on his chest scraping painfully against the rough flooring as he slid downward. But Kwasin was, if anything, a creature of stubborn determination. He thought of Weth's pale, lifeless face, picked himself up, and ascended again.

Light streamed through an opening above and ahead of him. Finally, his hands and knees bloodied, Kwasin pulled himself up to the lip of the opening and gazed into a spacious chamber. Three men, two of them bearing spears, stood with their backs to him in front of Awineth, who had drawn her long, jeweled ceremonial dagger. She was cursing the men, calling them traitors that the Goddess would wipe from the face of the earth like insignificant insects. On the other hand, she told them, if they put down their weapons and swore allegiance to her, she would make sure they were properly rewarded with *nasuhno* and positions of power in the government.

The man in the center, a mohawk-headed priest, laughed at her. "All that separates me from the kingship of Dythbeth is your death. By now my assassins have killed that loutish giant Kwasin—only Resu knows how he was allowed to ascend the throne—and I myself have just thrust my own dagger into the breast of Queen Weth."

A red haze filled Kwasin's vision as at last he recognized the man who stood before him—Taphiru, the treacherous priest and murderer of King Roteka. But how had the priest entered the city? Only the most loyal of sentries had been posted at the city's gates. One of them, however, must have betrayed his king and empress. He would interrogate the sentries later.

Rage broiling within, Kwasin leaped at the three men. He did not possess his ax, having left it under guard in his palace quarters when he had departed for his totem hall, but he still wore a short, heavy sword. He pulled the blade from its scabbard and slashed deeply into the neck of the soldier on his right, cutting clean through the man's leather neck guard.

Taphiru leaped forward toward Awineth, but the empress lunged viciously at the man with her dagger. Taphiru tried to retreat, but ran into the falling body of the second soldier, whom Kwasin had just cut down with his sword. The priest skidded to his knees, then moaned in panic as he tried to leapfrog away from Kwasin. But the man did not leap quickly enough. With the butt end of his sword's hilt, Kwasin knocked the dagger from the priest's hand and encircled his own giant hand around his victim's throat. Taphiru's eyes bulged in their sockets, but Kwasin only squeezed harder. He did not intend to kill the priest—not yet anyway. There was too much information that could be wrung from him, knowledge about who had participated in the plot to overthrow Awineth and the royalty of Dythbeth.

Then, unexpectedly, Taphiru's body jerked violently and his face underwent an abrupt metamorphosis. His lips, which had been pulled back over his teeth as he struggled for breath, went limp, and his eyes, just a moment before trying to leap from his skull, softened and became dull.

Kwasin looked down and saw the tip of a dagger disappear from where it had protruded out of the center of Taphiru's stomach. He released his grip on the priest, who toppled to the floor.

On the other side of Taphiru's corpse stood Awineth, clutching in both hands the bloodied ceremonial dagger, her dark eyes flaming with wild satisfaction.

15

Kwasin could not blame Awineth for killing the priest. Bloodlust in the heat of battle was not a thing to be second guessed, certainly not by him. Still, in the weeks that followed, he could not deny the problems caused that day by Taphiru's death. Not only had Awineth by her actions forever silenced the plot's chief instigator, but a short time later three bodies were found in the palace, their necks broken. The corpses were those of the priestesses who tried to prevent Kwasin from stopping Weth's murder. Someone in the palace from among the priests, priestesses, or military had silenced the three women, and that person—or persons—would be after Kwasin and his empress.

One thing did become simpler for Kwasin after the attacks: Awineth now seemed to trust him, at least more than she had before. And while she did not always include him in her decision making, she did summon him frequently to her royal offices. Once she even spoke of rebuilding the navy and sending a great fleet to plunder Hadon's outpost city after the war on the island was won. The city's great wealth, she said, would help the empire get back on its feet; and of course, she had an old score to settle with Hadon. She would give Kwasin command of the fleet, as well as half her share of the spoils, if he would bring back Hadon's head. Kwasin grinned with approval at the idea, and also pleased that Awineth now included him in her distant plans.

In the many meetings he attended, Kwasin fought to remain silent as Awineth voiced her decrees—for the Empress of Khokarsa did not consider her ideas about Dythbeth's future open for discussion, even with the city's king. Very often, however, Kwasin's patience wore thin. Upon one such occasion he erupted in protest at Awineth's unquestioning reliance upon the network of priestesses.

"You cannot use them!" Kwasin complained. "They can no longer be trusted!"

Awineth rose from her seat, her beautiful features made harsh with anger.

"The coup could only have succeeded in killing the queen," Kwasin went on before she could speak, "because some of your faithful priestesses have forsaken their sacred vow to Kho."

"The disloyal priestesses were not under my direct supervision," Awineth snapped. "I cannot be faulted if Queen Weth failed to properly screen her attendants.

But that is a minor issue compared to the larger one you raise. If the people believed that I, Kho's high vicar, had no faith in the network of priestesses, the entire resistance on the island would crumble in an instant. We are in a Time of Troubles unlike any other, Kwasin! My father seeks to establish the primacy of the male, and everywhere across the empire his irreverent priests are lifting up the sungod to the level of the Goddess. And my sources tell me this is not the worst to come, that my father not only seeks to make Kho the subordinate of Resu, but that he will ultimately throw Her from the pantheon altogether! He would have done so already but the people need time to adjust to his deceptions. While the townsfolk might go along with his blasphemy, those in the country—and they are numerous—are less willing to believe my father's lies. Already he places great strains upon their patience by recruiting the island's rural population to continue work on the Great Tower, even as he sends their fathers, brothers, and sons to fight and die in his profane war."

Kwasin shook his great mane of hair. "I have had enough!" he exclaimed. "As we sit cowering in the palace with our poison testers, Minruth the Mad will kill us in our sleep. You won't win this war until you have rid yourself of the rats your father has set among us!"

Awineth looked at him skeptically. "And how do you propose to do that?"

"I will bait them myself! Each traitor I find will wish he had never heard the name of Kwasin!"

"Or 'she,'" Awineth added mockingly.

Still smarting from Nelahnes' betrayal, Kwasin almost lost control of his anger. Then Awineth smiled.

"Do what you must," she said. "Military matters are your concern, and about that I can do nothing. There are provisions in the law, however, for those who interfere in religious matters. And until the priestesses decide the issue of Queen Weth's successor, I am the interpreter of the law."

As Kwasin turned to leave, Awineth added, "And watch yourself around Kho's daughters—they have all been ordered to steer clear of you. I know of your passions, Kwasin, but if you find a woman who seeks to entice you, she may well give you a kiss as welcoming as Nelahnes'."

Scowling, Kwasin left the room.

For the first time since he had been crowned king, the throngs of increasingly disgruntled citizens watched Kwasin leave the palace grounds unaccompanied by armed escort. General Hahinqo had blanched when Kwasin told him his plans and urged his king to reconsider. Kwasin, however, remained firm. The only way to fight an invisible enemy, he said, was to draw him out, to make him think one's guard had been lowered. Finally, sensing the battle over his king's notion lost, the general had shrugged and set off to oversee the construction of new siege defenses.

Kwasin felt for Hahinqo's great burden. Minruth's forces were already reassembling in the hills beyond the great plain, in numbers that daunted even the combined might of the Dythbethan and Mukhan armies. Hahinqo was in the process of drawing back the allied forces, while simultaneously organizing the remainder of his soldiers to undertake the excavation of great trenches in the earth on the perimeter of the city's outer wall. The trenches would make the enemy's task of storming the city much harder. Further, new spears, javelins, and oil-soaked missiles that could be hurled from the walls needed to be made, and the general was organizing a civilian auxiliary army—mostly made up of women and children—to help with the weapon-making. All that, Kwasin knew, would be a wasted effort if his plan failed.

The crowds parted before their king as he strode forth through the streets. Every now and then Kwasin noticed a familiar face in the crowd, but then he would look casually past the face and continue on. For the most part, however, he failed to see the men stationed in secret among the masses of pedestrians, or those who stood looking down at him from rooftops or out of high windows. The audaciousness of his plan, he thought to himself, was not that he allowed himself to walk among the people. Rather the plan hinged on the fact that the men of his secret guard were trustworthy and not in league with Minruth's conspirators. Hahinqo, however, had personally vouched for the men, and Kwasin made sure that each of them were handpicked from among those he had led into battle himself.

The first day Kwasin had gone out thus did nothing except to enflame the curiosity of the populace. Never had King Roteka walked abroad without escort among the masses, and he had certainly never mingled with the commoners in the taverns, as Kwasin did that afternoon and in the days that followed. At first, Awineth had chided Kwasin, warning him that he set a bad example for those in high office. Kwasin pointed out that his actions in no way broke any law, and that Awineth herself came dangerously close to committing an unlawful offense by interfering with a sensitive military operation. Awineth had fumed. She soon backed off, however, when she began to understand that an unanticipated benefit sprang from the king's unorthodox mixing with the lower classes. It seemed that Kwasin's descent into the coarser strata of Dythbeth's population, far from tarnishing his public image, only served to enhance it. The city's inhabitants were quickly coming to regard their king as one of their own, a real man of the people. This newfound enthusiasm for their king, Awineth realized, might be channeled into a potent weapon in winning the citizens' hearts and minds in this dark time of war, doubt, and famine. Meanwhile, gloating at Awineth's reluctant support, Kwasin proceeded with his plan.

The days passed and nothing eventful transpired. If any of the conspirators took note of Kwasin's habitual jaunts to the shops and drinking halls about the city, they did nothing to give themselves away. And then, just as Kwasin began to believe the traitors had either fled the city or were on to his game, an assassin drew forth from the shadows and struck.

Kwasin had been drinking one evening at the Inn of the Mute Hyena, a local watering hole frequented by palace servants not far from the royal citadel. He sat at a table in a semiprivate alcove overlooking the main room in which the tavern's patrons could be seen engaging in drinking, eating, and general merrymaking. The bar's clientele seemed especially jovial this night, despite the bad news coming in from the front. Kwasin was not greatly surprised. One reason might be that the tavern, serving the city's most wealthy, was still stocked with alcohol, a luxury that was becoming scarce in taverns that catered to the middle classes. But the real reason, he knew, was that the Dythbethan spirit soared freer than the spirits of the other cities in the empire. Next to the capital, Dythbeth ranked the second-oldest city on the island, and many times in its long history had its people stood up against would-be conquerors. This time, Kwasin reflected, might be different. The empire had expanded greatly since the days Dythbeth last thumbed its nose at the capital, and the forces wide and near that now assembled against the City of the Leopard God were unlike anything Kwasin's ancestors had ever faced.

And so, as he pondered the queendom's strengths and weaknesses, Kwasin failed to notice that the man who came to refill his flagon with sorghum beer was not the same who had served him earlier that evening. When he did realize it, it was almost too late.

Kwasin had just taken a deep swig of beer when shouts exploded from the kitchen. An instant later, two members of his secret guard burst out of the kitchen and into the room. Kwasin immediately spat out his mouthful of drink, believing his men had uncovered a plot to poison him. That, however, was not the danger.

As his men ran through the startled patrons to get to him, Kwasin sensed someone behind him. He grabbed hold of the table in front of him and whirled it behind. The table crashed into his server. A gleaming dagger flew into the air and clattered on the oaken floorboards. The mad lust of battle almost seized Kwasin as he leaped at his attempted assassin and throttled the fallen man. Then Kwasin remembered that the man must live or he would not be able to give up his secrets.

He released the man and thrust him at the guards who had now reached the scene. The assassin struggled, but Kwasin's men secured him in irons they had brought along for just this purpose. Before the captive was hauled off, Kwasin took a close look at the fellow. Though the man might have been mistaken for any bald-headed, middle-aged frequenter of the tavern, Kwasin noticed that his lack of hair was by design rather than natural; the man's pate, though bare, revealed a slightly darker shadow running down its center. It was obvious the man had recently shaved a narrow shock of dark hair from his head in an attempt to do away with the distinctive haircut that marked him as a priest of Resu.

That same day the traitor, a lower-echelon palace priest named Dykeko, was brought to a specially prepared cell beneath the palace citadel. Here Kwasin had arranged for a pet of the old king to be boarded and chained to a wall. This was a large and magnificent male leopard said to have been descended from the giant cat that once terrorized the inhabitants of ancient Dythbeth. Kwasin had discovered King Roteka's leopard by accident when a group of soldiers employed at the palace had carted out the proud, though half-emaciated beast. Since food was becoming scarce, the soldiers had intended to slaughter the leopard and divide the animal's meat among themselves. Kwasin, however, could not stand to see such a prideful creature killed with such disrespect, and certainly the spirit of Khukhaken would not look favorably upon Dythbeth's king if he allowed one of his leopard children to be dispatched in such a contemptuous manner. It was then that Kwasin realized he might have a way to use the animal that would at once please Khukhaken and also help root out the traitors.

Kwasin ordered the palace guard to have Dykeko chained to the wall opposite the leopard. The priest must have been frightened at the sight of the ravenous beast in the cell with him, but he managed to feign an air of indifference. Kwasin, looking through a barred window from an adjoining cell, asked the man to reveal his accomplices in the conspiracy to overthrow the rulers of Dythbeth. As he expected, despite the screams and thrashing about of the leopard, the priest refused to speak. Kwasin only smiled. Then he placed his hand upon the crank handle of the special winch he had had his people install in the cell.

Around the winch's spool wound a heavy chain that dropped into a hole in the stone floor. Beneath the floor, the chain crossed under the captive man's cell, up behind the far wall, and out through it. The end of the chain was attached to the leopard's bronze collar and was all that kept the beast from free rein of the cell.

Slowly, Kwasin turned the crank. One by one the links reeled out from the winch. When the leopard realized its chain had slackened, it leaped with wild frenzy at the man-thing shackled against the opposite wall of the cell. Dykeko yelled out in terror, causing the furious and hunger-driven leopard to hiss, scream, and yank harder against its chained collar.

With great effort, Kwasin reeled the animal away from the sweating man and back closer to its own wall.

Again, Kwasin asked the man to reveal his accomplices. Though the terrified captive had wet his kilt, he still refused to speak.

The leopard's chain again reeled out from the hole near the base of the wall. This time Kwasin spooled out even more slack, until the leopard's claws just grazed the captive man's torso and legs, leaving them streaked with blood. Then Kwasin reeled back the chain, but only by inches.

The beast's screams became so loud now that Kwasin had to shout to be heard above them.

"Tell me the names! Or I'll reel out the full length of the chain!"

The man sobbed. "You might as well!" he cried. "Minruth's spies will find a way to kill me even if you don't. And if I speak, you'll feed me to the leopard anyway!"

Kwasin grinned at the priest through the bars that separated them.

"Too bad then!" Kwasin yelled, and began inching forward the chain.

Suddenly Dykeko's will broke and he began shouting out names. Kwasin reeled back the beast but he asked how he could know for sure that Dykeko wasn't lying to save his skin.

"You'll find secret missives hidden beneath the flooring in my sister's home!" the man shouted. "They will reveal all!"

When Kwasin again began reeling forward the leopard, the man exclaimed, "What are you doing? I've told you what you want!"

"Khukhaken's son is hungry," Kwasin said dryly, but after gauging he had scared the man enough he pulled the leopard back to its side of the cell. The Leopard God's child would have to wait for his meal until Kwasin had verified the man's information.

Kwasin wasted no time in getting to the house of Dykeko's sister, since it was conceivable that the priest's accomplices, once they found out their colleague had been captured, would know to go there and destroy any evidence the man might have left behind. Kwasin waited in the house while his men pried up the floorboards and Dykeko's frightened sister and her husband looked on. Finally, one of the king's men called out, "Here! I think I've found something!"

Before Kwasin had time to cross the room to see what the soldier had uncovered, a low and heavy rumbling belched up from deep inside the earth's bowels. Then, the entire house shook violently.

"Kho awakes!" someone shouted.

16

The tremor lasted for thirty seconds. The room in which Kwasin stood rattled with such violence that his vision blurred. Halfway through the quaking, part of the building's roof collapsed, piling the soldiers on the other side of the room under a jagged heap of crumbled plaster and splintered cedar beams.

Little on earth frightened Kwasin, but the earthquake shot pangs of fear through him. He cried out to the Goddess and clutched the nearby doorframe as if he were riding the ferry that carried the dead to the dark depths of Sisisken's underworld.

Suddenly, the room ceased its terrible shaking. Kwasin ran to the pile of destruction that was the other side of the room and began heaving up beams and digging through the powdery plaster with his bare hands.

Finally he managed to reach those of his men who had been buried, only to find them all dead, crushed by Kho's wrath. But Kho, Kwasin thought, could not have been angry at him—at least not too angry. She had not only spared his life but also allowed him to pull up from the cracked and splintered flooring the evidence hidden by the priest Dykeko. After gathering up the papyrus scrolls, Kwasin and his surviving guards proceeded as quickly as possible out of the ruined building and into the streets.

The district's inhabitants were coming out of their houses and gaping at the destruction wrought by the Goddess. He had been lucky the building he was in had only partially collapsed. Down an adjoining street a long row of buildings had been thrown completely from their foundations. Each of these had collapsed one atop the next in an almost precise east-to-west pattern, as if Great Kho had flicked Her divine finger against a row of lined-up toy blocks. Perhaps in the west Khowot had again erupted and sent a shockwave eastward across the island. Standing amid the devastation of his own city, Kwasin could only hope this was the case, and that Minruth's capital lay smothered and utterly destroyed beneath a smoldering sea of burning ash and lava.

Kwasin and his men began thrusting their way through the throngs of distraught residents. Shock had turned to bitter anger. Having seen their king emerge from the half-ruined house, many began shouting at him, accusing him of bringing misfortune to their neighborhood with his ill-fated presence. Some yelled at him that he must surely be cursed, since their beloved King Roteka had been killed the very night Kwasin had returned to Dythbeth. And now, Queen Weth was dead at the hands of an assassin, and who knew how many had died in the earthquake?

Although they must have felt great trepidation, the guardsmen maintained a stoic demeanor and drew in closer about their king. Kwasin hoped they could reach a safer district before the mob got the notion to hurl at them the bricks, stones, and other debris that lay scattered across the street.

At last they arrived at the main road leading past the military barracks. Here a number of soldiers greeted him, giving their king a much different welcome from the one he had just received in the poverty-stricken environs behind him. Instead of feeling cursed by Kwasin's presence, the soldiers seemed heartened at the unexpected appearance of the king who had fought so valiantly at their side. Several men cheered out his name, but Kwasin could waste no time on adulation. As he jogged down the road, he shouted at those who were not already busy dealing with the earthquake's mayhem, telling them that any soldier who was able should make haste and accompany him to the palace, as their empress might be in desperate need of help. Immediately, the soldiers in range of his voice stopped what they were doing and joined their king.

When they neared the palace, Kwasin began to fear greatly for Awineth's safety. Even from a distance he could see that a massive fissure had cracked vertically down the face of the citadel's great dome, the dark, jagged breach looking like a lightning bolt in the negative. An enormous amount of granite must have tumbled down inside the palace's main chamber when the tremor struck. Anyone beneath the fissure—and Awineth's duties as empress brought her often to the throne room under the dome—would have been killed instantly.

By the time he was halfway across the bridge that spanned the moat, he could see a group of priestesses congregating near the base of the citadel's eastern side. He sighed heavily, surprised at the depth of his relief. Among them he spied Awineth. The queen's antechamber, which Awineth had occupied after Weth's death, was positioned along the eastern wall of the palace, and Kwasin guessed the empress and her attendants must have fled the room by means of secret tunnels of which he had no knowledge.

Kwasin's party had crossed half the distance between the bridge and the palace when without warning the earth again began to shake and rumble. The aftershock lasted for only a moment, but another mass of the royal palace's great dome tumbled inward, its crash thundering across the courtyard. Awineth and her priestesses could be seen fleeing down the rear steps of the palace, trying to get to a safe distance away from the damaged building.

Awineth's face was drawn and pale when Kwasin finally met up with her. She took Kwasin aside from the others and said, "I know you have much work to do, but the people will need to be reassured. They will need to see me as soon as possible, and I need you to arrange it. I have already instructed my priestesses to spread word that Kho is angry at the blasphemous traitors of Minruth who have infiltrated our city. If any among the citizenry know the names of the traitors, they had better surrender them immediately or they will be struck down."

"I have news on that front which will please you, O Queen." Kwasin held up the scrolls he had recovered from the house of Dykeko's sister. "I possess here the names of those who must be routed out."

"That is good news indeed," Awineth said. "But just before the temblor I received word from the oracle in the old temple. Wasemquth has revealed a dire prophecy from the Goddess." Awineth paused, and again Kwasin felt the unfamiliar fear course through him.

"Kho warns that if the old order is not soon maintained," Awineth continued, "She will destroy all the land, including Her faithful people. It is an ominous message, of which today's devastation is a clear harbinger, but I have begun to circulate the oracle's prophecy in the hope that it will rally the people of Dythbeth to fight even harder.

"And Kwasin," she said, surprising him by laying a hand gently upon his arm and looking up at him with softened eyes. "I will need to rely on you greatly in the days and months to come. As will the people. And for that reason, and that alone, it is best we are not at odds. Hadon, who would have been my king had he not turned and fled like a coward when I needed him most, has by his actions forsaken the Goddess. But there is no time to hold Great Games to determine who is worthy of Kho's high priestess. War, however, is a game greater than any staged contest, and in war you have indeed proven yourself a champion. Make no mistake, Kwasin, I do not love you, nor do I think that I, who have seen so much corruption and distrust, shall ever know love. The marriage will be one of convenience, and if I did not think it was necessary to win the war, it would never happen."

Even with her words of denial, she reached up and placed her hands about Kwasin's neck and, drawing down his head, kissed him warmly upon the lips. Kwasin, though he was later to lament the missed opportunity, was too surprised to respond.

When Awineth pushed him away a moment later, he found her eyes had returned to their usual cold gray.

"Your city is in ruins, O King," she said frostily. "Do not dally while your people are in need." And then she turned her back on him and rejoined the party of priestesses.

17

In the days following the earthquake, things became much worse for the Dythbethans. A series of violent aftershocks jolted the region over the next two weeks, bringing further devastation to the already reeling city. Soldiers had to be pulled from the task of fortifying the walls, and additional troops were recalled from the front lines to help with the reconstruction and restoration of vital services.

Further, it seemed the enemy had fared much better than the city-dwellers. The Khokarsans had weathered the quakes without significant damage, their structures at best consisting of a number of transportable tents. General Phoeken, sensing an opportunity, swarmed his troops into the vacuum left by the recalled Dythbethan armies. Before long, General Hahinqo and General Wahesa were forced to cede any gains made during the past two months, allowing the Khokarsan armies to close in on the city. Within a month after the first tremor, Phoeken's men once again loomed just beyond the city walls, on the eastern boundaries of the great plain.

The Dythbethans were also running out of food. The few remaining shops in the marketplaces lacked their usual abundance of local and exotic goods. No more the delightful aroma of freshly baked millet and emmer bread wafting in the air, nor the bountiful array of baskets bearing colorful fruits and vegetables; no pigs or domesticated buffalo waiting for slaughter; no ducks, partridges, ravens, and parrots left to quack, screech, croak, and whistle at the market-goers; and, perhaps worst of all, no casks of millet beer, sorghum beer, mead, wine, or *s"okoko*. Instead, driven to desperation by the blockade, the handful of merchants still in business had resorted to peddling the scrawny carcasses of domesticated animals such as dogs and cats, most of which had been rounded up from their owners by the merchants' henchmen. A great price was charged for the meat, which only the richest in the city could afford; and to prevent rampant thievery by the desperately hungry, the merchants were required to hire guards—paid in food, of course—for their shops. Even insects, that usually ever-abundant staple of the Khokarsan diet, seemed to have become scarce and were being sold at exorbitant prices by the merchants. But mostly it was every man, woman, and child out for his or her own family.

The feeble remnants of Dythbeth's once proud navy had also suffered significant losses during the tremors and afterward. Great waves caused by the initial quake had sunk five biremes and three uniremes with all hands aboard. Only three weeks later, Admiral Nemusaketh was forced to defend the harbor against an all-out attack by the Khokarsan fleet. While Nemusaketh managed to hold his position and drive Minruth's Admiral Poedy back out beyond the mouth of the harbor, he had little confidence he could hold the bay for long. He had lost another seven biremes to the deadly rams of Poedy's ships. Awineth, on hearing the news, flew into a rage and ordered Kwasin to assist Admiral Nemusaketh. But before he could do that, Awineth summoned a great rally and called on Kwasin to assist her.

Standing on the high steps before the crumbing palace citadel, with the starving and disconsolate masses thronging beneath her, the queen of queens announced the prediction of the oracle.

"Great Kho," Awineth's voice rang out, "is preparing to shatter the foundations of the world and lay waste to her people!"

The hordes of citizens gasped. Many prostrated themselves upon the ground, while others moaned and, in an expression of great distress, beat their fists against their own heads.

"But this need not be!" Awineth cried out to the crowd. "Dythbeth must remain strong! All is not yet lost! Kho is angry, yes, but she has also laid down the groundwork for our salvation. Almost ten years ago Kho ordered the oracle to exile a man to the empire's hinterlands. Kho did this not merely to punish the man for his crimes, but also because She wanted to mold him into a warrior so great he could one day lead the battle against Her son Resu. But the plans of the Goddess are often obscure in the moment, and for reasons then unknown She also sent the winner of the Great Games to the Wild Lands to locate a mighty weapon—an extraordinary ax, made of a metal forged and tempered by the raging fires of the stars themselves! A weapon of such potent strength that—in the hands of the right hero—it might smite down Resu's armies and slay the sungod himself!"

Kwasin, like many in the crowd below, stirred uncomfortably at Awineth's words. Her sentiment went against the centuries-old tradition that placed Resu second only to Kho in the holy pantheon, and on equal footing to the Goddess according to the strict liturgical interpretation, although the latter view was largely ignored by the populace. But voicing such thoughts of deicide was perilous indeed. Awineth had been cunningly careful—she had not said with certainty that Resu would be slain by the ax, but rather that he *might* be slain. Still, the implication remained clear: Kho's high vicar believed the Goddess was considering overturning the old order and removing Resu permanently from the pantheon. Somewhat to Kwasin's disbelief, a majority of the onlookers erupted in frenzied support of their empress, shouting out wild encouragements. The faces of the priests and their followers, however, turned white.

Awineth waited for the official criers to carry her message to the farthest reaches of the crowd and then continued.

"But the heart of Hadon—the winner of the Great Games of Klakor—turned treacherous under the temptations of a woman, Resu's pawn, the evil White Witch from the Sea, and Hadon turned his back on his queen. But Kho, Who sees all before it happens, foresaw this and caused the sky ax to fall to another, a mortal unlike any other—half-man, half-god—who might slay all Her enemies. The defender of the Goddess," she cried, "the great hero selected by Kho to wield Her mighty weapon, now stands before you! Behold, the future betrothed of Kho's high priestess, and the future king of kings over all the land! Behold, King Kwasin of Dythbeth!"

At this moment, a priestess drew back the curtain from a framed structure that had been erected to hide Kwasin while Awineth addressed the multitude. Instantly, a thunderous cheer rose up and the spectators began chanting Kwasin's name. As he had prepared in consultation with Awineth before the rally, Kwasin raised above his head the ax that had once belonged to the hero Wi, and then the manling Paga. Those in the audience who were not too weak from lack of food thundered out their adulations. The priests, of course, again refrained from applause.

While the ovations, smattered with the occasional jeering, reached a crescendo, the traitors named in the missives of the priest Dykeko were paraded out and made to lay their heads upon a long stone bench that had been set up at the top of the palace steps. The accused, consisting of four priests and two priestesses formerly serving in the palace, had stood no trial other than that in the mind of the high priestess of Kho. New provisions in the law permitted bypassing the usual court system in such cases during wartime. Awineth, Kwasin reflected, seemed excessively eager to consolidate any power she could.

A naked priestess, her face shrouded from view by a veil of black linen, stood beside the prisoners as guards secured them with iron chains to the stone bench. The veil represented the unknowable visage of Sisisken, goddess of the dead, and the great scythe the woman held symbolized the tool used by Sisisken to reap the spirit from the body of those she welcomed into her dark realm. Six times the scythe swung down. Then a soldier took the hair of the disembodied heads and tied them together with rope.

Later that day, by the king's order, the gruesome bundle of heads was loaded into a catapult high atop one of Dythbeth's crenellated towers and launched onto the center of the great plain. Kwasin had no doubt General Phoeken would understand the message.

18

After the rally, determined to prove himself to Awineth and reverse the series of losses that had besieged the city, Kwasin sought out Admiral Nemusaketh. He asked the admiral if he could hold off Poedy's navy and maintain his occupation of the bay for another ten days. Nemusaketh replied he could make no guarantees, but if his king so ordered it, he would hold the bay or die trying.

And so it was that ten days later, on the first moonless night of the month of the goddess Khukly in the Year of the Horned Fish, Kwasin sailed out with a fleet of twenty-two black-painted longboats onto the calm waters of Dythbeth's harbor. As hc paddled away from the docks he murmured a prayer to Tesemines, goddess of the night, and also sight and blindness. He would need her help if his plan were to succeed. He also prayed to Piqabes and Kho. It couldn't hurt to be too careful.

The longboats cut smoothly past Admiral Nemusaketh's stately trireme and the thirty-three surviving biremes and uniremes that patrolled the mouth of the bay. Leaving the galley fleet behind and paddling forth into the Kemu's impenetrable blackness, an almost overpowering sense of loneliness enveloped Kwasin. The enormity of the dark sea struck him, and he wondered at the incomprehensible game that was being played out by the deities while their mortal subjects struggled and died.

They rowed for a great while before Kwasin saw the first evidence of Poedy's fleet, a faint glimmer of light in the gloom that winked into and then out of existence. Probably the door to an officer's cabin on one of the galleys had swung open and closed, briefly revealing lantern light from within.

Kwasin looked back toward the bay. Nowhere could Nemusaketh's fleet be seen in the inky night, though he knew that by now the galleys had already begun rowing forth behind him. He was hoping for a one-two blow against Poedy's ships: first his own longboats doing the unexpected, and then, out of the pitch black of the moonless night, a strike by Nemusaketh's entire navy. Small though the latter might be, and even smaller the odds of the longboats' success, it was Dythbeth's best hope to weaken the Khokarsan blockade and possibly allow some supply ships to get through. If Kwasin failed in his mission, however, a good chance existed that Poedy would take the harbor. Then, Dythbeth would fall in a matter of days at most.

A charcoal-based pigment darkened Kwasin's skin and that of the other rowers in the longboats, effectively cloaking them from the enemy galleys. Kwasin himself could only barely discern the craft that cut the waters only a few yards away, though he could hear the paddles of its oarsmen slicing the water.

He whispered to the five oarsmen in his own boat and instructed them to head in the direction of the light that had briefly shone. The boat beside him followed dutifully, and Kwasin hoped it would continue to do so. It was a long swim back to the mainland.

Having emerged into the wider Kemu, Kwasin's boat loped forward on the crests and troughs of large, rolling waves. A few stars glinted through the breaks in the clouds and, as he rose up with the boat's bow, he caught the faint flicker of lightning on the southern horizon. The rainy season was about to begin again, when rapidly forming and often violent storms were known to sweep across both great inland seas over a period of one to two months. Though he hoped the cloud cover would remain, he did not want to be caught out on the Kemu in a storm. Further, if the lightning moved northward and intensified, it could easily reveal his boats to the enemy.

He bent into his oar and quietly urged the other oarsmen to do the same.

The wind shifted and Kwasin and his crew had a hard time keeping the boat upright and on course. As waves broke across the boat's windward side, and cold seawater splashed overtop them, Kwasin began worrying that the flammable oil and resin with which the boat had been doused would be rendered ineffective. He did not worry long, however. At that moment, the boat crested high above the other waves and he saw the enemy galley not twenty-five yards to port.

By Great Kho's teats, he was fortunate! The galley was a trireme. Tesemines must be looking down at him and stretching her toothless grin. Perhaps Kho or Piqabes would reward him too and the galley would turn out to be Admiral Poedy's ship.

He could no longer hear the paddles of the other longboat, however, and would have to trust that it still managed to pace them.

After much difficulty fighting the waves, Kwasin's boat pulled alongside the trireme. The oars of the large vessel were in their upward and locked position, which was fortunate. Otherwise, anchoring to the galley's side would have been impossible; the many oars, sinking down into the water from their three banks, would have gotten in the way. And of course, had they been at their banks, the oarsmen on the galley might have spotted the longboat. As it was, the lookout on the galley's deck must have been nodding off or else had failed to spot Kwasin's boat because of the rolling waves which hid it half the time.

The linen-padded bumpers on either side of the specially equipped boat thudded against the galley's side. Kwasin and his fellows scanned for their escort but saw nothing. Kwasin swallowed a curse and signaled his men to proceed. They did not hesitate, but what he could discern of their pigment-darkened faces showed worry.

Again the cloth bumpers thwacked the galley. As one, three of the seamen cast their ropes upward, each of the three-pronged, iron-legged grapples successfully catching over the lip of the lowest bank of oars. Immediately, Kwasin and the two men who had not cast grapples drove their foot-long iron hooks, which were attached to a short line of rope tied to the boat, into the galley's wooden side. Now for the tricky part…

As Kwasin stood there on the rocking boat with the waves repeatedly breaking over the vessel's side, his plan no longer seemed so smart. Nemusaketh had warned Kwasin that the dampness of open sea would make his task extremely difficult, and maybe impossible, but the idea to set afire Poedy's flagship, escape on a companion boat, and open the way for Nemusaketh's pitiful fleet to attack had been a desperate one to begin with.

Kwasin unslung the wax-sealed waterproof satchel from around his shoulders and removed from it a flint, a piece of iron, and a bag of dried tinder. The boat, though semi-anchored to the larger vessel, was throwing with the waves and knocking its port bumper repeatedly against the galley. He knew it was only a matter of moments before someone would come to investigate the noise and vibration.

He signaled one of the men to start dousing the galley's side with oil from three ceramic jugs they had brought along. When they were done, he motioned for all but one man—his backup, who also bore a wax-sealed satchel with kindling materials—to jump over the side into freezing sea water. They looked out into the darkness for the other boat and then back to Kwasin, the wide whites of their eyes appearing as pale circles against their blackened faces. Kwasin glared at them, then began striking his flint against the iron. Let them all burn with the galley, he thought.

Someone cried out above. Kwasin looked up, but seeing no one, he returned to his task of furiously striking the iron. Now he could hear the sound of men running across the deck. He cursed. The moist air had dampened the iron and he could get no spark.

"It's not going to light, we should cast off!" one of the men called quietly to Kwasin.

Still striking the flint, Kwasin swung out a leg and kicked the man backward into the sea. "Cast off then!" he yelled. He did not look to find out if the man managed to stay afloat or had sunk into Piqabes' cold bosom.

Realizing their king meant business, the other men in the boat jumped overboard, leaving behind only Kwasin and his backup. Then, the backup cried out and fell onto the bottom of the boat. Dim light shone down on the longboat as a lantern was hung over the side of the deck above, accompanied by more shouting. The sheen of metal, reflecting in the lantern-light, revealed a dagger's hilt protruding from the fallen man's neck. The man lay completely still.

Kwasin leaped belly-first across the longboat. In the dim light he had seen the dead man's iron drop on top of his bag of kindling—maybe the man's iron was drier than his own. He grabbed the iron from the bag and began striking it with his own flint, but the stone slid off the slick metal as if the latter were greased. It was no use.

He rose to get off the boat before the men above could cast another dagger at him. Looking up he saw an orange glow wisping above him in the sea breeze. It flitted first one way and then another, before a strong gust brought it quickly to the deck on the other side of the longboat.

The ember—which must have dropped from the wick of the lantern that had been hung over the galley's side—smoldered orangely for a moment, then grew steadily in intensity. Suddenly, flames were streaking across the oil- and resin-saturated wood, and Kwasin leaped from the longboat into the frigid waves before he became a part of the rapidly blazing pyre.

Kwasin, full of swagger and cocksure about his abilities when on dry land, suddenly found himself at the mercy of the waves. Or, rather, the mercilessness of them. Ceaselessly, the tall swells rolled over him, making it difficult to breaststroke without gulping down large amounts of sea water. He turned over on his back and began backstroking away from the ship. Once, lifted up high on a wave, Kwasin saw one of the men who had jumped off the longboat; but then the man was gone, hidden behind the wall of water.

Rising and falling, Kwasin also caught occasional glimpses of the trireme. Flames engulfed the galley's port side. Men were dumping buckets of water over the side in a futile attempt to extinguish the fire, but the oil- and resin-soaked longboat continued to burn, fueling the oil-doused wooden beams of the galley at the waterline. The ship was already beginning to take on water, keeling heavily to port.

One down, Kwasin thought. And then, as if responding to the thought, Kwasin saw first one and then another fiery glimmer through the choppy waters—and then four, five, six points of flickering yellow-orange on the horizon. At least six of the other longboats had succeeded in setting galleys afire!

A rhythmic sound came to him over the water, then disappeared. For a moment he thought he'd imagined it, but then he heard the deep booming again and could not deny it. He couldn't be sure about the direction of the sound, so tossed about had he become, but it seemed to come from the east. If that were true, then it could only be the drummers on the decks of Nemusaketh's fleet, their deep, steady beating synchronizing the strokes of the rowers.

Lightning erupted on the southern horizon. For a moment a strange image formed out of the darkness and imprinted itself on his inner eye. He saw a line of galleys—Poedy's fleet—on the open sea, some of the ships flaming in the night, others with oars extended into the sea and rowing rapidly forward toward the bay. But that was not the strange thing.

Three ships, unlike anything Kwasin had ever before seen, had materialized in the lightning flash. They appeared to be sailing through the opening left by Poedy's burning galleys, heading into the bay *against the wind!* The ships were of sleek design, with long, narrow decks, perhaps spanning sixty feet from fore to aft, but what stood out most were the vessels' strange-looking triangular sails. Not square, but *triangular.*

There! The lightning flashed again. There could be no doubt: the oddly designed craft were moving at a tremendous speed past Poedy's ships. Already they had far outpaced the blockade and were heading into the opening of the bay. He had never seen a ship move so swiftly. These would have left behind even the fastest galley, which could travel at speeds of up to fifteen knots. At first Kwasin was afraid Poedy had unleashed some new and terrible war craft against the Dythbethans, but then he saw illuminated in a lighting flash the symbol on the sails of the speeding ships: a stylized oak tree, the symbol of Karneth, daughter of Kho. The newcomers had to be allies of the Goddess!

Now the tempest to the south raged, bolts of lightning splitting the horizon and allowing Kwasin to see some of what was happening about him. The Dythbethan galleys were rowing forward to engage the enemy. Compared to the swift, triangular-sailed ships that sped past them, the galleys seemed painfully slow and awkward. Still, the latter were effective, he thought, as a unireme rowed on a collision course with a Khokarsan trireme. The larger vessel turned its rudder and tried to veer leeward. But the ship moved slowly, oh, ever so slowly. Before the trireme could get out of the way, the Dythbethan unireme swung sharply around in an impressive maneuver and laterally raked its ram across the enemy's stern, gutting an entire bank of oars. The unireme swung around again as it neared the aft of its opponent, a striking move that fully wrecked the trireme's steering rudder. Now completely disabled, the trireme floated dead in the water. The skilled captain of the unireme, now able to take his time, swung back out to sea. When he gauged he had attained enough distance to attain full speed, he brought his vessel back for the kill and rammed his enemy's broadside. Then the oarsmen on the unireme began rowing backward to extricate their ship from the trireme's side. Within minutes, the trireme sank.

Kwasin shouted for the unireme, but the crewmen could not hear him. He had little choice but to begin swimming for the southern mainland. There he would have to elude the many enemy troops which occupied the area, but what other choice did he have? He could not tread water forever.

Then came the evening's final blessing, though he was unsure whether to attribute it to Tesemines, Piqabes, or Kho. Out of the rolling waters before him lifted the bow of a longboat. Moments later, hands reached out to grab his cold-numbed arms and pulled him up onto the deck.

19

I am technically already employed by you, O Queen," the young redheaded man was saying. "Before the civil war, I had applied to the Naval Department, but that drunkard of an admiral I spoke with threw me out! He didn't believe my ships could do what I said. But the Temple of Kho had better sense and hired me to build my fore-and-aft sailing ships for the postal system of the priestesses. All under the banner of your name, so to speak."

Kwasin, Awineth, Admiral Nemusaketh, and the scrawny fisherman's son from Bhabhobes sat round a table in a small hexagonal, marble-walled room in the College of Awines. With the palace unsafe for habitation after the earthquake, the college now served as Awineth's headquarters. The acolytes in the college assured the queen that the building was the most secure structure in the city, impervious to the worst of Kho's upheavals thanks to an innovative design conceived by the genius Awines over a thousand years ago. Perhaps the acolytes' claims amounted to more than the mere bragging they seemed to be, for indeed, unlike many of the great edifices in the city, the college had suffered not so much as a cracked flooring tile during the recent quake.

"After war broke out," the young man continued, "I was sent across the Kemus on an important errand by the priestess at Kloepeth. We anchored at Rebha the very night the pile city burned, and my ship, the *Wind-Spirit*, was lost."

Awineth regarded the man askance. "The priestess at Kloepeth?" she asked, suspicion edging her voice. "Just what errand did Suguqatheth send you on, Captain Ruseth? What cargo did you bear for her, and what port was your destination?"

Ruseth's blue eyes looked coolly across the table at his queen. "The records at Kloepeth will confirm that my destination was the city of Wentisuh, and as to what secret message I carried from the priestess, only Piqabes might say. It was lost with my vessel."

Kwasin didn't believe the freckled youth; he was holding something back. Both Awineth and Hadon also had been at the temple at Kloepeth. Could it be that Awineth believed Ruseth had smuggled Hadon to the safety of his native city, only a short jaunt across the southern sea from the city of Wentisuh? Kwasin took an immediate dislike to the young sailor sitting before him.

Awineth seemed unfazed by Ruseth's apparent deception, at least outwardly. She smiled and said, "It is indeed fortunate you arrived when you did, captain." She picked up a pomegranate from a basket of fruit at the table's center. "The food you have brought on your ships is a blessing to the city, though it won't go far. We are beyond desperate, and if Dythbeth falls, so fall the hopes of all who love and worship Kho. Tell me, how did it come that you found a patron to fund the construction of your new ships, and is further aid on its way?"

"After my ship was lost," Ruseth said, "I managed to make it aboard one of the giant raft-islands of the K'ud"em'o, which took me to Wethna. From there I signed up as a deckhand aboard a merchant galley headed back to Khokarsa. I had already heard you were here, O Queen, and that Dythbeth was to be the last stand on the island for the worshipers of Kho. My trials to get to you, however, were many. Pirates attacked the merchant galley aboard which I served, and I was imprisoned and brought as a slave to Mikawuru. But Suhkwaneth, the goddess of the scales, tipped fortune in my favor, and the man to whom I was sold was a devout supporter of your cause. He had recently come into great fortune after sinking the *Haken*, the infamous pirate ship that has long stalked the seas around the Strait of Keth, recovering from its sunken wreckage the legendary diamond known as the Begetter of All Jewels. When this man heard my story, he realized my fore-and-aft ships might make all the difference in the war against Minruth. Immediately he granted me my freedom, commissioning the construction of three ships to aid the forces of the queen of queens and run supplies past Minruth's blockade. And now here I am at your service, Holy One."

Kwasin had heard of the legendary *Haken*, or Death Hawk, although some referred to it as the Red Death because of its crimson sail and the bloody toll it had taken in the strait over the years. That it had sunk was one fewer thing Kwasin had to worry about.

Turning from Ruseth, Awineth said, "Admiral, what is the status of your fleet?"

Though the wrinkles beneath Nemusaketh's eyes hung heavy with fatigue, the old seaman's lips stretched over a crooked-toothed smile. "We have achieved a victory I had not thought possible, O Queen. Thirty of Poedy's galleys have found their final resting place at the bottom of the bay, and though we lost five ships, we captured another seven. Two of these are supply ships bearing food and provisions meant for Phoeken's troops. We have requisitioned these for our own military, but as you say, the food won't go far. We must get a ship out of port to seek aid while Poedy still reels from our attack. But it will be dangerous even now. The enemy still holds the waters around the island."

"That's where you come in, captain," Awineth said, turning back to Ruseth. "I need you to take your ships and, as quickly as possible, return with help and supplies. One ship will go to Towina, from where we've received word that the allies of the Goddess yet manage to hold off the forces of Resu. The others will go to Qethruth and Bawaku to seek support from the priestesses there. It will be a difficult task because of the hard times suffered by all, but you must convince our allies to build many more ships of your new design. If they do not come quickly to the aid of Kho's high priestess, the island will fall to the supporters of Resu. And if that happens, Kho will certainly destroy all the land."

"Getting away from the island won't be a problem," Ruseth said, swagger now pumping his voice. "My ships can run circles around Poedy's fleet. And once those in Towina, Qethruth, and Bawaku see how much faster glide the sails of the fore-and-aft compared to the old square sails, they'll be clamoring to make more."

Nemusaketh's watery eyes carried doubt. "It is true I saw your ships break through the blockade, but they would not have been able to do so if we hadn't cleared the way with our attack. And your narrow vessels, which by their very design can't possibly mount rams on their bows and impact enemy ships without themselves sinking, are still vulnerable to Poedy's rams and missiles."

"I can far outpace any ram-headed galley, be it trireme or unireme," Ruseth replied. "And as long as my ships aren't lying at anchor, any missiles fired at them will be left far behind to fizzle in the sea."

The admiral grunted in disbelief. But Kwasin, recalling the speed of the triangle-sailed ships, thought Ruseth might not be bluffing.

"We have no other option," Awineth said. "The situation becomes grave. The Klemqaba warriors my father recruited from the southwestern mountains along the Kemu have begun pouring into the area. Though they are an unruly lot, more often apt to fight among themselves than attack outsiders, they are eager for loot and blood. If their commanders don't order them to do so first, they will attack the city on their own. And the wild mountain men brought in from beyond the coast of the northern mainland are not much more patient."

"I won't fail you, O Queen," the young sailor said.

"Don't. As of now, I authorize you to head the navy's shipbuilding department, feeble though it now stands. If you succeed in your mission, however, I shall make you a full admiral, answerable only to myself."

The admiral glowered at Ruseth, as if daring the freckled youth to think of himself as an equal. Then he said, "O Queen, if my business here is done, I need to get back to my fleet. I must begin drafting preparations to clear the way for this boy and his clever toys."

Ruseth's cheeks turned the bright red of his hair.

Kwasin erupted in laughter, slapping the wiry youth so hard on his back that he began to sputter with cough.

"Ho!" Kwasin exclaimed. "Fleet are your ships, Captain Ruseth, but nowhere near as fleet as the tongue of an old seaman! But I wouldn't worry, Admiral. As King of Dythbeth, I control the military and you are ultimately answerable to me. Ruseth might indeed be as smart as Awines, though I doubt it, but he certainly doesn't have the experience to outrank you."

"And does your experience as a whoring drunk who defiles temple priestesses qualify you to be king?" Awineth snapped icily.

Kwasin merely rolled his eyes, while Nemusaketh and Ruseth looked uncomfortable.

"Although I will do everything in my power to maintain the old order," Awineth went on, "some things must change if we are to win this war. We must begin to reward those who bring us results, and diminish the power of those who are ineffective. I am not speaking of you, Admiral. I am impressed with what you have managed to accomplish with so little."

Nemusaketh conceded a half-smile.

"And another thing that may change in the future," Awineth added, "is that the priestesses may have more say in military matters."

The room fell silent. The notion went against laws that stretched back hundreds of years, and precedents that dated to a time when the island was still inhabited by uncivilized barbarians.

Perhaps sensing she had gone too far, Awineth rose and said, "I have much work to do myself. Admiral, if you will please have your guards escort Captain Ruseth to his vessel. We can't risk anything happening to our naval prodigy." And then, as if to test her authority, she looked at Kwasin and said, "And you will go to the docks to see that the food is properly distributed. Half will be dispensed evenly between the Temple of Kho and the military, and the remainder will go to the people. Double the guards at the wharves. No matter how fairly we divide the food, there are certain to be riots. But I am trusting you, as king and commander of the military, to see that the protesters don't get out of control and erupt across the city."

Thus dismissed, Kwasin left the College of Awines, descending the wide, marble-hewn spiral ramp that encircled the building. Below him, the sound of shouting children broke from the darkness of the otherwise serene night. At the ramp's bottom, a group of Kwasin's guardsmen were in the process of forcibly removing from the premises a ten-year-old boy and a girl, half his age, who might have been his sister. The children cursed the soldiers with a vicious liveliness that brought a smile to Kwasin's lips, but when he heard what they were after and saw their small, pitifully emaciated bodies, his amusement faded. The two had apparently heard about the food brought from the newly docked ships and come to beg for their share. The boy hollered that his family hadn't had any food for a week, and all he wanted was a piece or two of fruit to divide among his sister, his mother, and his ailing grandmother. The guards, under orders to keep unauthorized individuals away from the college at all cost, were on the verge of forcibly removing the tenacious children when Kwasin arrived at the bottom of the ramp and confronted them.

"What kind of men are you?" he barked at the surprised guards. "You would resort to violence against mere children?"

The officer in charge opened his mouth to speak but at a dark glare from his king seemed to think the better of it.

"Take the boy and his sister into the college," Kwasin said, "and instruct my servants to give them my entire share of the new rations. Then take your guard and escort the children and their food back to their home."

The soldiers stared at him dumbstruck.

"Go!" Kwasin winked at the now smiling boy, who proceeded to strut up the ramp before the chastised soldiers as if he were the newly crowned king and his sister the queen.

Kwasin's stomach would growl tonight, but for the moment he would feel good about his act of charity. He also knew the feeling would not last long; soon he would begin thinking about the thousands of hunger-crazed inhabitants of the city who would starve to death unless Ruseth managed to return swiftly and successfully from his mission. He hoped the young captain knew how much was riding on him.

When Kwasin stepped into the street, the remaining guardsmen who had not gone with the children surrounded him in a defensive blanket. Kwasin growled quietly to himself, then ordered the men to remain at the college and protect the queen. He tired of the constant company, and besides, the threat of an assassin's dagger had been greatly reduced. The missives left behind by the priest Dykeko had revealed the names of those involved in the conspiracy to murder the city's royalty, and the traitors had been rounded up and executed. That was not to say some citizen displeased with the new king's rule might not take the law into his or her own hands and come after Kwasin. But that was a chance he was willing to take. His spirit roamed too freely to be forever caged; he would rather risk taunting death.

The storm brooding on the horizon the previous night had passed far to the south, and a glimmering of starlight now bathed Kwasin's great shoulders as he passed through the temple district along the Avenue of the Hero-King Toenuseth. The avenue was named after a man for whom Kwasin had garnered much respect over the past year. He could not help but identify with him. Toenuseth, who had been a mere consort of Dythbeth's chief priestess, had stood up to insurmountable odds when, almost five hundred years ago, the people of Towina had united with the savage Klemqaba and invaded the island of Khokarsa. But Toenuseth had prevailed against the enemy's massive fleet, and after his lover made him king, he went on to become one of the most revered rulers in the history of the queendom of Dythbeth. Of course, gallant King Toenuseth, slain by a spear cast by the chief priestess of Khokarsa when he attempted to take the capital, had been ultimately ill-fated. In the end, Kho had passed her judgment upon the man for his overreaching arrogance. Kwasin would not make that mistake. He had sided with Awineth, Kho's legitimate regent on the earth. If Awineth indeed married him as she had promised, he—not Minruth or Hadon—would share Kho's gratitude and favor. That is, as long as he didn't overstep his bounds.

As he looked up at the stars, Kwasin momentarily wished he could slough off the mantle of kingship and once again roam free across the trackless expanses of the Wild Lands. It had been lonely there, true, and hard to find a woman to whom he could sing, woo, and otherwise manifest the great urgings with which the Goddess had blessed him—or, as Awineth claimed, cursed him. But at the moment he felt sacrificing companionship for freedom would make more than a fair trade.

Above, an unearthly trail of orange-blue flame streaked across the night's dark canopy, and for some reason the heavenly apparition—an omen?—made Kwasin think of Sahhindar. When the god of time, bronze, and plants had made his appearance in the hills outside of Khokarsa, he had told Kwasin to make sure Lalila and the manling Paga headed south, far south. Before it was too late, the god had said. Too late? What did it mean?

Suddenly another fiery bolide lit the sky, this one so brilliant its eerie illumination cast a momentary flicker across the city. In the brief flash, Kwasin thought he saw movement along the eastern wall. It was probably just a shadow moving with the light of the falling star, but with Phoeken's troops looming outside the walls, it was best to be certain. He left the avenue and headed down a side street to investigate.

The late hour left the city deserted and mostly darkened. Fish oil and wood had been rationed since the siege, and even the great torch that normally burned high atop the temple of Piqabes had been extinguished. The moon appeared as only the barest of slivers. Moving forward toward the wall, he passed into the utter darkness behind a large, empty grain silo. Here he remained still and listened. Up over the rim of the inner wall, he could see the night sentry patrolling along the top of the higher outer wall. About twenty yards in from the inner wall another squat silo rose. From this direction Kwasin faintly heard what sounded like stone scraping upon stone. Then the noise stopped, and a moment later he heard a creaking, like the sound of a door opening.

A man crossed from behind the silo ahead, looking over his shoulder as if wary that someone might take note of his presence. White robes and a stiff roach of hair revealed the man to be a priest. He was running to catch up with another man, also a priest, who had just emerged from the shadow of a storage building adjacent to the silo.

Still hidden in the darkness, Kwasin crept forward. When he reached the silo, he discovered a door in the building's side had been left ajar, presumably by the first priest. Kwasin opened the door and passed inside.

The sweet after-smell of emmer wheat hung heavy in the empty building, and Kwasin's footfalls echoed strangely against the rounded walls as he advanced in the darkness. Near the center of the silo's round, hollow storage bin, he stumbled over something that projected several inches from the floor. He reached down until his fingers felt around what appeared to be a small, circular slab of some sort.

He lifted up the stone and peered down a shoulder-width opening in the floor. Dim flickerings came from the opening, revealing a ladder leaning against a shaft that descended approximately ten feet below the surface. Off one side of the shaft began what appeared to be the opening of a crudely excavated tunnel, jutting off in an eastward direction. Kwasin unslung the ax from his back and dropped into the hole.

Whoever had tunneled beneath the silo had worked fast. Piles of loose dirt lined the narrow, three-foot-tall passageway ahead, the walls of which were buttressed at intervals by freshly cut cedar beams. A jog in the tunnel before him prevented Kwasin from seeing the source of the light. Then, as he decided to return to the surface to get help, the light grew much brighter. Someone was coming, and quickly.

With no chance to climb back up the ladder, he quickly pressed himself against a wall of the entry shaft. The cedar frame of the tunnel's opening jutted out just enough to hide him from whoever approached. He gripped his ax and waited for just a moment, estimating the time it would take for someone to pass up the length of the tunnel. Then he leaped out, his ax swinging.

Kwasin's ax chopped into the helmeted head of a crouching man, a soldier. Because of the shaft's constricting space, Kwasin's blow did not carry enough force to cleave his opponent's helmet, but even so the man heaved forward upon his face, unconscious. The man's burning torch fell on the ground before him, illuminating the tunnel.

Kwasin almost could not believe what he saw next. Two faces, drawn long with surprise, peered from behind the body of the fallen man.

One of the men was General Phoeken—the other, King Minruth himself.

20

Kwasin took no time to think. Without room to make an effective swing, he thrust the ax's head forward with all his strength. The toe of the ax head cut deeply into the center of Phoeken's face. Blood fountained from the crushed bone and cartilage where the general's face had been, and then his body toppled forward onto the fallen soldier lying in front him. Kwasin jerked back the ax as his arm was singed by the torch the soldier had dropped. Minruth's surprised face had vanished from behind the bodies of the two men, and Kwasin could see the movement of multiple figures retreating hastily down the low tunnel.

Despite having killed Minruth's greatest general, Kwasin swore. That Minruth and Phoeken both personally occupied the tunnel could only mean one thing: a carefully timed, all-out attack on the city was underway.

Kwasin pulled himself back into the entry shaft and with his ax began furiously chopping at the cedar beams supporting the tunnel. After only a few swings, the tunnel collapsed, filling the outer shaft and nearly burying him in the process. Quickly, he pulled himself out of the deluge of dirt and clambered up the wooden ladder to the surface.

Bolting from the silo, he already heard the trumpeters sounding the alarm. Dythbeth's soldiers would be waking up in the barracks and hastening to the defense of the walls.

Kwasin began running along the inner wall, hoping he could get the soldiers at the next guard tower to lower a ladder for him to climb up. Otherwise he would have to go out of his way and cut through several side streets in order to pass through the gate that separated the military district from the temple and palace district.

As he ran, Kwasin heard a commotion behind him. Looking back, he cried out in anguish. About one hundred yards away, a large hole gaped in center of the street that ran from north to south along the inner wall. Stones pried up from the street were heaped in jagged piles around the perimeter of the hole, from which a great stream of men poured forth. Minruth's soldiers had excavated a second tunnel!

Getting on top of the wall no longer mattered. He must get to Awineth before the soldiers attacked the college. The priests he had witnessed leaving the tunnel beneath the silo indicated the enemy still had spies in the city. Surely the invaders knew where the queen was quartered and would make the college their primary target. They would also want to target the gates and storm them from the inside. Once the gates had fallen, nothing could hold back the Khokarsan hordes from flooding into the city.

An embattled turret farther down the wall exploded in a horrific conflagration. Kwasin ignored it and took off down the avenue toward the inner city. He would have to trust the men on the walls to do their best in the face of Minruth's catapults.

He ran past the temple of Piqabes, its great torch now lit and flaming in defiance of the attackers. Frightened priestesses, priests, and attendants stood on the temple steps, gawking at their king as he ran past them.

Kwasin stopped. The torch of the green-eyed goddess of the sea had given him an idea. Perhaps there was something he could do to stop the men coming from the tunnel after all.

He jogged back to the temple and asked a priestesses standing on the steps to fetch him a torch. The woman entered the temple and returned a few moments later, handing him what he had requested with a puzzled look. He thanked her and gave blessing to Piqabes, then ran as fast as he could back the way he had come.

When he again neared the hole out of which poured forth the human tide, Kwasin began lighting nearby buildings afire with his torch. Not all of the buildings, of course, could be lit; some were constructed of large stone blocks, and others from sun-dried bricks. But there were enough made of wood, or adobe and wood, for his plan to work. That is, if only Piqabes—who besides being goddess of the sea also controlled the winds—kept blowing her southwesterly breeze.

It took longer than Kwasin hoped, but eventually, one after another, the fires took. Within twenty minutes a raging inferno swept across the entire block. As the fires spread from building to building and lashed out across the streets, the Khokarsan soldiers in the area quickly found themselves trapped between the flames and the old wall. Despite frantic attempts by many soldiers to reenter the tunnel to escape the fires, the unrelenting droves of men still storming from the tunnel prevented them. And by the time the men leaving the tunnel could assess the situation, it was also too late. They too tried to get back in the hole only to find the way blocked by the onslaught of new soldiers pouring forth.

Peering through the flames at the doomed men, Kwasin grinned darkly. But he knew he had no time to gloat. Not all of the men had been trapped by the fires. He must get to Awineth as quickly as possible.

That turned out to be quicker than he estimated, for by the time he again reached the temple of Piqabes, he saw the queen and a small number of her guard running down the street toward him. Not far behind them surged a mass of soldiers, and from the anxious looks cast behind by Awineth and her guards, the pursuing men did not seem to be Dythbethan.

Kwasin ran forward and joined Awineth's group.

"What are you doing here?" Awineth screamed at him, her voice indicating she was on the brink of hysteria.

Ignoring the question, Kwasin said, "We must get you back to the palace. I am told there are tunnels which could lead out of the city."

Awineth nodded her head no. "Cut off," she said. "Too many soldiers. The bay's been taken and sailors are landing on the docks. The west gate has been breached, and the southern gate on the palace road has been closed off. We need to make it to a tower."

"There are soldiers ahead too," Kwasin said, "though many have been caught in the fires I've set. Still, we might find a way through."

They set off running back the way Kwasin had come. Behind them the enemy soldiers were coming on fast and making up ground. But soon Kwasin and his party were forced to stop. Fickle Piqabes had changed her mind and begun to blow her great breath seaward. A massive wall of flame confronted them.

"You idiot!" Awineth shrieked. "You've set the whole city on fire!"

Unable to argue with the scorching blaze that blocked their path, Kwasin said nothing. The woman was right that he had very probably made a fatal miscalculation. But the fault was not entirely his. If he survived this hellish night, he would never again put his faith in the capricious goddess of the sea.

Quickly, they ran down a slender alley behind an outbuilding that served as temporary housing for the influx of wartime refugees. If Kwasin and his party could make it to the next street over, they might be able to escape the flames.

They emerged onto the street and found the buildings on both sides of the way also on fire. Worse yet, the soldiers pursuing them had also cut across an alley and were running toward them down the thoroughfare they had just entered. Kwasin, staring ahead at the gauntlet of flames that licked angrily across the street, saw only one way out. Still holding his ax and giving no warning, he grabbed Awineth and threw her over a shoulder. The queen's guard, sensing what he was about to do, looked at him as if he were mad. Kwasin ignored them, as he did the desperate beating of Awineth's small fists against his back and her enraged screams to be put down. Without taking time to reconsider the brashness of his actions, or even to muster his courage, Kwasin charged forward into the scorching wall of fire.

Flames seared at his shoulders, arms, thighs, and legs, and the bitter tang of singed hair mixed with the sweet aroma of burning cedar almost smothered him. Awineth screamed wildly, and Kwasin himself shouted out in crazed defiance against the blistering heat of the fires raging everywhere about them. And then the flames were behind them and Kwasin was dropping Awineth to the stone-paved ground.

Immediately Kwasin and Awineth began blotting out the smoldering locks of their hair, which had caught fire in the terrifying gauntlet. Awineth's once beautiful jet-black tresses, let down from their tight knot, fell jaggedly across her burn-reddened shoulders. Kwasin, running a hand through his own singed hair, and patting gently the sweltering burns that spattered his body, thought they had been lucky. The burns, though painful now, were not serious and would heal. If they had stayed behind to face the large number of soldiers, they would certainly have been dead in short order. Or worse, captured.

For a moment, Awineth sat in the middle of the street glaring fiercely at Kwasin as she coughed and wheezed from the smoke she had inhaled while passing through the fires. She looked as if she wanted to claw out his eyes—and she might have done so if she could ever stop hacking—but finally she looked away, utter despair sagging her features.

She would be thinking that she had lost everything, that the Goddess had abandoned her and allowed Resu and her father to have the final, ruthlessly vindictive laugh. How she must have hated Minruth! Kwasin knew well the cold heart that lay at the core of Awineth's deceptively beautiful form, but seeing her in such a pitifully despondent state made his own heart go out to her. Minruth had denied her the husband she so rightly deserved—the hero of the Great Games—in order to maintain an aging grip upon his throne. And then, while the man who should have been king was sent off upon a fool's errand, Awineth had suffered the humiliation of being deposed and imprisoned by her own father. Now, after somehow managing to miraculously escape Minruth's dungeons, to face this! To flee, screaming in terror, from her father's soldiers as she ran through the fire-swept streets. Fate, it seemed, had only toyed with Awineth and would now leave her to die.

Kwasin hefted his ax—the mighty weapon that had at one time belonged to the hero Wi before a group of yellow-haired savages from the northern wastes took his life. Perhaps the manling Paga had been right: the luck possessed by the ax lasted only a short time for the weapon's bearer. But the oracle had claimed the ax was important, that it would either provide Kwasin's succor or his undoing, and that his fate would be shared with all the land. Summoning from somewhere deep inside himself a bleak faith for the oracle's more optimistic alternative, he pulled Awineth to her feet.

"Come," Kwasin said. "We have rested long enough."

He had no more than uttered the words when three figures leaped from the fires that tongued across the street, the flames fueled by the steadily increasing winds. The figures, three survivors of Awineth's guard, rolled on the ground moaning as they tried to snuff out their smoldering hair and clothing. Kwasin and Awineth leaped to help the men, patting them down with their bare hands. When the guardsmen had extinguished the small fires on their bodies and recovered from their fits of coughing enough to stand up on shaky feet, Kwasin asked them about the others.

One of the men, the captain in charge of Awineth's guard, nodded sadly and said, "Dead. Cut down by Minruth's men." The man coughed. "Need to keep moving. Don't think—" He coughed again. "Don't think they'll come through the flames, but not sure…need to protect the queen."

Kwasin managed to smile at the man, though he stopped himself short before he could clap the captain on his scalded back.

They took off jogging toward the wall. Kwasin turned to Awineth and said, "It's not over. We'll get you out of the city and off the island. Perhaps Towina still holds out." Then he smirked. "Or, if all the coastal cities on the northern sea have fallen to the sun worshipers, we'll go south and forge a resistance there." Briefly, he thought of Hadon, who Awineth suspected had returned to his backwater city. The thought of throwing himself at his cousin's mercy rankled Kwasin, and he quickly dismissed the idea. He would never be able to stomach the humiliation.

As if reading his mind, Awineth appeared even more dejected, if that were possible. She also had much reason to hate Hadon. Perhaps more than he did.

The street ended and they came out on a narrow, stone walkway that skirted the old wall. To the north a swarm of soldiers could be seen crossing into the city through a yawning hole in the wall. The emperor's siege engines had been at work, knocking clear through both fortified barriers. The Khokarsans would also be wheeling forth their massive towers of wood and, propping them against the walls, hurling down upon the defenders an onslaught of burning pitch. Hahinqo, having seen the wooden towers being constructed on the battlefield, had prepared for such a contingency and issued to the soldiers on the wall many leather hides under which they could protect themselves; but even with the hides, the assault would be horrendously appalling for the soldiers.

Kwasin barked at his companions to run south along the wall. Perhaps the military district had not yet been seized by the enemy. If it hadn't, Kwasin and the three men still might manage to flag down someone to lower a ladder, a rope—anything—to hoist Kho's vicar to safety. Awineth had said the gate on the palace road was closed. He could only hope that was a good sign, that the Dythbethan commanders had ordered it shut to prevent Minruth's troops from storming out of the central section of the city. Dythbeth, partitioned off into three fortified enclosures, would be extremely hard for any enemy, no matter how vast or well prepared, to take in a single night. One or even two sections of the city could fall, while a second or third might yet hold out. The three-in-one fortifications had been a key factor for Dythbeth in repelling her would-be invaders for over a millennium.

Kwasin grabbed Awineth by the hand and headed south along the wall, two guards flanking them and one protecting their rear. Awineth struggled to keep up with Kwasin's great strides, but at least she did not slow them down by bemoaning their fate or asking to rest. The Empress of Khokarsa was certainly made of stern stuff. Or perhaps she was merely too fatigued or shock-numbed to complain or think of doing anything other than follow Kwasin's lead. It made no difference as long as they were moving forward.

Out of the darkness ahead loomed another wall, this one nearly twenty feet higher than the old inner wall that traced the perimeter of the city. This was the interior cross-wall that separated their section of the city from the southern fortified military district. Kwasin scanned the top of the wall, looking for any sign the Dythbethans still held the area.

Awineth screamed, and the man on her right—the captain of her guard—fell facedown on the path.

"Slingers!" she shouted, pointing to the east. About fifty yards away several shadowy figures lurked in the darkness where Awineth had indicated. Kwasin could hear the whirring of slings as the figures advanced slowly down the street toward them.

With a rough jerk, he swung Awineth away from the oncoming men and to his other side, placing an arm about her waist. The captain lay unmoving on the ground, and they left him behind as they ran on. Awineth's two remaining guards, their broadswords drawn from their scabbards, drew in tight on both sides. Kwasin urged Awineth to run quicker, but speeding up only caused her to stumble and skin her shins badly on the stone road. As Kwasin helped her get back onto her feet, the soldier who had assumed the captain's position cried out and fell. A sling-stone had impaled itself in the man's leg. Though still alive, the man's injury was serious. He could not go on.

Kwasin, his nerves finally breaking, yelled out in frustration. "I won't be slaughtered like a lame ox! Take care of the empress!" he shouted at the remaining guardsman. Then, thrusting Awineth behind him, Kwasin took off down the street in the direction the slingers.

Though they still whirred their slings, the dark forms retreated as Kwasin advanced.

"By Kho, fight me, cowards!" he shouted, but the figures only continued to back away. It maddened him that the men would not face him. Clearly Minruth had issued orders that his daughter and Dythbeth's king were to be captured alive. The thought did not reassure Kwasin. Minruth would take sadistic pleasure in ensuring that their remaining days were filled with torment and humiliation. They had caused him too much trouble.

Since Kwasin could not manage to get near enough to attack his opponents, he turned back and returned to Awineth's side. Now he and Awineth, believing the enemy was likely under orders not to kill them, stood protectively in front of the remaining guard. The fellow with the injured leg now lay dead at their feet. He had crawled along the stone path in an attempt to rejoin them, but a slinger, advancing with Kwasin's retreat, had expertly cast a stone into the man's face despite his helmet's bronze nose guard. Kwasin bent down and took the man's helmet, placing it over his own head. Though the soldiers after them seemed not to be under orders to kill him, he didn't want to trust that a sling-stone would not go astray and hit him. Besides, the soldiers didn't seem to be all that careful. They had killed the injured guard while Awineth stood only a couple paces away.

Now Kwasin, Awineth, and the remaining guard headed east along the cross-wall. As they ran, a group of about twelve Khokarsan soldiers, some of them bearing torches to light their way, emerged from an alley. Three javelins flew out from the men and clattered forcefully on the stone path before the fleers. Awineth, frightened, tried to stop but Kwasin pulled her on even as he reached down to grab one of the iron-shanked javelins. Awineth's guard, he noted, was coolheaded enough to do the same.

The new group of pursuers now turned from the alley and ran furiously down the stone path behind their quarry. Kwasin turned to Awineth's guard and shouted, "Now!"

Simultaneously, Kwasin and the guardsman stopped and whirled on their heels. Kwasin dropped his ax to the ground. Then he planted his feet, raised the javelin, and swung back his mighty torso. Beside him, the guardsman released his missile at the same time. Kwasin cried out in delight as both javelins hit their marks, impaling two of the pursuers. But Kwasin, seeing the soldiers only a scant twenty yards away, did not pause. With furious speed he seized up his ax and charged, bellowing like a mad bull, his ax swinging above his head.

About half of the men broke upon seeing the enraged demon-giant storming at them. Five soldiers, however, stood their ground, though within moments they all lay strewn across the cobbled street, dead or mortally injured. Kwasin had cleaved down three in his initial onslaught with the ax, and while Awineth's guard—who had garnered Kwasin's respect by also launching himself at the soldiers—cut down one man with his sword, Kwasin barreled into the last standing man and tackled him to the ground. With a massive fist, Kwasin punched the man brutally in the throat, crushing his larynx.

Kwasin stood up. The enemy soldiers who had fled were hovering thirty yards back down the way, neither advancing nor retreating. But that wasn't what concerned him. Along the western wall he saw that one of the enemy's great wooden towers had been wheeled forward, and many figures now ran along the wall top. It was clear to him the battlement at the west end of the cross-wall had been taken by the Khokarsans.

No, not the Khokarsans. The figures storming over the top of the wall were short, squat, massive—Minruth's wild Klemqaba warriors were climbing up the wooden tower to assail the city. Kwasin raged when he saw a group of the savages take down a Dythbethan soldier with their bolas and then hurtle the man to his death over the wall. Now many ladders and ropes swung down from above as the hordes of Klemqaba began their descent upon the city.

Bolstered by the appearance of the savage Goat People, and perhaps thinking it wouldn't matter if they killed the king and the high priestess of Kho since the Klemqaba would undoubtedly slaughter them anyway, the soldiers who had been skulking at a distance advanced, swords raised menacingly above their small, round shields. And behind them came the slingers. Kwasin was on the verge of charging the entire group when Awineth appeared at his side.

"Leave them!" she cried. "By the time you kill them the Klemqaba will be upon us! Perhaps someone along the wall will see us and let us up."

Kwasin doubted it. The western wall was eerily absent of soldiers, Dythbethan and Khokarsan alike. If the military district had fallen, no one would remain on the other side to prevent the wild Klemqaba from moving forward across the wall. Still, Awineth was right. He might kill the advancing soldiers, but he would surrender what little chance they had of escape.

Again, they ran, angling somewhat to the east so they would be able to see anyone who might be running along the crenellated wall top. Awineth seemed to have recovered her breath, sprinting along with Kwasin and the surviving guardsman with renewed strength. For a moment, Kwasin allowed himself to hope. If only he could find a way to signal the soldiers on the opposite side of the wall—if, that is, his men had not all been slaughtered or subdued.

The guardsman running with them cried out and stumbled. A shallow dent on his helmet revealed where a sling-stone had hit him. Kwasin lifted the guard to his feet, but three more stones pelted the man in his back and he fell hard on the ground. He would not be getting up again. Kwasin picked up the poor fellow's wooden shield, handed it to Awineth, and urged her to keep moving.

When Kwasin looked up and saw a figure running east along the top of the wall, he thought he might weep. The man was one of their own, he was sure; otherwise the soldier would not be looking fearfully over his shoulder at the advancing Klemqaba. Kwasin and Awineth shouted and screamed, attempting to attract the man's attention.

The man looked down and slowed, but kept moving ahead along the wall.

"I am your king!" Kwasin cried out. "I order you to help your queen and empress, the holy priestess of Kho!"

The soldier stopped between two embrasures, looked back at the wild hordes, and then, as if weighing the wisdom of offering assistance, returned his uncertain gaze to Kwasin and Awineth.

"Kho will reward you if you help me," Awineth shouted above, "but She will curse you and all your kin if you abandon Her high priestess!"

Kwasin didn't believe the appeal would work, but the soldier surprised him by crouching at the foot of the embrasure as if securing something to the stone. A moment later a rope uncoiled down the wall.

"I have done my duty to the Goddess!" the soldier cried, and then he dashed northward, leaving his empress and his king to fend for themselves.

Quickly, Kwasin and Awineth ran to the dangling rope. Kwasin secured his ax to the harness on his back and pulled Awineth tightly to his chest. She wrapped her arms around his neck. Kwasin swung Awineth over a thigh and kicked off against the granite wall, his powerful muscles pulling them in fast jerking motions up the rope.

They climbed over the edge of the battlement just as a series of sling-stones barraged the wall face, the impact of the bulleting projectiles shooting off splinters of stone at high velocities. Keeping low, Kwasin and Awineth ran east down the walkway.

From his new vantage, Kwasin got a bird's-eye view of the assault on Dythbeth. Fire raged across nearly a third of the inner city, fanned by the heavy seaward breeze. A great portion of the fire would have been caused by Kwasin's defensive arson, but not all of it. A somewhat smaller though still substantial fire was sweeping through the market district in the southeast. Soon it would also expand with the winds.

On the southern side of the wall, three battlements blazed and billowed black smoke into the dark night, and an orange twinkling from the military barracks told him the garrison buildings had been attacked and set afire. The massive western gate stood wide open, with throngs of soldiers streaming through it in both directions. None of the soldiers seemed to be Dythbethan, and a number were certainly of Klemqaba stock.

Suddenly Awineth screamed. Ahead, a group of half-neanderthaloids swarmed over an embrasure and onto the wall's walkway. They surged toward the two, some holding small round shields and brandishing heavy bronze axes, others shieldless and bearing goat-hide slings and flint-headed spears.

Kwasin and Awineth stopped, but turning saw more men mounting the wall behind them. These were not Klemqaba but rather a swarthy, rangy-looking lot of humanoids—the wild mountain men brought in by Minruth from the Saasares. Kwasin would have charged them, since they stood a better chance against the mountain men than the fearsome, powerfully muscled warriors of the Goat People, but the Klemqaba were already upon them.

One of the hybrids—a hideously ugly and fearfully massive brute of a fellow—grabbed Awineth away from Kwasin and, seizing her by the shoulders, began to mock-rape her, pivoting his hips obscenely and repeatedly thrusting his long, rhino-tusk codpiece between her naked thighs. Awineth, looking surprisingly calm, did not scream or otherwise panic. Instead, with what seemed a cool and deliberate motion, she drew the dagger from the sheath on her thigh. For a moment Kwasin held his breath—even as he crushed the skull of a warrior who had charged him with a bronze ax—thinking that rather than be captured Awineth meant to take her own life. But instead, she stabbed the dagger deep beneath the edge of her attacker's cuirass, withdrew the blade, and stabbed him again and again, fighting like a cornered tigress. The brute, his theatrics done with for all eternity, clutched his chest and fell dead at Awineth's feet.

Having dispatched his immediate assailant, Kwasin recovered just in time to swing up his weapon and deflect the blow of a bronze ax that hurled at his face. His own ax, its head forged from the sturdy iron of a fallen star, glittered in the flames of the burning city as it struck the oncoming weapon, breaking its bronze head from the ox-bone haft in his opponent's hand. Kwasin rammed a giant fist into the fellow's chin, whose head swung back, his jaw cracking sickly from its joints.

Then Kwasin pitched forward on his hands and knees as something smacked his helmet and knocked all sense from his mind. The whole world clanged as if it had been struck by a mighty brass gong and, a moment later, deafness enveloped him. A biconical lead projectile, glistening darkly with blood, skidded on the granite walkway until it finally stopped between his knees. With perhaps the greatest single act of will of his whole life, he forced himself to lift his head. His vision wavered between varying degrees of blurriness before finally coming into focus. What he saw filled his heart with dismay. Awineth, blood freely streaming down her face from a deep gash on her forehead, lay crumpled on the ground before him. A black, shadowy wisp flickered to Awineth's left and then shot downward like lightning and disappeared in the ground. Was it her spirit, snatched away by the all-too-eager hands of dread Sisisken? Or perhaps it had been one of his own souls, for indeed the oracle had said he had two.

Kwasin shouted out in his mind for strength from the Goddess, but his once mighty muscles felt frail and wasted as he strained in the futile effort to will himself to his feet. Then the long, dark curtain of night fell about him and oblivion consumed him.

21

For a period that seemed devoid of time, Kwasin dreamed. Many faces and scenes—some familiar, some strange—passed before his inner eye. He saw his cousin, the tall, bronze-skinned Hadon, seated upon a golden throne beside Lalila, the fair White Witch from the Sea. At their feet sat Abeth, Lalila's daughter with the hero Wi, looking older than he remembered her and playing on the steps of the dais with a very young girl whose long, wavy hair shone golden bronze in a slanting shaft of sunlight.

The scene faded. Colors, forms, and shapes shifted nebulously upon the blackened background of Kwasin's mind. From them congealed the form of his mother, Wimake, laughing with great merriment as she sat upon a swath of scarlet moss near the banks of a babbling mountain stream. Beside her stood Pwamkhu, the man whom Kwasin once regarded as a father figure, running his hand along the gorged body of a serpent that curled down from a branch of a withering fir tree. Then that vision too faded, replaced by a series of images, scenes, faces, and events, passing by with such nauseating speed that Kwasin momentarily lost all sense of self. Suddenly the whirling stopped and one last scene materialized before his mind's eye: an ancient, stoop-shouldered crone bathed in moonlight—the oracle Wasemquth?—shaking her gnarled fist at a winged feminine form standing balanced atop a colossal, stone-hewn sphere.

Pain searing through his entire frame, but especially his back, Kwasin opened his eyes. At first he was unsure whether the dream still held him. What he saw and smelled certainly seemed nightmarish.

He was outside the city walls. The hot, white sun beat down upon a wide mountain of corpses heaped up outside Dythbeth's eastern gate. On top of the ghastly, fly-swarming, foul-smelling, sun-baked pile of slaughter was the death-stiffened body of a lone man, propped up and tied to a wooden post driven into the grisly foundation. Even from the great distance, Kwasin recognized the man. It was General Hahinqo. He had been stripped of his armor and clothing, and his penis had been cut off and stuffed inside his mouth.

Behind the mountain stretched the exterior of the city wall, from the merlons of which dangled down the disfigured remains of men, women, and children, tied to the ends of long ropes. Along the foot of the wall, human and Klemqaba soldiers heaved body after body into massive but unfinished trenches, the same great troughs Hahinqo had ordered to be excavated outside the wall in his failed attempt to thwart Minruth's siege engines. Two large clusterings of poles and spear shafts had been driven into the ground on either side of the gate's towering bronze doors, which were swung open to reveal the blackened and smoldering ruins of what had once been the city's military district.

The world was upside down for Kwasin, literally, and now his head cleared enough to understand the cause of his throbbing pain. Trussed up like a captured lion, his naked, blood-streaked body hung down by its wrists and ankles from iron-manacles attached to the center beam of a makeshift wooden A-frame. He felt nothing in his hands and feet, which had numbed due to a lack of circulation, and with each breath he took, torturous, jabbing pains stabbed through his neck and arched back and shoulders. Groaning, and almost choking on his parched and swollen tongue, he tried moving his fingers and toes only to find they barely responded.

A dark form moved in front of Kwasin, blocking out the harsh rays of the sun.

"I do not believe it!" a haughty male voice cawed. "This stinking lump of flesh cannot be the lauded exile-king of Dythbeth, and certainly not the wild demon who taunted my armies and caused them to piss themselves with fear. Ah, but still a hulking bull indeed! As powerfully muscled as an ox, although I understand cursed with a slowness of mind. But an ox doesn't need brains to pull a stone block up the ramparts around the Tower of Resu."

The obnoxious, swaggering voice could belong to one man alone. Kwasin had only once before seen Minruth, in the tunnel dug by the Khokarsan soldiers beneath Dythbeth's walls, but he recognized the emperor by his likeness, which had been minted into the gold coin known as the *nasuhnohehehe*, or one thousand piece.

Kwasin, his eyes having adjusted to the change in light caused by the shadow which fell upon him, stared up at his taunter. Minruth stood with hands on hips, his obese gut bulging out over the belt of his finely embroidered leather kilt. The man had his daughter's jet-black hair and dark eyes, but his otherwise regal features were marred by a large, somewhat curved nose. Though broad-shouldered, he certainly did not look like he ever had been a hero of the Great Games. Neither did he seem the valiant warrior famed for suppressing the bloody rebellion at Sakawuru, nor the powerful man who in his youth had slain the great black leopard of Siwudawa with his bare hands.

Minruth did look younger than his fifty-nine years, however. Rumors abounded that the king of kings was preoccupied to the point of obsession with maintaining his youthful appearance. Some even attributed his fanatical devotion to completing the Great Tower of Kho and Resu to a prediction supposedly made four hundred and fifty years ago by the high priestess Pwymnes. The prophecy stated that the man who sat upon the imperial throne of Khokarsa when the Tower was finished would ascend to the sky and be blessed with everlasting life. Whether that blessing came from Kho or Resu, the legend did not say, although many theologians over the years had tried to settle the debate. The philosopher-priest Qohawiten claimed the blessing obviously originated from the sungod, since the sky was known colloquially as the blue palace of Resu. The priestesses, however, refuted Qohawiten's theorem by citing liturgical stone carvings dating back to antiquity in which the sky was referred to as Kho's blue bowl, still a common expression today. Kwasin thought they were all fools, as the task of completing the tower was so vast it would never be completed during the lifespan of the debaters—especially if a new light-weight brick was not found, as the tower's structure could not bear much more stress. So what then was the use of arguing?

But looking up into Minruth's smug face, Kwasin found himself wondering. The man had achieved what no other king had even dared imagine. Now that the priestesses had been defeated and he controlled the purse strings of the empire, perhaps Minruth could truly succeed in his mad quest to complete the tower.

Then Kwasin had a wry thought. If the blessing of immortality were in fact Kho's gift, Minruth had very likely forfeited his claim on eternal life when he seized the throne from his daughter, demoted the Goddess in the pantheon, and removed from the base of the great ziggurat Awodon's masterpiece of sculpture, the frieze known as *Kho and Her Children*. And if that were not enough, Kho would be further angered that her name had been dropped from what was now known only as the Tower of Resu. It would be ironic if Minruth fulfilled his dream to complete the tower only to have the Goddess leave him an old man on death's door.

Kwasin tried to speak, to tell the mad Emperor of Khokarsa that he could shove his Great Tower up his corpulent backside, but his voice only croaked and grated like a bullfrog too long out of water.

"Look, it tries to form words!" Minruth sneered. "To think my daughter meant to marry such an ape!" And then the king of kings squatted so that his face hovered before Kwasin like a bloated moon. "But even an ape can be of some value if properly trained," he continued in a more appeasing tone. "You know, I would have welcomed you as a brother, a common ally of the sungod, upon your return from exile—had you only forsworn your loyalty to Kho. I would have made you one of my great champions, maybe even treated you as a son, but instead you ran amok and killed my soldiers. Still, Resu is generous and forgiving. After all, even that whore-goddess Bhukla was allowed to remain in the pantheon as goddess of the sword after she waged war against Great Resu. I will make you a one-time offer, here and now. Forswear Kho and I will let you live. I will even place you in charge of an important mission, one without which the city of Khokarsa could not hope to function. Of course, sweeping out the backed-up and stinking muck from the city's sewage canals would be an unpleasant task for most, but being as you already reek of ape shit, I think you will feel right at home."

His throat too dry and swollen to speak, Kwasin mouthed the foulest curse he could think of.

The Emperor of Khokarsa merely smiled. Then he stood up and said, "A pity. Then your stubborn soul will be given in sacrifice to the glory of Resu. But not just yet. First you will serve as a symbol to all those who yet oppose the sungod. Along with another who so unwisely rejected my openhanded offer."

Minruth motioned to someone behind Kwasin, and the sound of squeaking wheels and much grunting followed. A few moments later a wheeled, iron-barred cage, to the shafts of which were chained four long rows of slaves, was carted out in front of Kwasin. Seated on the floor of the cage and slumping against the bars was Awineth.

In the last moments of battle before darkness stole away his consciousness, Kwasin had thought he had seen Awineth die. Though relieved to find her among the living, her appearance distressed him. Dried blood caked one side of her face where it had streamed down from a horrible wound on her forehead. The other side of her face, though clean of blood, was badly bruised, and her naked body, streaked with dirt and blood, bore many cuts, scrapes, and bruises. What disturbed Kwasin the most, however, was the vacant look in her eyes. He could only guess that something had snapped in her soul under the cruel treatment she had endured. Perhaps his own eyes also carried the same hollow stare, but he doubted it. His entire frame coursed with as much rage as it did pain.

"Welcome to your new home," Minruth proclaimed loudly, "in which you and my daughter will be paraded across the island so that all may see what becomes of those who blaspheme against Great Resu!"

At last summoning a weak and rasping voice, Kwasin managed to croak, "You're mad... The people...won't stand for it." He truly believed they wouldn't. To place Kho at a lower station than Resu was unimaginable enough, but to enslave and publicly humiliate Kho's high vicar! Minruth pushed his game too far. If the Goddess Herself did not smite him down first, the people soon would.

Minruth merely laughed. "The people are docile cattle who desire to be herded. Your trust in them is as misguided as your devotion to the wife of Resu. But it is true there are still some supporters of Resu's estranged wife who yet hold out in the mountains and countryside. Therefore I won't execute my daughter, though she certainly deserves to die after what she has cost me. No, when my triumphal procession arrives at the capital, Awineth will have undergone a conversion of faith. There she will found a new order among the priestesses, one happy to recognize Kho's new and proper place as Resu's willing servant." Minruth leaned in closer and whispered, "Then my chief priest will announce that Resu has appeared to him and decreed that He is divorcing Kho and marrying a lesser goddess. Kho will be banished to the dark land of Sisisken, there to dwell for all eternity. It will take time, but those reluctant to accept Resu's dominance will eventually come around."

Kwasin had no doubt Minruth would do as he said, but would the people be willing to follow the new puppet religion? The more liberal city-dwellers might, if Kho's priestess ordered it, but he could not believe that Awineth, even looking as pitiful as she did now, would ever become an accomplice to such a plan. She hated her father too much to give into him, even under duress.

As if to contest Kwasin's thoughts, Minruth approached the caged cart and said, "Isn't that right, daughter?" Awineth only continued to stare vacantly through the bars of her prison, never once focusing her eyes upon Kwasin.

"Enough!" Minruth exclaimed. "I tire of the stench of death. Put the giant king of Dythbeth in with my daughter and let us begin the journey home. We must spread the news of my—I mean Resu's—victory."

Minruth retreated to the edge of the wall near the east gate, where he looked on, surrounded by close to forty soldiers. He must have worried that Kwasin might escape while being transferred into the cage, and attempt to kill him. Minruth was not wrong that Kwasin would have liked to have done so, but even had he the strength remaining, the subsequent actions of the emperor's men would have prevented him.

A group of twenty soldiers came forward, ten with spears pointed at Kwasin, and ten to assist in the transfer of the prisoner. The cage, only five feet wide and twelve in length, was opened. Kwasin's hopes for escaping the cage at some point in the future dwindled when he saw its unique construction. The door itself was actually two doors, one directly in front of the other, each consisting of iron bars set on massive iron hinges. The bars of the cage were not merely lined in a row but staggered in rows of three, so that even if he could pry loose a bar, several more would remain in place to block his way to freedom. For his great bulk to pass through them, Kwasin estimated he would have to remove six of the iron bars. Though the chassis on which the cage rested was wooden, a thin sheet of brass lined the floor of the cage itself. Escape through the flooring would be impossible without an implement hard enough to wear away at the metal sheet. And even if such a tool were smuggled to him, where would he hide it in the bare-floored cage? If they chained him, he might use his shackles to saw at the floor or the bars, but with all the thought that had gone into the construction of the cage he was sure Minruth wouldn't fetter him with metal.

For a moment he wondered how, with the heaviness of all that iron and brass, the bearers were going to be able to haul the cart all the way to Khokarsa without dying from exhaustion. Then he realized the question was the answer. The men would in fact die and Minruth would simply replace them. Of course, Minruth would want the bearers to travel slowly anyway, so that many would come to gawk at the prisoners and then spread the word of Kho's defeat across the island, and ultimately the entire empire.

Four of the men lifted the iron bar to which Kwasin was manacled, removing it from its wooden support frame; then they carried Kwasin into the cage and dropped him onto its blistering, sun-heated metal floor. When the second of the two men who had climbed with him into the cage attempted to exit, Kwasin bit the man in the calf as he was squeezing between him and the iron bars. The man screamed, then fell to his hands and knees and scrambled out of the cage as fast as he could. The other soldiers quickly yanked from the cage the iron bar they had used to carry Kwasin. He had no chance to grab it and use it against them.

Kwasin spat out a sizeable mass of flesh onto the floor. He felt a little better. The blood had wetted his mouth some.

Now the men came to release Kwasin from his fetters. He had been right; they didn't want him to be able to grate iron against brass, no matter how small a chance it would afford him of escaping. The soldiers were careful this time. They stood a distance back, tossed the keys through the bars to Kwasin, and ordered him to take off the manacles. If he refused, they said, they would spear him to death. Kwasin began to comply, but then, after some fumbling with the keys, he called out that his hands had been constricted for too long as he hung down from the manacles. He could not use his fingers effectively enough to undo the lock. There was some debate among the soldiers about what to do, until finally Minruth, his face as red as Resu himself, marched over and shouted at the officer in charge to carry out his orders or join the pile of the dead. The chastised officer hurriedly ordered a private to approach the cage and reach inside to unlock the captive.

Kwasin squirmed on his side to position his wrists and ankles up against the bars. Then the private, his face pale with fright, reached forth and retrieved the keys, first unlocking the chains around Kwasin's ankles, then sliding the key into the manacles on the captive's wrists. Suddenly Kwasin was on his feet. The private screamed as Kwasin yanked the man's left arm into the cage and levered it against the iron bars. There was a sickening crunch. The private slumped, keeling over from shock and pain as his left arm was torn from its socket.

Soldiers rushed the cage, their spears thrust before them. Kwasin withdrew against the opposite wall of bars as some of the men drove their spears between the bars to hold him back while the others dragged their fallen comrade away to safety. Their expressions a mixture of hatred and fright, the soldiers pressed their spearpoints against Kwasin's chest, pinning him against one side of the cage. Kwasin smiled at the men. He turned the key that still rested in the lock of his manacles, tossed the manacles outside through the bars. There was nothing he could do. If he resisted, he would be jabbed with the many spears until he passed out from loss of blood.

After the men had retreated, Kwasin looked down at Awineth, whose worn, reddened eyes stared dully at the floor. She had not even reacted to his attack. He squatted down beside her and began examining the wound on her forehead while she continued to gaze listlessly into space. The gash was deep, and a large lump rose beneath the broken flesh, but as far as he could tell her skull seemed unfractured.

The cart lurched and began moving, pulled along slowly by its human beasts of burden. Kwasin took one last painful look back at conquered and devastated Dythbeth, the city where he had been born and raised until the age of ten, and which he had always thought of as home. Then, after placing an arm around Awineth and leaning against the bars of his moving prison, he fell asleep to the creaking and rocking of the cart and the grunting of its bearers.

22

Almost a week passed while Minruth's triumphal procession waited outside the city only a few miles distant on the great plain. Though Minruth must have been eager to parade his captives before the island's population, he also wanted the grandest of processions to showcase his greatest of victories. Therefore Kwasin and Awineth sat glumly within their cage beside the dirt road to Khokarsa while slaves were gathered up from the city's surviving inhabitants and the caravan was assembled and provisioned.

Meanwhile, though they were given meager sips of water from a foul-smelling flask, the two captives starved. Dythbeth had already faced famine before the invasion, but with the Sixth Army raiding what little fare remained in the city, the food crisis worsened. Looking out over the great plain, Kwasin watched the mountains of the heaped-up dead grow taller with each passing day. But Minruth could not have his prized captives die before his procession even began, and so at last food was brought to them. Kwasin cursed, however, when the undercooked meat was tossed onto the floor of their cage. The soldier who had thrown it to them laughed.

"I hope you like your bear meat rare!" the man jeered.

Kwasin swore. As a member of the Klakordeth, he was forbidden from consuming the flesh of bears; to be caught doing so, no matter the situation, would result in Kwasin being cast out of the totem. The act was also considered ritually unclean to the population at large. Penalties for breaking the prohibition varied with local custom throughout the empire, and although bears were rare south of the Saasares, some did exist on the island in the backwoods mountains. The local priestess of an area where such an offense was committed typically sentenced the transgressor to be locked in a specially prepared and nearly intolerable hothouse until the impurities of soul and body were sweated out through the pores, usually to be followed by a thirty-day period of segregation from the community, either in solitary confinement or expulsion to the wilds. Not that many went out of their way to violate the taboo. Still, there were always fetishists among the totem who got their thrills from consuming bear flesh and were willing to endure the risk of being caught.

After staring for several minutes as the revolting morsel smoldering on the sun-baked brass flooring of the cage, Kwasin shrugged. He had eaten fouler things during his trek through the Wild Lands, and they had best eat the meat now before it spoiled in the heat of the afternoon. The rainy season, which normally brought a brief reprieve from the oppressive heat, had been delayed—yet another bad omen from Kho. In any case, the meat smelled so rank that he believed it to be that of a hyena, not a bear. And if in all honesty he believed he did not eat bear, would he truly have sinned? Of course, hyena meat was also considered unclean but at least eating it would not get him thrown out of his totem.

He tore at the tough, unpalatable flesh with his teeth, ripping off small scraps which he offered to Awineth before he consumed his own portion. At first she refused to eat, though she was not of his totem. It worried him greatly that she had not yet said a word to him since their capture, and he wondered if her languid spirit would ever wake up from its trance. But after he forced the meat into her mouth, Awineth began to chew mechanically. It gave Kwasin hope. Somewhere beneath the woman's broken outer shell, something wanted to live.

He couldn't blame Awineth for feeling so miserable. She had grown up pampered by royal attendants and instilled with the belief that her sanctity placed her high above the common riffraff. And now the high vicar of Kho was a prisoner, forced to eat unpalatable food and defecate in her own cage! The guards seemed to take a perverse pleasure in their former queen's discomfort, and often a full day, sometimes two, would pass before they would come with their buckets to wash away the filth. Kwasin resolved to watch Awineth closely, as he feared she might try to take her own life. Then he wondered if that might not be for the best, although for his part he intended to defy Minruth's humiliations until the bitter end. For good or ill, the deities had made sure that giving up just wasn't part of his character. There was always a chance, however unlikely, that he might escape someday and get his revenge. That thought more than anything kept him going.

Later that same evening a lieutenant in the Sixth Army came by to question Kwasin. Having heard of the trouble surrounding the imprisoning of Dythbeth's former king, the officer stood a good distance back from the bars.

"What has become of the great hatchet you carried when you returned from the Wild Lands," the man asked, "the ax formerly belonging to the dwarf Paga?"

The question took Kwasin off guard, but what surprised him even more was the reaction from Awineth. At the officer's inquiry, she suddenly sat up straight, her eyes glimmering with interest in the torchlight.

"Well, let's see," Kwasin said, eyeing the ceiling of the cage as if trying to summon a long-buried memory. "I must have stashed it in the city somewhere, but my head is heavy and my thoughts are slow from lack of good food. If I had a piece of that venison roasting over yonder I might be able to think better."

The officer folded his hands over his chest, but a moment later he walked to the soldiers' campfire and returned with a small, greasy cut of antelope thigh. He tossed it into the cage and watched while Kwasin and Awineth ravenously consumed the best meal they'd had in weeks. After they were finished eating, the soldier asked his question again.

"I must have left it somewhere," Kwasin said, scratching his head and rubbing a greasy hand upon a thigh. He stood up and began pacing the cage, inspecting each corner with what seemed a concerned diligence. Suddenly he jolted stiffly erect, as if seized by an unexpected illumination. "I remember now! Just as your cowardly slingman came up from behind and struck me on the head with his pellet, Lahhindar, the Archer Goddess, descended from the heavens on a silver string and plucked the ax from my hands for safekeeping!"

The officer frowned and then left, apparently convinced he would never get a straight answer from the wisecracking giant who was as much a trickster as Kagaga the raven. But the officer's visit intrigued Kwasin. Why did Minruth seek the ax? Did Minruth know the oracle's mysterious motives for demanding that the ax be brought back from the Wild Lands? And what about the officer's question had so struck Awineth that she temporarily awakened from her trancelike doldrums? Of course, Awineth had told the people of Dythbeth that the ax would be used in the war against Resu, but Kwasin had been led to believe that the claim was a false one. Perhaps she felt that if the ax was still missing, there was a chance it was in the hands of the network of priestesses and might be used as a symbol of the resistance. That is, if there even was a resistance any longer. He questioned Awineth about the matter when the officer was out of earshot, but she continued to be unresponsive, though she looked vaguely like she might be thinking.

The next morning the procession got underway. In addition to the twenty-four slaves manning the shafts of the prisoners' cart, a long line of courtiers, soldiers, and slaves both preceded and followed them. Near the front of the caravan rode Minruth, pulled along by human bearers in his red-painted, gaudily decorated covered wagon. Traveling with Minruth were his many young and beautiful consorts, brought from the capital to entertain the King of Khokarsa on his campaign. Like the corpulent Minruth, all were well fed.

The slaves, however, were provided barely enough sustenance to keep them going. By the time the caravan forded the Howahinly River and passed into the bee fields southeast of Qoqada—which took over two weeks as the bearers struggled to haul their heavy loads along the often agonizingly hilly road—nearly a quarter of the slaves had perished. Minruth was not fazed. He merely collected more slaves at Qoqada, and while his men rounded up the new additions from the region's already war-decimated population, he used the excess time to parade his captives through the city streets.

The supporters of Resu ran along with the processioners, shouting praises to the Emperor of Khokarsa for his great triumph and pelting the prisoners in their cage with rotting rubbish and, when they could find it, whatever dung they could scrape up from the few animals in the city that had survived Minruth's siege. They hurled no edible food, because they had none to spare.

Many stood back from the spectacle, peering from the front doors of their dwellings with looks both disapproving and despondent. These would be the loyalists to the Goddess, disgusted by what they saw happening but too afraid to voice their complaints for fear of what the soldiers would do to them and their families. Qoqada had faired better than Dythbeth, chiefly because the city had accepted Minruth's offer of amnesty in exchange for surrender. But still, many had died during the siege, either from starvation or from the skirmishes on the walls, and when the Sixth Army finally entered the city, Minruth's promises turned out to mean little. The soldiers took what they wanted, including food, women, and in the latter instance—when the Qoqadans came to the defense of their wives, daughters, and mothers—not a few lives.

Awineth made Kwasin proud as their cage rolled through the streets and they were heckled, cursed, jeered at, and barraged with refuse. She sat with regal bearing in the center of the cage, her chin held high and her eyes now haughty instead of dull, as Kwasin attempted to shield her from the rain of vile muck and often viler invectives. Certainly she was made of royal stuff, and was, as the saying went, as tough as a rhino's heel. But when the cart finally rolled away from the crowds, Awineth again slouched, and he saw in the corners of her eyes the first tears she had shed since their incarceration.

They stayed in Qoqada three days while the caravan rested and replenished itself with slaves. Then the procession continued its journey across the island. Kwasin overheard the soldiers guarding his cage say that Minruth was anxious to get back to the capital and see how much work had been accomplished on his tower. He had somehow continued the tower's construction despite the hardships and shortages of the war, and he was rumored to have commissioned a new architect who promised to speed things up. The soldiers to whom Kwasin listened laughed quietly among themselves, saying that Minruth could dream all he wished but the Tower of Resu would never be completed in his lifetime.

Late one night, well into the third week after their departure from the bee city, an incident occurred which made Kwasin shake with rage and frustration and sank Awineth even further into depression. The caravan was camped along the southern shore of the great lake to the northeast of Qoqada, and Minruth, intent on celebrating his own glory, had decided to open up the large store of mead, wine, and beer he had levied from the subjugated Qoqadans. As the drinking and merrymaking in the vicinity of the royal cart became ever more raucous, some of the soldiers stole into the supply wagons and made off with a share of the liquor in order to indulge in their own revelry. Thus, when a raging-drunk Minruth staggered up to Kwasin and Awineth's cage, the guards had already abandoned their post and gone to the lakeshore to carouse with their fellows. The guards were lucky. They would not be reported, at least not that night. Khokarsa's great king was far too intoxicated to care.

As he came forward, Minruth stumbled over a root and fell to one knee but still somehow managed to maintain his grip around his wine cask. After taking another swig of alcohol, he pulled himself up on shaky feet, lifted his kilt, and arched a stream of urine into the prisoners' cage.

The captives turned their backs to the warm showers and pressed themselves up against the bars on the far side of the cage. Kwasin swore under his breath but did not want to give Minruth the satisfaction of hearing his discomfort. Beside him, Awineth trembled with rage and, when the unpleasant deluge at long last ceased, threw herself up against the bars screaming that she would kill her father yet.

Minruth laughed, his face bloated and pale in the moonlight. "When you're angry you remind me of your mother," he said, beaming. "I wouldn't have poisoned her, but she had the gall to try and blackmail me into submission! My only regret is that I didn't get her out of the way sooner!"

Awineth beat her fists against the bars of the cage until Kwasin thought she would break the bones in her hands. It had long been rumored that Queen Wimimwi had been poisoned, and now here was Minruth, openly admitting his crime. The Emperor of Khokarsa had indeed become brazen.

As Awineth carried on, Minruth's eyes burned with a light that Kwasin recognized all too well. Kwasin tensed and anger made the blood in his ears pound.

"Seeing you so distraught, my daughter, titillates me. Indeed, you do remind me of Wimimwi, and I suddenly find myself enflamed with passion. Of course, I'll have to throw you in the river to clean you off, but then…"

Awineth stopped banging against the cage. Slowly, she backed away from her father, her expression now one of horror. Kwasin moved to position himself between her and Minruth, but stopped himself short. Awineth looked at him, as if to make a plea for protection, but Kwasin ignored her. Instead he walked to a corner of the cage, leaned against the iron bars, and folded his arms.

Keys jingled in Minruth's hands as he swayed an uneven course toward the heavily barred double doors. Now tears streamed down Awineth's eyes, and again she looked to Kwasin. "Please!" she said.

"Who am I to interfere in family matters?" Kwasin said with a shrug.

Awineth had begun to sob when suddenly the jingling of the keys stopped.

"By Kopoethken's sagging breasts!" Minruth cried, quickly backing away from the cage. "I'm drunker than I thought. Not that I wouldn't bed you, daughter—that can wait until we reach the capital—but to think I almost tried to open the cage with no guards present! Your mad ape of a lover might have killed me!"

Awineth regarded Kwasin, and for a moment he thought he saw understanding and possibly relief in her dark eyes. Kwasin had hated to deceive her, and found he almost couldn't. But he had been betting that Awineth's genuine terror would stimulate the twisted mind of her father enough that, in his drunken state, he would open the doors to their cage without realizing the danger to which he exposed himself.

Kwasin watched Minruth, swaying and stumbling, as he wandered off into the night. Then the two prisoners settled in for another unpleasant night. Kwasin drifted off to the sound of Awineth's weeping.

The two captives were awakened in the early morning hours by a great crashing and booming of thunder. Lightning streaked the heavens with its blinding anger, and within moments a torrential downpour was unleashed upon them. The Khokarsan rainy season had begun.

At first they welcomed the showers, and they stood willingly in the rain as it washed off the unpleasant blessing left upon them by Minruth, not to mention the odorous grime remaining on their bodies from the detritus hurled at them by the Qoqadans. Within a few minutes, however, they were so cold they began to loose the feeling in their hands and feet.

Shivering violently, Awineth pressed her naked body up against Kwasin's. Then she surprised him, as she had on the day of the great earthquake, by pulling him closer and pressing her cold, wet lips against his own. And for a period that seemed timeless, as the lightning struck about them and washed away the darkness, they gave themselves to one another.

They awoke again at dawn's first light in each other's arms. The rain now drizzled miserably and Kwasin could tell from the loud sawing snores coming from the guards' tent that the hung-over men had returned.

Then he started. A scrawny-looking youth of about sixteen years was emerging from the trees surrounding the meadow in which the procession camped. Behind the youth, who now padded stealthily past the guards' tent, a motley band of peasants carrying pitchforks, scythes, and other farming implements crept forward. One among the group stood out, an attractive, raven-haired, middle-aged woman whose distinctive Psyche-knot hairstyle, gold-ringed girdle, and ceremonial dagger identified her as a priestess of Kho.

The loyalists of the Goddess were staging a rescue!

Kwasin shook Awineth from her half-slumber and indicated the approaching group. Awineth gasped, and they both stood up and pressed their faces anxiously up against the side of their cage, their hands gripping whitely the iron bars.

The sandy-haired youth approached the double doors of their cage. In his hands he carried a large bronze skeleton key, which seemed to clank all too loudly when he slid it inside the lock of the outer door. Kwasin held his breath as the boy scraped the key's teeth against the wards of the lock. After experiencing some difficulty, the key turned and the outer door swung open.

The boy inserted the key into the second door's lock just as a cry erupted from the direction of the band of loyalists. Apparently not all of the guards had returned to their tent during the night. One of them had just staggered back and discovered the rescue attempt.

Surprised by the man's cry, the youth jerked back from the lock. The key dropped from his hands, clattering off the brass rim of the cage and onto the ground.

Kwasin growled and shook the iron door. The shocked soldier shouted out an alarm call loud enough to awaken the entire camp. At the same time, the man drew his sword from its sheath and cut down one of the loyalists before he could raise his scythe. A farmer, smarter than his fellows, began jabbing his pitchfork into the guards' tent, obviously hoping to buy time for the boy to unlock the cage. One of the men in the tent screamed, and another guard ran out of the tent only to be impaled by the farmer. But a moment later a group of soldiers armed with swords and spears—though clearly still half-drunken—charged in among the loyalists. Kwasin cried out in anguish as the farmer who had attacked the tent was struck down first. The man had been a true hero.

The boy at the lock picked up his key but in his nervousness dropped it again. Both Kwasin and Awineth groaned. Then the boy again rose from the weeds growing around the cart, the key in his hand and a smile on his face. A moment later the boy died, still smiling, when a soldier thrust a bronze spearpoint into his back.

Crestfallen, the two captives sank to the cold, damp floor of their cage and watched helplessly as the entire band of loyalists was slaughtered.

In the days following the incident, Awineth again lost the will to live. The procession went on, traveling over the hills and dales of the rolling Khokarsan countryside, while Awineth resumed her sullen and soulless staring through the bars of their cage. And now, despite Kwasin's attempts to force-feed her, she simply refused to eat.

On the evening of the fifth day of her fast, Awineth awoke, the dark eyes of her now gaunt face looking startled and surprisingly lucid. "The Goddess has blessed me with a vision!" she said, loudly enough that the guards took note and quieted their campfire talk. "Kho appeared to me in all Her terrible glory! She says that I must save myself, for in the end She will triumph! But She will only succeed in her struggle against the sungod if the people stand up and come to my aid. She has rewarded the spirits of Her followers who attempted to free us the other night, but those who imprison us will be cursed! When the spirits of the latter arrive in Sisisken's dark domain, they will be doomed to endure eternal torment!"

Kwasin shuddered. Had Awineth truly seen the Goddess, or had she merely made up the vision to frighten the camp guards? The guards certainly did seem subdued that evening, and he didn't think it a coincidence when the following morning he overheard the guards whispering among themselves that three of their fellows had deserted. Awineth seemed pleased with the development.

"Kho has rightly put fear into their hearts," she said. "She has sent the men running back to their families to spread the word of my vision."

That morning Awineth began eating once again the foul, ritually forbidden cuisine offered her, saying that she must remain strong for the moment when her followers would come to free her. But over the weeks that followed—weeks filled with humiliation and suffering as the two endured the cold, whipping rains and were paraded through the streets of various villages—no further attempts were made to emancipate Kho's high vicar.

At last the day came when mighty Khowot's smoldering volcanic summit rose up slowly upon the eastern horizon and the procession marched out of the rolling hills surrounding Khokarsa and past the fields and huts that marked the city's agricultural suburbs. Kwasin, but even more so Awineth, was shocked at the state of the capital since they had been there last, now almost a year and a half ago. At that time, when Kwasin had been imprisoned in a cell beneath the palace citadel and Awineth locked away by her father, the city lay devastated in the aftermath of Minruth's revolt. Thirty thousand died in the uprisings that followed, and much of the capital and its suburbs burned to the ground. Then Khowot had erupted again just as Kwasin—along with Hadon, Awineth, and their companions—managed to escape from Minruth's prisons. Once more the lava had descended on the city and set much of it afire. But now the charred rubble had been razed and the stinking piles of corpses disposed with, and in place of the wreckage, new stately buildings proudly lined the paved streets of Khokarsa. How Minruth had managed the city's renovation during the costly civil war baffled Kwasin, and he could only surmise the military had enforced a brutal policy of civil service, or perhaps enacted total slavery over a great portion of the population.

And by Kho, the Great Tower! When last they had seen it, the massive ziggurat stood only two-thirds completed, rising just short of five hundred feet into the heavens. But now, by some miracle of miracles, at least another fifty feet had been added to its height. Perhaps less than a quarter of the tower remained to be constructed.

Seeing the surprised looks on the captives' faces, a guard marching beside them said, "The tides have turned—Kho subsides, and Resu provides! King Minruth says the tower will be completed by the Year of Wenqath the Hero!" As the Year of the Horned Fish was now coming to a close, that meant Minruth planned to have his tower finished in only two years! Kwasin gaped at the impressive structure that loomed over the city, its base nearly a half-mile in diameter, its slanting stepped walls surrounded by massive earthen ramparts and enveloped by great billows of orange dust hanging ominously in the air—the latter raised by the travails of the thousands of men and oxen, looking ant-sized in the distance, working to haul cyclopean stone blocks up the ramparts. Up, down, and across the broad face of the tower, teams of workers labored to install elaborate friezes on the stonework. The carved figures rivaled in craftsmanship the work of Awodon, that bygone master of sculpture, and were in the form of many varied animals, men, heroes, gods, goddesses, and demons. The cost of commissioning the impressive sculptures must have been exceedingly vast, though it would have paled in comparison to the expenditure required to make such rapid progress on the entire structure.

"It wouldn't have been possible," the talkative guard continued, "without the emperor's new architect, Wenekaru. The man carries a genius to rival Awines, they say! I do not understand the high talk of mathematics, which is wearisome to me, but it is said Wenekaru is actually building a completely new type of structure on top of the old one. And he has at last found a light-weight type of brick, long sought by King Minruth, which will ensure that the tower will not collapse from its own heaviness."

They continued on, passing into the city through the outer eastern gate and crossing a stone bridge spanning one of the many canals of the great metropolis. Scores of residents and market-goers thronged about the procession to see their king returning from his great victory, and to gawk at the misery of his two famous captives. But Kwasin noted that only a portion of the onlookers cheered the king of kings, and that Minruth was careful to surround his royal wagon with an intimidating number of armed soldiers, who with the points of their spears sought to hold back both the overeager and the potentially dangerous.

When they passed through another gated wall and were carted past the tower workers' residences, Kwasin understood that his guess about Minruth's totalitarian tactics had been correct. Expansive stone-walled pens, marked at intervals by well-manned sentry towers, enclosed a vast district set aside for the workers. While slave labor had always been used for the construction of the ziggurat, it was clear now that Minruth had indentured a tremendous portion of the city's population to finish his dream once and for all.

"Get a good look," the guard who had spoken before said to Kwasin. "Because after the trial, which is likely to be quite a show, the slave pens are sure to be your new home. Oh, no, our beloved king wouldn't waste an elephant like you by executing you or letting you rot in the pits beneath the citadel—not when he can use you to set the blocks on his road to immortality."

Then the soldier looked up at Awineth and grinned. "And as for you, my former queen, I'm told your father has other plans."

23

The procession stopped on the edge of the Inner City and the soldiers, thrusting their spears inside the cage, forced Awineth to manacle Kwasin in heavy iron chains. When satisfied their giant prisoner was properly restrained, the soldiers swung open the iron doors of the cage and with additional chains secured Kwasin's arms, crossing them so tightly behind his back he could not move them at all. Then, to the sound of trumpets blaring, drums beating, and brass gongs clanging, Kwasin and Awineth climbed down from their cart and were led forward through the clamorous throngs of spectators.

Continuing on, the procession crossed over the arching stone bridge that rose above the moat, then climbed the wide, steep steps of the acropolis before passing through the huge bronze doors into the citadel. As they marched past the many temples and government buildings, Kwasin noted that all of the statues of Kho had been removed where possible and replaced with effigies of Resu, while those figures too large to move had been defaced by Minruth's vandals. The sight both outraged and disgusted Kwasin, and beside him Awineth's eyes burned with fury.

They approached the great domed, nine-sided palace, and Kwasin thought they would be led inside when suddenly the guards yanked hard on the chain around his neck and pulled him out of the procession. Kwasin roared and drove a massive shoulder into the group of soldiers who tried to restrain him, landing a number of them on their rears. Many in the thronging street cheered and hooted their approval, but more soldiers quickly overwhelmed Kwasin and forced him to his knees, nearly jumping over one another to assail the prisoner with the butts of their spears.

Kwasin caught one last glimpse of Awineth as she was led up the broad and steep steps of the palace. She looked back at him over a shoulder, but she was already too far away for him to discern whether her large, dark eyes were pleading or remained proudly defiant.

The soldiers drove Kwasin ahead of them with their spears, while at the same time retaining a firm grip on the chain about his neck. They prodded him around the palace to a rear entrance, and after passing up the steps of the building into a spacious hall, his captors unlocked an iron-grilled door and brought their prisoner down a series of winding stone staircases and narrow corridors. Kwasin already knew their destination, for Minruth had imprisoned him beneath the palace once before.

"What of the trial?" Kwasin asked one of the soldiers. "When will I be summoned to testify?"

"Trial?" The man laughed. "It's going on as we speak, but you won't be testifying. Our orders are to hold you here until you're sentenced. I don't think Minruth would have bothered with the trial at all, but he wants to give the appearance of fairness. Now get moving, you great oaf!"

The soldier jabbed his spear at Kwasin, forcing him inside a dark cell near the end of a long corridor. The iron door slammed shut, echoing against the hallway's stone walls like a sentence of doom. The turnkey bolted the door's heavy lock, removed his key, and left Kwasin to brood in the darkness of his cell.

Kwasin had just stood up to examine his prison when the turnkey returned with the guards and opened the cell door.

"What now?" Kwasin asked, scowling.

"Trial's over!" one of the guards exclaimed. "You've been convicted on seventeen counts of high treason and sentenced to death. But King Minruth will allow you to ruminate on your multitude of transgressions while you slave on the Great Tower."

"And what of the queen?"

"You mean the former queen," the guard said. "The criers have just announced to the city that she has denounced the College of Priestesses as corrupt. Because of her contrition and her father's great mercy, she will be allowed to retain her office as high priestess of Kho and will immediately begin initiating reforms among the priestesses. But there will no longer be an Empress of Khokarsa. King Minruth says that Resu has decreed it."

Disgusted by the sham trial, the lies about Awineth, and the blatant sacrilege, Kwasin said nothing. If Minruth was fool enough to let him live a little longer, then so be it. Meanwhile, he would try to find a means of escape. And after that, revenge.

But when the guards escorted him to the tower workers' district, he saw what a truly daunting feat escape would be. Not only were the workers' pens double-walled and kept under the ever vigilant watch of the sentries in the towers, but he was brought to a special heavily fortified pen which had been designed and created just for him. The pen was in reality more of a pit, fully thirty-feet deep, and a hundred feet in both length and width. The only way in or out of the pit was to be lowered or hoisted up by rope. A special wooden crane, from the sheave of which dangled a wooden platform, had been set up for the purpose of ferrying passengers from the base of the pit to ground level. When the crane elevator was not in use, it could be swung back away from the pit to prevent a person below from somehow lassoing the crane and thereby escaping. To further complicate matters for the would-be escapee, a tall stone wall had been erected from the base of the pit and rose thirty feet above the pit's rim, and a barrier of thorns wrapped along the top and sides of the encircling wall to discourage potential climbing. Not that there would be any climbing, a soldier told Kwasin, for at all times he was to be fettered in chains of bronze inside a stone prison that had been constructed in the center of the pit. And even should Kwasin escape his shackles, break through the door of the prison, and attempt to scale the walls or burrow beneath them, he would be spotted immediately by the soldiers in the overlooking towers, as the pit was lit by torches throughout the night.

Five soldiers accompanied Kwasin to the floor of the pit on the swaying platform that hung down from the crane. He would have tried knocking the men from the platform, but a noose had been slipped over his neck. A man stationed on top of the wall released the slack of Kwasin's noose from a winch as the platform was lowered. The captain in charge warned Kwasin that if he caused any trouble, the man above would draw up the noose. Then Kwasin wouldn't be creating any more trouble for anyone, the man had said with a smile.

When they reached the bottom, Kwasin eyed a number of small stone-lined holes spaced at regular intervals along the pit's perimeter. This would be a drainage system put in place to prevent the massive slave pit from filling up with rainwater, although it would not stop it from suddenly becoming a muddy hellhole once one of the violent seasonal storms struck the region. Because of this latter fact, a raised, stone walkway ran from where the crane dropped off its passengers to the stone prison where Kwasin was to remain chained to a granite wall when he wasn't working on the tower.

The soldiers escorted Kwasin down the walkway to the prison, unlocked and swung open the great bronze door, and brought him inside where he was secured with massive bronze chains to a wall. One of the soldiers took off the chains that trussed up Kwasin's arms behind his back, although he did not remove the manacles. A bowl of cold and watery millet gruel was set on the floor before Kwasin. Then torches in the wall sconces were extinguished and the door to the long, narrow cell was shut and locked behind the departing soldiers.

Kwasin leaned forward to lap up the contents of the bowl in front of him when a voice arose in the darkness, carrying from what must have been a cell behind his own.

"Strange is the road of fate laid down by the deities," the melodious voice rang out, "but stranger is the road from Dythbeth to Khokarsa! Indeed, it is as if Kho has inextricably tied us together, my king!"

Kwasin groaned upon hearing the singsong voice. Would he never be rid of the loudmouthed bard?

24

It turned out that Minruth, not fate or the Goddess, had paired up Bhako with his former king. The romantic bard, however, saw things differently.

"It is true," Bhako explained, shouting through a ventilation shaft in the ceiling that connected both of their cells, "that Minruth has placed me in your pit because he wishes me to punctuate my epic verse, the *Pwamwotkwasin*, with a record of your final and humiliating days as a slave. But it was really Kho, acting through Her high priestess, Who orchestrated the events that led me to be once more at your side. For on the very night shining Dythbeth fell, Queen Awineth ordered me to the walls to entertain with song the war-weary soldiers serving night duty. Had she not done so, I would surely have joined the pile of the dead upon the great plain. Because on the night before that great battle of battles had yet begun, I was plucking my lyre and reciting a minor cycle in your heroic epic when suddenly, drunk on song, I stumbled and hit my head. I must have done this and lost consciousness just as the invaders attacked, for when I awoke I found it was morning and that I had fallen behind the wooden supply crate on which I had been standing as I performed. I say it must have been at the moment the Khokarsans struck, for if I had fallen earlier, why wouldn't the soldiers to whom I was singing have pulled me up from behind the crate and brought me to a priestess of medicine?"

"Perhaps they'd had enough of your tuneless singing!" Kwasin growled.

Bhako ignored the jibe and continued. "Only because I was hidden behind the crate had I escaped the enemy's notice. When I got up and peered from the wall, I saw my once proud and fair city smoldering in ruins and the Klemqaba busied with their looting and raping. I even saw you, O King, trussed up before Minruth's tower of dead. Oh, how I agonized that I could do nothing to help you!"

"I am sure saving my hide was your highest priority," Kwasin murmured skeptically.

"It was, O King," Bhako replied, who must have been as keen of hearing as the fabled long-eared hare in the verse of the priestess-bard Hala. Certainly the bard was as annoying as that mischievous, although widely renowned leporid. "But by the time I had donned the trappings of a fallen Khokarsan soldier," Bhako continued, "and made it outside the walls, it was too late. Minruth had already begun to transfer you to the cage in which, to my horror, Queen Awineth was also imprisoned. And yet I did not give up. I infiltrated the army and joined Minruth's great triumphal procession. Yes, my king, although you did not know it, I remained faithfully at your side all the way to the capital! Unfortunately, only a few weeks into our journey, I was found out when I attempted to filch the key to your cage from a guard. Despite my status as a sacred bard, Minruth threw me in irons. At first I thought—and hoped, so I might soothe your suffering and woe with song—that he would put me with you in your cage. But Minruth the Mad said the sharp wit of a bard's tongue revealed his devious nature and feared I would somehow help you escape.

"Yes, the Emperor of Khokarsa is quite interested in you, O King! Almost to the point of obsession, for he has heard of your many feats of bravery and knows too well the great losses you have caused him. He even had me recite to him my great epic of your adventures, saying he has in store for it a most fitting conclusion."

Kwasin had no comeback to the bard's last comment. He was sure Minruth had long contemplated how best to dispose of Dythbeth's great hero.

Feeling even more sullen after hearing Bahko's story, Kwasin pushed aside the bowl of gruel left by the guards and, leaning against the cold granite wall, fell into a restless sleep filled with nightmares that upon awakening he could not remember.

The days, weeks, and months that followed stretched on wearily for Kwasin. The Year of the Horned Fish came to a close, and the Year of the Honey Bee progressed as the once defiant King of Dythbeth slaved away on the Great Tower, waiting anxiously for word from the outside that the forces of the Goddess had at last rallied against Minruth. But no such news ever arrived, and what little information Kwasin did garner from eavesdropping on his guards, or from rumors spread among the tower workers, was not good.

His guards' whispers confirmed that Minruth had kept true to his word and given his daughter her life but not her freedom, permitting Awineth to live out her days in a heavily barred apartment within the palace. Probably he feared the public outcry, and quite possibly all-out revolt, that would be sure to follow if he killed Kho's high vicar. But while Awineth was more or less comfortably imprisoned and otherwise well treated, rumor had it that Minruth took great pleasure in periodically entering her chambers and raping her, despite the fact that she was said to be pregnant with Kwasin's child. Kwasin could not dismiss the disturbing stories as fiction. He had seen for himself Minruth's unhealthy infatuation with his daughter.

Upon hearing the news, Kwasin became distraught. In his wanderings, he had spread his seed far and wide with little thought of consequence for either mother or potential offspring. But now Kwasin began to feel differently, and a great worry seized him at the possibility that Minruth would murder his future son or daughter, or worse yet, raise the child as his own. He was not sure what had changed in him to cause these unfamiliar pangs of conscience, but the more he thought of the danger looming over his unborn child, the deeper also seemed to grow his feelings for the child's mother. That realization shook him more than anything. Kwasin, while always a great lover, had never known love. Always had he been a free spirit, eager to share his insatiable desire with as many women as he possibly could. Why then should his heart gallop like a crazed rhino at the merest thought of Awineth? With perhaps the exception of the fair Lalila, the woman was as beautiful as any he had known—but the world was full of beautiful women! And besides, Awineth was a bitch, a she-devil like none other! Still, though the mind argued, the heart—always the strongest of beasts—won out. He could not deny that, against his better judgment, he had somehow lowered his emotional guard to the woman.

The hearsay from the palace only made Kwasin work harder to grate his bronze chains against the granite walls of his prison as he attempted to saw down his fetters. Once he had weakened them enough, he would wait for an opportune moment. Then he would strike and, even if he did not escape, at least many guards would die before he was killed or subdued.

Kwasin also learned through the grapevine that the newly ordained order of Kho, propped up in Awineth's name, had all but caused the College of Priestesses to collapse. This did not prevent the priestesses' network from going underground and operating in clandestine fashion among the common people. Vague murmurings of the network's existence came occasionally to Kwasin through his fellow slaves, though he received no direct communication from the priestesses. Then one day something happened that made him realize he had merely been too deaf to hear the priestesses' messages. It also made him reevaluate the worth of Bhako, that constantly chattering, ever bothersome bard.

Kwasin had been single-handedly pulling a massive granite block up one of the great ramparts of dirt that angled up along the walls of the Great Tower, trying to ignore the dozens of spectators who congregated on a large wooden viewing platform and often volleyed insults at him. Minruth had ordered the platform to be constructed atop the massive stone wall penning in the tower workers, desiring to broadcast to the island, and indeed the entire empire, that the once mighty Kwasin was now his slave. The King of Khokarsa had gone so far as to issue travel vouchers to anyone who wished to come from afar and see his famous captive. That Minruth had placed a heavy tax upon the vouchers, one which served to cancel out any benefit to the travelers, was not advertised. In fact, many of those ensnared by Minruth's voucher program now resided in the capital as indentured servants, forced to become slaves themselves because they had spent too many *nasuhno* on their trip and gone into debt. In this way, Minruth increased his already great number of stonemasons, brickmakers, carpenters, foundrymen, ropemakers, surveyors, artisans, stevedores, warehouse workers, scribes, bakers, brewers, and cooks contributing to the effort to finish the tower.

But on this day, without warning, all work on the tower suddenly halted. The guards yelled up at Kwasin to leave the granite block he had been hauling where it lay. This despite the fact he had dragged his burden only halfway up its rampart and stopping now might cause the block's wooden sledge to become lodged on the dirt-and-gravel concourse. Cursing because he knew he would later be the one ordered to get the block unstuck, Kwasin slipped out of his harness—though not his heavy bronze chains—and joined the other slaves who were being herded back to their pens. Kwasin was escorted under heavy guard to his pit, where he was lowered down by the crane and shackled to the usual wall inside his cell.

"Is that your stink I smell, bard?" Kwasin yelled up at the ventilation shaft in his cell's ceiling.

"Yes, but I am surprised you can smell me, O King, over your own spicy excretions," Bhako replied from his own cell.

Because Kwasin wanted an answer from the nosy bard, whom he had come to rely on for much of his gossip, he held back a crude retort and asked, "Why have all the slaves been given reprieve from today's labor? Surely you've heard something?"

"The word among the workers," Bhako replied, "is that a number of traitors loyal to the Goddess have been planted among the camp guards. The traitors are here, the gossipers say, not to free the slaves, but rather to transmit intelligence from the network of priestesses." Then Bhako laughed and said, "But they only have it half right."

"What do you mean?"

"Perhaps I have already said too much," Bhako said. "What if guards have been stationed outside to eavesdrop on our conversations?"

Kwasin would not normally egg on the gregarious bard, who never seemed to tire once he began talking or singing, but now Bhako's words piqued his curiosity. "I can see the crane through the iron grille in the door of my cell," Kwasin said. "The guards who brought me here all stood upon the crane's platform when it was last lifted above. There are no guards to overhear us."

When Bhako did not reply, Kwasin cried, "Now you choose to remain silent, when you might actually have something of value to say! I am your king, as you ceaselessly remind me—never mind that I reside in a slave pit, fettered and hobbled so that I must shuffle about like an old woman. And as your king, I order you to speak!"

Kwasin was about to threaten the bard with an unpleasant accident the next time they were assigned to the same work gang when suddenly Bhako spoke up.

"I only hesitate to confide in you, my king, because if we are overheard, the well-laid plans of the network of priestesses will have all been for naught. And besides, you've been receiving their messages anyway—through me! Haven't you wondered why I'm such a good gossip? It's not from listening to the rumormongers or even traitorous guards. No, the secret communications come instead from the very spectators Minruth so vainly parades before us! But King Minruth and his guards are too stupid to understand the messages, even though they are transmitted in plain sight. Or I should rather say within earshot, for the messages come to me through my chosen medium, that of song. Certainly you have heard the women who often come to hector us workers with their derogatory rhymes? But while the insults of the women are only the shallowest sort, much deeper beneath their verse lies a secret message, coded in a type of rhyme, allusion, and meter that only a bard would understand."

"You're saying the priestesses have hidden a message in the obscene limericks hurled at us by the spectators?"

"Precisely, O King! It is another legacy left by Awines, Dythbeth's favorite son, and I only know of the secret language because I was once employed by the Temple of Kho in our native city. The priestesses know this, and only today I received a new message from them, one which bears great hope."

"Out with it!"

Bhako paused, and then with joy ringing clearly in his voice proclaimed, "The priestesses say that Awineth has given birth to your child, a boy who because of the thunder of his cries she has named Deth!"

Kwasin felt as if a god had struck him. "Has it been that long?" he said, his breath suddenly short and his extremities tingling with shock.

"Indeed! In fact it has been longer than nine months since our imprisonment as slaves to the tower. Queen Awineth gave birth a full month ago, but Minruth has clamped down so hard that the network of priestesses dared not send any messages, even in code." The bard went on to relate that, on the night of the birth, Minruth had sent two women to take the newborn away from its mother. Awineth's attending priestesses, however, killed the women and attacked the guards, slaying them. Though most of the priestesses were killed in the struggle, they managed to get both mother and child out of Awineth's locked room, spiriting them from the palace through secret passageways and tunnels known only to the initiates of Kho.

"Minruth flew into a rage when he found out," Bhako continued. "He immediately threw a cordon around the city and began a house-to-house search. But now, a month later, he has still found no one, or at least not those he was looking for."

"What do you mean?" Kwasin shouted up at the shaft. His heart pounded and he had broken into a sweat, notwithstanding the fact that the edges of the great pit shielded their enclosure from the hot glare of the sun and left it relatively cool.

"You've noticed the influx of new slaves of late?" Bhako asked. "They're the most shameful lot of humanity I've ever seen, but now I understand why. The new slaves are composed of the criminal rabble Minruth rounded up during his search of the city. Slaves by nature make poor workers, which is one reason it has taken so long to build the tower—that and the efforts of the priestesses over the centuries to slow its construction. But criminals make even worse slaves than—"

"Save your philosophizing!" Kwasin bellowed. "What do you know of the queen?"

"Sadly, nothing more than I've already told you," Bhako replied. "Even the priestesses who delivered the intelligence to me know nothing. It's assumed that she is being concealed in a house, or possibly beneath one in an underground room, somewhere in the city. Minruth is still patrolling the city's residential districts and suburbs, and he has sent spies everywhere, even among the tower workers. No one can be trusted, my king, absolutely no one."

Suddenly Bhako announced he had come to a decision. Though it was forbidden to do so without authorization from the priestesses, he had no other choice than to teach his king the secret metaphorical language of Awines. When Kwasin asked why he must learn the code when Bhako could simply translate for him, the bard replied, "What if Minruth should separate us or something unforeseen happened to me? I might fall from the tower by accident or be murdered by someone in the slave gangs. While I am a sacred bard, we are among many felons who would not think twice about harming me. If I were to be killed, you would have no way of communicating with the priestesses."

And so for the remainder of their day off from working on the tower, Bhako prattled on about rhymes and riddles and secret messages. Kwasin tried his best to understand the bard's explanations and examples but, by Hala, what did the man mean when he said that the intervals between the words often meant more than the words themselves? Frustrated by the depth and sophistication of the ancient code, and also anxious because of the information he had received about Awineth, Kwasin finally gave up. He told the bard he would just have to make sure he did not get himself killed.

Four months passed while Kwasin waited for further word from the priestesses. Meanwhile Minruth redoubled his efforts to complete the Great Tower, bringing in thousands of additional workers utilizing policies that involved bribery, deception, and frequently outright blackmail. The latter consisted of threatening to shut down crucial trade routes and thus deprive both the local island queendoms and those across the two Kemus of vital supplies. During the civil war, access to the salt mines in the Saasares had been disrupted, forcing the empire's queendoms and outposts to deplete their stores of this essential dietary mineral. Shortly after the war ended, however, the salt trade had been reestablished, and now Minruth garrisoned the mines, denying salt shipments to any city that did not provide for him a certain percentage of their population to serve as laborers on the tower.

Kwasin's guards, talking among themselves but loudly enough to be overheard, said that the king's advisors feared to question Minruth the Mad, even though his obsession with the tower threatened to bankrupt the entire Khokarsan economy. Minruth had begun to propagate the idea that he, as king, was in fact Resu himself, the sungod incarnate. Therefore anyone who questioned the king's decisions was in reality expressing their lack of faith in Resu. Under the new order imposed by Minruth and his priests, doubt in the sungod itself was an unlawful and punishable offense. If prosecuted, it could lead to imprisonment, heavy fines, and even a sentence of death.

The guards also brought news from across the island that only worsened Kwasin's already black mood. It seemed that the northern mountaineers, who had been allowed to colonize Dythbeth after the Klemqaba were through with their pillaging, had proved extremely poor administrators. Inexperienced in the complexities of running a city, they had run Dythbeth's former prosperity into the ground while the local population died off by the thousands from famine and disease. One of the guards remarked that it would take another hundred years for the population to expand before the city could be rebuilt and restored to its past glory.

Kwasin's heart sank upon hearing of the catastrophic demise of his native queendom, and as he heaved load after load of bricks up the tower's great ramparts, he began to question what he could have done differently to save his city. Perhaps he should have swallowed his pride and sought help from his cousin Hadon. News had recently spread among the tower workers that Hadon was now king of his outpost city. Further, King Hadon supposedly claimed that, as winner of the Great Games, he was still rightfully the king of kings, and it was said that he was rallying the cities along the southern sea to unite against Minruth and attack the island, although the latter may have just been hearsay. But Minruth, according to Kwasin's guards, believed the rumor. Even now, as the Khokarsan treasury strained under the weight of the tower project, he was raising an army among the subjugated cities of the Kemu to face the alleged threat from the south. Minruth had also ordered Admiral Poedy and his navy to blockade the Strait of Keth, thus preventing any vessels from entering the northern sea.

But while all of the coastal cities along the Kemu had been vanquished, one of them would not be assisting Minruth in either his military operations or his mad quest to complete the tower. Mukha's entire population was said to have been slaughtered in retaliation for having secretly sided with Dythbeth during the war while at the same time outwardly claiming allegiance to Minruth. Old King Qanaketh and the entire royal family of Mukha now resided in the dungeons beneath Minruth's citadel, awaiting a fate unknown.

The months passed among the tower workers. Twice Kwasin became so frustrated with his situation that he attacked the guards overseeing his work gang, killing three soldiers. Two of the men had been hurled by Kwasin down the face of the tower, while the third soldier's skull was crushed with a well-slung brick when he made the mistake of removing his helmet in Kwasin's presence while trying to get at an itch. Normally any such display of violence would have resulted in immediate death for the offending slave, but Minruth had issued orders that Kwasin was not to be harmed.

Or at least so Kwasin assumed. While he was being escorted back to his pit after the first incident, he asked a guard why he had not been killed on the spot.

The man, grinning, looked at Kwasin and said, "From what I hear the king has something special in store for you."

When Kwasin asked what this was, the man only continued to smile and said no more.

25

One day, well over a year and a half into his captivity, Kwasin looked up at the Great Tower and realized much to his surprise that the colossal structure was almost complete. Nearly half a millennium had passed since the first stone of the massive ziggurat had been laid down by King Klakor and blessed by Queen Hiindar. Since that time many thousands of men and women had died working on the monument, not a few of them over the past three years alone. The Great Tower of the Kho and Resu—now simply the Great Tower of Resu—soared majestically into the heavens, its staggered sides rising well over six hundred feet from the half-mile wide base.

Kwasin shook his mane of hair, as angered and saddened as he was awestruck at the breathtaking testament of blood, sweat, tears, and obsession. He took no pride in the fact that he had contributed to the tower's construction. To him it represented only the intense anguish of his captivity and the longstanding suffering of the people. Because of the tower—because of Minruth's mad quest for immortality—Great Kho had been dethroned, many of Her people slaughtered, and the priestesses and their college propped up in a hollow mockery of their former glory. And yet the world went on. The oracle's prediction of doom for all the land had not come to pass. The sun and moon continued rise and set, the rains came and went, and the great flocks of birds still winged their way across the horizon.

Now that Minruth's great project neared its final stages of completion, the majority of the hired artisans and craftsmen working on the tower, as well as a good number of the skilled slaves and indentured workers, were being redeployed to other critical duties in the reconstruction of the postwar empire. Kwasin and Bhako, however, were not posted away from the tower, but rather assigned to the burdensome and backbreaking task of deconstructing the massive ramparts of earth that squared the enormous ziggurat.

The vast quantities of dirt that needed to be moved out of the city posed a significant logistical problem for the king and his advisors. As the Year of Wenqath the Hero rapidly approached, Minruth wanted the area around the tower cleared posthaste. There was no time to allow for the dirt to be loaded onto galleys and freighted off, especially when the number of ships needed to do that would have choked off both the Gulf of Gahete and the Gulf of Lupoeth for months, appreciably impacting the influx of supplies and foodstuffs necessary to keep the city operating. Besides, Minruth's navy had suffered greatly during the war and the majority of his remaining fleet was currently occupied in patrolling the southern Kemu.

A solution was found when a priest in the royal court facetiously remarked that there was enough dirt left to build another great wall around the capital. Minruth seized upon the idea, immediately ordering his engineers to design a broad and tall earthwork barrier beyond the eastern walls of the city at the bottom of Khowot's slopes. The volcano had last erupted only three years ago, and at that time a sea of lava had washed over and destroyed the sacred oak grove and inundated the large stone-block Temple of Kho. Many yet feared that a future eruption might belch a deluge of death-dealing lava directly into the Inner City itself, killing tens of thousands. So now Minruth sent out his criers throughout the capital to proclaim the barrier to be his gift for the citizens' patience during the construction of the tower. But the building of the lava wall only added more aggravation to the citizens weary of both war and their king's vain engineering projects. For months they would have to put up with disruptions caused by the bearers as they hauled one cartload of dirt after another eastward through the heavily populated commercial and residential district on their way out of the city.

Slowly, the Great Tower of Resu began to emerge from behind the mountainous ramparts of earth that surrounded it. Now the spectators came not to jeer at the slave-king of Dythbeth but rather to peer up in awe at the successful completion of the greatest engineering feat ever undertaken by human hands. Kwasin only glowered. He knew that the tower's completion only speeded him on the way toward his impending doom. He had long ago given up on receiving help from the priestesses. Since Bhako first informed him of the secret language of Awines, they had received no further coded transmissions. He could only assume that the conspiring priestesses had been rooted out and put to death.

Then, just as he finally determined he had nothing to lose and would attack barehanded and hobbled the forty spear-, sword-, and sling-armed guardsmen who routinely escorted him to and from his pit each day, a message arrived at last.

Kwasin had been shoveling dirt into a wagon from the shallow remains of the tower's last rampart when suddenly, carried to him on the wind, a musical voice rang out.

"Sisaweth-ken-keth-qa-sin-kwa!"

He stopped what he was doing and cocked an ear toward the observation platform that rested on top of the stone wall enclosing the work area. In the distance he could see the tiny figure of a woman gesturing obscenely at him, doubtless hoping that her vulgarism would serve as a decoy to distract the guards from the secret message she imparted.

"Phekwakwo-dy-komumim-wona-namosi-wapoebi!"

Silently, Kwasin cursed. Bahko had just taken ill with the most recent plague to sweep through the slave district and had been excused from the day's labors while he recovered in the pit. Kwasin would have to hope he could memorize the priestess's message and recite it to the bard later for translation.

"Roqaqa-dy-wona-wenti-wokomku!"

While Kwasin stood before his wagon intently listening, one of his keepers approached from behind. Kwasin ignored the man and concentrated on the woman's words.

Suddenly a whip cracked loudly. Blistering pain lashed across Kwasin's naked back. Raging, although not vocally because he was still trying to listen to the priestess, Kwasin reached out with lightning speed, grabbed hold of the slave driver's whip, and yanked it from his tormentor's hand.

"Kekete-ti-gati-gar-terisiwuwu!"

The driver, seeing the seven-foot-tall giant now armed, blanched and hightailed it back to the large contingent of guards overseeing Kwasin's work gang. When Kwasin turned back to the observation deck, the priestess was gone.

He dropped the whip and resumed his shoveling, running the priestess's words over and over in his head. The guards, relieved to see their dangerous charge surrender his weapon with no struggle, retrieved the fallen whip and left Kwasin to his toiling.

Kwasin was nearly exploding with anticipation by the time the sun set and the soldiers returned him to the enclosure at the bottom of the pit. Still, he waited to make sure his guards had ascended to the surface by means of the crane elevator before calling out to the bard in the adjoining cell.

Silence met him. "Bard, do you hear me?" he shouted again. "I bear what must surely be urgent news from the priestesses, if only I could understand the message! Wake up!"

A great fear seized Kwasin. What if Bhako had died, or was so sick that he had been moved to the surface? Now Kwasin berated himself for not taking up the bard's offer to teach him the secret language of the priestesses.

A strangled moan arose from the darkness, and a moment later came a feeble cough.

Hope leaped in Kwasin's heart. "Bhako, my friend!" Kwasin cried out, using the bard's given name for the first time since they had met. "You are still alive!" But no matter how Kwasin tried to engage the ailing troubadour, Bhako would not—or could not—reply.

Finally, tired of hearing his own voice echoing hollowly from stone, Kwasin slumped against the side of his cell and once again began diligently grating his fetters against the granite wall. Only another week, he judged, and he would have weakened a single link on each of his bronze chains just enough that with great effort he might break them with his oxlike strength. He was being careful this time to keep the worn-away areas of the links as modest and unnoticeable as possible. Three times before, just as he all but sanded down his chains to the point of escape, his guards had detected his handiwork and replaced his fetters.

One line of the priestess's melodic heckling, which Kwasin ran over and over in his head as he sawed at his chains, made him wonder if his work on the fetters would all be for naught. *"That which you dread comes in seven days!"* the woman had taunted. But Bhako had said the priestesses' messages were not what they seemed on the surface, that a deeper, less obvious meaning lay within. Seven days might mean seven months, or even seven years. Or perhaps the number seven was misleading altogether, as *namosi-wapoebi*—which could mean both the seventh day of the week or a period of seven days—was originally named after the ancient priestess Wapoebi before being replaced a couple hundred years ago with a term more commonly employed, *namosi-sahdar*, which literally translated to *gray-sky-day*, or more commonly, *cloud-day*. Why had the priestess not used the more modern idiom? Or for that matter, why had she not said *namosi-go*, a term that translated unequivocally to a period of seven days? Was the priestess merely utilizing archaic language to make her verse more poetic, or did she mean to make subtle reference to that day of the week's ancient namesake? Kwasin wracked his brain trying to remember anything he could about Wapoebi before finally surrendering to the fact that he knew nothing. He also reflected on the phrase *"Kekete-ti-gati-gar-terisiwuwu,"* which in the vernacular meant *"Gird your loins"* but literally translated to the more vulgar *"Witness thy strength in the great python."* What could it mean?

It was no use! Kho had created him to fight, rage, and make love, not dabble in a troubadour's poetry!

Five agonizingly long days passed and still Bhako uttered no word from his cell. The last mighty rampart of earth had at last been cleared away from the tower, and now Kwasin sat idle in his cell, singing aloud in appalling tones the message from the priestess, praying to Qawo, goddess of healing, that it might wake Bhako from what was in all probability his deathbed. Though Kwasin could hear the guards force water into Bhako's mouth twice each day, and once a day clink down a bowl of gruel upon the stone floor of his cell, the bard could not last much longer.

On the evening of the sixth day after the message from the priestess, the door to Kwasin's prison rattled open and a group of guards entered. They carried with them new, even heavier chains of bronze which they placed on Kwasin's wrists and ankles, laughing as they observed the work that had been done to his old restraints. Kwasin thought the guards would leave him alone after this, but instead they unchained him from the wall of his cell and forced him to hobble at spearpoint out into the open pit.

He asked the officer in charge where they were taking him.

"Haven't you heard?" the guard replied. "Tomorrow morning at sunset, as the Flaming God rises in all His glory upon the eastern horizon, you are to be sacrificed at the consecration ceremony of the Great Tower."

26

Early the next morning—three hours until dawn if the water clock he observed as he passed the guard station was correct—Kwasin was awakened in his cell beneath the royal palace and brought above to an antechamber. Here, surrounded by the ever-present guards who stood ready to spear him upon the least provocation, he was ordered to bathe in a great marble tub, after which he was administered ablutions by the robed and thickly bearded priests of Resu in preparation for the morning's ceremony on top of the highest level of the Great Tower.

Kwasin considered hurling himself at the guards, even though that would mean certain death. If he were slain now, he would thus deprive Minruth the satisfaction of seeing his great enemy die to nurture the spirit of the sungod. According to the priests attending him, Resu required for the tower's consecration the blood sacrifice of the greatest hero of the devout Goddess worshipers. The priests claimed this would return the land to prosperity after the devastating war between arrogant Kho and Her righteous son and husband.

The idea of cheating Minruth of this final symbolic victory did appeal to Kwasin. If he martyred himself, the cause of the Goddess might yet live on in the hearts of Her followers, and one day Minruth, or whatever tyrant assumed the throne after him, would have a bloody revolution on his hands.

The priests also told Kwasin that he should be honored and filled with great joy. He would bear witness to an event unparalleled in human history, the very ceremony in which the blessed king and high priest of Resu would set the final capping stone in place atop the great ziggurat. At that moment the sungod would bestow eternal life upon the reigning king of kings. Of course, Kwasin would be dead before that part of the ritual occurred—his beating heart having been cut out and laid upon the altar—but it was an honor nonetheless to be present at this most hallowed of occasions.

Perhaps Minruth truly was mad enough to believe he would become immortal upon the tower's completion. But more likely, the spectacle on top of the tower was designed to bolster Minruth's image among a population rapidly turning against him. Though subdued, the followers of Kho were still many. They must have believed that the recent bout of plagues sweeping the city, as well as the tremors which still continued to rattle the island, indicated that Kho was displeased with the people's allegiance to Minruth.

But while Kwasin had sat in his cell beneath the palace, he discovered something which gave pause to his thoughts of martyrdom: the latest set of massive bronze chains placed upon him by the soldiers had been peculiarly fashioned. When he tapped the individual links of the chains against the stone floor of his cell, he found the link at the joining of each manacle clinked at a different pitch than the others. He could only conclude that his shackles bore hollowed-out links at the gyves! If this was true, then the network of priestesses, or someone loyal to them, might still be in a position to help him. More likely, however, the conspirators only planned for Kwasin to break free of his restraints for one last, suicidal rampage among Minruth's soldiers. Certainly there was no way the priestesses could hope to spirit away Kwasin through their secret tunnels as they had Awineth, not when he was flanked by dozens of guards and the palace and the streets swarmed with soldiers on high alert for the tower's consecration ceremony.

Nevertheless, it would be pointless to throw his life away attacking the palace guards now when he could cause Minruth much more grief by breaking free during his cherished ritual on the tower. Perhaps he could actually get close enough to attack Minruth himself. But for now he would keep an eye open for the moment when he could do the most damage. He had waited two excruciatingly long years toiling in Minruth's slave pens; he could bide his time a little longer.

When the priests were done with their ablutions, Kwasin was given a new, but plain white linen loincloth. While he discarded his old tattered loincloth and put on the new one, Kwasin asked that, as was traditional for prisoners about to be executed, he be permitted to make a last offering to Kho in the presence of a priestess. The priests only laughed at him. Then, with their sacrificial victim now bathed and properly clothed, they turned Kwasin over to the soldiers, who escorted him through the palace, out the great bronze doors, and onto the streets, where he found the grandest of processions awaiting him.

The darkened streets had come alive with celebrators, awakened early by Minruth's criers to witness at long last the historic completion of the Great Tower, and to rejoice in their emperor's symbolic ascension to the heavens. Despite the early hour, wine and beer flowed freely among the revelers and many shouted out lewd invectives at the legendary Kwasin of Dythbeth. Others in the crowd, however, refrained from the name-calling and, with expressions that might have been sullen or even embarrassed, turned their faces away and disappeared among the other spectators. These would be the citizens still loyal to the Goddess, unwilling to show dishonor to the great hero of their movement and yet afraid to exhibit their discontent. Right now Kwasin hated them more than the king's soldiers.

The large contingent of guards, stemming off the crowd with stern looks and raised spears, quickly positioned their famous captive behind the long line of priests in the street. Without delay the procession began moving. King Minruth, Kwasin noted, was not among the entourage. Presumably he had already been escorted under heavy guard to the Great Tower and ascended the monument so he could partake in special rites with his priests.

The procession soon passed from the citadel, descending the steps of the acropolis and crossing over the moat into the Outer City. Tiny pinpoints of reddish-orange light bled through the black morning sky in the west, evidence that the priests' rituals were already underway on the tower's uppermost level. Before long Kwasin and the cavalcade of priests and soldiers began wedging their way through the vast human sea that had congregated in the open area east of the Great Tower. Many in the tremendous crowd, waiting to witness the final act of the monument's completion, would be disappointed. Most would be too far back to see anything worthwhile, while those closer to the base of the tower would be unable to see up over the edge of the tower's highest step.

As they forged ahead, Kwasin looked up. The outline of the enormous monument angled down, black and ominous, against the dark morning sky. A great sense of dread now enveloped Kwasin. He knew his ultimate fate lay at the tower's apex, that he had lived his entire life—fighting and drinking and bragging and lovemaking—to arrive at this very moment. But what would any of it matter when his heart no longer thrummed with the exuberant joys and the agonizing trials of life? Perhaps Minruth was not so mad after all to seek immortality. In the face of death, did anything but life hold any meaning? Alas, in a short time Kwasin would be in the shadowy presence of Sisisken, who would perhaps be able to answer his question.

Suddenly Kwasin's great frame trembled and he shook free of the dark foreboding. In his thirty years of life he had cheated death more times than he could remember. He would not surrender to destiny just yet. Warm blood still coursed through his veins, and as long as it did, the fire raging inside him would roar with the will to live.

Eventually Kwasin and the others left the clamoring multitude behind, passing through an opening in the base of the tower and descending a staircase until they stood in a chamber walled by huge granite blocks. Many of the priests darted wide-eyed glances at Kwasin. They must have been fearful of being trapped in the enclosed space with the terrible giant, the bringer of death and woe to so many of the followers of Resu.

A number of the guards filed into a low, narrow passageway at the back of the chamber, and then one of the priests placed a black linen hood over Kwasin's head. The priests must have still held great fear that he would escape; otherwise they would not have been concerned about him seeing the secret tunnels that wormed throughout the enormous ziggurat. He wondered if the soldiers knew they would also be considered a risk and that their king would probably order them killed after the morning's ceremony. Kwasin himself had witnessed the execution of the slaves who had worked on the tunnels.

Sharp spearpoints jabbed at Kwasin's back as the soldiers forced him into the passageway. He swore loudly as his forehead smacked hard against the doorway's decorative epistyle. The tunnels were not built for a seven-foot-tall, extremely broad-shouldered, big-boned man.

The passage proceeded only a short distance before it jogged to the left and its previously level floor rose to an angle of twenty-five degrees. Before long, the soldiers in front of and behind Kwasin began puffing loudly. Kwasin, however, did not become short-winded, having become used to such steep ascents while hauling mammoth loads of bricks up the tower.

The higher they climbed, the quicker came the tunnel's turns and the steeper became its incline, until the shaft slanted at a frightful thirty-five degree angle. Now, in addition to his back and shoulders scraping painfully against the ceiling and sides of the constricting corridor, after every few steps he tripped over his hobbled ankles and slid two or three feet back down the shaft. The soldier following at his heels cursed each time this happened, as Kwasin's flailing feet would strike him and knock his own footing out from under him. Though the tunnel was cool, Kwasin began to sweat. He did not want to slip and accidentally be skewered by the spear of the man behind him. But soon the soldier, tired of repeatedly being kicked in the face, backed off and widened the distance between them.

Finally the hellish climb ended and Kwasin's hood was removed. Before him was a small, brightly painted, stone-walled chamber, the size and shape of which indicated that he likely stood directly beneath the tower's twenty-seventh and highest level. In one corner of the room a staircase rose to an opening in the ceiling, through which the chanting of priests could be heard. A man in his mid-fifties, a beautiful middle-aged woman, and three boys ranging in age from five to twelve years old were already in the room when Kwasin and the others entered. Standing with their hands manacled behind their backs, and adorned in nothing but plain, white linen loincloths, the five huddled together in a corner as the teary-eyed woman whispered in falsely reassuring tones to the obviously terrified children. The man's expression, however, looked proud and unyielding. His hazel eyes and long, hawk-beaked nose hinted at his Klemsaasa ancestry. Because of this, and also the man's regal bearing, Kwasin guessed this must be old King Qanaketh of Mukha. The woman would be his wife, the high priestess of Mukha, with the children being the couple's offspring.

Kwasin felt great pity for the woman and children, but not much for the man. Qanaketh's decision to feign allegiance to Minruth, while at the same time backhandedly sending his general to attack the Khokarsans, had sealed his fate. Because of his spineless double-dealing, his family would die with him on the tower, sacrificed to the ravenous hunger of the sungod.

Still, when the old king looked up and solemnly bowed his head at him, Kwasin returned the gesture of respect. He did not know if he would have acted any differently than the king under the circumstances. Kwasin had never known the joys or the worries of having a family. And now he never would.

They waited in silence for what seemed a great while. Kwasin, taking pity on the children, began imitating to comic effect the sour expressions of the priests who stood waiting at the base of the stairs for a signal from above. Finally, the corner of the youngest boy's mouth upturned and a moment later broke into a full smile. Seeing this, Kwasin guffawed loudly, and soon all three children were giggling.

The release from worry did not last long for them. Suddenly a priest descended the staircase and announced with a sickeningly cheery voice that it was time for their part in the ceremony to begin.

As the soldiers escorted the royal family of Mukha up the stairs, King Qanaketh turned and smiled grimly at Kwasin. Perhaps the man was no coward after all.

Next the soldiers took Kwasin above. He climbed the steps eagerly, feeling a rush of energy now that the long wait was over. Too long had he been caged and abused by his ruthless keepers in the emperor's slave pens. And though he might now be bound in chains, he would face death as he had always lived, as a man free in spirit.

He emerged from the tiny hole in the ceiling onto the ziggurat's highest step, the base of which measured thirty feet in diameter. Torches burned at regular intervals on all sides of the great square of brick and stone except to the east. This was the side which in a short time would welcome the brilliantly shining and blood-red face of Resu. Already the dark sky had begun to lighten with the sungod's coming.

A tall, blunt-topped, pyramidal block of carved granite rose from the center of the tower. Wooden steps had been placed before the monolith, in front of which sat a small, blue marble pyramid, bearing on each side an image of the sun in bas-relief. It was the Great Tower's capstone, which Minruth would carry up the steps and place on top of the monolith to finish the tower and thereby be blessed with immortality.

On the eastern edge of the tower's summit loomed a large rectangular altar stone. The altar's surface was concave, and a narrow channel ran down its granite face, beneath which sat a broad-lipped, artfully decorated ceramic urn intended to catch the blood of the sacrificial victim. A number of golden goblets sat upon a low block of stone beside the altar, doubtless waiting for the emperor and his priests to dip them into the urn after it filled. Human blood rites like those planned by Minruth had not been witnessed in nearly six hundred years among Kwasin's Klemsaasa and Khoklem ancestors. The practice had ended with the death of King K'opwam II at the hands of the priestesses after he murdered his wife and, like Minruth, attempted to strengthen the power of the priesthood. Ironically it had been the priests, playing upon the emotions of a distraught populace, who had brought pressure on the priestesses to ban human sacrifice from their rituals. Now the priests had resurrected the bloodthirsty custom they once reviled.

Kwasin surveyed the others who stood before him on the tower's summit. There was Minruth, standing upon a raised platform behind the altar with a group of his priests, looking grand and triumphant in his long white robes and crown of gold. The effigy on the crown's face, representing one of Resu's many incarnations, bore the likeness of an eagle of the mountains. Just below the crown, on Minruth's brow, was painted in red ochre an inverted arrow on top of a horizontal bar, another symbol of the sungod. Minruth's dark eyes burned redly in the torchlight, and for a brief moment his smug expression transformed into a satisfied sneer as he condescended to acknowledge Kwasin's gaze.

Also on the tower, lined up along the king's left, were a number of richly dressed men. Kwasin learned their identities a moment later when the priest of ceremonies called out their names, blessing them in the name of Great Resu. The men were ambassadors from the cities across the Kemu: Qethruth, Wethna, Bawaku, and Miklemres. And even a king's son from as far south as Wentisuh had come to pay homage to the king of king's staggering achievement, leaving Kwasin to wonder what inroads Minruth had made among the revolting cities of the southern sea. Strangely absent was a representative from Siwudawa. Perhaps, like the population of Towina, Minruth's soldiers had committed wholesale slaughter against the worshipers of the parrot-headed androgyne god, who were known to be fiercely provincial.

Kwasin himself stood lined up with fourteen other prisoners, including the king and queen of Mukha and their children, the others having been brought up from a lower level after Kwasin's party had ascended. As soon as the chief priest finished blessing the ambassadors, he began announcing the names of the prisoners, stating that Resu would judge them fairly but harshly for their crimes. The accused included two priestesses who had served in the Temple of Kho at Khokarsa, three important figures from among the College of Priestesses in Dythbeth, Asema, and Oliwa, and General Karuphe and Captain Nowiten, both formerly of the queen's army—all of them steadfast heroines and heroes of the resistance.

Kwasin wondered what had become of the oracular priestess at Khokarsa. With the exception of Kwasin and Awineth, she had been a greater symbol of the resistance than any other. Did the oracle still lie low in the hills outside the city, hidden among the peasants and hoping for an opportunity to one day strike back at Minruth? Or had Minruth already killed her as his troops stormed across the countryside? Kwasin did not know.

Surprisingly, three priestesses not among the prisoners also stood witness with the ambassadors. All appeared to be very young and were in all probability token representatives from Minruth's fraudulent College of Priestesses.

Suddenly Kwasin reeled forward as pain exploded in the back of his head. A soldier standing behind him had brutally struck him with the butt of his spear. Momentarily stunned, Kwasin fell to his knees while the soldiers secured a bronze collar about his neck. By the time he recovered from the blow, he found himself restrained by the collar, which was secured by means of a heavy bronze chain to a metal ring embedded in the stone floor. He had waited too long to break his weakened chains.

At a signal from the chief priest, two of the soldiers seized King Qanaketh's children and pulled them roughly from their protesting and clearly heartbroken parents. Kwasin cried out in frustration and outrage while he strained futilely against the collar around his neck.

Then, much to Kwasin's surprise, Minruth raised his arms high in the air and shouted to the guards to stop.

"Let it not be said that I am not merciful!" Minruth cried. "I shall not hold these children responsible for the crimes of their parents. They are young enough that my priests should yet be able to correct any misguided notions placed in their heads by the enemies of Resu. Take the youths below!"

But when the soldiers moved to comply, Minruth shouted, "No! I've changed my mind. There's no better medicine for ill-advised youth than a good example. Let them witness what happens to those who dare oppose a living god!"

The guards held the children in place, and Kwasin and the other prisoners watched in horror as two soldiers took King Qanaketh by the arms and brought him forward to the altar. Qanaketh for his part did not flinch but went willingly, not even objecting as the soldiers made him lie outstretched upon the altar stone and held him down.

A long, jewel-hilted dagger appeared suddenly in the hand of the chief priest. The blade flashed under the burning torches. King Qanaketh cried out softly, his body jerking violently, and then went limp. Then the priest plunged dagger and hand within his victim's abdomen and, after several moments of gruesome surgery, emerged with the prize he sought—Qanaketh's glistening, blood-dripping heart. The priest, dark crimson streaking his white robes, held the excised organ aloft so that the crowds below might see it. A thunderous, and Kwasin believed disapproving, clamor carried up from the multitudes of onlookers below. Then the priest, holding the organ in his blood-soaked hands, carefully cut the heart into pieces, which he passed one by one to the attending priests. Lastly, he knelt before a small iron hearth burning at the base of the altar and thrust the last remaining sliver of the heart into the flame. When smoke began to wisp up from the hearth, the man removed with ceremonial tongs the now charred bit of heart; then he rose and proffered the grisly delicacy to Minruth, whose eyes danced with a mad light as he took the offering, put it in his mouth, and chewed with what seemed great relish. The priests then did the same with their own raw morsels.

Kwasin, growling fiercely as he strained at his collar, saw disgust upon the faces of the visiting ambassadors. Clearly they, like the horrified crowds below, were ashamed to see a thousand years of civilization end in such a repulsive, loathsome spectacle. The priestess from Mukha and her children had shielded their eyes, but Kwasin could see and hear their wailing.

One by one the other champions of the resistance were led to the altar by the soldiers. Slowly the urn beneath the altar filled with blood, until it finally spilled over its brim and pooled upon the stone floor. The worst death, Kwasin had to admit, was that of Qanaketh's wife. So distraught became the children at seeing their mother brought forth that Minruth relented and ordered his soldiers to take them from the tower. With great eagerness, the soldiers complied. They too seemed sickened by their king's morbid ritual, as they tried but failed to keep their eyes from straying to the grim stacks of bodies that continued to grow higher on each side of the altar.

Suddenly Resu's blindingly brilliant eye peered up over the horizon, casting its scarlet gaze upon the hideous scene. Now at last it was time for Kwasin to go the way of the others and surrender his precious life force to the sungod. The soldiers clustered thickly about him, warily unfastening the bronze collar from about his neck. But Kwasin did not attack yet. He wanted to get closer still to Minruth. Weaponless, he would only have a single moment to kill the king before he himself was killed.

As he walked with the soldiers toward the altar, he could make out upon the altar's facing the chiseled image of a monstrously fanged python eating its own tail. The words of the oracle at the old temple of Kho in Dythbeth suddenly rang through him. *"The serpent and the ax will be your undoing or your succor, and so shall it be for all the land."* Recalling the prophecy, he felt as if struck by a thunderbolt from the heavens. The curse of the ax had indeed fallen upon him, as witnessed by his capture and the fall of Dythbeth, and he could not deny the truth of the land's downfall at the hands of Minruth's profane followers. And now to see the serpent slithering across his stony deathbed! Surely it was a sign from the Goddess that death's long hunt for him was at last at an end.

Then a thing so strange, so unexpected happened that Kwasin felt as if all time had stopped. A soft and humming melody rose up behind him in a female voice. At once Kwasin recognized it, for it was the same tune that during the past week he had recited ceaselessly in his head. But now the singsong insults that the priestess had hurled at him in the slave pens jarred something in him. Missing words and implied meanings suddenly fell into place and the hidden message of the priestesses revealed its secrets.

"Phekwakwo-dy-komumim-wona-namosi-wapoebi! Roqaqa-dy-wona-wenti-wokomku!" became not *"That which you dread comes in seven days to destroy your world!"* but rather *"Kho-komumim-phekwakwo-dy-namosi-wapoebi! Roqaga-dy-lahbi-wenti-wokomku!"* That is, *"Dread Kho comes in seven days to destroy all the land!"* And now Kwasin realized that the phrase *"Kekete-ti-gati-gar-terisiwuwu!"* was to be taken literally—instead of translating to *"Gird thy loins!"* it meant *"Witness thy strength in the great python!"* It could only refer to the snake effigy carved into the altar's facing!

The realization sparked in Kwasin's mind for but an instant and then, as if blessed with a vision from the Goddess—which surely this was—he made the creative leap that had for the past week eluded him. It had to be that the words of the priestess were so crafted that only he, not Bhako or anyone else, would understand them. He, whose mother had died under the fangs of a snake because of his own youthful carelessness. The song transmitted a threefold metaphor. By referencing a python in their message, the priestesses not only sought to draw his attention to his own ill-fated past, but also to the stone altar before him, as well as the prophecy of the oracle: *"The serpent and the ax will be your undoing or your succor."* Seeing the serpent carved upon the face of the sacrificial stone before him, and at the same time recalling the oracle's prophecy of the ax, he could come to only one startling conclusion: the Ax of Victory lay hidden by agents of the priestesses beneath the altar stone!

Without taking the time to second-guess himself, Kwasin barreled forward to the startled cries of his guards and the priests before him. As he leaped forth, he pulled with herculean strength at the chains restraining his arms behind his back. Though the manacles tore painfully at his wrists, the hollowed-out links broke. His mightily muscled arms, now free, swung up and knocked down the guards leaping at him from either side.

Minruth and the priests scattered in the face of Kwasin's mad charge. Kwasin leaped over the altar just as several spears flew at him. Temporarily protected by the altar, he pushed up against its upper edge and groaned. For a moment he feared he would not be able to lift the immense table of stone, but then the two years spent straining his muscles on the tower paid off and the great altar lurched up and over, crashing on its side with a tremendous boom. There, glinting in the bright morning sunlight where the altar had stood, was the ax of Wi.

Kwasin snatched up the ax and began swinging, his first blow striking down three soldiers coming around the toppled altar. As more soldiers advanced, he chopped the ax against the chains binding his ankles. Bronze gave way before meteoritic iron and the chains split. Without pause, Kwasin jumped on top of the altar's now horizontal side, swatting out of his way with his great weapon the jabbing spears of the soldiers and splintering them as if they were mere slivers of wood. Three more soldiers went down under three powerful blows of Kwasin's ax.

In the midst of the panic on the tower, Kwasin saw blades flashing in the hands of the three priestesses of Kho. They must have had the daggers hidden beneath their robes. Now their blades lashed out viciously at the priests, the smug expressions of which had transformed into masks of terror. Kwasin had been wrong about the priestesses. They had not forsaken their vows to the Goddess but were rather agents of a well-planned conspiracy against Minruth.

More soldiers fell before Kwasin and his ax as he stormed forward. He spied Minruth, fleeing toward the hole that led into the tower.

For a moment the soldiers held back, daunted by the mad, ax-swinging giant that hulked over them. Kwasin, taking advantage of the lull, swung back the ax, then hurled it forward and released it. The ax, because of its great size and weight, did not make a good throwing weapon, but Kwasin was desperate. In another moment Minruth would escape into the tower.

The ax lobbed toward its target, spinning handle over head. Minruth was now at the opening in the floor, turning to access the staircase. Kwasin thought the ax was going to miss, but then the weapon's handle spun around, the large bone knob on its end smacking with great force into Minruth's left eye socket. Blood spurted, and Minruth collapsed into the hole.

Kwasin howled with disappointment. He had hoped to fully crush Minruth's skull. Still, the reindeer-bone ax handle might have struck with such force that his attempted regicide had succeeded. Or deicide, from Minruth's point of view. But Kwasin would have to see the body to be sure. And he needed to retrieve the ax.

He grabbed the *tenu* of a fallen soldier and made for the dark hole into which Minruth had fallen. The soldiers, who had been regrouping on the western edge of the tower, now rallied and surged forward. Kwasin laid his hand on the ax just as the soldiers closed and, bellowing like an angry god, raised his massive weapon, brandishing it at the soldiers.

The scare tactic worked. The advancing soldiers paused just long enough to give him the advantage. He barreled ahead, laying low three more soldiers.

From behind, a priestess cried out his name. Kwasin whirled. Now a stream of soldiers was rushing up from the stairs. The priestess who had warned him fell to the ground, cut down by a priest's dagger.

Kwasin sprinted to the center of the tower and stood before the tall, spiring monolith. Then he knelt down, set down his ax, and with both hands lifted up the marble pyramidal capstone that Minruth was to have set upon the monolith and thereby seal his godhood. He raised the stone above his head, took aim, and lobbed it at the opening out of which ran the soldiers. The forty-pound stone thumped into the chest of a soldier who had just come up, knocking him and those behind and beneath him down the staircase.

But it would only be a matter of moments before additional reinforcements came. Seeing the bodies of the three heroine-priestesses lying before him, bloodied and unmoving, Kwasin slung the ax's leather thong over a shoulder, ran to the summit's northern edge, and slipped over the side of the Great Tower.

27

Scaling the many carven deities, monsters, heroes, and heroines that decorated the face of the great ziggurat, Kwasin felt as if he had passed into an ethereal world. Here the present day vanished and the myths of ancient times sprang to life. The rising sun glanced its rays across the diverse assortment of bold and sometimes craven or hideously disfigured faces on the friezes, creating an eerie combination of shadows and red-golden light that only intensified the surreal effect. Each of the twenty-three-foot-tall levels down which he climbed placed him in the midst of a new set of fabulous legends. It was said that the stonework carvings depicted not only the gods of every nation on earth, but also every species of bird, beast, and creature of the waters that had ever lived. The claim, of course, was ludicrous, but climbing down them Kwasin thought the sundry collection of beings, both real and fabled, did indeed seem infinite.

Having descended three levels, he looked down to see a large number of soldiers cutting through the crowds of gawking pedestrians, swarming toward the base of the tower. If he continued descending, the soldiers would eventually be able to take him down with their slings, spears, and javelins. Though the tower was considered holy, he didn't think fear of damaging the artistry on the tower's face would stop them from hurling their weapons at him. And the soldiers above would soon do the same. That they had not yet done so could only be a result of the havoc left behind by his violent attack.

Only fifteen feet below him the decorative stonework opened around a window. This he knew led into a ceremonial chamber used by the priests. Although he had never been in the room, he had seen it practically every day while working on the tower. It might not provide access to the many tunnels snaking through the monolith's interior, but it was worth investigating. Continuing to scale the tower would only get him killed.

He climbed down and swung in through the window, startling three soldiers who stood near the back of the medium-sized room. One soldier charged Kwasin with a spear, while the other two followed at the man's heels with drawn swords.

Kwasin ran to meet his aggressor. His ax splintered the man's bronze spearhead from its shaft. Simultaneously, Kwasin struck the man in the face with his fist. The man reeled and fell to one side. Directly behind his unmoving form stood one of the other soldiers, his sword cutting broadly at Kwasin.

Suddenly the sword flew wildly out of the oncoming soldier's hand. The man pitched forward, a surprised look on his face. Behind his fallen body stood the third soldier, his own sword dripping darkly with his companion's blood.

"My name is Tenswath," the man exclaimed in response to Kwasin's shocked look. "I am an ally of the daughters of Kho, planted among the king's guard by the Queen Mother herself. Follow me if you wish to live!"

Kwasin wanted to ask Tenswath if that meant Awineth still lived, but the man had already grabbed a torch from a sconce and was bolting down a passageway located at the rear of the room. Kwasin took off after him.

When he caught up with the fellow, Kwasin said, "You are fleet of foot, ally of the daughters of Kho." Although Kwasin was both long of stride and in excellent shape, the man could doubtless beat him in a sprint.

"In my city's competitions I was second only to my brother Gobhu, who represented Dythbeth in the Great Games," Tenswath said proudly.

Kwasin clapped the man on his back. "Lo! A fellow brother of my native land. I thought I recognized the accent. Now let us show these Khokarsan straw men what it means to oppose the men of Dythbeth!"

"Stealth is better than strength in this case," Tenswath replied, keeping his voice low as they continued down the low-ceilinged corridor. "The king's guard is stationed throughout the tower, and if we encounter them, all will be over for us. But I know of a secret way, an underground tunnel that leads out into the city. We must hurry. The king may also try to use it to escape."

"Escape what?" Kwasin asked. "Is Minruth such a coward that among his multitude of warriors he would flee before a single man?"

Tenswath grinned. "The king of kings has more than you to worry about, O King." The man did not elaborate, but for the first time in what seemed ages, Kwasin allowed himself to hope.

Eventually the passageway opened into a bare, granite-walled room. Tenswath pushed against the ordinary-looking wall. A moment later the section of stone grated forward and revealed a hidden passageway. Tenswath disappeared within and Kwasin followed.

The tunnel descended sharply, taking many dizzying turns. When they came to a cross-tunnel, Tenswath led them to the left. A short time later they arrived at another tunnel. They continued past it, but stopped a moment later when they heard the sound of many running feet echoing through the passageway. Someone was coming.

"Go on, O King!" Tenswath cried, passing Kwasin his torch. "Take no more turns but continue on and the tunnel will lead you out into the city!"

Before Kwasin could stop him, the man was running back to where the two tunnels met. Then he disappeared around the corner of the adjoining tunnel.

Ignoring Tenswath's order, Kwasin ran back to the intersection. When he turned the corner, Tenswath was already speeding far down the passageway. At the end of the tunnel Kwasin could see Minruth, one eye darkened by the blow Paga's ax had dealt him, running ahead of a long line of torch-bearing soldiers.

Tenswath stopped running and began pressing his hands against the tunnel wall in a peculiar fashion. A deep rumbling shook the tunnel and then blackness cut off the scene as the entire tower seemed on the verge of shaking apart. Then the rumbling ceased.

Kwasin swore. By pressing on the wall, Tenswath had triggered a huge stone block to fall from above, thereby sealing off the tunnel and trapping himself on the other side. He had sacrificed himself for his king. Kwasin shook his head sadly, promising himself that if he ever made his way to freedom, he would have a hero's pylon erected for the courageous Tenswath.

He turned back and continued down the tunnel. When after many turns he had descended to a point that must have been near or possibly below the tower's base, a peculiar smell filled the passageway. The rank, spongy odor grew stronger as he forged ahead. He came to a side tunnel and stopped. The stench was now almost suffocating. He thought he might have stumbled onto a branch of the city's sewage system when suddenly, out of the black throat of the intersecting tunnel, a hideous shriek arose. The hair on the back of Kwasin's neck stood erect. He had heard that same trumpeting, spine-tingling scream once before, as a youth camping with his uncle in the gloomy jungles of the southern sea. Phimeth had told him the shrieking belonged to the legendary dragon of the Kemus. Though as brash a youth as the adult he would become, the adolescent Kwasin had known he never wanted to encounter the dreaded *r"ok'og'a* in the flesh. The nightmares that followed the incident had been terrifying enough for the boy.

But now, memories notwithstanding, Kwasin was unable to resist his burning curiosity. He recalled what General Hahinqo had once told him—of how at backbreaking expense Minruth had captured a great and terrifying serpent of the hinterlands, which he had then imprisoned in the tunnels beneath the Great Tower. Kwasin had not believed the rumor then, but now a chill passed through him that was not due to the dampness of the underground tunnels.

He left the main passage and treaded cautiously down the side tunnel, the broken chains that dangled from his manacles scraping against the stone floor. After proceeding only a short distance, the tunnel ended at a heavily reinforced iron-barred gate. A few feet beyond this he could dimly make out what looked like bronze grillwork. He slid open the bolt that secured the door and, noting a large ratcheted winch built into the corridor's flooring, approached the grilled wall.

Kwasin peered through the spaces between the wall of crisscrossing metal but saw only blackness. Then, he heard a rustling. A moment later he gasped when, at the back of the immense chamber beyond the grating, a scaly sheen momentarily caught in the dim light cast by his torch. He strained his eyes into the darkness. It might have been his imagination, but he thought he could just make out a nebulous shape, dark and bulky, in the far reaches of the chamber.

He pulled back from the grating. Fascinating though this distraction might be, he had no time to waste on it. But then, seeing the winch on the floor, he wondered. The winch must open something nearby, and what if…

Kneeling, he seized the crank handle and began turning. The sound of ratcheting chains and groaning metal came from the adjoining chamber. After turning the crank for a minute, he stopped. He hoped he had achieved what he thought he did, but he had to get going.

He headed back out through the barred doorway and into the main passageway. Now the tunnel leveled out and proceeded straight forward. He jogged onward for what must have been a half-mile before the tunnel ended abruptly at a narrow flight of spiral steps. He climbed up the steps and, reaching the ceiling, pushed up with his free hand against the stone plug above him. It lurched up and he slid it to one side. Leaving his torch burning on the stone stairs, he pulled himself up through the hole and found himself in what seemed to be a musty storage cellar filled with assorted masonry tools. He didn't take time to look around but vaulted up the cellar's creaking wooden steps, emerging into an empty, one-roomed house.

Screams and shouting sounded through the thin walls of the house. Kwasin threw open the dwelling's front door and ran outside to find a city in chaos.

He was in a residential district just west of the Inner City. Citizens ran wildly down the street before him. Farther up the street a small group of spear-bearing soldiers was fighting off a much larger band of residents armed with pitchforks, kitchen knives, and even brooms. To the southwest loomed the Great Tower, its lofty, stepped face illuminated brightly in the golden morning sunlight. In the east, a thick pall of gray smoke rose from the wall surrounding the acropolis. The Inner City was on fire.

Beyond the wall of the acropolis, Khowot belched its dark smoke skyward. But Kwasin did not believe the volcano was the source of the fires, especially since Minruth's new earthworks should have prevented the flow of lava into the city. Rather, the insurgent citizens must have set the blazes.

Kwasin ran south along the street, weaving his way through the bedlam of pedestrians. Many of the panicked inhabitants were running in the opposite direction, carrying in their arms their most cherished possessions. He guessed that the area's residents had decided to flee the city to avoid the possibility of additional fires being set. They had survived the holocaust that followed Minruth's revolt and didn't want to risk being burned to death in this one. They were probably leaving the city to join up with relatives in the country who might support them until the violence of the rebellion quieted.

He jogged out of the human tide onto a less densely trafficked avenue, intent on avoiding the military district that ran along the city wall. He could not afford a confrontation with soldiers. His plan was to head west until he reached the great canal that had been used to ferry supplies from the Gulf of Gahete during the construction of the Great Tower. There he would scale down the canal's stone-paved banks, jump into the waters, and swim across the gulf to the western shoreline. He already knew the land route he would take from that point, having gone that way once before, after escaping Minruth's prisons with his cousin Hadon and their companions.

A terrifying shriek arose in the southwest. Kwasin froze, but grinned a moment later with the realization that the winch in the tunnels had done what he had expected. The *r"ok'og'a* had been loosed from its prison beneath the tower. Now the beast would be running amok, raising hell for Minruth's soldiers and anyone else that got in its path. At least Kwasin hoped. So far the Goddess had rewarded his morning with success. Kho only knew it had been an eternity since luck had turned in his favor. He could only hope it was time for Kho's daughter Suhkwaneth, the goddess of the scales, to pay her debt.

He continued on. The farther west he traveled, the fewer citizens he saw in the streets. By the time he got close enough to smell the water, the area was completely deserted. Ahead he saw the stone foundation that edged along the canal. A few moments later he was slipping over the side of the foundation and dropping fifteen feet to the bank. A barge was docked on the opposite side of the waterway. It appeared to be uninhabited.

Looking to the north he saw two ships lying at anchor in the mouth of the canal. Upon seeing them, he almost shouted out with elation. Instead of the typical wide hull and square sail of a galley, the anchored vessels each sported a narrow body and a large, triangular fore-and-aft sail. Ruseth, that skinny-armed redheaded fisherman's son from Bhabhobes, had come through!

Kwasin headed north along the bank of the canal, the city's fortified wall towering on his right. As he ran, voices shouted at him from above. Soldiers stationed on top of the wall had spotted him. He increased his speed. When he reached the end of the stone walkway, he stopped and looked out across the waters. In the distance, a great battle was being waged on the Gulf of Gahete between Minruth's galleys and the priestesses' fore-and-aft ships. The nearest of the two ships hung at anchor roughly forty feet beyond the canal's entrance, its crew not yet noticing him. Over a shoulder he saw the soldiers above coming rapidly in his direction along the wall top. He would have to make a swim for it.

He unslung the ax from his shoulder—the heavy-headed weapon would slow him down in the water, but he could not bear to part with it. He spared a precious moment to gauge the distance from shore to the nearest of the priestesses' vessels. Then, using every ounce of his great strength, he swung back the ax and cast it out over the water.

Kwasin held his breath. Iron head toppled over bone-carven handle as the ax hurtled above the watery gulf toward its target. He shouted in joy when the ax head impaled itself with a heavy thud into the ship's portside hull.

A spear sailed past Kwasin's head as he dived into the cool embrace of the Gulf of Gahete. His thickly muscled arms cut the waters with powerful strokes and sped him forward. Only moments later he found himself at the ship's side. He yelled up to alert the crew to his presence but already a thickly braided rope was coiling down toward him from above. He grabbed the rope and hoisted himself up hand over hand.

Climbing over the ship's side, he started.

"Awineth!" he cried. "Long have my eyes waited to see the brilliance of your shining face!"

But the queen, flanked by a heavy contingent of fierce-looking guards, was not smiling. Instead, her eyes a cold gray, she turned to a guard and said, "Secure the ax from the ship's side. The oracle, who has made much of its importance, will want to see it."

Kwasin stepped forward and faced Awineth. "The ax remains with me," he said. "With it, I shall lay low our enemies and liberate the people from the sullied hands of the priests. If, after that time, the oracle still wishes to see the ax, I will permit it. But the ax—"

Before he could finish, soldiers surged from behind and clamped iron fetters on Kwasin's already manacled wrists. A man screamed, bone cracking loudly and sickly as Kwasin gave him a vicious kick to the hip. Kwasin bellowed his rage, trying to pull free of the men that sought to hold him. Several soldiers fell hard on the deck as Kwasin barreled into them with his shoulder, but then a spear shaft smacked roughly into his forehead. Stunned, he buckled to his knees, and before he could summon the will to regain his feet, additional irons were fastened upon his wrists and ankles.

He looked up at Awineth, whose face, though still cold, was smiling.

"Admiral Ruseth," she said, "have your men take the traitor below! I will deal with him after my forces have won the city."

"Yes, O Queen." The redheaded Ruseth, his bronze helmet now proudly fanning the plumage of his new rank and station, appeared at Kwasin's side. "Bring the prisoner to the hold!"

Kwasin got up of his own volition and was about to rail into his guards again when Ruseth said, "It's pointless to resist, as you're already in chains. You might kill some of my men even so, but in the end they'll overcome you and toss you overboard. Unless the deities miraculously release you from your shackles, you'll sink to the bottom of the gulf and drown."

Then Ruseth did a curious thing. He turned just far enough away from Awineth that she could not see his face. Then he winked one of his pale blue eyes.

"Let's move it, seadogs!" Ruseth shouted at his men.

"Wait!"

Awineth strode forward and looked up at Kwasin. For a brief moment her frozen expression softened with emotion. Then, hate twisting her features, she slapped him hard across the face.

"That is for moaning in your sleep for that witch Lalila, even as my father had us caged and you professed your love for me! Just as with your cousin Hadon, the woman has bewitched you! I was a fool to ever place my trust in you—a mistake I shall never make again. With Kho as my witness, my next strike at you will be final!" Awineth fingered the jeweled dagger that hung from the golden-ringed girdle encircling her shapely hips. Then she turned and strode off with her guards, leaving a bewildered and disbelieving Kwasin standing on the deck.

28

Say nothing until we are below," Ruseth said quietly as he and his soldiers escorted Kwasin to the hold. The young sailor looked as if he had just swallowed a pail of sour goat's milk.

Still smarting from Awineth's bitter reception, Kwasin fought to hold back the surging tide of his outrage. Throughout his long imprisonment, he had many times imagined how his reunion with Awineth might play out if he ever escaped, but never had he considered that the woman would betray his trust and charge him with high treason! Of course, it was indeed possible he had spoken lustful words regarding Lalila while he slumbered, but what did it matter? He loved Awineth as he had loved no other. And besides, no matter how much he loved her, was she foolish enough to think his mind would never stray to another? He cursed Adeneth, the goddess of sexual passion and madness. Truly was she a bitch goddess.

Restrained by the chains that bound him, Kwasin shuffled angrily down the steps to the hold. When they reached the bottom, Ruseth ordered his men to remove Kwasin's shackles, including those that had been put on him prior to the tower ceremony.

"Explain!" Kwasin boomed, turning on the young admiral. Ruseth's soldiers jumped into action, crossing their spears protectively in front of their superior.

"Keep your voice down!" Ruseth whispered. "If you draw the attention of the queen's guards, I won't be able to get you off the ship and take you to the oracle."

Kwasin knocked the soldiers' spears out of his way and throttled Ruseth in his powerful grip.

"Tell me what's going on," Kwasin said forcefully, though he lowered his voice. "If you don't, you'll never again utter another prayer to Piqabes!"

Ruseth waved off his men, who were on the verge of running Kwasin through with their swords and spears. "We don't have time," Ruseth replied with some difficulty because of Kwasin's unyielding grip, "but if you insist."

Kwasin released his hold.

Rubbing his neck, Ruseth said, "A madness has seized the queen. The priestesses tell me her mind went when her baby died of plague, only shortly after she—" Ruseth stopped, his wincing face showing that he only now realized Kwasin knew nothing of the death of his and Awineth's child. "Forgive me, O King!"

Kwasin felt as if a leopard's claws had raked out his bowels, but he told Ruseth to go on.

"Because all sense has left the queen's mind, the oracular priestess has secretly taken charge of the army my ships have carried from Siwudawa. But the oracle knows you have become quite a folk hero among those in the resistance. She wants you by her side, O King, when she announces to the people that Queen Awineth has been deposed."

Kwasin shook his head, not comprehending. "You say Awineth is mad, and truly she must be, for I have seen it with my own eyes. But the oracle must have lost her own mind to think the queen can be dethroned. Kho's followers won't stand for it! After enduring the hell Minruth has caused them, they would rather see the land torn asunder!"

"You wouldn't be wrong, O King," Ruseth replied, "except that Awineth has gone too far. She is not content with the priestesses' contention that Resu must be restored to his rightful position on an equal footing with Kho. No, she has actually declared Resu to be a false god and thrown him completely from the pantheon! And that is not all—she has called for an end to the priesthood and death to its entire clergy. The oracle—the holy voice of the Voice of Kho—was outraged when she learned of this. She says the queen's position is as unhinged as Minruth's scorning of Kho. Both positions, the oracle says, create an imbalance among the deities that threatens to give rise to a terrible calamity, one from which the land will never be able to recover."

"Will the empire never be at peace?" Kwasin cried.

"No, O King," Ruseth replied. "The priestesses tell us that war has existed since the time Kho's mortal offspring first fell from Her divine branches. I expect it always will. But then, your question is rhetorical, isn't it?"

"What is the oracle's plan?" Kwasin asked before his patience exploded.

"I am under orders to take you across the gulf to the Terisiwuketh Peninsula, where the oracular priestess awaits with her army. A brief ceremony will be held there in which Awineth's bond to the throne will be officially annulled. Thereafter, you will be wed to Awineth's young cousin, the priestess Awamethna, who is next in line to the queenship. Subsequently you will be named king of kings and lead the oracle's army to victory against the last remnants of Minruth's forces."

Kwasin's head reeled, overwhelmed by both the rapidity and the staggering gravity of the new developments.

"But what of Awineth?" he asked suddenly. Though sanity had fled the woman, he still could not shake his feelings of concern for her. He had spent too much time while imprisoned worrying about her fate. Now not only to discover that she hated him, but also that the priestesses and their followers conspired against her—it was too much.

"Leave that to me," Ruseth replied ominously. At Kwasin's threatening look he added, "She won't be harmed, O King."

Kwasin sighed heavily. "Take me to the oracle then."

"Aye, sir!" Ruseth said. "I mean, follow me, O King."

They crossed to the back of the hold and passed up another set of wooden steps to the ship's stern. Here Ruseth already had a boat manned and ready, waiting to be lowered into the waters. As Kwasin boarded the boat, Ruseth frequently looked over his shoulder. The young sailor must be keeping an eye out for any members of Awineth's guard who might come to investigate the unauthorized activity. Fortunately, no one came. They were probably all too busy coordinating the campaign to retake the capital.

"Goodbye, O King, and may Piqabes watch over you," Ruseth said. A few moments later Kwasin was watching the still, blue waters of the channel peel back before the bow as the oarsmen propelled the boat forward.

It should have been a short trip to the peninsula, but because of the battle on the waters, the officer in charge of the boat insisted on taking the long way around, passing south of Mohasi island and up and around the coast. Even so, traffic on the gulf was high, and when one of Minruth's uniremes spotted them, the officer ordered his men to row as quickly as possible for shore. Seeing that Kwasin's boat would make it to land before it could be intercepted, the unireme turned about, heading deeper into the gulf for easier game. Still, the officer directed the seaman manning the rudder to make for shore. He told Kwasin they would have to wait until the way north had cleared, or until after the battle had been pitched in favor of the priestesses' fleet, before again setting out on the waters. Kwasin steamed but he could do nothing.

As they neared shore, the high walls of the coliseum of the Great Games, silhouetted against Khowot's smoking cone, rose upon the horizon. Kwasin wondered how things might have been different if he, and not his cousin Hadon, had been able to compete in the Lesser and Great Games. He liked to think that after winning the bloody contests, as he unquestionably would have, he would have been man enough to stand up to Minruth when he refused to step down from the imperial throne. If he had, then the years of misery and suffering that followed might have been avoided. And perhaps Awineth would still love him. If she ever had.

He growled and shook off the hopeless dream. Even had he won the Great Games, the oracle would have sent him on the same quest as she had Hadon. And during his absence, Minruth still would have seized the reins of the empire.

They pulled up on shore, hid the boat and themselves in a thick copse of trees near the beach, and waited. An hour later Kwasin was about to set out north on foot when a scout returned to announce that the priestesses' navy had drawn the enemy to the eastern channel. The way was again clear. Kwasin jumped up and, single-handedly, began dragging the boat back to the beach. A short time later they were again rowing northward.

At last they rounded the southern jaw of the two-pronged Terisiwuketh Peninsula, whose name aptly meant the Python's Head. Kwasin shuddered, remembering old Wasemquth's prophecy about his fate being tied to that of a serpent and the ax. Did the oracle of Khokarsa send Kwasin a subtle message by summoning him here? He hoped not. He tired of prophecies and the vague, often manipulative meanings of the priestesses and priests.

When the boat rounded the southern tip of the peninsula, Kwasin saw the oracle, surrounded by her priestesses and soldiers, standing high upon a hill above the shoreline. The woman made an impressive sight, the white shrouds of her robes fluttering in the intense winds and both hands clutched around a tall golden spear. Indeed, she looked as grim and terrible as the statues Kwasin had seen of the priestess-heroine Lupoeth.

After they had landed and climbed the hill, Kwasin prostrated himself before the oracle, making his supplications to the Goddess.

"Rise, O King," the oracle cried, "and meet your wife-to-be! Behold, high priestess of Kho and of her daughter, Lahla the moon—behold, Awamethna, future Queen of Khokarsa!"

Kwasin rose. Beside the Voice of Kho—who, being in her early fifties, was nowhere near as ancient as he had imagined—stood a young priestess whose face seemed as familiar to Kwasin as her name. Then he remembered. The girl, Awamethna, had been one of the initiates who had attended him in the old temple of Kho in the marshlands outside of Dythbeth.

Truly was Awamethna a radiant thing, every bit as stunning as her cousin, though her features ran softer than Awineth's more cutting beauty. But right now, on the heels of his stinging fallout with Awineth, Kwasin was in no mood for thoughts of women or marriage.

"Tell me, O Priestess," Kwasin said, addressing the oracle, "what do you see in the future? Will the actions we take today finally bring peace to the land?"

The oracle leaned into her golden spear and fixed Kwasin with the dark pools of her inscrutable eyes. "Your frustration, O Long-Suffering King, is not without warrant. But even though the forces of Kho have today struck a terrific blow against Her enemies, word has come that Minruth—that greatest of blasphemers—has been driven out of the city and now flies with his decrepit followers toward Khowot. He clearly hopes to escape into the wilds beyond the volcano, where he can seek to foster a resistance of his own. Great forces whirl all about us, O King, pulling us within their furious current. There is nothing we mortals may do but remain steadfast to the Goddess and follow the flow."

"There is one thing I may do, O Holy Oracle," Kwasin said. "And that is to bring you Minruth's head!"

"Kho will bring you great blessings if you do so," the oracle replied. "But first we have other matters to attend."

"Respectfully, O Priestess," Kwasin said, "you will have to wait to wed this child to me. Perform what ceremonies you must to annul Awineth's power, but do not try to stop me from going after Minruth. If I wait around for the ceremony, he'll be sure to escape. And that I can't allow."

The Voice of Kho looked grave, but she said, "Do what you will, O Impatient One, for even I would not think to stop a spirit as mighty as your own. But be warned, what you find on Khowot's fiery slopes may not be all that you have longed for."

And with those final enigmatic words, the oracle turned her back on Kwasin, departing with the soon-to-be high priestess of Kho to begin their rituals. Meanwhile, Kwasin assembled a light team consisting of fifteen men and set out to pursue Minruth and his followers.

By the time they had marched south along the peninsula, and crossed the canal and river that stood between them and the volcano, morning had worn into afternoon. As they drew nearer to their destination, the great billows of smoke rising from Khowot's cone grew darker and thicker, all but blotting out the sun. Bolts of lightning streaked the backdrop of the swelling black clouds, and the edges of the volcano's lofty crater glowed bright orange as lava threatened to spill down the mountain's cracked and angry face.

The soldiers accompanying Kwasin paled at the terrifying sight, but he urged them on, telling them that Kho Herself had belched forth the great clouds of smoke. She did this, he said, in order to hide them from Resu's arrogant gaze and thereby allowing them to sneak up on the enemy. The frightened faces of the soldiers, however, indicated they doubted his words.

As they skirted the northwestern base of the mountain, one of the soldiers cried out. "There!" Kwasin followed the direction of the man's pointing finger. To the south he saw a number of pale dots moving across a field of hardened lava, the same area where once had stood the Temple of Kho and the sacred oak grove. The tiny figures were ascending the face of the volcano, clearly intent on circling around its southern side. From what he could tell, the party consisted of only seven or eight members.

Again, Kwasin urged his team on. Now, as they climbed upward, the terrain became rougher and more dangerous. The deep furrows of the increasingly steep cone, and the ridges arching across its surface from previous lava flows, made for slow going.

They had made painfully little progress when Kwasin spied a second group ascending the volcano. He counted only five figures among the new party, which followed only a short distance to the south of the first group. At first he thought the newcomers might be more of Minruth's supporters, but eventually, as his own group drew nearer, he was not so sure. One member of the new group was clearly a woman. Further, the first group seemed to have put on speed, as if desperate to escape the followers. Surely Minruth led the first group, but who led the second?

Kwasin got his answer a short time later when a runner approached from the southeast. Kwasin recognized the puffing and perspiring man as a member of Ruseth's crew.

"Admiral Ruseth sends word that he has failed in his mission, O King!" the man exclaimed when he arrived. "The queen, aided by those most loyal to her, has escaped!"

Kwasin cursed. The second group, then, must be led by Awineth. After her own priestesses turned against her, she must have fled the city and spotted Minruth also trying to escape. Awineth was making one last attempt to wreak vengeance upon the father who had taken everything from her.

"Why hasn't your superior sent his men after her?" Kwasin growled.

"He presently has his hands tied, O King," the runner replied. "Queen Awineth's men have managed to sink Admiral Ruseth's flagship, and though it is certain the queen's loyalists will be subdued, they're still putting up a hell of a fight. The admiral received word from the oracle and knows of your plans to go after the king. He wanted to warn you to keep an eye out for the queen." The man looked to the south. "But it looks like you've already found her."

Kwasin charged up the slope, his great strides leaving the soldiers under his command far behind. The group led by Awineth was rapidly closing on Minruth and his men. Within ten minutes, the two groups clashed.

Only two hundred yards now separated Kwasin from the skirmishing factions. Awineth's soldiers, though fewer in number, seemed to have gained the upper hand. He could see the bodies of three of Minruth's men strewn across the craggy incline, dead or severely wounded. Minruth, seeing the tide of battle turning against him, now fled the melee, heading farther up the slope. Awineth broke away from the fight and began following her father, dragging something behind her which seemed to be slowing her progress. When Kwasin got close enough to see what burdened her, his heart blackened. Awineth was towing the Ax of Victory behind her up the steep side of the volcano.

Kwasin altered his course, veering toward Awineth.

Suddenly, the ground beneath Kwasin's feet trembled, and the thick stench of ash wafted over him. He looked up to see a river of red-hot lava searing down the mountainside, following a jagged channel in the volcano's deeply rutted shell. Now the smoldering current hit a gouge in the slanting terrain, forming a tributary that snaked down and cut off Minruth's path. The Emperor of Khokarsa, his hawkish face carven in a look of desperation, looked down to see both Awineth and Kwasin running toward him. But Minruth could go no farther up the mountain. Already he winced with pain at the severe heat emanating from the lava flow. Blood streamed down from his left eye socket and the wound caused that morning by the handle of Kwasin's ax.

Awineth reached her father before Kwasin. She dropped the ax and, drawing a long, slim dagger from the jeweled sheath at her waist, attacked the man who had ruined her world.

The struggle did not last long. Minruth, though unarmed and out of shape, still remembered how to fight from his old days as a champion of the Great Games and a hero of the empire. He grabbed his daughter's wrist and twisted her arm and the dagger behind her back. Awineth, shrieking with pain and anger, fell to her knees. Minruth plucked the dagger from his daughter's grip and shoved her forward on her face. Sobbing with rage, Awineth whirled about to look up at her father, who grinned down devilishly at her. In his hands, he held Kwasin's ax. He looked as if he meant to swing it down and crush his daughter's skull.

Kwasin cried out, and now both Minruth and Awineth turned to face him.

"Come no closer or I'll kill her!" Minruth cried, brandishing the great ax over Awineth's head.

"Why should I care if you do!" Kwasin roared. "The woman has betrayed me!" But despite his words, he stopped his ascent. He stood not half a dozen yards from the two. All about them, heat waves from the surrounding lava flows wavered through the air, lending an eerie, nightmarish quality to the scene. Surely some mysterious force beyond the understanding of mere mortals had led the three to this hellish showdown.

Then Awineth began to laugh, her look of amusement only adding to the uneasy feeling in Kwasin's stomach.

"Kill me, father," she said, her piercing gaze still locked on Kwasin. "Or try. The Goddess will not permit it. She will smite you both down for your offenses against Her."

Minruth shook his head sadly, but his eyes were smiling. "My daughter's wits have cracked like the golden eggs of Korudeth out of the old legends. But I know that you love her, Kwasin—I can see the passion burning in your black eyes!"

"And your own eye," Kwasin said, "the only one left to you, burns with madness!"

Minruth only smiled and fondled the knob on the ax's handle. "For the wound you have given me," he replied, "I express my gratitude, as your vicious attack this morning has not in fact blinded me but rather allowed me to see! For when the haft of your mighty weapon smote out my eye, I was blessed with a vision from Great Resu! You will remember, the ax was brought back from the Wild Lands by the explicit order of the oracle...a fact which I find of extreme interest. But be that as it may, in that moment, half-blinded by your blow and toppling head over heels down the stairs of the Great Tower, I saw the future! And what do you think I saw in my vision? I saw you, Kwasin! You, the mad giant who has been the bane of my elder days, and the man who, according to the secret records I uncovered from the Temple of Khukhaken in shattered Dythbeth, was fathered by none other than Sahhindar himself! Do not look so sickly, my great opponent—or should I say ally, since everyone knows Sahhindar is the loving son of Resu." Minruth's wide grin cracked his bloated, heat-reddened face. "Have you not long wondered why your wild temperament burns hotter than any other in the land? It burns so fiercely because the blood of the Flaming God sears your veins!"

Though Khowot's wrath flamed hotly about him, Kwasin felt as if a cold hand had seized his bowels and squeezed them with its icy grip.

"Your forked tongue is only less deceitful than your daughter's!" Kwasin yelled. "With such lies you tore apart the land! And what if I am Sahhindar's spawn? Many a son has turned against his father, as this last war has shown. I have been, and forever shall be, a devout supporter of holy Kho!"

Minruth laughed mockingly. "That is not what I have seen! Did not your precious oracle pronounce that you have two souls, one which struggles against the other?"

Kwasin wondered how Minruth had learned of his visit with the oracle, and the contents of their conversation. Then he shrugged off the idle speculation. Minruth must have tortured a priestess to gain the information.

"Yes, and you must have wondered why I've been so interested in you," Minruth continued. "I can say now that it was because in my heart I always sensed the truth—and now my vision has confirmed it! You, Kwasin of Dythbeth, are my heir. No, maybe not my literal blood kin, but even more poignant, you are the blood kin of Resu Himself! And because His divine blood beats in your heart, you will live longer than any man. And one day—perhaps many years from now, my vision did not reveal the exact time—the part of your divided soul which is the strongest, that which you have inherited from your divine father, will overcome your mortal half. On that day, as my vision has shown me, you will lead Resu's followers to battle against arrogant Kho Herself!"

Now it was Kwasin's turn to laugh. "They don't call your father Minruth the Mad for nothing," he said to Awineth. "Then again, madness seems to run in your family.

"But enough! I will hear no more from either of you. Minruth, come at me with your weapon, if you still have the courage to wield it. But do not weary my mind with your deranged visions! I have had enough of such delusions! You are all mad—kings, queens, priestesses, priests, and maybe the very deities themselves!"

Feeling in control of his own destiny for the first time in years, a grinning Kwasin drew his broadsword and advanced on Minruth and his daughter. He would spare Awineth and bring her back to the oracle. Minruth would come back with him as well, but only his bloody head.

But then suddenly, as if responding to Kwasin's blasphemous soliloquy, Khowot—the Voice of Kho—began to rumble violently beneath their feet. Sickening fumes filled the thick, sweltering air and Kwasin and the others gasped for breath. Then a deafening thunder bellowed up from the ground, which now rattled so brutally that Kwasin lost his footing and began skidding down the rocky scape. He let go of his sword and flailed out his arms, finally grabbing onto a large rock and stopping his fall.

He looked up. He had slid almost thirty feet down the mountainside. Awineth was still upslope of him, but where was…

Then he saw Minruth. Or at least part of him. His legs and feet jutted out horizontally from behind a ridge of black dirt. Awineth was rising up from the ridge. In her hands she held her bloodied ceremonial dagger. Her eyes looked wild.

Awineth looked down at Kwasin, her expression a twisted mix of disgust and demented joy. She sheathed her dagger, which she must have recovered during the volcano's tumult, and again bent down. When she rose a moment later, her back was to him. She was skirting the slope, trying to make her way around a lava flow. Behind her, by its leather thong, she dragged the ax.

Kwasin started after her but again the mountain began its violent shaking and rumbling. Once more he fell and slid several yards down the volcano's rugged flank. When he looked up, he could no longer see Awineth. Perhaps Khowot's flames had engulfed her.

Finally, with the ground rattling beneath his feet, and his tears burning from the fumes that nearly smothered him, Kwasin headed down the mountainside.

29

Many hunts have I led for King Mahedana, O Great One, but never have I seen tracks like these."

"Do not doubt your skills, Urudu," Kwasin replied to the tall Wan"so tracker, who sat on his haunches examining the rhino-sized, talon-like prints frozen in the black mud. "You have never before laid eyes upon such a spoor because the animal that left it lives a great distance to the south of your kingdom, in a land so far away that the very fires burning in the night's dome look strange."

Kwasin thought of the odd markings he had seen long ago in the wet sand along the shores of the southern sea, footprints his uncle had said belonged to the legendary dragon that stalked the area. But how had the beast come to be here, on the northern coast of the Kemu, high in the frozen reaches of the Saasares mountains?

There could be only one reasonable explanation—it was the same *r"ok'og'a* that Kwasin had freed from the prison beneath the Great Tower and that had later rampaged through the streets of the capital before escaping into the island's wilds. Awineth, who had somehow managed to survive Khowot's tremblings, must have ordered the ragged band of followers who had come to her aid to capture the beast. Then they had brought the *r"ok'og'a* with them when they fled the island and crossed over to the mainland coast. But why? Did she hope one day to unleash the fearsome beast against her enemies?

Kwasin shook his head at the bizarre development. Squinting into the fierce, bitterly cold winds, he pulled his thick otter-fur cloak tighter about his shoulders and beckoned Urudu to rise. It was time to resume their dangerous ascent into the mountains. The only way to find an answer to the mystery was to trudge on.

He hoped coming across the *r"ok'og'a*'s spoor meant that Urudu would once again pick up the trail left by Awineth and the men who accompanied her. Already Kwasin had spent far too long stalking his quarry across the northern coastline. Far to the south, King Hadon's impudent coalition was amassing its great fleet. Kwasin did not want to return to the island only to find that Hadon had snatched the throne of Khokarsa out from under him. He only hoped Bhako's expedition to woo the pirate king of Mikawuru into an alliance would succeed, thus granting the Khokarsans a foothold on the southern sea. Surely Kwasin's promise of complete control of Hadon's golden city and its mining operations—including the new settlement of Kartenkloe, the gateway to the southern savannas and the lucrative ivory trade—would satisfy even Mikawuru's greedy king.

Kwasin sighed. He knew he could not return to the capital and Queen Awamethna's loving embrace until after he had completed his mission. The oracle had been clear on that point. Then again, there was nothing in the oracle's words to say he must return, nothing to stop him from setting out toward the trackless expanses of the Western Lands, where he could lose himself in the wilds and roam free for the remainder of his days. He recalled the hardships he had suffered during his eight long years of exile in the wilderness, and the loneliness that had assailed him. But was any of that worse than the deceptions, manipulations, and political backstabbing that ceaselessly plagued the life of the king of kings of Khokarsa? He did not think so. Not after all he had endured since his return from exile.

Nevertheless, he knew he would never gain peace of mind until he found and confronted Awineth. Though he had tried to bury his feelings for her in the dark pit of his soul, he could not escape the fact that he had somehow come to love her. Perhaps that was it. He loved her because her soul was made of the same darkly streaked material as his own. Awamethna, beautiful though she was, would never fill the emptiness in his heart left by Awineth's absence. But maybe, if he saw Awineth one last time, he would wake up to the madness that had seized him. Then he might be able to forget her.

Two days later, Kwasin and Urudu entered a mountain pass and came upon the carcass of the *r"ok'og'a*. It was the strangest creature Kwasin had ever seen. About the size of a large rhino, the beast's sleek, half-frozen body was covered in reddish-golden scales. A thin mane of short, bristling hair ran down its long, serpentine neck, upon which was mounted a smallish, snakelike head. From the center of the skull, between a pair of beady, lidless eyes, projected a straight, flat-sided horn, ivory in color and about two and a half feet long, which narrowed to a sharp point. In contrast with the hoof-like appearance of the *r"ok'og'a*'s front feet—each of which was in reality a bundle of short toes retracted around a thickly calloused heel—the hind feet bore long, talon-like, clawed toes that were unmistakably reptilian and without doubt quite deadly when the creature had lived.

Kwasin felt pity for the beast, which lay curled up in a shallow cleft gouged into the side of the boulder-strewn valley. It must have escaped its human handlers and crawled here, where it had died of exposure. Urudu wanted to poach the *r"ok'og'a*'s glossy, ivory-colored horn, saying it would make him a rich man, but Kwasin told him to let the dead beast be. It had not asked for the fate that had been thrust upon it, and that was a sentiment Kwasin understood only too well.

They continued on, passing higher into the mountains. Throughout much of the next day, the sky darkened overhead as great flocks of birds winged their way northward. The birds should have already flown north by this time of year, but for the past two months the migratory patterns of many species of animals had been strangely disrupted. Urudu, who had spent much of his life in the wilds, said the animals' unusual behavior was an ill omen, although he could not say exactly what it portended. Kwasin told the tracker that he wanted to hear no more of omens. He was tired of letting the deities control his destiny. If ill fortune came his way, he would meet it and deal with it head-on, but there was no sense in brooding over vague forebodings.

Early on the third morning after finding the *r"ok'og'a*, Urudu awoke Kwasin from his slumber, joyfully exclaiming that he had again picked up their quarry's trail. Kwasin eagerly packed up his belongings and set off following Urudu into the frigid morning. Later that day, they found Awineth's camp.

Kwasin's heart sank as he ran forward on top of the ice-crusted snowfield that blanketed the mountain valley before him. On the valley's western side, the tops of several deerskin tents steepled out of the blinding white snow. He knew from what Urudu had told him that the trail they had been following was at least three weeks stale. That could only mean one thing. For those three weeks Awineth and her people had been forced to hole up in this valley, probably caught in a sudden snowstorm. That nothing rose from the smoke holes of the buried tents was an ominous sign. But then, they were above the timberline. Awineth's party would have burned through any wood they carried in just a few days. And that too made Kwasin sick with worry.

He headed for the tent in the center of the cluster. Reaching it, he began digging furiously through the snow, oblivious to the searing cold that numbed his bare hands. Urudu arrived at Kwasin's side and also began digging. When they had cleared away a good portion of the snow, Kwasin used his knife to slash an opening in the tent's side. He raised the flap and looked inside.

Snow-refracted light from outside gently illuminated the tent's interior. In the center of the tent two forms, one larger than the other, lay cradled together beneath a thick pile of furs. Kwasin could not see the faces of those under the coverings, but raven-black hair, shining softly in the snow light, spilled from beneath the furs. Neither form was moving.

Urudu laid a hand on Kwasin's shoulder. Kwasin shrugged it off and entered the tent.

Kneeling beside the smaller of the two forms, Kwasin pulled back the furs and looked down at Awineth. She could have been sleeping, but her unmoving breasts, and the bloodless cast of her fair skin, told him otherwise. Kwasin leaned forward and kissed her cold, bluish lips.

Suddenly a coldness settled over Kwasin—not a physical cold, but rather an iciness that cut deep into the soul. He sat and absorbed the feeling, letting it sear through him, and then pulled back the coverings from the form lying beside Awineth.

It was Wahesa of Mukha, a fact which did not surprise him. According to intelligence Kwasin received before leaving the capital, Wahesa had escaped the fall of Dythbeth and gone renegade in the island's mountains. After Awineth fled into the backcountry behind Khowot, Wahesa and his band of outlaws had sought her out and offered their assistance in getting her off the island.

Next to Wahesa's corpse lay the Ax of Victory. Kwasin felt tempted to leave it there. True to the dwarf Paga's prediction, the weapon had brought him nothing but trouble. Then Kwasin shrugged. He removed the great bronze-headed club from the harness on his back and replaced it with the ax. The latter had saved him more times than he could recall and it would be a pity not to take it with him after he had come all this way. Besides, he didn't believe the superstitious manling knew what he was talking about.

Outside the tent, Urudu was uttering a curse upon Wahesa's spirit. The Wan"so tracker had been sent along with Kwasin at the request of King Mahedana, who wanted to avenge the man who had so wronged his daughter. It seemed that Daka had broken with her husband after her affair with Kwasin. Kwasin did not know the details of the dispute, nor did he ever care to, but thereafter Daka had sworn to kill Wahesa.

Since Wahesa was dead, Urudu would be denied the honor of defeating King Mahedana's son-in-law in combat. He would also be unable to enhance his reputation as a warrior by adding Wahesa's hands to the others he wore about his neck. But he could still deliver Wahesa's head to Daka, and because of that Urudu began softly humming a song of joy.

The coldness in Kwasin's soul retreated. He now felt only numb despondency. He had not known what would happen when he finally caught up with Awineth, but this was certainly not an outcome he had foreseen.

Gently, he wrapped Awineth's body in furs and carried it from the tent. He hated the thought of leaving her in the lonely, snow-swept terraces of the Saasares. But then, Kho was the Mother of All, and all the land was Hers. Even in death one could not hope to evade the earthy embrace of the Goddess. One burial place could be no worse than another.

And so Kwasin carried Awineth out of the snow and laid her down upon the mountainside, where he buried her beneath a crude pylon of rocks overlooking the sea. After he had finished, he spent some time searching for an animal he could sacrifice to Awineth's spirit. Finally, he looked down to see a white-furred mouse burrowing its way into the snow. He reached down and scooped up the mouse. The tiny thing sniffed at his fingers and looked up at him with its round, black eyes.

Kwasin exhaled gruffly and then set the mouse free. Too many had died already in the costly war between Kho and Resu. Why needlessly snuff out another life, even one this small? Awineth's spirit would not go hungry in any case; there were still those loyal to their former queen who would sacrifice to her upon learning of her death.

He waved down to Urudu, who was placing Wahesa's head in his pack. Without waiting to see if the tracker would follow, Kwasin turned and began his slow descent toward the sea.

The day wore on as Kwasin and Urudu climbed downward. By the time they reached the timberline later that afternoon, they knew something was wrong.

To the south, the shadowy outline of the island of Khokarsa floated upon the seaward horizon. From the center of the island's hazy blue form a dark plume of smoke billowed skyward, blanketing the entire eastern half of the island. At the source of the black plume Kwasin could just make out a faint orange glow. Moments later a thundering boom cracked through the air and the mountain shook beneath their feet.

Khowot was erupting.

Kwasin stopped his descent, watching in horror as the distant volcano jettisoned red-hot lava into the heavens. The shock of the initial explosion must have been horrendous. He wondered if anyone in the capital could have survived it.

Then all words dropped from his mind. The flames shooting from Khowot burned brighter, until the entire midsection of the island seemed to radiate with an intensity of orange and red hues. He closed his eyes and opened them again, thinking his vision deceived him. It could not be. The whole island seemed to be lifting up out of the sea!

The Saasares boomed as if a giant heart thrummed beneath them. Kwasin reached out to grab at the jagged black rocks jutting from the side of the mountain, but as he did so he found himself thrown high into the air. His arms and legs flailed in empty space. Then he smacked hard against the face of the mountain.

Freezing-cold water was pouring down from above. A mountain lake must have shaken loose from its foundations and spilled its contents down the mountainside. Kwasin floundered to grab hold of something but the force of the downward-pouring water was too much. He slid downhill, carried along in a roiling flood of water, snow, and ice.

The mountain buckled beneath him as he plummeted downward. For a moment he found himself thrown out into the air. Then he was again sliding. His entire body throbbed with pain. Rocks, both large and small, battered against his arms, legs, torso, and head. Something large and long was falling alongside him. He reached for it and encircled his arms about it. It was a mammoth-sized tree trunk, careening down the mountainside like some kind of gargantuan sled. For a moment Kwasin thought he might ride it all the way to the sea. Then the mountain hammered against the trunk and Kwasin was once again bucked into the air, only to slam into the mountain a moment later.

He screamed but he could not hear his own voice over the roaring of the flood and the deafening thrumming of the mountain. Suddenly the angle of his descent leveled off. Instead of being carried almost vertically down the face of the mountain, he now slid at a forty-five-degree angle. Though the deluge still gushed over him and propelled him downward, its flow had lessened somewhat. If only he could find something to grab hold of to stop his fall, he might survive the tremor yet. But the mountain tore past him too quickly.

His back ached, doubtless because the ax slung across his shoulders had been hammering against it.

The ax!

He whirled about so that now he was on his chest, scraping along the rocks and dirt that hurtled beneath him. Though his entire body rattled with the mountain's furious shaking, he reached behind his back and firmly gripped the handle of the ax. With the greatest effort he had ever made, he pulled the ax from its harness. Then, with an even greater effort, he swung the ax forward.

The ax bounced away from the mountainside and almost flew out of Kwasin's hand. He gripped it tighter and, crying out for Kho to give him strength, again thrust the ax at the mountain's rocky face. Twice more he repeated the motion, each time thinking that the ax would tear loose from his grasp. But he did not let it go. If he did, he knew he would be dead.

Then, just as he looked down and saw nothing but empty air yawning below him, he struck the ax at the black rock with such force that the weapon's iron head shattered. A large shard pierced his shoulder, while other glittering splinters of iron shot out past him into the air. And yet Kwasin no longer fell. Part of the ax must not have broken. Whatever remained of its iron head had impaled itself in the rock.

He was dangling above a precipice that dropped five hundred feet to the sea. Hanging on to the leather thong attached to the handle of the ax, he twirled about in the air as mud and water rained down upon him. Then, as suddenly as it had begun, the flood ceased, and as he swung about he saw a sight that almost made him lose his hold.

Like some mighty leviathan of the ocean, the island of Khokarsa was rising up out of the waters of the Kemu. But the island was now two. It had split down the center, and its two halves, east and west, were toppling to either side, sinking into the sea. All about the island the sea churned violently, whirling in a counterclockwise direction as if a Brobdingnagian sinkhole had opened up deep beneath the waters. Then the island was gone, swallowed by the raging sea.

Kwasin bellowed with terror. Kho was at last fulfilling her promise and destroying the land! What hope did he have, a mere mortal, against such inconceivable power? Had his entire life been but a dream in the mind of the Goddess?

Now his terror turned to rage. Rage that his destiny, and that of all the land, had come to this. That Kho would smite down the whole world in Her righteous anger.

As Kwasin hung there, looking out over the edge of the broken mountainside at the end of his world, a golden-crowned fish-eagle glided directly in front of him. He watched it soar to his right—the good luck side—drawing his attention to something he had not noticed while engrossed in the horrifying events transpiring upon the sea. Fifteen feet above him to his right, jutting out over the broad, five-hundred-foot drop to the boulder-strewn shoreline below, was a narrow, triangular-shaped wedge of rock. Beyond the overhang, he could see a broad and apparently stable tableland.

The mountain continued its violent quavering as Kwasin dangled from his precarious position. He knew that at any moment the head of the ax might shake loose from the rock and plummet him to his death.

He looked up at the narrow shelf of rock to his right. To make it to the ledge, he would have to swing twenty feet across the chasm from where he hung. But he would also have to hurl himself fifteen feet upward. It was an impossible feat, one which even a hero of the Great Games would never dare to attempt. But then Kwasin had never been one to compare himself to others. And he could not go on clinging to the ax forever. Not when the mountain thundered its rage all about him.

Kwasin began rocking back and forth above the yawning chasm, his entire being screaming out with the will to live. If he died, then all his life would be meaningless. And that was a concession he was not willing to yield even to Kho Herself. Somehow, somehow he would achieve the impossible.

Roaring, Kwasin swung out into the abyss.

Epilogue

Seasons passed. The great stone walls, gilt domes, and stately minarets of the outpost city lay cracked and tumbled in the midst of the encroaching jungle. The people waited, pulling together their shattered lives as best they could. Still, many thousands died from the pestilence and famine which followed the unparalleled devastation that was Kho's wrath. Some said that if things kept going the way they were, Sisisken would soon have to close her towering gates. The grim ruler of the underworld would not have enough room in her dark house to board all the dead.

But though the citizens waited, not a single ship sailed into port. No sail had been sighted upon the sea since the foundations of the world rattled with the fury of the Goddess.

And so it was that on the first moon day of the Year of the Fish-Eagle, the oracle of the city stood high upon the steps of the Temple of Kho and called forth for the greatest hero of the land to begin construction of a great galley in which to seek out the fate of the motherland. The oracle did not name the hero who would lead the expedition, but there could be no doubt whom she meant.

Two months later King Hadon stood upon the docks at the port of Nangukar, kissing the fair-skinned, violet-eyed Lalila goodbye, and also Abeth and little La. He looked about for his son, but did not see him. Kohr was no doubt still angry at him because he would not be coming on the expedition. Hadon had told the boy he wanted to bring him along, but these were dangerous times. Only a short time ago, Gamori and his priests had attempted to imitate Minruth's blasphemy. Someone had to look after Kohr's mother and two sisters in the king's absence. But the boy had not wanted to hear it and had stalked off in anger.

Hadon hoped the youth would not run off and do anything rash. But he did not think he would. Like his father, Kohr was too even-tempered and duty-bound. The anger would blow off in time.

Hadon boarded the galley, which he had christened the *Taro* in memory of his now long-dead friend, and watched from the deck as the priestess poured libations over the bow. He surveyed the two dozen or so spectators standing below upon the stone wharves. Among them no bullroarers or trumpeters commemorated the vessel's departure, nor did any of the onlookers clang together brass cymbals or shout out words of encouragement to their king. Since the great calamity, there had been no celebrations. Too many had died to be joyful about anything.

As the vessel pulled away to the sound of the beaters and the splashings of the rowers, Hadon returned his gaze landward. Kohr was now standing on the wharves, one arm around his mother and the other about his two sisters. Hadon stood tall upon the deck, fighting back his welling tears, until the tiny figures on the wharves dwindled out of sight. It might be a year before he saw his family again. Or it might be never.

The *Taro* followed the coastline due north while Hadon and his crew marveled at the devastation which seemed to go on with no end. Everywhere great, thick-rooted trees knotted the sandy beaches and the jungles beyond. Here, as along the wharves of Nangukar, the sea had receded several yards from shore. There could be only one explanation for the low level of the water. The banks surrounding the far-western arm of the southern sea, known as the Bay of Dythphida, must have collapsed during the earthquake, thereby allowing the sea water to drain into the Aquthly River, and from there out into the world-ringing sea. If Hadon's theory was correct, the two great landlocked seas could very well drain to the bottom of their basins.

"Captain Rewenkwo says we should have reached Sakawuru by now."

Hadon broke his trancelike staring at the ruined coastline and regarded the barrel-chested manling. Though powerfully muscled, the squat fellow beside him stood no taller than an eight-year-old child. But Hadon would never make the mistake of misjudging the maturity of his friend's keen mind. Paga was as wise as the hills.

"Are you saying the whole city is gone? That all its citizens are dead?" Hadon shook his head. Although he had witnessed with his own eyes how Great Kho had thrown down many of his own city's impressive structures, he could not fathom a whole population obliterated.

"Indeed, the red-granite city is no more," Paga replied gruffly. "It has been swallowed by its black cliffs." And then he pointed to the coastline that trailed behind them.

Hadon looked out over the waters at a dark clumping of rocks along the distant shoreline. Could those really be the towering cliffs of Sakawuru, hurtled into the sea by Kho's quaking fury? He could not believe it. But then, as the days wore on with no sign of the city or its people, neither could he deny it.

The galley continued up the coast to Wentisuh. Here they found survivors of the earthquake, but Hadon and his crew were not able to stop and talk with them. Almost as soon as the *Taro* drew anchor, Wentisuh's starved and wretched inhabitants leaped into the water and began swimming for the galley. At first Hadon allowed the swimmers to board, thinking they were simply eager to get news from beyond their native port. But then, as more and more of the rawboned, wild-eyed survivors swarmed up the sides of the galley, Hadon realized their true intention. The hunger-crazed men meant to take the *Taro* and all its spoils. Hadon shouted to the coxswain to get his rowers moving and, with swords drawn, advanced with his men to clear the deck of the invaders.

After they had beat back the last of those trying to climb up the galley's sides, Hadon withdrew to his small cabin. Several hours later, unable to sleep, he got up and returned to the deck. There he remained, staring off into the waters, until Kho's blue bowl grew black with night and the heavens glittered with brilliant starlight. He felt great remorse at not being able to help the famine-stricken inhabitants of Wentisuh, but there was nothing he could have done for them. The survival of his own people lay in question in the aftermath of Kho's wrath. He knew he would face many more hard decisions in the years to come. The fact that life went on at all was itself a blessing from the Goddess.

The latter thought returned to Hadon as the galley proceeded onward and entered the Strait of Keth. Everyone but the rowers came out on deck to marvel at the awesome sight. The sheer walls and choppy waters of the once gloomy chasm were no more. Now a serene, mile-wide channel ran between the southern and northern seas, punctuated upon occasion by rocky outcroppings protruding from the calm waters. The small islands were all that remained of the strait's formerly towering cliffs, which Kho had also smote down in Her great anger.

"Now that the strait has been widened," Paga remarked to Hadon, "the Kemu will drain even quicker into the southern sea. Within a single generation, both seas will be gone."

Hadon did not argue with his friend's breathtaking pronouncement. The destruction of the cliffs above the strait was all the evidence he needed to convince himself that their world was dramatically changing.

Leaving the broad seaway behind, Captain Rewenkwo now headed the galley north-by-northwest. Whereas the southern sea had been a beautiful blue-green, the waters of the Kemu quickly turned a muddy brown. Paga claimed this indicated that the earthquake had in reality been a seaquake. The fact that the waters had not yet cleared of the churned-up sediment, he said, was proof that great forces were still at work beneath the seabed.

Several times each day Captain Rewenkwo consulted his lodestone compass, and at night compared his notations to the patterns of the stars. Soon it became clear that the man was agitated about something. Hadon asked him what was wrong.

The old seaman shook his compass as if it were broken. Then he swore and said, "I took my first voyage to the capital when I was only eight years old. Since then I've made the circuit across the Kemus every year of my life, even during the war when I commanded a smuggling ship for the Temple of Kho. Next week I'll be fifty-two. Every bone in my body tells me the island should be looming off the fore. But what do I see?" He waved an arm at the brown waters stretching from horizon to horizon. Again, the gray-haired sailor swore.

Hadon told the captain to keep his voice down. There was no need to alarm the crew until they could prove, one way or another, what had or had not happened to the island.

But Hadon's concern had been needless. By the time the tall ridges of the Saasares rose upon the horizon, it became evident to everyone onboard that they had either overshot the island or that it had altogether disappeared beneath the Kemu's murky depths. Hadon ordered the captain to follow the coast eastward. Two days later the ruins of Miklemres appeared off the port bow.

Unlike the survivors of Wentisuh, the inhabitants of the northern mainland posed no danger to the crew of the *Taro*. Too few of them remained to be a threat. Eager to exchange gossip, Hadon brought aboard the half-dozen dirty and emaciated men and women who had waved from shore. Their story was as shocking as it was grim.

The entire island, they said, was gone. One of the men claimed he had seen Piqabes herself, Kho's green-eyed daughter, reach forth her great hand from the waters and pull the island down to her cold bosom. A woman, the man's wife, disagreed, saying that it was Resu who had destroyed the island. She knew this because she had witnessed his fiery breath split the island in two. The couple argued at great length over what they had seen while Hadon and his stupefied crew looked on in astonishment.

The survivors from Miklemres also told Hadon that many of their fellow citizens had survived the catastrophe, although many had also died, both during the great tremor and afterward from disease and starvation. And then, shortly after the earthquake, a wave of previously unknown foreigners stormed into the valley from the west. These were a fierce people, small in stature, but numerous and deadly, wielding forbidden bows and poison-tipped arrows. The king of Miklemres, who had survived the earth's upheaval, fell back before the attacking tribes and led those citizens who would follow him higher into the mountains. The four men and two women sitting on the deck before Hadon were all that remained of those who had stayed behind to face the fierce hordes. Hadon asked why his crew had spotted none of the encroaching warriors along the coast, but his new guests replied that the invaders, with no one remaining in the area to fight, had moved on.

"What of Queen Awineth?" Hadon asked. The last news his people had received from the island was that the College of Priestesses had annulled Awineth's authority and placed her cousin upon the throne. And Kwasin! Hadon's spies said he had been named king of kings!

Suddenly Hadon's guests looked uncomfortable.

"They are aware you are the winner of the Great Games, O King," a slim, white-robed man standing next to Hadon whispered.

Hadon looked questioningly into the large, russet-brown eyes of his bard Kebiwabes.

"They know you were planning to invade the island," the bard said, "and they are unclear whose allegiance they should follow. Even now, with the land destroyed, they do not wish to betray the man who defeated the tyrant Minruth."

Finally understanding, Hadon assured his guests that he no longer had any interest in the crown of Khokarsa. Kho had shattered his ambition along with the world. And besides, Hadon said, he had not formed the coalition of southern cities in order to attack Kwasin, but rather to stand in defense against him.

The distrustful looks softened and eventually Hadon weaned from the survivors of Miklemres the information he desired. It seemed the oracular priestess had sent Kwasin off on a quest to find Awineth and her followers in the eastern Saasares. For all his guests knew, the two had both survived the destruction of the island.

The news did not exactly please Hadon. Kwasin and Awineth had each given him more than a fair share of trouble. Still, he could not shrug off his sense of obligation to them. If it remained possible they still lived, then he must search for them—to satisfy his own curiosity if nothing else. He ignored Paga's advice that it would be better to leave them in the wilds, although he agreed that, if found, the two would only complicate his already difficult life.

For weeks Hadon's expedition searched the coastline along the eastern Saasares without success. Then, on the very day Hadon decided it was time to turn the galley about and head home, a search party led by Paga reported in with the news of an exciting discovery. When Hadon asked what this was, Paga replied, "You had better come see for yourself."

His curiosity mounting, Hadon accompanied Paga and his men back to shore and up the treacherous face of a broken mountain. Having climbed to an altitude of five hundred feet, they mounted a broad plateau overlooking the sea. Here Paga pointed across a twenty-foot-wide chasm to the face of an adjoining mountain. At first Hadon saw nothing but rubble and debris. But then he gasped.

Across the chasm, a huge shelf of the mountain had collapsed into the sea below, leaving a narrow ledge of rock and dirt jutting out over empty air. An object, embedded into the face of the overhanging rim, glittered brightly in the sunlight.

"Your eyes are not mistaken," Paga said in response to Hadon's incredulous look. "But how did the ax of Wi come to be here, thrust into the face of a shattered mountainside?"

Hadon edged closer to the brink, trying to get a better look. Truly it seemed as if the ax had been purposefully driven into the rock. Could Kwasin have been caught on the mountain when the great catastrophe struck? Had he tried to stop his fall by impaling the ax into the mountain's stony face?

"I can tell by your expression that you are thinking the same thing as I," Paga said. "But it would be foolish to believe that even someone as strong as your cousin could have held onto the handle of the ax during the earthquake that knocked down half this mountain. And even if he had, not even a *nukaar*, one of the long-armed hairy halfmen of the trees, could have swung the twenty feet up and across the chasm."

Hadon scanned the distance from where the ax lay embedded in the rocky overhang to the ledge where he, Paga, Kebiwabes, and the other members of their party stood. Not only would Kwasin have had to jump across the twenty-foot gulf, but he also would have had to swing himself fifteen feet upward to the ledge. Paga was right. No man could make such a leap, not even a Great Gamester. But then again, if anyone could have done it, it would have been Kwasin.

Looking down at the waves crashing against the rocks below, Kebiwabes exclaimed, "Alas, goodbye to Kwasin! Never again shall I know a man as strong... nor as mad!"

Hadon was about to lead his men back down the mountain when suddenly he turned and again looked out over the chasm. It would be a shame to leave the ax behind, he thought, especially when he had the means at hand to procure it. And besides, it would make a good souvenir for Kohr. It might even make the boy forget his anger at not being allowed to accompany the expedition.

Thankfully Hadon's training for the Great Games had made him a skilled lassoer. But even so, it took all seven men in his party to pull the ax from the black stone after he had ensnared it. When at last he hoisted up the rope and examined the ax, Hadon feared the effort had all been for nothing.

"It's ruined," he said. "The head of the ax must have splintered when it was thrust into the rock."

Paga asked if he could see the weapon, which had been crafted by his own hand many years ago in a faraway land. Hadon handed him the worthless ax.

"There is still enough iron left," Paga said, rolling the glittering weapon in his hand. "I might yet be able to rework the head, although it will never be the mighty cudgel it once was. Still, stature is not everything. If I'm lucky, I might fashion it into a kind of pole ax, one better used for pecking than chopping, although still a weapon to be reckoned with."

Pleased with the manling's assessment, Hadon announced that it was time to return to the ship. They had already lingered too long on their journey and the time had come to head home.

Later that day, as Resu set in the west and Lahla the moon rose over the eastern mountains, Hadon stood alone upon the bow of the *Taro*. He looked out over the rolling waters of the Kemu, waters that one day in the not too distant future would disappear, replaced by exotic jungles, yawning deserts, and rolling savannas. He was anxious to get back to his city. His people would face many daunting challenges in the years ahead. The city would have to be rebuilt, new sources of food and other vital materials would have to be obtained and exploited, and defenses would have to be built up to fend off invaders seeking for their own his queendom's relative wealth and stability. The staggering enormity of the work threatened to overwhelm him.

But it was also, he knew, an exciting time to be alive. And he was not alone. He would have his friends and family to help him endure the many trials and tribulations that would assail him in this newly remade world. For what more could he ask? The world had always been made up of hardship, and it was a fool's dream to think it would ever be otherwise.

He watched a fish-eagle plummet to the surface of the water, only a moment later to soar up gracefully into the sky with its bounty.

Kho had spared his city when She had laid waste to so many others, and for that Hadon was thankful. He would return to the city of gold and little jewels and, with Lalila by his side, rule over it for the good and well-being of his people. And who could say? With the blessings of the Goddess, some luck, and a lot of hard work, his descendants might yet gaze upon the city's gilt domes and soaring towers for many thousands of years to come.

Addendum 1

DESCRIPTION OF MAPS

Map 1 shows the major part of Africa circa 10,000 B.C. This is a modification of the map presented by Frank Brueckel and John Harwood in their article: *Heritage of the Flaming God, an Essay on the History of Opar and Its Relationship to Other Ancient Cultures,* The Burroughs Bulletin, Summer, 1974.* Their map, in turn, was based on that in Willy Ley's *Engineers' Dreams,* Viking Press, 1954, though also much modified.

The world in 10,000 B.C. was in the dying grip of the last Ice Age. The present Sahara was mountains, plateaus, vast grasslands, parks of trees, rivers, and freshwater lakes. Elephants, rhinoceroses, hippopotami, crocodiles, lions, antelopes, and ostriches numbered in the millions. The two inland freshwater seas actually existed, though their boundaries as shown here are highly speculative.

The outlines of the mountains won't satisfy a professional cartographer; they're provided to give the reader a rough idea of their extent. The Mediterranean coastline was from 100–200 feet lower than its present level.

While the rest of the world was in the late Old Stone Age, a maritime civilization had risen around the northern inland sea, the Kemu (the Great Water). Some colonial cities, including Opar, had been founded in the Kemuwopar (Sea of Opar). Excluding the cities of Khokarsa Island (see Map 2), the major cities were: 1, Mukha; 2, Miklemres; 3, Qethruth; 4, Siwudawa; 5, Wethna; 6, Kethna; 7, Wentisuh; 8, Sakawuru; 9, Mikawuru (the pirate stronghold); 10, Bawaku; 11, Towina; 12, Rebha (the pile-city). A - Klemqaba country. Opar and Kôr are called out on the map, but Kôr was built after Hadon was born.

Note: The Khokarsans had their own system of measurements and weights, but in the novels only the English equivalents are given.

---

* Although scheduled for publication in *The Burroughs Bulletin* in 1974, Brueckel and Harwood's article went unpublished until it appeared in the collection *Heritage of the Flaming God: Ancient Mysteries of La and Savage Opar*, ed. Alan Hanson and Michael Winger, Waziri Publications, 1999.

Addendum 2

CHRONOLOGY OF KHOKARSA

INTRODUCTION

About 13,500 B.C. the coasts of the two seas of Central Africa were inhabited by a hundred small groups of paranthropoids, neanderthaloids, and human-neanderthal hybrids. The latter dwelt on the northern coast of the north sea; the neanderthaloids, on its west and east coasts; the paranthropoids, farther south. The total population along a coastline (including both seas) almost equal to that of the present Mediterranean was perhaps ten thousand.

The inland seas were the last refuge of the neanderthaloids. Elsewhere they had been exterminated or assimilated by *Homo sapiens*. The paranthropoids were hairy subhumans related to the *yeti* and the *sasquatch* of today. These were more numerous than now. Paranthropus lived in the forest and jungle areas, retreating before the advance of *Homo neanderthalensis* and *Homo sapiens*.

Some time before 13,000 B.C., a number of Caucasian tribes wandered down from the lush savannas of what is today the Sahara. These people called themselves the Khoklem. They gradually pushed out the hybrids and the neanderthaloids to the south, or else assimilated them.

About the same time, another group of Caucasians, the Klemsuh, began drifting into the middle-eastern coast of the north sea. These had physical characteristics which, if history had not decreed otherwise, might have seen the Klemsuh develop into a separate race. Their skins were a yellow-brown; their hair was straight, coarse, and dark; and they had slight epicanthic folds. These are Mongolian characteristics today, but the Klemsuh (the Yellow People) were definitely a stock of the Caucasian race.

The hybrids, who were to be called the Klemqaba (People of the Goat) by the Khoklem, eventually settled along the coast and in the hilly and mountainous interior northwest of the strait between the two seas. Though very peaceful in the beginning, many hundreds of years of belligerency by the Khoklem taught them the art of war. Until the end of the Khokarsan civilization, they were to be a thorn in its side.

The Khoklem, like the others, subsisted mainly on fishing, hunting, and food-gathering. Most of their protein came from the Kemu (the Great Water). Due to the absence of cereal plants in this area, it is doubtful that they would ever have amounted to anything if it had not been for the appearance of the man they called Sahhindar.

This mysterious man was regarded as a god by the Khoklem, and with good reason. He brought with him a variety of plants (apparently during a number of visits in a period of fifty years) and taught them how to domesticate these as well as the animals and birds of the area. Sahhindar also showed them how to mine copper and tin, how to make bronze tools and weapons, and how to make bricks and mortar. He also instilled in them a respect for sanitation and taught them the concept of zero. It is no wonder that he held a position in the Khokarsan pantheon analogous to that of Thoth in the Egyptian pantheon.

These gifts explain why the Khokarsans anticipated the Agricultural Revolution of Mesopotamia by about four thousand years. It also explains how these Old Stone Age tribes leaped over the Middle and New Stone Ages into the Bronze Age.

Eventually, groups in dugouts and on rafts landed on the island of Khokarsa, which was about the size of Crete. These were Khoklem belonging to a tribe known as the Klemreskom (People of the Fish-Eagle). Their chief goddess, Kho, was a fertility deity titled the Bird-Headed Mother. She was represented in rock paintings and on bone and hippopotamus-ivory carvings as a steatopygic, huge-breasted woman with the head of the fish-eagle. Other tribes came in a little later, and some of these represented her as having the head of a parrot. No doubt this was because the island was swarming with parrots.

Sahhindar was also the god of Time, though the religion had it that he stole Time from his mother Kho and that was why She exiled him from the land. Sahhindar was said to have been able to travel in time before Kho had taken away this power. Undoubtedly, he was a time traveler from the twenty-first century who had been stranded about 12,000 B.C. (See my *Time's Last Gift*, Ballantine, 1972.) Apparently he was not in the least responsible for the development of civilization elsewhere (in the Near East and on the Indus), but regarded Khokarsa as a private project. He will be referred to throughout this series but will play only a minor role in a few of the novels.

That Sahhindar appeared a number of times in Khokarsa over a period of two thousand years can only be attributed to an age-delaying elixir of some sort.

MAJOR EVENTS

12,000 B.C. — Khoklem spreading out on northern shore of the Kemu. Appearance of Sahhindar.

11,800 B.C. — The hero Gahete is the first man to land on uninhabited island of Khokarsa. On succeeding trips, brings his tribe, the Fish-Eagle Totem. Their chief priestess dedicates a sacred oak grove high on a volcano, Khowot (Voice of Kho). Khokarsa (the Tree of the Hill of Kho) gives its name to the island. Painted fire- or sun-hardened pottery used.

11,700 B.C. — Other tribes have also landed elsewhere on the island. First beer from millet and sorghum made. Priestesses develop an early pictographic writing. Village of Khokarsa becomes the first walled area in the world. Potter's wheel invented. Trephining of skull to relieve chronic headaches introduced.

11,600 B.C. (1 A.T.) — Large stone-block temple to Kho built on plateau by the sacred oak grove. King Nanla seizes the town of Miklemres, the gateway to the tin, copper, and salt mines in the Saasares mountains (the present Ahaggar and Tibesti). Mead-making becomes a major industry, controlled by the chief priestess, Nanwot. Alkaline-glazed pottery. Ox-drawn wagons.

11,550 B.C. (50 A.T.) — Chief priestess, Awineth, establishes a chronology, starting from completion of temple to Kho fifty years before. (A.T. stands here for After Temple.) Wine from grapes first made.

11,530 B.C. (70 A.T.) — The priestess-bard Hala composes the first epic poem, *The Song of Gahete*, based on folk songs. Painting and sculpture are more lifelike but still stiff.

11,520 B.C. (80 A.T.) — The sundial and the processing of olives invented. First temple-tomb (for Awineth) built. (The kings at this time were still being sacrificed at the end of a nine-year reign. They were buried under large mounds of earth on top of which was set a bird-headed monolith. Heroes and heroines—that is, extraordinary men and women—were buried under mounds with a pointed monolith on top.)

11,450 B.C. (150 A.T.)	King Ruwodeth of Khokarsa crushes the revolt in Miklemres. First appearance of the Klemsaasa, a tall people speaking an unknown language, in the mountains north of Miklemres. Lead-glazed pottery.
11,400 B.C. (200 A.T.)	Expeditionary fleet led by King Khonan founds the port of Siwudawa in the country of the Klemsuh. This marks the beginning of a long series of campaigns against the Klemsuh of the rural areas. Lost-wax process for casting bronze invented.
11,350 B.C. (250 A.T.)	Port villages of Towina and Bawaku flourishing. The "oikos" system of settling the coast frontier is founded. (Bands of adventurous men and women build little wooden forts along the coast and dig in. These were led by men of the hero category whose residences later became small palaces and who ruled large estates. They founded the leading families of these areas, and many of the "oikos" became thriving towns in time.) By this time all six cities of the island have become powerful trade centers. Population of the city of Khokarsa: 15,000. Dythbeth, Saqaba, Kaarquth, Asema, and Kunesu have populations of from eight to ten thousand. Glass invented. Salt-glazed pottery and porcelain.
11,250 B.C. (350 A.T.)	Barter is still the basis of economy. Gold and silver first extensively mined in the northern mountains. From their villages in the Saasares, the Klemsaasa raid outlying districts of Miklemres. They incorporate their patriarchal sun god with Kho's son, Resu. Hourglass using sand invented.
11,153 B.C. (447 A.T.)	The genius Awines born in Dythbeth.
11,118 B.C. (482 A.T.)	By the age of thirty-five, Awines has invented a syllabary, founded the science of linguistics, created a theory of atomism (much like Lucretius'), discovered the circulation of blood, formulated an elementary algebra, and invented wooden printing blocks, catapults, Greek fire, the water clock, the magnifying glass and a solar calendar.

11,113 B.C. (487 A.T.) Awines is exiled to Bawaku because his syllabary and calendar are considered sacrilegious. Bawaku revolts and defeats the Khokarsan fleet with Awines' catapults and Greek fire.

11,111 B.C. (489 A.T.) Awines is killed while trying to fly with artificial wings from a mountain.

11,110 B.C. (490 A.T.) Keth of Kenesu reports discovery of the strait of the southern sea. Apparently, however, others had preceded him. The port village of Mukha becomes a city due to salt mines discovered near it.

11,000 B.C. (600 A.T.) The Klemsaasa, having adopted agriculture, have become more numerous. They seize and control for a decade some tin and copper mines and require tribute from some outlying provinces of Miklemres. First mint established with coining of electrum.

10,985 B.C. (615 A.T.) Under King Madymin of Khokarsa, Bawaku is retaken, its citizens are massacred, and it is resettled with colonists from Khokarsa. A group of Bawakans, led by the hero Anesem, escape and found the first City of Pirates, Mikawauru. (In Khokarsan, *mi* means *city*, and *kawauru* means both *crocodile* and *pirate*.) This was on the fjord coast northwest of the strait into the southern sea (still little known at this time). First silver and gold coins. First recording of use of brass.

10,968 B.C. (632 A.T.) A great earthquake and tidal wave. The Klemsaasa seize the city of Miklemres. Towina, Bawaku, Dythbeth, and Kaarquth revolt successfully. Aboriginal population of Siwudawa revolts, massacres Khokarsan troops and merchants, and establishes independent state.

10,954 B.C. (646 A.T.) The Mikawuru are driven from their stronghold by the Klemqaba. Led by Wethna, they cross the Kemu and found Wethna on its eastern shore. Use of perspective in art begins to spread.

10,915 B.C. (685 A.T.) A Bawaku expedition under the hero Nankar travels the length of the Bohikly (the Niger River) and brings back from West Africa the red protein berry mowometh* and the ebony, African mahogany, and okra trees. These begin to spread rapidly around the Kemu. First biremes built. First contact with the Negroes of the west by the hero Agadon of Towina. King K'opwam of Khokarsa retakes Dythbeth and Kaarquth.

10,878 B.C. (722 A.T.) The first great plague. (Smallpox, previously unknown, was probably brought in by black captives.) A quarter of the population of the island and of the cities of Towina and Bawaku die. A few years later, smallpox ravages all the population of the other areas.

10,875 B.C. (725 A.T.) A chief of the Klemsaasa leads them and an army of Miklemres allies to Khokarsa and seizes the city. He marries its sole surviving priestess and ascends the throne. He adopts the Khokarsan name of Minruth; assimilation of the Klemsaasa begins. Those left in the mountains become known as the Klemklakor (Bear people).

10,866 B.C. (734 A.T.) Minruth I completes the conquest of all the cities of the island and Towina and Bawaku. He refuses to honor the age-old custom of sacrifice of the king after nine years of rule and institutes custom of sacrificing a substitute. The Klemsaasa pantheon is entirely incorporated into the Khokarsan. Resu, the sun god, is proclaimed to be the equal of Kho. Nevertheless, in practice, most of the people for a long time regard Resu as secondary to Kho. This year marks the beginning of the long struggle between the priestesses and the priests. Old lunar calendar is abandoned and Awines' solar calendar is adopted. New one has twelve months of three ten-day weeks each, with five festival days at end of year. Year starts on the vernal equinox.

10,846 B.C. (754 A.T.) Syllabary of Awines adopted. Governmental postal system, based on that of the temples, is adopted. First copper coins stamped.

---

* *Dioscoreophyllum cumminsi*. A recently discovered red berry, native to West Africa. It's three thousand times sweeter than sugar on a weight-for-weight basis. It is a protein, not a carbohydrate. See *Signature* magazine, March, 1973.

10,832 B.C. (768 A.T.)	First trireme built. Coastal highway of stone blocks begun from Miklemres east and west. The hero Kethna circumnavigates the southern sea. This was originally called the Kemuketh but later became known as the Kemuwopar (Sea of Opar).
10,824 B.C. (776 A.T.)	The city of Kethna founded. This will eventually control the strait and be a source of trouble to Khokarsa.
10,810 B.C. (790 A.T.)	The priestess-heroine Lupoeth discovers gold-, silver-, and diamond-bearing clay at site of Opar and founds a mining village. Depiction of deities as human-headed in art and sculpture spreads from Khokarsa.
10,800 B.C. (800 A.T.)	First Negro slaves brought into Opar.
10,757 B.C. (843 A.T.)	A second Mikawuru (City of Pirates) founded on northwest shores of the Kemuketh. These settlers were not from Wethna, which had become respectable, but were criminals and political refugees from all over the northern sea.
10,700 B.C. (900 A.T.)	Colonists from Mikawuru establish a stronghold on east coast of the Kemuwopar. It grows in later years into a city called Sakawuru.
10,695 B.C. (905 A.T.)	The city of Opar completed in all its grandeur. The port of Wentisuh founded by colonists from Siwudawa.
10,600 B.C. (1000 A.T.)	The climate is warmer and drier. The ice sheets in the Saasares are dwindling. A great plague and a series of earthquakes usher in another Time of Troubles. Revolts of tributary states and falling apart of the empire. K'opwam II murders his wife in attempt to impose patriarchy and flees to Miklemres during the uprising that follows. He is captured and sacrificed at the great temple. For a hundred years the chief priestesses of Khokarsa have husbands who are denied the kingship. Many temples of Resu torn down or converted to temples of Kho. Human sacrifice, except in times of great tribulation, is abandoned. This custom spreads throughout the two seas, except at Sakawuru.

10,560 B.C. (1040 A.T.)	Beginning of the *numatenu* (heroes of the broadsword), a warlike class similar to the samurai. By custom, only the members of the *numatenu* are allowed to use the slightly curved, blunt-ended broadsword lately introduced, but this is not strictly observed.
10,499 B.C. (1101 A.T.)	The Klemqaba take Bawaku and massacre its citizens.
10,490 B.C. (1110 A.T.)	A combined Klemqaba and Towina fleet attacks Dythbeth. A *numatenu*, Toenuseth, consort of Dythbeth's chief priestess, destroys the fleet. His wife makes him the king, and he sets out on the conquest of the island of Khokarsa.
10,485 B.C. (1115 A.T.) to 10,480 B.C. (1120 A.T.)	Toenuseth conquers Saqaba and Kaarquth. The city of Towina, now an enemy of the Klemqaba, drives the Klemqaba from Bawaku with the aid of revolting Bawakans.
10,478 B.C. (1122 A.T.)	Toenuseth killed by a spear thrown by the chief priestess of Khokarsa during the siege of that city. This is considered a judgment of Kho, and it discourages the idea of the kingship for some years.
10,460 B.C. (1140 A.T.)	The chief priestess of the city of Khokarsa institutes the Great Games (later known as the Great Games of Klakor, after the winner of the first games). These mark the return of the kingship. By the Law of Pwymnes, the victor of the Great Games becomes the husband of the chief priestess (if she accepts him) and is crowned king of Khokarsa. Any man is eligible to compete unless he is a slave, a neanderthaloid, or a Klemqaba. The Games occur when the old king has died or the chief priestess dies. However, the reigning king may keep his kingship if he can induce the dead wife's daughter to marry him, or if she lacks daughters, the nearest relative to assume the priestess's throne. Pwymnes, too old to bear children, retires after the hero Klakor wins the Games, and he marries her daughter, Hiindar (meaning Gray Eyes). It must be kept in mind that the king governed only military, naval, and engineering areas. The queen controlled the judicial courts, the law-making, currency, religion, taxation, and commerce. It had, however, long been recognized that men were responsible for the impregnation of women, that Kho or her sons and

daughters (gods and goddesses) were not the agents of fertility of women (except that they might cause a man or a woman to be sterile). That men caused pregnancy was the main argument of the priests of Resu for the superiority of Resu and for the dominance of males in society. Officially, the fact was ignored, and it took a long time for the idea to be accepted in rural areas. Work on the Great Tower of Kho and Resu begun by Klakor.

10,452 B.C. (1148 A.T.) Klakor completes the reconquest of the island of Khokarsa. Kwamim, the greatest of the epic poets, born in Miklemres. At the age of twenty-eight, she will create the *Pwamwotkethna*, or *Song of Kethna*. This is based on the wanderings of Kethna and the founding of his city but is historically inaccurate. The songs of much earlier heroes and heroines are incorporated in it, making them contemporaneous with Kethna, and much mythological matter is embodied. The language is based on that of the city of Khokarsa, but Kwamim borrows words from other dialects and even coins new words.

10,449 B.C. (1151 A.T.) Fleet of Miklemres destroyed by Klakor, and Miklemres capitulates. This event marks the beginning of the conquest of the queendom of the coastal Kemu.

10,448 B.C. (1152 A.T.) Opar conquered by Sakawuru pirates under Gokasis. They control the precious metal and jewel trade. Plumbing invented and installed in the palace of Khokarsa.

10,443 B.C. (1157 A.T.) Klakor's herald, the bard Roteka, arrives in Opar to demand surrender. His head is sent back to Klakor, arriving there in 1159 A.T. But Klakor has died.

10,440 B.C. (1160 A.T.) Kethna seized by allied Oparians and pirates of Mikawuru and Sakawuru.

10,427 B.C. (1173 A.T.) Gokasis proclaims himself king of kings of the Kemuwopar after taking Wethna. The first Khokarsan expedition against the alliance destroyed outside the Strait of Keth. Awodon, the Praxiteles of Khokarsa, born. Owalu, Qethruth, and Mukha become major Khokarsan cities. The poetess Kwamim, a guest at the court of Wentisuh, is taken prisoner and carried to Opar.

10,423 B.C. (1177 A.T.) to 10,420 B.C. (1180 A.T.) — The hero Rimasweth, leading a Khokarsan expedition, strikes Kethna from overland and, leaving a holding force, bypasses Wentisuh, and Sakawuru and raids Opar. He slays Gokasis (son of the first Gokasis) in hand-to-hand combat, massacres the citizens, and takes Kwamim. His fleet is caught at the Strait of Keth and destroyed, but he and Kwamim, with three *numatenu*, escape.

10,417 B.C. (1183 A.T.) — Kwamim first sings the *Pwamwotrimasweth*, the *Song of Rimasweth*. This is the second-greatest epic of Khokarsa (some critics consider it the greatest). It is the first to sing of living heroes. The barbarian Klemklakor are numerous enough to require large punitive expeditions.

10,397 B.C. (1203 A.T.) — Awodon begins work on his masterpiece, *Kho and Her Children*, a frieze of sixty-four figures along the marble base of the Great Tower of Kho and Resu. A fourth expedition levels Kethna and Wentisuh but is destroyed in the Battle of the Bay of Opar.

10,390 B.C. (1210 A.T.) — Siege of Opar begins. Mikawauru and Sakawuru blockaded but resist storming. Expeditions sent out to West Africa, the Mediterranean, and Nile Valley. (But none return.)

10,389 B.C. (1211 A.T.) — Opar taken. Spectacles invented.

10,387 B.C. (1213 A.T.) — Sakawuru taken, its citizens executed, and a ship sent out to arrange for colonists from Khokarsa to repeople it. Mikawuru resists successfully.

10,386 B.C. (1214 A.T.) to 10,266 B.C. (1334 A.T.) — A hundred and twenty years of comparative peace, prosperity, and expansion of population. Awodon completes his great work at the age of seventy, dies two years later, and is buried in a hero's tomb. Work on the Great Tower proceeds apace. Networks of stone roads built out from coastal cities along the shore and inland, and a network completed on the island of Khokarsa. Census in 1334 A.T. shows that population of the two seas is an estimated two million. (This was the peak.) The town of Rebha, built on piles in a shallow spot in the southeastern Kemu, becomes important in sea commerce. Border forts built to strengthen defense against Negroes of the Western Lands. Another unsuccessful expedition against the troublesome pirates of Mikawuru. The explorer Dythphida discovers that an arm of the Kemuwopar is about to cut through the middle-west mountains on the western shore. This portends the eventual drainage of the two seas, but this should not start until another estimated two or three hundred years have passed. The chief priestess of Khokarsa, Aquth, proclaims that this drainage can be averted only by a downgrading of Resu and a return to more conservative forms of religion. Minruth III considers building a gigantic dam, but since this will halt work on the Great Tower, he takes no action.

10,265 B.C. (1335 A.T.) Opar half-destroyed by an earthquake, but rebuilding begins at once. The Whooping Plague first appears in Towina.

10,261 B.C. (1339 A.T.) The plague has spread all over the empire. Crop failures and a deadly disease among the fish cause great famine. The Klemqaba devastate Bawaku but are themselves struck down by the plague. The city of Khokarsa is half-destroyed by an eruption of Khowot, and the citizens flee.

10,257 B.C. (1343 A.T.) The population has been reduced to three-quarters of a million. The empire has fallen apart. The majority of the royalty has died. A *numatenu* from Opar, Riqako, marries the only surviving priestess able to bear children in the city of Khokarsa. He becomes Reskomureeskom, the king of kings, literally, the Great Fish-Eagle of the Fish-Eagles.

10,061 B.C. (1539 A.T.) Heliqo discovers connection between malaria and mosquitoes.

10,050 B.C. (1550 A.T.) The climate is getting warmer and drier. There is, however, still ice and snow in abundance on the peaks of the Saasares. The level of the Mediterranean has risen. Khokarsa is once again in the ascendancy. All states of the Kemu acknowledge its suzerainty, but in fact are semi-independent. Kethna sends tribute but acts as if it were independent. Though the population has increased, there are still some areas that have not recovered. The pirates of Mikawuru are giving more trouble, and there are pirate bases in the Kemu. There has been little progress in technology. Iron weapons and tools were introduced circa 1340 A.T., but since the main iron-ore deposits are deep inside the Saasares, it is expensive. Bronze weapons and tools are still much used.

10,049 B.C. (1551 A.T.) Minruth IV wins the Great Games of Klakor, marries Demakwa, the chief priestess.

10,042 B.C. (1558 A.T.) Bissin, inventor of a crude steam engine, is born.

10,036 B.C. (1564 A.T.) The herculean and ill-fated Kwasin, Hadon's cousin, is born in Dythbeth.

10,034 B.C. (1566 A.T.) Demakwa dies. Minruth marries her cousin, Wimimwi, and so no Great Games are held.

10,031 B.C. (1569 A.T.) Hadon of Opar born. His father, Kumin, is a crippled *numatenu* who has been reduced to sweeping the floors of a temple. His mother, Pheneth, is the daughter of an overseer of slaves, so Hadon has a poverty-stricken childhood, and his parents are of a low social class. Both parents are members of the Ant Totem. Awineth, daughter of Minruth and Wimimwi, born in temple of Kho on the slopes of Khowot. Electroplating of metal by means of a primitive battery is invented.

10,018 B.C. (1582 A.T.) Kwasin, drunk, ravishes a priestess of Kho and kills some temple guards. He is exiled instead of being executed when the oracular priestess of the temple of Kho at Dythbeth (where the sacrilege took place) says he should be sent out of the land but permitted to return when Kho so decrees. He wanders off into the Western Lands carrying his great brassbound oak club.

10,013 B.C. (1587 A.T.) Wimimwi dies. Awineth becomes the chief priestess. The Great Games are scheduled to be held within three years. (Enough time has to be given for all states to be notified, the preliminary Lesser Games held to choose three main contestants and their three substitutes from each state, and for the contestants to journey to the city of Khokarsa.) Minruth asks his daughter to marry him, but she refuses. Minruth (called the Mad behind his back) plans to keep the throne by hook or crook. Ruseth, a fisherman, invents the fore-and-aft sail.

10,012 B.C. (1588 A.T.) Hadon becomes one of the winners of the Lesser Games in Opar.

10,011 B.C. (1589 A.T.) The events of *Hadon of Ancient Opar* begin.

Acknowledgments

Special thanks to Michael Croteau for resurrecting the manuscript and outline of *The Song of Kwasin*, and for his key role in giving its hero a chance to live again. Thanks again to Mike, and to Win Scott Eckert, Dennis E. Power, Paul Spiteri (who went above and beyond the call of duty), and S. M. Stirling for reading various drafts of the novel and offering their valued feedback; Rick Lai for his keen insight; Alan Hanson and Michael Winger for bringing into print Frank J. Brueckel and John Harwood's *Heritage of the Flaming God*, and for their own fascinating speculations; Christopher Lotts and William K. Schafer for believing in this project; Philip Laird Farmer and Kristan Josephsohn for their generosity and seeing the project through to publication; Charles Berlin for his painstaking work with the maps; Judy Bauer for her feedback on Khokarsan linguistics; Yanni Kuznia for all those eleventh-hour changes; Tobias S. Buckell for an encouraging early talk; my colleagues at Planet Stories—Erik Mona, Pierce Watters, and James L. Sutter—for keeping the old flame alive; David Lars Chamberlain, Henry G. Franke III, Hans Kiesow, Zacharias Nuninga, Art Sippo, and Bill Thom for their enthusiasm and good cheer; Mark DeNardo, David Herter, Karl M. Kauffman, Jon A. LaBore, Thomas S. McGraw, and Heidi Ruby Miller for their friendship and inspiration; Henry S. Carey, Jr., Velma R. Carey, and Diana M. Carey for their indefatigable support; and Laura Wilkes Carey for standing by me through it all.

Above all, neither *The Song of Kwasin* nor the present omnibus would have come to pass without Philip José Farmer's gracious blessing and advice, and Bette Farmer's encouragement and determined support. I'll always cherish the good times we had in Peoria.

—C.P.C.